D0281183

Principal characters in Kingshaven

At the Palace

Liliana King, matriarch and widow of Basil King who became proprietor of the Palace Hotel in 1937 after the scandalous elopement of his older brother, Rex.

Ruby Farmer, Liliana's former dressmaker and friend, now in permanent residence.

Libby King, dutiful daughter of Liliana and Basil, who took over the running of the hotel on her father's death in 1952.

Eddie King, Libby's husband.

Christopher King, their eldest son.

Angela King, their daughter.

Adrian and Edwin (known as Winny), their younger sons.

Jolly Allsop, heir to the Castle and recently divorced from Ruby Farmer's daughter. Now living in the Summer House in the Palace grounds.

Julia Allsop, his youngest daughter.

Joanna, Jacqueline and James Allsop, his other children.

At the Castle

Sir John Allsop, eccentric philanthropist aristocrat and father of Jolly.

Professor Liebeskind, refugee offered shelter by Sir John during the war.
Claudia Dearchild, the professor's daughter.
Michael Quinn, left-wing novelist and lover of Claudia.
Bruno and Fiammetta Dearchild, their illegitimate twins.
Winston Allsop, Sir John's adopted mixed-race son, now a music promoter.
Iris Quinn, Michael Quinn's older daughter.

Town People

Sylvia Quinn, Michael Quinn's ex-wife, now a successful department store owner.
Millicent Bland, daughter of publican Percy Bland.

THE THINGS WE
DO FOR LOVE

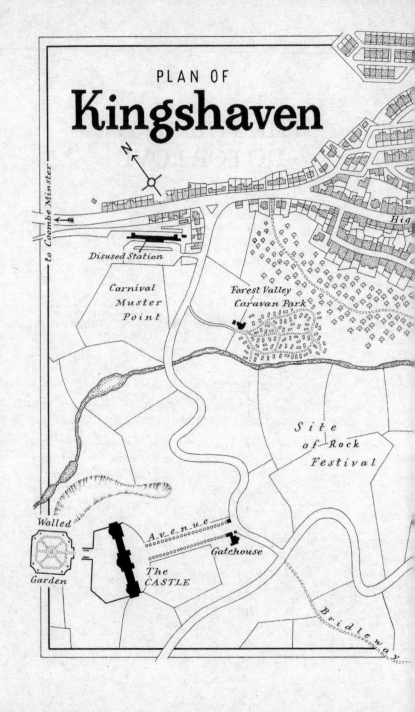

PLAN OF
Kingshaven

N

to Coombe Minster

Hig

Disused Station

Carnival
Muster
Point

Forest Valley
Caravan Park

Site
of Rock
Festival

Walled

Avenue

Gatehouse

The
CASTLE

Garden

Bridleway

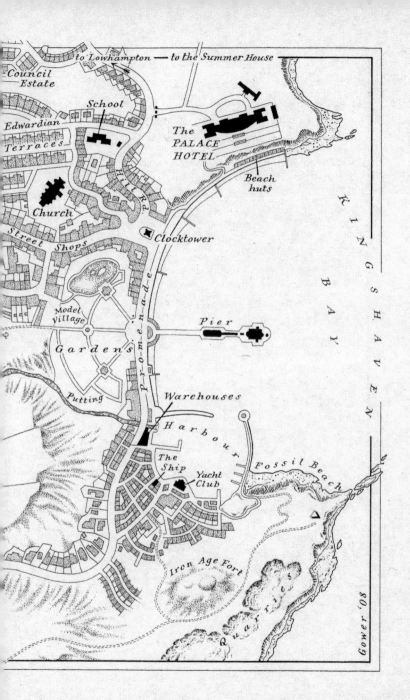

Prologue

1992

It had been a horrible year, thought Libby King, a year in which everything she believed in and held dear had been destroyed. In the misty, grey dawn, with the acrid smell of burning still hanging in the air, Libby King picked her way through the piles of wet rubble that had been the Hall. The charred remains of the grand staircase stopped at the first landing, the Tudor-style oak banister now just a blackened stump. The fire had completely destroyed the main body of the hotel, almost like a physical manifestation of the turmoil that had rocked the Palace in recent months.

And it had all happened in the name of love.

Libby blamed the sixties. People had proclaimed that love was the answer to everything. But her generation knew that love was a notoriously unreliable foundation on which to build the future . . .

Chapter One

19 July 1969

Like most new things, the Summer of Love arrived rather late in the small South Coast town of Kingshaven. Nineteen sixty-nine was already a momentous year: Concorde had flown for the first time, men were about to land on the moon, and, almost as mind-blowing, Kingshaven was hosting its first rock festival. The DJs on the radio were calling it England's Woodstock; there was a mass migration of young people to the South Coast. Kingshaven was where it was at.

Iris stared through the windscreen. The seafront with its pier and clocktower looked exactly as it always had: the beach littered with striped windbreaks; a Punch and Judy show; families splashing in the surf and random shouts of children on the air – but, as Winston's VW van ground its way up the steep High Street towards the site of the Festival, passing straggles of young people with long hair and hippy clothes, Iris became increasingly aware of the thump of bass and the screech of an overstretched sound system. She glanced along the bench seat, wondering how Winston managed to get away with it.

Winston's adoptive father, Sir John Allsop, who owned the fields where the Festival was taking place, had a record of flouting tradition. He had taken in Winston, an abandoned mixed-race baby, who was generally assumed to be the product of a local girl's liaison with one of the

15

black American GIs stationed in Kingshaven during the war. He had also given refuge to a Middle European Jewish professor and his daughter, Claudia. Recently, more scandalously, Sir John had allowed Claudia's lover, Michael Quinn, to live in sin with his mistress and their illegitimate twins at his mansion, known locally as the Castle. But for the residents of Kingshaven, allowing Winston to hold a rock festival in the grounds, bringing hordes of unwashed 'foreigners' to the town, must surely be the final straw.

Iris and Winston had been friends since her first year at grammar school in nearby Lowhampton when she was the only person prepared to sit next to him on the school bus. When Winston had gone off to Oxford University, Iris had penned him weekly angst-ridden screeds detailing the breakdown of her parents' marriage, her father's elopement, and her miserable life in Kingshaven. They'd fallen out of touch when Iris had run away from home, only bumping into each other the previous year in London, on an anti-war march. Now, Winston was letting her doss in the Victorian house he had bought in the run-down area of Clapham until she got her life back together. She was one of the few people who knew how much work had gone into setting up the Festival, and about the only young person in the country who didn't want to go to it, having vowed never to return to Kingshaven when she ran away, five years before, on the back of a Mod's Lambretta. But that morning the phone had rung as Iris was about to leave for work. One minute later and Winston would have been unable to contact her.

At first, she'd assumed he was calling to give her an update.

'You've gotta come down,' said Winston.

The mere thought of the town she'd grown up in seemed to strip away the years, turning Iris back into a bolshy teenager.

'If it were anywhere else—' she began.

'Not for the bloody Festival,' Winston interrupted. 'It's Claudia.'

'Claudia?'

The mention of her father's girlfriend made Iris feel even more brittle.

'Iris, she's very ill . . .'

Iris stared at the diamonds of colour on the floorboards created by the sun streaming through the stained glass in the front door of Winston's house.

'Iris?' Her silence had made him wonder whether she was still listening.

'Yes?'

'Iris, I think she's going to die.' Now Winston was whispering, as if frightened that someone might hear him at his end of the phone.

'Going to die?' Iris repeated, unable to comprehend what he was saying. She knew Claudia had recently had an operation, but she was little more than thirty. Far too young to die.

'The twins are only two years old . . .' Winston's normally smooth voice was choked, staccato.

It sounded almost as if he was crying. Iris couldn't imagine Winston crying.

'I'm on my way,' she'd told him.

The VW van bumped up the long avenue of beech trees and braked outside the front of the Castle, throwing up a spray of gravel. Iris got out, stretched and looked up at the decaying grandeur of the frontage. From an upstairs window, her father stared down at her as if she were an apparition, and then the front door burst open and two tiny children came running out.

The little boy was beautiful and buoyant, with dark curly hair and huge brown eyes, the little girl more wary. She had creamy unfreckled skin but her long red ringlets were exactly as Iris's had been when she was a little girl.

'My name Bruno, mean brown in Italian,' the boy announced. 'Fee Metta mean little flame.'

'My name's Iris,' Iris told him, adding, since he looked as if he expected a reason, 'I don't know why, really.'

She followed them into the house. Out of the glare of sunshine it was unnaturally chilly inside, but the children seemed unaware of the oppressive atmosphere of foreboding. With touching trust, they each slipped a hand into hers as they climbed the great curving marble staircase.

'Mummy,' announced the little boy, as he led the way down a dark corridor to the bedroom. 'This I Wish. She don't know why really.'

The room was furnished with ornate black furniture with gold inlay. The walls were covered in dark wallpaper painted with Chinese scenes. On the bed lay a very pale, thin young woman whose beaming smile made Iris understand instantly how her father could have fallen so irrevocably in love. Although Claudia was frail and unable to move, there was an enchanting energy around her that seemed to radiate life in this strange mausoleum.

When Claudia asked Michael to take the children away so that she and Iris could get to know each other, Iris observed how tightly she clasped Bruno, even though it was clearly excruciatingly painful to do so, and how she demanded a kiss from Fiammetta, the little girl's sombre face lighting up as her mother told her that it was the best kiss in the world. Claudia waved them all the way to the door, only letting go of her smile when the children's voices were safely distant down the passage.

'Could you try to love my children?' she asked Iris abruptly, as if she knew there wasn't enough time for the niceties of polite conversation.

'I already love them.' Iris surprised herself with her instant response.

On the train journey down, she had thought that because she wasn't involved, she might be useful if everyone else went to pieces. But the moment she'd set eyes on the children, joyfully innocent of what was about to happen, and her father, pole-axed by fear, Iris realized that she was involved after all.

'I don't want them always to be surrounded by gloomy old men,' Claudia declared, so categorically that Iris blurted

18

with nervous laughter. 'I want them to have an intelligent woman who cares about them . . . just sometimes . . . ?'

'I'm not sure I'd be any use,' Iris stammered, at once flattered and frightened by the responsibility.

Claudia was struggling to sit up, to plead her case, her beautiful face now a terrible contortion of eagerness and desperation.

'I'll try,' Iris tried to reassure her. 'I promise I'll try,' she said, backing towards the door, calling for her father.

In the small hours of the following morning, Winston, Michael and Iris sat staring at the television screen. Iris wondered if either of the men was finding it difficult to believe, as she was, that the scenes they were witnessing were really taking place on the moon and not in some television studio. The set looked almost amateur, a plain black backdrop, a sandy floor, a stiff, squat doll in a spacesuit climbing down from a rickety stick-and-squeezy-bottle spaceship.

'That's one small step for man; one giant leap for mankind,' crackled the voice of Neil Armstrong.

Michael Quinn jumped suddenly to his feet as if he'd just woken up.

'I must get back to Claudia,' he said.

The whole house seemed to shake as he ran up the stairs, then there was a moment of stillness. Iris held her breath, trying to separate the quiet dread in the house from the excited squawking on the television.

'I'm going outside,' she said to Winston.

He nodded, his eyes still glued to the screen.

The balmy summer air had cooled, and Iris shivered. The moon was still high, still pearly white, much nobler than the images of dusty rubble beaming back to Earth. Iris couldn't get her head around it. Could there really be men up there where mankind had only ever gazed and wondered?

A waft of lavender blew over from the walled garden, settling her fidgety thoughts for a moment, then suddenly the chill, silent air was rent by a terrible primal howl more profound than anything else in the universe.

Iris ran inside, taking the stairs two by two, racing down the corridor to Claudia's room, then stopping outside, the sound of her panting breath drowned out by her father's stricken cries.

She hovered for ages, wondering whether to leave him, or go in. Eventually, she put her head around the door and saw him kneeling beside the bed, gasping and snorting back tears and mucus, asking Claudia's shockingly lifeless body, 'What am I going to do?'

The Morning After

Libby King stood at the window of her mother's day room on the second floor of the Palace Hotel, wondering if everyone her age considered the next generation rather feeble. By the time Libby was twenty-one, she'd lived through a world war, survived on rations, learned to adapt to the constant fear of invasion. If you had faced the imminent overthrow of everything you believed in, it certainly made you think about what you valued and what you were prepared to stand up for. The young men of her generation hadn't had time to indulge themselves singing songs about peace because they'd been too busy fighting for it.

From the bay window, which was a good vantage point for observing the hotel's arrivals and departures, Libby watched as the pop group who had been staying in the Tower Suite for the weekend loaded their gear into Winston Allsop's brightly painted VW van. They were a scruffy bunch with long hair that hadn't been brushed, and cigarettes dangling from their mouths. Libby found it astonishing that crowds of bedraggled young people had travelled long distances to hear this lot at Kingshaven's First Rock Festival (not that there would be a Second, if the King family retained any influence over the district council).

According to Libby's younger sister, Pearl, who followed the latest trends, the lead singer was a sex symbol. He'd brought a girl back with him in the early hours of the morning, and Libby had been so exhausted from the dreadful racket booming across the valley from Sir John Allsop's fields all night, she'd been unable to summon the energy to enforce the hotel rule forbidding overnight guests. Now she recognized the girl as Millicent Bland, the publican's daughter. She was lolling in a mini-skirt against the psychedelic paintings on the van. A carefully chosen word or two from Libby would have seen her off sharply, but it was Libby's eldest son's first day as duty manager, and Libby didn't want to intervene again unless it was absolutely essential.

At least Christopher showed no interest in pop music, Libby thought. One should be grateful for that. Christopher showed very little interest in anything much. Sometimes Libby wondered whether her husband, Eddie, was right about the abolition of National Service. At the time, it had been a huge relief not to have to think of waving off her son in uniform, but now she wondered if a spell in the forces might not have stiffened Christopher up a bit. Despite all the money they'd spent on his education, their eldest son appeared uninterested in finding a viable profession of his own. Libby's hope was that making him deputy manager of the hotel would enable Christopher to learn on the job, and take a little of the responsibility off her own shoulders.

The last few years had not been the easiest in the English hotel trade, an unpredictable business at the best of times. Today had been particularly trying, with the unfortunate, though not unexpected, death in the night of Eddie's ancient mother, Adela. In fact, it was something of a relief that the band had slept in late (which would, in usual circumstances, have incurred a supplementary charge), what with the doctors and the police having to make their reports. And even though for the last few years of her life Adela had been a colourful presence, the departure of a psychedelic VW van at the same time as the hearse would have been an undignified exit. Luckily Mr Adams, the undertaker, had conducted arrangements with his usual courteous efficiency. Sad though it was to say goodbye, Libby couldn't help feeling that the atmosphere in the hotel would be a lot less fractious now. Her own mother, Liliana King, and her best friend, Ruby Farmer, who had a permanent suite at the hotel, had found Adela very trying.

Inadvertently, Libby sighed so heavily that Liliana, who was standing beside her at the window, her steely eyes fixed on the pop group, asked, 'What's wrong now?'

'I do worry about Christopher,' Libby confessed, trying to voice her thoughts tactfully because Christopher was Liliana's first and favourite grandchild. She had taken care of him as a baby in those wonderful early days, when Eddie was still in the Navy and he and Libby had been posted to Gibraltar.

'Sometimes I wonder whether he's really cut out for all this.' Libby waved her hands round. 'He seems to lack the necessary—'

Liliana's famous blue eyes stopped Libby mid-sentence.

'There's only one thing Christopher needs,' she announced with her characteristic assuredness. 'And that's a suitable wife. You and I both know that the Palace Hotel has always been run by women.'

Libby didn't think she had ever consciously thought this before but now that her mother had pointed it out, it did seem rather obvious.

Indeed, the Palace Hotel had been established by a woman, Libby's great-great-grandmother Beatrice, and Libby's resourceful grandmother Maud, who survived several of her sons, and dressed right up until her death in a long black Edwardian dress, had kept the place going against the odds through the First World War. Liliana herself had almost single-handedly restored the Palace's reputation after the scandalous departure of Uncle Rex in the thirties, successfully steering it through a period of requisition by the Air Force during the Second World War, and doing her utmost to keep up an appearance of respectable luxury in those frugal post-war years. And since Libby and Eddie had taken over in 1953, the responsibility of running the place had, in all honesty, fallen to Libby. Eddie was a convivial presence at the bar, but couldn't be trusted with the boring detail of regulations and balance sheets. For a moment, Libby found herself wondering whether it would have been better to have groomed her daughter, Angela, for the role of future proprietor, but she doubted whether Angela could be prised away from Kingshaven Stables, where she spent every waking moment of her life.

The idea of Christopher getting married had never properly occurred to Libby before. He still seemed very young for his age, although she calculated that he was already three years older than Eddie was when she first fell in love with him. At eighteen, Eddie had been a man, but even he, she reminded herself, hadn't been ready to marry for eight long years after that, and she'd had to wait patiently while he played the field before finally seeing the sense in settling for her. Was Christopher playing the field? He had never brought a girlfriend home, but that didn't necessarily mean anything, did it? Now that Liliana had put the idea in her head, Libby could see that with the right girl to support him, Christopher might make a go of it. He was perfectly presentable, after all, and patient with old people, animals and children. Not qualities that were particularly valued in this day and age, but useful in a hotelier, and a husband, for that matter.

There was always the tiny nagging doubt that Christopher was actually interested in girls, but Libby hardly dared even to think it in her mother's presence, for fear of raising the dreadful spectre of Uncle Rex, which always brought a red mist down over Liliana.

The pop group finished loading their equipment into the van and Christopher finally emerged on to the steps of the hotel to see them off. Winston Allsop, who styled himself a music promoter these days, shook Christopher's hand. Against all odds, Winston had become a very smooth operator indeed, and Libby hoped that Christopher was not so charmed that he'd forgotten to check the Tower Suite for breakages or stains on the carpet.

Millicent Bland draped herself over the lead singer in a final, explicit embrace, then prised herself away. As she passed Christopher, she obviously made a cheeky remark because his face immediately turned pink, and then she sauntered nonchalantly down the gravel drive waving her hand in the air without looking back.

With mixed feelings, Libby noted that Christopher's eyes were firmly glued to Millicent's swinging mini-skirted bottom.

Perhaps there was hope after all.

'A *suitable* girl, obviously,' said Liliana King, as if she had been reading Libby's thoughts.

The best section of the beach for building castles was near the water's edge, Iris remembered, as she picked her way through the crowds of sunbathing holidaymakers, tightly gripping her small half-brother and half-sister in each hand, aware that they were attracting curious glances from the locals.

'Wet!' said Bruno, plonking himself down on the flat sand.

'Shall we take your shorts off?' Iris asked.

She really wasn't sure what you were supposed to do, but there were other small children running around naked.

She lay Bruno's shorts on a towel and helped Fiammetta out of hers. The children immediately started to dig with their small shovels while Iris scraped handfuls of sand with her fingers and deposited them into the tin bucket.

It was one of those glorious English seaside days, the sky almost mockingly bright blue, the sea a deeper navy. In the sunlight, the pretty pastel façades of Kingshaven's seafront cottages looked so toy-town perfect, it was impossible to imagine any private tragedies going on behind them.

'Mummy can't come to beach.'

Iris was suddenly aware that Bruno was addressing her, as he determinedly patted sand into the bucket.

What had their father told them? This morning, he had been adamant about getting them out of the house before the undertakers came, saying he wanted them to remember her alive, not as a pale still husk, not in a coffin sliding into the back of a hearse, but it worried Iris that the children's inquisitive brains would wonder why their mother hadn't waved them off, and perhaps they would always expect her back. But when Michael had gone in to speak to them, they had emerged from their bedroom smiling and Iris had remembered how good her father had always been at explaining things when she was little, and how he had welcomed her myriad questions, unlike her own mother, Sylvia, who called her a little nosy parker, or warned her, darkly, that curiosity killed the cat. (The reason Iris had never dared ask for a pet when she was a child was that she believed she had inadvertently murdered one she couldn't even remember.)

'Mummy gone,' Bruno now said.

Iris's heart pounded in her chest waiting for the inevitable moment she would be called upon to speak.

'Heaven,' Fiammetta chipped in.

'Where heaven, by the way?' Bruno suddenly demanded to know.

His language was much more advanced than his sister's, and Iris noticed that he often repeated phrases he had heard adults using without properly understanding why.

What was she supposed to say?

For a moment, Iris was irrationally annoyed with her father for introducing heaven, a convenient comfort provided by a faith he had spent his life denying. He had insisted on raising Iris and her brother, Anthony, as atheists, which had not only been a major cause of dispute with Sylvia, but had singled them out at school, making life difficult, although not quite as bad as his denial of Santa Claus.

Now that very lack of religious education made Iris

ill-equipped to answer the inevitable questions from his younger children. Where was heaven supposed to be anyway? If the children asked her, should she just say that it was in the sky?

'Mummy say heaven in garden.' Fiammetta came to the rescue.

'In garden?' Bruno seemed happy to accept this answer.

Iris breathed again, and turned out a perfect truncated cone of sand.

She was not going to be very good at this. She'd told Claudia, 'I'm not sure I know what to do . . .'

'The children will show you,' Claudia had replied, sinking back into her pillows.

'I cream?' Bruno now asked, his ears tuning into the unmistakable music-box jingle of the ice-cream van a second before anyone else's.

In the distance, Iris spotted the Mr Softee van inching along Kingshaven's pedestrian promenade.

'Yes, let's all have an ice cream,' said Iris.

Julia Allsop stared out of her bedroom window under the eaves of the Summer House, which stood right at the edge of the Palace Hotel grounds, waiting for guests to arrive for her eighth birthday party.

Julia sometimes felt as if she spent most of her life waiting: waiting for Daddy to say something at supper (sometimes he was interested in what she and her brother, James, had been doing, but sometimes he forgot they were there behind his newspaper, and they would sit through both courses in silence, with James making faces across the table at her, trying to get her to laugh). Waiting for her sisters to come home from boarding school, when the house would suddenly feel full again. And, for as long as she could remember, waiting to move out of the Summer House and up to the big house on the other side of the valley, which was called the Castle, even though it didn't look like a castle at all.

Waiting was a funny thing, Julia thought, because you

were doing something but not doing anything at the same time. At the beginning of each school holiday Julia and her brother always waited on platform five at Lowhampton Station. As soon as the rails began to whirr softly with the approaching train, the responsibility of holding on tightly to her little brother's hand took over. They would find an empty compartment, and sit with their legs sticking out over the edges of opposite seats. Only when the train began to move did relief rush through Julia, almost as if she'd wet herself, her body would feel light and flexible again, instead of heavy and solid, and it would finally be safe to get excited about seeing Mummy.

Julia had long ago given up waiting for her mother to come home. Now she understood what she had overheard the gypsy lady saying.

They had been walking along the promenade together when Mummy had spotted the little striped tent.

'Come on!' she'd said excitedly. 'Let's see what the future holds.'

Waiting outside, Julia could hear a strange voice through the fabric.

'A choice lies ahead,' it said.

'Yes?' said her mother.

'To follow the path of true love means turning away from what you most wish for.'

'Are you quite sure?' her mother had asked, sounding distressed, and Julia had put her head round the flap to see that she was all right.

'Give me your hand!' the fortune-teller had drawn Julia in.

Not knowing whether this was the type of stranger one should be kind to or ignore, Julia decided on balance to obey.

'Do you believe in fairy tales?' the old woman had asked.

'Of course!' Julia replied.

'Well, little princess, you will wait a long time for love. But if you are very good, it will come one day.'

'Do you think she meant "Sleeping Beauty" or "The

Princess and the Pea"?' Julia asked as Mummy dragged her along the promenade, but she could tell that Mummy wasn't really listening.

'I'm trying to think!' she'd snapped.

And, the next day, Mummy had gone.

Julia spotted her guests at the far end of the avenue they called the Rhododendron Mile. There were more people in the group approaching the house than Julia had counted when she had helped Mrs Crouch, their housekeeper, lay the plates for tea, but as they drew nearer Julia could see that the extras were not really guests at all, but just two of the hotel porters, who were carrying a very large parcel between them. The group made stately progress, determined by the pace of Julia's Granny Ruby, who lived at the hotel and whose proper name was Mrs Farmer. Accompanying her was Auntie Libby (who wasn't really an auntie at all), who was usually far too busy to attend to anything as unimportant as a children's birthday party, together with her two younger sons, Adrian and Winny.

Julia's brother, James, was first downstairs to open the door.

'What's in that?' he demanded of the two men as they placed their burden on the floor. They were both dressed in black trousers, white shirts and maroon waistcoats with gold buttons and the hotel's insignia in gold embroidery. They were sweating from the heat of the day.

'It wouldn't be your birthday today, now, would it?' one of the men addressed Julia's brother.

'No, but what is it?' James couldn't stop himself asking again.

'Perhaps Julia should open it?' suggested Auntie Libby.

Julia looked to her grandmother for confirmation.

'Are you going to take all day?' huffed Granny Ruby, still breathless from the walk, but Julia knew that if she hadn't deferred, there would have been some sharp comment about manners.

Feeling rather uncomfortable with everyone's eyes upon her, Julia bent down and tried to unpick the knotted string. She could feel the collective impatience in the room pressing on her back, and then James, unable to wait any longer, jumped forward and ripped the paper away in violent jagged strips, leaving the object standing with the string still loosely tied around it.

'The dolls' house!' Julia exclaimed.

Over the top of the roof, which had had a fresh coating of red paint, she noticed that five-year-old Edwin was biting his lip, trying very hard not to cry.

'It's Winny's dolls' house!' protested James, with his usual lack of tact.

'Don't be silly. Boys don't have any use for dolls' houses,' interrupted Auntie Libby. 'As a matter of fact, it was Angela's dolls' house, but she never played with it. We could have sold it, of course. It is worth quite a lot of money, I believe. You couldn't buy one like this nowadays.'

'I've made new curtains,' Granny Ruby announced.

Granny Ruby was very good at sewing because she used to be a dressmaker.

'Look inside,' Adrian chipped in. 'Mummy bought a new family of dolls, so you can pretend it's really new.'

Winny suppressed a sniff.

'Well,' said Mrs Farmer. 'What do you say?'

With trembling fingers, Julia opened the front of the house. The inside was all neat and tidy, as if someone had given it a good spring clean, and everything was in order, not the mess it was when Winny played with it, doing silly things like putting a rubber cow from his farm in the kitchen. On the chairs in the parlour sat a family of dolls. A mummy, a daddy, a boy and a girl. They were all smiling at her.

'Thank you!' Julia turned round, smiling at everyone in turn to impress the sincerity of her gratitude.

'I'm starving!' said James suddenly.

'Is the tea ready?' Mrs Farmer enquired in a loud enough voice for Mrs Crouch to hear in the kitchen.

'Shouldn't we wait for Daddy?' Julia said.

'Yes, where is Jolly?' Auntie Libby asked.

'He's out on business,' James said, repeating the important-sounding phrase their father had used that morning.

'Better start without him, in that case,' Mrs Farmer decided. 'I know what men and business are like . . .'

There was a choice of egg or fish paste sandwiches, and Mrs Crouch had let James make shortbread cut in the shape of stars, which, like most of James's attempts at baking, closely resembled concrete. Granny Ruby had something called dentures in her mouth, which looked like teeth but came out at night and were put into a glass beside the bed (Julia had last Christmas morning made the mistake of going into her grandmother's room while she was still asleep, and been terrified by the sunken parody of her face), which made even the offer of chewy or hard food a cause for complaint. Julia spent most of teatime passing the biscuit plate down the table out of her grandmother's reach, while her brother, aided by Adrian and Winny, passed it back up.

It was quite a relief to get to the cake, a Victoria sponge covered in white icing with a circle of lilac sugar flowers interspersed with eight pink candles.

Julia didn't understand why she always found her eyes brimming with tears when her birthday candles were lit and people started singing 'Happy Birthday' to her. At other children's parties she watched the birthday child's face and saw only the excited anticipation of cramming their mouth with cake, but Julia thought it was a shame that something so pretty and perfect could be so quickly destroyed.

'Make a wish!' Granny Ruby ordered in the moment of hush after Julia had blown out her candles.

Tiny plumes of smoke rose from the still-glowing wicks.

Julia closed her eyes and wished her mother was there.

Mummy had always done a lot of wishing. In autumn, she used to chase falling leaves with childish determination, shrieking with good fortune when she caught one. But she would never tell Julia what she was wishing for, warning, 'It won't come true if I do!'

Whenever it was Julia's turn to wish, she had always wished for whatever it was that Mummy wanted because Mummy seemed to want it so much more than Julia wanted anything.

But when Mummy went away, Julia wondered whether it was the double wishing that had made it happen.

'What are the dolls called?' James asked, kneeling down to play beside her after all the birthday guests had departed.

'Mummy and Daddy,' Julia said, picking up an adult doll in each hand. She remembered all the times she had played with the dolls' house in the nursery in the private wing of the Palace Hotel and wished it was hers. And yet, now that it was, she didn't feel quite as happy as she thought she should, which sometimes happened with surprises. It was one of those things that felt as if they were both hers and not hers at the same time, and made her feel guilty, like her face, which people always said was her mother's. Sometimes, when Julia looked in the mirror, she didn't recognize the face reflected back as anything to do with her at all until she touched her cheek with her hand.

'What shall we call the doll children?' she asked James.

'Julia and James!' her brother shouted.

'I don't think so,' said Julia.

'Why not?'

'I don't think Daddy would like that.'

'Why?'

Julia couldn't answer that. She simply knew it to be true.

Julia got James into his pyjamas, made him clean his teeth and stroked his head until the headlights of her father's car swept round the walls of James's room, signalling that the car had turned off Hill Road and was coming down the track that led down to the Summer House.

When Daddy put a hand on her shoulder and bent to kiss her goodnight, Julia pretended she was asleep, recalling the previous year, when he'd asked why she was crying on her birthday and she'd sat up and tried to explain, and even though she'd been careful to leave out any mention of Mummy, she'd got it all wrong and Daddy had been cross and told her that she was far too young to be so melancholy.

In the days after Claudia's funeral, a minimal ceremony at Lowhampton Crematorium, attended only by Michael, Claudia's father and Winston, there was a peculiar succession of visitors to the Castle.

First, Iris opened the door to Millicent Bland, who was as surprised to see Iris as Iris was by her request.

'I'm glad it's you,' said Milly with a little giggle, after they'd got through the standard tongue-tied condolences. 'It's just . . . well, I was wondering if anyone had found a pair of knickers . . . ?'

'Are they lilac?' Iris asked.

A pair of nylon lace knickers had been hanging from a cup hook in the kitchen since Winston found them in the backstage area when he was clearing up after the Festival.

'Bit embarrassing, but they're new, and they cost me seven and six,' Milly explained.

In her schooldays, Millicent had always been one of the girls who sat at the back of the school bus with a compact mirror in one hand and a wand of blue mascara in the other, attempting to apply make-up as the bus bumped along on the coast road back from Lowhampton. At weekends, Iris remembered, Milly and her gang used to hang around the amusement arcade on the seafront, skinny rib sweaters stretched over their burgeoning pointed breasts, awarding marks out of ten to the 'talent' that went by. Although they were several years older, the gang had acknowledged Iris because she had achieved the school record of detentions, and had been made to stand alone at the front of the school during assembly every day for a whole term.

As Iris handed the panties over, she was dying to ask what Milly would have said if the door had been opened by her father or even Sir John himself, but she was still a little in awe of Milly. When Milly suggested she should come down to the Ship for a drink if she was sticking around in Kingshaven for a while, Iris felt flattered, as if she was in the first form and Milly in the fourth all over again.

The next day's visitor stirred very different emotions. Iris was upstairs tidying the children's bedroom when she heard the sound of a vehicle rolling slowly up the avenue. A black saloon car drew up outside the front door and the back door opened, revealing a pair of slim legs with black patent leather chisel-toed shoes. A woman wearing a silk headscarf and sunglasses eased herself out of the car, smoothing down the skirt of her black suit.

Sylvia Quinn.

Iris had not seen her mother since the day she ran away from Kingshaven. Instinctively ducking down below the window sill, Iris hoped that Sylvia's eyes had missed her as they made a peremptory sweep of the Castle's neglected frontage.

The doorbell rang.

Iris could hear her father's weary footsteps across the hall.

Iris opened the door of the nursery just a crack, as curious as she had been as a child, crouching at the top of the stairs, listening to her parents talking in the front room.

'Sylvia.'

'Michael.'

There was a long silence.

Finally her mother said, 'I came to say how sorry I am . . . for your loss.'

Hearing her mother's disembodied voice, Iris noticed for the first time that Sylvia's accent retained no trace of the North, as her father's did still. It made her wonder whether Sylvia had been taking elocution lessons.

There was a long silence. Iris could almost hear her mother fidgeting.

'Well, you've said it,' her father said coldly.

'Michael!'

This was more of a scream.

Iris suspected he had gone to shut the door, and this was the only way Sylvia could keep it open.

'I'm sorry . . .' Her mother's tone was slightly desperate now.

Her father's sigh was so heavy, Iris could hear it from upstairs.

'What do you want, Sylvia?' he asked.

'Honestly, Michael, I feel terrible . . . I didn't know, you know . . . honest I didn't . . .'

'It's too late now,' he told her.

'But there must be something I can do to help . . . something with the kiddies . . .' Now her speech was racing, the occasional short vowel slipped in.

'I can't help you, Sylvia,' he continued.

'But it's me that wants to help you,' she protested.

'Is it?' Michael asked. 'Do you really think I'd let you near my children?'

Iris winced for her mother.

There was a long pause, then Sylvia lashed out.

'God, I'd forgotten what a self-righteous bastard you are! So bloody high-minded, you don't even think what it might be like for them, poor little mites, with no mummy . . .'

Iris could stand it no longer. She pushed open the door, came out on to the balcony at the top of one of the staircases in the huge hall and shouted, 'Stop it, both of you, for God's sake!'

The words echoed up and down the two majestic marble staircases.

Shocked, Sylvia looked up, lifting her sunglasses.

'Iris?' she said, sounding so bewildered that for a second Iris was filled with the urge to rush down and grab her mother's hand and her father's hand and make things all better like she used to.

'I might have known you'd come running . . . Daddy's girl!' Sylvia sneered.

'Please go,' said Michael.

'Daddy didn't need you when *she* was alive, though, did he? Daddy didn't need anyone else then,' Sylvia yelled up at Iris, who cowered as if the words were striking her, as if the past five years had simply collapsed.

'Get out of my house!' Michael gave Sylvia a sharp push, which caught her unawares and made her stagger backwards and sit down abruptly on her bottom.

Iris came running down the stairs, linked her father's arm, and they both stared as Sylvia's face pulled itself from shock through fury to determined dignity. Her mother picked herself up and brushed the dust from her skirt.

'Perhaps you'd be wise to remember it's not actually *your* house, Michael,' she said, with chilling composure.

Michael closed the door and brushed his hands together, giving Iris a lopsided grin.

'Claudia wanted us to get married, but Sylvia refused to give me a divorce, and now I think she feels guilty,' he explained.

How stupid men were, Iris thought. Any woman could see that Sylvia had refused to divorce him because she'd never stopped loving him. She'd come today, risking humiliation, because she'd thought there was a chance that he might learn to love her again.

For a moment, Iris felt almost sorry for her.

After a week, Winston went back to London.

The Isle of Wight Festival was coming up, Bob Dylan's first concert in three years, and everyone who was or wanted to be anyone in the music business had to be there.

As she waved her friend's painted VW van down the avenue, Iris was more preoccupied by how on earth was she going to carry the weekly shopping up from Kingshaven than by how much she was going to miss him. It was weird how quickly human beings adapted to a different routine. In London, Iris had been waitressing during the day and studying at night school to get the O levels she'd missed out on by running away from home. That all seemed unimportant now. For the time being, she knew she was needed here, and she quite liked the feeling that gave her, even though caring for two strong, bright toddlers was much more demanding than she could ever have imagined. At the end of each day, when Iris tucked them up in bed and left Michael telling them a bedtime story, she was sometimes so tired, she yearned to curl up on the nursery floor herself and drift away as she used to, with her father's voice becoming more and more distant as dreams enfolded her. But it was only after they were asleep that she could attend to the piles of washing-up and washing and ironing two small children generated.

'I feel like I'm doing the washing for the entire world,' Iris hinted heavily one evening as she fed the towels through the mangle ready to hang out on the line the following morning. Her father looked up from his newspaper for a moment, smiled wanly, then returned to it.

There were certain chores that men wouldn't even attempt. Sir John's housekeeper came up twice a week to 'do' for Sir John and the professor, and if Iris hadn't been there, Mrs Burns would probably have done for Michael and the twins as well, but because Iris was a female relation, Mrs Burns allowed her, and Iris would in any case have refused to participate in the exploitation of an old woman with lumbago.

One morning, when Iris was struggling to carry the zinc pail of vegetable peelings to the compost heap, her father called, 'Here, let me take that for you!'

And Iris shouted at him, 'It's *for you* too, you know!'

He shrank back with a wounded look, which she recognized from long ago at home, when Sylvia had nagged him, and which made her feel guilty, because he seemed such a sad figure now, and the last thing Iris wanted to do was make it worse for him.

Michael's loss pervaded the house, almost as if part of him had disappeared as irrevocably as Claudia. Even when he was watching his children, whose delightful antics, Iris had noticed with a strange feeling of pride, made even the crabbiest and most disapproving of Kingshaven residents smile, Michael's eyes didn't seem properly to focus. When the children pestered him or held out their hands to tug him into one of their games, he often did not appear to hear or see what they were asking. Sometimes, Iris caught herself looking at his face with no idea what he was thinking or what the limits of his grief might be, and it frightened her.

Iris suspected the many kindnesses offered by the ladies of Kingshaven were motivated by curiosity as much as charity, or possibly even courtship, since her father was still a very good-looking man and his tragic status appeared to have erased memories of previous misdemeanours. There was a constant supply of home-made cakes from the Women's Institute and hand-knitted winter jumpers for the children; a hideous plastic flower arrangement from the vicar's wife; a set of Tupperware boxes from the wife of the undertaker; a promise of free milkshakes for the children at the Expresso bar, and finally, a goat, although the goat was really more of a guest than a gift.

Its owner, Barbara, appeared at the front door one fine September afternoon. She was a large middle-aged woman whose face was red and sweaty from the exertion of walking the recalcitrant beast up from town. She spoke in a loud, rather well-to-do voice, which initially Iris found off-putting, but there was an endearing vulnerability about her too, as she stood there, with her windblown hair sticking to her damp forehead, trying to control the inquisitive goat and introduce herself at the same time. Barbara explained in rushed detail that she had just been getting to know Claudia when she got ill. Barbara and her husband, Peter, were newcomers to Kingshaven. They too had decided to get out of the rat race. They had both been teachers, but now they were trying to make a go of the Riviera as a guesthouse for vegetarians. Claudia had promised to supply the guesthouse with free-range eggs from the Castle chickens, but with all that had happened – Barbara gestured in a vague way – they hadn't wanted to bother Michael. In fact, they had bought their own chickens now, as well as a goat, but the goat was much smellier and more inquisitive than they could have predicted from the books on goat husbandry, and actually quite unsuitable for the garden of an Edwardian terraced guesthouse.

Iris could barely stop herself laughing.

This morning, Barbara went on, the goat had squeezed through a hole in the fence and demolished next door's prize dahlias, and now the neighbour was threatening to get the guesthouse closed down.

'And so, well, I was hoping, praying, really, that you might see your way to letting the goat stay here . . . Of course I'd come and milk her twice a day . . . The milk's supposed to be terribly good for children—'

'It's really not up to me.' Iris finally managed to cut her off. 'But if you wait there, I'll ask . . .'

Iris was virtually certain that her father's response to this barmy plan would be negative, but by the time she had found him in the library and brought him down, the twins had discovered their visitors, had named the goat Mary, and were clamouring to keep it. To Iris's astonishment, her father agreed.

'Why?' Iris asked him later.

'Claudia would have wanted it,' he said simply.

Iris was burning to tell him that there was no way she was going to add a goat to her responsibilities, but she said nothing, sensing that something in her father had changed, that he was beginning to look outwards again, and that the goat might in some strange way be their salvation.

A few days later, Michael went to collect Claudia's ashes from the crematorium, and when he returned to the Castle, he asked Iris to bring the children into the walled garden.

It was a beautiful late summer afternoon, and inside the walls, the sunshine seemed warmer and more golden. The vegetable patch was beginning to show signs of neglect. The spinach had gone to seed and there was ragwort and cow parsley among the root vegetables. Brown papery heads interspersed fragile overblown blooms of pink and yellow roses that rambled along the red-brick walls. Iris held a child by each hand and walked them around the outer paths, inspecting the herbaceous borders, which were becoming overrun with convolvulus, pausing to pinch lavender and rosemary bushes and sniff the fragrance on their fingers. Michael had not explained to the twins what was happening, but they seemed to know instinctively that they must be quiet. Iris glanced at her father as he opened the tin of ashes, his face frowning with concentration as he tried to scatter them over as much ground as possible. There was no breeze to blow the dust around, no sound except the occasional buzz of a bee. When he was done, he stood, as men sometimes stand, with his hands behind his back, and Iris looked away, not wanting to intrude on his silent farewell.

Then Fiammetta spotted a particularly fine rose.

'Daddy, lift!' she called, and Michael came across to them. He picked his daughter up and tipped her forward to smell the rose, just as he had held her over Claudia to give her a kiss.

Fiammetta closed her eyes and sighed deeply, as if mimicking a particular action she had witnessed, and said, 'Heaven!'

Chapter Two

1970

On the fourth floor of her new department store in Lowhampton, Sylvia Quinn sat watching what was going on in her shop on her closed-circuit television security system. Sylvia Quinn's shop comprised three storeys and a basement. The basement had been used for storage in the shop's previous incarnation as Gillie's of Lowhampton, but Sylvia had it converted into The Underground, a darkened boutique with a separate entrance, loud music and clothes for the younger generation. The three storeys above were laid out more or less traditionally – the ground floor a miscellany of jewellery, haberdashery, perfumery and a small florist's barrow, which gave it a lovely smell; the first floor ladies' fashions; the second, men's and children's; and the third homewares. The décor itself was famously luxurious and original, designed around the art deco fittings of a decommissioned cruise liner, which had been broken up in one of the many backwater inlets of Lowhampton Harbour.

Sylvia suddenly sat forward to get a better look at the image from the children's clothing department where there was a man holding a dress on a hanger up against a little girl.

'It's Mr Allsop, isn't it?'

Sylvia swooped towards him.

He turned round, startled and, she thought, a little flushed to recognize her.

'Mrs Quinn!'

'Sylvia, please,' she said, holding his eyes for a second before turning her attention very deliberately to the little girl. 'And you must be Julia!'

The little girl averted her huge blue eyes shyly.

'She's growing so fast,' said Mr Allsop, with a helpless shrug of his shoulders.

'Daddy doesn't know what to buy me,' the child explained.

'Most daddies don't know one end of a department store from the other,' said Sylvia, smiling knowingly at Mr Allsop. She could almost feel the whoosh of relief from his body that she had come to his aid.

'We'd value an expert opinion . . .' Mr Allsop went rather red.

Sylvia felt a blush creeping across her own face. She'd always wondered if there was a genuine spark between them or whether it was just good manners on his part.

'It'd be my privilege, Mr Allsop,' she said, addressing herself to the task in hand.

'All my friends call me Jolly,' he said, which sounded odd because of him looking so serious and earnest.

'This is new in for the autumn season,' said Sylvia, picking out a shift dress made of purple needlecord with a border of giant orange rickrack. It was part of what Sylvia called her sub-teenage range, but Julia was quite tall for her age. The child sucked in her breath as if she feared that the slightest wrong move might put the desirable garment beyond her reach.

'Would you like to try it on?' Sylvia asked her.

Julia nodded emphatically.

'It's washable at a low temperature, and has that little bit of warmth for those chillier days,' Sylvia explained, pulling the curtain across the cubicle.

The shift was lovely on Julia, but even lovelier was

the broad smile that spread across her forlorn face as she looked in the mirror.

'Isn't it a little bright?' Jolly finally said.

'You could always wear it with a nice white blouse instead,' said Sylvia. 'But perhaps Mrs Farmer wouldn't approve?'

She had an idea that purple and orange would be as objectionable to Mrs Farmer as swearing on television. She might even consider it worthy of a letter to the paper.

'It's really not up to her,' responded Mr Allsop quickly. 'She's a . . .'

'. . . different generation?' Sylvia suggested tactfully.

'Exactly. A completely different generation,' said Mr Allsop. 'We'll take it then, shall we, Julia?'

The little girl nodded eagerly.

'What's the damage?' Jolly asked Sylvia.

Sylvia looked at the label. 'Two guineas,' she said, ignoring his wince. For a split second she weighed up whether to offer a discount, but decided not to risk offending him.

'Are you still living in Kingshaven?' Jolly Allsop asked, as Julia disappeared behind the changing-room curtain again.

'If you can call it living,' said Sylvia. 'What with this place and the little shop to keep an eye on – I've got Millicent Bland looking after things, but she's not really management material – I barely get a chance to sleep there before I'm back here!'

'Hard work,' said Jolly.

'I enjoy it, though,' said Sylvia. 'Anyway,' she added, 'takes my mind off things, and when you've had your problems, it's not so easy to socialize.'

'It certainly isn't,' said Jolly, leaping on the common ground of divorce.

'People see you differently,' Sylvia said.

'You don't want their pity,' Jolly confirmed with feeling.

'A divorcee in her thirties is not everyone's first choice to invite to their cheese and wine party,' Sylvia added, with a tinkle of light laughter.

'Especially not one as attractive as you,' Jolly blurted, and then reddened, as if he had overstepped the mark. 'You'll be moving to Lowhampton then?'

Was there a glimmer of disappointment in Jolly Allsop's eyes?

In her dreams, Sylvia imagined a day when the office space on the fourth floor would be converted into a dream penthouse for her to live in. The floor-to-ceiling windows around its curving frontage presently leaked great patches of rusty dampness on the floor, but they could be repaired. She rather liked the idea of sitting up there looking out over Lowhampton like the captain of one of the tall liners in the docks.

'I can make a fresh start here,' said Sylvia. 'Tomorrow will be better than today!' she added, quoting the Conservative Party slogan that had recently brought Mr Heath into power, although with the dockers about to go on strike, it already seemed a bit of a hollow promise. 'If I can keep this place going,' she added.

Right now, her store with its art deco fittings was all the rage, but fashions changed. She remembered a time when she'd thought Gillie's of Lowhampton the height of class and luxury, but she'd been the one who ended up buying it from the liquidators.

'I'm sure it will be a tremendous success with you at the helm,' said Jolly, with a very flattering smile.

It was a long time since Sylvia had flirted with a man. She'd been married at eighteen. Married before she was old enough to vote. When the law had changed recently to allow everyone to vote at eighteen, Sylvia had wondered whether it wouldn't be more sensible to raise the age you were allowed to get married instead.

For a moment, Sylvia was tempted to pour out all her plans, but instead she held out her hand and said, 'Well, it's been a pleasure . . .' and was pleased to register a look of disappointment on his face.

'Try to leave them wanting more,' was the advice she'd read in an article entitled 'Is There Love After Divorce?'

in one of the more go-ahead women's magazines she subscribed to.

Women's magazines were one of the few bonuses of being single, Sylvia thought. If Michael had caught her reading that sort of thing when they were married, she would have had to put up with all sorts of sneering.

Millicent Bland had locked up the shop on Kingshaven's High Street before she noticed that the sign hanging inside still said 'OPEN' in pink art deco-style letters on a black background. She sighed, opened the door again, and turned it over. It was pretty obvious that the shop was closed – blinds down, door closed – but Sylvia Quinn was finicky about details, and Miss Potter, who saw everything from the post office across the road, was always looking for a black mark to put against Milly's name. Audrey Potter disapproved of girls who wore short skirts, or long skirts, or trousers, or make-up, or smoked, or chewed gum, or did any of the things Milly could never imagine Miss Potter doing, even in her youth, if she'd ever had one. Milly, who was twenty-two, couldn't remember the postmistress ever looking any different from how she looked now. She was a dried-up old spinster, probably a lesbian, Milly and her friend Una had decided recently when it had been sheeting down with rain so hard they could shriek and giggle under the shelter on the promenade with no fear of anyone overhearing them.

This evening, the weather was more suitable for the low murmur of pleasantries, as the air was balmy and full of the kind of sunshine that made you smile.

Una Adams, Milly's best friend since the infants' class at St Mary's Primary School, was sitting on their usual bench near the pier, dressed in the navy skirt and patterned blouse she had to wear as a cashier at the bank. That was one thing about working for Sylvia Quinn, Milly thought, at least the uniform didn't look like a uniform because Sylvia Quinn designed it herself, and changed it every season. This year's summer outfit was a pinafore dress in a printed lawn, with crisscross straps, which you were supposed to wear with a white shirt underneath, but before leaving the shop Milly had taken off the shirt, and her bra, making the pinafore into a sundress, leaving her shoulders and back mostly bare.

Una smiled as Milly approached and offered her a cigarette from her box of ten Consulate.

'Good day?' she asked.

'Quiet,' said Milly. 'How about you?'

'Busy,' said Una. 'Mostly foreigners.' Which was the way the people of Kingshaven referred to holidaymakers, daytrippers, and anyone who had lived in the town for less than twenty years. 'You don't know how lucky you are,' said Una. 'Reading magazines all day.'

'You're the lucky one, meeting all those people,' Milly replied.

Working in the bank, Una was always first to know when anyone moved into town, where they lived, and approximately where they stood on the social ladder.

Milly could count on the fingers of one hand the number of evenings in the year where their conversation did not start in exactly this way. The first day of the Summer Sale was usually busy for Milly because Mrs Quinn offered some very enticing bargains, and in the run-up to Christmas there was a lot of trying on of outfits for the dinner dance at the Yacht Club that was the highlight of Kingshaven's social calendar, but most days it was quiet, because anyone who wanted to wear Sylvia Quinn clothes now tended to go to the big new store in Lowhampton, which carried the full range. Milly wondered whether Sylvia wouldn't be better off selling things in the Kingshaven shop that there was a demand for, like school uniform, stockings, and sanitary towels under the counter, as Mrs Farmer had always done when she had owned the shop. But Sylvia Quinn had built the business up herself and wasn't about to listen to anyone else's opinions.

Milly and Una stared down at the beach. There were a few families with small children making the most of the

45

sunshine. The caller's megaphone in the Bingo Hall on the pier was just audible in the still air.

'Legs eleven! Doctor's orders, number nine!'

'Why is nine doctor's orders?' Milly asked idly.

'The new doctor was in today,' said Una, who often sounded like she knew things even though she didn't. 'Seems very nice,' she added.

'How old?' Milly immediately wanted to know.

'Youngish.'

'Married?'

'Married with a baby,' Una confirmed. 'He's got a beard. Neat and trimmed because he's a doctor, obviously.'

'Still, a beard,' said Milly.

Neither of them were keen on hairies, though Una's fiancé, Simon Ironside, had recently been experimenting with a moustache, which Una had demanded he shave off after her face was so scratched, her manager had asked if she'd caught the sun.

'Talent alert!' Milly nudged Una.

Walking in their direction along the promenade towards the Harbour End was a young man they'd never seen before.

'He's working at the Palace,' Una whispered. 'His name is Mr Balls.'

'Mr Balls. Are you taking the mickey?'

'Shush!'

They both fell silent and looked straight out to sea as the man sauntered past, whistled appreciatively under his breath, then performed an about-turn, as if something had just occurred to him. He leaned against the railing between their bench and the pier.

'I wonder if you ladies would be able to help me?' he called.

'What with?' Milly asked, making Una giggle.

'Is there anything to do here in Kingshaven?'

Una giggled even more.

'Depends what you're after,' said Milly.

'There's putting,' Una volunteered.

46

'Putting,' echoed the man.

'And bingo,' she added, as the call 'Two little ducks, twenty-two!' drifted over from the pier.

'I've never been much of a one for the bingo,' said the man.

'There's walking,' said Milly. 'If you like walking.'

She allowed herself to look at him directly, and saw that her boldness surprised him. He held her eyes, challenging her to be the first to look away.

The thought shot into her brain from nowhere. 'This is the man I am going to marry', and then she did look away, unnerved, almost believing that he had heard her think it too. When she dared to look at him again, he was smiling at her as if they'd known each other for ever.

'There's always the pubs,' said Una, oblivious to all this.

'It's too nice an evening for sitting in a pub,' said the man, still looking at Milly.

'The Anchor has a beer garden,' said Una.

The nerve of it, thought Milly. Bad enough that Una was muscling in like some eager tour guide, let alone recommending the rival pub to Milly's dad's.

'Aren't you supposed to be meeting your fiancé this evening?' Milly asked her friend pointedly.

His name was Gerard Balls.

'Gerard,' Milly repeated.

'Everyone calls me Gerry,' he said.

He came from Tipperary, he told her as he walked her back along the promenade to the Harbour End.

'That's a long way,' Milly said, not intending to make the joke she immediately realized everyone must make.

His uncle had managed Kingshaven Stables years ago, and his cousins had all grown up here. Their name was Carney.

'The Carney boys!' said Milly, remembering her old school class. 'There were dozens of them!'

Most of the family were in horses now, and Gerry had set his heart on being a jockey himself, but he'd grown too tall,

47

so he'd had to look for something else as his passport to the wider world. Mr Carney had written to Mrs Libby King to ask if she needed any help at the hotel and she'd written back to say they needed a bartender for the summer.

'So you're just here for the summer?' Milly felt unaccountably disappointed. The air was chillier now. Gerry took off his jacket and hung it around her shoulders, and she could feel her bare skin puckering into goose bumps against the rough tweed, and smell the horses in it. Ridiculous, she thought, to be regretting his leaving when they'd only met an hour before.

The twins were getting a bit big to push up the hill in the twin pushchair, and if Iris let them get out and walk, Bruno always ran off and Iris never knew whether she should run after him, leaving Fiammetta obediently holding the side of the pushchair, or trust that he would find his way back.

They had been to the beach and the Victoria Gardens so often that one day Iris decided to take them on an adventure to Lowhampton. It was the first time the children had been on a bus and they both waited at the bus stop unusually quietly. When the bus pulled up beside them, emitting a loud sigh as the doors opened, Iris felt the grip of both small hands tighten with alarm, and a certain hesitance as they moved forward in the queue to climb aboard.

'It's green like a great big dragon!' As usual, Bruno found a way of articulating their fear.

He sat very nicely next to Iris on the journey, looking eagerly out of the window, describing things that were new to him.

'Look at that house with a haystack on top! Look at that elephant cloud!'

But when they reached Lowhampton bus station and began to walk towards the quay, Iris could feel his tug becoming more impatient as she and Fiammetta paused to look in the shop windows along the cobbled street. The delicious smell of hot pasties drew them up a couple of steps into an old-fashioned baker's, and as Iris was distracted for a moment searching in her purse for the right change, Bruno slipped her hand.

The press of people queuing to buy their lunch hadn't noticed a three-year-old boy wriggling through their legs, and exchanged glances as Iris called his name with increasing disbelief.

Out on the street, there was no sign of him.

'Which way?' Iris asked a bewildered Fiammetta, grabbing her by the hand and running towards the sea.

The terror was like nothing Iris had ever experienced before as she called Bruno's name with increasing volume and desperation. Nothing in her life had ever been as important as finding him.

There were fishing boats tied up along the quayside, their holds a long way down because of the low tide, and between them, wells of water as dark as oil into which Iris peered, both wanting and not wanting to see Bruno.

No sign. No indication of where to look. No hope.

'Bruno!'

Hearing Iris's voice full of tears, Fiammetta began to cry too, and then she stopped and pointed.

A hundred yards further down the quay, next to a ticket kiosk for boat trips to the Isle of Wight, a small crowd had gathered. Iris barged breathlessly to the centre where Bruno had climbed to the top of a pile of empty lobster pots and was precariously balanced and singing, 'I'm the king of the castle!'

A concerned mother with a child in a pushchair was asking, 'Where's your mummy?'

'I don't have a mummy. I have an I Wish!' Bruno yelled.

Clambering up to reach him, Iris grabbed his hand so hard he screeched with offence that she was hurting him, and her heart beat twice as fast as usual as she hugged him tightly and shouted with relief into his dark curly hair, 'Don't you ever do that again!'

Occasionally, at weekends, Winston came down in his van and drove them along the coast to Havenbourne, buying them hamburgers in a steamy Wimpy bar, and providing an endless supply of pennies for the children to drop into the Penny Falls machine in the amusement arcade.

In the evening, Iris and Winston walked down to the Harbour End together, bought fish and chips in newspaper, and sat on the harbour wall talking as they had done as teenagers. There was something profoundly calming about the rhythm of waves, the smell of seaweed, the mournful call of a seagull. Even with the cold of the stone seeping through her corduroy jeans into the base of her spine, Iris tried to make her chips last as long as possible. It was so good to talk to someone of her generation.

'When are you coming back?' Winston asked her.

'I'm not sure,' Iris told him.

Privately, she'd decided that she would leave once her father started to work again. Writing had always been his way of coping – through the unhappiness of his marriage to Sylvia, through his anxiety when Iris disappeared. If he started writing, she would know that he was beginning to deal with his grief, but so far her father had shown no signs of wanting to work. Whenever she took him a cup of tea in the library, she would find him simply staring into space.

'I don't like to think of you here,' said Winston.

'I promised Claudia.'

'Yes, but . . .' Winston clearly wanted to say something, but stopped.

'But . . . ?' Iris pressed him.

'Claudia chose this daft lifestyle . . . you don't have to. I mean, for heaven's sake, Iris, a goat!'

'I've grown quite fond of Mary,' Iris told him. 'And Barbara.'

'What's Barbara?' asked Winston, fearing another animal.

'Barbara's the woman who owns Mary. She comes to milk her every day. She's trying to convert me to vegetarianism. Apparently, it's healthier.'

Winston rolled his eyes skywards, as if Iris had gone a bit mad too.

'You can't get stuck here with all these cranks.'

'I'm helping Dad get back on his feet.'

'Maybe he'd get back on his feet quicker if you weren't here.'

'Bloody hell, so it's my fault, is it?'

'I didn't mean that.'

'Sorry,' she said.

'No, I'm sorry,' said Winston, putting his hand over hers.

Iris stared at it, feeling the warmth of his palm on the back of her hand, remembering how she had longed for him to hold her hand when she was in the first form and he in the fifth, even though (or perhaps because) her mother would have had a fit. But he never had. When she'd run into him again on the anti-war demo in Grosvenor Square she had seen his surprise that she had become a woman. They'd shared a stoned snog back at his pad, but she'd pulled away confused, because she'd been Clive's girlfriend at the time.

Winston had never tried again. Now, she didn't know if she'd even want him to. It was almost as if they knew each other too well, and their friendship had gone beyond the point where they could risk it for sex. But sometimes she ached for the touch of another person's skin against hers, the heat of another person's body to warm the sheets that were always so cold at the Castle.

'You can't be their mother, you know,' Winston said, lifting his hand to eat another chip.

Her hand felt suddenly exposed, stranded.

'I'm not trying to be their mother,' Iris replied sharply.

'OK, OK . . .' Winston realized he had touched a nerve. 'It's just I've got an empty room in my house . . .' he attempted to lighten the exchange.

'If it's rent that concerns you, let someone else have it,' Iris lashed out at him. 'It's always money with you, isn't it?'

She knew this was unfair since he'd never asked her for any contribution.

51

'I didn't mean—' Winston recoiled.

'Why d'you keep saying things you don't mean?' Iris snapped.

'I'm sorry,' said Winston, screwing up his chip paper and throwing it at a bin.

It went in. Winston was the sort of person whose litter always went in the bin. Iris didn't even bother trying to throw hers. They walked all the way back to the Castle in silence.

Millicent Bland was lying next to Gerry Balls on top of the counterpane on Sylvia Quinn's bed in the apartment above the shop on the High Street. Although it was understood that she was allowed to use the toilet in Sylvia's flat upstairs, and make herself a cup of tea in the kitchen, Milly knew very well that the living quarters were strictly out of bounds, even though it had never been explicitly stated. She wondered now why she had resisted the idea of getting in between the sheets. Sheets could be laundered, whereas she doubted any marks on the counterpane would come out without drycleaning, and that would mean taking it to Lowhampton. Sylvia would be bound to notice the counterpane gone for a week. Milly would probably lose her job, but what the hell! It was worth it. She'd known from the moment she first set eyes on him.

They both stared shell-shocked at the ceiling, as if the ferocity of their passion had flung them apart.

'How many blokes have you had?' Gerry broke the silence.

Milly longed to be able to reply that he was the first, because the feelings she had for him were so over-whelmingly different from anything she had previously experienced, but the true number, she suspected, was three. She wasn't sure whether the rock star, Dexter Strange, technically counted. After giving her the snog of her life at the backstage party at the end of the Rock Festival the previous year, he had become disappointingly philosophical when they returned to the Palace Hotel and

52

had insisted on reading her a poem he had written. After that – or possibly during – she must have fallen asleep and woken the next morning to find him in bed beside her, phoning down to reception to announce that he was intending to stage a Love In for Peace. But just as they'd begun to get down to it, foreplay had been curtailed by the arrival of the police, albeit on a routine visit following an overnight death at the hotel, and not in search of drugs as the suddenly cowardly Dexter Strange had feared. Milly still felt slightly cheated that the predominant memory of her brush with rock and roll's wildest man (as *NME* had dubbed him), was Dexter Strange whimpering 'Have they gone yet?' through the keyhole of the ensuite bathroom.

Now, after Gerry, Milly finally understood what it was her girlfriends meant when they talked about saving themselves for The One, which had previously seemed a pointless restraint when you'd gone to all the trouble of getting yourself on the Pill.

Milly turned her head on the pillow to look at him. What they had just done had been so marvellously, deliciously accomplished – everything fusing together as if their bodies were one – there was no way he, who clearly had a great deal of experience, could mistake her for a virgin.

'One or two,' she heard herself saying in a shy voice, which somehow made it sound like many more.

'Just the one or two!' Gerry echoed. 'Now, tell me, would that be one or two? Am I the second or the third?'

His Irish way of pronouncing a 'th' made it sound like 'turd'.

Milly giggled. 'What about you?' she challenged.

'Let me see,' said Gerry, screwing up his face in concentration, and holding out both hands to count silently on his fingers.

Milly watched horrified as, having counted all ten digits, he started on his right hand again. She found herself growing jealous of each representative finger as it pointed in the air, each little smile of memory that flashed across his face, each little blink and sigh of 'Oh, yes!'

'How many?' she demanded, grabbing his hands.

'Just the one,' he said, leaping on top of her and kissing her again, sending a shudder of happiness right down the centre of her body.

'Or two! he added with a wink, as he rolled off again, swung his legs over the side of the bed, and bent over to pick up his Y-fronts. Milly gazed at his long white back, wanting to feel each bump of his vertebrae, to press against him, grab his thick fair hair and yank his mouth on to hers. Tentatively, she touched his spine. Watched the skin pucker and go smooth again.

'They'll dock my wages if I don't get back now.'

He turned round and looked lustfully at her still lying naked on the bed.

'I'll be seeing you, then,' he said.

Every sinew of her body wanted to shout 'When?' at him, but she knew what sort of a man he was. Knew she had to play it cool to stand a chance.

'Suit yourself,' she said.

A gorgeous half-knowing, half-bashful smile spread across his face. It was a bit like being in bed with Robert Redford himself. Nobody should be as good-looking as he was, she thought.

'Well, aren't you just the little minx?' he said approvingly, and then he leaned over and rewarded her with another extravagant, tonguey kiss. 'I'll be seeing you, Milly Minx,' he said.

Minx was a nickname she could get used to, Milly thought, lying as still as she could, trying to hold the memory of his voice, his taste, his smell in the room for as long as possible. Much better than some of the names she'd been called. People said the Pill gave women freedom, but sometimes Milly thought it was more like freedom for the men. If you slept with them, they thought you were fast, and if you didn't, you were frigid.

Just as she remembered that she should tell him to use the back door, the bell pinged over the front. Now, she'd

54

really be for it, Milly thought. If Audrey Potter hadn't been suspicious when he sauntered in, she'd certainly have registered that he hadn't left when Milly shut the door for early closing. And even if she'd missed all that, she was bound to have seen him leaving. The thing was, Milly didn't seem to care. Her body felt so wonderful and her head felt so happy, nothing else mattered. It suddenly occurred to her that this was what it felt like to fall in love, and instead of wanting to hide it, she could barely stop herself rushing naked on to Sylvia Quinn's balcony and proclaiming it to everyone on Kingshaven High Street.

The saloon bar of the Ship Inn was empty, but the noise and laughter coming from the public bar seeped over the top of the frosted-glass panelling that separated the two bars. Milly poured two halves of lager and lime and brought them over to the table.

'Don't be silly. On the house,' she said, as Iris got out her purse.

Milly's dad, Percy, was the publican.

They both sat sipping their drinks in the empty room, neither of them quite knowing how to begin a conversation. Milly lit a cigarette, blew a long stream of smoke out through her nostrils.

'Dad doesn't like me going in there,' she said, indicating the public bar with her thumb. 'Doesn't think it's very ladylike!'

Iris smiled.

On the other side of the partition, an Irish voice was regaling the bar with amusing anecdotes.

'Do you know Gerry Balls?' Milly asked Iris.

Iris shook her head.

'He's the bartender at the Palace.'

'Isn't it a bit coals to Newcastle?' Iris asked.

'What?'

'Bartender going to the pub,' Iris explained.

'What else is there to do in Kingshaven?' asked Milly.

They both laughed, as if conscious of the irony that if

there were anything else to do, they would probably be doing it, rather than having a drink with someone they had little in common with.

'How are those kiddies?' asked Milly, sucking on her cigarette again. 'Everyone thinks you're ever so good to look after them.'

'I didn't really have a choice,' Iris said, uncomfortable with the compliment.

In all the time she'd lived there, Iris had never enjoyed the approval of Kingshaven people. Being a redhead was bad enough; being clever was worse. At primary school, Iris had always come top of the class, despite all Sylvia's warnings about tall poppies. As a gangly teenager, she'd consorted with the half-coloured boy, then run off with a gang of Mods who'd kicked down Little Kingshaven, the model village in the Victoria Gardens. She was quite sure she'd never be entirely forgiven for that.

The conversation had come to another standstill.

'Gerry's so funny,' said Milly, straining to hear what was being said in the public bar. 'Do you have a boy-friend?'

'Not at the moment,' Iris told her.

'Aren't you going out with Winston Allsop?' Milly asked. 'Saw you together the other day . . .'

Nothing went unnoticed in Kingshaven.

'We're just friends,' Iris said, although in fact she still felt slightly aggrieved by Winston's remarks.

'Have you ever been in love?' Milly asked.

'I was once,' Iris told her.

'Come on, who was it?'

'His name was Clive,' Iris told her, a shiver running down her spine.

'Isn't it the best?' said Milly, oblivious to Iris's discomfort.

'At first,' said Iris warily.

'Why did you split up?' Milly wanted to know.

'He went to prison,' Iris said.

'Blimey. What for?'

Iris could see Milly was impressed. 'Conspiracy to murder,' she said.

Milly stared at her in awe.

Clive was in prison, so it wasn't a complete lie, Iris told herself, even if that wasn't the reason they'd split up. But she felt awkward now, like she used to standing at the front in assembly at Lowhampton Girls' Grammar School, because she'd gone too far in her attempt to impress with her badness and would now have to live with the consequences, condemning herself to the role of Kingshaven's renegade all over again, when there was a moment when she could have been the prodigal daughter.

'I'd prefer you didn't tell anyone,' she said to Milly.

'Cross my heart,' said Milly.

'What about you?' Iris asked finally, and then it was Milly's turn to reveal what she'd obviously been dying to tell her, Iris belatedly realized, when she'd enquired about Iris's love life.

Milly's new boyfriend was standing on the other side of the partition, but it was still a secret because her dad thought Irish was almost as bad as coloured, even though he had to admit that Gerry had the gift of the gab.

The unmistakable look of giddy triumph on Milly's face made Iris remember what it had been like with Clive in the beginning.

'You won't tell, will you?' Milly asked. ''Cos I'd get into all sorts of trouble and I'll probably lose my job!'

'Why?' Iris wanted to know. Surely you couldn't get sacked for engaging in pre-marital sex.

'The thing is . . .' Milly beckoned Iris's ear to her lips and whispered about the damp patch on Sylvia's counterpane.

'Oh dear, Sylvia won't like that,' said Iris, laughing.

'Oh God! I forgot she was your mother!' Milly said. 'You won't tell, will you?'

'Cross my heart,' Iris assured her, sealing the bond of confidentiality between them.

As Iris walked back up to the Castle from the Harbour End in the fast falling dusk, she found she kept looking instinctively over her shoulder, as if by allowing herself to say Clive's name, she might have conjured his presence.

It was over two years since she'd left him now, but she'd never quite felt safe since, especially after he'd been arrested, and she'd read about the extent of the criminal activity he'd been involved in. The tentacles of the organization he worked for had a long reach. When one of the brothers who owned the Zebra Crossing nightclub, which Clive managed, was taken down, the papers reported that he'd shouted 'See you later!' menacingly up to the public gallery.

In London, Iris had never quite rid herself of the feeling that Clive, or one of his associates, was watching her. Sometimes she wondered if her stay in Kingshaven was the selfless sacrifice with which people credited her, or just a different form of running away.

Chapter Three

1971

The last day of Kingshaven Regatta Week was traditionally celebrated with a parade. What had originally started as a simple procession involving the military band, and members of the lifeboat crew rattling buckets for donations, had developed over time to include a dog show, fun events, and a ram roast at the Harbour End culminating in a fireworks spectacular.

Julia Allsop awoke that morning tingling with excitement about her chances in the Swimathon. She knew she must be in with a chance in the children's section of the race between Harbour and Pier because she could swim a hundred lengths of the Palace Hotel pool without stopping and had even taught herself to do butterfly stroke, though her brother, James, said she looked more like a mad hippopotamus than a butterfly. Perhaps they would win the sandcastle competition. James was good at finding the right spot on the beach where the moat would fill up with water when the tide came in. She was good at finding shells to decorate the castle with. In that cosy moment just after waking up, when she was still pretending to be asleep, Julia pictured a photograph in the *Chronicle* with the two of them standing on either side of a magnificent crenellated creation.

When Daddy took them up to the Palace Hotel, however, to get into the costumes that Granny Ruby had made for them, Julia suddenly realized that she was never going to be allowed to go on the beach in the long velvet dress, and Daddy had probably forgotten her swimming costume anyway.

'Who am I supposed to be?' she asked, as Granny Ruby, placed a stiff little embroidered cap on to her head and stood back to assess the costume.

'You're Guinevere,' Mrs Farmer replied through a mouthful of hairpins. 'Adrian is King Arthur. Winny and James are knights.'

'This is Excalibur!' said James, brandishing a wooden sword, which had been painted silver.

Julia held her breath as the sturdy blade, which was far too heavy for James to wield with any control, sliced dangerously close to their grandmother. One inch further, she thought, and it would have jolted Granny Ruby's head, and she might have choked to death on the hairpins.

'Who's Guinevere?' Julia asked.

Granny Ruby heaved a sigh. 'Don't they teach you anything at that school?' she asked. 'King Arthur was England's first king and Guinevere was his lady. Or was she Sir Lancelot's? Oh, anyway,' she concluded impatiently, 'one of that lot.'

The hotel foyer looked a bit like one of those busy illustrations in Julia's history book at school of a cross section of a house and all the different types of people in it. Auntie Libby was wearing a ruff round her neck and a dress with a huge skirt; Uncle Eddie had big padded breeches. There was even a costume for Daddy – a red tunic and big velvet hat resembling a knitting bag turned upside down. Julia took a picture of him in her head, so that she could describe the silly outfit to Mummy when she next saw her. It was just the sort of thing that cheered Mummy up.

When Mummy had lived with them, they always used to go down to watch the Carnival, but Julia couldn't remember Daddy ever bothering with it before because the Carnival was more for town people. This year the Palace Hotel was entering a float for the first time – something to do with keeping an end up – and Daddy always did what the Kings did.

Julia wasn't quite sure why town people were different from the Kings, but they definitely were. Privately, Julia and James often wished they could be town people, because town people seemed to have more fun. They had come to the conclusion that they must be half, or at least a quarter, town people anyway, because Mummy had grown up in a flat above a shop on the High Street, but it was not something they could confirm with Daddy, because he didn't like it when they talked about Mummy.

Julia sometimes felt as if they were in-between kind of people. Neither town, nor King.

Europe, the theme of this year's Carnival, had been the subject of heated debate on the letters page of the *Kingshaven Chronicle*. The idea had been suggested by the mayor, Mr Moor, in honour of the successful twinning negotiations with Reine La Plage, a similar-sized town on the French coast. It was enthusiastically supported by the younger members of the council, who looked forward to opportunities for wine-tasting weekends and other cultural exchanges between the two towns. But there had been vehement opposition from the generation who believed that Kingshaven had enjoyed its finest hours resisting European influence.

Iris's only dilemma had been thinking of costumes for Bruno and Fiammetta to wear. She was no seamstress, and had an antipathy to the whole idea of dressing up, stemming from a childhood being stitched into ever-more-ambitious costumes by her mother, Sylvia Quinn. At the same time, Iris knew just how uncomfortable it felt as a child to be different (they had always been seen as 'foreigners' by Kingshaven society, because of coming from the North and her father's unorthodox views) and she thought Bruno and Fiammetta already had enough to cope with, being both motherless and illegitimate, without being the only ones without costumes.

Fortunately, Winston, who was down for the Bank Holiday weekend, came to the rescue. Winston spotted the blue and white striped T-shirts in the window of the chandlery at the Harbour End and drove her down to buy two of the smallest size for the twins and three adult ones for Iris, Michael and himself.

'We're back!' Iris called when they returned.

There was a woman with her father in the parlour. She was tall and rangy, with long thick brown hair, which she tossed around a lot, and she exuded a kind of glamour, even though she was dressed in jeans and a plain white shirt.

Initially Iris mistook the palpable air of tension between her father and the woman for attraction. All sorts of questions ricocheted around her head as she tried to work out how she would feel about Dad having a new woman. Would it be good for the twins? Would it affect the special closeness Iris had developed with them?

'My daughter, Iris,' her father said. 'And Winston Allsop. This is Josie. Josie was a friend of Claudia's,' Michael Quinn explained, as if to distance himself from her.

Josie smiled. She had very straight even teeth.

'Claudia left instructions for me to save the children from a life dominated by gloomy old men!' she announced with a faint American accent. 'And I was on my way back from friends in Cornwall when I saw the sign to Kingshaven and thought I'd drop by.'

'Claudia said exactly the same thing to me!' Iris blurted out, astonished.

'Did she?' Michael frowned at this revelation.

The atmosphere in the room grew invisibly more awkward.

'Claudia and I were at Cambridge together,' Josie explained. 'Long before she knew Michael.'

'As a matter of fact,' Michael corrected, 'I knew Claudia before she went to Cambridge.'

'Did you?' asked Iris. Now it was her turn to be surprised.

'I met her at the Palace Hotel, at their Coronation Party.' Michael smiled distantly as if the memory gave him pleasure.

'In nineteen fifty-three? You knew her all the time we were here?' Iris demanded.

'Just about. Obviously we weren't . . .' Her father prevaricated, conscious that he had revealed too much.

'Even so,' Iris snapped.

She'd always dated her father's knowledge of Claudia from that time they met her on the promenade in the terrible winter of 1962, when the snow was knee deep and Kingshaven had been cut off from the outside world. Had he known her almost ten years by then?

'Well,' said Winston diplomatically. 'None of that matters now.'

'No,' both Iris and Michael agreed quickly.

But what a different complexion it put upon the steady decline of her parents' marriage, Iris thought, and the hell they had all been through. Strangely, it seemed to matter quite a lot.

'Coffee, anyone?' said Winston.

'I'll help you,' said Michael quickly.

This public display of good manners further irritated Iris, as neither of them ever usually lifted a hand to make a pot of tea or help with the washing-up.

'How very domesticated,' said Josie, winking at Iris, as if she knew.

Josie was a journalist whose full name Iris recognized as the by-line on some provocative articles she'd read in the Sunday newspaper. She had been one of the organizers of the first Women's Liberation March from Hyde Park to Downing Street the previous spring. The police had estimated that there were four thousand demonstrators, but Josie claimed there had been many more.

Eager to prove her own left-wing credentials, Iris told her about how she had been on the Anti-Vietnam march when she lived in London and how she'd recently asked Kingshaven library order a copy of *The Female Eunuch*.

'What on earth are you doing in this dump?' Josie demanded to know.

Iris wasn't quite sure whether she meant the Castle, which was badly in need of some repairs, or Kingshaven itself.

'Dad was in pieces and the children were so little . . .' Iris stuttered.

'And you thought you could make things right? People from a broken home often try to be healers.'

Was this true? Iris hadn't consciously thought of the last couple of years in that way. When she was little she had always been the one in the family who could cheer her father up when he was in one of his moods, enjoying the joint reward of his smile and her mother's gratitude for her efforts. But as she'd grown older, the challenge had increasingly eluded her, and when he'd eloped with Claudia, Iris had been left with a sense of guilt, as well as the feeling that Sylvia blamed her for failing to keep her father with them. Was her selflessness now really a selfish attempt to re-establish that special bond with her father?

'Or perhaps you were trying to make amends . . .' Josie speculated.

'Make amends?' Iris echoed.

'. . . for running away and upsetting everyone so much. Poor Claudia. Just when she thought she'd finally landed her man, then you disappear and he turns into a misery guts. But I suppose that's what you wanted,' Josie smiled.

Iris found it disconcerting that Josie seemed to know so much about her, even though they'd only just met. Had she been trying to punish her father when she ran away? Iris wondered. Had she thought that it would serve him right for abandoning her when he went to live with Claudia? Had she wanted him to know what it was like?

'Perhaps it was,' she admitted, feeling rather undermined by Josie's insights.

'I'm only joking,' Josie told her. 'Michael's always been

good at getting women to feel sorry for him. Scratch an "angry young man" and you'll find a misogynist.'

How amazing to be so confident in your opinions. Iris suddenly wanted more than anything else for Josie to think she had interesting thoughts too.

'Winston and I were founder members of the Kingshaven Civil Rights Movement,' she said, as Winston returned to the room bearing a tray of coffee mugs.

'The only members in fact,' Winston said, smiling his broad smile across at Iris.

'And Winston used to live in a squat, didn't you?' said Iris.

'But now you're a fully paid-up property-owning capitalist,' said Josie.

'As I imagine you are,' Winston responded coolly to the implicit challenge, and there was suddenly a frostily competitive atmosphere in the room rather like the unease Iris had detected between Josie and her father.

On the whole, Iris thought, men, however liberal-minded, did not really like forthright, intelligent women.

She went to the door and called out, 'Bruno! Fiammetta! Come and look what we've got you!'

The twins came running in, filling the room with smiles.

'What are we supposed to be?' Bruno asked, tugging his T-shirt over his head.

'French,' Iris said. 'Go in the kitchen and ask Dad for some strings of onions.'

'We only bought five,' she apologized to Josie.

'Josie can have mine,' Winston offered. 'Someone ought to keep an eye on the old boys, anyway.'

'Oh . . .' said Iris, filled with the peculiar sensation that she was betraying Winston by her instant friendship with Josie.

As Iris, Josie, Michael and the twins all set off for the Carnival in their Gallic stripes and onions, Iris turned round to wave to Winston at the front door, but he had already gone inside, and she felt suddenly foolish with her arm raised, like a child putting a hand up at school, then forgetting the answer to the question.

Sunlight filtering in through the slits between the boards on the windows lit the dust motes dancing in the air. The interior of Kingshaven's disused railway station still retained the slight smell of coal. A resident sparrow flew in unpredictable bursts around the ceiling joists, stopping to perch occasionally, as if to listen to the conversation as Millicent Bland leaned through the ticket window of the booking office.

'How far do you want to go?' she asked, holding up a roll of unused tickets.

'As far as I can,' replied Gerry, who was standing on the other side of the hatch.

Milly's heart skipped a beat.

'Day return?' she asked.

'I'd like a season ticket, please.'

Could this be a romantically disguised proposal? Or was it just that he couldn't think of any other type of ticket? Milly found it was often a mistake to read too much into what men said.

'Where to?' she asked, hoping he would reply, 'Wherever you want!'

'Lowhampton?' he said.

'That's a bit boring, isn't it?' said Milly. 'Who'd want a season ticket to Lowhampton?'

Now she was irrationally disappointed.

'You're right,' said Gerry. 'I'd rather stay right here.'

He took off his riding hat to duck his head through the hatch and kiss her quickly on the lips.

'Why there?' flirted Milly, pointing her finger out of the hatch. 'It's much nicer on this side. Why don't you come and see?'

''Fraid I can't,' Gerry sighed.

'Why?'

'It says "Access Prohibited to Passengers",' Gerry pointed to the notice on his side of the door.

'In this instance, I'm prepared to make an exception,' said Milly in a stationmaster kind of voice.

Gerry opened the door and caught her hand, dragging her out of sight of the ticket window. They kissed again, for longer.

'What if someone comes?' Milly asked.

'What if two people come?' Gerry replied, with eyes closed, his voice already slurry with the prospect of sex. He held her face in his hands and kissed her deeply, his tongue flicking in and out of her mouth.

'What about my dress?' Milly asked, breaking off for breath. The long white sleeveless gown was open at the front, fastened only with a wide gold belt. 'It'll get all dusty if I lie down in here!'

'Who said anything about lying down?' asked Gerry, manoeuvring her gently back against the door. He pushed aside the dress, and unzipped his jodhpurs. Milly couldn't help staring at it, wanting it inside her as urgently as he did. His fingers began to play with her crotch. She could feel herself becoming suddenly slippery, and when he smiled at her again, she felt embarrassed to be so clearly ready for him.

'Take your knickers off!' His voice was a little croaky, his breath warm next to her ear, making her shoulders shrug and shiver with pleasure.

'I can't!' she said.

'Why not?' His head pulled back in surprise.

'I've got a bathing costume on underneath,' she said. 'People would see everything in this dress,' she explained, with absurd modesty.

'Access prohibited?' he whispered, pushing the crotch of the white costume aside, bending his knees a little. With one shocking thrust, she was off the ground, wrapping her legs around his back, unable to tell how it was that she was able to defy gravity, unable to think of anything except him right up inside her.

'God, Milly,' Gerry breathed as her grip on his shoulders turned to a caress as she soothed the final judders from him, stroking his hair, kissing his face, battling the urge to say anything that might reveal how much she loved him.

'Are we going steady?' a small voice inside her wanted to ask, but didn't. Wasn't it enough that he'd decided to stick around in Kingshaven?

As he withdrew she felt a rush of wetness between her legs, and she knew that she would twitch down there all day as she sat on the float in her white dress with her purple Miss Kingshaven sash and her virginal attendants.

'Better be getting back,' said Gerry, fitting his riding cap on again. 'I told Angela I was just going for a slash.'

'Angela King?' said Milly, trying to keep her voice calm.

'We're riding at the front of the Palace float to make it look like a carriage or something.'

'What's Angela King going as then, Lady Godiva?' Milly tried to make a joke out of the discomfort she always felt when Gerry mentioned her. And then she thought, Oh bugger, as a predatory glint flashed across Gerry's blue eyes and Milly kicked herself for putting the idea of Angela King naked into his head.

Perhaps he already knew what she looked like naked. Surely Angela was too posh for him, although he was good at imitating those horsy types, making himself sound like the man who did the commentary on *The Horse of the Year Show*. He had everyone at the bar of the Ship in fits.

'I'll go first then, shall I?' Gerry interrupted the crescendo of jealousy escalating inside Milly's head.

The booking-office door creaked as he opened it a crack to check the lie of the land. 'Don't want everyone to know what we've been up to, do we?'

He kissed her quickly on the nose, and then was gone.

Milly looked at all the initials of other couples scratched on the dark panelling as she began to count slowly to a hundred.

*　　*　　*

Unusually for Bank Holiday weekend, it was a very hot day, so hot that most of the musicians in the band had taken off their uniform jackets and were sitting on the grass smoking cigarettes with their instruments around them. Julia's dress was tight across her chest and the long velvet sleeves and skirt felt as if they were dragging her down.

There were still floats gathering in the field next to the disused railway station, which was used as the Carnival muster point. Two hefty members of the lifeboat crew, their faces wet with sweat under shiny yellow sou'westers, had taken up position on the road holding a large banner reading: 'KINGSHAVEN: EUROPEAN SINCE 51 BC'.

Julia gazed at the white silk banner with red writing, which was strung from poles at the front and back of the Palace float: 'CELEBRATING ENGLAND'S HERITAGE'.

'Why do you think it says that?' she asked her best friend, Adrian King.

'Obvious, isn't it?' said Adrian. 'Our float is the history of England. Mummy is Queen Elizabeth the First, Daddy is Henry the Eighth who had six wives, Granny Liliana is Queen Victoria. She always used to wear black. Christopher was supposed to be the Prince Regent, but he refused to wear embroidered breeches and a powdered wig . . .'

Julia thought that Christopher King looked almost more out of place in his casual clothes – a navy blazer and cream slacks – than he would have done if he'd put on a costume like everyone else.

'Your granny is Florence Nightingale or someone like that,' Adrian continued. 'Your father and some of the men are the Beefeaters . . .'

'I thought the Carnival was supposed to be about Europe,' Julia said.

'England *is* part of Europe,' Adrian informed Julia.

'Don't be silly!' Julia laughed.

Adrian was always trying to trick her, but she'd heard Granny Ruby and Granny Liliana saying on many occasions that England hadn't fought and beaten Europe for nothing.

Julia looked enviously across at her school's float, which was supposed to represent Austria. The infants' teacher, Mrs Evans, was dressed in Austrian national costume with her hair in coils like earphones. The pupils had spent most of the summer term making the costumes – kitten ears lined with pink felt and black pipe-cleaner whiskers, boxes, with holes for legs and arms, covered in brown paper and tied with string. Denise Jones was wearing a white dress with a blue satin sash. She looked cool and pretty and when she saw Julia staring at her, she gave her one of her little smirks.

Julia and James attended the school, but they didn't mix with the other children outside school hours and when the time came to go on to big school, Julia would be sent away to board like her sisters. The time for James to go would arrive even sooner. It was important for boys to have a proper education, her father had told her. Especially when the responsibility of the Castle would one day fall to him. But Julia didn't know what she was going to do without her brother for company.

Nothing was moving and it seemed to be getting hotter and hotter.

'I wish there wasn't always so much waiting.' Julia squinted at the sun.

There was a song in the charts, which she and James listened to on the radio on Sunday afternoon if Daddy was out, about a little girl waiting patiently for love which would surely come one day, and Julia always thought it was about her.

The wet black nose of one of the King Charles spaniels sitting at the feet of Auntie Libby's throne, twitched as it caught a scent on the breeze. Nobody except Julia seemed to notice the dog jumping down from the float. She stared as it zigzagged through the crowd, until she lost track of it.

'Granny Ruby?'

'Not now, Julia.'

'Come along, Gerry,' called Angela King. 'The judges are here.'

Angela knew a lot about judges because she often did something called Horse Trials and everyone was always congratulating her when she walked into the hotel in her smart black jacket and hat and tight white jodhpurs with the smell of the stables wafting around her. Like everyone else, Julia was a little bit afraid of Angela, and of horses, because she'd made the mistake of falling off when Angela was teaching her to ride.

The judging committee, consisting of the vicar, the mayor and the editor of the *Chronicle* inspected the float and went on without making any notes on their clipboards.

'Bloody hell!' exclaimed Eddie King. 'Don't we even get a bloody rosette?'

'Shush,' hissed Auntie Libby, tapping his padded breeches with her broom-handle sceptre. 'It makes local people feel we're part of the town,' she reminded him.

'It's not the winning, Eddie, it's the taking part,' commented Julia's father.

'Try telling that to Captain Moor when he's skippering *Evening Mist*,' snarled Eddie.

Still nothing moved. Angela King sat on her horse swatting at flies.

'Which is your favourite float?' Julia asked Adrian King.

She liked Tulips from Amsterdam because it had a windmill with red sails that actually turned.

'Probably Spain,' said Adrian.

The ladies of the Women's Institute were dressed in tiered skirts with black lace fans and there was a real beach donkey with a big straw hat.

All the dressed-up people reminded Julia of the shelf of wooden dolls in different national costumes, which Granny Ruby had made out of remnants for Mummy during the war, and which now sat on a shelf in Julia's bedroom, their open eyes staring at her as she slept.

'What are we waiting for now?' Julia asked Adrian.

'They can't find Miss Kingshaven,' he informed her.

'There she is!' said Julia.

Emerging from the dilapidated station building with her tiara askew, Miss Kingshaven picked her way in high heels through the forest of wild hollyhocks growing on the forecourt towards the first float in the procession, which had big white columns at each corner and men dressed in short leather skirts and sandals. The white banner fluttering above it read: 'UP POMPEII!'

'Sorry, call of nature!' shouted Miss Kingshaven.

Granny Liliana turned to Granny Ruby and remarked acidly, 'Not exactly your typical Vestal Virgin, is she?'

'What is a virgin?' Julia asked Adrian, as the procession finally began to move off.

It was the first time the Palace had entered a float in the Carnival and nobody had thought to nail down the furniture for the steep incline at the top of the High Street. It was quite an effort, even for the grown-ups, to keep everything from slipping right down to the front of the float. Auntie Libby was clearly irritated with this lack of practical forethought, and her smile was forced through gritted teeth.

'Has anyone seen Baroness?' she suddenly asked.

'She's probably bunked off to the dog show,' Eddie replied.

'Angela, have you seen Baroness?' Libby called to Angela, who was chatting to Gerry at the front, their heads close together.

'Baroness!' repeated Libby desperately. 'She's gone!'

'Probably thought there were enough bitches on this float,' Eddie King remarked with a glance at the two grannies.

'Gerry and I will go and look for her,' Angela called back to her mother.

On the Roman float in front of theirs, Julia noticed that Miss Kingshaven, who was reclining on a kind of sofa with her attendant holding a bunch of grapes above her mouth, suddenly sat up, swatted the grapes away from her face, and glared as the two horses veered off the procession route, taking the left fork, which led up to the schoolfield where the dog show was being held.

There were crowds of people lining the main bit of the High Street where the shops were. Julia was surprised to find it was actually quite nice to be up on the float with everyone looking up and clapping as they trundled past. She tried a little wave, like Auntie Libby's, and people waved back and smiled. Town people!

As the float rolled past Granny Ruby's old shop, Granny Ruby and Granny Liliana both looked determinedly in the opposite direction. Julia looked up and saw that Mrs Quinn was staring down from the balcony.

Mrs Quinn didn't come to Kingshaven very often because she now lived in an apartment on the roof of her shop in Lowhampton.

'Like a goose on top of her golden egg,' Granny Ruby said.

Daddy had taken Julia and James to see Santa Claus there the previous Christmas and Mrs Quinn had spotted them in the queue and invited them up for tea afterwards. Julia didn't think Mrs Quinn had been very pleased when James told her Father Christmas smelled horrible.

But now, thankfully, Mrs Quinn's critical eyes were trained on the group of people walking behind the Palace float, a man, two women and two small children all dressed in blue and white striped T-shirts with strings of onions draped round their necks. The man, who had a beret on his head, and a long thin moustache inked on to his face was Mr Quinn, who used to be married to Mrs Quinn, but now lived up at the Castle with Julia's grandfather, Sir John Allsop. The twins, Bruno and Fiammetta, were his children. On rare occasions, Julia and James were taken to the Castle to visit their grandfather. Usually, Daddy and Sir John would start shouting at each other, and Julia and James would have to go outside with the twins, who were nearly four years old and had lots of animals. As well as the chickens, which were actually allowed to come inside the house – a health hazard, in Granny Ruby's opinion – they had cats that caught shrews and lined the bodies up on the back doormat, a nanny goat called Mary, and, on the last visit, a kid goat called Jeremy, which Granny Ruby didn't think was a suitable name.

The twins were looked after by their big sister, Iris, because their mother had died when they were babies. Iris was very tall and thin with lots of red curly hair, which looked a bit like wool and reminded Julia of a rag doll. Iris was always inventing brilliant games for them to play and Julia often wished that she could have an older sister like Iris, instead of one who thumped her and called her runt.

Throughout her life, Iris had observed other girls forming attachments so close they almost seemed like secret societies with languages of their own, but her only two close friendships had been with men. Winston and Vic. Having a good friend who was female was something she'd never, somehow, learned to do. Sometimes Iris went to the cinema with Milly Bland and her friend Una, but they talked about nothing but fashion and fiancés.

Josie was exactly the sort of woman Iris expected to encounter if she ever got to university, a confident, intelligent woman who had opinions and asked searching questions.

'What do you want to do when you get out of here?' Josie asked her.

'I'd like to read English at university.'

'And after . . . ?'

'I think I'd like to write.'

'Don't you have to have lived a bit before you can write?' Josie asked.

For a moment, Iris was felled, but then her fighting spirit rose to the challenge.

'What makes you think I haven't?' she countered.

Josie looked surprised that someone should come straight back at her, and then she smiled warmly, and Iris smiled back. Finding female friendship was almost as giddy and exciting as falling in love.

'So, let's have the guided tour,' Josie said, casually linking Iris's arm.

'The Kings,' Iris whispered, pointing discreetly at the Palace float, which was bedecked with Union Jack bunting and a determinedly patriotic banner. 'They virtually own the town.'

'Claudia told me about them,' Josie replied. 'Didn't Michael have an affair with the daughter?'

'Dad? No! They represent everything he can't stand!' Iris whispered. 'He only used to play the piano for their tea dance . . .'

Josie raised a sceptical eyebrow and Iris's voice trailed off, aware that the words sounded ridiculous.

Surely Dad couldn't have . . . ? Not with Libby King, who was so tweedy and middle class Iris couldn't imagine her having sex at all, not even with her leering husband, Eddie. Then she remembered there had been a younger sister, Pearl, who had taught Iris to swim one afternoon. Her father had accompanied her. He had sat beside the Palace pool in a suit, causing Iris acute embarrassment by refusing to take off his brown leather lace-up shoes. When they'd got back home, he and Sylvia had an awful row.

Or was that a different day? There had been so many rows.

'The church was narrowly missed by the only bomb dropped on Kingshaven during the war,' Iris said, pointing at the tower visible above the High Street rooftops. 'My mother used to take us to the Sunday service whenever Dad was in London,' she went on. 'She said that if God didn't exist, as Dad claimed, then she couldn't see the harm in going, and if He did, it was better to be on the safe side.'

As the procession moved slowly down the High Street, they passed the library where her father used to go to write when they were making too much noise as children.

'Where he used to meet Claudia, you mean,' Josie told her.

'What?'

'Claudia and Michael used to compose poetry and pass

it to each other across the desk in the reference section. Sweet, no?'

Was this true?

'That's my mother's original shop,' Iris nodded, suddenly aware that Sylvia was standing there on the balcony above the arcaded frontage of the shop, glaring down at all of them. Iris looked anxiously across at her father, who was holding Fiammetta by one hand and Bruno by the other. Fiammetta was like a doll, with her china-white face and bubbles of red hair; Bruno had dark almond-shaped eyes like Claudia's. They looked so cute in their stripy T-shirts and shorts, people couldn't help smiling at them. Michael, who was usually grim-faced, was smiling proudly too, unaware of Sylvia's evil glare.

'I'd rather like to meet Sylvia Quinn,' Josie said. 'I'm doing a series of profiles of women with influence.'

Iris laughed at the idea that Sylvia had influence, and then saw that Josie was serious.

'Well, don't expect an introduction from me,' she said. 'We've barely spoken since I left home, and I'm a traitor now, of course.'

'You'll have to kiss and make up one day, you know,' Josie told her.

If anyone else had made such an observation, Iris thought she might have hit them. She glanced up at the balcony again at the exact moment her mother looked the other way. Had she been unfair to Sylvia, she wondered, with her assumption that it was her mother's bourgeois, narrow-minded attitudes that had been the cause of her parents' incompatibility? Now Iris recalled Sylvia's distress when Michael used to go to the library, and the way she'd round on Iris, demanding hysterically why Michael couldn't stay with his family like any normal husband, as if it was somehow in Iris's gift to stop him.

Had she known about the poetry?

The idea of doing an *Up Pompeii* float, based on the television programme, had been leaped upon with enthusiasm by the

76

regulars in the Ship, who considered it a suitably mocking two fingers up to the Carnival Committee. Still, from her reclining position on the couch, Milly had to concede that the generally unpopular theme of Europe had inspired some imaginative ideas. The Kingshaven Amateur Dramatic Society had recycled the costumes from an old production of *The Gondoliers* and Mr Murphy, a carpenter by trade and a nervous tenor, had fashioned two ends in hardboard to make the float look like a gondola. The Ship's rival pub at the Harbour End, the Anchor, had decked out their float as a German beer tent. The bar staff were all wearing lederhosen and it was proving a popular float as there was a beer keg on it and they were handing out free ale. Milly's own father had provided drinks only for the people on the float.

Milly took a long gulp of Martini and lemonade, which she was drinking because it looked like red wine, which the Romans used to drink. As the float rolled past Sylvia Quinn's shop, she was momentarily alarmed to see her boss staring down at her from the balcony above the shop. Milly quickly slid her glass under the couch on which she was reclining, fanned by her attendants with palm branches.

Why was Sylvia in the flat? It was unoccupied now, except by Sylvia's son, Anthony, in his holidays from university. Had Sylvia detected the lingering smell of Gerry's aftershave in the bedroom – Brut, by Fabergé? Milly breathed a sigh of relief as she realized that on this occasion she wasn't the cause of Sylvia's displeasure. How cutting it must be for Sylvia to see her ex-husband and Iris and the kiddies walking down the street in the sunshine, all so happy together. She felt a pang of sympathy for her boss, but then she thought about the way Sylvia had docked her wages when she'd accidentally shrunk her uniform, and she told herself not to be so daft.

The front of the procession reached the clocktower and was about to turn on to the promenade.

'Gerry's gone off with Angela King,' Una announced.

Una had never been Miss Kingshaven herself and this

year had been her last chance before getting married. Milly detected a slight feeling, although Una had never said anything directly.

Stretching and shifting her position on the couch, Milly watched as Gerry and Angela clip-clopped up Hill Road away from the parade. There was something about the angle of their heads that induced an urgent stab of jealousy, which seemed to shoot straight down the centre of Milly's body where she could still feel him.

'Don't worry,' said Una, as if she was reading her thoughts. 'She's not as pretty as you.'

'He loves horses. She's got a horse,' said Milly despondently.

'Why don't you learn to ride?' Una asked.

'It's not just that. They talk a different language, horsy people, and I don't have a clue,' said Milly.

'Neigh,' said Una.

Milly looked at her crossly for a moment, as if she wasn't taking it seriously enough, and then a laugh burst out of nowhere.

'Two can play at that game,' Milly told Una, with a confidence she didn't quite feel.

'You wouldn't?' squealed Una. 'God, you would as well . . .'

The procession slowed to a standstill as each of the floats manoeuvred to get on to the promenade and the twins began to get restless. They jumped down on to the beach to watch the Punch and Judy show. Everyone booed as Mr Punch hit first Judy, then the baby, then the policeman, and then the crocodile who came to steal his sausages.

'It's not a real crocodile,' Bruno assured all the other children in a loud, brave voice.

'There's nothing the English like better than a bit of domestic violence for entertainment,' Josie remarked as the curtains in the little red and white striped tent closed and the Punch and Judy man went round with a hat.

'It's part of the same tradition of surrealist humour as *Monty Python*,' Michael countered. 'Being American, I doubt you'd understand.'

'I can assure you that women who are being beaten up by their husbands find it neither surreal nor funny,' Josie said crisply.

'I'm surprised they have the time for Punch and Judy shows,' Michael quipped.

'How very droll,' Josie said sarcastically.

Iris, feeling curiously stranded between the two of them, took a twin in each hand and walked over to view the winner of the sandcastle competition, an elaborate four-towered structure with battlements, a moat and a working drawbridge made from ice-lolly sticks roped together with long green strands of angel-hair seaweed.

'Daddy and I made one just like that,' Bruno told Iris loyally after inspecting the winning entry in awe.

'Really?'

Iris had made enough sandcastles with her father to know that this wasn't quite true.

''Cept ours were bigger.'

'"David Coe".' Iris read the name that had been written on the flag flying from one of the towers. 'Do you know him?'

'He's probably a foreigner,' said Bruno dismissively.

'A holidaymaker,' Iris corrected. 'You mustn't call them foreigners.'

'Everyone else does,' Bruno told her.

'That doesn't make it right,' Fiammetta chimed in. She was so quiet in comparison to Bruno, you could forget she was there, and then she would say something so grown up, it was like an adult speaking out of her doll's face.

The crowd began to move in the direction of the pier as a crackly voice announced with a scream of feedback that the prize-giving was about to begin.

'I think they're judging the children's fancy dress,' Iris said, standing on tiptoe to get a better view over the packed beach.

'Are we going to win?' Fiammetta wanted to know.

'I don't think you'll win, sweetie,' said Josie. 'Some of the mommies have spent months on these costumes . . .' Her voice trailed off as she realized too late that she was being tactless. There was an awkward moment as her words hung in the air and none of the adults knew what to say.

'Can we watch the swimming race then?' Fiammetta asked brightly.

Iris recognized the anguish in her father's eyes. Of course it was better that the twins did not miss their mother all the time, and yet sometimes it was shocking that they could be so contented without her.

'Of course we can,' she said.

Iris suddenly looked round anxiously.

'Where's Bruno?' she asked.

The incomprehensible voice on the loudspeaker droned monotonously over the jangle of shrieks and splashes from the swarming beach, as the Carnival procession inched along the promenade. The noise was so loud, Julia felt as if it was engulfing her, taking over all her senses so that she couldn't think properly. As soon as she saw the sea, her dress seemed to become even heavier and more itchy. The air was hot and swirly, and as she squinted at the pier, its spindly black legs wobbled, like a mirage. The tide was coming in now. She could see the silver crest of it, pushing further up the beach. The children in the water were all jumping in unison over the incoming waves. The Swimathon would soon begin.

Julia's eyes focused on a small figure standing under the pier slightly apart from the main swarm of children. Julia put both her hands up to shade the glare. It had gone. Maybe it was the sun playing tricks on her eyes? The pier was dangerous when the tide was on the turn. The water made invisible holes round the legs and if you weren't careful you could get sucked down. She looked again. There *was* a lone child, she was sure of it. For a moment, all the other noise went silent in her ears and she could hear him calling for help, and she suddenly knew that of all the thousands of people on the beach, she was the only one who had seen him.

There was no time to ask for permission. Wrenching off her best black patent bar shoes, Julia jumped down from the float with two leaps on to the promenade and then on to the sand. She picked up her long velvet skirt and charged towards the pier, jumping over sandcastles, flailing through the middle of a cricket game, kicking up sand over bodies shining with sun oil.

'Oi!' several people called after her, but she did not stop, not even at the water's edge where she waded into the waves towards the spot where she'd seen the child. Tucking her dress up into her knickers Julia scoured the sparkling silver surface of the water. Suddenly, the child bobbed up. Bruno! Julia dived head first into the surf, swimming as she'd never swum before, knowing that she could save him if only she tried hard enough. When she reached the leg of the pier, she dived down into the deep bottomless pool and grabbed him, bringing him to the surface and keeping him afloat with an arm around his chin. With the other arm, she held on to the iron leg of the pier, treading water for what seemed like a very long time.

Afterwards, Adrian told her it was only a couple of seconds before the lifeguard got there, and she was probably in her depth anyway. Nevertheless, the following Monday, Julia's photograph appeared on the front page of the *Chronicle*. The headline read, 'Brave Julia in Mercy Dash!'

And after that, whenever Julia went into Kingshaven, town people said hello to her, and Denise Jones even asked if she would be her best friend.

When she was called on to remember it later (as Milly was more often than she wanted) the afternoon was a bit of a blur. There was the kerfuffle with the rescue on the beach, Julia Allsop posing dripping wet for the photographer from the *Chronicle* and everyone forgetting that it was supposed

81

to be Miss Kingshaven's day. It was so hot, and there was all that Martini and lemonade.

Then there'd been the humiliation of the tug of war final between the Ship and the Anchor, with the Ship losing for the first time in five years, because they were one man short. Gerry. Her father was gracious in defeat, but Milly knew how much his pride had been wounded from the way he banged around getting the oil drum barbecues set up on the forecourt of the Ship for the ram roast.

Gerry didn't turn up until the first batch of lamb chops and sausages were sizzling over charcoal, offering some pathetic excuse about searching for a dog. Angela King clung on to his arm, gazing adoringly at him like she was the one who was on heat. Milly's father handed Gerry a long-handled two-pronged fork without a word, and, unable to contain her pique and act cool, Milly marched off, without quite knowing where she was marching to.

She often wondered later whether it was fate or just an excess of booze that had produced that crystal-clear moment when she had spotted Angela's older brother, Christopher, standing beside the chandlery, looking as out of place in his light-coloured slacks and navy blazer as black tie at a barn dance.

Their paths had crossed before – notably the morning after the Rock Festival, when Milly had woken up with Dexter Strange in the Palace Hotel. On her way out, she'd cheekily asked Christopher King to let her know if the chambermaids found a pair of lilac knickers, which she seemed to have mislaid. Even with a hangover, she'd noticed that Christopher's blue eyes stared at her with admiration rather than disapproval and she'd thought that he was quite sweet really, and perhaps not as queer as everyone in town thought.

They'd never been formally introduced and with the absolute certainty that alcohol inspires, Milly decided that now was the time.

Checking to see that Gerry had a clear view of her from his position from behind the smoking barbecue, Milly adjusted the shoulders of her gown, and sauntered sexily over to where Christopher was standing.

'Hello. I'm Miss Kingshaven, the Carnival Queen!'

Her title just came out without thinking.

'So I see,' said Christopher, staring at her cleavage so brazenly, she looked down to check that nothing had popped out, before realizing that he was just looking at the purple sash with Miss Kingshaven embroidered on it.

'As a matter of fact,' Milly continued, 'my real name is Millicent Bland.'

Her voice felt somehow disconnected from her lips, as if it was coming from another place.

'I know,' said Christopher.

Milly glanced back at the barbecue and was gratified to see Gerry staring at her, a metal spatula in one hand, paper plate in the other. She turned back to Christopher, trying to summon up a witty remark.

'You're a King and I'm a queen, so how about it?' she heard herself suggesting, pushing her fingers flirtatiously back through her hair, forgetting that it was coiffed up in a lacquered top knot with a tiara on top.

'I . . . I . . .' Christopher stammered.

It was like Una always said: sometimes she went too far.

'I was only joking.' Milly squeezed his arm sympathetically.

Christopher smiled at her gratefully.

'C . . . c . . . can I get you another drink?' he managed.

'Ooh, yes, please,' said Milly, glancing over at Gerry again. 'Martini, please. Like it says on the adverts, any time, any place, anywhere!'

Flaming torches were lit on the quay. The forecourt of the Ship was packed with Roman soldiers drinking pint pots of beer. The Palace float was parked outside the Yacht Club, where the Kings and their retinue were sipping gin and tonics on the terrace, looking out over the water, away from the riffraff amassed in the street.

The air began to fill with the smell of charcoal and

83

the evening chill made everyone suddenly wish they had brought a cardigan out with them.

Bruno and Fiammetta were each holding a balloon with 'Chronicle News Group' printed on it in red. Their eyes were wide open, but they looked as if they were sleep-walking.

'Come on, Iris!' said her father. 'Bruno's still a bit wet, and this gloomy old man has had enough excitement for one day.'

'It's still early,' said Iris.

'It's their bedtime,' said Michael.

'Yes, but it's not mine!' said Josie, which made Iris giggle.

'Do you mind?' Iris felt ridiculous asking her father as if she were a child seeking permission to stay up late.

'Of course not,' said Michael, struggling to hold on to Bruno, and twitching Fiammetta's arm as she stood mesmerized as if already asleep.

'Where do you think the best place to see the fireworks is?' Josie asked, as they waved Michael up the street, which rose steeply from the bay towards the ridge.

'They usually float a barge out in to the bay,' Iris said. 'Most people crowd on to the harbour wall . . .'

She hesitated, suddenly wishing she had gone home with her father after all. Getting to the wall would involve walking past Sylvia, whom Iris could see talking to Jolly Allsop in the flickering light of the flaming torches. Even from a distance, Iris could tell that she was flirting with him, and he was lapping it up. They were perfect for each other, Iris thought. An aspiring nouveau riche divorcee meets a soon-to-inherit divorced member of the gentry. Having conquered the fashion world, Sylvia had set herself the new challenge of insinuating her way into the English upper classes.

'Come on,' said Josie, slipping her arm through Iris's. Iris's heart was pumping so fast, she thought Josie must be able to feel it.

Sylvia's laughter tinkled prettily as they approached. She

was staring at Jolly Allsop's mouth as if pearls of wit were dropping from his lips, which, having encountered Jolly on a couple of occasions when he came to visit Sir John, Iris thought was pretty unlikely.

'Mum?'

Sylvia turned and looked at her. Instinctively, Iris glanced down at her blue and white striped T-shirt to check that she hadn't spilled ice cream or ketchup down her front, remembering suddenly all the costumes her mother had created for her as a child in an effort to win her the title Little Miss Kingshaven. Iris had always managed to tread on the skirt or jump in a puddle, and ruin all Sylvia's work. The only title Iris had won was Little Miss Easter Bonnet in 1956, and even that had been spoiled by Angela King doing bunny ears behind her in the photo that appeared in the *Chronicle*.

'I thought I spotted you earlier,' Sylvia said in the sing-song voice Iris remembered her putting on for customers when she used to serve in the shop. 'Quite the little mother to those poor children, aren't you, Iris? Do you know Mr Allsop?'

'We have met,' Jolly Allsop responded with classic public-school manners. He shook Iris's hand, then looked at Josie.

'Josie,' Iris introduced her companion. 'Sylvia Quinn and Mr Allsop.'

'Jolly's daughter rescued your little boy,' Sylvia pointed out.

'Yes, I know. She was very brave . . .'

'Well, I'm not sure it was quite as heroic as all that . . .' Jolly protested.

'You want to keep an eye on that one,' Sylvia warned Iris.

Iris tried to keep a lid on all the emotions frothing up inside her.

'I've promised Julia she can come and pick out any dress she wants in my shop,' Sylvia added.

'You're too kind,' Jolly told her.

'I'm such a fan of your designs,' Josie snatched the opportunity to address Sylvia.

A little blush of pleasure spread over Sylvia's face.

'And you're . . . ?'

'A journalist,' Josie told her. 'As a matter of fact, I've been wondering whether you would agree to do an interview for my series on liberated women.'

'Women's Liberation?' A frown spread across Sylvia's face, as if the words were not quite the thing for polite conversation. She half turned to Jolly Allsop. 'I've never understood why anyone would want to burn their bra, have you?'

Jolly chuckled obligingly.

'Not that you've ever really needed a bra, have you, Iris?' Sylvia added with an instinctive shimmy to emphasize her own perfect proportions.

Iris's face burned with the acute mortification only a parent can induce.

'Enjoy the fireworks,' she said flatly, forcing herself to maintain her dignity.

Iris walked hurriedly to the darkened end of the harbour wall, keeping just in front of Josie, making it clear that she didn't want to talk. It was only when they were so far away that Sylvia's white jumper was merely a flash of iridescence in the darkness, that Iris felt she could breathe again.

'Well done,' Josie said finally. She put an arm round Iris and gave her a quick supportive squeeze. 'If it makes any difference, she probably found it as tough as you did.'

'No, she finds it easy being nasty to me,' Iris said, hating her mother for embarrassing her in front of a new friend she was trying to impress.

'She's probably jealous,' said Josie.

'Jealous? Why would she be jealous of me?'

'You're young.'

'She's still young . . .'

'She must be coming up for forty. In my experience women like Sylvia do not like being forty.'

It was a balmy evening. The wash from the boat tug-

86

ging the fireworks' barge out into the bay lapped softly against the harbour wall. The hum from the quay was like the sound of a distant party. As the appointed time for the display grew closer, a murmuring crowd of shadows began to make its way along the harbour wall, but Iris and Josie had the best position, right at the end, like standing on the prow of a sailing ship when the wind has dropped and moonlight turns the ocean to molten silver. Iris felt calm again, steady.

As the first rocket whooshed into the sky and fanned into a soundless palm of glittering light, followed in a heartbeat by the bang of its explosion, Iris turned to smile at Josie.

The kiss felt the most natural thing in the world. Not sexual, not even particularly intimate, only celebratory.

Iris was suddenly aware of her name being called and when she turned round, she found herself looking directly into the only face in the crowd that was not looking up to the sky.

Winston's eyes were bright with horrified disbelief.

Iris brought her hand to her lips in surprise, and for one peculiar moment she was certain that Josie had known he was there.

Chapter Four

1972

The sun was sinking in the west, but the mossy ramparts of the Iron Age fort were still as warm as a just-slept-on mattress. Surrounded by daisies, buttercups and bright-blue speedwells, Milly's golden hair fanned out like a halo around an angel's face. She smiled sweetly as Christopher dipped his lips towards hers. A different kind of smile, he thought. Her mouth softened under his, allowing his tongue to probe that delicious wet softness within. She tasted of mint toothpaste. He could feel her nipples hardening against his chest, her ankles digging into his buttocks, as she pulled him into her. Christopher tried to hold back, but her breath was in his ear.

'Yes, yes, yes . . .'

And suddenly, all his senses were enveloped by her, taste and touch and smell, and there was nothing he could do except shout, 'I love you!' and explode with pleasure so acute it was suddenly painful.

She said, 'I love you too.'

His heart began to race because he knew that now was the moment. There was nothing else he would ever want or need but her.

'Will you marry me?' he stuttered.

And then the alarm clock went off, and Christopher awoke in his room at the Palace Hotel, the sensations of the dream still so present in his head, his body, and, to his dismay, the sheets, that he was almost unable to believe that they had not been on the South Cliffs just now, nor that Milly, tucked up in bed in her room above the saloon bar of her father's pub, had not been having the same dream. How amazing that one's brain could trick one like that, he thought, although in the dream he had almost known that it was too perfect because some of the details were wrong, as if his unconscious mind had been trying to give him clues. But there was a sense in which the dream was profoundly true, he thought. He loved Milly Bland and he was sure she loved him, perhaps in a deeper way than she was even aware.

It was so early, Christopher's sister, Angela, was the only one at breakfast, which was a relief, because Angela approved of his relationship with Milly. Angela was in an uncharacteristically good mood these days because she'd got a new boyfriend called Miles Fogg, who owned horses and was, she had shamelessly informed Christopher, pretty well endowed in every sense of the word.

'What do you think Milly would say if I asked her to marry me?' Christopher asked his sister in a low voice so that there was no possibility of being overheard.

'Suck it and see,' said Angela, through a mouthful of Shredded Wheat, which looked a bit like hay.

Sometimes Christopher wondered whether Angela was actually changing into a horse.

'She's not still keen on Gerry Balls, is she?' he asked.

The bartender was unaccountably popular with all the local girls. Angela herself had been smitten for a while. Now she looked annoyed that Christopher had dared mention his name.

'I can't see what people see in him,' Christopher said, hoping to make amends.

'Treat 'em mean, keep 'em keen,' Angela told him, throwing the spoon back into her empty bowl.

Christopher didn't know whether this was an explanation of Mr Balls' attraction, or simply a piece of advice.

Surely someone as gloriously rational as Milly couldn't

really be serious about a penniless Irishman, who appeared to have slept with just about every girl in Kingshaven? Angela had hinted that he had a colossal member, but it was Milly herself who had assured Christopher several times that it was the quality not the quantity. One thing Christopher was quite certain about was that he and Milly were sexually compatible. Perhaps more importantly they shared the same sense of humour. His impersonations of the silly walks in *Monty Python's Flying Circus* always made her laugh.

Christopher scooped up the last of his cornflakes and threw his napkin on the table. There was only one way of finding out what Milly felt, and that was to propose before his confidence ebbed away. He knew what it was like to hear her say she loved him, only in a dream, but it must be an auspicious sign.

When he later looked back on that morning, Christopher always thought ruefully that five minutes might have changed the course of his life. Had he run down the hill to Milly as she walked along the promenade to work, dropped to his knees and proposed, who knows what might have happened?

The coast was clear, the sun was shining, Christopher was about to step out of the front door. And then the telegram arrived.

It wasn't a particular surprise that Uncle Rex was dead. When Libby King had seen him a couple of weeks before, he was clearly on his last legs, although he'd done his best to stand up when she came into the ward, displaying the natural good manners bred into people of his generation, even though he was attached to all sorts of tubes. Libby had been so touched by the gesture, she hadn't had the heart to refuse him his final request, which was to be buried in the family plot in the churchyard of Kingshaven's parish church, alongside his brothers.

It was only now, with the telegram in her hand, and her mother, Liliana, staring expectantly at her down the breakfast table, that Libby began to fear the consequences of her generosity.

'Well?' said her mother.

'Uncle Rex is dead.'

'Good!' said Liliana.

Perhaps as one grew closer to death oneself – Liliana was in her seventies now – one didn't have time for sentimentality, thought Libby.

'The body will be arriving tomorrow,' she said, trying to keep her voice level, as if it was entirely natural to expect Rex to be brought home for burial.

'I beg your pardon?' said Liliana.

Liliana's companion, Ruby Farmer, who was always alert to any potential trouble, cocked her head in Libby's direction, a forkful of bacon poised midway between her plate and mouth.

'Rex is going to be buried in the churchyard. I didn't really see how I could say no,' Libby faltered. 'He seemed so sweet and eager to make amends . . .'

Liliana let out a long, portentous sigh.

'I knew I should have stopped you going to visit him,' she said.

'For God's sake, Liliana! Libby's forty-six years old. You could hardly have prevented her,' said Eddie.

Libby did wish that her husband wouldn't intervene on occasions like this. It only made things worse, and she didn't particularly like having her age shouted all over the hotel.

'Naturally, I extracted some guarantees,' Libby went on.

'Guarantees?'

'About the return of your jewellery.'

Liliana's face softened slightly, then hardened again. 'Did you get it in writing?' she asked.

'He was so frail . . .'

'Well, that'll be about as much use as the paper it's not written on,' Liliana snapped.

Mrs Farmer nodded in agreement.

'I'm sure Regina can be prevailed upon . . . if we're all civilized about it . . .' Libby said.

'Civilized!' Liliana spat out the word. She pushed back her chair and stood up as if about to make a speech.

'I find it an affront that you have seen fit to invite that person to this house. I will be taking meals in my room until the whole thing is over.'

Ruby Farmer also stood up. 'Me too!' she said.

'Good!' Eddie muttered under his breath as the two old women left the room.

Libby frowned at him.

'If it makes any difference,' Eddie leaned across the table and patted his wife's hand, 'I think you did the right thing.'

'Do you?' Libby brightened.

'For God's sake, the poor bugger's dead – what harm can he do now?' said Eddie.

'I don't suppose Mummy will ever speak to me either unless I get the jewellery back.'

'Why don't we get Cyril over?' said Eddie, referring to his uncle. 'He's always good at wheedling things out of people.'

'What a good idea!' said Libby.

Sometimes it needed a pragmatist like Eddie to cut through all the emotion that could build up in a family.

Iris's fingers were shaking as she wound Fiammetta's silky red hair into two tight plaits. She was anxious that the twins looked as clean and tidy as possible so that no one would be able to tell that they hadn't got a proper mother. Then she brushed her own dry, ginger hair, which never shone like Fiammetta's, and tied it into a ponytail, wanting to look neat as well, in case the infants' teacher was in the playground when they arrived. Iris shushed the children impatiently, trying to remember all the things they would need – handkerchief, pencil case, satchel, dinner money – and seeing their perplexed faces, she was stung by an unwanted memory of Sylvia doing exactly the same thing to her on her first day at primary school. Perhaps her mother had been nervous too, eager for Iris to make a good impression.

It was only when Michael came down dressed in a shirt and tie that Iris realized that he intended to take the children himself on their first day. Whilst part of her was glad because it was the right thing for him to do, part of her felt oddly disappointed, as if she was suddenly redundant.

'Come on, then, you two!' her father said.

Not, 'you three', Iris noted, hanging back, annoyed with herself for feeling so childish.

'Have a good day, then!' she called, watching the little triangle of figures disappear down the avenue of golden beech trees.

The house echoed with the children's absence.

'Claudia!' called the professor.

Claudia's father was completely on the ball about some things – only the other day, he had been explaining the make up of the Roman army to Bruno – but his mind was clearly failing in other ways.

'Claudia's not here,' Iris told him patiently, putting a cup of tea beside his usual chair in the draughty Victorian conservatory.

'No. No, of course she's not,' he said.

Iris washed up the breakfast bowls, and brushed the toast crumbs off the kitchen table. Unable to bear the silence, she turned on the radio and tuned it to Radio One. 'School's Out', the song that had caused so much controversy earlier in the summer, was playing. For some reason, it made her feel even sadder. Suddenly, she wanted to get out of the house before her father returned. She pulled on a jacket, slipped out of the back door and cut across the fields of stubble towards the bridleway along the top of the South Cliffs.

It was a typical September day. The sunshine was bright but there was a slight edge on the air that hinted at frost and smoky autumn days to come. The sea was vast and blue, with the wind whipping up white horses, but it was already too cold for yachts to be out. Iris turned three hundred and sixty degrees. In all the vastness, she could see no other person. A wisp of smoke rising from one of the cottages down in Kingshaven was the only sign of human activity. Iris sat down tentatively on the bent-over tree on the cliff top that she used to bounce on when she was a child and began to rock backwards and forwards, thinking about how the twins were getting on. She pictured them both in the circle of chairs in the nursery class. Fiammetta would be listening and sitting up nicely, with her knees together and her socks pulled up. Even though she looked very like Iris had done as a child, she was such a different character, so quiet and controlled, she sometimes made Iris feel like the childish one. Bruno would be finding it more difficult to sit still, and if Mrs Evans was anything like she had been when Iris was in her class, Bruno would already have been singled out as a naughty boy, because Mrs Evans wasn't keen on children with opinions. But even Mrs Evans would find it difficult to resist Bruno's charm. Iris realized that the strange ache inside her was because she was missing their chatter, and their sheer physical presence. There was no better feeling in the world than when Bruno charged up and flung himself against her chest, or when Fiammetta's small hand slipped quietly into hers when they were about to cross a busy road. Now, all that was over.

Iris sniffed, patting the pocket of her jeans, hoping that she'd remembered a handkerchief for herself – that would be an irony – and tried to think about what she was going to do now. The more time she spent away from London, the more she felt that time in London was rushing on, whereas time in Kingshaven stood still. Here, everyone seemed to know everything about everyone else in the town, but nobody cared about the Vietnam War, or Civil Rights in Northern Ireland. In Kingshaven, feminism was as dirty a word as socialism.

In London, Iris and her friend Vic had always gone to the latest plays and films. In Kingshaven, now that the Pier Theatre had been turned into a bingo hall, the only cultural events were the Amateur Dramatic Society's annual production of Gilbert and Sullivan in the church hall, and the occasional WEA lecture and slide show on subjects like local Romano-British treasures, and Thomas Hardy's Wessex. The Regal cinema got films so late they hadn't even got round to showing *A Clockwork Orange* before Stanley Kubrick had withdrawn it. Iris had read that the film portrayed England as a sixties paradise becoming a violent dystopia, but Kingshaven hadn't yet moved out of the fifties.

Winston was so busy, he rarely came down now, and her other great friend Vic didn't even know where she was. Iris's only real friend was Barbara, who came every day to milk the goats. She was pleasantly unconventional, a bit batty really, but Iris had come to regard her almost as family since Barbara's husband had eloped with a vegan folk singer who had arrived the previous summer with an acoustic guitar in the expectation of another festival. Peter had left Barbara the Riviera Guesthouse and custody of the goat, even though both ventures had been his mad idea in the first place. Instead of selling up, Barbara was determined, with her very English, jolly-hockey-sticks resilience, to make a go of it. Sometimes Iris went down in the evenings to keep her company, and Barbara opened a bottle of wine and poured out her troubles.

'The irony is, I thought he was safe because he was boring. I used to go for moody difficult men,' Barbara would tell her. 'Still waters run deep and all that. Then suddenly I was thirty, and along came Peter, and I thought, he'll do, but almost as soon as we were married, he grew a beard . . .' She burst into self-mocking laughter, and almost as suddenly folded into tears.

'We couldn't have children, you see,' Barbara said dismally. 'It probably affected him as much as me. Just came out in different ways.'

Iris's only friend of her own age was Milly Bland, who was a laugh, but recently Milly had been trying to persuade Iris to get off with Christopher King so that she could go out with Gerry Balls again. Iris didn't fancy Christopher King, and she was pretty sure he felt exactly the same way about her, and Milly was a bit cross that Iris wasn't prepared to play the game and help her out. Invitations to come for a drink at the Ship had become less frequent.

In the last days before going off to their new boarding schools, Julia and James spent a lot of time playing in Granny Ruby's suite at the Palace Hotel. James made up a game where the pattern on the carpet was a road and a marble he had found in his pocket was a car. The idea was to push the marble along, staying on the blue bit, otherwise you lost your go. Julia kept having to stop James making brum-brum noises because Granny Ruby didn't like children being heard.

Now they both ran to the window at the sound of tyres on gravel. A big black old-fashioned car was inching up towards the hotel. When it finally came to a halt, Julia could see it was one of those horrible long glass cars used to carry coffins. The driver got out. He was dressed in black. He put a top hat on to his head and went round to the passenger side of the car to open the door. Out stepped the strangest-looking woman Julia had ever seen. She was extremely tall and thin but with very broad shoulders, and huge feet in shoes with narrow heels, which made her wobble on the gravel. Her head was covered with a veil like a bride, except it was black, and when she pulled it up from her face with her big square hands, her face was as white as a Pierrot clown with black eyes, and bright red lips. She stood on the steps of the hotel as the hearse started up again and watched it all the way down the drive.

'Why is that lady waving to her trunk?' James wanted to know.

Her name was Regina Wallace, Julia found out from Adrian, and she took meals in her room and stared sadly out of the window. Julia's father explained that she was the wife of Uncle Rex, who was dead, and when James asked why her name wasn't King too then, Daddy muttered something about her being American. Granny Liliana said that wild horses wouldn't drag her to Uncle Rex's funeral, and the image of the old lady being pulled along in a cloud of dust as if she was in a Western appeared in Julia's troubled dreams.

Nobody was allowed to talk to Regina Wallace except Great-Uncle Cyril, whom Julia overheard shouting as she hovered outside the lady's room.

'Look, it's perfectly simple,' Great-Uncle Cyril was saying. 'Give back what you took and he can stay. You can even stay with him when the time comes. If you don't give it back, then the two of you can . . . well, bugger off!'

'But I keep trying to tell you, there's nothing left . . .'

Julia wondered if all American women had such croaky, deep voices.

'Well, what happened to it?' Uncle Cyril demanded.

'We sold it, of course! How else do you think we survived? I told Rex we should get a legal opinion, but he was so full of loyalty and shame – utterly misplaced, I might say. Of course . . .' the funny deep voice paused for a moment, 'now he's gone, there's no reason for me not to take legal advice.'

'I'm sure there'll be no need for that,' said Uncle Cyril quickly, and then Julia heard footsteps approaching the door and ran down the stairs in case he caught her eavesdropping.

Bruno and Fiammetta took to school immediately and were always full of chatter about which *Janet and John* books they were on and what they had painted or made of clay.

'Samantha Coral and Darren Coral are twins too,' said Bruno, as he went through the children in his class at the end of the first week. Iris thought they must be the children of Carole Coral, who had been in Winston's year at Kingshaven Primary School.

'And have you made any friends, yet?' she asked Fiammetta.

'My friend is Nikhil.'

'Nicky?' Iris repeated.

'No. Nick ill,' said Fiammetta, enunciating both syllables loudly. 'He got a brown face.'

'What victed mean?' asked Bruno suddenly.

Michael put down his newspaper. 'Victorious? It means winning.'

'No, *victed*!' Bruno insisted. 'Had to leave Ganda.'

Iris and her father looked at each other for help translating this, but shrugged.

'Hang on,' Michael asked, glancing at the headline about Idi Amin's expulsion of Asians from Uganda. 'You don't mean Uganda?'

'Ganda. Been victed,' said Bruno.

'Evicted?'

'Yes, victed!' Bruno shook his head as if his father were impossibly slow. 'Nikhil been victed.'

'Where is he living?'

'In guesthouse till the money runs out,' said Bruno. 'Then victed again.'

'Poor things,' said Michael. 'I think I'd better see if they need any help.'

Mr Patel and his wife had two sons: Nikhil, who was the same age as the twins, and Sonny, who was eleven. They had owned a prosperous import–export business in Uganda but had left with almost nothing, having been robbed even of the valuables they carried with them by General Amin's soldiers as they boarded the plane from Kampala. Despite all this, they were relieved and happy to be in England.

'He's a very intelligent, well-read man,' Michael told Iris when he returned later that evening from visiting them. 'When I asked him why on earth they'd come to Kingshaven, he said he'd read what a beautiful place it was in a British Council library book by someone called Daphne W. Smythe. I've never heard of her, have you? As you can imagine, they haven't exactly felt welcome here, although he's far too well mannered to say it, and they're living in one room. I told him I would ask Sir John if they could have the gatehouse for a while.'

Her father was more animated by the plight of the Patels than Iris had seen him for ages. It was a big step for him to think of other people living in the gatehouse, which was where Claudia and the professor had lived when they first came to England, and where the affair with Michael had started. Iris felt suddenly that he had taken a big leap forward.

Una Ironside, née Adams, who was the undertaker's daughter, told Milly that the Kings were a heartless lot when it came to the loss of their loved ones. According to her father, people of their sort would usually choose the middle range of coffin with polished oak and nice brass handles at the very least, but he reckoned that if there'd been a cardboard option they'd have taken it for Uncle Rex. In a way, it wasn't surprising, after what had happened, but even so . . .

'What happened?' Milly asked.

'Don't you know?'

Sometimes Milly found Una's smugness a bit annoying, and she was sure it had got worse since she married, as if Una suddenly saw herself as that little bit more sophisticated than Milly.

'Oh, that!' said Milly, not wanting to give Una the satisfaction of asking.

When Milly met Christopher later on, in the disused station building, which was the best place now that it was getting dark earlier and there was a chill in the air, she could barely contain herself from asking straight away, but she let him kiss her first. In public, Christopher never touched her, but in private, he was just like any other man.

'Hear you've got relations staying,' she said, as Christopher tentatively began to open her blouse. He was very polite, but sometimes she just wished he'd rip the buttons open and get on with it.

'What?'

Milly found it was often difficult to have much of a conversation with a man when his mind was on the other.

'Your uncle's widow?' she pressed a little further, lying down on the floor to encourage him.

'My goodness, word gets around,' said Christopher, kneeling on the floor between her legs.

'What's the big problem about her, then?' Milly asked, reaching up and pulling him down on top of her. She wasn't in the mood for any fumbling.

'Problem?' said Christopher innocently, but his breath was beginning to quicken.

'There was a scandal, wasn't there?'

'I'll . . . tell . . . you . . . later . . .' Christopher panted urgently.

Afterwards, Milly lit a cigarette, and lay on her back in the fast-greying light, blowing smoke rings into the air.

'Well?' she said eventually.

'If I tell you, you must absolutely promise . . . because I would never say a word to anyone I didn't completely trust . . . ?'

'Cross my heart,' said Milly.

In the half-light, she could feel how difficult it was for him to speak of it and she had to stop herself saying, 'Come on!' like she would automatically have done with Una.

'The f-f-f-f-fact of the matter is that Uncle Rex's marriage was not exactly legal.'

'How come?'

'Well, he didn't exactly get married. Not that there's necessarily anything wrong with that,' said Christopher.

'You've lost me,' said Milly.

'Regina, the woman who is presently our guest, was, ahem, actually, Reginald.'

Milly prided herself in knowing more about the world than most people in Kingshaven, but she could feel herself going red as a beetroot. She was absolutely sure that Una didn't know this because Una could never have resisted telling something as bad.

'You are kidding me?' she said.

Christopher shook his head.

'So this Reginald calls himself Regina and wears a dress?' Milly wanted to have the details absolutely clear.

'Actually, I think he had an operation . . .' Christopher said.

'You mean . . . ?' Milly mimed the fall of a knife above Christopher's flies. It was much worse than she could possibly have imagined.

'People do. Some quite normal people, I believe,' said Christopher.

'Normal?' shrieked Milly.

'I meant people who appear normal . . .'

It was quite dark now inside the station building apart from the glowing arc of Milly's cigarette.

'In a way, you know,' Christopher mused, 'I rather admire Uncle Rex. It must take very great love and devotion to go against the wishes of your family.'

'I suppose so,' said Milly doubtfully.

'Actually . . .' Christopher paused as if there was something he wanted to say, but wasn't sure whether he dared, 'I've been struggling with something similar myself.'

In the darkness, he groped for Milly's cigarette-free hand.

'You what?' said Milly, pulling her hand out of his reach. She wasn't sure she liked where this was heading.

'If one is sure, however unsuitable the person might be . . .' Christopher paused again. 'What I mean to say is, however unsuitable the person may be thought to be, by certain narrow-minded individuals . . . surely one is duty bound to be true to one's feelings?'

Milly couldn't believe what she was hearing. She knew Christopher wasn't very experienced with women, but he seemed to enjoy it all the same. Only the other day, she'd been assuring Iris Quinn that there was no truth in the rumours about him being a poof. Was he now going to make a complete fool of her?

'What I'm trying to say, Milly, is . . .' Christopher rolled over on to his side to look at her.

101

Milly had had enough. She was on her feet in an instant, stubbing out her cigarette with the toe of her shoe, and without stopping to button up her blouse, running out of the station building.

'Milly!' Christopher ran after her. 'Milly, stop! I wanted to ask you something . . .'

'Keep away from me,' Milly shouted at him.

A letter had come from Josie, a treat Iris decided to save until after she'd walked the children down to school. She and Josie had corresponded sporadically since the weekend of the Carnival the previous summer. Josie sometimes sent Iris early copies of books she'd been asked to review, and once, when Iris had read Josie's column in the Sunday paper, she had been thrilled to recognize a phrase she had written to Josie quoted as the opinion of a friend.

Now she wrote:

A group of us are putting together a feminist magazine. We haven't got any finance yet, so we need all the help we can get! We're all working and none of us has a lot of time for research. I've told the group about you and everyone agrees that you'd be the ideal person to help us out. You could live here, rent free – I have lots of empty rooms – and when the magazine hits the newsstands and is the runaway success we all expect it to be, we would pay you wages . . . What do you think? At least I could feel that I'd rescued someone from those gloomy old men . . .

Iris could hardly contain her joy. Running all the way up the avenue of beech trees to the Castle, she found her father still sitting at the breakfast table.

'I'm going to go back to London,' Iris told him, waving the letter about. 'Josie's asked me to join her women's group. They're putting a magazine together and they need some help.'

'But what do you know about magazines?'

The response completely floored her.

'Josie's a top journalist. I'm sure she'll teach me . . .' Iris faltered.

'But I thought you were going to study to go to university,' Michael said.

'Yes, well, other things got in the way, didn't they?' said Iris pointedly. 'And I'm twenty-two now; I'm getting a bit old for university.'

'I'm sure it's not too late . . .'

'London's where it's happening. And opportunities like this don't come along every day. Josie says I can stay at her place.'

'I'm just not sure it's such a great idea—' Michael said.

'You know what? I don't really care what you think,' Iris interrupted him. 'Because I'm not asking your permission, I'm telling you. I'm going. And that's the way it is.'

She stared at him as defiantly as when she was a teenager and he had tried to stop her going to one of Winston's gigs. But this was a confrontation she wasn't going to lose.

'God, I'm sorry, Iris,' he finally said. 'Of course you must go, if that's what you want to do. Bruno and Fiammetta will miss you, of course. And I'll miss you,' he added.

'There are two types of girl, I'm afraid,' said Uncle Cyril, tapping the side of his nose knowledgeably, 'and I suspect this Millicent Bland falls into the second category.'

They were walking in the garden together. Christopher often found his great-uncle Cyril a useful sounding board, full of experience and good advice, more like a father to him than his own father ever was.

'What do you mean?' asked Christopher.

'There is the type of girl a man would want to marry, and, well, there's the other type.' Uncle Cyril winked at him.

'The thing is, I do want to marry her,' Christopher explained.

'Is she up the spout? Because there are ways, you know—'

'No!' Christopher interrupted.

The man-to-man chat was not going at all as he expected.

'You want to watch out, my boy,' Cyril continued. 'That's the way they'll get you to sign on the dotted line.'

'But she doesn't want to sign on the dotted line! That's the whole problem,' said Christopher, exasperated.

'She doesn't want to marry you?' asked Uncle Cyril, as if it was the first time Christopher had said it.

'She won't even speak to me,' said Christopher.

'The oldest trick in the book, I'm afraid,' said Uncle Cyril.

'Do you think she's treating me mean to keep me keen?' Christopher asked.

'Course she is! Know the type.'

'And what should I do?' Christopher wanted to know.

'Steer clear,' said Uncle Cyril. 'It would kill your grandmother if you got a girl like that in the family way . . . after all this business with Uncle Rex. I don't think she could survive another scandal.'

'But that's really not the problem,' said Christopher, increasingly aware that they were talking at cross-purposes. Why did no one ever understand?

The day of the funeral was particularly sunny and bright, and many of the town people came out of their houses to look as the long glass car rolled past. At the church, the coffin was taken out and everyone had to line up behind Regina Wallace. The graveyard was so silent, Julia thought that even the birds had stopped singing, but then, as clear as a bell, a child's voice rang out from beyond the church wall.

'Daddy, look! It's a man lady!'

And Julia turned to see a small boy about the same age as James, with brown skin and brown eyes standing watching with his father. Foreigners, Julia thought, probably the Indians who had moved into her grandfather's gatehouse, which Daddy was so exercised about.

Everyone turned and scowled so hard at the boy that his father quickly led him away, which was a shame because Julia thought he looked nice, and anyway he had only said what everyone else was secretly thinking.

It reminded Julia a bit of a story she'd read in which there was an emperor who needed a new suit and some naughty tailors tricked him into thinking that they had made him a suit from the finest silk and the finest lace, and the emperor was so silly he'd believed them and went out into the street wearing nothing at all. And all the town people were so afraid of the emperor that they didn't dare tell him that he had no clothes on, but then a little boy said it and everyone else felt stupid.

'Did you meet the man lady?' Milly asked Gerry, as he lit two cigarettes simultaneously and handed one to her.

He blew a smoke ring, then turned to look at her lying naked on Sylvia Quinn's old bed. Milly felt her nipples contracting as if his eyes were actually touching her, and instinctively covered her breasts with her hands.

'No,' he said. 'She wasn't allowed down for cocktails.'

'I'm surprised Angela didn't introduce you,' Milly said, blowing a funnel of smoke vertically into the air.

'Angela King? She's engaged to Miles Fogg,' Gerry revealed casually.

Did this mean Angela had finally renounced her claim? Was he disappointed? Milly couldn't tell.

'I've missed you, Milly Minx,' Gerry nestled closer to her, kissing her bare shoulder, using his pet name, which sent shivers trickling down her spine.

'How long is it?' he asked.

'What?'

'We've known each other?'

'I've no idea,' she said.

It was three years, three months and four days, from the first time he asked her if she'd like to go to the flicks with him (*Women in Love*, funnily enough – he'd looked sideways at her during that wrestling bit by the fire as if he thought she might be embarrassed, and they'd had a laugh after about Alan Bates's thingy bobbing around), and three years, three months and three days, if you counted from when they'd first . . .

A gorgeous twinkly smile spread across his face.

Nobody should be as good-looking as he was, she thought.

'Isn't it about time we got engaged, then?' Gerry said.

Milly had tried ever so hard not to imagine this moment, but inevitably she had, and it hadn't been like this at all.

'All right then,' she heard herself saying casually, beneath the deafening noise inside her shouting, 'Yes! Yes! Yes!'

At the weekend, Iris took the children down to the fossil beach, and showed them the stones most likely to have ammonites inside, just as her father had showed her when she was their age. They broke a couple open with the fossil hammer, but didn't find anything, and they soon lost interest, so she gave them each a length of string with a piece of bacon tied to it, and they sat on the big rocks by the sea, pulling up little crabs and putting them into a bucket. Then they ate the sandwiches she had prepared with lettuce and Barbara's latest batch of goat's cheese. Barbara's first few attempts had come out tasting like fetid bath sponges, but this was creamy and rather delicious. They all fell quiet as they ate it.

Iris knew she couldn't put it off any longer but her heart was suddenly beating in her head like a metronome, drowning out the lapping waves.

'I'm going to go back to London,' she announced, trying to make her voice sound like it wasn't a big deal.

'How long for?' Bruno asked through a mouthful of sandwich.

'I'm not sure . . .' Iris said.

'I 'spect you'll be back tomorrow,' Fiammetta said, clearly relating Iris's trip to London to the times when their father went up for lunch with his publisher. Michael usually spent the night in London because there was no longer a late train that linked up to a bus to Lowhampton, but it had been a while now since he'd made the journey at all. Iris had not answered the phone to the distinctive voice of Roman Stone for some time either. She wondered whether his publisher had given up hope that her father would ever produce another novel.

'I won't be back tomorrow, but I will come back for holidays . . . and sometimes at weekends, maybe . . .' Iris explained.

It wasn't going according to plan. She had decided to say as little as possible, but the twins were looking at her mystified.

'Who will cook our supper?' asked Bruno.

'Daddy will, I expect,' Iris told him.

Bruno made a face. 'Daddies don't cook!' he said.

'Yes, they do,' said Iris. 'You'll see. Daddy is a brilliant cook who makes different things.'

She hoped they wouldn't enquire further. She could only remember her father making beans on toast, or scrambled egg on toast. He sometimes dug up the potatoes, but she'd never seen him peel one.

'Maybe Barbara will make supper for us, sometimes?' Fiammetta suggested.

'Drop scones!' said Bruno, remembering when Barbara had stayed for tea, but they'd run out of bread, and she showed them how to make drop scones. When Michael had come in, he had pretended to drop his on the floor, which had made everyone laugh.

'Maybe she will,' said Iris.

'Can we have a crab race now?' Bruno asked.

They poured the contents of the bucket on to the sand and watched the tiny creatures making their way back home to the sea.

Chapter Five

1973

Josie owned a tall Victorian house in Camden Town, a neighbourhood, like many in London, where deprivation and shabby elegance lived side by side. In the sixties it had been a sort of commune, but one by one the others had moved on to properties of their own, and now Josie lived alone, but it was always open house, with people staying over, or visiting from the States. There were ethnic wallhangings and Indian bedspreads, and a vaguely hippy atmosphere lingered with the smell of patchouli oil.

Occasionally Josie would bring home a man or a woman, but her relationships never seemed to last longer than a few days.

'Still searching for a zipless fuck,' she told Iris one day after an awkward breakfast with a young man who clearly wasn't comfortable with the intimacy of pancakes, bacon and maple syrup the morning after.

The expression, Josie explained, came from a sensational new novel called *Fear of Flying*, which she had bought on a recent trip to New York. What she, like the author, Erica Jong, was looking for was pure, molten passion, the briefer the better, no involvement and preferably anonymous.

'Do feel free to bring someone back, if you want,' Josie told Iris.

'I'm fine, thanks,' Iris replied.

'Did you have a bad experience with a man?' Josie asked,

making Iris wonder whether she could read her mind, or whether her own expression had given her away.

'Sort of,' she admitted.

'Were you raped?'

'No!'

The casual way Josie said things that were generally taboo sometimes made Iris feel very young and unsophisticated.

'But you were hurt? Bastard!'

'It was complicated,' Iris said.

It wasn't really Clive's fault, but Iris couldn't begin to explain.

'If you ever want to talk about it . . . I'm right here,' Josie offered.

'Thanks,' Iris said, but she knew she never would, because the only possible hope of forgetting what had happened was never to mention it.

During the day, Iris couldn't get used to the idea that the space and the silence of the house was hers alone. Once Josie had gone off to work in the morning, Iris experienced the same feeling of almost sinful liberty she could remember when as a child she had sometimes come home from school to an empty house and found herself able to choose which chair to sit on, what cupboards to look in, what to read, when to eat, without anyone telling her.

On her own, time seemed to expand. She went for long walks, pushing her knowledge of London a few streets further each day. From the top of Parliament Hill, the city looked like an endless sprawl stretching as far as the eye could see in every direction. To the east, she could pick out the high-rise tower where she had lived with Vic and his brother, Clive, when she first arrived in London. She could remember the precise sensation of awe and exhaustion climbing off the back of Vic's scooter, her knees stiff with cold after the long journey, looking up at the tower looming above. In those days, she had known only the estate in Hackney where they lived, and the area round the back of the theatres in Shaftesbury Avenue where she worked as a waitress in a café called the Luna Caprese. She had been much younger then, and more frightened. She would never have dreamed of getting off the number 38 bus, which linked the two locations, for fear of getting lost in unknown territory. She'd never quite got over the feeling that she wasn't supposed to be there, and would one day be found out.

Now, Iris discovered that London was like a series of villages. Belsize Park had a different identity from Hampstead; Swiss Cottage from St John's Wood. The area where Josie lived was so vibrant with different languages and music and smells, Iris found even mundane tasks like shopping interesting. Each week, Inverness Street market displayed exciting new fruit and vegetables for Iris to experiment with in the spacious basement kitchen.

In Kingshaven, the Castle orchards produced apples and pears, and at Christmas, Mr Sweetman, the greengrocer, sold nets of clementines, and sticky boxes of dates. Here, there was exotic fruit all year round, mangos, pineapples and avocados, fresh dates, and dusty purple figs, which split open to reveal gleaming crimson flesh inside. In Kingshaven, Iris had taught herself to cook through necessity. Here, folding fistfuls of spaghetti from blue paper into bubbling pots of water and creating sauces from shiny aubergines, ripe tomatoes (which the stall holders sold off by the tray towards the end of the day) and papery globes of garlic, gave her a sense of achievement and pride that she was contributing to the community she was lucky enough to be part of.

In the evenings, Josie's kitchen fizzed with talk. The editorial cooperative of the magazine met regularly and energetically debated all aspects of design and content around Josie's long, pine kitchen table.

There were those, like Josie, who saw their mission as raising awareness; for others, like Maeve, who was setting up a women's refuge, the most important objective was the dissemination of practical advice and services such as pregnancy tests and contraception. Some wanted the magazine to be overtly political like the underground press of the sixties; some, like Shelley, who worked in publicity at a publishing house, were in favour of creating a glossy product that would sit alongside *Cosmopolitan* but offer a subversive feminist perspective, although she was rapidly persuaded that advertising needed to finance high production values, like cosmetics companies, would be completely at odds with the editorial.

As far as the content was concerned, some favoured a balanced forum that encouraged discussion; others saw it as their mission to promote alternatives to the traditional gender roles for women as virgin, wife, mother or whore.

In an effort to respect the different approaches, it was decided that the editorship of the magazine should rotate among the founder members.

For Iris, who had never had the opportunity of mixing with educated women before, the ebb and flow of intelligent conversation, the confidence with which they expressed their opinions was an inspiration. Occasionally she would chip in; mostly, she listened.

'For the first time in my life, I'm with people I aspire to being like,' Iris tried to explain the exhilaration she felt to Winston, when she met him for lunch one day in a cramped sandwich bar on the Tottenham Court Road. The café was near his record shop, which sold singles and albums imported from all over the world. The shop was a big success story and Winston had recently launched his own independent record label called No Worries. He was often travelling, looking for new sounds, and recently, one of the bands he'd signed in Jamaica had appeared on *The Old Grey Whistle Test*. Whenever he was in London, he called Iris and they would grab a sandwich together, eating in Russell Square if it was fine weather, or crushed against the steamed-up window of the sandwich bar if it was raining.

'But what's your role?' Winston enquired.

Iris sometimes wished he would unquestioningly support her enthusiasms, just as she always did his, instead of coolly analysing everything.

'Research,' Iris offered. 'General backup . . . I'm learning lots,' she said, seeing the scepticism on his face.

'You should go to university,' Winston told her.

Sometimes Iris wondered whether Winston was a little bit offended that she had not returned to his house when she came back to London.

'You were going to do the sensible thing and be a barrister,' Iris reminded him. 'But you threw it all up to go into the music industry. I've been given this opportunity, so I'm gambling too.'

'I had something to fall back on,' said Winston.

'That's so paternalistic!' Iris told him, using one of her new words.

Winston laughed, then he scrunched up his empty white paper sandwich bag, and gave her a kiss on the cheek before squeezing out past the queue and leaving her to finish her sandwich alone.

Iris found herself walking towards her old haunts in Soho. The Luna Caprese was exactly as it had been, with the same menu of pasta and twenty different ways with a veal escalope, and the same mural of the Bay of Naples on the back wall. Her old boss greeted her as if she was a long-lost relation and insisted that she sit down and eat a plate of *spaghetti alle vongole* even though she told him she had just had lunch.

'You were the best waitress ever, Sarah,' he said, with exuberant Italian exaggeration. 'You want your job back, yes?'

Nobody had called Iris Sarah for years. It was the name she had given herself when she first came to London. Now she didn't feel like that person any more. She would have liked to explain, but she knew that Stefano, with his limited English, would not understand. She wasn't sure she even understood any more.

'Do you ever see Vic?' she asked tentatively.

'Vic, yes, of course,' Stefano laughed. 'He has orange hairs now.'

'Orange?'

Stefano's smile was a mixture of affection and disapproval. Vic had always been a dedicated follower of fashion.

'He work in theatre with pop groups,' he explained.

'Pop groups?'

'Rainbow, I think is the name. Sometimes he get tickets for Anna Maria. Vic a very nice man. His brother, no!'

'No?' Iris tried to keep her voice even.

'Clive, very bad. Very bad man,' Stefano told her.

There was still a faint palpitation of fear when Iris thought about Clive, the logical, rational part of her mind telling her that Clive was safely in prison and would have forgotten all about her by now, but, as she walked through Soho's sleazy streets, where every other premises was a peep show, she could almost feel his presence lurking in the doorways of the seedy clubs where the bouncers still wore dinner suits and Brylcreem in their hair.

The new Big Biba store in the art deco building that had been Derry and Toms on Kensington High Street, had been open only a couple of months when Mummy took Julia there during the first half-term holiday from boarding school.

It felt more like being inside a film than a shop, one of those black-and-white films that were always on television on Sunday afternoons with Fred Astaire and Ginger Rogers tapping intricate routines down grand staircases and over marble terraces. The luxurious old-fashioned look of the place made the customers behave differently too – as if they were not just trying on new clothes, but new lives as well.

'What do you think?' Mummy asked, wrapping a purple feather boa around her shoulders, and pouting.

'You look like a film star!' Julia told her truthfully.

Mummy liked that description. She blew a silent kiss over her shoulder, then frowned and unceremoniously unwound the boa, throwing it back on the hatstand. One of the feathers detached itself and floated slowly to the floor where it lay like an accusation.

'When do I ever have an occasion to wear a feather boa?' Mummy asked crossly.

'Not very practical,' Julia agreed.

For a fraction of a second, her mother looked annoyed, then put her arm round Julia's back and gave her a squeeze.

'No, not at all practical,' she said with a strange little laugh.

It was lovely just being with Mummy – girls together, Mummy said – without James for once. James always made a nuisance of himself in department stores, trying to run up down escalators or speed up revolving doors, whirling bewildered elderly customers back out on to the street.

They had lunch in the Rainbow Room Restaurant on the fifth floor, which Julia said was the most beautiful place she'd ever seen and Mummy looked pleased.

'There's a roof garden, you know,' Mummy told her. 'With real flamingos! I bet Sylvia Quinn doesn't have real flamingos in her roof garden.'

Julia chose the moment to take another pull on the fat black plastic straw in her chocolate milkshake. She wondered how Mummy could have found out about the roof garden Daddy had created for Mrs Quinn, on top of the department store in Lowhampton.

'I think Biba is the best place in the whole world,' Julia tried to switch the direction of the conversation.

'Do you, darling?' Mummy said, reaching across the table and clutching her hand. Then she went very silent, and Julia tried not to make unsophisticated slurpy noises as she neared the bottom of the milkshake, desperately willing her mother not to start crying.

Mummy had met her off the train this morning and they'd caught a bus straight to Biba instead of going to freshen up at Mummy's little flat in the red-brick mansion block like they usually did. It was quite a relief, really, because normally, as soon as the door to the apartment closed behind them, Mummy would start to wail about how awful it was that she wasn't allowed to see her children. Whilst she did her best to comfort Mummy, Julia did sometimes think it was an awful waste of the precious time they did have together to spend it all crying, then checking her face in her compact mirror demanding to know if she looked as if she'd been crying. Once, when Julia dared to suggest this, Mummy had rounded on her and accused her of ganging up on her just like everyone else, and then it had taken even longer to make her happy again.

Mummy lit a cigarette.

'How are things in Kingshaven?' she asked casually.

Julia had her answer ready. It was one of the good things about being at boarding school.

'I don't really know,' she said.

'Doesn't Daddy write to you?' Mummy's eyes gleamed in expectation of fault.

'Yes he does,' stammered Julia.

She knew Mummy would love her to say that he didn't, but she simply wasn't able to lie about Daddy, who sent a letter to her every single week (which was actually more than Mummy did).

'But you know Daddy,' Julia added.

His letters never said anything much except about the weather (which usually wasn't very different from the weather at the school, since it was less than fifty miles away).

Mummy glared at her, then softened.

'I do,' she said curtly, stubbing out the half-smoked cigarette.

Julia racked her brain for some neutral titbit of news from Kingshaven that Mummy would be able to pounce on and toss about mercilessly like a cat with a mouse, until she had completely exhausted it.

'Angela King is getting married,' she ventured. 'Her fiancé's name is Mr Fogg.'

'Mr Fogg? I've never heard of him,' said Mummy, as if Julia was somehow to blame for her ignorance.

'Angela met him at the Horse Trials,' said Julia. 'He won a prize.'

'Someone would have to love horses,' Mummy mused, 'to marry Angela.' She looked up and smiled, as if she had made a joke.

'Yes,' said Julia, pleased to have hit on a subject that might cheer Mummy up. 'Auntie Libby says she wouldn't be surprised if Angela and Mr Fogg have children with four legs!'

'Did she really! Good old Libby!' Mummy laughed.

Phew! Mummy now seemed much brighter.

'Are you going to the wedding?' she suddenly demanded.

Julia nodded, wishing now that she had saved some of the chocolate milkshake so she wouldn't have to elaborate further.

'Well, then,' said Mummy, taking her napkin from her lap and throwing it down on to the table decisively, 'we must get you something to wear!'

Julia knew she had missed the moment to reveal that she was going to the wedding as a bridesmaid, and that Granny Ruby had already made her dress in white satin from the same pattern as the Guinevere dress, with a bodice that squashed the tender buds of breasts that had recently appeared on Julia's chest.

Back on the first floor, Mummy held various dresses up against Julia and, squinting, estimated that Julia must be a proper ladies' size twelve. She picked out a clingy dress in plum jersey. To Julia's amazement, it fitted, and she emerged shyly from the changing room, not recognizing herself for a moment in the full-length mirror. Her mother was waiting for her with a pair of boots in the exact same plum-colour suede with platform soles and heels much higher than Julia had ever been allowed. She looked at least fifteen. Julia felt a smile stretching right across her face.

'What you need,' said Mummy, staring at Julia's chest, 'is a bra.'

Outside she hailed a taxi to Sloane Square, justifying the extravagance because it was a special occasion. There was no one like Mummy for making a special occasion even more special. As they sped along beside the park, Julia kept touching the black and gold carrier bags beside her, unable to believe that the clothes and boots inside now belonged to her.

The lingerie department of Peter Jones was almost more exciting than Biba itself. The lady shop assistant showed Julia into a cubicle all of her own and explained how to do the back of the bra up at your front first and then twist it round to your back. When she emerged with two white Gossard junior bras – size 32A – Julia felt she had crossed a very special boundary.

Her mother had arranged for them to meet her new husband, Alan, for supper in the self-service Spaghetti House and Julia was allowed to choose cannelloni and profiteroles. There was a candle in a round bottle in a basket on the checked tablecloth, and Mummy's eyes shone, not with tears, like they usually did, but with happiness.

When Alan asked them what they'd been up to, they both said shopping, and then giggled simultaneously, as if they had a woman's secret that they couldn't possible share with him.

'How were the flamingos?' Alan enquired, and Julia realized they'd been so intent on their quest, they'd forgotten all about the roof garden.

When Iris turned up at the Rainbow Theatre in Finsbury Park, Vic did a double take, then rushed out of the box office to give her a hug. He was taller than she was now because he was wearing silver platform boots under his loons, and his hair was dyed bright orange and styled short on top and longish at the back. He was wearing silver eye shadow and a lot of mascara.

'I can't believe anyone would choose to have hair this colour,' Iris teased him.

'It's an homage,' said Vic.

'To?'

'You,' quipped Vic. 'Well, you *and* David Bowie. He played here last August. Him and Roxy Music on the same night – can you believe it? There were dancers and mime artists crawling all over the stage. A Mazing!'

Vic spoke differently, with a camp archness in his voice. Clive's imprisonment had given Vic his freedom too, Iris realized. Vic had finally 'come out' as a homosexual, something he would never have dared to do with his older brother around.

They sat together in a dingy empty pub, Vic's flamboyant glam-rock clothes looking incongruous against the dark Victorian furnishing and the pictures of the double-winning Arsenal football team behind the bar.

'I thought you might have gone back home,' Vic told her, when Iris told him she had been in Kingshaven.

'It wasn't like that . . .' Iris explained about Claudia and looking after the twins.

'Excuse me.' Vic squinted at her. 'No. Can't quite see it,' he said.

'What?'

'You as a mother figure.'

'You'd be surprised,' Iris said.

'I certainly would!' Vic laughed.

They picked up as if it was hours, not years, since they'd seen each other.

'How long is it?' Vic asked, as he bought her another lager and lime.

'Five years,' said Iris.

'Five years,' Vic sang. 'God, you should have been here for Bowie. We've got Sweet coming soon. I'm friends with one of their roadies . . . What about you?'

'What?'

'Boyfriends?'

'There's been nobody since . . .' she confessed.

'Clive?' Vic sounded surprised.

'Men don't fancy me,' Iris told him. 'I'm too tall, I've got no tits and I don't know how to simper.'

'Me neither,' said Vic. 'Except . . . oooh . . . men do fancy me!'

He said it in such a camp *Are You Being Served?* kind of

voice, a couple of workmen, who were sitting at the bar downing pints of beer, turned and gave him a threatening kind of look.

'And the ones who jeer from building sites are often the worst,' Vic whispered. 'With their arses hanging out of their trousers . . .'

'Stop it,' said Iris, but she couldn't help laughing.

'What about that black guy?' Vic asked.

'Winston? What about him?'

'He had the hots for you, didn't he?'

'How do you know about Winston?' she asked, suddenly suspicious.

When she had lived with Vic and Clive, she had kept her past completely secret. She had been Sarah Bird. Vic knew where she had come from, because he'd given her a lift out of there on his Lambretta, but he did not know Winston.

'Clive had you followed . . .' Vic looked a bit sheepish. 'I was going to try and find you, tell you, but then Clive got arrested . . . I reckon your Winston had a lucky escape,' Vic told her.

'He's not my Winston,' said Iris.

Back at school, Julia's mind began to rehearse the possible consequences of misleading Mummy about the dress. There would be hell to pay if Mummy were to find out that Julia hadn't worn it to Angela's wedding. Julia would have to make sure that Mummy never saw a photograph. She could rely on Daddy and Granny Ruby because neither of them had spoken to Mummy since she left. She was sure that her sisters would keep it under their hats, because they were quite clever at using the divorce between Mummy and Daddy to their advantage. The problem was going to be James, who sometimes let things slip.

Julia stowed the dress and boots in their Biba bags under her bed in the dormitory, but she couldn't resist showing them to her friends Cee and Bee. Cee, whose real name was Celia, could be trusted not to tell tales, although she envied the bra, because it made her the only one in the dormitory without one. Bee, whose real name was Belinda, was one of the more grown-up girls, who smuggled copies of *Jackie* magazine into the school and had already got the curse. She was an unlikely friend for Julia except that they both had divorced parents and Bee had come to Julia's defence when the other girls were teasing her about it. Bee's mother, even more scandalously than Mummy, had run off with a Latin American ballroom dancing teacher, but Bee was completely unrepentant and said she didn't blame her mother because José was gorgeous and her father was an old bore. It was Bee who offered a solution to the dilemma of the dress.

'It's quite normal to change for the party in the evening,' she told Julia.

The name of the magazine was eventually agreed. *Siren* was chosen for its dual meaning of an urgent alarm call and a mythological woman who lured men on to the rocks, overruling Maeve, who thought it sounded like a newsletter for the Union of Firemen. With all the discussion, Iris sometimes wondered whether they were ever going to get down to actually producing the magazine, but gradually the agenda for the launch issue began to emerge. After strenuous arguments in favour of launching with the theme of work, which would put down a marker that they were serious, they decided instead to launch with the theme sex. As Shelley put it, sex sells.

Iris's first proper assignment was to survey the availability of contraception in the local area. She visited clinics, pretending to be a mother of two who didn't want any more children, and was outraged to be told that she would need her husband's permission if she wanted to have an IUD fitted. She discovered that contraception was often difficult to obtain because of the restricted opening hours, which meant that women who worked could not easily access the services. She traipsed round the local council estates with questionnaires, knocking on doors and asking women about their needs. Iris quickly learned which doors had angry dogs behind them, and which had men who worked night shifts and didn't relish being disturbed during the day. Women who were initially suspicious of another woman asking personal questions gradually grew to trust her. Some of them used the anonymity of the forms as a kind of confessional, and Iris ended up learning more than she wanted about their lives.

Whenever Iris found herself climbing up cold flights of concrete stairs, she was reminded of the tower block where she had lived with Vic and Clive. Their building had been relatively new then, and there had been a sense of optimism among the residents, who felt fortunate to have swapped crumbling Victorian slums for gleaming modernity. The lifts had generally worked, and the stair-cases hadn't smelled of piss. Now the graffiti-ridden towers and the power cuts seemed like the symptoms of a general malaise. And when Iris listened to the women's stories, she often found herself thinking that this was how she would have ended up herself if she had stayed there, struggling to find the money to feed the children, and waiting in terror for a violent man to return home.

The initial print run of the first issue of *Siren*, with the banner headline 'SEX – THE FACTS OF WOMEN'S LIVES' sold out, even though W. H. Smith and a number of other newsagents refused to stock it. Iris was concerned that the cover price would be unaffordable for many of the women she had spoken to, who had little or no financial independence. After some discussion, she and Maeve tried to distribute free copies around the estates, but Iris was disheartened to return with only four copies taken, as most of the women took one look at the cover and did not dare give the magazine house room for fear of what their men would think.

'Nobody ever said it was going to be easy . . .' Josie told her.

Iris had to squash down her natural outrage and impatience. Things didn't change overnight, but they had made a start. She threw herself into the celebrations, cooking a huge tray of vegetable lasagne for everyone to eat and toasting the future of *Siren* with rough red wine called (appropriately, said Josie) Bull's Blood. Later, by the flickering light of two fat orange Habitat candles, Iris looked down Josie's long kitchen table at the animated faces of her colleagues and felt a kind of peace settle on her as if she had finally found a place in the world where she belonged.

After everyone had gone she and Josie stood side by side at the window doing the washing-up together. It felt completely right when Josie put her arm around her and planted a kiss, first on her hair, like a parent would, and then, when Iris turned to smile at her, on her lips.

Julia spent the night before Angela's wedding restlessly worrying about her bridesmaid duties. When she came down to breakfast yawning, she was surprised to find Sylvia Quinn sitting at the breakfast table, lending credence to James's preposterous claims that Mrs Quinn sometimes stayed the night at the Summer House and slept in Daddy's room.

'Good morning, Julia.'

'Good morning, Mrs Quinn.'

'You can call me Auntie Sylvia if you want.' Mrs Quinn offered her cheek for Julia to kiss.

'No, thank you,' said Julia politely.

Julia guessed that Mrs Quinn must be about the same age as Mummy but she never looked young like Mummy sometimes did, and she never looked old like Mummy sometimes did. Mrs Quinn's lipstick was never chewed off and there were never little black bits under her eyelashes. And even though Mummy often smelled a bit like the smoking compartment on a train, Julia preferred that to the smell of Mrs Quinn. Julia guessed that Mrs Quinn must use every single one of the Fresh'n'Dainty deodorant sprays on the advert that ran down the side of the problem page in *Jackie*. There were sprays for breath and feet as well as antiperspirant for underarms. There was even something called intimate deodorant for your knickers. Mrs Quinn was the kind of person who liked to have the latest thing and it would explain clouds of competing scents that seemed to precede and follow her around.

Julia poured herself a bowl of cornflakes from the box. The noise of munching cereal was loud inside her head, but at least it meant she didn't have to try to make conversation. Mrs Quinn watched with an insincere smile fixed to her face, her cold blue eyes alert for any crumb of cereal or dribble of milk that might escape the corner of Julia's mouth.

At last Daddy appeared, his cheeks still pink from his shave. There was a little fleck of shaving foam still clinging to the top of his right ear, which Mrs Quinn dabbed away with a pressed white handkerchief.

'Good morning, Julia.'

'Good morning, Daddy.'

'Good afternoon,' said James, because he was still at the age when he thought that was funny.

'Looking forward to today?' Daddy asked brightly.

'Not really,' Julia replied.

'I think madam got out of the wrong side of the bed,' Mrs Quinn remarked.

Julia hated her most of all when she called her madam.

'There's only one side,' James pointed out. 'The other side is wall.'

'Nervous?' Daddy asked Julia kindly.

'Very,' Julia replied.

Daddy gave Mrs Quinn a reprimanding sort of look.

'I've got something that might cheer her up.' Now it was Mrs Quinn who was eager to get back in his good books.

'What's that?' Daddy smiled his big adoring smile at her.

'I would have supplied your bridesmaid's dress, if I'd been allowed to,' Mrs Quinn explained, producing from beside her chair a large stiff pink carrier bag with her name and a shell design in black. 'But I wasn't, so I thought you might like this to wear for the party instead.'

Julia's heart began to beat faster as privately she prayed to God that the bag would contain embroidered denim hot pants or some trendy outfit the Kings would consider entirely unsuitable. Instead, it was a perfectly appropriate smocked cotton dress with a pattern of little lilac sprigged flowers on a navy-blue background. The high Victorian collar was edged with cream lace and there was lace round the cuffs of the long sleeves. A year, or even a month before, Julia would have been thrilled, but since she had been to Biba, it just looked like a little girl's dress.

'Aren't you lucky?' said Daddy.

Angela King, Eddie King, Susannah Snow, who was the other bridesmaid, and Julia all travelled in a horse-drawn carriage to the church. Because of Angela's dress, there wasn't enough room for Eddie to sit next to her, so Julia squeezed in beside the bride, with Eddie in the opposite seat with Susannah Snow, who was almost exactly the same age as James. When they arrived at the church, there was a line of cars outside puffing clouds of exhaust into the already misty November air. A biting wind swirled brown papery leaves around the churchyard.

'Turn your bloody engines off, for Christ's sake!' Eddie shouted. 'At this rate, the petrol'll cost more than the bloody champagne.'

He climbed down from the carriage to see what was going on.

'Apparently, the Rev's booked another wedding in before us,' he reported back.

'Bloody nerve!' exclaimed Angela.

Julia shrank back against the seat. Whenever voices were raised or swear words used, she always somehow felt as if it was her fault.

'Who's getting married?' Angela King demanded.

'Percy Bland's daughter,' said Eddie. 'Millicent, isn't it?'

'Who to?' Angela demanded.

'That bartender fellow,' said Eddie King.

Angela went rather pink.

'I didn't think he was the marrying kind,' she said, tossing her head so forcefully the garland of flowers holding the veil in place went a bit wonky. She looked cross.

'I expect he's got his eye on taking over the Ship,' said Eddie.

'Poor Christopher . . .' said Angela.

'Christopher? What's it got to do with him?' Eddie asked.

'He's besotted with Millicent,' said Angela.

'He's kept that one secret,' said Eddie.

It sounded to Julia rather like one of those photo-stories in *Jackie* magazine, featuring boys called hunks, who appeared not to be in love with girls, but really were. The title was normally something like 'What Becomes of the Broken Hearted?', and there was usually a happy ending after all the misunderstandings.

Julia's own favourite bit of the magazine, apart from the pin-up of David Cassidy, which she had torn out and Sellotaped to the inside of her locker door, was the Cathy and Claire page where girls wrote in with their problems.

As they waited shivering in the cold outside the church, Julia composed a letter in her head about her own present difficulty.

'Dear Cathy and Claire, My mother has bought me a lovely dress to wear for a wedding, but so has my father's lady friend. Which one would it be better to offend?'

Cathy and Claire would be bound to come up with some sensible advice, but Julia couldn't imagine what it might be.

'He's a bit of a dark horse, isn't he?' Eddie was saying.

Julia found herself staring at the tail of the horse harnessed to the carriage as it suddenly rose to reveal a steaming dollop of dung, which thudded to the ground and enveloped them all in the pong of fresh manure. She hardly dared look at Angela, in case Angela somehow thought it was Julia's fault. And then suddenly Angela and Eddie King were laughing their heads off, and Julia and Susannah joined in, not really knowing why they were laughing.

*   *   *

In the end, Julia decided it would be easier to wear the dress that Mrs Quinn had given her than to explain where the Biba dress had come from. Then it turned out Mrs Quinn wasn't invited to the party after all, but it was too late to change.

The disc jockey in the former ballroom of the Palace Hotel had two turntables, coloured lights that spun round, and a blobby pattern projected on to the wall that painted people's faces psychedelic if they moved in front of it. Everyone sat at the tables round the edge of the ballroom, staring at the empty space in front of them and tapping their feet awkwardly until 'I Love You Love Me Love' came on, and Angela and her new husband took to the floor. After that, most of the grown-ups joined in the dancing, except Granny Ruby and Granny Liliana, who retired to the lounge saying it was a terrible racket. Christopher King stood staring out of the window, even though it was quite dark outside, while Julia's older sister tried to flirt with him. According to Adrian, Joanna 'fancied' Christopher, which made Julia feel a bit sorry for him. When there was something Joanna wanted, she was usually horrible until she got it.

All the Kings were there, including Great-Uncle Cyril, who was making strange robotic attempts to dance to 'All the Young Dudes'. Pearl Snow, Susannah's mother, was wearing an embroidered cheesecloth smock over a long wrap-around skirt, which flew out when she twirled, revealing very white, rather lumpy legs. Susannah shrank with embarrassment as her mother tripped on her skirt and almost overbalanced as she approached their table. Pearl had black lines painted all the way round her eyes, which made her look like an ancient Egyptian, and there was a smell wafting round her a bit like the joss sticks her sisters sometimes burned so Daddy wouldn't know that they smoked.

'Come on, Jolly!' Pearl Snow snatched Daddy's hand as the DJ said something over the loudspeaker, then put on Wizzard's recent hit, 'See My Baby Jive'.

126

'I don't think . . .' Daddy stuttered.

'Oh, for God's sake,' Pearl insisted, 'you used to be the best jiver on the South Coast!'

As Pearl pulled him on to the dance floor, Julia could hardly bear to watch in case Daddy was embarrassing too, but she was proud to see that he was a very good dancer, much better than Pearl, who kept getting tangled up. Poor Susannah. Julia wanted to tell her fellow bridesmaid that it didn't matter, but she wasn't very good at lying.

'The trouble with you, Pearl, is you won't be led,' Daddy scolded, as they returned to the table. Pearl picked up a glass of wine, drank it in one gulp, then poured herself another.

'I simply can't bear being told what to do!' Pearl laughed. 'It goes against my nature. Fancy a smooch?'

'I need a breath of air,' said Daddy, unpeeling Pearl's fingers from his arm and making a swift exit from the ballroom. Pearl stood staring at the space where he had been for a couple of seconds, as if she hadn't realized he had gone.

'Goodness me, Julia, you're growing up,' she remarked, then staggered off in search of another victim to dance with her to the slow record, 'Without You' by Nilsson, which had stayed at the top for the longest time ever.

A blue light swept around the room making Angela King's wedding dress glow as if it was radioactive. The lace at the edge of Julia's sleeves was the same bright white too.

'It's called ultraviolet,' Adrian King explained. 'Picks up anything light, makes you look as if you've got a suntan, would you like to dance?'

'Pardon?' Julia wasn't sure that she'd heard him correctly. At school, she was good at dancing. She'd got her Grade 3 ballet with Merit. But it was different dancing with boys. Julia wasn't sure she'd know what to do.

'Who do you hate most?' James suddenly asked. 'Mrs Quinn or Pearl Snow?'

Susannah Snow burst into tears and fled the table.

'At least Daddy doesn't like Pearl Snow,' Julia said.

'Nobody likes Pearl,' said Adrian authoritatively. 'Not even her husband.'

Julia watched as Pearl seemed to melt on to the young man she was dancing with, as if she would slide down his body into a cheesecloth pool on the floor if he took his arms away.

'What do you mean?' Julia asked.

'He's left her.'

'Are they going to get divorced?' Julia asked, suddenly brightening. If they did, then she would be able to look after Susannah when she came to boarding school, just like Bee had done with her.

The last record was 'How Can I Be Sure?' by David Cassidy, which was Julia's favourite of all time.

All the couples were holding each other very closely, moving very slowly. Julia tried not to stare, nor catch anyone's eye, especially not Adrian's. She was terribly aware of him standing next to her, and half of her wanted him to ask her to dance again, while the other half was wishing, hoping, praying that David Cassidy himself would suddenly miraculously appear in the ballroom and sweep her into his arms.

She looked across the ballroom and caught Christopher King staring at her chest. No embarrassment she had ever felt before came close to her utter mortification as she realized that the ultraviolet light had penetrated her dress and picked out her precious Gossard junior bra, spotlighting it for the whole room to see, like a bright white bikini.

As Sir John Allsop grew progressively more frail, and the inevitable day drew closer when the motley assortment of people who lived at the Castle would have to leave, the traditional celebration of Christmas seemed to take on a disproportionate significance, as if both atheist and Jew had decided to suspend belief and make merry in case this year was the last.

Watched over by the naked statues of the Roman gods Mercury and Mars from their niches on either side of the grand staircase, the children carefully lit the candles on the Christmas tree with long tapers. Michael and Winston dug up the tree each year and planted it in a zinc dustbin in the lofty hall.

Christmas Eve at the Castle was open house, with any intrepid carol singers who felt like braving the steep walk up from the town welcomed in for refreshments, and Michael playing ragtime on Sir John's grand piano.

This year's surprise additions were Iris's brother, Anthony, and a girl in a purple midi coat who arrived pink-faced after their brisk walk.

'Happy Christmas!' they chorused, stamping their feet on the mat.

'Happy Christmas,' said Iris.

She let them in with a smile, but Anthony's presence reminded her immediately of Christmases when they were children.

Anthony and Iris had never been close, and since Iris ran away as a teenager, they had hardly been in contact because Anthony had been away at boarding school. Now Anthony was at St John's College, Oxford, and his girlfriend, Marie, was studying Law at St Hilda's College. Apparently, they had met at their first lecture in the University Schools when she had asked to borrow a rubber. (Which, as Josie was later to point out, was somewhat ironic in the circumstances.)

Marie talked in a soft Liverpool accent that just occasionally slipped into harsh fishwife and made her sound, Iris thought, like both of the Liver Birds at the same time. Although there was no reason she could point to, Iris took an instant dislike to her. Marie seemed to make herself at home far too quickly.

Barbara arrived with a big tin of mince pies, and she and Iris went to the kitchen to make mulled cider. Iris found it slightly alarming how easily she had fallen back into the traditional female role at the Castle.

'Does my father actually do anything?' she asked Barbara.

'I help out a bit with the cooking,' Barbara admitted.

'I dread to think what they'd do without you.'

'No, it's lovely for me, really . . .' Barbara said, with bright eyes and a smile spreading across her face that made Iris wonder whether it was only the children Barbara had grown fond of.

'How is the Riviera?' Iris asked her.

'Just about ticking over,' said Barbara. 'I've got a few regulars who come back each year. I'm thinking of getting a French student next summer who could help me out in exchange for board and speaking English.'

'Sounds like a good idea!' said Iris.

'What about you?' asked Barbara.

'It's going well,' Iris told her.

'You're happy?'

Iris nodded and handed Barbara a tray of mugs.

Was she happy? Sometimes Iris wondered why the things she imagined would solve her life never quite did. When she was fourteen, she thought everything would be perfect if she could be in Swinging London; when she was sixteen, her dream had been to be Clive's girlfriend, but she'd quickly realized that wasn't enough, because she wanted to change the world. When she met Josie and discovered feminism, it seemed more like the answer than anything else had, and yet, was she happy? Was this what happiness felt like? If it was, then it wasn't how she thought it would be, and yet she didn't know what would make her more so.

Back in the hall, presents were being opened. For Barbara, Fiammetta had painted rather a good picture of the goat, and Bruno had found a cow bell in one of the trunks in the attic to hang around Mary's neck. There was also a box of expensive soap. A blush of pleasure spread across Barbara's face as she nodded her thanks to Michael.

Barbara had bought Bruno a set of biscuit cutters in

130

animal shapes, and Fiammetta a tapestry set. For Michael, there was an expensive leather-bound notebook.

'I thought perhaps it might inspire some writing—' she said, stopping mid-sentence and going rather pink, sensing immediately she might have overstepped the mark.

Michael frowned.

'Are you working on anything?' Josie asked him.

'No,' said Michael, with the finality of someone who did not want to discuss it further.

The silence was a little uncomfortable.

Iris knew that her father sometimes received royalty cheques from foreign editions of his first two novels, but she wasn't sure that they were still in print in England. One of the Christmas cards on the mantelpiece was from his publisher. Under the printed message of seasonal greetings, Roman Stone had scrawled in fountain pen, 'Will 1974 be the year? Do hope so.'

Anthony and Marie had brought presents for the twins.

'Thank you,' said Fiammetta very politely, as she pulled the wrapping paper off a little pink handbag made of moulded plastic with a pretend lipstick and powder compact inside. 'What is it?'

For Bruno, there was a cowboy hat, and a plastic gun in a holster, which he turned over a couple of times in his little hands before handing it back with the solemn words, 'We don't believe in guns in our family.'

An almost tangible wave of pride lapped through Iris.

Bruno offered a plate of snowflake biscuits with white icing decorated with silver balls and tiny thumbprints.

'How delicious,' said Marie, nibbling one. 'Did you make these?'

Bruno nodded proudly.

'Are you going to be a chef when you grow up?'

''Spect so,' Bruno replied, then asked his father, 'What's a chef?'

In the ensuing laughter, Iris seethed with irritation.

'You wouldn't dream of saying that to Fiammetta,' she said, throwing down an implicit challenge to Marie.

The large hall went quiet.

'What do you mean?' Marie asked softly.

'If Fiammetta cooked something delicious then you'd probably tell her she'd make someone a lovely wife!' Iris declared combatively.

Marie's eyes held hers. 'You've no evidence on which to base that assumption,' she responded, with a lawyer's insistence on accuracy.

Iris felt everyone's eyes were going from one to the other like spectators watching a rally at Wimbledon.

'We just think it's important to think about these things,' Josie said.

'Oh, lighten up, for God's sake!' said Winston, under his breath.

Anthony suddenly got up from the chair he was sitting in and said, in a voice Iris thought he had probably been taught for speech days, 'My Lord, ladies and gentlemen, I've an announcement to make . . .'

Everyone was quiet again with not even a rustle of wrapping paper from the twins.

'I'm delighted to tell you that Marie and I are engaged!'

Winston started clapping and Bruno enthusiastically followed his lead, and then Marie went round the room kissing everyone in turn, including Sir John, who clearly had no idea who she was, and the professor, who was so deaf he hadn't heard a word of the announcement.

Iris slipped out to the kitchen to reheat the cider.

'Need any help, sis?'

Anthony had followed her out.

'I'm fine, thanks,' said Iris.

There was steam coming off the saucepan and Iris's forehead broke into a sweat.

'Do you approve?' her brother asked.

'You're a bit young to be getting married, aren't you?' Iris replied, side-stepping the question she knew he was asking.

'We're only getting engaged. We won't marry until we've both finished at uni.'

132

'So why the big deal?'

'Marie's a devout Catholic . . .'

'For heaven's sake!' Iris couldn't help laughing. 'She's not still a virgin, is she? Not in nineteen seventy-three!'

Her guess was confirmed by her brother's blush.

'I'm surprised she's prepared to be deflowered by some-one from such a family of sinners,' Iris went on.

'So are you and Josie . . . ?'

'What?' asked Iris sharply.

'Together?'

'We're friends,' said Iris.

'Marie thought you were. She doesn't mind . . .'

'Well, bully for Marie!'

How quickly adults who had been children together be-came children again, Iris thought, slightly ashamed of her easy slide into bickering.

'What do you think's going to happen to Dad?' Anthony asked. 'I mean when . . .'

'When he can't live here any longer?' Iris filled in.

Now they were talking as if they were the grown-ups responsible for him.

'Do you think he even realizes Jolly Allsop will throw them out?' Anthony went on. 'If Mum gets her way, he won't even be allowed in the gatehouse when the Patels move out,' said Anthony.

'And will Mum get her way?' Iris asked.

They were speaking in a kind of shorthand, but they both knew what she was asking.

'Looks pretty likely, I'd say,' said Anthony.

'Lady Allsop,' said Iris sarcastically. 'She'll like that.'

'She deserves it,' said Anthony loyally.

He had always been their mother's favourite.

'When someone says, "My motto is live and let live," you can bet your bottom dollar that you're dealing with a bigot,' Josie remarked later, as she brushed her hair, looking in the round Georgian mirror at Iris, who was lying in bed behind her.

It was at moments like this that Iris was certain she did love Josie. She could be deliciously caustic.

Josie put the hairbrush down. The room they were sleeping in was so cold, Iris could see her breath.

'Can I come in and get warm?' Josie asked.

Iris lifted the heavy layer of blankets, which smelled of mothballs, so that Josie could climb into the bed with her. The room had two single brass bedsteads with sagging mattresses with creaking springs. The only way they could both fit in a single bed was if they lay side by side like spoons. Josie's long back pressed against Iris's chest, the firm contour of her buttocks warming against the concave hollow of Iris's pelvis, Josie's icy toes jabbing against her warm shins. Josie's left hand sought hers, drew it towards her thick tangle of pubic hair.

'At least Marie didn't ask what we do!' Josie whispered.

Iris felt a little contented surge of achievement as Josie's breath quickened. She liked making Josie come. It was like a gift she could offer in return for everything Josie gave her.

Afterwards, Josie dropped a kiss on Iris's shoulder and was soon snoring softly against her back, but Iris remained wide awake, gradually picking out shapes of the furniture in the room as her eyes grew used to the darkness.

As tradition demanded, the entire King family assembled in the lounge on Christmas Eve. This year, due to the fuel crisis and lack of demand, the hotel was closed for Christmas. It was so cold in the public areas that several of the family were wearing coats and looked like proper carol singers about to stamp through the snow to sing on people's doorsteps.

As Christopher King looked at his shivering clan, he wondered if the King family would celebrate many more Christmases there. How long could the hotel go on limping from one financial crisis to another? The fact was that nobody wanted to come to Kingshaven any more and everyone who was here wanted to leave. The local children were used to going to Lowhampton for their senior schools, and so it was natural that they would look for work there and further afield. Many of them, even the girls, seemed to regard further education as a right. No English people wanted to work as chambermaids or dishwashers any more. In the face of opposition from certain quarters, Christopher had employed Mr and Mrs Patel as cleaners, although Mr Patel had quickly become involved in other aspects of running the hotel, and even Granny Liliana had been obliged to warm to him when she saw the ledger books. But having reorganized the operation of the kitchen and negotiated far better deals with the suppliers than Christopher had ever managed, Mr Patel had informed him just before the hotel closed for the winter that he wouldn't be returning to work in the spring. Apparently, he had bought the lease on Mr Sweetman's greengrocery. The Sweetmans had lost both their sons in the war, so there was no one to take over the family business when they retired. Christopher had wished Mr Patel well, although privately he doubted that even Mr Patel could make a viable business out of Sweetman's, with the state of the local and national economy, but it had been a personal blow as well as a professional one, because Mr Patel had treated him more like a son than an employer, and Christopher had come to rely on his wisdom.

'It's a shame no one thought to light a fire,' said Libby King, with a pointed look at Christopher.

'The chimney hasn't been swept,' Christopher explained. 'I didn't think it was worth the expense with no guests.'

He could see that his mother, who had a tendency to be frugal, accepted the excuse, but his father, Eddie King, harrumphed loudly, and made a big drama out of fetching an electric bar fire from the private quarters. A faint smell of burning dust filled the room before the glowing orange element of the fire faded to grey as the power went out again. The three-day week made candlelight a necessity rather than a seasonal decoration.

'Where are the Allsops?' Granny Ruby suddenly asked,

as Adrian handed round the dog-eared songsheets that had been printed in better times when the hotel had been filled with warmth and Christmas cheer.

'Jolly was a little put out by your refusal to entertain the idea of Mrs Quinn joining us. Perhaps he's making a point,' Libby King informed her.

'The nerve of the woman,' said Granny Ruby. 'First she insinuates herself into my shop, now she's after my grandchildren . . .'

Nobody spoke, and Christopher could tell from the quality of the silence that many of them were thinking, as he was, that Granny Ruby was the last person who should talk about people insinuating their way into places. He'd never understood how his otherwise sensible grandmother Liliana had been so indulgent with the dreadful woman, who had been allowed to become a permanent guest at the hotel. Female friendship, with all the secrets and giggling, was a mystery to Christopher.

'I hardly think it's your grandchildren she's after, Ruby,' said Granny Liliana tartly. 'Shall we get on with the first carol?'

Christopher's youngest brother, Edwin, whom everyone called Winny, had recently started learning the cello, but it was really too soon for him to be playing in public. As he painfully scraped out the introduction to the first song, everyone looked at each other in the hope that someone would work out which carol it was they were supposed to be singing. Uncle Cyril leaned so far to the left in an attempt to crane his neck round Winny's music stand, that he almost tottered, and Christopher had to grab his arm and hold him upright.

Suddenly, Libby burst out decisively in her clear soprano, 'Ding dong merrily on high . . .'

And everyone joined in with uncharacteristic gusto, drowning Winny out, whether he was playing the right tune or not.

Sometimes Christopher wondered why they bothered with the carols at all since they all saw it as a duty rather than a pleasure, a tariff they had to pay before being allowed a Christmas tipple. With no means of heating it, even the possibility of mulled wine seemed remote this evening. Looking across at Angela and her new husband, Miles, Christopher suddenly wondered if everyone except him *was* enjoying themselves. Angela still had a honeymoon glow around her and she smiled every time her husband looked at her. Candlelight and love made his sister almost pretty, thought Christopher. Marriage had given her a presence, a status in the world she had not enjoyed before. It suited her.

Christopher had noticed that marriage had had a similar effect on Milly Bland – Milly Balls, as he must think of her now. The other day, he'd been standing behind her at the bank and seen her beam when the cashier had called, 'Good morning, Mrs Balls!'

Whenever he passed by the shop where she worked – he tried to limit it to twice a day – she seemed to be talking with confidence to the customers. Marriage had made her a woman.

In contrast, he felt so lonely he was almost invisible. Marriage had robbed him of his soul mate, and now that Angela was married, marriage had also robbed him of the only person he could talk to about it. There was no one in the world who understood. Not even Uncle Cyril. Even Granny Liliana, who, he sometimes thought, saw everything, had a blind spot when it came to his feelings for Millicent.

'Plenty more fish in the sea,' she said, waving her hand at the bay as if she meant it literally.

'She wasn't good enough for you. You'll see that one day,' Uncle Cyril assured him, but it was cold comfort.

What right did anyone have to tell him who was good enough?

Christopher found himself staring at Granny Ruby, directing all his pent-up anger towards her. The two grannies had dropped enough hints that 'good enough' meant a girl like Granny Ruby's granddaughter Joanna

Allsop, because she had the right background. It didn't seem to matter that that background was riddled with madness and scandal, as long as the accent was right. Never mind that Millicent was the adored daughter of perfectly respectable parents who loved one another, she spoke like a local, so that ruled her out. Joanna's father was a landowner. Millicent's was a publican. Joanna knew which knives and forks to use at table. Milly ate chicken and chips in the basket.

Christopher tried to suppress the image of the love of his life licking ketchup off her fingers.

Chapter Six

1975

Although Julia's family had been waiting to take over the Castle for as long as any of the children could remember, and the oldest of them, Joanna, was nearly twenty by the time Sir John Allsop finally died, nobody, not even Jolly, seemed in any particular hurry to stake their claim.

For Julia, rare family visits to the Castle to see their grandfather had always been tinged with dread in case Sir John, or his friend the professor, started asking her questions she couldn't answer, like what was the capital of Denmark, or who her favourite composer was. Once, when she'd replied Gilbert O'Sullivan, because 'Clair' was at the top of the charts, her grandfather had unaccountably made her listen to a crackly LP of a tedious opera called *The Pirates of Penzance*.

Even though the twins were six years younger than Julia, they always seemed to know a lot of things, and sometimes spoke in a funny language to each other (Latin, Julia presumed, since the professor was quite keen on it) so that other people couldn't understand what they were saying.

The only time Julia had really enjoyed visiting the Castle was at Christmas, when there was a huge Christmas tree in the hall, with candles, which all the children were allowed to light, leaning over the banisters of the two curving staircases with tapers and transforming the huge room into an enchanted grotto.

There was always lots of lovely food at Christmas (except for the time when Julia asked politely after Jeremy, the baby goat, and Bruno told her she was eating him). Bruno and Fiammetta's father, Mr Quinn, would play bouncy music on the piano and organize team games like musical statues, which Julia was always good at; pass the parcel (even if the prize, after layers of newspaper had been removed, was always something slightly disappointing, like an apple); and the orange game, where you had to stand in a line and pass an orange under your chins all the way down to the front.

But absolutely the best thing about visits to the Castle was that Mrs Quinn never came with them. Mrs Quinn had once been married to Mr Quinn (who told Julia and James to call him Michael, although they never dared), which meant Mrs Quinn wasn't allowed at the Castle, just like Mummy wasn't allowed in Kingshaven.

When Sir John died, and the Allsop family were preparing to move to the Castle, Julia somehow managed to delude herself that the Castle would remain a Mrs Quinn-free zone, but unfortunately that wasn't to be the case at all.

At the beginning of the Easter holidays, Mrs Quinn took the whole family out to lunch in the Grand Hotel in the next resort along the coast, Havenbourne, and asked them with one of her horribly insincere smiles, 'Haven't you all waited long enough?'

The children, who had made a pact that none of them would speak to her that day, since she was always saying that children should be seen and not heard, remained silently focused on their plates.

'You'd have so much more space,' Mrs Quinn continued, her eyes searching each of their faces for a response. 'Trees to climb.' She nodded at James. 'You could have a swimming pool all of your own in a garden that size,' she said to Julia.

Their father coughed awkwardly.

'The trouble is there's an awful lot to be done and no money to do it,' he explained. 'What with death duties . . .'

'Have you really gone into it properly, Jolly?' Sylvia wanted to know. 'I find it hard to believe that there's no money when you're sitting on a pile like that, with all that land. Any bank would lend against that.'

'But in these times, with the pound sinking . . .' Jolly faltered.

'It's not a bad time to get a mortgage with inflation rising,' Mrs Quinn informed him. She knew about something called economics because she read a pink paper that had lots of graphs and initials like IMF, instead of the normal type of newspaper Daddy read, which was all about murders and disappearing lords and that sort of thing.

'I can hardly mortgage my inheritance,' said Daddy.

'Well, you'll have to sell some of those awful paintings then. They should bring in a bob or two,' Mrs Quinn told him.

'But that's our heritage . . .'

'Bet you don't even know who half of them are,' said Mrs Quinn.

'Actually, I don't see that it's any of your business,' ten-year-old James suddenly piped up, breaking the children's vow of silence.

It was one of those moments when the whole room suddenly seemed to go silent just before he said it, so everyone in the restaurant heard.

Mrs Quinn visibly reeled and Daddy's face looked so angry, Julia couldn't stop herself giggling with fear.

'Don't you ever speak to Sylvia like that again!' Daddy told him. 'You too, Julia . . . and the rest of you. I'm ashamed of you all!'

Suddenly, Julia's oldest sister Joanna got up and threw her napkin on to her plate, which still had most of her dinner on it. Julia, not daring to look up, stared as a brown stain of gravy seeped into the white fabric.

'I've had enough,' said Joanna, and walked out, taking

full advantage of the fact that they were in a restaurant and public manners would prevent Daddy from chasing her.

There was a moment when the rest of them could have followed her, but Daddy glared so horribly at them, they all froze. And actually the food was rather nice, much better than Sunday dinner at school.

'I apologize for my children's unforgivable behaviour,' Daddy said gravely.

Mrs Quinn patted his hand and smiled at him. 'Don't you worry, Jolly, there's nothing I don't know about stroppy teenagers,' she said.

Sir John's will had stipulated a wish that should his friend Professor Liebeskind survive him, he would be provided with a home for the rest of his life. There had been some dispute as to whether this was binding, but in spite of advice obtained by Sylvia that Jolly was under no legal obligation, he willingly offered the use of the gatehouse and agreed that Michael and the twins could live there too in order to look after the old man.

'For the time being,' Jolly warned, giving Michael a significant look, which Michael wasn't sure how to interpret. Did Jolly mean until the professor died, or until Sylvia got her own way? Although he and Jolly had about as much in common as a prince and a pauper, they did share the knowledge of intimacy with Sylvia, and Michael couldn't help feeling a kind of sympathy for the new Sir John.

From the outside, the little faux-gothic house, which stood at the end of the beech tree avenue, looked more like a folly with its disproportionately tall chimney and mullioned windows. The door made an exaggerated creaking noise when Michael budged it open, like a sound effect in a horror film, but inside sunlight streamed in through the leaded windows, making rainbows on the floor, which the children immediately started jumping on, like a hopscotch court. It was one of those spring days, just after the clocks go forward, where a quality of warmth in the air suddenly makes you remember what summer feels like again.

An aroma of spices from the Patels' cooking remained, but they had taken all their possessions with them, and the only thing in the kitchen was an old biscuit tin with a Wedgwood design printed on it, and sharp, rusty corners. Claudia had never been able to get the lid of it off, and had always handed it over to him, Michael suddenly remembered. He was sure he hadn't thought about the biscuit tin once in fifteen years, but holding it in his hands conjured such a specific memory of her passing it to him, it was like touching the past. He clasped the cold metal box to his chest, as if it somehow connected her to him, then prised the lid off, and stared at the ancient crumbs inside, wondering whether they were from a cake that she had baked.

Upstairs, in the attic room in the roof, the same blanket of knitted squares lay folded neatly on the child's bed where they had made love together for the first time. He picked it up, burying his face in it, trying to detect the sweet light fragrance of her skin again, but the blanket smelled only of dust, and when Bruno picked it up, imitating his father's actions, it made him sneeze.

'I want to sleep in this room,' Fiammetta said.

'OK,' said Michael.

'So do I,' said Bruno.

Which was just as well, Michael thought, since it was the only bedroom in the house. If the professor had his old study back, then Michael could sleep in the living room.

'It's going to be a bit of a squash,' he warned them. 'But when you come back from London, it will be all nice and bright.'

Josie and Iris had offered to have the children while Michael got the gatehouse ready, and arranged for Mary, the goat, to be taken away. He knew that saying goodbye to the goat would be the most difficult thing and he didn't want to have to answer their inevitable questions about where the goat had gone and whether they would be able to visit it.

At Waterloo Station they met up with Iris. The children

were so excited about this new adventure that neither of them turned round to wave at him as they headed with their big sister and their large suitcase towards the exit for the tube. His children's equilibrium in the face of such a huge change to their lives was gratifying, but Michael couldn't help finding it slightly alarming at the same time. Their welfare was the sole reason for his existence, and yet, when he saw them walking away from him without looking back, it made him feel as if they didn't need him at all.

'That must mean you're doing a good job,' Barbara told him, when he made a black joke later about how he was helping to push up the unemployment figures, which had been recently announced as over a million.

Barbara was standing on a stepladder painting the ceiling of the main downstairs room of the gatehouse. There were tiny globules of white paint suspended in her mousy hair, and spattered across her forehead, which smeared when Barbara wiped away the sweat with her sleeve. Michael found the paint on her face almost endearing. He didn't know if he should point it out to her, but decided not to, because he didn't want to deal with her flustered embarrassment.

'It's very good of you to help like this,' he said.

'Oh, it's no trouble, at all,' Barbara assured him. 'I've got Pascale making a vegan cassoulet for the guests. I don't think she's been in a kitchen before. And the French don't understand what vegetarian means, of course. She asked where I kept the duck fat . . . didn't seem to realize that might be a problem . . .'

'What's she like?' Michael asked.

The French student had recently arrived to help Barbara with the summer season.

'Early twenties, rather glum,' Barbara told him. 'She's one of those perpetual students with rich daddies you get in Europe. Far more serious than I was at her age, but then I was always a bit of a flibbertigibbet . . . I don't know how she's ever going to learn any English if she doesn't speak, but as far as I can tell she's happy enough in a French kind of way . . . obviously, it's early days . . .'

Barbara had a habit of chattering on, then trailing off mid-sentence as if she'd suddenly run out of steam, or confidence, or ideas. Michael found it intensely irritating, and he often found himself wanting to stop her, but Barbara was hard enough on herself without anyone else doing her down. Even though she was one of those sturdy, well-bred English women who prided themselves on being capable, as Michael had got to know her he had begun to realize she was oddly vulnerable. Instead of feeling properly sympathetic, he found it made him even more uncomfortable around her.

Michael picked up a paintbrush, dipped it into the tin of white emulsion and painted a huge M on the wall, like a child with a paintbrush and a blank sheet of paper, he thought, making the M quickly into a series of giant loops.

'Aren't you going to strip the paper?' Barbara suggested.

'The paint sticks to this all right,' said Michael.

Barbara went quiet, as if she had taken his answer as implying criticism of her suggestion.

Sometimes Michael could see exactly why Barbara's husband had left her, even though he hated himself for thinking it because she was a generous person, who'd been enormously supportive to his family.

'I don't think we'll be here very long,' he said, to explain why he was not taking her advice about the paper. 'It hardly seems worth it.'

The professor surely wasn't going to survive much longer. The intervals between his bouts of dozing were becoming shorter and shorter. He was still disarmingly alert when he was conscious, although he seemed to be living in another time. Michael hoped that the return to the gatehouse would bring him peace, rather than making him constantly ask for Claudia, as he did whenever he woke up, as if hoping that the last few years had all been a bad dream.

'On which subject, I have had an idea,' said Barbara suddenly and slightly too loudly, as if she'd been rehearsing the statement quietly in her head before coming out with it. 'The thing is . . .' She tried to moderate her voice to just above a whisper. 'The thing is, the Riviera, well . . . quite frankly, I'm not sure whether it will ever be viable financially . . . and, even if it does suddenly, miraculously . . . well, there's loads of room . . .'

Barbara looked at him, as if she might be expecting him to help her out. Michael had no idea what she was driving at.

'And it's so near the school . . . there's the attic room with a dormer window with a fabulous view . . . I always thought that it would be a wonderful place for a writer . . . I mean, we all seem to rub along quite well, don't we? I'm terribly fond of the children and I assume they are of me . . . ? It seems so obvious, really. So sensible . . . pool our resources . . . with Mary gone now . . . don't see that the neighbours could object to a few chickens . . .'

Was she asking them to move into the Riviera with her? Michael couldn't be quite sure, and he didn't want to offend her.

'I'm not sure what you're saying . . .' he said.

'It's just that . . . well, I wondered. Would you all like to come and live with me?'

Barbara's face turned bright pink as she said the last three words, and Michael suddenly wished he hadn't asked for clarification because he could have found a way, if he'd thought about it for a couple of seconds, of avoiding the question, whereas now he was going to have to turn her down.

'Obviously, I don't expect an answer straight away . . . something you'd have to think about . . .' Barbara was saying.

He wanted to say, no, I don't have to think about it at all. It's simply out of the question, but the paint smear on her forehead wouldn't let him.

'That's a really thoughtful and generous offer—' he began, but she interrupted him.

'No, not at all, because it would be lovely for me too. I mean, we've sort of become like a family, haven't we? To me, it's just the obvious thing to do . . .'

Michael began to panic. 'You're right. I am going to have to think about it,' he said, hating himself for his dishonesty. He could almost feel Claudia watching him saying, 'Coward!'

'Of course,' said Barbara, reddening again. 'Sorry to spring it on you, it's just that, well, I didn't want to say it in front of the children in case they got excited and, well, you know . . . and we're never usually alone together, and well . . . obviously . . .'

'I hadn't really thought beyond doing this place up,' Michael finally offered, trying to force a smile.

'Big coward,' said Claudia's voice in his head.

'Of course not. Absolutely,' said Barbara, all flustered again. She looked at her watch. 'I'd really better go and see how that cassoulet is coming along.'

As the three of them struggled across London on the Northern Line, Iris rued the confidence with which she'd said, 'Of course', when her father had asked, 'Are you sure you'll be able to cope?'

Usually Iris avoided the tube, preferring to walk, but there was no way she could traipse across London from Waterloo to Camden Town with two seven-year-old children and a heavy suitcase. Tube travel had become a more fearful experience in the past couple of years. Since the recent Moorgate train crash, alarm glimmered in passengers' eyes whenever the train braked unexpectedly, bodies almost imperceptibly bracing against impact. There were bomb warnings everywhere urging travellers to view luggage with suspicion. People kept glancing at the huge suitcase Iris had placed by the doors, so she decided to stand next to it to reassure the rest of the compartment. It made her wonder how watching the suitcase would help if it were actually a bomb. What were you were supposed to do anyway? Get off the train? Pull the emergency handle?

Challenge your fellow passengers to claim ownership of the luggage?

Unaware of the peculiar vow of silence Londoners take when travelling on the tube, Bruno and Fiammetta chattered away, the two of them so untouched by the cynicism of city life that involuntary smiles broke over several of the gloomy faces in the compartment.

'Tottenham Court Road,' spelled Bruno as the train screeched into a station.

'What's that?' Fiammetta asked.

'It's where we are,' said Bruno.

'How do you know?'

'I read it!' said Bruno. 'Look!'

He pointed at the pattern of tiles on the station wall opposite where they were sitting.

'Oh, yes,' said Fiammetta. 'Tottenham Court Road,' she said with exactly the same grave intonation as Bruno.

Looking after the children in London was harder work than Iris anticipated. In Kingshaven, they were used to having their books and their toys, a huge garden to play in, with familiar trees to climb and a hammock to swing on. If they ever needed a change of scene, there were wildflowers to gather in the fields, trout to tickle in the stream at the bottom of Sir John's land, and a sandy beach less than a half an hour's walk away. Bruno was like a dog who needed to be exercised each day, and when he was cooped up too long, he would go a bit wild when let off the leash. In Kingshaven, it was usually easy enough to spot where he'd gone from the ripples in the wheat field, or to follow the jingle of the ice-cream van and find him licking the free cornet he had managed to cadge, but when Iris took them to London Zoo she spent most of the day standing on tiptoe, looking for him in the crowds, or dashing after him, yanking Fiammetta along beside her. Once, when she and Fiammetta had looked everywhere and retraced their steps calling his name, they were alerted by cheering from the penguin enclosure only to find that Bruno had climbed in and very nearly caught the fish the keeper threw at him.

'Don't worry, Iris,' Bruno told her, as she looked as cross as she could and then hugged the breath out of him as the keeper handed him back up to her. 'Penguins don't eat you like lions do.'

He proceeded to recite all eighteen verses of 'The Lion and Albert', a cautionary tale, which an adult – the professor, Iris suspected – had read to him as a warning.

Bruno's smile made it impossible to be cross with him for very long, but Iris quickly realized that if they weren't going to spend the rest of the holiday in Josie's house with its courtyard garden, she was going to need assistance.

Winston was the obvious person to ask, since the twins knew him well, and he was good at running fast. They arranged to meet in Regent's Park with a picnic lunch, and afterwards Winston promised to row them round the lake, something Iris would never have dared offer for fear of Bruno deciding he fancied a swim.

It was still a bit cold for picnics and there weren't many people around, so they were able to find the perfect place on the slope near the bandstand. The children gobbled the inside bit of their sandwiches as quickly as possible so that they could take the crusts to feed the ducks, leaving Iris and Winston alone together.

Iris could tell straight away that there was something Winston wasn't telling her from the way his eyes, usually so direct, were refusing to meet hers.

'Well?' she asked.

'Well?' he repeated, pretending to be watching the children.

'Is it some vile new capitalist venture you're too embarrassed to tell me about?'

'What?'

'Must be something you're ashamed of,' Iris pushed.

'Not at all. The fact is I'm getting married,' said Winston, now giving her his full attention.

For a moment, Iris wished she hadn't fished. It was as if control of the conversation had been abruptly wrested from her.

'Well?' Winston asked now, giving the words the exact same taunting intonation. 'Aren't you happy for me?'

'It's just it's a bit of a weird way to tell me,' said Iris.

'Should I have asked your permission first?' Winston seemed to be enjoying teasing her now.

'Of course not!'

Now Iris stared at the lake. The sunshine reflecting off the water made her eyes blur. She blinked hard.

'So, who is the lucky woman?' she asked.

'Valencia Cooper,' Winston told her, as if she would know who that was.

Iris shrugged.

'She's a model,' said Winston.

'Doesn't she have a title?' Iris asked, then kicked herself for revealing that she had heard of her. Josie, who got all the magazines at work, had brought home a picture of Winston and the woman in a recent edition of *Tatler.*

'She does, but she doesn't use it,' said Winston.

'How very egalitarian of her,' said Iris, knowing that the sarcasm made her sound as if she was bothered, but unable to stop herself.

The two of them stared at the lake.

'Why is everyone getting married?' Iris asked suddenly.

'Who else is?'

'Anthony and Marie.'

'Well, that hardly points to a universal trend,' Winston said. 'I think it's usually something to do with the feeling that you want to spend your life with someone,' he added.

'I suppose I can understand it from the man's point of view,' Iris conceded. 'You get guaranteed sex and someone to wash your socks. What I can't understand is why a woman would ever submit to it.'

'Isn't that a rather old-fashioned view of the woman's role?' Winston challenged her.

'No, just a realistic one,' said Iris. 'I wouldn't have anything to do with it. That's what I told Marie. Can you believe she asked me to be her bridesmaid? Can you see me, in a lilac frock, parading down the aisle of a Catholic church with a posy?'

'Horrible thought,' Winston agreed. 'I don't suppose there's any point in asking you to be my witness then? Ours will be a registry office. And I'm pretty sure Valencia won't want any lilac frocks around . . .'

Despite herself, Iris was touched, and she wished that Winston had flagged up what he was going to ask, instead of slipping it into the conversation almost unnoticed. Now, her pride wouldn't let her lose face by agreeing.

'You'd like me to give you away?' she joked.

'To be my best man,' Winston followed up.

Iris wasn't sure whether this was an attempt to acknowledge her equality, or a snide reference to her sexuality.

'Sorry, but if you want to tie yourself up in a patriarchal arrangement designed to promote the suppression of women, that's your funeral,' she told him.

'I believe it's normally referred to as a wedding,' said Winston, with an easy-going smile, but she could see in his eyes he was disappointed. 'Pity,' he added.

There was a moment when a light of opportunity for her to change her mind flickered, then went out.

'Sorry,' she said.

Her self-righteous refusal seemed suddenly to goad Winston.

'Do you even realize how negative you've become?' he asked.

'What?'

'You know what I mean,' said Winston. 'The women you hang around with always banging on about being exploited by men. It's all so negative, negative, negative . . .'

'We're very positive about affirmative action,' said Iris, pleased with herself for this response, which she thought Josie would be proud of.

'Affirmative action! You call yourself a feminist, but you spend half your life cooking and cleaning for Josie. I certainly won't expect my wife to be a drudge for me.'

151

'I do that because I can't pay rent.' Iris was furious at the insinuation.

'And why's that?'

'Because the magazine can't afford to pay me much yet.'

'Come and work for me, then,' said Winston suddenly.

'What, along with all the other women you employ in significant positions?' said Iris sarcastically. 'Tell me, is it the lack of money I earn that you object to, or the gender of my lover?'

It was the first time she'd referred to Josie publicly as her lover. The word surprised her as much as it obviously did Winston. For all his liberal credentials, she thought, he was just as chauvinistic as the next man.

'You've never liked Josie, have you?' she demanded.

'I don't like the way she makes you!' he said hotly.

'And how's that then?'

'Hostile, unreasonable . . .'

And then, suddenly retreating from the brink of saying things that could not be taken back, he reached out for her hand.

'I'm just trying to help you.' He tried to soothe things down.

Iris snatched her hand away. 'What are you, all of a sudden, the Salvation fucking Army? Do you think you can save me?'

The ugly words hung in the air. Winston said nothing.

And then the twins came running back to them, shouting, 'Is it time to go on the boat yet?'

And Iris spent the next hour avoiding Winston's eyes, as he rowed determinedly round the cold black surface of the lake.

Whenever Millicent Balls had pictured herself as a wife and mother, she'd seen herself with an apron tied round her waist, like her own mother, or one of the ladies in *Peyton Place*, taking a cake out of the oven, fanning away the steam, and smiling at a group of eager children sitting round the shiny kitchen table.

152

Now, as she tried to spoon a mushed-up Farley's rusk into her baby son, Sean's, mouth, she didn't know why she had ever thought her life would be like that, given that she had never baked a successful cake in her life. And even though she'd learned to wield a mop, and bought the right products, her kitchen floor always seemed to have lines of dried dirty water left on it, and never sparkled with little pinging stars as it did on the adverts.

It had been very good of her parents to hand over the running of the pub, along with the roomy flat upstairs, to her and Gerry after they got married, but sometimes Milly wished that her mother was still there, humming along with the tunes on the radio and cooing at the baby, leaving Milly to sort out the ploughman's lunches and chat to the customers in the saloon bar. Instead, her mother seemed to spend her entire life playing golf and ballroom dancing along the coast in Bournemouth where she and Milly's father, Percy, had chosen to retire.

'Sugar Baby Love,' sang the Rubettes on the radio.

It was amazing how many pop songs had the word baby in, Milly thought. Sean smiled toothlessly at her. He was good at taking the mushy rusk into his mouth, but equally good at letting it slop back out again. Milly had no idea how he stayed as chubby as he was when most of his food appeared to end up on his bib. And whatever colour the food was when it went in his mouth, it always left brown stains on his clothing.

He was, by all accounts, a dear little chap. People were always telling her. But he was such a bad sleeper, Milly felt as if she had lost the part of her brain that could make such judgements. She knew she must love her baby. It was automatic, wasn't it? But she hadn't really thought of him yet as a person, just something that had to be endlessly fed, and changed, and fed and changed. Sometimes, when Sean was asleep, she did find herself thinking how sweet he looked with his little hands stretched up in the air, but then he would wake up and make that grating awful sound that it was impossible to ignore, and she would feel like throwing him against the wall.

Gerry was a very good father. Everyone said so as they watched him tossing Sean in the air and catching him. Once Sean had sicked up all over his dad in the public bar and Milly had slightly thought that it served him right, but Gerry had wiped off the sick with a tea towel and kept smiling, and now people never stopped talking about it, as if Gerry was some kind of hero. Gerry told everyone that Sean took after Milly because he was blond and beautiful (leaving it unsaid, though obvious, that Gerry himself had fair hair and was objectively far better-looking than Milly). When it was just the two of them together, though, Gerry told Milly that the baby took after her because he was a light sleeper, implying that it was her fault and therefore her duty to get up in the night. Milly was so exhausted, she couldn't seem to find a way of contradicting his argument, although she knew something was wrong with the logic. Gerry slept, never waking up when Sean wailed, nor even when Milly, at her wits' end, elbowed him hard in the ribs.

In the morning, however, her husband was always very alert indeed. During the first few months of their marriage, Gerry's Morning Glory, as he called it, had been a wonderful surprise, a bonus of marriage Milly had never anticipated, since it wasn't the sort of thing you could know unless you lived with someone. The ever-ready erection wasn't just pleasurable in itself, but seemed to symbolize something unexpectedly romantic – that even when her husband was lying unconscious beside her, his body knew that it wanted to make love to her. Even when her body was at its most enormous stage of pregnancy, Gerry still desired her, which had been very reassuring.

Obviously, they'd had to stop while she was healing up down there, but very quickly Gerry had become as insatiable as ever. Whilst Millicent could feel her body returning gradually to normal, her mind didn't seem to have caught up, and about the last thing she wanted in the mornings, when she was trying to grab a few moments of peace, was Gerry's thing stabbing against her back. Sometimes, she allowed him, keeping her eyes closed in an effort to hang on to sleep, but Gerry always wanted her to join in, which made her feel a bit cross.

As she'd told him this morning, 'I don't mind doing it, but you can't expect me to enjoy it too,' and he'd got out of bed in a huff, and then she hadn't been able to get back to sleep because she was worried. Gerry's need of sex was like his need of water, and she knew that if he didn't get it at home, he would certainly have to look elsewhere.

As she scraped the last spoonful of babyfood from the bowl on to the spoon and popped it in Sean's mouth, Milly found herself thinking that it might not be such a bad thing if Gerry got someone else for the time being, because it would take the pressure off her. Then she couldn't believe she'd caught herself thinking such a thing.

'My brain is as mushy as this,' Milly said out loud to Sean, who smiled at her, leaking food from each corner of his mouth.

When she heard the other mothers, like Una who had two children now, talking to their babies, and often answering for them too, Milly thought they sounded stupid. It was a terrible combination, lack of sleep and endless time with no grown-ups to talk to. Milly looked back to her days as a shop assistant with nostalgia, although conversations had been pretty few and far between towards the end. Now Sylvia Quinn had finally closed her Kingshaven store down and rented it to a family of Chinese who had opened a restaurant and takeaway called the Happy Dragon, which seemed to be doing a roaring trade, leading Kingshaven people to mutter darkly about the only people able to make a living out of the town being foreigners.

'Come on, you little smiler,' said Milly, untying Sean's bib. 'Let's get you out in the sunshine.'

They usually went for a walk at lunchtime. There was nothing worse than picking up a baby for a cuddle and smelling cigarette smoke instead of Johnson's baby powder.

As it was impossible to push a pushchair on the beach, and Sean had a tendency to try to eat the sand, she usually took him to the Gardens instead. A bit of a damp bottom from the grass was a lot better than a nappy full of sand, and there was a lot of space for Sean to crawl around. The one thing they missed, living at the Ship, was a garden, but, as Gerry was always saying, theirs was only two minutes' stroll and they got the lawns cut and the beds weeded for them.

Milly put the brakes on the pushchair, unstrapped Sean and put him on the grass, then sat down on one of the painted green benches with curving wrought-iron ends.

'Ba Ba!' said Sean.

Gerry always insisted he was saying 'Da Da!', but it was definitely a B sound. Milly suspected that Sean was actually trying to sing 'Bye Bye Baby' which was at the top right now and was always playing on the radio.

'How about Ma Ma?' she asked Sean now, checking to see that there was no one around to listen to her talking nonsense.

'Ba Ba!' said Sean.

'Please yourself,' said Milly.

In this sheltered spot, the sun was really warm and bright for the time of year. Milly closed her eyes to block the glare, and then she opened them with a start, realizing that she must have dropped off. It could only have been a couple of minutes, she thought with relief, because Sean had got only as far as the main ornamental bed, which had been stripped after the spring bulbs and prepared for the gardeners to create their annual picture out of bedding plants. Sean had a fistful of earth, which he was about to eat.

'No!' Milly rushed at him, and brushed away the soil from his palm.

'Honestly!' she said. 'Are you still hungry?'

Her breasts felt huge and hard, which was usually a sign. Milly looked about her. There was no one in the gardens behind her, and only sea in front. What would be the harm of giving him a quick feed? Quickly, she unfastened her bra and slipped Sean's face under the stretchy pink jumper she was wearing. His gums locked on hungrily. Milly closed her eyes again, but this time, when she jolted awake, the sun appeared to have gone in. Sean had fallen asleep at her breast. As her consciousness sluggishly returned, she saw that it wasn't a cloud that was blocking out the sun, but a person. Christopher King.

Their paths sometimes crossed when she was out walking, and they said hello, but usually they both looked at their watches to indicate that they were in a hurry, and walked quickly on.

'You frightened me!' she said now.

'I didn't mean to.' He looked worried.

'No,' she reassured him. 'No. Actually, I'm glad it was you . . .' She attempted a joke. 'After all, there's nothing you haven't already seen!'

Christopher went so pink, she wished she hadn't bothered.

'Can you hang on to him a minute?' she said, passing the baby like a parcel to Christopher, who held him away from his body with stiff arms, as if he had no idea what to do. Milly quickly tucked her boob back into her bra and pulled her jumper down again, then took back the sleeping baby.

'He looks very peaceful,' Christopher said.

'Oh, he's fine at two o'clock in the afternoon. You should hear him at two o'clock in the morning!'

'You look tired,' Christopher said with such genuine sympathy, Milly almost felt she was going to cry.

'You can say that again,' she said.

'You look tired!' repeated Christopher.

Milly laughed obligingly. It was one of his jokes that used to irritate her, but now she wondered why. It was harmless enough.

She patted the bench next to her. 'Why don't you sit down? If you're not in a hurry . . .'

'No. Well . . . No, actually . . .' Christopher sat down.

'Beautiful day, isn't it?' she said.

157

'Beautiful,' he agreed.

'So what have you been up to?' Milly asked.

It was the sort of thing you said without really expecting a full answer, but Christopher didn't understand things like that. Milly thought it was the way he'd been brought up. They were so full of airs and graces up at the Palace, they didn't really know how normal people talked.

The fortunes of the Palace Hotel had been steadily declining, except for a brief flurry of interest the year before, when a man with a moustache, who looked very much like Lord Lucan, had checked into the Tower Suite. In fact, he'd been an inspector for the Michelin guide.

'Or so he said,' Christopher recounted. 'Because we never did receive a rating.'

'Interesting,' said Milly.

There had been talk, Christopher told her, of developing some of the hotel grounds, but plans had fallen through when the developer had gone bust and the planning officer had resigned almost simultaneously.

'Very dodgy,' Millicent agreed, trying to suppress a huge yawn.

Christopher had had an idea, he told her excitedly, which he'd only shared with his family so far, which was to turn the hotel into an educational holiday centre for children. Kingshaven was the ideal place to learn worthwhile things like hiking, climbing, natural history and archaeology, wasn't it?

'Where would be the money in that?' asked Milly.

'That's what my family said,' said Christopher dismally. 'I thought that the Scouts might want to get involved.'

The sun felt so kind on her skin, and Sean was like a blanket sleeping on her lap. Christopher's voice murmured on, and . . .

Suddenly, Millicent woke up. Her head must have nodded against Christopher's shoulder. He was gently stroking her hair, but his hand froze mid-air, as she looked up into his eyes. He looked guilty.

'What's the time?' she asked drowsily.

'Not sure. You're lying on my watch!'

She sat up.

'Just gone four,' he said, shaking the pins and needles out of his arm.

'That's the longest sleep I've had in weeks,' Milly told him. 'And the nicest,' she added. 'Thank you!'

'Any time!' he said with a short, nervous laugh.

Winston's words were branded indelibly on Iris's psyche and would not go away. Hostile. Unreasonable. Drudge. They were there when she opened her eyes in the morning, and they always returned at moments whenever her mind was not furiously engaged in some other activity. It made Iris remember her mother's advice when she was teased at school for being ginger, or clever.

'Sticks and stones will break my bones, but words will never hurt me!' Sylvia used to chant it as if it were a self-evident truth, the kind of motto she might have embroidered on to a sampler, but Iris could never see the logic. Bruises and cuts were painful at the time, but then they healed up and you forgot they had ever been there, but words stayed in your head and tormented you, from the moment you became fully conscious in the morning to the moment when sleep carried you away at night.

Iris hated the accusation that she was wasting her life, but the implication that she was Josie's wife touched an even more painful nerve. She depended on Josie for accommodation and work and she would never be equal partners with her, because somewhere between being a stroppy teenager and becoming an unreasonable woman, Iris had missed out on getting an education. Without a single O level to her name, let alone A levels or a degree, Iris would never have the intellectual confidence of Josie and her friends, and it was too late to start going to night school now. By the time she ever got to university, she would be thirty, and anyway, she'd still have to rely on Josie's goodwill. The opportunity had gone.

She admired Josie hugely, found her funny and witty,

and when she told Josie that she loved her, she meant it, but Iris was not sure that it was the same kind of love that Josie felt for her. They lived in the same house, sometimes slept in the same bed, but Iris didn't know if she was actually a lesbian. Though her whole life revolved around women talking and empowering each other, there was no way she felt she could mention any of these doubts to anyone, least of all Josie, in case they thought her a fraud or a liar. And yet having the thoughts and not sharing them made her feel like a liar too.

'I mean, I am absolutely a lesbian politically,' she tried to voice her unease to Vic, as they sat together at one of the back tables by the mural in the Luna Caprese.

'What's that supposed to mean?' Vic asked.

In spite of Vic's unconventional lifestyle, Iris always found him politically naïve.

'I don't really fancy any other women . . .' Iris tried to put it in a way he could understand. She wasn't even sure that she fancied Josie in the way that she had fancied Winston when she was an adolescent, or Clive when she was in her teens. Sometimes they turned each other on, but Josie was always the instigator, and Iris wasn't convinced that her own lack of enthusiasm for sex was simply a physical manifestation of subconscious guilt, as Josie claimed.

'Maybe you're frigid,' said Vic in his loud, camp voice, which made Iris want to shrink into the leatherette padding of the seat even though they were the only two people in the café.

'Just because I don't want to bonk every person I set eyes on,' she retaliated.

The gay scene he moved in was all about having numerous lovers, sometimes more than one a night.

'Did you know Winston Allsop got hitched?' Josie asked the next morning, flapping her newspaper down on to the table.

Iris's chest deflated, as if all the air had been sucked out of it. She suddenly felt very close to tears.

'Yeah. He did mention it,' she said, as casually as she could.

'Didn't he invite you?'

'Sort of . . .'

'What's that supposed to mean? That he invited you and not me?'

'Something like that,' said Iris non-committally, pretending to be fascinated by the latest opinion polls predicting the outcome of the Common Market Referendum.

'I always thought he fancied you,' said Josie, continuing to stare at Iris.

'Me? When he can have Valencia Cooper?'

'Lovely dress!' said Josie, handing over her newspaper.

The model was wearing a floor-length dress made of gathered tiers of fabric with different patterns. Her hair was long and smooth, not a single split end in sight.

'I wonder how long it took to create such a perfectly natural look,' said Josie bitchily. 'So, did you two have a row?' she asked.

'Sort of,' Iris admitted, then, unable to hold back any longer, the whole story came bubbling out of her like an unstoppable lava flow.

Josie came round to her side of the table and kneeled on the floor beside her.

'Why didn't you just tell me, instead of bottling it all up?' she asked tenderly.

'I thought you'd be angry,' Iris sniffed.

'I am angry,' Josie said. 'I've every right to be angry, and so have you! We'll be as angry as we bloody well please!'

Iris smiled at her.

'But maybe he has a point,' Josie went on. 'Maybe you should be more independent. It's difficult for you living here and working here too. Why don't you join Shelley?'

Shelley had quit her place on the board of *Siren* to set up an all-female publishing company, Harridan Press. The company's plan was to establish a reputation and cash flow by reviving forgotten classic novels by women, and follow

161

this with a list of novels by as yet unknown contemporary female writers.

'But I don't know anything about publishing,' Iris said, slightly frightened now about the prospect of emerging from Josie's shadow.

'You read, don't you?' Josie asked.

What she loved most about Josie, Iris realized, was her complete absence of fear.

There were buckets of tulips outside the Patels' shop, which gave the street a continental market kind of feeling.

'What are they for?' Bruno asked him.

'They're for giving to someone,' said Michael.

'Why?'

Michael had a memory of picking daisies in the scruffy bit of recreation ground where he and his brother, Frank, used to go to play, the happiness on his mother's face and her extravagant kiss when he presented them to her. It was one of those tiny moments of family intimacy his children would never know.

'If you give someone flowers, it brightens up their day,' he said, his voice thick with sudden sentiment.

Fiammetta looked at him with her serious navy-blue eyes.

'Can we give some to Barbara?' she asked.

'What a good idea!' said Michael.

He'd been feeling a little guilty about not going to see Barbara since her suggestion. With no goat for her to milk, there was no automatic reason for her to come anywhere near the gatehouse. The flowers would be a kind of apology for his lack of contact. And with the children there, the conversation couldn't become too personal.

Bruno chose a bunch of purple tulips and Fiammetta a red bunch, and Mrs Patel wrapped them in dark-green paper, gave the children each a banana, and refused to let Michael pay.

'You were very kind to us,' she said, smiling.

The front door of the Riviera Guesthouse was open, the

162

black and white tiled hall floor stretching right back to the kitchen, making it look a bit like a Dutch interior. The bell, which Bruno was just tall enough to reach, echoed loudly, making it sound as though the building were empty.

Michael and the twins looked at each other, and then stepped across the threshold.

'Barbara!' he called.

'Barbara! Barbara!' shouted the twins.

Silence.

And then, a floorboard upstairs creaked and there were footsteps along the landing, so light that Michael knew straight away that the person about to appear at the top of the stairs would not be Barbara.

He looked up.

The girl was in her early twenties. She had short black hair. Her complexion was sallow, her face slightly cross, as if they'd disturbed her in the middle of something important. She was very slim and wearing jeans and a navy-blue tennis shirt with a little crocodile appliqué. When she shrugged her shoulders he caught a glimpse of olive skin, a belly button on a flat stomach.

Michael felt a small shudder in his groin, like a tiny yawn, as if some dormant instinct had stirred.

The girl looked down at him and said, 'Can I 'elp you?'

For a moment, he held her eyes, and then suddenly the cool, empty entrance hall was full of Barbara as she rushed in from the back garden, wiping her hands on her gathered skirt, and bending to accept the flowers from the children, bundling them up in big hugs, and asking all the right questions about their trip to London.

When Michael glanced up again, the girl had gone.

'I'm putting in bedding plants,' Barbara told him. 'I know they say you should wait till May, but really, there isn't going to be another frost, is there? What do you think? It'll serve me right if there is, I suppose . . . Come and have some tea. I've got a fruit cake. I'm sure Bruno and I could rustle up a Victoria sponge if you're staying. You will stay, won't you?'

She looked at Michael, and he couldn't help thinking that he had inadvertently sent the wrong message again. Arriving with the children and flowers had been a more meaningful gesture than he had intended.

'We'll stay for tea, yes,' he said. Then, remembering his manners, added, 'Thank you, Barbara,' and smiled at her, which made her blush.

'Can we go in the garden?' Bruno asked.

'Of course you can,' Barbara told them.

The entrance hall seemed suddenly very quiet without them.

'Shall we sit in the kitchen?' Barbara asked.

'Wherever you like,' Michael said, following her down the hall.

'Tea? Coffee? A glass of wine? Or is it too early in the day for you?'

Michael wasn't much of a drinker. Occasionally, when Iris had been staying, he used to stroll down to one of the pubs at the Harbour End for a pint of an evening, but he hadn't missed it. Now, he thought a glass of wine might help to relax him.

'Why not?'

'Pascale's father owns a vineyard, so we have our own private supply.' Barbara winked at him.

The corkscrew was on the draining board. She pulled the cork out with a flourish, as if she was quite used to opening bottles. He noticed that her face flushed pinker than usual at the first sip, and she became rapidly more loquacious. It made him wonder whether Barbara was a drinker. It would explain her peculiar distractedness, her tendency to break into a sweat.

Michael sipped the red wine cautiously. Although he knew nothing about wine, he could taste that it was smoother and more rounded than the stuff he had drunk at his publication parties in London, or even at the lunch at the Savoy, where he had once been presented with an award.

'I think we met Pascale on the stairs,' he said.

'She spends most of her time in her room reading,' said Barbara. 'I get the feeling,' she lowered her voice, 'that she sees England more as a punishment than a holiday.'

Michael heard himself laugh exaggeratedly, and realized that the wine had gone straight to his head.

Barbara had already finished her glass, and topped his up while pouring herself a second.

'So,' she said. 'What have you decided?'

He could tell that for her the question was rhetorical. She assumed the visit was to confirm they wanted to move in with her.

'About what?' he asked.

Coward!

'Well, um . . . about my proposal . . . not that it was that sort of *proposal*, obviously!'

She paused so that he could say something if he wished. Michael sipped some more wine.

'Do you remember that I asked if you and the children, and the professor, of course . . . would like to . . . ?'

'Yes. Yes. I've been meaning to have a chat, but . . .' Michael hesitated.

The space as he paused was filled with the sound of Bruno and Fiammetta chasing each other in the garden.

'They seem to like it here, anyway,' said Barbara. 'And I think you probably know how I feel . . . I don't want to boast, but I do think Fiammetta likes a woman around. I seem to be able to bring her out of herself—'

She stopped mid-sentence, as if she had only just realized she was meant to be listening to him.

'Barbara,' Michael leaned across the table and put his hand over hers, 'You are a lovely person and it's not that I don't appreciate everything you do. Of course, you're important to us, but the thing is, I think I ought to try and stand on my own two feet for a while, at least . . .'

'But I wouldn't stop you. You could do whatever you wanted . . . I can't pretend it wouldn't be nice to have a man around the house again, changing light bulbs, that sort of

. . . but if you get back to your writing, it would be easier for you—'

'Barbara!' His voice came out sharper than he intended, and he saw her flinch. He tried again, gently. 'I know it's probably mad . . .'

'Don't writers have to be a bit mad?' Barbara smiled.

He knew she was nervous and didn't mean to annoy him, but he felt like grabbing her by the arm and shaking her, and saying, 'Don't you understand? This is why nobody wants to live with you. Because you never stop bloody talking.'

The violence of his thoughts took him back to the awful arguments with Sylvia, when the balance of power had always been on his side and he'd been capable of inflicting terrible verbal cruelty.

'I'm not trying to replace Claudia, you know,' Barbara suddenly said. 'I'd never try to do that.'

It was Barbara's fault for mentioning her, he thought. Barbara had almost set it up for him.

'The fact is, I could never live with another woman after Claudia,' he said decisively. 'But, thank you,' he added.

'No, I perfectly understand,' she said. 'And I want you to know that the offer stands . . .'

'No,' he said.

'Yes, really,' she assured him.

Then they both pushed their chairs back from the table at the same time.

'We'd better be getting back,' Michael said, walking towards the door and calling to the twins.

'Why do we have to go so soon?' Bruno asked. 'I want to make a sponge cake.'

Barbara hugged him. 'We'll do that next time you come,' she promised.

'Where is Mary?' Fiammetta suddenly asked.

Barbara and Michael exchanged glances.

Barbara took responsibility. 'I'm afraid she's passed away.'

'Does that mean she's in heaven?' asked Fiammetta.

'I suppose so,' said Michael.

'Mummy won't be so lonely now,' said Fiammetta.

As Michael tried to imagine what his daughter must be thinking, an absurd image of Claudia and the goat sitting on a cloud together floated through his mind and made him want to smile.

Chapter Seven

1976

It was the year of the long hot summer. The heatwave began in June with sustained high temperatures across Southern England inspiring a kind of desperation to absorb every moment of sunshine in case it suddenly stopped. Office workers took their packed lunches out on to fire escapes and melting rooftops; tables appeared on scorching pavements outside restaurants; anyone with transport headed for the white glare of the beach.

Quite soon, nobody could remember a time when it had not been hot. Lethargy began to replace joy. It was too hot to do anything, too hot even to think. The community spirit of shared good fortune mutated into an increasing sense of unease. Heath fires spontaneously ignited; subsidence cracks appeared in buildings that had stood solid for centuries; the air seethed with apocalyptic swarms of ladybirds.

Transistor radios beside sunbathers in London's scorched royal parks blared out ABBA hits during the hot summer days, but at night, a musical revolution was fomenting in pubs and underground clubs around the city. Iris, who had never felt any empathy with the bands that defined her generation, like Pink Floyd and ELO, went to see Patti Smith at the Roundhouse in May with Vic and came away feeling her life had changed. The music was so raw and pared down, it spoke to her as no other music had, and Patti Smith was unlike any other female singer, fearless and in control. Seeing Patti Smith gave Iris confidence in her own androgynous style. Patti Smith was not about gratifying men's expectations of what a woman should be, but she was still powerfully female and sexy. Iris cropped her long red curly hair to her scalp, dyed it black and wore only skinny black jeans and black or white vests in boys' sizes.

At Harridan Press, nobody minded how you dressed for work. Iris's job was reading and writing reports on manuscripts women sent in as word about the company spread.

'She reads all day and gets paid for it,' was Vic's way of describing her job, and put like that, it did sound almost too good to be true. Because the philosophy of the company was founded on making it possible for women to succeed in publishing, Shelley was sympathetic to her taking the school holidays off to see Bruno and Fiammetta, and although her salary was only just enough to pay her own way and go out for an occasional drink, it was no worse than any equivalent job in the book trade.

A hunch that there was talent out there waiting to be discovered was overwhelmingly confirmed by the hundreds of unpublished novels that piled into the cramped top-floor offices in Soho. To begin with Iris, who had no formal qualification in English Literature, had been uncertain whether she would be able to judge whether one book was publishable and another not, but after reading over two hundred novels, and writing equivocating reports, trying to balance criticism with praise, she opened a novel entitled *Sandwiches and Samosas* by a young Indian woman, and from the first sentence knew that she was reading an original new voice. The book needed work. It was too short and the ending was rushed, as if the writer had suddenly lost her nerve. But it was funny and gave a fascinating glimpse of what life was like for a Sikh schoolgirl in a Southall comprehensive school.

There was nothing like the buzz of discovering a new

writer. Iris imagined it was something like a pioneer must have felt when, after weeks of panning gravel, he suddenly spotted a nugget of gold glinting out of the mass of grey stones.

Once or twice a week, Iris met Vic after work before going on to some sweaty basement where a new band was playing. With his impeccable sense of the *Zeitgeist*, Vic, who'd heard the band rehearsing in a room above Denmark Street, was one of the first people to see the Sex Pistols. London's punk scene was more about anger, less about art than its New York counterparts, the visceral stripped-down chords and revved-up tempo, the edgy violence and anarchy an exquisite two fingers up to the Establishment. Sometimes, when Iris was dancing wildly to the ear-splitting thump of overstretched speakers, she felt like she was on a cliff edge screaming her life's frustrations to the wind, and for a second, she would feel free and able to do anything she dared.

The sex started with an amyl nitrate-fuelled snog with a boy with green hair outside a pub on Wardour Street. It felt as if an empty place inside her was being filled ('Yeah, right,' said Vic, when she attempted to explain). And then it became like a drug itself. The more she had, the more she needed. Soon Iris was frequently having sex with men whose names she didn't even know in the alleyways of Soho. The anonymity was part of the pleasure.

'*Very Last Tango in Paris*,' Vic teased. 'Lucky Clive's not around, though . . .'

In the more glamorous days of champagne bars, floor shows and men in tuxedos, the streets of Soho had been Clive's territory. Occasionally, Vic went to visit his brother in Parkhurst. Iris always knew because she wouldn't see him for a few days, but Vic never offered an explanation. It was as if he had decided that it would be disloyal to mention Clive to Iris, if, as she hoped, he never mentioned Iris to Clive.

What terrified Iris more was the idea of Josie finding out about the men. Josie viewed Iris's changed appearance as an indulgent parent might view their rebellious teenager, making her parade like a sulky catwalk model in front of the editorial board of *Siren*, who still met in her front room, but sometimes Iris saw her looking at her alarmed, and once, when she woke up for water during an endlessly hot night, she found Josie propped up on one elbow, staring at her naked body, and wondered if she had been talking in her sleep.

Julia wished that Daddy had never inherited the Castle, and her family had kept on living in the Summer House because she knew that Sylvia Quinn would never have married Daddy if they had stayed there.

The summer holidays, which Julia normally looked forward to, seemed to stretch endlessly ahead, each day hotter than the last. The sea was the temperature of soup. There was talk of rationing water. At the Castle, the water was usually off anyway because the house was being replumbed as well as rewired and refurbished.

True to her word, Sylvia had organized the construction of a swimming pool and a tennis court. The walls of the walled garden had been razed to the ground and there was now a huge hole in the sunniest spot, but there was no water to fill it.

In an interview in the local newspaper, the *Chronicle*, which appeared under the title 'Lady of the Manor's Facelift', Julia's stepmother talked about how she planned to return the Castle to its former glory.

'Former doyenne of the department store Sylvia Quinn,' read the caption under the large photograph of the new Lady Allsop, reclining on a reupholstered chaise longue, 'says the Castle is like a beautiful woman who has let herself go, but now she's going to get some lovely new make-up and clothes.'

Sylvia's own choice of clothes, Julia couldn't help noticing, had changed since she had closed down her shops and married their father. Whereas she always used to wear her own trendy designs, now she bought clothes she considered more befitting for a lady, with flounces and frills, and quite unnecessary matching hats.

'As if she'd be ready at a minute's notice to have her portrait painted by Gainsborough,' James remarked, and Julia knew what he meant, even though she wasn't exactly sure who Gainsborough was.

To spite their new stepmother, Julia's older sisters lived in cut-off jeans and the cache of collarless shirts they'd discovered in one of the late Sir John's old chests of drawers. Joanna and Jacqueline refused to change for dinner as Sylvia demanded, provoking bouts of frustrated tears. Their father didn't like it when Sylvia was upset but, now that they were no longer little girls, he could hardly force them into clothes they didn't want to wear. Joanna pushed it even further by refusing to eat with Sylvia. In fact, Julia wasn't sure when Joanna did eat and she became so thin that you could see her hipbones jutting out over her bikini bottom when the Allsop children were invited to swim in the Palace Hotel pool, which, owing to the sudden popularity of the English coast as a holiday destination, had been filled for the first time in several years.

While Julia and James played with Adrian and Winny King in the water, splashing and bombing each other as they had done when they were young, Joanna arranged herself in different poses on her sunlounger, occasionally lifting her sunglasses to look hopefully up at the hotel.

'Aren't you coming in?' Julia asked her.

Joanna glared as Julia dripped fat drops of chlorinated water over the copy of *Cosmopolitan* spread over her concave stomach.

'No,' said Joanna.

'Why did you come then?' Julia wanted to know.

'Piss off, fatty,' said Joanna.

'She's hoping Christopher will come out,' Adrian whispered to Julia.

'Granny Ruby says Joanna would be the perfect bride for Christopher,' twelve-year-old Winny's voice rang out like a bell.

It hadn't really occurred to Julia before that her sister was old enough to get married, even though Joanna had had a big silver key to the door on her last birthday – not a real key, obviously, but it was still the mark of being grown up.

'Christopher fancies a barmaid,' Winny continued in his unbroken singsong voice.

'Shut up,' said Adrian, pushing his brother into the pool.

'If he really loved her, it wouldn't matter that she's a barmaid,' Winny persisted, when he came up for air. Adrian plunged into the pool and held his brother's head under the water until he had extracted a spluttering promise to say no more.

Did Christopher King really love a barmaid? Julia wondered. She wasn't exactly sure what a barmaid actually looked like, and the picture that kept coming into her head was a smiling young woman with golden plaits and red cheeks, carrying a yoke of pails on her shoulders. She couldn't really blame Christopher if her sister Joanna was the only other choice. Was unrequited love the reason that Joanna was so thin? Julia wondered.

It sounded rather like one of the romantic novels Julia often slipped inside the book by Dickens or some other old bore they were supposed to be reading at school. The books she liked best had poor or plain-looking heroines who won the hearts of rich or handsome men because of their sweet nature. Sometimes the heroines were surprised to discover that they were actually beautiful after all, but nobody had been able to see it, either because they were wearing glasses or because they had a lot of puppy fat. In novels, the weight miraculously fell off because the heroines were so in love they forgot to eat. Julia had tried to simulate the effect by staring at a picture of Bjorn Borg Sellotaped inside her rough book, but it was impossible to follow a diet of cottage cheese and Ryvita when you were at boarding school where the smell of spotted dick and custard was always wafting up from the canteen.

The heat made everyone tetchy. As Sylvia no longer had her own business to occupy her, she made a business of running the Castle and constantly complained about the slackness of the builders and carpenters just as she used to moan about her idle shop assistants. When the workmen finished for the day, Sylvia started on the children and their lack of manners. Sylvia was tremendously insistent on things being done in the proper way, but James, who was only twelve but very clever, quickly realized that she didn't know very much about etiquette and delighted in devising elaborate teases. It began harmlessly enough with him insisting at the breakfast table that the correct way to eat Weetabix was with a knife and fork, but soon progressed to more public humiliation, like when Sylvia held her first dinner party for some of Jolly's friends, and James convinced her that the hostess always indicated it was time for the ladies to retire from the table by standing up and singing 'Ave Maria'.

James got away with a lot because boys were supposed to be naughty, but sometimes Daddy snapped and shouted at him really loudly, and the noise echoed round the great empty house, with its sour smell of brick dust, and reminded Julia of the way Sir John used to shout at her father. It made her wonder if her family passed down arguments from one generation to the next, just as they passed down the dark portraits of forbidding men with round eyes like Daddy's, which covered the walls of the Castle's huge entrance hall.

On the first blisteringly hot afternoon of the heatwave, Claudia's father, Professor Liebeskind, nodded off as usual in an old wicker chair under the shade of a beech tree beside the gatehouse and didn't wake up.

An eviction order arrived shortly after, and, accepting the inevitable, Michael rented a caravan for the summer in the newly opened Forest Valley Caravan Park.

When Iris and Josie arrived in Kingshaven at the beginning of the school holidays, they found grubby

174

brown children with matted, sun-bleached hair. The water supply at the camp site was from a standpipe, and there was only the sea in which to get clean. Josie took one look, and promptly checked herself into the Riviera, explaining that being American she couldn't face a day without a bath. Iris elected to stay in the caravan with her family.

For Bruno and Fiammetta, now eight years old, who had grown up in an enormous house with miles of corridor and acres of land, cramped quarters where the dining table turned into a bed, and the Calor gas hob hid under the breadboard, were fantastically exciting. And, they informed Iris immediately, they were permitted to walk the half-mile down to the beach on their own, because the path went straight through the woods to the Victoria Gardens and there were no roads to cross.

'What will you do when the summer's over?' Iris asked her father one afternoon when they found themselves alone together because Josie had taken the bus into Lowhampton to see if she could buy an electric fan. A fly buzzed intermittently against the caravan window, the only sound in the still, sluggish air.

'I've become a property owner,' he admitted slightly sheepishly. 'Come on, I'll show you.'

It was strangely familiar walking beside her father down the shady wooded path towards the Victoria Gardens just like they used to do, and strangely unfamiliar too, because Iris didn't think they had been for a walk together, just the two of them, since she was much smaller than him. As they talked, she kept turning to him, expecting his face to be higher, not on a level with hers. Her father appeared happier somehow, in a way she couldn't quite define, and his step was as bouncy as it had been when he was a young man.

The stone walls of the three-storey warehouse were fundamentally sound, and it was situated in what estate agents call a prime location, right near the Quay at the Harbour End, but the timbers were rotted and a new roof required. The building had been due for demolition and there was planning permission for flats, but the developer had gone bust in the wake of a scandal, and the liquidators had put it on the market at a knock-down price. There was a mains water supply but no plumbing and the wiring was obsolete. The cellar was damp and the ground floor stank because the local fishermen had recently used its cool dank rooms as a wet fish market.

'Where are you going to begin?' Iris asked her father, biting back the urge to tell him he was mad. Unlike the fathers on the adverts at Christmas for Black and Decker power tools, her father had never attempted to put up a shelf, let alone renovate a derelict property.

'Help is on its way,' her father replied with an enigmatic smile.

A couple of days later, a white van pulled into the caravan site at dusk, driven by a burly man whose muscular arms were almost black with tattoos. Crowded along the front seat were Iris's brother, Anthony, his new wife, Marie, and a very tall, lanky youth. In the back of the van, among ladders and toolkits, sat another man whose build was midway between the hefty one and the skinny one.

'These are my brothers,' said Marie, introducing the big one as Little Tony.

'Because my dad's Big Tony,' she explained, making Iris think it was just as well Anthony had never shortened his name.

'This is Declan, and this,' Marie pointed at the skinny youth, 'is Little Mal.'

Michael rented them another of the caravans and any initial hostility amongst the other caravanners to the three bulky Scousers was quickly assuaged when Little Tony and Declan found a way of making the showers work.

During the day, everyone worked at the warehouse, to the constant blare of Radio One. At first, the building was too dangerous for Bruno and Fiammetta to be inside, and so the unskilled workers took it in turns to take them to the beach, in between brewing endless cups of tea, and ferrying pints of chilled cider over from the Ship.

At night, it was so hot everyone would give up trying to sleep and emerge from the caravans to play games of moonlit rounders on the beach, with mad plunges into the warm sea to retrieve the ball. A kind of camaraderie developed, like a disparate group of people marooned on a desert island.

Sometimes Pascale, the French girl who was still staying with Barbara at the Riviera, joined them. At first, everyone found her a bit standoffish, but it was impossible to remain aloof with Marie's brothers, and she gradually moved from disinterested outfielder to the top scorer of home runs, as crazily competitive as the rest of them.

Josie, who wasn't particularly keen to spend her vacation mucking in with the renovation and found mindless beach games incomprehensible, was increasingly the outsider in the group. She suddenly seemed a different generation from Iris and the others. Her sophisticated urban irony sounded contrived and snotty in comparison with the quick-witted Scousers, and Iris was beginning to find her constant complaining about the heat as irritating as the nocturnal insects, who seemed to prefer the taste of Iris's skin to anyone else's and patterned her legs with flaming red polka dots which itched like mad in the heat. It came as a relief when Josie made water rationing her excuse to return to London.

'At least I'll be able to bath with a friend,' she said pointedly to Iris, who waved the bus to Lowhampton out of sight before sticking her tongue out at it.

That evening, Iris got very drunk in the beer garden of the Anchor and ended up round the back of a beach hut with Little Mal, with whom she had developed a bantering flirtation as he ribbed her relentlessly about her hair, which was now stiff from bathing in salt water. He was eighteen, stank of Brut, and kissed her with the hungry wet lips of an adolescent.

In the morning, Iris woke up with such a self-loathing hangover that she couldn't face him, or anyone else, least of all Marie. Iris remained in her bunk in Michael's caravan, pretending to be asleep even when Bruno blew in her ear, and got up only after the noise of them all going off to the Harbour End had faded into silence.

The cold shower made her shivery, despite the already oppressive heat of the day, and she decided to walk up to the top of the cliffs in search of a breeze to blow her headache away, but the air was as sluggish up there as it was down in the town, and the heat haze was so thick it was almost yellow and seemed to muffle the sound of the sea. It was almost as if there'd been a nuclear explosion, Iris thought, and this was the fallout of hot radiation in which human beings could only survive a limited time. Sitting on the bent yew tree, Iris suddenly found herself crying. She wept until her body felt as desiccated as the parched grass and dust around her, then she walked along the top of the ridge, her face tight with salt, making resolutions in her head: she must not drink so much; she must show more respect for herself; she must not have casual sex with men.

From the top of the ridge, Iris could see the Castle estate, where her mother was now chatelaine. The old walled garden had been demolished and a large swimming pool dug out, its turquoise lining bright and alien in the scorched, brown landscape. There were four young people playing a desultory game of tennis on the new tarmac court with its bright white markings. The Allsop children, Iris thought. The gossip in town was that they all hated Sylvia. Anthony and Marie, who had been invited to the wedding, weren't sure whether the Allsop children had declined to go, or whether they hadn't been asked, but apparently it had been a very low-key affair in Lowhampton Register Office. The picture in the *Echo* showed Sylvia in a pale suit with a tense smile, and Iris had felt a pang of sadness for her, remembering all those Saturday mornings during her childhood that the two of them had spent peering over the wall of the churchyard. Her mother's excuse for going to have a look when there was a wedding on was that it gave her ideas for her own designs, but, even as a small child, Iris had observed Sylvia's excited shining eyes, and known that she was imagining herself in one of those pretty white dresses.

Now, Iris crouched down and crept along the side of a beech hedge at the edge of the garden, hoping she couldn't be seen through the gaps where prematurely autumnal leaves had already withered and dropped.

At the front of the mansion, there was a great deal of activity and several big removal lorries were parked in the drive. Iris could see her mother directing operations with a frilly white parasol, which served both as sunshade and a pointer as Sylvia decided the destination of each item the men were bringing out of the house.

Statues and portraits were loaded into a pantechnicon that had the name of an auctioneer in nearby Havenbourne on the side; four men were trying to manhandle the grand piano into another lorry, but it wasn't designed to be carried by its legs and as the back one broke, the keyboard tipped to the ground, making all the wires jangle discordantly as if in pain.

Sir John's entire library was being thrown into a skip, pages fluttering like the wings of a dying dove as each book flew through the air and landed with a thud.

Jolly Allsop came out of the house.

Iris strained to hear what Sylvia was saying to him.

'We can't have our new life dominated by dusty old books!'

Jolly put his arm around his new wife. 'They'll all be gone soon,' he said.

Iris's reappearance at the warehouse was greeted by such an uncharacteristic silence that if her face hadn't already been red from running, she knew it would have turned red from embarrassment. Everyone was clearly aware of what had happened the previous evening, except the twins, who rushed up to greet her.

Their hugs were gratifyingly tight and, for a moment, they obliterated her shame.

'Where's Dad and Anthony?' she asked.

'In the roof,' Bruno told her.

'Go and get them for me, would you?' she asked, sitting down on the floor, the heat, dehydration and exertion of running all the way from the Castle grounds suddenly too much to endure. Her brain felt like a balloon being pumped up inside her head.

'They can't be throwing Sir John's library out,' said Michael when Iris reported what she had seen. 'Sylvia's not as philistine as that, is she?'

'I'm only telling you what I saw.' Iris was defensive.

'Are you sure?'

Iris wondered whether Marie's expression of distrust was a result of her behaviour the previous evening. She had a vague memory of an altercation outside the ladies' toilet in the beer garden of the Anchor Inn, and the word 'slut' being used.

'Of course I'm sure,' she said angrily.

'Well, what do you think we should do?' asked Anthony.

'Rescue them, of course,' Iris snapped at her brother.

'Legally, they're Jolly's to do with as he sees fit,' Marie counselled.

Iris stamped her foot. 'But if they're just being thrown away, surely you've got a moral right . . . ?' she appealed to Michael. 'Or are you going to just stand by and watch Sir John's life's work thrown into a skip?'

Suddenly Michael's expression changed, and for a moment there was a flicker of the rebellious young man Iris remembered from the sixties.

'Let's liberate those books!' he said, giving a salute with his right arm and grabbing Iris with his left.

'If Sylvia thinks you're conspiring against her, she won't let you touch them!' Marie cautioned.

And even though she wanted her to be wrong, Iris's shoulders slumped with the knowledge that her sister-in-law had a point.

'It'll have to be me, then,' Anthony suddenly volunteered.

Iris was so surprised, she didn't know what to say.

180

Stepping out of the cool interior of the warehouse into the blazing glare of the sun, Anthony lunged back to give Marie a quick impromptu kiss on the cheek, as if he were a soldier leaving for the Front, and said, in a solemn voice, 'I may be some time.'

The books – all five van loads – virtually filled the ground floor of the warehouse. Michael and his family stood looking at towers of boxes in triumph.

'What are you going to do with all these books?' Bruno suddenly piped up, which was a question nobody had asked.

All of Michael's children – Iris, Anthony, Bruno and Fiammetta – looked at him expectantly.

'I suppose some of them will go to museums,' he ventured.

'It'll give you something to do,' said his daughter-in-law Marie. 'Sorting that lot out.'

Although he knew that she probably hadn't meant anything by it, the comment cut Michael to the core. Whereas he thought of himself as a writer who just didn't happen to be writing at the moment, Marie, who had never known him work, obviously thought he was a waster. An almost childlike impulse to prove her wrong throbbed in his brain.

Upstairs, all that was left to do was to paint the plaster and sand the floorboards. Marie, who knew about home furnishings, having recently equipped the small flat she and Anthony had purchased in North London on a tight budget, accompanied Michael to Lowhampton to look at kitchen and bathroom fittings, advising that avocado was the colour of choice nowadays, and was clearly put out when Michael opted for white instead. He ordered the bare minimum of simple pine furniture – a kitchen table and chairs, beds for the children, and some beanbags covered in fabric with geometric shapes – which would be delivered.

'I'll miss the emptiness,' Michael said to Iris one evening.

The two of them were finishing off painting a wall and the others had already gone down to the pub. With the windows curtainless, and no furniture except a sink and a kettle, the vast first floor was bathed in golden light from the tall windows.

Iris turned to him. 'You really like it here, don't you?'

Michael nodded, and then felt guilty.

'I don't see Claudia here,' he confessed in a whisper. 'At the Castle, I couldn't look at the kitchen table without seeing her sitting there, or walk in the garden without hearing her calling me. I don't mean a ghost,' he tried to explain, as Iris's eyebrows shot up suspiciously. 'It was never a supernatural thing, more like an imprint of memory stamped on every object . . . and it just doesn't happen here because this is new . . . and it's . . . it's such a relief.'

Iris remained silent, allowing him to continue his thoughts if he wanted. He had noticed that she had become a better listener. Sometimes he missed her constantly butting in with her opinions.

'Do you think that's bad?' he asked.

'No, I don't think so,' Iris said hesitantly. 'I think it sounds . . . healthy.'

'Thank you, Iris.'

For a few seconds Iris beamed at him like a child, as if his confiding in her had made her very happy. He thought how pretty his daughter's face could be when she was untroubled, and he wondered what it was that made her want to make herself ugly with her ridiculous spikes of two-coloured hair and her black clothes. But he didn't dare ask her, partly because it was none of his business, and he feared she would tell him so, and partly because he didn't know if he would be able to deal with knowing the answer if she did want to tell him.

'Here's another idea for you,' he said, trying to prolong the moment of closeness between them. 'What do you think of having a party, a big party while it's still empty? To thank the Liverpool boys, you . . . everyone, and well, to celebrate this amazing . . .'

'Freedom?' Iris suggested.

'Summer,' he said. 'The long, hot summer of nineteen seventy-six.'

'Julia?'

Julia was almost asleep when she heard the whisper at her door. James tiptoed into the room. He was dressed in long colonial shorts and an old green string vest of Sir John's, which was one of the garments they'd unearthed in the attic that most offended Sylvia. He was barefoot so as to make the minimum noise, but holding a pair of plimsoles in his hand. He had a torch.

'Let's go to the party?'

It was the most sluggish, oppressive night so far, but occasionally a gust of warm stormy wind blew up from the town like a reprieve, carrying on it the sound of pop music. Julia had already caught snatches of David Bowie and the loud operatic bit in the middle of 'Bohemian Rhapsody'.

'What do you mean?' Julia sat up in bed.

'Mr Quinn's party . . .'

'I meant, what do you mean, go?'

'It's open house, I heard Anthony Quinn telling Joanna.'

'That doesn't mean us,' said Julia. 'It's for adults.'

'You could pass for sixteen,' said James.

'Could I?' Julia was flattered. She'd only recently celebrated her fifteenth birthday.

'I could pass for fourteen, couldn't I?' James asked.

In the circumstances Julia didn't really feel she could disagree.

'You can go in a pub when you're fourteen,' James informed her.

How did he know things like that? They seemed to teach all sorts of different things at boys' schools.

'The trouble is, Mr Quinn knows how old we really are,' Julia pointed out.

'He won't mind,' said James. 'Remember how he used to let us taste the mulled cider at Christmas?'

This was undeniably true.

'And Bruno and Fiammetta are bound to be there, and they're younger than us.'

Julia could see that she was going to have to come up with something very good to stop James.

'Mrs . . . Sylvia would have a fit . . .' she began.

'That's the whole point,' said James triumphantly, then delivered the ultimatum: 'But if you're too yellow, then I'm going by myself.'

Julia knew that he would too. What if something terrible happened to him like he fell down a quarry shaft that had opened up in the drought, like that foreigner's dog had done the other day? If they got caught, as Julia thought they were bound to be, she could explain to Daddy that she had only gone along to protect James.

'Come on!' James urged.

It was too dark to hunt in the wardrobe for a suitable party dress, and even though her father's room was on the other side of the Castle, they didn't dare turn on any lights. Julia pulled on the tennis dress she had been wearing that day, and fumbled about on the floor for her plimsoles, then tiptoed down the stairs after her brother and out into the hot night.

Barbara had made a great pyramid of mushroom vol-au-vents, which looked as if they were sweating in the heat. The guests were much more interested in the bottles of Blue Nun and the cans of Party Seven on the drinks table.

An almost translucent flake of pastry stuck to Barbara's upper lip.

'I haven't really had time to eat or drink today,' she told Iris. 'You don't really feel like eating when it's so hot, do you? Not that it seems to have made any difference to my waistline . . .'

Barbara was wearing a tent-like dress made out of Indian cotton with a black, red and ochre pattern. It was the sort of garment plump people bought because they imagined that if people couldn't see their exact shape inside they might think them slim. The trouble with this theory, Iris thought, was that everyone knew that slim people never wore tent-like dresses.

'You know what the really weird thing is?' said Barbara, draining her glass of red wine. 'The fatter you get, the more invisible you become.'

She looked at her so earnestly, Iris didn't know whether she was meant to laugh or not.

'Nothing more invisible than a fat, middle-aged woman,' Barbara went on. 'Shop assistants look the other way. You might as well not exist as far as men are concerned . . .'

Barbara looked as if she was about to cry, and Iris felt a bit panicky.

'I thought it was a relief not to live with a man.' She recalled the bittersweet conversations they'd had when Barbara's husband had left her.

'You're right,' said Barbara distractedly, refilling her glass.

At the other end of the huge room, Michael was dancing with Fiammetta to the song 'I Love to Love (But My Baby Loves to Dance)'. She couldn't remember ever seeing him dance before. At previous parties, her father had provided the music playing the piano. Iris recognized the expression of delight on Fiammetta's face. When their father was in good form, there was nobody else in the whole world you wanted to be with because he was so wonderful.

'I don't think Michael pays Fiammetta enough attention, do you?' Barbara remarked suddenly.

Iris was startled by the comment because it was the exact opposite of what she had been thinking.

'Bruno demands attention, so he always gets it, but Fiammetta needs more time,' Barbara went on.

'But they both get lots of his time.' Iris's instinctive re-action was to leap to her father's defence, just as she did whenever Josie criticized Michael. It occurred to her that Josie must have been talking to Barbara about him.

'Fiammetta can't read, you know,' said Barbara. 'She pretends she can because she's clever, and she gets away

185

with it because she's got such a good memory, but she can't . . .'

'But she's very intelligent,' Iris protested. 'You just said so yourself.'

She didn't want to believe that Fiammetta couldn't read, and yet, now that Barbara had said it, it did explain Fiammetta's slightly odd behaviour at times, and the relief that had flooded her serious little face when Bruno had asked whether they had to read all the books stacked up on the ground floor, and Michael had laughed, and said no, not immediately.

'Of course, I can't say anything because he already thinks I interfere too much,' said Barbara, drinking the glass of wine down as if it would quench her thirst.

A conversation Iris had had with Josie just before she left repeated in Iris's mind. Josie had asked her why Michael hadn't simply moved in with Barbara instead of converting the warehouse.

At the time, Iris had thought it just a chance remark. 'Barbara's not Dad's type,' she had replied instantly.

'You mean she's not young enough or thin enough?' Josie had remarked tartly, and Iris had been embarrassed to admit it was exactly what she had meant, even though it made him sound so superficial.

Now she realized that something must have put this idea into Josie's head. Had Barbara asked her father to move in, and been turned down? Had Barbara and Josie been sitting up all those long hot nights drinking and bemoaning men's lack of logic?

'My father really appreciates everything you do for the children,' Iris said carefully.

Barbara shrugged. 'The invisible interfering woman!' she snorted.

Barbara had got to the point of drunkenness where brittle laughter suddenly turns to maudlin self-pity.

On Declan's cassette deck, Elton John and Kiki Dee were singing 'Don't Go Breaking My Heart'. Across the room, Little Mal was looking at Iris. He had been trying to get Iris on her own ever since the night when they'd had sex, but so far Iris had managed to avoid him. Mal's hang-dog expression made her feel a bit guilty, but there was no way there could be anything between them. She hoped he wasn't going to make her spell it out to him.

'I need some air,' Iris told Barbara, squirming her body through the crowd.

The distinctive smell of cannabis floated up the stairs. Iris followed the scent through the labyrinth of boxes on the street-level room and found Pascale smoking a joint. The French woman looked at her coolly. Pascale was probably a couple of years younger than her, Iris estimated, but the French woman seemed infinitely more sophisticated. Once or twice she had caught Pascale looking at her hair in bewilderment. She wasn't sure she could begin to explain.

Pascale came from a very rich family, but Barbara thought that there must have been some sort of scandal, which was why her father was paying for her to live in England. Everyone was intrigued, but Pascale gave little away. Whenever anyone asked her a probing question, her English became suddenly non-existent.

'You want?' Pascale asked, offering Iris the joint.

'Sure,' said Iris, sitting down on the box next to her.

'Are you enjoying the party?' Iris said, taking a toke of the joint. It was high quality and strong.

Pascale shrugged.

'How long do you think you'll stay in Kingshaven?' Iris asked.

'Depend,' said Pascale.

They both fell silent at the sound of footsteps coming down the stairs.

'Iris? Iris?' Little Mal's voice called into the maze of books.

Iris had just inhaled. She held her breath, and put her hand over her mouth for what seemed like an age. And then the footsteps went back upstairs again, and both Iris and Pascale exhaled an explosion of stoned giggles.

* * *

187

In the end it had been easier to give in to the pressure to ask Joanna Allsop out, than to keep making excuses, Christopher thought. But he should have made more extensive enquiries when Joanna Allsop suggested they go to a party. It was a completely disorganized affair, with the doors wide open so that anyone could walk in off the street. Upstairs, people were drinking wine out of paper cups, one burly tattooed man was drinking straight from a giant can that looked as if it contained at least a gallon of beer. The pop music was deafening, and there was a distinctly funny smell, which Christopher suspected indicated the presence of drugs.

What if there was a police raid? The newspaper would be bound to pick up on Christopher's presence. The editor didn't seem to like the Kings, and never missed an opportunity to criticize. Christopher could almost see the headline in the *Chronicle*: 'Heir to Palace at Drugs Party'.

The grannies would have a fit. It would serve them right for making him go out with Joanna, thought Christopher.

'We should have brought a bottle,' said Joanna, trying to identify faces in the dark throng.

'A bottle? What for?' Christopher asked.

'To drink. Everyone does!'

'Doesn't the host provide?'

'That'll have run out by now! Do you think the Ship does off-sales?' Joanna asked.

'I'm quite sure they don't,' said Christopher.

There were some things he would never do, whatever the pressure, and taking Joanna into the Ship was one.

They pushed their way around the side of the room.

'Aren't you going to ask me to dance?' said Joanna.

She had a lot of eye make-up on and some of it had smudged in the heat.

'I wouldn't know where to begin with this sort of dancing,' said Christopher.

'Oh, for God's sake!' said Joanna.

He could tell she was becoming disenchanted with him, which could only be a good thing.

'Wanna dance?' the burly tattooed man asked Joanna.

'Wouldn't mind!' she said, giving Christopher a told-you-so kind of look.

Christopher glanced at his watch. Just gone ten thirty. Only another half an hour before it would be perfectly acceptable to take Joanna home. He stood watching the dancing. Occasionally one of Joanna's thin arms would shoot out from beyond the gleaming chest of her burly dance partner, and then the music changed to a slower tempo, and the big man led Joanna back to Christopher's side.

'Enjoying yourself?' asked Christopher.

She said something he didn't catch, and when he bent his ear closer to her face, she suddenly shouted, 'What the fuck are they doing here?'

Christopher turned to look at the latest arrivals at the top of the stairs. Joanna's little brother and sister, James and Julia, were staring, wide-eyed with amazement at the heaving mass of people.

The fishermen in the public bar of the Ship were bemoaning the noise coming from Michael Quinn's party, but Millicent Balls thought that the sound of people enjoying themselves was infinitely preferable to salty sea-dog tales of woe everyone had heard a thousand times.

When Michael Quinn and one of the Liverpool lads who'd become good customers over the past few weeks, came in to try to negotiate the purchase of a barrel of beer, she supplied it for only just above cost.

'Come round the back to pick it up, Mr Quinn,' she said, never quite able to bring herself to call him Michael because he'd been her teacher for two years at primary school.

'Why don't you join us when you're closed?' Mr Quinn asked.

It was nice, Millicent thought, to see him smiling for a change.

There wasn't much opportunity to go to parties when

you had children and she hadn't been out of the pub once in the past week because Gerry was at another family funeral in Ireland, as he often was these days, what with having such a big family and his parents' generation reaching that sort of age. It wouldn't really be like leaving Sean and baby Lucy, because it was only a couple of yards across the street. Millicent thought she deserved a treat after dealing with the children and the flat and the pub and everything all on her own.

Fiammetta didn't think Barbara smelled very nice. Normally, when Barbara gave her a cuddle, her apron smelled of washing powder, and when Fiammetta kissed the soft loose flesh of her cheek, it usually smelled of carnation soap, except when Barbara was dressed up for a special occasion, like when she came to see them in the nativity play at school, when her face tasted sort of chalky. When Barbara had been gardening, there might be a waft of manure, but Fiammetta didn't mind that, because it reminded her of the smell of Mary the goat, who'd gone to heaven with Mummy. When Barbara baked a cake, she smelled sweet and buttery and warm, like her kitchen did, and often there were blobs of cake mixture in her hair and on her apron, as if she'd made a whirlwind of the batter when she was beating it with a wooden spoon. But tonight, when Barbara bent down to talk to her, her breath smelled like poo and rotten mushrooms, and her hair was all sticking to her wet, sweaty face. Fiammetta tried not to jerk her nose back, but it was so much effort trying not to be rude that she didn't really take in what Barbara said to her. From the expression in Barbara's bloodshot eyes, it was obvious Barbara had asked her a question, so Fiammetta decided to say no, even though she was not sure what she'd been asked. And Barbara looked a bit sad, then released her hand and left Fiammetta standing on her own.

Grown-up parties were not at all like children's parties, which involved games followed by sandwiches, sausage rolls and orange squash, and a piece of cake wrapped in a serviette when you went home. At grown-up parties, it was too dark to play games, and there wasn't enough room to sit down and eat, so grown-ups danced to very loud music or stood shouting at each other and drinking. When they'd drunk all the bottles and cans on the table, Dad went off and came back with a metal barrel that was so heavy, Declan had to carry it as well, and then Little Tony, who was actually the biggest person Fiammetta had ever seen, knocked a tap into the barrel with a hammer and everyone cheered as beer came frothing out. The music got even louder and more people started dancing even more wildly. Fiammetta had promised Barbara she would keep right against the wall, so it wasn't dangerous, but Bruno took no notice, as usual, and went on dancing with the grown-ups.

Iris was dancing with Declan. Dad was dancing with Pascale. Suddenly the music went slow. Some people stopped dancing. For a moment, Dad and Pascale stopped too, standing opposite each other, completely still. There was a gap between them through which Fiammetta could see James Allsop standing at the other end of the room. He raised his hand to wave at Fiammetta, but then looked away, as if he hadn't meant to. And then there wasn't a gap any more, because Dad and Pascale were dancing in a sort of cuddle, and Fiammetta felt very strange, and didn't want to look at them. She glanced around the room, noticing that other people were pretending not to look as well, like Iris and Declan, and Anthony and Marie. Then Barbara came back up the stairs into the room, and stared straight at Dad and Pascale with a look on her face that was not at all smiley like her usual one, and made Fiammetta feel a bit frightened.

'Bruno has an eye for the older woman, I see,' said Declan, as he and Iris watched Bruno pulling Julia Allsop in close, imitating what Michael had just done.

Iris was glad of the opportunity to laugh because she felt as if she had been holding her breath since Dad had taken Pascale in his arms. It was such an unexpected and uncharacteristically public declaration, and she wondered if everyone in the room felt as awkward as she was feeling, or whether it was just the embarrassment of a child seeing a parent displaying intimacy.

'I've got a poster that looks a bit like her in my room at home,' Declan said, and it took Iris a moment to realize that he was still talking about Julia Allsop, whose tennis dress had ridden up her backside and caught in her knickers, like a junior version of the ghastly Athena poster you saw everywhere.

Iris laughed weakly, not wanting Declan to think she approved of the way he was looking at Julia, who was barely out of puberty, let alone that it was acceptable for him to have soft porn on his walls, but the Liverpool boys were so good-humoured, she'd learned to put up with their sexism, and she thought she'd probably miss the perpetual banter when they'd gone.

'My brother Mal says you've been avoiding him,' Declan was saying.

'No,' lied Iris.

'Talk to him then,' Declan urged her. 'Look at him, standing over there on his own like a spare prick in a nunnery.'

Before she'd had a chance to reply, he was beckoning his brother over.

'I suppose we ought to take them home,' said Christopher King to Joanna. Oddly, Christopher felt rather fond of Julia for giving him the perfect excuse to leave.

'Can we come back after?' Joanna grabbed his arm and looked pleadingly into his eyes.

'I think it's probably winding up . . .' Christopher stuttered.

'It's not! There are still people arriving!' said Joanna, pointing with her other hand towards the top of the staircase, where the latest guest had just appeared and was staring straight at the two of them.

What on earth was Millicent doing here?

*　　*　　*

'Can we go somewhere a bit quieter?' shouted Mal above the music. 'There's something I have to tell you.'

'No!' Iris shouted back. 'Tell me here!'

'It's private,' he shouted. 'I don't think you'd want me to tell you here.'

'Oh, all right then,' Iris agreed, thinking he was really rather sweet and chivalrous. If he wanted to tell her that he loved her, it would be embarrassing, but no more than that. The Liverpool boys were leaving in the morning.

'Hi, Milly!' Iris brushed past, as she made way for them at the top of the stairs, thinking how matronly Millicent looked these days. She'd put on a lot of weight since having her two children one after the other, and her thick blonde hair was cut in a long page-boy style with the ends carefully flicked up with curling tongs.

There was no relief from the heat. The temperature in the street was as hot as it was inside, and heavy with humidity. As Iris and Mal walked along the quayside together, the party music became a background noise to the rumble of thunder around the bay.

Now that he had got Iris on her own, Little Mal seemed reluctant to speak. They walked silently side by side along the harbour wall, at a safe distance from one another so that there was no possibility of their hands accidentally touching. Suddenly, a sheet of lightning lit the sky.

'God!' said Iris. 'Do you think it's safe to be out?'

They stopped walking.

He was one of the few men tall enough to make her look up into his eyes when she spoke to him. She quite liked it.

'Don't know how to tell you this,' said Mal eventually.

'You really don't have to,' Iris said, smiling at him.

'No, I think I do.'

Iris prepared herself for some dreadful cliché. How keen was he? Surely he wasn't going to go down on one knee?

'The thing is, Iris,' Mal finally looked directly into her eyes, 'the thing is, I think you've given me the clap.'

Iris waited for the inevitable punchline; her brain felt

slightly out of sync with reality as an aftereffect of the joint she'd smoked with Pascale. She didn't know whether it was a couple of seconds or a couple of minutes before she realized that he wasn't joking.

'What?' she asked.

'It burns when I piss, and I've got this muck coming out of my—'

'I don't want to know!' Iris stopped him.

'Sorry,' he said.

'How do you know it's . . . ?' Iris, who prided herself on being able to match the Liverpool boys' language, found herself lost for words.

'Declan told me.' Mal looked a bit sheepish.

'Bloody hell! Who else have you told?'

'Only my brothers.'

'What are you going to do?' she asked.

'I'll get myself checked out at the clap clinic when I get back home,' Mal told her. 'And you need to do the same.'

It hadn't properly sunk in that if Mal was infected, then she was too. She felt suddenly filthy.

She went on the offensive. 'What makes you think it was me?'

'Because . . . because I never slept with anyone else,' he admitted.

'Slept with' was such a euphemism for what had taken about two minutes and hadn't even involved lying down that it made Iris laugh.

'It's not funny,' said Mal.

'Sorry,' said Iris, now feeling horribly guilty.

The heaviness of the air was unbearable. Flashes of lightning lit up the town like flares, and the thunder grew louder, angrier. Filled with the urge to cleanse herself, Iris began to run towards the beach, pushing her body through the humid air as if she was running in treacle. As the thunder crashed above, the air grew suddenly cold, as the humidity condensed into delicious splatters of rain. She lifted her face to the heavens, feeling a glorious cold wetness on her eyelids and in her mouth, daring the storm to strike her down.

The party wasn't as good as Millicent had hoped. By the time she got there, the music was the slow stuff and everyone had paired off, and it wasn't much fun being the only one in the room who wasn't drunk. Millicent was quite used to having conversations at work with drunk people who thought they had just had the most interesting idea in the world, but she didn't fancy it on her night out and she didn't feel like having a drink herself. It put you off when you lived with the smell of beer all day.

Christopher King ushered the Allsop children out almost as soon as Millicent arrived, mumbling something to her under his breath about having to look after them, as if he was their babysitter or something. Millicent didn't quite know why that annoyed her so much. She'd told him enough times that they could only be friends, but she'd grown used to the idea that he only had eyes for her. It was a kind of refuge when her brain was tormented with images of Gerry and what he might be getting up to in his frequent absences from home. It was nice to feel you had options, even if you had no intention of taking them up. Now, seeing Christopher with Joanna Allsop on his arm gazing at him adoringly was a bit of a shock because they looked like a couple. To be fair, Christopher had mentioned Joanna's pursuit of him, aided and abetted by the two grannies, as if it was a kind of joke, but Millicent couldn't help feeling a little bit betrayed and let down. It was disappointment, she told herself, not jealousy. She couldn't be jealous, could she? That wouldn't be logical at all.

It was so hot, Michael wondered if he was imagining that Pascale's hipbones were pressing slightly more insistently against his belly. He drew his head back and looked at her quizzically, but her cool gaze was unflinching. The song faded away and for a moment they were standing still. He couldn't seem to wrest his eyes from her mouth. Her soft lower lip protruded slightly. What would it feel like to kiss it? A pulse of desire shivered through his groin; he could feel acceleration of his heartbeat and a long-forgotten mist of urgency beginning to blur his reason. Aware that people were looking at him, his hands dropped from her waist, but he couldn't take his eyes from her face, that lower lip, more brown than pink, how soft would it feel . . .

'Come,' said Pascale. She led him downstairs, through a secret passage among the towers of books to the little den where she had stashed her tobacco tin. She sat down on a box, patted it so that he would sit next to her, took out a slim wallet of Rizla papers and began to construct a joint, licking the sticky bit of the cigarette papers carefully with the very tip of her tongue.

'No,' he suddenly said, grabbing her wrist.

Her hands were long and slim, her arms so thin her wrist bone jutted out. He drew it to his mouth, and kissed the nobble of bone, chastely, almost reverently, his nostrils inhaling the scent of skin that smelled very slightly of Ambre Solaire. Her other hand reached out and fingered the top button of his jeans. Knowing he would explode if she went any further, he found himself grasping both her wrists, staring at her. Her arms were rigid and then they suddenly slackened, allowing him to pull her upper body against his. His mouth finally discovered that lower lip, and she kissed him back as hungrily as he kissed her, like he had never been kissed before, his equal in passion and strength.

Between kisses, he heard himself repeating her name: 'Pascale, Pascale, Pascale . . .'

And as lightning splintered between the towers of boxes, and thunder rolled around the bay, he forgot all about time passing, and anyone else in this world or beyond.

When they eventually came back upstairs, the huge first-floor room was dark. Everyone had gone home. The cassette deck had been switched off. A flash of lightning lit up the debris of the party. Cups with cigarette butts floating in the dregs littered the floor, spillages of red wine looked like bloodstains on the sanded boards.

'Let's leave all this,' he said, taking Pascale by the hand, leading her towards the spiral staircase that went up to the bedrooms.

Her sandals made the metal clang, and Michael was suddenly aware that there was someone there in the party room.

'Michael?' said Barbara's drowsy voice. She had obviously fallen asleep waiting. 'I put the children to bed.'

'Thank you,' he whispered back into the darkness.

'Are you all right?' she asked.

'Fine,' he said, feigning a yawn, hoping she would drop back to sleep again.

And then another flash of lightning lit the room, and he could see Barbara sitting propped against the wall below the high window, a wine bottle still in her hand, shielding her eyes from the sudden brightness. Even though he instantly let go of Pascale's hand, she was standing just below him on the spiral staircase, and it was as obvious as if Barbara had caught them in the act itself.

'Oh! . . . I'm sorry,' Barbara said, with peculiarly English manners, before clambering to her feet and running head-long downstairs and out into the storm.

For a moment, Michael wondered if he should go after her, but he knew there was nothing he could say to make things different now.

And then there was a sound like machine-gun fire close by, and Pascale grabbed his arm, suddenly vulnerable, frightened.

'What is it?' she asked.

'It's rain,' he told her. 'Rain on the roof. The summer's over.'

Chapter Eight

1977

From the skylight in Fiammetta's bedroom in the roof, Michael could see the twins in the distance walking back along the promenade on their way home from school. They were still too far away for him to distinguish their facial features, but he could tell from the angle of their heads that they were talking, and he longed to know what they were saying. He had read that some twins developed a language of their own to exclude other people, but his children had never done that, except that time when their grandfather had attempted to teach them Latin and they had thought it great fun to put 'us' on the end of almost every word. Bruno had always been the articulate one, Fiammetta the quiet observer, but they had communicated with each other and the outside world perfectly effectively until recently. Michael couldn't decide whether Fiammetta's withdrawal had been sudden, or whether he hadn't noticed a gradual change because he hadn't been paying proper attention.

The children were almost home now, and he did not want them to suspect he'd been spying. He turned away from the window and picked his way through the arrangement of paintings laid out all over the floor. They were mostly slightly disturbing abstracts, painted in thick purple, grey or black paint, but at the centre was a simple charcoal sketch. The portraiture was very accomplished for a nine-year-old. The woman had long hair and was smiling. The woman's hands enfolded the two other figures, who were less well drawn, with lots of scrubbings-out and smudges, but recognizable nevertheless. The pyramidal structure of the drawing was iconic, but the smiling animal's face and the child's flat perspective made it look like the Botticelli altarpiece copied by Chagall. *Madonna with Barbara and a Goat*, Michael thought sadly.

One of the worst aspects of Barbara's tragedy was that, until her body was washed up on a shingle beach near Lowhampton, nobody had noticed she was missing for five days.

When Pascale had returned to the Riviera the morning after the party to collect clothes and toiletries, Barbara's absence had seemed like a lucky escape, a cause, even, for guilty celebration. Those heady first days were such a whirlwind of intense pleasure, there had been no space for the idea of someone else's pain.

When Fiammetta asked to go and see Barbara, Michael had promised to take her at the weekend, privately hoping that, with the beginning of a new school year, his daughter would forget, but forgetting himself that little girls have very precise and tenacious memories.

Sometimes, Michael wondered if it was the way his daughter had learned, as much as the fact itself, that had affected her so badly. They were just leaving the warehouse on their way to visit Barbara, when Millicent Balls, returning from town with two bags of shopping, asked them if they had heard the news.

The shock had frozen Fiammetta. She seemed to stop growing, while Bruno, who had always been a boy of appetites, shot up and began to put on weight, almost as if he was growing for himself and Fiammetta too. Intellectually, Bruno continued to develop, devouring books as he devoured food, and asking questions all the time, sometimes uncomfortably profound questions. Fiammetta said nothing and seemed to do nothing but paint these strange dark pictures. Michael had always assumed that, left alone, his daughter would progress to reading in her own time, but now time was running out. With the twins' move to senior school fast approaching, Michael knew that it would be difficult to shake off the label of low achiever if Fiammetta arrived at Lowhampton's new combined comprehensive unable to read or write competently. Occasionally the worry and frustration made him shout at Fiammetta as she stared at him impassively as if challenging his competence as a parent, the very foundation on which he had built his life since Claudia died.

Ironically, with Barbara gone, there was no one he could talk to about it, and he feared that if he acknowledged Fiammetta's problems openly by talking to her teacher, or to Kingshaven's young GP, it would only give people another reason to heap further disapproval on him.

Nobody would ever know what was in Barbara's mind when she fell or walked into the churning sea that night. The coroner recorded a verdict of accidental death, and Michael tried to persuade himself that it was a tragic accident as a result of the heat and alcohol, but privately he was convinced it was suicide. And even though he knew the reaction was unfair, he was primarily angry with her for inflicting such a burden of guilt and grief, even though he knew that Barbara couldn't have been in her right mind, because she would never have deliberately hurt his children. The residents of Kingshaven had their theories, and it was clear that any sympathy that had accrued to Michael after Claudia's death, disappeared with Barbara's, as people inevitably linked her tragedy with his new love affair that had started so publicly at his notorious party.

Michael was as surprised as anyone else to find himself involved with a woman half his age, and yet Pascale seemed more equal than any woman he had ever known. Her poor English and his even poorer French meant that their communication was intuitive, physical and felt, in some almost primal way, pure. There was a self-sufficient quality about her. She never nagged nor demanded his attention as Sylvia had done, nor even frightened him with an adoring gaze, as

Claudia sometimes had, and she made it clear that she had no interest in becoming a parent to the children. Right at the beginning of their relationship, he'd felt obliged to tell her that he didn't want ever to have any more children.

She'd told him, 'I don't want either.'

Then, as if to show that she meant it, she had told him her story in touchingly bad English. Her parents were powerful people in the region she came from. Her father, a rich man, and a prominent Catholic, had turned a blind eye when a local politician flirted with her as a teenager, even, she thought, considering his daughter's attractiveness something of a feather in his cap. But when she became pregnant, he had only wanted to make her disappear. She had been sent to a convent far away from home. The baby would have been given away to some good Catholic family at birth. But Pascale had escaped, stolen money to have a backstreet abortion, and, afterwards, even worse, gone to Paris to join the students on the streets in 1968. Her father had paid for her to stay in the capital, study at the Sorbonne, just to keep her away from the family home, but a relationship with a drug dealer had eventually landed her in trouble with the police. Fearing she would bring disrepute on the family, with the help of the politician who was now in government, her father had packed her off to England.

'He pulled string,' Pascale had told Michael, 'so I not stand trial.'

The confession had bound them even closer together.

When the children were at home, Pascale left Michael with them as if she was a lodger renting a room in the same space. At night, they were as close as any two people could be. With Pascale, he explored fantasies he had never imagined, the strength of sensation wiping his memory of sex with anyone else, as if he had leaped straight from the ache of adolescence to exquisite fulfilment. The release was profound, making him both powerful and powerless, as if he had just been freed from prison, but didn't yet know where he would go.

*   *   *

'How was your day?'

The question was directed at both of his children, but Fiammetta slid silently past him and up the spiral staircase to her room.

'I wrote a story,' Bruno told him, sawing at a loaf of bread, and making a doorstep sandwich with a hunk of cheese from the fridge and a smear of horseradish sauce left over from their Sunday lunch instead of butter on the bread. Bruno was always experimenting with different combinations of flavour.

'Did Fiammetta write one too?' Michael asked as casually as he could, trying to sneak information about one from the other.

'Fiammetta is the best in the class at making stories up,' Bruno informed him authoritatively, through a mouthful of sandwich, 'but she's not so good at writing them down.'

It sounded like something an encouraging teacher might say.

'Why do you think that is?' Michael asked gently.

'The letters jump around the page,' said Bruno, taking another bite.

'Did Fiammetta tell you that?'

He'd made his eagerness to know too obvious. Bruno merely shrugged in response.

Then Fiammetta came downstairs with an empty jam jar in her hand to get water.

'Those are interesting paintings in your room,' Michael told her, realizing that it was no use pretending that he hadn't seen them. 'Will you explain them to me one day?'

She went to the sink and filled it with water from the tap. Then went back upstairs.

The following day, when he went to look, he could no longer find the Madonna painting, just another blue and purple mass with a few milky grey streaks where the paint was still wet. It made him wonder whether all the paintings over the floor had once started out as careful drawings, then been painted over, and he stared at them as if by looking long enough, he would find the answer to his anxiety.

'I'm sorry, I can't,' Iris told Vic, when he rang to invite her to a gig featuring a singer calling himself Elvis Costello.

'But he's going to be big,' said Vic.

'Not with that name,' said Iris.

'Don't you think so? I kind of like it . . .'

'These days Elvis means a big sweaty bloke in a white jumpsuit, not a lean, mean boy in black drainpipes,' said Iris.

'Suit yourself,' said Vic. 'You're no fun any more!'

The silence after a phone call always seemed much emptier than before it rang, Iris thought, staring at the phone on her desk. For a moment, she was tempted to change her mind. She picked up the receiver and dialled Vic's number, imagining the phone ringing in the flamboyantly decorated flat just a few streets away in Soho, which he shared with a gay student from St Martin's School of Art. It was a council flat in a small block tucked away behind Old Compton Street, and Vic's neighbours were nearly all prostitutes with young children, except for an old woman called Molly, who had ten cats.

Vic must have gone out, Iris decided, or was calling from a phone box. These days Vic called himself a promoter and he was paid for tip-offs about new bands. But his day job was running round the major outlets buying copies of singles record companies wanted to get to the top of the charts.

Iris looked at the pile of typescripts stacked up on the floor beside her desk. It was, she estimated, about four feet tall, which was an afternoon's reading and rejecting, unless one of them was a gem. How strange, she thought, that she now measured the unsolicited manuscripts by the yard, able to tell, almost from the first page whether something was going to work.

'Isn't it arrogant to judge whether people will like a book just because you like it?' Vic had asked her once.

'Wouldn't it be more arrogant to judge that other people might like something that I don't?' she had replied.

After the critical success of *Sandwiches and Samosas* in England, and the sale of rights to Germany and the Netherlands, as well as a film option, Iris had been made a junior editor at Harridan. Sometimes Iris couldn't believe that she was being paid to have opinions. At the beginning of the year, she had been one of the 'New Faces in Books' featured in the *Observer Magazine*, with a memorable photo of her standing beside a single tower of books as tall and thin as she. (Iris told no one, not even Josie, that they'd glued the books together.) As well as dealing with authors, which she enjoyed because after years of dealing with her father's sensibilities she was a natural at saying what artistic temperaments wanted to hear, Iris had to master new skills, like what to eat when lunching with literary agents (soup was too slurpy; steak involved too much chewing, and spaghetti was to be avoided, particularly if you were wearing a white blouse, because you would certainly splash Napoletana sauce on it, even though this never ever happened when you were eating spaghetti at home).

It was the social side of publishing that Iris found hard work. Even though people in the industry constantly bewailed the parlous state of the finances, there were always parties to launch books and parties to celebrate mergers, as smaller publishers were subsumed as imprints of larger publishers, everyone downing cheap white wine by the gallon to put a brave face on the changes. Publishing was full of upper-middle-class young women with names like Miranda or Lucinda, whose daddies financed their dabblings, and whom Iris resented because they helped to keep salaries abysmally low. They were also much better than she was at moving around a party, chatting to people whilst looking over their shoulders for who to talk to next. Shelley called it 'working the room'. To remain with the same person for more than five minutes, even if you were having an interesting conversation, was social death. At the same time, you had to monitor how often your glass was refilled. Two glasses of wine made Iris witty, three tempted her into indiscretion. It was all much harder than editing a manuscript and – Vic was right – not exactly fun, but it suited Iris, because fun was dangerous. Fun had given her VD, and she never ever wanted to repeat the humiliation of visiting the Sexually Transmitted Diseases clinic again, nor the sustained deceit of having to hide a course of antibiotics at home. It had been bad enough trying to conceal packets of the Pill from Josie in her wild, punk days, but she never wanted to have to explain the antibiotics to anyone. Now Iris was clean, and she intended to remain so. No drugs had passed her lips since the madness of the long hot summer, nor had she had sex. Her hair was cropped really close to her scalp. She still wore black, but her clothes were smarter now, befitting her new status as a career woman.

'Are you taking vows?' Vic had asked last time he saw her. 'Because you're beginning to look like a bloody nun!'

The phone on Iris's desk rang again.

'If it's Vic, can you tell him I've popped out?' Iris asked the receptionist, knowing it would be harder to resist his invitation a second time.

'It's Mr Stone,' said the receptionist. Her voice contained a slight question.

'Mr Stone?' Iris echoed, mystified.

'I think it's Roman Stone,' whispered the receptionist, as if the caller was so important, he might be able to hear her through the switchboard.

Roman Stone was chairman of the Portico Books Group, which had recently taken over several old-established hardback publishing houses, set up exclusive links with a leading paperback house and was jokingly referred to by publishing insiders as the Roman Empire. Roman Stone was one of the most powerful men in publishing.

'Put him through,' said Iris, assuming he was ringing to talk about her father.

In the early sixties, Michael Quinn's first novel, *The Right Thing*, had been Roman Stone's first commercial success as a fiction publisher. It had become a minor classic, ranking alongside iconic novels like *A Kind of Loving* and *Saturday Night and Sunday Morning*. Her father's second novel, *Hide and Seek*, based on his search for Iris when she had run away from home, had also won critical acclaim, and, though Michael had not written anything since, Roman Stone had continued to take him out to lunch once or twice a year, more out of loyalty than with any real hope of getting another novel out of him, Iris suspected. When Claudia had died, Roman had rung the Castle every month or so, keeping a friendly eye on his protégé, and more often than not, it had been Iris who answered the phone. They had developed a bantering phone friendship, based on the shared exasperation of dealing with a morose writer, but Iris hadn't spoken to Roman Stone since she had moved to London.

'Iris?'

The publisher's voice resonated with authority, but Iris always thought she could hear an ironic kind of smile in it too.

'Roman Stone!'

She didn't feel she could call him Roman because they'd never met, and yet they knew each other too well for her suddenly to become deferential and start calling him Mr Stone.

'How are things?' he asked.

'Things are fine, thank you,' said Iris. 'What about you?'

'Yes . . .' said Roman.

She sensed he was attending to something else, signing letters or reading a review some minion had placed in front of him.

'I was wondering whether you were free for lunch?' he asked.

'Now?' Iris asked surprised.

'I expect you're greatly in demand . . .'

'Very greatly . . .' said Iris, with mock seriousness, as she struggled to recover her dignity.

'How about next Monday?' Roman asked.

Iris paused to flip through a mostly empty desk diary.

'Actually, Monday's not great for me,' she lied.

It was the sort of thing she'd heard Shelley say.

'Shame!' said Roman. 'I'm off to New York on Tuesday, and I really didn't want to wait till I got back.'

There was something about his automatic assumption she would change her plans (not that she actually had any) to fit in with him that irked Iris. He was only trying to find out whether her father was writing anything, so it was hardly urgent. Or perhaps, Iris suddenly thought, he had heard about Dad's affair with Pascale and wanted the inside story. Roman Stone was famed both for the longevity of his marriage to Pippa Stone, with whom he was often photographed in *Tatler*, but also for his penchant for pretty girls with names like Lucinda and Miranda. Perhaps he was the type of middle-aged man to feel a little competitive? All the more reason not to jump when he called.

'I'm afraid you'll have to,' Iris told him.

'In that case,' said Roman, the smile back in his voice, 'I'll have my secretary call you to arrange something.'

'Fine,' said Iris, putting down the phone and staring at it, wondering why she couldn't work out who had won, or why anyone would want to win a telephone conversation anyway.

With the refurbishment of one wing of the Castle now complete, Sylvia's bid to host *the* Kingshaven Silver Jubilee celebration was launched so early and with such fanfare, it almost looked as if she was trying to pre-empt any plan the Kings, who traditionally celebrated significant dates in the royal calendar, might have had to hold a big party at the Palace.

Unable to think of a single event that would adequately demonstrate her largesse, Sylvia eventually decided to host two parties: a children's tea party in the afternoon, and a much grander and more exclusive black-tie Jubilee Ball in the evening.

After what seemed like endless discussions over the

refreshments – Sylvia was sure that Harvey's Bristol Cream would be appropriate, whereas Daddy favoured champagne – and arguments over the guest list, with Daddy wondering out loud if Audrey Potter, the retiring postmistress, would really fit in and Sylvia saying she couldn't really leave her out because she'd been a loyal friend in difficult times – silver-edged invitations to the Jubilee Ball were sent to everyone who was anyone in Kingshaven and the surrounding area, with the exception of the Patels and the Wongs, because, Sylvia said, they weren't British, after all.

Another giant invitation, also edged in silver and decorated with Union Jacks, was delivered to the primary school commanding all the children to the Castle for the afternoon of 7 June. A photograph of the presentation duly appeared in the *Chronicle* beside an article that made it sound as if the Allsops themselves were graciously granting the children the day off, although the date was already designated as a national holiday.

When James Allsop remarked how nice it would be for Bruno and Fiammetta to come to see their old home again, Sylvia succumbed to one of her migraines before getting on the phone to her own son, Anthony, to instruct him to tell his father not to send the children to the party because it would be embarrassing for everyone. Word had come back that Michael wouldn't in any case be allowing his children to participate in an afternoon of flag-waving jingoism, which Sylvia said was just typical of him.

'She thinks she *is* the Queen,' James said scornfully on the afternoon of the party, as Sylvia walked up and down the long trestle table, watching the children eat their sausage rolls and crisps from red, white and blue paper plates, occasionally stopping to pick up a dropped silver cardboard crown in her gloved hand.

By luck or intuition, Sylvia's outfit for the afternoon was the exact fondant pink that Her Majesty was wearing for her own walkabout, although in the evening, she changed into a pale-lemon ballgown.

Julia and Jacqueline Allsop dutifully ironed their Laura

Ashley pinafores, which were virtually part of school uniform, to be worn on the rare 'social' occasions when the older girls were bussed to hops at boys' public schools in the vicinity. James, to everyone's surprise, came down to the ball with his thick fair hair wetted and combed back from his face, and looking amazingly grown up in full black tie. Only Joanna defiantly wore a hip-length orange kaftan (which was just about long enough to be described as a dress) over jeans.

The marquee was swathed in silver fabric and garlanded with Union Jacks and clusters of red, white and blue balloons. Julia tried her best to shrink into the folds of silver lining and not to be noticed. The Laura Ashley dress made her look fat and nobody asked her to dance. She was always the one left standing like an idiot at the boys' school hops and sitting silently on the coach back to school while the other girls chattered on about who fancied whom.

Whatever their opinions about Sylvia, everyone had to admit that she did throw a blissful party. No expense had been spared. The carousel and dodgem cars hired for the children in the afternoon made the Castle grounds look like a magical fairground when all lit up at night with coloured lights. The terrace was floodlit and the band played sophisticated tunes like 'Chanson d'Amour' by Manhattan Transfer. The silver lining made the marquee too hot to dance, so guests spilled out into the open air like the wonderful party in a film Julia had seen starring Robert Redford called *The Great Gatsby*.

The only person who didn't seem to be enjoying it very much was Sylvia herself. Whenever Julia overheard Sylvia talking to Daddy, her stepmother was moaning about the guests who hadn't turned up.

'You would have thought Libby King would have had the decency, seeing James is her godson . . .'

'I believe there's a do at the Yacht Club,' said Jolly.

'At least she could have sent Christopher . . .'

'Adrian and Winny are here, though,' Jolly tried to soothe her.

'But they're just children!'

'Angela's vastly pregnant, you couldn't really expect her—'

'I don't mind about her,' snapped Sylvia.

'And I heard that Pearl was in the Caribbean with her young man.'

'Good. Because I wouldn't have her in my house!'

There seemed to be no pleasing her.

Julia was standing with Adrian and Winny when James sidled up.

'Do you think I should ask Sylvia to dance?' he asked.

Secretly Julia felt slightly ashamed that they were always so mean to Sylvia when she'd tried so hard to make everything so nice for them, but she never dared say so in case James accused her of taking Sylvia's side. Now she leaped at the suggestion.

'Oh, yes, do!' said Julia, knowing that it would be the thing to cheer Sylvia up.

Julia watched proudly as her little brother, who was taller than she was now, in his first proper dinner suit, walked across the terrace and bowed to his stepmother. At first, Sylvia looked bewildered, but then Daddy, positively beaming with pride, gently nudged her into his son's arms, and the two of them moved off in a slow formal waltz. Gradually Sylvia's face began to break into a smile, which made her look prettier than Julia had ever seen her looking before. Sylvia allowed herself to be twirled a little faster, and faster, the two of them laughing and whirling in the twinkling spangled lights as they spun closer and closer to the edge of the swimming pool.

Julia realized what was going to happen only a split second before. She heard herself yelling, 'No!!!'

And in that instant, Sylvia's pretty smile disappeared and terror descended over her face as James, with the precision of a winning competitor on *Come Dancing*, slipped his leading foot in front of Sylvia's and tried to throw her headlong into the pool. But Sylvia was stronger than he'd imagined and clung on to him, taking him down with her.

The splash was followed by an awful shocked silence and then the two of them bobbed up, Sylvia flailing, screaming, 'I can't swim!'

Luckily Adrian, who had a proper life-saving qualification, was there to dive in.

'We're calling it the Downstairs Jubilee Party,' said Millicent Balls, standing at the front door of the warehouse. 'You know, as in Upstairs . . .' she pointed her finger in the direction of the Yacht Club, 'Downstairs.' She pointed at the cobblestones beneath her feet.

Michael smiled at her.

'It's open house,' she said. 'Free bar, free barbecue, and there's music,' she added unnecessarily, as the local band played a raucous encore of 'I am a Cider Drinker'.

'Thanks, but . . .'

'Oh, go on! The kids are hanging out of their bedroom window,' said Millicent, pointing up again. 'They won't sleep while it's still light.'

Michael stepped out of the warehouse door and saw the heads of his children, who must have been standing on chairs to reach the skylights, suddenly duck out of view.

'Bruno? Fiammetta? If you want to go to the party, get some clothes on and come down,' he shouted up.

There was a frantic scrabbling above like the sound he used to hear of rats in the Castle attics, and then his children appeared, with unfastened sandals and buttons done up in the wrong holes.

'Go on, then!' he said, ruffling Bruno's black curly hair. 'But be careful near the harbour.'

'You're very welcome too,' said Millicent. 'Both of you,' she added.

Even though she hadn't felt able to use Pascale's name, it was a friendly gesture, and Michael was touched.

'Maybe we'll come along later,' Michael told her. 'Thank you.'

In the big first-floor room, he found Pascale staring out of the window at the crowd of revellers outside the Ship.

'It's like the Day of Bastille,' Pascale remarked. 'With all the – how you say?'

'Flags? Except you're celebrating getting rid of royalty, whereas we're all happily toasting our servitude!'

She turned and half-smiled at him. He caught her arm, pulled her gently away from the window, bringing the underside of her wrist to his lips and kissing the delicate skin tenderly. Then he pulled her against him, his knee pushing between her thighs. Her breathing began to quicken, as they dropped to the floor. He forced her arms up over her head, pinning both hands back, while his other hand methodically opened the buttons of her plain white shirt. Then the doorbell rang again and they looked at each other, silently calculating the odds of it being the children returning already.

'Let me just see who that is,' Michael said, clambering to his feet.

Sonny Patel had suddenly sprouted up from a little boy to a youth, and it took a moment or two for Michael to put a name to the face. He'd been meaning to pop into the post office to wish the Patels well as they'd recently taken over after Audrey Potter's retirement.

When they arrived in Kingshaven, nearly five years before, the Patels had struggled to survive in a town that had little experience of immigrants, but sheer hard work, well-mannered children, and their resigned dignity in the face of racist graffiti sprayed on the window of their first shop, appeared to have brought the town round. Letters in the *Chronicle* made it clear that the people of Kingshaven would never tolerate swastikas in their midst. Mr Barratt in the hardware store refused to sell cans of aerosol paint to anyone under twenty-one. As if to compensate for the town's collective guilt, no objections had been raised when the Indian family applied to take over the post office.

There was a letter in Sonny Patel's hand.

'Is that for me?' Michael prompted.

'Yes!' said the boy, remembering his errand. 'We found it down the back of the counter when we were cleaning up. Technically, Daddy thinks it should probably go back to the sorting office, but it's been so long, he thought you wouldn't want to wait any longer . . .'

'Special delivery!' Michael said.

The letter was addressed to 'Michael Quinn, care of The Primary School, Kingshaven'. The postmark was September 1968. Michael immediately recognized the untidy handwriting, and he knew exactly when he had last seen the writer of the letter. In 1956 on the first Aldermaston march. At the Atomic Weapons Centre, they had linked arms and sang 'Auld Lang Syne' together, but as he had watched her threading through the crowds back to the station, he had known that they would not meet again. Now, it was as if her hand had reached into the present and touched him, and he felt a shiver run through his body.

Rachel.

Michael suddenly realized that Sonny Patel was waiting for a response of some sort.

'Please thank your father for me,' he said, stuffing the letter into his pocket. The boy still stood there.

'What about you, Sonny? Have you come to the party?'

'I should be studying. I'm in the middle of O levels,' said the boy.

'A few hours off won't do you any harm,' Michael told him.

The boy smiled at him, but his eyes were directed round the corner of the door at the boxes of books, most of which hadn't been touched since they'd come down from the Castle.

'Are you interested in books?' Michael asked.

Sonny nodded.

'Perhaps you'd like to come over when your exams are done and help me sort these out?'

Sonny nodded again.

'Good lad! Please give my regards to your father.'

Sonny finally took the hint.

'And he sends his regards to you too, Mr Quinn.'

'Michael.'

213

'Enjoy the Jubilee!' said Sonny.

Michael closed the door, pulled out the letter again, slumped down on the stairs. He stared at the handwriting on the envelope, as if looking long enough would give him a clue about what was inside without him having to open it. The school would have been the only address Rachel had for him, but by the time the letter was written, he'd long since stopped being a teacher. Someone must have handed it in to the post office, and Audrey Potter put it to one side – accidentally or deliberately? – the postmistress had always been very thick with Sylvia.

There was a phrase going round and round in his head, but he couldn't work out where it had come from.

Didn't you get the letter?

Had he dreamed it?

Didn't you get the letter?

Then he remembered.

Rachel's children had come to Winston's Festival in 1969. Every young person in England seemed to have made their way to Kingshaven that weekend. It had been such a strange, unreal time, with thousands of hippies camping in the grounds, and Claudia dying at the Castle.

Michael had stumbled upon the two of them on one of his walks, when he had to get out of the house. The girl had recognized him from the Aldermaston march. Her name was Clare. She was in her early twenties. The boy was younger. About the same age as Anthony, Michael seemed to think. His name was Keir or Karl, something socialist, anyway. When they'd told him Rachel, their mother, his former lover, had died the year before, Michael had burst into tears and it had been embarrassing for everyone. He'd felt a fraud, because really he'd been crying for Claudia, but Rachel's children didn't know that, and he couldn't explain.

Now he remembered Clare asking, 'Didn't you get the letter?'

Michael stared at the envelope.

Why would Rachel have written to him? To say goodbye? To tell him that she loved him? Some primal instinct told him that he shouldn't open the letter. Like Pandora's box, it should be left sealed. The past was the past. Rachel was dead. And yet, he knew that he would open it. He was a writer and there was something irresistibly Hardyesque about receiving a letter from a former lover almost ten years after she had died.

As he carefully levered his finger under the flap, breaking the seal of glue that was brittle with age, his hands shook with a presentiment that he was about to receive the inevitable payback for any happiness he had recently allowed himself to feel.

Dear Michael,

I didn't mean to tell you this, but I didn't think I was going to die either. It's not like it is in the movies, by the way. Much uglier and smellier. You imagine there will come a moment of serene acceptance, but it's taking its time with me. I'm still raging . . .

Michael found himself smiling, because the words were unsentimental and abrasive. Rachel.

The first time he'd seen her at Etherington Labour Club, she was like no woman he'd met before. Strong, funny, unwilling to hide her intelligence. They'd hit it off straight away – a similar sardonic sense of humour, an undercurrent of attraction despite her being at least fifteen years older than he. He hadn't known whose wife she was.

He was only recently married to Sylvia at the time, living with her parents, occasionally having sex on the living-room floor as the white dot in the centre of the television faded to grey, because their bedroom was next to Sylvia's parents' and Sylvia couldn't bear the idea of her mother hearing.

Michael had felt more at home at work. He was doing his first teaching practice and had been lucky with the headmaster of the school, who was both a brilliant educator and a progressive. He'd told Michael to call him George, lent him books, talked about the arts. At a time when the only art in Michael's life had been Sylvia's mother's prized collection of porcelain figurines, George had invited him back to his house to listen to opera. And he had introduced him to his wife . . . Rachel.

Their affair began in a rain shelter in the park on the way home from the Labour Club, with the smell of creosote, and the scrawled initials of other lovers all around them. It had gone on for over a year.

When Sylvia found out, it was the doomed attempt to save their marriage, start afresh, that had brought them down from the North to Kingshaven. He'd taken the first job he was offered, in St Mary's Primary School.

Rachel, Michael mused, was ultimately the reason he was here in this conservative little town in the South, with its constant lament of seagulls.

Michael, I don't know what's best to do. You may officially call me a coward after all the times I have called you one, but I am too selfish to allow my son to hate me just now. Our son, I should say, Michael. Your son.

I thought I could get away with it, but puritanical death is saying no, I'm not allowed to die with my secret.

He looks SO LIKE YOU!

Sometimes I think that George must have known all along and forgiven me, but I daren't ask him, in case he hasn't, and he stops loving me too for this little time we have.

I thought about telling you on the march. Do you remember how I went on and on about George being a wonderful father to our son (which he is), and I thought perhaps you would think . . . ? But you didn't. Perhaps it's only women who do that kind of second guessing.

So why tell you now? Because our son is not a shabby secret. He is a fine young man, and he came from love. We did love each other, didn't we, Michael? I know the answer already, by the way, because I read *The Right Thing*. And it made me feel more beautiful than I ever felt in real life. I wouldn't dream of telling you this, of course, unless I was about to die. But, thank you for that.

What will you do with this fact? If you believe in nurture over nature, as you used to, you will do nothing. Are you still a good Marxist, Michael?

Perhaps you will even write a novel about it?

Goodbye, Michael.

Love, Rachel

Millicent always knew when Gerry was hiding something, but in recent weeks, she hadn't been able to work out what was going on. First of all, there was his purchase of a bloody great motorbike, which she'd put down to the emergence of a few grey hairs around his temples and the distinctly middle-aged thickening round his waist. Now there was the spontaneous decision to throw a Jubilee party for all the people of Kingshaven who weren't posh enough to be invited to the Castle or the Yacht Club.

It wasn't that Milly objected, far from it, but such blatant *bonhomie* was usually a sign her husband was feeling guilty about something, and normally he had no time for the Royal Family.

There were none of the usual indications, like lovebites on his neck, stubs of unfamiliar brands of cigarette in the ashtray of the Hillman Imp, the reek of unfamiliar perfume in his chest hair, and she knew better than to ask because there was nothing worse than an interfering woman. She'd heard him saying so often enough in the bar.

'I always come back to you, don't I?' he'd told her once, and Milly knew that was as near to fidelity as she was going to get.

Now, as she stood watching people dancing in the street outside their pub, Gerry suddenly appeared behind her, smelling of sweat and charcoal from the barbecue, and led her down from the steps into the midst of the crowd. She could tell from the way he leaned against her during the slow tunes that he'd drunk quite a lot himself and he hadn't had his usual early evening shave. The stubble on his cheeks was more grey than gingery blond these days.

'Don't give up on us, Mil-ly,' Gerry sang along, puffing wet beery breath into her ear, his sandpaper cheek scratching against hers. 'Don't be cross with me, Mil-ly . . .'

'Why should I be cross with you?' Milly asked, suddenly aware he wasn't singing David Soul's exact words.

'I've got a horse!' said Gerry with a big stupid grin. 'I've always wanted a horse of my own . . . you wouldn't be denying me that, would you, Milly Minx?'

Gerry's Irish lilt always came out when he'd been drinking. It was one of the reasons she tried to moderate him. People got uncomfortable hearing Irish voices in pubs these days.

'How did you pay for it?' Milly demanded to know, still not certain if he was joking.

'My old uncle left me some money and a horse . . . so I've brought it over from Ireland, now.'

Milly stared at him. The story fitted the facts, and she thought her husband was probably too drunk to have made up such an elaborate ruse, but there was a confusion of reactions to his confession whirling round her head. She was elated, because a horse was better than a woman – although, she knew from experience that one often led to the other – but furious that he hadn't told her about the bequest. How much money was it anyway, and why hadn't it crossed his mind to ask her what they should do with it? It annoyed her that he'd cannily chosen his moment so that she couldn't make a scene in public. Wasn't it her parents who had given them their livelihood (along with the advice that a publican should never drink)? Didn't she work as hard in the pub as he did? Where was her reward?

Milly left her husband standing with his arms still outstretched, staring into space, as if he couldn't work out where she'd gone, and ran straight through the pub to the kitchen at the back where she slammed the door behind her and shouted at the top of her voice, 'A bloody fucking HORSE, for God's sake!'

'Milly?'

Milly was suddenly aware that someone was in the little courtyard outside where the dustbins were, looking in the window.

'Christopher?' she said. 'What are you doing here? I thought you'd be hobnobbing with the upper classes.'

Milly wiped her nose with her sleeve, pointing with her elbow in the direction of the Yacht Club.

'I brought you something.'

'What?' Milly wanted to know.

Christopher was holding a perfect long-stemmed red rose. He offered it to her shyly, like one of the children she'd seen earlier on telly with the Queen.

'It's from my garden,' he told her.

It was such a sweet, romantic gesture, Milly felt her eyes suddenly filling with tears.

Michael closed his eyes, trying to block out the murmuring hum of the nearby parties, the random shrieks of laughter and feedback from speakers, as he concentrated on thinking his way back to the Festival in 1969. It was almost like developing a photograph, sitting in the dark, gradually seeing the picture emerge.

The daughter, Clare, had Rachel's voice, but not her looks. She was quite plain, and suspicious of him. He couldn't remember the boy at all, hadn't noticed anything different from any of the hundreds of lanky, long-haired teenagers milling around. There had been no spark of recognition between them, he was sure of that. Nurture had triumphed over nature.

'Didn't you get the letter?' Clare had asked.

Now, when he recalled it, the words seemed to carry an intonation of relief. Had she known what the letter contained? Had she gently taken it from her mother's hands and read it while her mother slept her morphine sleep? He could picture Rachel waking up, seeing her daughter reading, imploring her to send her message, and not to tell; a daughter's pact with her dying mother;

the girl's sigh as she dropped the letter in a red postbox, fulfilling her mother's last request with a heavy heart.

But he was imagining all this, he realized, creating a melodrama from the tone of one sentence spoken with relief, if relief was what it had been.

Didn't you get the letter?

Perhaps Clare's surprise was simply due to the fact that she expected him to be aware of Rachel's death. Maybe it was as simple as that.

Michael tried again to picture the boy.

He seemed to think long fair hair, shoulders shrugging, eyes unwilling to engage. About sixteen.

Now, he would be in his twenties. Twenty-four or twenty-five, Michael calculated, because Rachel must have fallen pregnant before they left Etherington in 1952.

When had conception occurred? Where? Had it been that last time?

They'd never used contraception. She said it had taken years to conceive her daughter, and he'd believed her. No chance, she said, when he'd worried. I'm too old! Had she been telling the truth? Was she even telling the truth in the letter? Perhaps Rachel's mind had been wandering. Perhaps the drugs . . .

Michael remembered their last walk in the park when he'd told her that Sylvia had found out about them, absurdly keeping a distance from her so there could be no possibility of their bodies touching, as if his wife's discovery had made him suddenly chaste. But inside the park shelter, with its powerful memories and the smell of creosote, neither of them had been able to resist. It had been the only way of saying goodbye.

The boy – Karl, he thought it was – would probably have children of his own by now. Michael couldn't think of a single reason why a young man would want to learn that he was his father. He wasn't very good at being a father. Iris had run away from home, and now his twins were distant from him. Of all his children, the only one who appeared relatively stable was Anthony, whose upbringing Michael had had least to do with. Why would anyone want Michael as a father instead of George? At the time, Michael had wished he had had a father like George, a father who knew about things.

Michael took a last look at the letter.

What will you do with this fact?

He would do nothing. He ought to do nothing. Wasn't that what Rachel was saying?

For George's sake, if not his own.

He would do nothing. It was not cowardly, he told Rachel silently, it was right. He would at last do the right thing.

Michael was suddenly aware of a presence on the stairs behind him.

'What is it?' Pascale asked.

Michael didn't know how long he'd been sitting there, the letter clasped in his hands.

'It's a letter,' he said. 'From someone I used to know . . .'

Pascale frowned, not understanding. 'A woman?'

'Yes.'

She thinks I am telling her something about us, Michael thought, something that has a bearing on our relationship. He pointed to the postmark.

'A long time ago,' he said, reaching out for Pascale's hand. 'It was a long time ago. The letter was lost. And now . . .'

His shoulders began to shake.

'Everyone I love dies,' he said helplessly.

Holding his head in both her hands, Pascale tilted his stricken face to look at hers.

'I will not die,' she told him, and then, as if remembering her grammar, 'I am not going to die.'

She held his eyes for a long time until the loud bang, like a gun going off, bounced them out of their miserable trance.

'What is it?' Pascale asked.

'It's the fireworks at the Yacht Club,' Michael said, opening the front door, and looking up at the sky.

*　　*　　*

221

'Do you remember the first time?' Christopher asked.

'The first time what?' said Milly.

They could hear the oohs and ahhs of the crowd gathered on the quayside, but standing together in the tiny courtyard at the back of the pub, it felt like the firework display was just for them.

'The first time we kissed,' said Christopher, speaking to the sky because he was too shy to say it to her face. 'Nine-teen seventy-one. There were fireworks and I felt as if my head was going to burst . . .'

'Your head?' Milly teased.

'And something else,' admitted Christopher.

There was something very endearing about Christopher, Milly thought. The way he blushed at the hint of anything rude, the way he always said the wrong thing, and how he never jumped from A to Z when telling a joke, but always had to go all the way through the alphabet.

Milly caught a waft of his aftershave. It was an expensive citrus fragrance, and his shirt was clean and dry, not all sweaty and rank as Gerry's was (although the horse went some way to explaining the distinctly animal body odour she had detected recently). Gerry was sex on legs. Christopher was a romantic soul.

Milly stepped a fraction closer to him. Christopher looked at her, surprised, put a tentative hand around her waist, touching that tender part at the small of her back which always made her yelp inside.

'How was it again?' she asked.

'What?' he asked.

'When we kissed the first time?' she said, her voice sud-denly a little croaky.

'You were wearing a white Roman dress and you looked, well, gorgeous, and you said, "You're a King and I'm a queen, so how about it?"'

How embarrassing!

'And then what happened?' Milly asked.

'Well, we kissed,' said Christopher. 'And after that . . .'

'Show me,' Milly whispered, tilting her face towards his.

He kissed her hesitantly, as if he didn't believe her. She could feel him trembling. She put her hands around his neck and pulled his lips against hers, his body against hers. As the firework display grew to its climax, ever bigger rockets whooshing into the sky and exploding cascades of tiny stars above, she could feel his manners giving way to desire, as he began to kiss her back with hungry, unguarded passion.

Sylvia unwound the towel from her head and looked despairingly in the mirror of her Louis XIV-style dressing table. It had taken hours in Carmen rollers to get her naturally straight hair into waves that flicked back from her face and now she couldn't even get a comb through because the firm-hold hairspray had gone all sticky. The yellow silk ballgown filled the bath like a heap of crumpled custard because she couldn't think where else to put it. It was dry clean only, and would certainly be ruined by its soaking in chlorinated water. Even though her long fair hair could be washed and conditioned with Wella products, and her husband could buy her a new dress (several, in fact), Sylvia didn't know if she could ever live down the humiliation of flailing and spluttering for her life in her own swimming pool, while the band (who were inside the marquee and didn't know) went on singing their cover of the recent hit 'Float On'. Had that little beast James Allsop chosen the song deliberately?

Sylvia stared into the mirror, as if by looking long enough she would be able to see where she had gone wrong. With a successful business behind her (granted it had been more a matter of having to sell up than deciding to, as she'd had people believe, but that was the fault of the useless Labour government mismanaging the economy) and now marriage to a man with a title and a mansion, Sylvia had thought she had everything she'd ever dreamed of.

'Life begins at forty,' she'd told Audrey Potter.

'Or thereabouts,' Audrey Potter had remarked tartly, and they'd both laughed at that.

'Be careful what you wish for,' Sylvia could remember her mother saying when she was a little girl. 'Because it might come true.'

But her mother had always been a cup-half-empty kind of person and Sylvia had tried not to take too much notice. Now she thought how wise her mother was, and it made her feel guilty for not visiting her more often in the old people's home in Etherington. But she couldn't think about that right now.

Sylvia realized she had a decision to make. Either she could lock the door of the dressing room and have a good old cry, or she could quickly get herself dressed again, repair her make-up, and return to the party. A simple choice, but it felt a watershed moment, because it would signal defeat or victory.

Sylvia picked up her hairbrush and pulled it determinedly through her hair, then wound her tresses up, pinning them into a chignon. Stepping into a classic black boat-necked cocktail dress (a little black dress will always be your friend, a magazine article she'd read recently had claimed, and how true that was), she smoothed it down over her slim figure. They could sneer, she thought, picturing an amorphous baying mass of Kings, Allsop children and Jolly's county friends, whom she'd overheard calling her 'the shopgirl', but not one of them had a figure like hers.

Defiantly squirting herself with Je Reviens by Worth, and applying a slick of Champagne lipstick, Sylvia dabbed her mouth with a hanky, and pepped herself up with her mother's words.

'Sticks and stones will break your bones, but words will never hurt you!'

As Sylvia strolled back into the marquee, the band was playing 'So You Win Again', and she was delighted to see James Allsop's face sink like a stone.

In a small French restaurant called Mon Plaisir, just off Shaftesbury Avenue, Iris toyed with an *omelette aux fine herbes* while Roman Stone regaled her with his thoughts about a new play called *Abigail's Party* he'd seen the night before at the Hampstead Theatre Club.

'It's a clinical dissection of the peculiar strata of the English middle classes,' he was saying. 'Like all great comedies, it makes you wince at your own pretensions as you laugh at this dreadful woman who thinks herself a cut above with her nibbles and her Demis Roussos LP . . .'

'Sounds like my mother,' said Iris bitchily.

'I never met your mother,' said Roman. He leaned forward slightly as if to encourage her to elaborate.

Iris speared a curly frond of bitter lettuce from her side salad with her fork. The omelette was perfect for eating while talking, simple to cut, whereas the frisée lettuce seemed to have a mind of its own.

'Sylvia is always keen to be seen to do the right thing,' said Iris, unwilling to be drawn further.

'*The Right Thing!*' said Roman.

Which brought them neatly, Iris thought, to the subject of her father's writing, which was presumably where Roman had been leading, although he was such a skilful conversationalist, Iris hadn't been aware of the manipulation. Recalling her brief spell as an actress in the television film of Michael's second novel, *Hide and Seek*, Roman had sought her opinions about current productions on the London stage: had she seen *Separate Tables* at the Apollo Shaftesbury Avenue? The setting of a seaside hotel was rather as Roman had always imagined Kingshaven; what had she thought of Ian McKellen's Romeo in the RSC's production at the Aldwych?

Iris couldn't help feeling flattered that a man with so much knowledge and background was listening to her opinions as if they mattered. Roman Stone was as attractive in person as his distinctive caramel-smooth voice was on the telephone. Long before she'd ever seen a photo of him, she had pictured him as a tall, debonair man, conscious of his own attractiveness, with humour playing in his eyes, like Cary Grant, perhaps. In person, he was stocky, a good deal shorter than her, and very Jewish-looking, with thinning black hair and eyebrows so dark, it crossed her mind that he might dye them. He must be at least forty years older than her, Iris calculated, but he was still a sexy man, from the firm handshake that went on just a second or two longer than she expected, to the knowing eyes, which danced with curiosity and fun.

'Can I offer you a dessert?' the waiter asked as he removed her plate.

'No, thank you,' said Iris.

'Coffee?' Roman asked.

'Yes . . . if you have time?' she replied.

Roman looked surprised. Obviously the wrong thing to say, Iris thought.

'Two coffees,' he instructed the waiter.

'I really don't know if my father will write again,' Iris told him.

'I wonder,' said Roman.

'Sorry,' said Iris with a shrug.

'It's hardly your fault!' he laughed.

'It's probably not what you wanted to hear, though . . .'

He looked at her like he wasn't sure what she was saying and then suddenly understood.

'But my dear Iris! It's you I'm interested in!'

His eyes held hers so directly, she had to be the first to look away.

'I hear very good things about you,' he continued. 'I'm interested to hear your ambitions . . .'

She found herself telling him about her ambition to publish commercial women's fiction with a feminist message, books that lots of women would read, like some of the blockbusters that came out of America, like *Kinflicks* or even *Valley of the Dolls*.

'You're the first person I've met who thinks that *Valley of the Dolls* is a feminist work,' said Roman. 'Isn't it about women being ground down by ambitious men?'

'Well, it is, but surely it could be read as a critique? Because it's written by a woman everyone just takes it at face value instead of seeing an underlying message. Nobody thinks *The Stepford Wives* is a simple tale of suburban life, do they?'

Roman laughed heartily.

'Iris, I was rather hoping to use this lunch to sound you out about working for me. Having met you now I realize . . .'

That you're rather young and inexperienced . . . Iris finished his sentence in her head.

'I should come straight to the point,' Roman interrupted her thought. 'What would it take?'

There was a nuance in the question that made it sound as if he was inviting her to be equal partners in some delicious caper.

'I think we get along rather well together,' he went on.

Now, it was almost as if he was offering an illicit weekend. Was he flirting with her?

An unwanted image of him standing at the bay window of a hotel bedroom looking out to sea flashed through Iris's mind, rendering her uncharacteristically lost for words. The clever, witty, attractive person she'd become over the past couple of hours would quip back with some equally ambiguous response, but she couldn't now think of anything that wasn't either crude or prudish. Some instinct was telling her that if she said yes to his proposition, she would somehow put herself at a disadvantage.

In any case, Iris reminded herself, she liked working at Harridan and she believed in what they were doing. Even if money was tight, and progress was slow, they were all in it together and they were getting there, changing the culture, book by book. How could she even consider abusing the trust of women she'd known for years, after just a couple of hours with this man?

Iris decided to be straightforward.

'I'm flattered, of course,' she said, 'But I don't feel I know enough about the business yet. I've got a lot to learn.'

'What you've got, you can't learn,' he told her.

'And what's that?' She couldn't resist hearing what he thought of her.

'Gut instinct,' he said. 'It's something you've either got, or you haven't. You've got it. I want it.'

He didn't say it in an overbearing way and yet it was a demand, and faced with demands, Iris's immediate gut instinct was always to say, 'Well, you can't have it!' but she stopped herself.

'But I'm happy where I am right now, thank you,' she said.

Roman thought about this for a moment or two.

'Well, I'm glad to hear that. It's always useful to discover that you're happy . . .'

'In my work,' Iris qualified.

Roman seemed to suppress a grin.

'It's been a great pleasure,' he said, throwing his napkin down on the table, signalling that the meeting was at an end.

Chapter Nine

1979

In later years, whenever people talked about how ghastly a decade the seventies had been, citing disco music and the Winter of Discontent as an unarguably awful combination, Julia would think nostalgically that some of the best times of her life had been spent dancing round a tiny candlelit kitchen, to the strains of 'You're the One that I Want' playing on a battery-operated cassette recorder.

Julia's fondness for disco music was in fact one of the principal reasons for those happy times just after leaving school and before the demands of adulthood took over, when she lived in the gatehouse with her old schoolfriends Cee and Bee.

In 1978, Daddy had suffered a stroke that was so serious that nobody, not even the doctors, believed he could recover. Sylvia had made Daddy's recovery her new project, dedicating herself to it as professionally as she had done the restoration of the Castle, researching the finest doctors, paying for the best hospital, and sitting beside Daddy's bed encouraging him, ordering him almost, to get better. The Allsop children reluctantly had to admit they had reason to be grateful to her, but once Daddy was well enough to return home, their father's rest and recuperation became Sylvia's excuse to prevent the children engaging in any pleasurable teenage activity involving noise or friends. It was no coincidence that both older sisters, Joanna and

Jacqueline, accepted proposals of marriage from property-owning men within months of Daddy's return, but as Julia had only just left school and had never had a boyfriend, that option wasn't open to her. Unexpectedly, it was Sylvia who came up with the idea of Julia moving into the gatehouse. Her stepmother gave her a budget to decorate the little house exactly as she wanted, with primrose walls and blue and white gingham curtains, and it was Sylvia who suggested she invite her old school chums to keep her company (for a moderate consideration), so they could play their Bee Gees LPs as loudly as they liked.

Bee, who had been expelled from the Swiss finishing school she'd been sent to for unladylike conduct with a ski instructor, found receptionist work at Kingshaven Stables, which was now owned by Angela and Miles Fogg, whose baby son, Piers, Julia sometimes babysat. Cee was training to be an estate agent in Havenbourne, just down the coast, and was the proud custodian of a brand-new Mini Metro. Julia, who was good at looking after young children, having such a lot of experience with James after Mummy left, was employed as a helper at Kingshaven's nursery school.

Although the girls enjoyed the independence of sharing a house and the novelty of earning a small salary, all of them saw it as a temporary step on the way to finding a husband. Men were the constant subject of conversation and speculation. Fortunately, they all had very different requirements for the perfect beau. Bee, who occupied the upstairs bedroom, wanted to have as many thrilling encounters with handsome hunks as possible before settling down. Cee, who shared the downstairs bedroom with Julia, was looking for someone rich enough to buy her the kind of nice, detached neo-Georgian house she showed her clients, but who would not pinch her bottom (as most of the property developers did) or expect her to make coffee (as her boss did). Julia, who still remembered her parents shouting at each other downstairs in the Summer House when she was supposed to be asleep, thought the most important qualities were kindness and reliability.

'We'll pass all the wimps on to you, shall we then?' said Bee.

The evenings were as larky as the midnight feasts they'd had at school, although celery and cottage cheese had taken over from baked beans on toast, cucumber face packs replaced Pond's cold cream, and they'd moved on from *Jackie* to *Cosmopolitan*. Julia found the *Cosmo* quizzes slightly intimidating. It had been fun picking answers that revealed whether you were a shrinking Violet, a gentle, shy flower with a quiet inner strength, as Julia (mostly Ds) turned out to be, or a beautiful and sensitive Lily like Cee (mostly Bs) or a brave, bold, popular Sunflower like Bee (mostly As). When it came to more sophisticated investigations such as 'Are You Good in Bed?' Julia could only guess at the appropriate answer, sometimes eliciting howls of mocking laughter from Bee.

The great thing about Bee's outgoing personality was that she got them invited to all the parties. On Saturday nights, Cee would drive the three of them to the venue in the Metro, with Julia trying to read the map in the dark. On the way home, it was usually just Cee and Julia in the car, because Bee would have got off with someone. Cee and Julia worried out loud that their friend was getting a reputation, whilst privately yearning for a little of her sense of adventure. None of them would have predicted that Bee would be the first to fall in love.

It all started as a bit of a laugh when Bee came home riding pillion on a motorbike, joking about the throbbing mass of power between her legs, but soon they knew it was serious because she was staying in every evening, waiting for him to ring. He was married, but had apparently confided in Bee that things hadn't been right with his wife for a long time, and he was only waiting for the right moment to leave. Privately Cee was dubious, and Julia concerned, but since Bee was by far the most worldly of the three of them, they hardly dared voice their doubts, and when the doorbell rang unexpectedly and the two lovers disappeared in a cloud of exhaust, Cee and Julia would gaze enviously

231

after them, as if it was the most romantic thing in the world.

The Winter of Discontent was as much a description of the country's mood as it was about the physical signs of grievance, like rubbish building up on the street, and coffins piling up in the morgues as council gravediggers went on strike. When a rat gnawed its way into Josie's basement, even Iris found it difficult to be resolute in her support of the striking dustmen.

Late for work, she was eating a bowl of home-made muesli, which wouldn't be hurried, when she became aware of a rhythmic sound other than her own chewing that sounded like someone sawing in the next house. Detecting movement in the corner of her vision, Iris saw the rat's whiskery face emerge from the hole in the floorboards in the recess where the boiler stood. When Iris screamed, the rat turned and went back down. Frozen with panic, but knowing that she must seal the hole, Iris searched the room for something to block it up with. The space was too small to get a saucepan in but an empty wine bottle, neck down, wedged in perfectly. Iris ran upstairs, shutting the door to the basement firmly behind her, but logic told her that the rat, finding his original route blocked, would think nothing of gnawing another hole. Maybe he had a family, or friends. Already late for work, Iris grabbed her carrier bag of manuscripts, and her Annie Hall hat, and closed the front door behind her, pausing to breathe, as if she'd made an escape.

The hardware store had sold out of rat poison. There'd been a run on it, the man in the brown overalls explained, and now the lorry drivers were going on strike, who could say when more supplies would arrive? People said you were always within thirty feet of a rat in London, he told Iris, as if that would be some comfort.

'It's only a tiny little fur ball,' Josie said, when Iris got hold of her on the phone at work. 'It's far more terrified of you than you are of it.'

232

'Why doesn't it stay in its sewer then?'

'He's probably just cold and hungry,' said Josie.

'There's plenty of food in the streets.'

'Perhaps he's a Hampstead rodent who prefers ratatouille,' Josie joked lamely.

Every hour, Iris tried the Environmental Health Department at the Town Hall, but the phone always rang unanswered. The council office workers were probably on strike too, she decided, shouting 'Bastards' into the receiver before slamming it down. It rang again immediately, making her think for a moment that they'd heard the profanity and were ringing back to ask her to explain herself, but it was only Vic, who wanted her to come and see a band called The Tourists.

'You can always stay at my place, if you like,' Vic offered, when she told him about the rat. She could even have her own room, he told her, because his flatmate, Gav, an art student who was studying at St Martin's School of Art on Longacre, had gone to New York for the weekend on Freddie Laker's Skytrain.

'The thing is, you're only thirty feet from a rat wherever you are in London,' Iris informed him dismally.

'They probably keep their distance from Molly's cats, though,' Vic pointed out.

'I can't anyway,' Iris told him. 'I said I'd go to the group tonight. Apparently, they're discussing an important resolution which affects me.'

'No shaving in the shower?'

'Stop it!' said Iris.

She hated the way men automatically belittled feminist organizations, and yet she couldn't say she was exactly looking forward to the meeting herself. The views of Josie's women's group had become increasingly radical in recent months. Last time they had debated whether they should ban language that contained the masculine root, spending a good half-hour seriously considering whether they should spell the word 'women' as 'wombyn' or refer to 'history' as 'herstory'.

Several of the original members, including Shelley and Maeve, no longer came, pleading pressure of work as their excuse, but Iris was pretty sure that they found some of the discussions as ludicrous as she did. As a socialist, Iris essentially believed in equality, and she saw feminism's struggle for equal rights and pay as part of that. What she was less sure about was the separatist view that all of society's problems resided with men, even though on the surface it seemed a persuasive argument at the moment, with all the unions led by men, the Cabinet dominated by men, and, as Josie pointed out, as if to appeal to Iris's CND affiliations, 'Men take countries to war.'

'But only women bleed, apparently.' Iris couldn't resist an irreverent reference to the song they played before every meeting.

That didn't go down well. The meeting was supposed to be an open forum, but Iris had noticed there was a quiet, punishing hostility if you happened not to agree with the majority.

This evening, one of the new members whose name Iris couldn't remember announced that she was wondering whether to leave her husband and her two children to live in an all-female house. Apparently, the other members of the house would accept the female child, but not the male. What did the rest of the group think?

'You don't want to live with a man, but it's OK to leave your children with him?' Iris couldn't really believe it was a serious suggestion.

'I just don't feel I can separate my children. They're very close . . .'

'But it's OK for them to grow up without a mother? That's completely absurd,' said Iris.

'Some children do,' Josie intervened. 'Bruno and Fiammetta, for instance.'

'They have to. Not because Claudia chose it,' Iris protested, unable to believe that Josie could have said such a thing.

'My friend Claudia was never very sound when it came to

men,' Josie explained to the rest of the group. 'She let her first husband walk all over her, and then—'

'And then she died, at the age of thirty-two,' Iris interrupted. 'Men weren't to blame for that, were they?'

Iris was aware of the rest of the group watching. It felt too personal a fight to have in public, and yet she couldn't let Josie's remarks go by.

'I was just making the point,' said Josie calmly, as if Iris were the one who was being unreasonable.

'So, if Claudia were alive, you would be trying to persuade her to leave Bruno with Dad and take Fiammetta into an all-female house . . .' Iris clarified.

'If she wanted to,' said Josie.

'But that's ridiculous!' Iris shouted, lost for words. She often found it difficult to argue with Josie, who was so articulate she could turn anything on its head and make it appear logical.

Why shouldn't a woman choose to behave differently from society's accepted version of what a mother should be? Iris asked herself. She knew it was just wrong, even though she couldn't explain why.

'I support a woman's right to decide to choose what's in her best interest. You choose to live in an all-female house, after all,' Josie pressed home her point.

'I choose to live with you,' said Iris, trying to think calmly. 'That's not the same thing.'

'It will soon be,' said Josie. For once, she looked away, her eyes unable to meet Iris's.

'You are joking?' Iris said quietly.

'It won't make that much difference.' Josie tried to lighten the threat.

'Are you saying you wouldn't allow Bruno or Vic in the house?' Iris wanted to make quite sure she understood.

'They hardly ever come, do they?'

Had she intended the announcement as a public humiliation, Iris wondered, or was Josie suddenly a coward, who didn't dare tell Iris without the support of her friends around her.

'Well, I can't stay here, then,' said Iris, bewildered by the turn of events.

'Honey, you haven't really been here for years,' Josie said. 'Have you?'

Iris left the house straight away, while the rejection and bewilderment were still raw and Josie hadn't had a chance to analyse the conversation and make her feel like it was all her fault. She caught the Northern Line to Leicester Square, bought two bottles of red wine from the off-licence in Old Compton Street and waited outside Vic's flat until he returned from his gig.

'I knew it was more than just a rat,' Iris told him, halfway down the second bottle. 'It was a kind of sign. A metaphor for our relationship . . .'

'Oh, please!' said Vic, who hated it when she used long words.

'I'm not running away, am I?' Iris asked, clinging to his hand.

'Well, you are,' Vic told her. 'But not in a bad way,' he added.

'Can I stay here for a bit?' Iris asked.

'Till Gav comes back,' Vic agreed.

Before Gav moved into Vic's flat, the brown flock wallpaper and the black plastic sofa left by the previous tenant made the place feel dark and dingy. Vic had cut out a couple of prints from a second-hand book about modern art he'd bought from Zwemmers and stuck them on the wall with Blu-Tack, but they'd looked like a couple of prints from a book stuck on to a brown wall, until Gav added an artistic spin, sticking up lots more prints and painting ornate gold frames around them, so that the room suddenly became a kind of faux art gallery. Gav had arranged the sofa along one wall, and painted a frame on the opposite wall just big enough to surround the television. It was a cheap, simple idea, but now sitting in the living room felt like actually being inside a work of art.

The *trompe-l'œil* theme was continued more ambitiously

in Gav's bedroom, which was like stepping directly into one of the prints of a Matisse interior. The walls were painted daffodil yellow with black vertical stripes, the floor covered with off-cuts of carpets with different patterns. Finding a folding screen in a skip on Brewer Street, Gav had cleverly etched a blue-on-white design that made it look like an arched Moorish window with light coming through. He had even painted a little table with a vase of purple tulips on the wall beside his bed, and a chest of drawers on the wall opposite.

Iris loved sleeping in the room so much, she was dreading the day she would have to look for somewhere else to live. Everything she wanted or needed in life was no more than a five-minute walk from the flat: the office, the bookshops on Charing Cross Road, the library just south of Leicester Square, theatres, cinemas, Chinese restaurants, a French patisserie with a mosaic of iced and glazed pastries in the window, an Italian delicatessen with an aroma of salami and fresh-ground coffee, and Luna Caprese just round the corner, with its never-changing menu and garish mural of the Bay of Naples.

When you lived in Soho, it seemed more like a village than the den of sleazy iniquity it was famous as. Bouncers on the doors of the peep shows said hello to her, the newsagent handed her a *Guardian* when she called in each morning on the way to work. Neighbours looked out for each other. Occasionally, Iris agreed to look after the next-door prostitute's children in the evenings while Lulu went out to work, and every week she purchased Molly's order from the off-licence, even though a half-bottle of whisky cost considerably more than the crumpled fiver the old woman pressed into her palm. Living among the pimps and prostitutes and lurid neon signs, Iris felt strangely safe. One day she found herself walking past the doors of what had been the Zebra Crossing nightclub, now a strip club, and realized that she had lost the automatic twinge of fear that Clive, or one of his associates, was watching her.

There were no more crowded tube journeys, and no

more hauling bags of vegetables all the way up the Camden Road, and Iris found she didn't miss Josie at all, which made her feel a little bit guilty, because Josie had only ever been generous and kind to her, and she had probably repaid her shabbily.

When she tried to describe how happy she was to Vic she said, 'It's like for the first time in my life, I feel like a proper person.'

'It's taken you long enough,' Vic said. 'You're nearly thirty.'

'Do you feel grown up, then?' Iris challenged him. Vic was a couple of years older than she was.

'No way!' he said.

Ever since the day in 1964 when they'd first met, and Vic had offered her a lift out of Kingshaven on the back of his Lambretta, they'd got along as if they'd known each other all their lives. He was the only person who'd known where she came from. She was the only person he'd told he was gay. It was a strong bond of trust, which she had broken by getting off with his brother, Clive.

At the time, she'd been so young and infatuated, she hadn't understood why it mattered to Vic, because he didn't fancy her. Now she understood that it must have felt like he was losing his best friend and his brother at the same time.

Now, as they sat side by side on the sofa, watching *Edward and Mrs Simpson* on the telly, like an old married couple who were fond of each other but didn't have sex, Iris caught Vic looking at her out of the corner of his eye and she knew he was wondering whether he could trust her again.

'What?' she asked.

'Gav's not coming back,' Vic told her. 'He called to say he's fallen in love with a guy who works at the Factory, and he's staying out there in the Big Apple.'

'So . . .' said Iris carefully.

'I'm thinking of putting an ad in *Time Out* for a gay flat share,' said Vic.

'Does it have to be a gay man?' Iris asked.

Vic looked at her quizzically, a bit like that first time in Kingshaven, but he knew what she was asking.

'As long as you don't try it on with any blokes I bring home,' he said eventually. 'And I don't want any political lesbians or metaphorical rats in the flat either . . .'

'He treats this place like a hotel,' Sylvia told Jolly, stroking her husband's hand, one spring afternoon, as he lay resting in bed.

The distant but intrusive sound of James Allsop braying down the phone to one of his Hooray Henry friends, underlined this statement. James had suddenly shot up, changing almost overnight from a smug, irritating youth into a smug, arrogant man, who seemed to take up more space than he ought to whenever he was home from school. He left things lying around, like books and coffee mugs, and discarded bits of dirty laundry in the bathroom, as if he expected Sylvia to pick them up and wash them.

'He'll be off to Oxford soon,' Jolly said with an indulgent smile. 'I don't suppose we'll see much of him after that. It'll be just the two of us,' he added quietly, giving her hand a little squeeze. 'Won't that be wonderful?'

'It will,' said Sylvia, smiling.

Her husband had become much more docile and even-tempered since his stroke and Sylvia thought she probably preferred him a little less active. During their courtship, he'd always been the perfect gentleman, but as soon as the ring was on her finger, he'd become a lot more demanding in the sex department. Sometimes, when she'd opened her eyes to see him straining and puffing on top of her, she'd wondered if he wasn't going to do himself a mischief.

It was quite a relief not to have to share a bed any more. There was no pleasure quite like the chill of fresh new sheets, crisp, neat and smelling of Persil, and nobody to make it too hot, or too cold by pulling off the blanket.

'Just the two of us,' Jolly repeated as he dozed off for his afternoon nap.

Sylvia watched him fondly for a few moments, checking the temperature of his forehead with the back of her hand, tucking his hand under the covers. So much of her energy had been spent keeping her husband alive, she hadn't given a lot of thought to what would happen when they'd finally got rid of the last of his vile children.

Before they were married, she'd naïvely imagined them spending half the year in posh foreign places like St Moritz and Monte Carlo, or cruising down the Nile on a steamer. She'd had no idea how tight their finances would be. To be fair, Jolly had always told her that he wasn't a rich man, but she'd assumed that was just aristocratic affectation, like the Royal Family always claiming that they hardly scraped by on the Civil List, even though they were sitting on top of all that land and all those jewels.

In the first honeymoon flush, Sylvia had managed to persuade her husband to sell most of his horrible family portraits, but they weren't worth nearly as much as she'd thought, what with the auctioneer's commission and the Inland Revenue taking their slice. Neither of them had reckoned on private hospital bills to keep Jolly alive. Sylvia hadn't allowed herself to think about the financial situation she'd be in if he'd died. They'd only had the money to do up the East Wing, not the West Wing, where Michael had lived.

He treats this house like a hotel. The words buzzed round in her head, as Sylvia stood at an upstairs window, watching James swimming lengths in the pool.

In point of fact, the Castle was big enough to be a hotel, she thought.

As if the idea would melt away as rapidly as it had crystallized in her mind, Sylvia rushed to her desk to write it down. She began to make notes on a jotter. The pool was actually bigger than the Palace's, and there was a tennis court too. The roof was sound now, the plumbing new, so it wouldn't be such a big job to create ensuite bathrooms. It had proved impossible to get the bank to loan money for the renovation because they couldn't see a return, so she'd had to use up every bit of her own money, but loaning for a hotel was an investment, and investment was going to get a lot easier under a Tory government, which there was bound to be when this lot finally called an election. Sylvia's name was still worth something, wasn't it? Especially now that she was a lady. She'd design the interior, paper over all that vile old wallpaper, make it all modern and bright. When he was a bit stronger, Jolly could landscape the garden. He'd enjoy pottering about. He'd be good at greeting guests, particularly Americans. They liked a bit of history.

'Situated in one of England's most picturesque spots and steeped in history, the ancient home of the aristocratic Allsops has all the period charm with all the modern conveniences . . .'

The words seemed to be tumbling from Sylvia's pen.

'The Castle. The last word in luxury.'

She could already see a full-colour brochure, its thick, shiny pages smelling of printer's ink and slightly sticky with newness. She would personally deliver one to the Palace and see the expressions on the Kings' faces. That would show them! She'd close them down, Sylvia thought, ambition running riot in her head like a drug. Just like she'd closed down Mrs Farmer. That'd teach them to snub her Jubilee party!

She looked out of the window. James was pulling his big strong body out of the pool, shaking himself like a dog who'd been in the sea, tossing his head, sweeping his thick hair back with his fingers.

She imagined him turning up at the front door, and her telling him, 'I'm sorry, but we're fully booked.'

That'd wipe the smile off his smug face.

Bruno and Fiammetta came up to stay for the Easter holidays. Almost as tall as Iris, and with an endearing squeak in his breaking voice, Bruno was more of a young man than a boy now. Fiammetta was still tiny, but she was developing the body of a petite woman rather than a little girl. With her serious gaze and her hair tied back in a tight long plait, Iris thought she looked rather like one of the ballet dancers who could sometimes be seen late at night in the Luna Caprese, wolfing down improbably huge plates of pasta after a performance at Covent Garden.

Although she had organized time off at work, Iris discovered that the twins had changed since the previous summer and were no longer children who needed constantly amusing, but young adults with ideas of their own. It took a bit of getting used to. Her automatic instinct whenever they crossed a street was still to put out both hands for the children to hold, but they shrank away now, leaving her feeling foolish. Iris was so used to Bruno running off that when she turned round in the newsagent and saw he wasn't there, she charged into the street screaming his name, then spotted him through the window of the next-door delicatessen, pointing at something behind the counter.

On the first afternoon, she took them to the National Gallery, which was only five minutes' walk from the flat. While Bruno followed her on a quick tour of the galleries, more with a sense of obligation than interest, Iris suspected, Fiammetta sat looking at a single painting by Degas for over an hour and, when they returned, she pointed out aspects of technique that Iris would never have seen however long she had spent looking. The next day, when Iris asked what they would like to do, Fiammetta said she would like to return to the gallery.

Noticing Bruno's less than ecstatic face, Iris suggested a riverboat trip.

'Couldn't I go to the gallery by myself?' Fiammetta asked.

'And spend the whole day there?'

A smile lit up Fiammetta's face.

It was an irony, Iris thought, that Fiammetta's smile was very like Michael's in the way it magically changed her face from self-contained to outgoing, making its recipient feel somehow privileged. It made Iris wonder whether a smile could be inherited, or whether the facial muscles simply learned to imitate a particular configuration over time.

Bruno had an engaging smile too, but its effect was to put you at your ease, rather than make you feel blessed, and it was far less stressful being just with him, Iris thought a little guiltily, as the riverboat pulled out from Westminster Pier.

'How are things at home?' she asked.

'Not bad,' said Bruno. 'Dad's still sorting out the books. Some bloke from a university came and took the really old ones away. Dad's going to try to sell the ones he couldn't give away.'

'Sell?'

'Dad took some of the books to an auction, but he came back with even more books . . . He says the ground floor would make a perfect second-hand bookshop . . .'

'If he can bear to part with them,' said Iris. 'It'll give him something to do, I suppose.'

'Oh, and he's started writing,' said Bruno.

'Writing what?' Iris demanded, intrigued.

'Stories, I guess,' said Bruno.

'Did you read any?'

Bruno looked at her like she was mad, reminding Iris that he was not yet twelve, even though he looked almost a man.

'How's school?'

'I'm captain of the football team . . .'

'What's your favourite subject?'

'French, but I really want to learn Italian, like Mummy.'

'Do you speak to Pascale in French?' Iris asked before she realized how tactless that was.

'Sometimes,' said Bruno cautiously.

'Does Fiammetta like French?'

'She hates it!' said Bruno.

'What's her favourite subject?'

'Art,' said Bruno instantly. 'Fiammetta's always top in Art.'

Iris knew she would get no more from him about Fiammetta. The twins had always been utterly loyal to one another like that. Iris thought it must be good to have

243

someone to share your anxieties with. There had been another woman in Dad's life when Iris had been about their age, but she'd had no outlet for all her confusion and pent-up rage. Anthony had never been on the same wavelength, probably hadn't even realized that Dad was having an affair.

It was a different situation with Pascale, because Michael wasn't deceiving anyone about it, but Iris wondered whether the twins felt the same sense of betrayal as she had that someone else could make him happy. She guessed that was why Fiammetta barely spoke to her father. Even though Iris was almost thirty, the memory of Michael leaving when she was thirteen still stung.

'On your right,' the commentary informed them, as the riverboat chugged down the Thames, 'the site of Shakespeare's famous Globe Theatre, which a group of actors is presently trying to rebuild. Another writer who lived near here was Samuel Pepys, who described the Fire of London across the river from that house.'

So her father was writing again. Iris thought it was probably because of Pascale. A kind of contentment seemed to have settled on him since he'd been with her. Even though it felt odd that her father had a girlfriend almost the same age as herself, Iris quite liked Pascale, although she couldn't really work her out.

Was Michael only able to write when he had a woman's love to protect him? Iris wondered. Having met a lot of writers now, she realized that his insecurity about his writing was not uncommon. All writers seemed to need constant devoted encouragement.

It would be interesting to read his work as an adult. When she'd first read *The Right Thing*, secretly under the bedcovers with a torch for fear of her mother finding her, Iris was only twelve. She hadn't understood some passages, although she'd suspected they were rude, but she'd found other bits funny, like the character of the mother-in-law, who was very strict about manners, and had reminded her of Sylvia's mother – whose visits to Kingshaven Iris always dreaded because her presence seemed to magnify all the crossness in the house and put everyone on edge. It hadn't occurred to the adolescent Iris that her father had actually based the character on Sylvia's mother. At the time she had thought that novels were all made up, like the stories about elves she wrote at school. That was what fiction meant, wasn't it?

When *Hide and Seek*, her father's book about a runaway teenager, had been published and Iris had read it as a runaway teenager, it had finally dawned on her that writers did not really make things up at all. It wasn't that they wrote the truth exactly, but they drew on material in their own life to create other lives – perhaps ones they would have preferred or feared.

Now Iris viewed the relationship between novelists and autobiography as a bit like a tapestry that the writers were constantly unpicking, using the same threads to create different pictures. *Hide and Seek* hadn't been about Iris exactly, but it had been Michael's way of exploring what it meant to be a parent.

Iris wondered whether she would read Michael's work differently again as an editor. Would she be able to judge it objectively? Could she rely on that gut instinct that made her feel physically excited as she turned the pages of a new typescript she just knew she had to publish?

The seed Roman Stone had planted in her brain appeared to have germinated and taken root. It came as a shock to realize that she was ambitious, and she hadn't yet decided what to do about it, although she knew that to ring Roman Stone and tell him she had reconsidered would put her at a disadvantage. When her phone rang at work, Iris had developed a habit of clearing her throat and composing herself, just in case it was Roman calling to ask her out to another lunch, and she was becoming better at publishing parties, flirting and gossiping, and looking over other people's shoulders, in case she spotted Roman Stone working the room towards her.

*   *   *

'I'm starving!' said Bruno, as they stepped off the river-boat with slightly wobbly legs. Even though it was a sunny day, being out on the water had made them both cold and hungry.

'Where would you like to eat tonight?' Iris asked, expecting the answer 'McDonald's', which had been one of the city's major attractions since its arrival in London. There was nothing like McDonald's anywhere near Kingshaven.

'Could we try cooking some of those little parcels of fresh pasta?' Bruno asked.

Iris didn't know what he was talking about.

'From Camisa's,' he said, referring to the Italian delicatessen. 'Some are filled with spinach and ricotta, which is a kind of cheese, and some have dried mushrooms inside,' he explained.

'How do you know all this?'

'I asked the owner, when you went to get a paper.'

'And did he tell you how to cook them too?'

'Only take-a cinque minuti in big pan-a boiling water,' Bruno said, mimicking the man's Italian accent, '*poi* a little butter, parmiggiano, *e basta* . . . *mmm*!' He pinched his forefinger and thumb together and blew a kiss.

'We could get one of those fruit tarts from Patisserie Valerie for afters.' Bruno gave her his most winning smile.

'You've been planning all this, have you?' Iris asked.

'You need to be organized when you're cooking,' he told her.

'Do you cook at home?'

'Pascale's useless,' said Bruno.

'It's not necessarily the woman's job to do the cooking,' Iris felt obliged to point out.

'Dad's useless too,' said Bruno.

Which made Iris laugh out loud.

They picked Fiammetta up from the gallery, and did the shopping on the way home. While Bruno took over the kitchen, Fiammetta moved the sofa round in the living room and sat staring at Vic's print of *The Scream* by Edvard Munch.

The following day, Fiammetta asked if she could go to the Tate Gallery, and every day after that Fiammetta would look at pictures while Iris and Bruno wandered around Fortnum and Mason, Selfridges or Harrods Food Hall, tasting free samples.

'That was the best holiday we've ever had,' Bruno said, when they kissed Iris goodbye at Waterloo Station, old enough now to travel by themselves back to Kingshaven.

The last thing on Julia's mind at the moment they met – 'as if for the first time', Christopher later remarked – was romance.

Julia was not dressed up, nor even wearing make-up, but playing the fool. It was a lovely April morning, with just enough warmth in the air for her to suggest a walk to the Victoria Gardens with the nursery-school children. They had played 'Ring a ring o' roses', skipped to 'Here we go, Looby Loo', and now, after repeated requests, she had agreed to sing 'The Ugly Duckling'. Julia was very good at doing loud nasal quacks, which made the children shriek with laughter. When the song finally came to an end, after several encores and clamours for more, they all collapsed laughing together in the sunshine. A couple of the children clambered on to her legs, demanding bounces, while another hugged her tightly round her neck.

Lying on the grass, covered in children, Julia was suddenly aware of a man looking down at her with an amused smile playing around his lips.

Christopher King.

'You look like Lippi's *Madonna and Child with Two Angels*,' he told her, and though Julia had no idea what he was referring to, she had no doubt from his face that it was a compliment.

'It's a painting we studied in the WEA class on Renaissance art,' he explained. 'Some people think it is the most beautiful painting in the world.'

Julia felt the blush rising in her cleavage and suffusing her neck and face.

'Do you ever go?' he asked. 'To the WEA classes?' he added as she stared at him bewildered. 'They're sometimes rather good.'

'I'm not much good at classes,' Julia admitted.

'Perhaps you're a better teacher than pupil,' said Christopher with a gesture that took in all the children around her.

Julia sat up, trying to look a bit more dignified, wondering whether she should explain that she wasn't exactly a teacher.

'Where are you off to?' she asked.

'I go for a walk every afternoon,' Christopher replied.

There was an awkward silence. She'd known Christopher all her life, but he seemed to be looking at her in a different way with his eyes so firmly on her chest, she quickly checked to see that a button hadn't popped open.

'I was so sorry to hear about your uncle.' Julia suddenly remembered that the previous week Christopher's great-uncle Cyril had died of a heart attack. He was seventy-nine, which was quite a good age, but Julia knew how much of a shock it was when someone you loved died. It had almost happened with Daddy. 'You must be ever so sad,' she said.

Christopher King looked surprised. Would it have been more polite to avoid the subject? She'd probably said the wrong thing, as usual.

'He meant the world to me,' he said, and then turned his face away, looking out to sea as if there might be tears in his eyes he didn't want her to see.

Julia felt the onus was on her to pay an appropriate tribute.

'Uncle Cyril was such fun,' she finally said, knowing the words were probably inadequate, but unable to come up with anything else to describe the old man who Granny Ruby always said could bore for England.

'How very sweet of you to say so,' Christopher said, now looking at her again.

Julia felt herself colouring.

'Isn't it a bit lonely?' Julia stammered.

'Desperately lonely. He was a great friend.' Christopher stared earnestly into her eyes. 'I feel quite lost without him . . .'

Embarrassed now, Julia said, 'I meant on your walks.'

'Oh, I see,' said Christopher distractedly. 'With the ever-changing vista of sea? With the rustle of trees?' He paused as if expecting a response.

Julia smiled uncertainly, not quite sure whether he was joking or not.

'I think the feeling is at one with nature,' he said, 'rather than lonely.'

'Oh, quite!' Julia agreed fervently.

'Yes, they do say he likes a bit of the *au naturel*,' Bee remarked that evening, after Julia had given her flatmates a second-by-second account of the encounter.

'What do you mean?' Julia asked.

'He's been known to take the occasional roll in the hay,' Bee said in a mean way that made Julia think she was probably a bit jealous. Christopher King was, after all, the town's most eligible bachelor, not that it had ever occurred to any of them to list him amongst their most-wanted because he was so much older.

'I'm hardly likely to be the only girl he's ever asked out. He's at least thirty,' said Julia.

'Oh, are you going out?' Cee asked excitedly.

Julia felt herself blushing. 'He said he hoped we'd bump into each other again,' she admitted.

'Well, that's hardly a bloody proposal,' said Bee.

Which both Julia and Cee thought was a bit of a cheek in the circumstances.

'Iris! Iris!'

When Iris turned round on Old Compton Street and saw Winston, his smile was so familiar and warm, for a moment she completely forgot why she had ever been cross with him. He stopped a yard or so away and they both hovered, as if they weren't sure whether a kiss would be appropriate.

'Dig the hair!' said Winston.

After many attempts, in the course of which she had achieved enough degrees of salmon pink to fill a book of Dulux paint shades, Iris had finally got her cropped hair peroxide white like the lead singer of The Tourists.

'The Tourists?' said Winston.

'You ought to sign them,' Iris told him. 'The lead singer is called Annie Lennox and she's got a really unusual voice.'

She was surprised to see him take a slim leather notebook and a silver pen from the breast pocket of his expensive-looking suit, and write the name down.

'Memory's going,' he explained, giving her another broad smile.

'It happens with old age,' Iris teased, calculating that Winston must be mid-thirties now.

His hair was really short too, and he was clean-shaven, which was much better than the Afro and moustache he'd been sporting when she last saw him.

'How's Valencia?' she asked.

'Very well, I hear,' said Winston equably. 'We're divorced now.'

'I didn't know. I'm sorry,' said Iris, trying to sound like she meant it.

'How's Josie?' he asked.

'Very well. I hear,' said Iris.

'Oh.'

'Oh,' Iris echoed.

'How are the twins?' asked Winston, as if he too had suddenly been transported back to the cold black lake in Regent's Park where they'd last seen each other.

'Growing up fast,' said Iris. 'They're all in the warehouse on the Quay now.'

'Yes. Yes. I'd heard,' said Winston distractedly.

'How's the record label doing?' Iris asked.

'Very well,' he said. 'We're talking about a record station . . . as the next step . . .'

'On the road to world domination?' Iris said.

He smiled again, tilting his head, half bashful, half rather pleased with himself.

'Still can't tempt you to work for me, I suppose?' he said.

'I've got a job, thanks,' said Iris.

'Yes. I'd heard,' said Winston.

She wondered who he'd heard from.

'Listen,' said Winston, looking at his watch, 'I must dash, but look, we're having an election party at the house on Thursday. Why don't you come? I'd love to catch up properly.'

'Where?' Iris asked.

'Same place,' said Winston. 'Do you remember?'

'I remember,' said Iris.

'And you'll come?' he pressed. Winston was used to getting his own way.

'I'll see,' said Iris.

'Bring someone, if you want,' he told her, as he stuck out his arm to hail a cab.

'I'll see,' said Iris, but she couldn't help smiling as Winston turned round in the back seat and waved like a child until the cab turned the corner.

'Maybe the phone box has been vandalized,' said Julia, rather pleased with herself for coming up with an original excuse to explain why Bee's man hadn't rung. Obviously he couldn't ring from home, because of his wife.

'Maybe he's lost your number,' Cee offered.

Bee glared at her as if that was a pathetic excuse and she wasn't putting enough effort in.

'It's not fair because he absolutely promised!' she said desperately.

Julia felt so sorry for her. She racked her brains for another reason.

'Maybe he's had an accident on his bike and he's been taken to hospital,' she suggested.

'Oh God! Do you think so? Do you think I should ring Casualty and ask?'

'No!' said Julia, alarmed by the way Bee leaped up. It was only an idea, after all.

'It's not a proper emergency, is it?' she tried to back-track.

'What if he's hit his head and he has amnesia and he doesn't remember who he is? They may be wanting some-one to call,' Bee was off, 'to identify him.' Her face filled with horror.

'But you don't really know he's had an accident,' Julia tried to calm her down.

'But why else wouldn't he call?' Bee demanded.

'Maybe his wife has found out and forbidden him to ring. Maybe one of his children is ill,' Cee suggested.

Bee and Julia glared at her. Cee just didn't seem to get the rules. You were meant to support your friends. Bringing his wife and children into it wasn't very supportive, was it?

'Sorry,' said Cee.

'All men are bastards anyway,' said Bee.

She got up from the sofa and switched on the hi-fi, then examining the wire rack of 45s, as if she genuinely wasn't sure what she would like to hear, she finally chose the single she put on every evening, slipping it out of its paper sleeve, placing it on the turntable and dropping the needle on.

All three of them stood up on the first arpeggio, and spoke the opening line together, and then Bee turned the volume right up as the disco beat started, and they all danced wildly around the room, twirling like the girl on roller skates in the video on *Top of the Pops* did, and shout-ing 'I Will Survive!' along with the chorus, so loudly that none of them heard the phone on its first ring.

On the second ring, Julia leaped to the volume knob, and Bee stared at the telephone as if she had suddenly frozen.

'You answer it!' she whispered to Cee.

'Why?'

Ring, ring.

'Tell him I'm not home!'

Ring, ring.

'But you've been waiting in all week!' Cee protested.

Ring, ring.

'Answer it, for God's sake, or he'll ring off!' Bee gestured frantically.

'I'm handing it straight to you,' Cee warned, picking up the receiver and saying, in her best estate agent voice, 'Hello? Can I help you? Would you mind holding the line one moment?' Ignoring Bee's ever more frantic arm waving, Cee calmly handed the receiver to Julia. 'It's Christopher King for you,' she said.

'Oh,' said Julia.

Feeling slightly guilty because of poor Bee, Julia took the receiver and listened.

'Yes. Yes. Yes. Fine. Bye, then!'

'Well?' both Bee and Cee demanded as soon as she'd put it down.

'He's invited me to the opera!' she said, jumping up and down on the spot.

'Please come with me!' Iris pleaded on election night.

'You know I'm not interested in politics,' said Vic.

'You can't not be interested. It'll affect you, you know. Thatcher's very right wing.'

'Look, I've voted, all right, but I don't see why I have to sit in front of the television watching a load of suits with a swingometer.'

Vic's camp way of saying things could give any word of more than one syllable rude innuendo.

'It's just . . . Winston might offer you a job. He always offers me a job and everything I know about music is down to you. I'll tell him you were the first person to see The Clash, and The Tourists, and—'

'I hardly think Winston Allsop is going to be interviewing for staff at his own party,' Vic interrupted.

It suddenly dawned on Iris from the way Vic called him Winston Allsop that he saw him as the smooth-operating successful entrepreneur who sometimes appeared on the television, and not as the boy on the school bus, as she did. Vic didn't want to go to the party because he thought he would be out of his depth.

'He's just an ordinary bloke, you know,' said Iris, now feeling slightly nervous herself. 'Oh, please come,' she wheedled, wanting a friend beside her more than ever now.

'I was quite looking forward to having the flat to myself for one night without you flirting your arse off.'

'Me, flirting?'

'You're such a fag hag,' said Vic.

'I'm not a fag hag!'

'Well, you're a fruit fly, then!' said Vic good-humouredly.

Iris could hear the noise of the party all the way up the street. Outside, she paused for a moment, looking at the silhouettes of guests against the brightly lit sash windows on the ground and first floors. Winston had bought the double-fronted house on a wide street leading directly off Clapham Common long before anyone had thought of Clapham as an up-and-coming area for property. During Iris's brief stay there at the end of the sixties, the house had contained at least ten bedsits, all sharing one bathroom. Winston had occupied the large, high-ceilinged rooms of the ground floor, which were always cold. The previous owner had knocked out the fireplaces and replaced them with ugly gas fires with meters, and boarded over the panelled doors with hardboard. The only original feature remaining from the early Victorian period when the house was built had been the coloured glass in the front door.

Now, the front door was open, with a waiter in black tie holding a silver tray of wine glasses standing sentry. Winston had certainly come a long way from the days of leading a squat, Iris thought, remembering less formal parties that had happened spontaneously whenever someone in the house had managed to get hold of half an ounce of black. Inside, Iris could see women in long dresses, and was immediately conscious she was underdressed in her long black T-shirt knotted at the hip, and black leggings, which she was wearing with a pair of black ballet pumps from Anello and Davide because it was impossible to buy smart shoes that didn't make her look like a giant. Shrinking slightly inside, Iris felt like heading straight back to Soho, but she knew that Vic wouldn't appreciate that. Anyway, she was a proper person with a proper job now and she knew how to do parties. Taking a deep breath, Iris walked up the short path to the front door.

'Red or white?' asked the waiter.

'Most definitely red tonight,' said Iris, expecting him to smile, but his face remained expressionless.

Winston waved and came across to welcome her.

'I'm so glad you came,' he said, kissing her first on one cheek, and then the other. 'Now, who do you know?'

At first glance, there was no one in the room at all who Iris recognized, but then she spotted her brother, Anthony, chatting with a group of people in one room, and his wife, Marie, in another. Though she could think of no reason why they shouldn't be friends with Winston, Iris felt oddly possessive. She might not have seen him for four years, but Winston was her friend, not her brother's.

Iris occasionally met Anthony for a drink in a pub in one of the little Dickensian alleyways near the Inns of Court. He was a barrister now, and Marie a rising star in their chambers. They'd recently moved from their first flat to a terraced house in Islington, which had three bedrooms and a small basement studio, which would be perfect for a nanny, he'd told Iris, leading her to believe they were about to breed. Iris really must come round to dinner some time!

Although they could talk for a couple of hours without bickering these days, Iris always came away wondering why she bothered to keep in touch with her brother at all because they had absolutely nothing in common, not even their parents. For Anthony, Sylvia was an extraordinary, strong, generous woman who'd pulled herself up from nothing against all odds, whereas Iris saw her as scheming, manipulative and mean. Anthony's father was an eccentric leftie, with an unconventional, almost laughable lifestyle, whereas Iris's was a flawed, damaged, but deeply charismatic man.

'This place looks a bit different,' Iris told Winston, with a gesture that acknowledged the restored fireplaces, the original panelled doors. She desperately didn't want Winston to move off and leave her stranded.

'Like it?' It was a rhetorical question.

'Darling!' A very slim woman, whose lightly tanned body was displayed to perfection in a sleeveless royal-blue catsuit, joined them.

'I don't think you've met Candy,' Winston said. 'Iris is my oldest friend,' he explained. 'Candy and I got married last week.'

'Congratulations,' said Iris without enthusiasm.

Iris could feel the woman's expert eyes sizing up her short peroxide hair, her freckly arms, the black T-shirt and leggings, deciding that she didn't constitute a threat, and disappearing into the throng as suddenly as she had emerged.

'The triumph of hope over experience?' Iris asked.

Winston smiled again, slightly uneasily.

Iris glanced at her watch. It was nine thirty. Only half an hour to go to the close of polls and that moment when the BBC would project the result from an exit poll. She fervently hoped it wasn't as clear-cut as all the papers were predicting. Surely the conservative elements of the British public would never, when it came to the crunch, vote in a female Prime Minister.

'Where's the telly?' she asked Winston.

Winston pointed at a huge white screen in the room where Marie was.

'We're projecting it on that so that everyone can see,' he said.

'Are those real Andy Warhols?' Iris asked, noticing a sequence of Elvis screen prints along the wall beside it.

Winston nodded.

'A friend of my flatmate is working at the Factory,' Iris said, feeling a need to keep her end up.

'Where are you living, by the way?' Winston asked.

'In a flat just round the corner from where you saw me,' Iris said.

'Cool,' said Winston. 'How much does it cost to buy a flat round there these days?'

'No idea. It's a council flat,' Iris told him, draining her glass.

'You're renting?' he asked in disbelief.

'All property is theft, remember?' said Iris.

Winston looked at her, then laughed as if she'd made a very good joke. She was aware of several people looking at her, not quite able to place her, she realized, because she was too old to be a rock chick, not pretty enough to be a model, and yet she had made their suave host laugh like a drain.

Winston went to greet a guest at the door. Another waiter offered Iris another glass of wine. She took it and glanced at her watch again. The television would be on soon, and then she wouldn't have to worry about finding someone to talk to because she could be absorbed in the results programme. Ever since she was old enough, Iris had always liked staying up on election nights watching events unfold. It made her feel she was there as history was being made. All the elections she had witnessed had been too close to call, and she expected this one to be the same, whatever the papers were saying. People weren't stupid enough to vote for a person whose main achievement was to have stopped free school milk when she was Education Secretary. They might blame the unions for the general feeling of malaise, but surely they didn't want a return to the dark ages?

'It's ten o'clock and the polls have closed,' said Robin Day. 'On the basis of our exit polls, we are predicting a win for the Conservatives.'

An excited scream went up round the party. Everyone started jumping up and down and hugging each other.

Blue balloons, which must have been strung in nets from the banisters upstairs, cascaded down in the entrance hall. There was loud stamping as a cohort of waiters filed in carrying trays laden with champagne flutes.

Iris was aghast. Surely they were kidding? Her eyes roamed the room, searching for Winston, and found him arm in arm with his blue-clad wife. As if he felt Iris's eyes piercing in to him, he looked around. His eyes held hers for a second.

'You're a bloody Tory now?' Iris shouted at the top of her voice, although there was so much noise in the room, there was no way he could hear. His shoulders shrugged almost imperceptibly, as if to say there was nothing he could do about it.

A waiter offered her a glass of champagne.

'There's nothing to celebrate, as far as I'm concerned,' Iris said, pushing past him, fleeing from the warm hubbub of self-congratulation into the cool night air outside.

The shock seemed to have made her legs wobbly as she stumbled up the street, glancing over her shoulder a couple of times, half-expecting to see Winston chasing after her, like he had the other day in Old Compton Street, but she was quite alone. Gradually the distant hum of the party was replaced by the rumble of traffic on the main road along the north of the Common. It was a similar feeling of displacement to the night she'd left Josie's house, as if the axis of the world had shifted and all the people she thought she knew best, she didn't know at all.

Where the street joined the road, Iris paused for a moment and looked at her watch under a streetlamp. It was only ten thirty, too early to walk in on Vic, too late to go to the cinema, too dark to walk on the Common. In the distance, she could see a double-decker bus, but it wasn't a number that would take her back over the river. She stared as it came closer, then passed her, an empty rectangular box of light. It would be safe and warm on a bus, a kind of limbo in which to sit quietly and collect her thoughts for an hour or two until she could decently return to Vic's. Iris decided to run for the bus stop a moment too late. The bus pulled away just as she reached it.

'Bastard!' Iris shouted impotently, stamping and shaking her fist at it.

She didn't see the orange light of the taxi heading towards her, nor the headlights dimming as it slowed down, nor did she look at the face of the driver as he wound down his window and asked, 'Are you all right, love?'

She got in, slumped down on the back seat, and said, 'Soho, please.'

'Sarah?'

Now, Iris looked in the rear-view mirror, into the eyes of someone she hadn't seen for over ten years. Terrified, she grabbed the door handle to jump out, but the cab was already moving.

'Long time, no see,' said Clive.

Every year since Christopher could remember, the Kingshaven Amateur Dramatic Society joined forces with the church choir to stage a Gilbert and Sullivan operetta in the church hall. Whilst none of the King family, except Uncle Cyril, ever showed the slightest inclination to participate, they always demonstrated their support by buying a row of half a dozen tickets, which were customarily allocated to Granny Liliana, Granny Ruby, Libby and Eddie, and two of their children.

As a boy, Christopher had found the seats so hard and the boredom so interminable, his legs would become jerky with restlessness as his brain struggled to create games to make the time pass quicker. He could still remember the considerable joy of spotting a mouse scurrying in and out of a hole at the base of the stage during *Iolanthe*, enabling him to predict and time the mouse's exits and entrances on his watch, whilst appearing to be following the plot, and so avoid sharp, disapproving nudges from his mother.

As he had grown older and wiser, Christopher had found ways of being absent during the distribution of tickets, letting his stupid younger brothers take the rap. But this year he willingly stood up for his duty, seeing it as a kind of homage to Uncle Cyril, who had been an enthusiastic, if unreliable, baritone, and whose performances, honed from years of practice in gang shows during his time in the Raj, had always made up in gusto what his voice lacked in pitch.

Sadly, none of Christopher's siblings seemed to feel a similar need to show respect. Angela pleaded the excuse of her baby, although maternal duties hadn't prevented her from going to the Cheltenham Races, Christopher noted. Adrian was in the Navy now, but Winny, who usually came home from school at every opportunity, elected on this occasion not to get a weekend exeat.

To Christopher's mother, Libby King, an empty seat would be an indication of money wasted, which was distasteful enough, but Christopher felt it would also symbolize his uncle's absence in a way he might find too poignant to bear.

'Well, ask someone else, if you're so bothered,' his mother said impatiently. 'Someone suitable, obviously,' she warned.

To Christopher's surprise, the first person who popped into his mind was the person whose large blue eyes had looked sadder as she offered her condolences than most of Uncle Cyril's close relations had at his actual funeral.

'How about Julia Allsop?' he asked.

'Julia Allsop would be suitable,' said Granny Liliana immediately.

'Ever so suitable,' echoed Granny Ruby.

'I've always been very fond of Julia,' said Libby, with a smile.

Christopher wasn't used to such unanimous approval.

'Well, I'll give her a ring, shall I?'

'Do you really think a young girl like her would want to come?' asked Eddie, as Christopher dialled.

'She does,' he told his father at the end of the conversation, suppressing the desire to add, 'So there!'

*   *   *

260

Now, halfway through the first act, as Christopher glanced at his watch, unable to believe that only seven minutes had passed since the last time he'd looked, he wondered if his father hadn't had a point. It did seem rather unfair to subject anyone else to this agony. Julia was so polite that every time he glanced anxiously at her she gave him a little smile, as if to reassure him that she was enjoying herself, but now he rolled his eyes skywards to indicate his boredom, he felt her body tremble with a little illicit giggle, and her smile became a shade less innocent, a shade more complicit.

Julia really had become a very pretty girl, he thought. Curvy and soft, unlike her sister, Joanna, who was all bony angles. As he smiled at her again, he couldn't help noticing at the other end of the row that Granny Liliana's attention had also wandered from the stage. Both she and Granny Ruby were leering at him in the most peculiar way.

In the interval, after ferrying cups of tea to the two old women, Christopher and Julia went outside for a breath of air and stood silently reading the church notice board as if it contained information of great fascination.

'*Patience* is certainly an appropriate title,' Christopher finally remarked, trying out a pun that had come to him during the performance. 'You need an awful lot of it to stick this one out!'

Julia's laugh was gratifyingly loud and sincere.

'I'm feeling rather guilty about subjecting you to it,' he said.

'Not at all. I'm enjoying myself,' she said.

He waited for an inevitable barb, but none came.

'Well, I hope you'll allow me to make it up to you one day,' he said.

Julia blushed so deeply, he could detect the flush of colour in the darkness.

'There's really no need,' she protested.

'Nevertheless,' he said, 'I promise I'll try to come up with something much more fun next time.'

'Well, that would be very nice,' she said.

Again, he found himself expecting a snide aside, but she simply looked at him with her huge, innocent eyes, then looked away, modestly, and, oddly, he felt himself blushing too.

Was it sheer bad luck that her first boyfriend, Clive, happened to be driving past or had he been following her? Had he seen her coming out of Winston's? Fear escalated inside Iris's head.

'I reckon your Winston had a lucky escape!' Vic, Clive's brother, had told her long ago.

'He's not my Winston!' she'd protested.

Even less so after this evening, Iris thought, but Tory or not, she didn't want any harm coming to him.

'What's in Soho then?' Clive called back from the driver's seat.

Did he already know? Was it a trick? Had Vic told him? Did Vic know that Clive was out of prison? Why hadn't he told her?

'I live there,' Iris mumbled at the floor.

She didn't like looking at Clive's reflection; somehow, his dark eyes were more menacing in the mirror.

'Live there?' Clive echoed.

'Not that!' said Iris, guessing what he meant. 'I just live there.'

Tentatively Iris slid her hand on to the handle of the door, but Clive seemed to go a little faster every time she tried.

'So when did you get . . . a cab?' she asked, trying to keep it as normal as she could.

'Couple of months back. I passed the Knowledge first time, what with having done a lot of driving. It was a choice of back to business, or this . . . Like I said, you get a lot of time to think inside . . .'

He kept looking at her in the mirror, and braking suddenly because he wasn't concentrating on the road. As far as she could tell, he was taking a direct route to Soho, not whisking her off to Epping Forest or any of his East End haunts, but she was conscious that could change in an instant. She felt completely at his mercy.

'I did a lot of thinking about you, Sarah,' he suddenly said.

If he still called her Sarah, Iris worked out, he couldn't know that much about her.

'I call myself Iris now,' she told him.

'Iris?' he said.

'It's my first name,' she added quickly. 'When I was young, I thought Iris was a bit old-fashioned.'

'The thing is, though,' he said, staring at her in the mirror, clearly set on telling her something, 'I worked out why you did what you did . . .'

She didn't know which particular thing he was referring to, but she wasn't going to stop him mid-flow.

'You always were smart, and you'd sussed out what was going on. You didn't want to be around when the police knocked on the door. Did you?'

Iris said nothing.

'Don't blame you for it now. It's in the past, as far as I'm concerned . . .' He smiled at her in the rear-view mirror.

Was this absolution? Iris wasn't sure.

'I'm sorry for leaving without telling you,' she offered by way of response.

'It's me that owes you an apology,' said Clive, 'for putting you through all that.'

Iris didn't dare to speak. The silence seemed to go on for ever. She felt she had been holding her breath all the journey and now she could release it.

'What have you been doing south of the river, then?' Clive suddenly asked, as if he'd just seen there was a piece of the jigsaw missing.

'I was at an election party,' she said.

'They say it's going to be Mrs Thatcher,' he replied.

'What do you make of that then?' Iris asked him, unable to believe that they were having a conversation about politics.

'She's the woman who can save Britain,' said Clive decisively.

It had been the *Daily Mail*'s headline.

In later years, when Iris looked back at that night, the sign that things had fundamentally changed was not the unexpected cheer that went up at Winston's, nor the blue balloons cascading down from the ceiling, not even the incoming Prime Minister's pious speech on the steps of 10 Downing Street, but those moments as Clive's cab sped past the Houses of Parliament when she could see his face in the rear-view mirror greeting the idea of a female Prime Minister with a smile.

Chapter Ten

1980

From time to time, the ghosts of previous inhabitants tossed up evidence of their lingering presence beneath Kingshaven's surface, from the fossilized skeletons of lizard-like creatures that occasionally appeared during erosion of the South Cliffs, to the jewelled Celtic brooch that had been found lying pristine at the foot of a ventilation shaft in one of the disused quarries, as if its former owner had dropped it down from her resting place in the Iron Age fort above, like a child dropping a shiny penny into a wishing well. In 1947 a cache of Roman coins had been unearthed by labourers digging the foundations for the council estate above the New End, but nobody was prepared for the discovery revealed during the laying of a new gas main to the Palace Hotel.

What had first appeared to be the straightforward excavation of a trench had been complicated by the ground being much harder underneath than anticipated, and, Christopher King suspected, a certain bloody-mindedness on the part of the labourers. On the pretext that the flat green lawn might disguise the treacherous terrain of an abandoned quarry below, the foreman, Sid Farthing, had called a stoppage pending a full survey. A geological drill had found only sandstone under a layer of stones, which, it was assumed, had been stockpiled in the mid-nineteenth century to supply the construction of the New End of town.

When work had resumed, worryingly behind schedule as far as the impending summer season was concerned, Libby King had charged Christopher with the responsibility of keeping an eye on the men. He could feel another delay looming, when he heard the mechanical digger suddenly stop one morning long before the men were due a tea break.

As Christopher approached the site, Sid picked up a handful of the spoil they'd just excavated.

'It's a funny kind of gravel, this,' he told Christopher, shaking his head. 'Looks almost like it's been cut special. It's a bugger to get the shovel through.'

Sid splayed his fingers to allow the little cubes of black and white stone to spatter back on to the ground.

'Was there anything else?' Christopher asked.

'I don't suppose,' said Sid, shrugging and indicating to the driver of the yellow digger that he should resume operations.

The shovel rose, like the angry head of a tyrannosaurus rex, Christopher thought, and fell on to the ground with a thump, biting and scraping a channel of earth with its jagged teeth.

'What the . . . ?'

Sid held up his hand to call a halt again. He was staring into the trench.

'What have we here?' he asked, jumping down.

Christopher approached gingerly and peered over. 'What is it now?' he asked with slight impatience.

'Looks like face,' said Sid.

Whether to love or to be 'in love' was the constant topic of conversation amongst the girls at the gatehouse. Loving someone was the companionable state enjoyed by Cee, who was going steady with Justin, the senior cashier at the Havenbourne branch of Lloyds Bank but, as Bee said, you could 'love' anything – a dog, a dress, a friend – but you could only be 'in love' with a man (or a horse, she added wickedly, if you happened to be Angela Fogg).

Being 'in love' was more a compulsion than a choice, according to Bee, and Julia was sure that the agony she suffered waiting for Christopher King to call and the sinking feeling of inadequacy she felt in her chest whenever she saw him, was definite proof that she was 'in love' too. Officially, they'd 'been out' twice since the opera, once to the ABC Lowhampton to see a film called *Being There*, which he'd chosen because the star, Peter Sellers, was apparently hilarious, but Julia didn't laugh once and, truth be told, would have much preferred *Kramer vs. Kramer*, which was showing on the other screen. Christopher had also taken her to the opening night of Kingshaven's new Indian restaurant, the Taj Mahal, on the site that had once been the Coffee Bean. The proprietor was Mr Patel's cousin, who'd recently moved down from Sudbury to help Mr Patel's growing business. Cee and Bee both thought it was rather brave of Julia to go, but actually the food had been delicious, even if it had made her mouth taste funny afterwards, which probably explained why Christopher hadn't tried to kiss her.

There were several other occasions when Julia had bumped into Christopher on one of his walks and he invited her to join him, but she wasn't sure whether those actually counted as dates. She persuaded herself that his failure to ask her out on a more regular basis was down to the fact that he obviously had a lot on his mind, and she drew hope from all the times he told her that she was a good listener. Having grown up next door to the Palace herself, she was familiar with the foibles of his family, and Granny Ruby was her own grandmother, so she understood his frustrations without him having to explain all the time.

Julia was quite good at cheering him up. Sometimes he actually apologized for being such a melancholic old thing, but she always assured him that thirty-two wasn't old at all, and that made him laugh. Julia and her friends were convinced that if Christopher could once stop worrying for long enough, he would see that she could make him happy all the time. They invested a great deal of creative energy dreaming up ways of putting her in his path.

Liliana King's impending eightieth birthday presented one such opportunity. The old lady's birthday, coinciding as it did with the age of the century, was marked each decade by the town. Julia encouraged the children at the nursery school to make a card and she was on her way to deliver it personally when she experienced something that felt like a macabre premonition.

For the past few weeks, there'd been a lot of activity and plant on the gravel drive leading up to the Palace, but today there was silence, the machines stood idle.

Three generations of Kings and Granny Ruby were standing in a line along the edge of the trench. From a distance they gave the appearance of mourners at a graveside, smartly dressed in dark suits, their heads bowed.

Julia approached cautiously with a mounting feeling of foreboding.

'What is it?' Eddie was saying.

'It's a woman's head,' said the man in the pit.

Julia stopped in her tracks.

'Yes, we can see it's a head, but is it attached to anything?' asked Libby King.

Julia gulped.

Suddenly, Christopher jumped down into the trench. 'Do you think it's Roman?' he called up.

Calculating that the mood was neither horror nor grief, but curiosity, Julia took a step closer.

'Roman? If it's Roman, I may have to curtail disturbance of the site pending investigation,' said the man.

'Investigation?' repeated Eddie King. 'What sort of bloody investigation?'

Libby King drew in breath sharply at the swear word.

'How long is that likely to take?' Granny Liliana asked Mr Farthing, the foreman.

The formidable old lady was still very much involved in the running of the hotel.

'Could be days, could be weeks,' opined Mr Farthing ominously.

'Excavations are still going on at Fishbourne. And it's years since that was discovered!' Christopher shouted up.

'Oh, do be quiet!' said Eddie. 'I can't hear myself think.'

Julia took a timid step closer. They were all so involved in the trench nobody had yet noticed her presence. She was half-expecting a skull, or a skeleton, so it was with relief that she saw that the object appeared to be just a dusty stretch of mosaic.

'Look, there's another one!' said Christopher, brushing away the dry earth with his forearm.

The lady's face was now joined by another, and a hand holding a bunch of grapes, and then another in profile with an open mouth about to eat . . . Christopher brushed a little more earth away . . .

'Oh!' cried Julia.

When she regained consciousness, not quite sure what had happened, she was lying a few feet away from the trench with her grandmother, Granny Ruby, fanning her distractedly with her hand, and straining to hear what was being said.

'There are definite safety issues . . .' Mr Farthing was warning.

'Quite,' said Granny Liliana. 'It's clear to me that it should be filled in, don't you think? We certainly do not want to run the risk of anyone sustaining an injury. And in the circumstances I do think it would be wise to keep it under our hats, so to speak. I'm sure we can rely on you, Sid.' She gave the foreman the benefit of her famous smile.

'Are you all right now, Julia?' Granny Ruby asked impatiently.

'Fine, thanks,' said Julia, getting up and brushing the dust from her skirt.

'Perhaps you'd care to come inside for a glass of lemonade,' Granny Liliana was saying to Mr Farthing. 'Must be such warm work in this weather.'

The family moved as one back towards the hotel, leaving Julia alone with Christopher.

'Are you OK?' he asked Julia.

'Absolutely fine,' said Julia, trying to look anywhere but the trench. She'd never felt so embarrassed in her life.

'I've always wanted to go on a dig,' Christopher told her excitedly. 'What a bit of luck to find one in one's garden, so to speak!'

'Yes,' Julia agreed uncertainly. Her head still felt a bit woozy. She wondered how she might get him to ask her in for a lemonade too. She wished Bee was there to whisper strategy into her ear.

'What's this?' Christopher picked up the giant card the children had painted, which must have slipped from Julia's hand when she fainted.

'It's for Granny Liliana,' stuttered Julia.

'I'll take it then, shall I?' he said. 'Look, are you sure you're OK? Should I walk you home?'

'No, I'm fine,' said Julia, seeing that he was eager to get back in.

'Well, I'd better be off. Things to discuss . . .' Christopher was beaming like a child with a new toy. She'd never seen him so animated.

'Of course,' she said.

'You know, this could be the thing that turns everything around!' he said, suddenly leaping forward and giving her a spontaneous kiss on the cheek. 'See you soon!'

Shelley gave the staff of Harridan Press the news the day before *The Times* reported it with the headline 'Women to Join Roman's Empire'.

The deal negotiated involved no redundancies, she told them as they all crushed into her office, and no editorial interference. All it meant was that the financial future of Harridan was assured and the staff would have all the benefits of working for a big company, such as word processors and a pension scheme.

'And I'll be the first woman to have a seat on the board

of Portico, which is progress, isn't it?' Shelley was quick to counter any suggestion that she'd sold out.

The announcement was greeted with a general sense of resignation. They'd all moaned about their rickety desks and ancient Adler typewriters, and the attic offices in Covent Garden were impossibly cramped, with only one loo, two flights down, which was also the only place with a sink where the kettle could be filled, but now they were reluctant to leave. However much they told themselves that it was a mark of the company's success that an entrepreneur like Roman Stone would want to make it his, the fact remained that Harridan wasn't financially sustainable without a man's intervention, and that was hard to stomach for some of the women who'd been there right from the start. Even though Shelley insisted that Harridan was going from strength to strength, it felt like the end of an era.

'He liked you so much he bought the company,' Vic quipped when Iris gave him the news that evening.

'It wasn't anything to do with me,' Iris told him, gloomily opening a bottle of wine she'd picked up on her way home. 'Drink?'

'Not tonight. I'm going out.'

'Again?' said Iris.

'I'm not really your husband, you know,' Vic retaliated.

'It's just I never seem to see you these days,' she said, sounding even more like a parody of a nagging wife.

It wasn't that she'd actually told Clive that she and Vic were together, it was just that Clive had assumed, and they'd allowed him to. Both of them. It was Vic's fault as much as hers, she thought.

On the night of the election in May the previous year, Clive had dropped Iris on Shaftesbury Avenue as she'd asked, refusing to take any money for the fare. She had watched the cab driving off towards Cambridge Circus becoming just another in a line of black cabs stopping at the lights.

The encounter had been so unreal – surreal, almost

– that when she'd woken up the next day, Iris was convinced she'd dreamed it, until she saw the card with the telephone number of the cab company printed on it, which Clive had pressed into her palm, saying, 'If ever you're stuck . . .'

It wasn't a number she could ever imagine herself calling.

Clive had been nothing other than friendly, but she couldn't rid herself of the idea that there was some other agenda.

Vic had told her that she was paranoid. He assured her that he hadn't known that Clive was out of prison, but he had known that he was coming up for parole. So, he was out and driving a cab. What was the big deal?

'So why didn't he contact you, then?' Iris asked.

'You know Clive. He's proud. He wouldn't want anyone to think he was asking for help,' Vic said.

So, there was nothing suspicious at all then, Iris told herself repeatedly. However, it came as no surprise when, a couple of weeks later, a black cab slowed alongside her as she walked home from work along Old Compton Street. To bump into a former lover in a city of six million people once might be coincidence, to bump into him twice was definitely planned.

'Need a lift?' he'd asked, winding down the window.

'I'm right home, thanks,' she said.

'I wouldn't say no to a cup of tea.'

She'd forgotten how big Clive was standing up. Not just tall, but kind of built. As she walked up the stairs to the flat with him following just behind her, she'd felt acutely aware of his huge presence and the fact that he would be able to crush her with one hand if he chose to, and she found herself wishing that either Molly or Lulu would step out of her flat and witness who she was with, but there was no one on the staircase or the balcony they walked along to the front door.

Sitting in the living room in his short-sleeved shirt and tie, and dark-grey trousers, Iris thought Clive looked like

272

one of the security guards on hard chairs in art galleries, the only people not looking at the paintings.

'An art student used to live here,' Iris said.

'Oh, I see.' Clive was relieved to have an explanation for the weirdness of the decoration.

Iris made him a mug of tea, put a couple of biscuits on a plate, and hoped that his curiosity would be satisfied. He'd left the cab on a yellow line. Surely he couldn't be away too long?

'You live here on your own, then, do you?' Clive asked.

'No, I share,' said Iris, trying to calculate whether it would be better to come clean or try to get away with it, when, as if to solve her dilemma, she heard the rattle of Vic's key in the door.

Clive looked from one to the other, put two and two together and immediately came up with five.

'Oh, I see,' he said again, pushing past both of them, leaving his mug of tea steaming on the floor.

'What the hell did you think you were doing bringing him back here?' Vic asked her.

'I didn't mean to. He asked for a cup of tea . . .'

Vic looked at her as if she'd gone mad. 'Why didn't you tell him to get himself one in a café?' he demanded.

'I didn't think. All right? I couldn't think. I got in a panic.'

'You silly tart!'

'Why are you so bothered? I thought I was the paranoid one?' Iris launched into a counterattack.

'I would have thought it was obvious why I wouldn't want him knowing about my life.'

'Well, he doesn't, does he? He thinks you're with me . . .'

'You stupid bloody cow!' shouted Vic in her face.

There was a moment of fury when she thought he was going to tell her to leave. But then he put his head in his hands and started laughing.

'Oh my God!' he said, as if only just realizing the implications.

'You'll have to marry me now.' Iris risked a joke.

It had been funny, at first.

The discovery of images of explicit sexual acts just a few feet beneath the surface of Kingshaven's topsoil came as little surprise to Christopher King, who had felt a kind of primal connection with the turf ever since his first sexual experience on the mossy ramparts of the Iron Age fort on the South Cliffs, when Milly had remarked with a lazy smile, 'The earth most definitely moved!'

Perhaps the mosaics belonged to a temple. Perhaps they had something to do with fertility rites. Or maybe their purpose was merely decorative, designed to titillate the guests at an orgy. How amazing to think there might have been a palace on the very site of the Palace since Roman times!

'It could be just the tip of the iceberg,' he said, as the King family discussed what to do over dinner. 'Kingshaven might be another Fishbourne!'

'What's Fishbourne?' asked Granny Ruby.

'It's a very important archaeological site near Chichester,' Christopher informed her loftily. 'I thought everyone knew that!'

Mrs Farmer gave him one of her irritating half-defiant, half don't-be-cruel-to-me-because-I'm-an-old-lady looks.

'People come from all over the country!' said Christopher, trying to remember some details of the television programme he'd watched about it. 'The archaeologist's called Barry Cunliffe. It's terribly significant.'

The rest of the family stared at him, waiting for him to come to the point.

'Can't any of you see?' he asked exasperatedly. 'It's almost as if our ancestors have gifted us the means to stay.'

'You're not seriously suggesting that we pursue the idea of an excavation?' said Eddie.

'I think we have an obligation to,' said Christopher a little pompously.

'Obligation to whom?' said Eddie.

'Well, to history, I suppose,' Christopher said, faltering slightly under his father's hostile glare.

'History be blowed! If we start digging stuff up, there'll never be an end to it.'

'If we start digging things up, it will ruin this season and the next,' said Libby gloomily.

'But, don't any of you get it?' shouted Christopher. 'This is the way of attracting a new clientele.'

'What sort of clientele?' Granny Liliana intervened. 'Who would come? Parties of schoolchildren, that's who. There's no money in schoolchildren.'

'Anyway, you couldn't let schoolchildren see those . . . things!' Mrs Farmer chipped in, still smarting from Christopher's rebuke.

'Exactly! That's the most sensible thing anyone's said today!' Eddie pronounced, bestowing a rare compliment on Granny Ruby.

'But . . .' protested Christopher, feeling it all running out of his control again.

'Exactly what sort of reputation do you want this place to have?' asked Eddie hammering his point home. 'Your outdoor activities are bad enough, without putting on a display of Roman porn in our own back yard.'

'Eddie!' Libby warned.

Both grannies stared unblinkingly at Christopher.

So, they all knew. He knew he should at least try to defend himself, but with the stark truth out in the open, he couldn't think of anything he could say that would get anywhere near satisfying his family. He was having an affair with a married woman. The fact that her husband was a bit of a cad himself made it worse, not better, as far as they were concerned. Unaccountably, they had all been fond of Gerard Balls when he'd worked at the Palace. Granny Liliana had presented him with a silver cocktail stick when he left.

'It's possible there's some sort of legal obligation to report a site of historic interest.' Christopher tried to refocus the conversation. 'Has anyone thought of that?'

'Not if nobody knows about it,' said Granny Liliana crisply.

'But we all know . . .'

All of them stared at him, closing ranks.

'Mr Farthing . . . ?' he offered desperately.

'I think Mr Farthing is perfectly aware of the value we attach to confidentiality,' said Granny Liliana with an enigmatic smile.

Christopher had to admit that his grandmother did have a way with the working classes. He thought it must be something to do with the war. She'd been stalwart in the face of an impending invasion and welcomed the troops into her home. He'd often noticed that people in the town seemed to regard her, astonishingly, as one of them.

'What about Julia?' Christopher played his last card.

'Julia is perfectly trustworthy, thank you very much,' said Granny Ruby, folding her arms defensively.

'I don't doubt that, but she won't actually know not to say, will she?' said Christopher, hating himself for succumbing so pathetically in the face of opposition. Should he have stood up against them, reported it to the appropriate authority, written to Barry Cunliffe, even? But what if there was no legal obligation after all? Then they'd be back to square one and the hotel would probably have gone out of business, and it would all be his fault.

'You'd better ring Julia up and tell her, hadn't you?' said Eddie.

All of them looked in unison at the telephone, then back at him.

'Why me?' said Christopher.

'You can just drop it in casually,' said Libby King in a more emollient tone. 'We don't want to make a big thing about it, do we?'

Christopher picked up the receiver.

'Make it look like you're calling about something else,' Eddie barked at him, as the phone started ringing in the gatehouse.

'Julia?' said Christopher. 'Just calling to see how you were after . . . oh, good . . .'

All eyes were on him.

'Look, we . . . I was actually wondering whether you'd like to come to the party Angela's arranging for Granny Lily's eightieth . . .'

Christopher's father now smiled and gave him the thumbs-up sign.

'Oh, and, Julia, the thing you saw in the trench, probably best not to mention it in the circumstances . . . I'm sure you weren't going to. Quite . . .'

'I have a question for you,' Roman Stone said to Iris a couple of days after Harridan had moved into Portico Books.

The offices occupied the top three floors of a characterless glass and concrete block off the Euston Road, slightly beyond the listed Georgian squares of Bloomsbury, the traditional territory of publishing, where such old-established firms such as Michael Joseph, and Hodder and Stoughton still resided. Iris wondered whether the location of the company headquarters was based on economics, since Roman Stone was renowned for the tight grip he kept on finance, or whether there was a subtle message of difference intended. Roman Stone had built his reputation publishing books that the more established lists had rejected.

His office, however, was exactly as Iris imagined the traditional workplace of a publishing grandee to be. Although the rectangular shape, low ceiling and plate-glass window were modern, it was furnished with a huge leather-topped walnut desk, a Persian rug on top of the fitted beige office carpet, which made it feel slightly like walking on a mattress underfoot, and two plump leather sofas, which sank you to a lower level than Roman, who sat at his desk, with a backdrop of sky behind him, like God, she thought.

'And what might your question be?' she asked, wondering why it was that she always felt like a favoured, but cheeky pupil in the presence of an indulgent, but shrewd headmaster when she was with him.

'My question is, what would be a good name for a new imprint?' Roman asked.

'Depends what market the imprint was aimed at,' said Iris cautiously.

'Well, let's say we were talking about a list of books someone like you might be interested in taking on holiday. The thinking woman's beach read, shall we say?'

There was a very thin line between being patronizing and flattering, and Roman walked it like no other man Iris had ever met.

Iris considered the question.

'I've always thought Penelope Books would be a good name for an imprint,' she said.

'Penelope? That sounds rather more headscarf and wellies in the shires than trendy girl about town, doesn't it?'

'I suppose,' Iris conceded. 'I was thinking more of the wife of Odysseus. I've always seen her role in the Odyssey as a metaphor for story-telling . . .'

Roman raised his eyebrows.

'She's constantly reworking the same material, unpicking it every night, creating a new image . . .'

'How interesting,' said Roman. 'I didn't realize we had a classical scholar in our midst. Have you read Homer in the original?'

'No, but I was always a great fan of Roger Lancelyn Green's *The Tale of Troy*,' Iris told him, mocking herself before he had a chance to.

'Penelope Books,' Roman pondered the words. 'I see where you're coming from, but even so, isn't it a little docile and domestic?'

'That's such a tired way of putting female writers down, don't you think?' Iris challenged him. 'Women write well about the domestic, yes. That doesn't make their novels less universal. Or would you call Jane Austen docile and domestic?'

Roman smiled indulgently. 'Sometimes you sound so like your father,' he said.

'Really?'

'The zeal of the autodidact.'

Roman was exquisitely good at leading victims to the bait, then observing as their vanity allowed them to snatch at it. And yet, however much he might despise her lack of education, her absence of finesse, Iris was aware that there was a certain way in which he prized those rough edges, acknowledging perhaps that all his had been smoothed away.

'If I were you, I'd think again about Penelope,' said Roman.

'What do you mean?' Iris asked.

'Your own imprint. I'm thinking in the region of a dozen books a year, if you can find them. If you only find three, fine. Thirteen, fine. Thirty would mean you were losing your touch, I think . . .'

'My own imprint?' Iris waited for the sign that he was teasing her.

'Do feel free to publish any universal men you might find, as well as women.'

'You are joking?'

'I never joke about business,' he said and, for a moment, Roman's face was so deadly serious it was almost spooky. Then the charming smile returned.

'I thought you might want to call it Iris Books,' he mused. 'I believe she was goddess of the rainbow. But you'd of course know more about that than I do . . .'

Cream and salmon pink would be the principal colour ways, Sylvia finally decided, with discreet touches of jade such as occasional scatter cushions or piping around the tiebacks and pelmets of the salmon-pink curtains. They were classic colours, as English as cream teas and cucumber sandwiches, and yet they were light, airy and modern, not like all those old-fashioned maroons and golds she could remember from her one visit to the Palace Hotel.

The first room to be done was the large bedroom at the front of the North elevation, with its hideous Chinese wallpaper and ornate black and gold lacquer furniture, which hadn't been touched since she and Jolly arrived. It had given Sylvia the creeps then, so she'd locked the door and tried to forget it was there, and she'd had the same feeling of dread when she opened it up again when an expert had come to value the furniture. There was the bed at the centre with an ornate black and gold headboard, two huge wardrobes and matching tallboys. She couldn't imagine anyone wanting the stuff and would happily have made a bonfire of it, but the valuer said some people actually collected it, adding the bittersweet qualification that the higher prices were generally achieved by smaller pieces because, he said, looking round the room enviously, there weren't many people with places as big as this.

Sylvia went to have a last look before the auctioneer's lorry arrived. An involuntary shiver trickled down her spine. All the musty-smelling drawers or cupboards were empty, but Sylvia opened and closed each one nevertheless, then she kneeled down to check that there was nothing hiding under the curlicues of gilded carving around the bottom section of the tallboy, which tapered into the four strange paws – Chinese lion's feet, Sylvia presumed – that acted as legs. It was too dark to see anything, but if she lay flat on the floor, Sylvia's hand could just about stretch to the back. Her fingers skimmed the thick blanket of dust, but there were no sharp outlines of single earrings or collar studs mislaid by an earlier occupant. Just as she was withdrawing her hand, it touched something lodged just behind one of the lion's feet. Sylvia drew out a scrunched-up ball of paper, which looked like it had been aimed at a litter basket and missed.

There were three sheets of pale-blue paper, Basildon Bond, Sylvia thought, uncrumpling them carefully and shaking the dust out of the creases. The ink must be Quink royal blue, because that was the one that would wash out if your fountain pen leaked in the pocket of your blouse, she remembered from school, and the words on the paper had run.

Sylvia sat down on the bed to read. It didn't occur to her until she was halfway through the first letter that the cause of the blotting was tears. By the time she had finished, there were tears running down Sylvia's own face, and she had to wipe them away with her sleeve to stop them wetting the ink again.

Claudia Dearchild must have written the letters as she lay dying, Sylvia thought, suddenly jumping up from the bed, realizing that this must have been where she died. No wonder the room had a chill.

'It's like a funeral parlour,' she could remember saying to Jolly when she first saw it.

Of all the places to put her!

There was a letter for each child, but neither was finished nor signed, and Sylvia could picture Claudia's frustration as she bunched up the inadequate screeds and hurled them away from her. How terrible it must have been to know that those little children wouldn't even remember her. It felt too intimate, too intrusive, somehow, to be reading words written for them. The first, to the girl, was longer, more considered, Sylvia thought, like when you were writing a composition at school and had to remember to get all the points in. The second, to the boy, was rushed, as if Claudia was racing to put everything in her head down on paper. The third piece of paper appeared to be just a scrawled list of book titles.

Sylvia went over to the window and looked out at the avenue of tall beech trees that led down to the road. It was raining and the town was shrouded in cloud. Through the rivulets of water drizzling down the windowpanes, she could see the auctioneer's lorry turning into the drive.

Perhaps they were just early drafts, Sylvia tried to persuade herself, thinking of all the bits of writing Michael used to tear up before he finally had a version he was happy enough to type up. You often needed several goes at any kind of letter before you got it right, didn't you? Perhaps

Claudia had written proper letters later that said exactly what she wanted.

But what if she hadn't? What if she'd left nothing? Wouldn't her children want to read these? Wouldn't she want them to?

Sylvia was suddenly cross. Why her? Why was she, of all people, the one who had to decide what to do with Claudia's letters? She who'd never even spoken to her, who'd hated her, who'd even wished her dead. Not that she'd meant it literally, Sylvia silently assured the imaginary presence on the bed.

For a moment, Sylvia thought the thing to do would be to discuss it with Jolly. Let him take responsibility. It was his house, after all, and all the property in it his. But she knew exactly what her husband would say. He would tell her to destroy them. Jolly thought that the past was past and best forgotten. The trouble with that was that in Sylvia's experience, however hard you tried to erase it, you never did quite get rid of the past. It always found strange ways of coming back, when you least expected it, and imposing itself on the present.

There was no reason Jolly needed to know at all, Sylvia thought, glancing at her watch. She would be back before he had even woken up from his afternoon nap. She was halfway down the avenue of beech trees with water splattering off her umbrella before she realized that she hadn't put a jacket on. In her rush to leave she hadn't even checked her make-up in the mirror. The cobblestones of the Harbour End's narrow streets were slippery, and Sylvia wasn't wearing very sensible shoes. Her ankle went over painfully and she limped the last few yards to the former warehouse.

The girl who opened the door looked like a miniature version of Iris. Twelve, or thirteen, Sylvia calculated. At that age, Iris had been almost as tall as she was. This one was prettier, as if Iris had been a prototype with a few imperfections still to be ironed out, but she had a similar look of defiance on her face.

Poor Michael, Sylvia couldn't resist a smirk. Two difficult redheads for daughters. Served him right!

'Is your father in?' she asked.

'Dad!' called the girl.

Michael came down the stairs, stopping when he saw who it was.

After all this time, Sylvia's heartbeat still accelerated when she saw him. He was still so handsome. Even though his hair had lost its tawny colour it wasn't grey but a bright shade of white, and he still wore it long, swept back from his face. His features were still chiselled, if a little weatherbeaten, and his eyes were as pale and as blue as they had ever been, dancing the line between amusement and anger. When they were young, Sylvia remembered, she'd sometimes been able to tip him towards smiling, but that hadn't happened for a very long time.

'Come in,' he said.

Sylvia put her umbrella down and propped it by the door, making an instant pool of water around the spike.

'Terrible weather,' she said.

'To what do we owe the pleasure?' Michael asked.

'I'd like to speak to you alone,' she said.

He looked as if he was weighing up whether to make another sarcastic comment. Sylvia promised herself that if he did, she'd just turn round and go.

The girl went silently back upstairs.

Michael came down the last couple of steps, opened the door into the downstairs shop and showed Sylvia in. It was like a library with all the rows of bookshelves. In a corner by the door stood a wooden desk with a cash drawer on it, and a chair. Michael indicated she should sit down. He remained standing. She wondered whether he'd taken her in here because he didn't want her in his living quarters, or whether his French girlfriend was upstairs.

'How's business?' Sylvia asked.

'Somewhat slow,' said Michael with a slight, self-mocking shrug.

'Is there any money in second-hand books?' Sylvia

picked up a paperback with an orange cover; the pages were dry and yellow, like an autumn leaf that would crumble in your hand. She put it down quickly.

'Just enough to pay the bills. A bit more in summer,' said Michael. 'Occasionally, a rare first edition turns up, and that helps.'

He'd never be a successful shopkeeper. It took more than a love of your product to keep a business going. They both knew that.

'How are you getting on?' he asked.

'Very well, thank you,' said Sylvia.

The rain pelted down on the cobblestones outside.

'How does it feel to be a grandmother?' Michael asked.

Anthony and Marie's baby son was two months old now. Sylvia had been up to see them in the hospital, but Marie's mother was the one they'd asked to help. Sylvia thought she'd probably be more use to them when the baby was a bit older.

'I'm happy it's a boy,' Sylvia said, ignoring his grandmother taunt. 'Boys are so much easier.'

She was surprised when he replied, 'I think you may be right about that.' She'd expected him to jump to Iris's defence.

'Have you seen him yet?' she asked.

'Not yet. No. I expect they'll bring him down in the summer,' said Michael.

The silence seemed to last an age. They'd run out of anything they had in common.

'Well, I'll be brief,' Sylvia resumed, as if it was a bank manager she was talking to, and not the man she had loved and married. 'I found these in that room with all the black furniture.'

She handed him the letters and looked away discreetly as he read.

Finally daring to glance, she saw he had the letters clasped against his chest. He was looking up at the ceiling as if the tilt of his head would hold the tears back in his eyes.

'I'm sorry,' she said.

'I didn't know . . .' he said. His voice was quavery.

'I brought them straight away,' Sylvia said.

He didn't appear to hear.

'I didn't know if it was the right thing . . .' She was trying her hardest to be a gentle sympathetic presence. 'I didn't—' she tried again.

'Would you mind going now?' he said.

He didn't mean to be rude, she could see that. It was just his male pride that wouldn't let him cry in front of her. But it hurt still that she was no use to him.

Her hand was on the door, when he said, 'Syl?'

He was the only person who'd ever shortened her name. It had driven her mother mad. His using it now was like an echo from happier times.

'Yes?' she said.

'Thank you.'

He held out to her the hand that wasn't clutching the letters. She grasped it and gave it an infinitesimally brief squeeze. And then she left, not able to look at him again.

As she limped back up the road from the Harbour End, Sylvia noticed that the chink chink of the yachts and the sound of cars revving up the first steep bit of hill were louder than usual. The rain had stopped and the air felt as if it had been rinsed. All the trees along the road towards the Castle were dripping with silvery light. Her shoes were so wet, they couldn't get any wetter. Checking to see that she was alone, Sylvia splashed right through the centre of a puddle. The water was cool and soothing on her painful ankle. As she neared the gatehouse, the auctioneer's van was just turning out of the drive. Sylvia stood watching it all the way down the road.

The room did look huge with the black lacquer furniture gone, and sunlight poured in with that particular brilliance that sometimes comes after rain.

The question of what Julia should wear for Liliana King's eightieth birthday party occupied all the girls at the gatehouse. It seemed unlikely, with the dilapidated state of the ballroom, that it would be the sort of occasion that required her to hire a proper gown. After much discussion and experimenting with outfits, Julia was persuaded to try Bee's black strapless dress with a low décolletage and a full calf-length chiffon skirt. The first surprise was that the dress actually fitted her. It was a size 10, and Julia hadn't been in anything less than a 14 for years. The idea of going on a proper public date with Christopher had made her too excited to eat anything apart from an occasional slice of toasted Slimcea that Cee urged on her at breakfast. The second surprise was that she looked good in black, the tight bodice gave her a waist, and her bare shoulders were remarkably smooth and creamy. Julia was not quite able to believe her own reflection. She squinted at the mirror as she used to do as a child and touched her exposed flesh just to make sure it was real.

'What if everyone else is in jeans?' she asked Bee and Cee, who were sitting on her bed in a pile of all the outfits they collectively owned.

'At the Palace?' said Cee with awe, which made Julia realize that an invitation to the Palace was probably a bigger deal to them than it was to her. Julia had virtually grown up in the Palace and called the proprietor Auntie Libby. All the more reason to wear a grown-up dress now, she thought, trying to hang on to her confidence.

'I'll never be able to dance in this.' Julia pointed to her cleavage, suddenly aware that she had just made the decision to wear the dress, and was now merely making up excuses for them to shoot down and confirm her choice.

'When he sees you in that,' said Bee authoritatively, 'dancing won't be the first thing on his mind!'

Cee drove her there in the Mini Metro.

The lawns on either side of the drive had been turfed over. Only someone who knew would have noticed the slight difference in the quality of the turf.

'Where were the dirty mosaics?' Cee asked.

'Shush. Nobody's supposed to know,' Julia whispered as

if someone might be able to hear their conversation in the car.

Cee pulled up outside the main entrance, where Christopher King was standing on the steps.

'Now, listen,' said Cee, leaning over and giving her a kiss, 'you can't be a shrinking violet in that dress!'

Julia nodded. Tonight she had to be an English Rose, proud, sophisticated and a little bit haughty. Taking a deep breath, she opened the car door.

'Good luck!' said Cee.

Julia gingerly put one foot out on to the gravel and then the other, careful not to catch the yards of black chiffon on the heel of her shoe. As she bent forward to step out, her breasts felt as if they were going to fall out of the stiffened velvet bodice, but they didn't quite. Finally standing up straight, she was pleased to see that Christopher was looking admiringly at her.

'I say, Julia!' he exclaimed.

The ballroom at the Palace Hotel smelled faintly of horses. In an attempt to create an authentic setting, the usual chairs with their threadbare claret velvet seats had been removed and hay bales had been brought in from Angela's stables. A barn dance, Julia realized immediately with dismay, although the ballroom would never look like a barn. In her dress, she felt as eye-catching and inappropriate as the mirrorball twirling in the centre of the ceiling.

As if sensing her distress, Eddie King immediately came over and asked her to dance, but Julia said she thought she'd wait a bit. She sat on a hay bale next to Christopher and felt it was going to be a very long evening. Auntie Libby smiled at her encouragingly from the other side of the room and Eddie King occasionally winked on his way past, stripping the willow. The room was full of people she'd talked to ever since she'd known how to speak, but she felt they were looking at her in a different way somehow, and she had no idea what to say.

The Gay Gordons had just finished and everyone was

clapping, pink faces gleaming with self-congratulation, when a slight chill seemed to descend on the room. Two new guests arrived, one of whom, Julia recognized with horror, was Bee's lover, Gerry. At first she couldn't place the woman who was with him, but then she remembered she'd had her picture taken with her long ago, on Carnival Day when Julia had saved Bruno Dearchild from drowning and the woman had been the beautiful Roman Miss Kingshaven. Millicent Bland. She was older and fatter now, but her hair was still blonde and her smile still broad and full of fun. She certainly didn't look like a wife whose husband was yearning to leave her. As Gerry walked past Julia he had the absolute nerve to wink at her.

'What the hell . . . ?' Christopher jumped up so suddenly from the hay bale they were sitting on that Julia almost lost her balance and fell off.

'Who invited them?' he hissed at his sister, Angela.

'Granny Lily's always liked Gerry,' said Angela defensively. 'He mixed her gin and Dubonnet just as she liked it.'

'Where's Granny Liliana, by the way?' Julia asked Christopher as he sat back down on the bale.

'What?' he asked distractedly, as if he'd quite forgotten she was there. 'Probably in the bar. With your grandmother . . .'

'I ought to go and wish her happy birthday,' Julia suggested, glad to have an excuse to do something rather than just sitting there.

'What? Yes. If you want . . .'

She found both the old ladies sitting at a table with their usual cocktails. Granny Liliana was wearing a lilac evening dress. She smelled slightly of moth balls as Julia bent to kiss her.

'Goodness me, Julia,' said Granny Ruby, staring at her chest. 'Where did you get that dress? Not Sylvia Quinn's, is it?'

'No, it's Wallis, I think,' said Julia.

'Wallis?' echoed Granny Liliana sharply.

'It's a dress shop,' Granny Ruby explained. 'Like Dorothy Perkins, but a bit more expensive.'

'I borrowed it, actually,' Julia said, sensing disapproval as both old ladies stared at her. 'I didn't realize it was a barn dance, you see.'

'We used to have one every year, didn't we, Ruby?' said Granny Liliana slightly tearily, draining her glass.

'Those were the days,' said Granny Ruby, and started singing the tune in a thin old-lady voice.

They both sounded as if they'd allowed themselves more than just the one cocktail on this special occasion, Julia thought.

'If you'll excuse me . . .' She extracted herself from their presence.

Julia didn't actually need the loo, but it was a way of being on her own and not having to make conversation for a few minutes. The downstairs ladies' toilet was engaged but Julia didn't think anyone would mind if she used one of the guest facilities upstairs, although it did feel slightly like trespassing as she quickly ran up the grand staircase.

The ensuite bathroom of the Windsor Suite was almost big and grand enough to be a ballroom itself, Julia thought, jumping up and down as fast and energetically as she could in front of the mirror. Her breasts bobbed, but remained inside the dress. Next, she twirled round at great speed as if an imaginary partner was spinning her. Still no spillage. She practised holding out her hand for a chain, first left then right, promenade, twirl and start again. It all stayed in place. Finally an *arabesque en l'air* in fifth position. In this dress, she could almost be Odile, the black swan, in *Swan Lake*, she thought. With slightly more confidence, Julia let herself out of the bathroom, giving one last shake of her bodice at the mirror.

She was about to come down the grand staircase into the Entrance Hall when she spotted Christopher talking in a corner to Millicent Bland, or Millicent Balls as she must be now, Julia thought, recalling how she and Cee had fallen about laughing when Bee had revealed Gerry's surname.

289

'Aren't you going to offer to show me your remains?' said Millicent, her voice full of innuendo.

'What remains?' Christopher sounded flustered as he attempted to dissemble, then ruined it completely by saying, 'How on earth do you know about that?'

Julia held her breath. She had told Cee and Bee before Christopher had called and said not to. They'd both promised not to tell, but now she wondered. Had Bee told Gerry and Gerry told his wife?

'A little bird told me,' said Millicent Balls.

'What little bird?'

'Tweet tweet,' said Millicent.

Any moment he was going to look up and see her, thought Julia. She took a step back from the banister.

'Who'd have thought it?' said Millicent. 'All that going on underneath us!'

'I'd better get back to the party,' said Christopher.

'Before your new girlfriend starts missing you?' asked Millicent in the same teasing voice.

As their voices receded, Julia strained to hear Christopher's response, but could not.

Did Millicent mean that Julia was his new girlfriend? Julia wondered, her heart beating fast again as she flew down the grand staircase, feeling a bit like Cinderella at the ball.

'Where have you been?' Christopher asked as she joined him on the hay bale again.

'Nowhere,' said Julia.

'Shall we get a breath of air?'

He sounded almost cross with her, but as he led her towards the French windows, he took her hand, and Julia suddenly felt as if her whole being had somehow concentrated itself in her hand. For a moment, the world stopped turning, everyone stopped talking, and all eyes were focused on it. Julia didn't need to see Winny's face to know that he was staring, nor look at Granny Ruby to know that she was nudging Granny Liliana. Libby and Eddie King, Angela and Miles Fogg, Millicent and Gerry Balls

– they were all looking. Holding someone's hand while barn dancing was one thing, but holding it when going outside for a breath of air was quite a different matter. She was now Christopher King's girlfriend!

What would Cee and Bee think? What would her sister Joanna think? And Daddy? And Mummy?

When she was ever so little she'd told Mummy that she was going to marry Adrian King when she grew up and live happily ever after at the Palace, and Mummy had laughed and told her that she'd have to marry Christopher if she wanted to do that.

Had that been a sort of premonition?

Sometimes Julia thought she did feel things before they happened.

Now Christopher King was holding her hand and looking up at the stars. It was the most romantic moment of her life, but Julia was terrified that Christopher was about to start asking her to spot and name the constellations, as James always did. Orion had three stars on his belt and the Great Bear looked like a saucepan, James said, but Julia was never quite sure whether her brother was having her on.

'It makes one feel rather humble, doesn't it?' said Christopher finally.

'Absolutely,' she agreed quickly.

Then, she wasn't sure how, they were facing each other.

'Were you always beautiful, or have I only just noticed?' he asked.

It was just like the moment in a novel when the troubled hero removes the shy heroine's glasses. Julia was so nervous she giggled, which made Christopher frown as if he thought she was laughing at him. She had to fight the instinct to tell him that she wasn't beautiful at all, it was just the borrowed dress, but with great difficulty she managed to say nothing.

He glanced back at the hotel terrace, as if to check that no one was looking, and then he said, 'I'd like to kiss you.'

'After that,' she told the girls when she arrived home

later, lifting up her hair to proudly display her first bruise-purple love bite on her milky shoulder, 'he was all over me like a rash.'

'Was it nice?' Bee asked.

'Of course,' said Julia.

In truth, her first proper kiss had been much wetter than she had expected, and nothing at all like the passionate kisses she had shared with David Cassidy or Bjorn Borg in her dreams, nor even as determined and ardent as the actual kiss she had with Adrian King on his first Mirror dinghy when they were both twelve and hadn't realized that you were supposed to open your mouth. But Julia had liked the feeling that shivered right through her when Christopher touched her breasts, although she wasn't sure she should let him, and she had been terrified in case someone came out on to the terrace and saw two white orbs cupped in his hands, shining in the moonlight as if lit by ultraviolet light.

My darling Fiammetta,

I don't know how to start this letter because you are so little now, and I am so sad that I am going to miss finding out what sort of person you will become. I already know that you are clever, because you can recite nursery rhymes. Your favourite is 'Mary, Mary' – I think because you like the soothing rhythm of the words, not because you are contrary. You are a very cooperative little girl. Everyone remarks on it. They say you look like a china doll because of your pale skin and your beautiful red curly hair and bright-blue eyes, and because you sit still. Dearest Fiammetta, it is good to be well behaved, but always remember that you are just as important as anyone else, and don't let anyone boss you around. My hope is that you stay as sweet-natured as you are, but grow up strong too.

There are so many things I wanted to show you, like mountains with snow on top, and Alpine flowers so tiny and perfect you think that fairies have made them, and the

Mediterranean sea as blue as ink, with porpoises playing in
the wash of an island ferry, and Venice, and all the places
I wanted to go with you for the first time, Athens, India,
Egypt, Mexico . . .

Fiammetta, when I was a little girl, I sometimes felt very
sad and lonely that I didn't have a mother, and sometimes
I forgot about it completely. I want you to know that if you
forget about me, I will understand and I won't mind at all.
And one day you will understand that we have experienced
the same thing, and that I am close to you, even though I'm
not there . . .

Fiammetta traced her forefinger over the writing for the
thousandth time, as if she would miraculously connect
with her mother's hand and understand the meaning that
always seemed to elude her. Usually, once she'd managed to
decipher the words on a page, or somebody had read them
to her, she could hear them in her head, as if she was saying
them over (like 'Mary, Mary' she thought), and she understood the meaning that way. But this collection of words
didn't mean anything. They were mostly a description of
how she'd looked when she was little. Fiammetta already
knew that from photographs.

If her mother only had such a little time, like Dad said,
it was pretty stupid to write about what she looked like,
wasn't it?

Instead of feeling sad and lonely, as her mother predicted
she would, Fiammetta was angry, and that made her feel
horrible inside. It wasn't that she had forgotten her mother,
she tried to excuse herself, it was that she'd been too little
to know her at all. It hadn't even crossed her mind to feel
bad about it, until Dad had given her the letter.

Bruno didn't understand what she was going on about.
Bruno's letter was different, but he refused to see that it
was. They'd fallen out for the first time in their lives, and
now he'd taken his letter and hidden it because he said
Fiammetta had ruined it for him. Fiammetta remembered
all the words anyway.

My darling Bruno,

You are such a bundle of energy, and you love to laugh. Listening to your laughter is the best sound in the whole world. You give me the tightest hug, and then you fall asleep so peacefully that I have to put my hand on your cheek several times a night, just to check that you are warm, and also because I can't quite believe my luck in having you. You love music and jumping and the dustbin lorry. Your first words were ''Ello, mate!', which is what the dustmen said to you. And that is how you greet people and it makes them laugh every time. You give me such joy because I thought I wouldn't know what to do with a boy baby, but you make it so easy. You are so affectionate, standing up in your cot to kiss me goodnight, so that I don't have to bend over when my back hurts . . .

It was true that Bruno's letter was shorter than hers, Fiammetta conceded. He'd counted up the words for her. Hers had 293 words and his had 159, so hers was almost twice as long.

'So what's the problem?' Bruno said.

It wasn't a question of length, but Fiammetta couldn't explain why. His letter just proved that their mother had loved him more. But then everyone loved Bruno more, except Barbara, who had loved them both the same.

And if their mother had still been alive, she would still like Bruno better. It was obvious from the third piece of paper with the reading list of books.

Children, these are the books I most loved because they made me think, or dream, or sometimes just laugh: *Persuasion, Middlemarch, Ulysses, Great Expectations, Far From the Madding Crowd, Anna Karenina, Women in Love, Howard's End, Brideshead Revisited, Our Man in Havana, Love in a Cold Climate, The Girls of Slender Means, Lucky Jim, The Country Girls, The Golden Notebook . . . Mrs Tiggy-Winkle, Flower Fairies, Milly-Molly-Mandy, The Family from One End Street, Emil and the Detectives, The Tale of Troy, What Katy Did, The*

Secret Garden, A Traveller in Time, The Far-Distant Oxus,
Little Women, Anne of Green Gables . . .

'. . . Read that, read that, read that. That's for girls. Read that. Girls. Girls. Read it, girls, girls!' Bruno ticked off the list of children's books as if it was homework he'd been set and completed.

For Fiammetta the list was a catalogue of failure. The only title she recognized was *A Traveller in Time*, which Barbara had read as a bedtime story when they still lived at the Castle. It was the story of a little girl who stepped back to Elizabethan times. Barbara always said she could imagine Fiammetta doing the same in the walled garden where it was sometimes so peaceful it felt as if time had stopped still.

The walled garden wasn't even there any more, because Lady Sylvia had knocked it down, Fiammetta thought. Lady Sylvia who'd brought the letters.

'I just found these in that room with all the black furniture . . .' she'd said as Michael had closed the door to the shop, making their conversation inaudible.

When he came upstairs a long time later, Fiammetta had known it was something to do with their mother, because he was staring at nothing like he always used to, and when Bruno started asking him loads of questions there was that delay in responding, as if he didn't quite register.

He had handed the letters over to each of them, saying, 'Your mother must have written these just before she died.'

Fiammetta looked at her letter again; the words were jumping around even more than ever because of the hot tears in her eyes. But it wasn't because she was sad. She was furious. With everyone: Lady Sylvia and Dad and Pascale and Bruno . . . and her mother.

'I don't miss you!' Fiammetta shouted at the letter. 'So there!'

There was a knock at Fiammetta's bedroom door.

'Go away!' Fiammetta shouted.

'Can I come in?'

It was Iris's voice.

'What do you want?' Fiammetta asked, her hostility now a little half-hearted. Nobody had told her that Iris was coming down for the weekend. Iris hardly ever came these days because she was so busy with her job.

'Can I come in?' Iris asked again.

Fiammetta unlocked the door.

'I didn't know you were coming down,' said Fiammetta.

'I thought I would,' said Iris vaguely, turning pink.

'Dad asked you, didn't he?' Fiammetta guessed immediately.

'Yes, he did,' Iris admitted. 'So, what's up?'

She listened for ages, and then Fiammetta let her read the letter. And Iris didn't say anything for ages.

Eventually she looked at her and said, 'Why don't we go out?'

They sat on the cold harbour wall together while Bruno and Nikhil Patel played beach cricket on the cold, wind-swept sand.

Iris didn't say that Fiammetta was being silly, or imagining things, or reading too much into it, like everyone else did. Instead she said she knew exactly how horrible it was when you know your mother loves your brother more. But then she said that even though she hadn't known Claudia very well, she didn't believe that was true with her.

'I only saw Claudia with you for a few minutes,' Iris said. 'And she was being very brave because she didn't want you to know she was in pain, but the main thing I remember is that she was totally determined that you and Bruno should both be equal. She asked me to be your friend because she was concerned about you.'

'Both of us?' Fiammetta interrupted.

'Particularly you,' said Iris. 'I think she knew Bruno would be OK, because Bruno was always a bit of a show-off . . .'

Just at that moment Bruno bowled Nikhil out and

celebrated by running around with his jumper stretched over his head and his arms in the air.

Fiammetta and Iris exchanged little smiles.

'But she worried about you, because she knew it was going to be tougher for a girl,' Iris went on. 'I think that's what she's trying to say in the letter.'

It sounded more plausible than anything anyone else had said to Fiammetta.

'She had lost her own mother when she was just a little bit older than you were,' Iris went on. 'She didn't want you to be surrounded by gloomy old men like she had been. That's what she told me.'

'She actually said that?'

'Absolutely,' Iris assured her.

Fiammetta found that strangely consoling.

'What was she like?' she asked.

'She was incredibly beautiful, not just because she was pretty, if you know what I mean, but because she was so alive. I know that sounds really weird, but there was this vibrancy about her, even when she was lying dying in that dark Chinese room . . .' Iris hesitated. 'This image I have of her . . . it's very sad, right? Do you want to know?'

'Yes . . .' Fiammetta said uncertainly.

'Claudia was in so much pain, but she kept smiling when Bruno hugged her, and then she realized that you hadn't hugged her too, and I think she knew it might be the last time, and so she absolutely demanded that Michael hold you over her so that you could give her a kiss, and she said it was the best kiss in the world . . .' Iris wiped away a tear with her fist.

Fiammetta couldn't remember ever seeing her cry before.

'One thing I do know for certain,' Iris said, 'is that Claudia would have absolutely hated to think she had made you miserable.'

'Would she?'

'Maybe that's why she threw the letter away. Because she knew that nothing she could write would be adequate

'. . . and she didn't want you to get the wrong impression. Come on, let's walk. My bum's freezing,' Iris said, jumping down from the wall.

Walking was a good idea because each pace brought a kind of order to all the bits of information whizzing around in Fiammetta's brain, slotting them into place. She had never had a proper memory of her mother before, only a few photographs – one on the Ponte Vecchio in Florence with Dad, which they must have asked a stranger to take, and the one picture of her with the twins when they were babies, all of them lying asleep in a hammock. Now the new image Iris had provided was so strong, Fiammetta almost felt she could remember being lowered over her mother's face to give her a kiss.

'Why didn't Dad tell me all this?' she asked.

'He didn't see it from the perspective I did,' Iris said.

'Why does he love Pascale?' Fiammetta asked Iris suddenly.

'I don't really know,' Iris said. 'It's better that he isn't sad for ever, isn't it?'

Fiammetta wasn't sure about that, she felt better than she had done for ages. Iris made everything seem so logical.

'My mother obviously thought books were the most important thing.' She tried to find something to hurt herself with again.

'You do know that Claudia wanted to be a painter herself?' Iris said.

'Nobody told me!'

'You don't talk to anyone except Bruno.'

It was just a statement. Not like Iris was blaming her.

'I can't,' said Fiammetta.

'I understand,' said Iris.

But Fiammetta knew she didn't.

'Think of all those things she describes in your letter, like mountains and flowers and porpoises. It's all very visual,' Iris was saying.

'And Venice,' said Fiammetta. 'Lots of artists have painted Venice.'

She picked up a pebble and threw it into the sea. They both watched as a silent circle of ripples spread across the water.

'Tell you what, why don't we go there one day?' Iris suggested.

'When?' asked Fiammetta.

'As soon as we've got the time and the money,' Iris promised.

'What else do you know about my mother?'

'She was a feminist . . . of sorts,' Iris qualified. 'She was left wing, concerned about the arms race . . .'

'I'm concerned about the arms race,' said Fiammetta.

Iris looked at her and smiled. 'Me too,' she said.

'Do you think,' Fiammetta whispered, hardly daring to ask, 'do you think that I'm at all like her?'

Iris looked at her for a long time, and then she finally said, 'I think maybe you have her honesty. She struck me as a very honest person.'

Chapter Eleven

1981

With no previous experience of relationships, Julia was never certain whether things were proceeding on the physical side at the pace they were supposed to. Although there was expert advice on hand from Bee, Julia was reluctant to confide in her friend in case Bee made her feel more stupid and naïve. She could vaguely remember hearing the sixth-form girls on the back seat of the coach that used to ferry them to and from the boys' school hops discussing whether they had 'gone all the way there' with their latest conquest, which Julia had taken to mean full sexual intercourse, but she didn't really know what the stages in between kissing and 'all the way there' actually were. How far should she let Christopher go and how quickly? Was he disappointed when she pushed his hand away as it strayed close to the zip of her jeans? Was he beginning to think that she was too young and silly for him, or did her innocence have a certain old-fashioned appeal after some of the girls he was rumoured to have slept with, her sister Joanna among them.

Christopher's facial expression gave little away. Sometimes he seemed a little cross, but mostly his eyes had the same faintly amused gleam as that first time he had looked at her properly in the Victoria Gardens.

'Still waters run deep,' was the way that Granny Ruby put it.

Almost the best bit about going out with Christopher was getting invited every Sunday for lunch at the Palace Hotel. It was lovely to have food cooked for you after living mainly on Vesta meals. Sitting at the big table in the private dining room with the whole King family reminded Julia of Christmas lunches when she was a child. There were subtle differences in the way the Kings treated her now. Eddie King pulled her chair out for her as if she was a lady. Granny Ruby and Granny Liliana watched her from the card table with fixed smiles that reminded Julia for some reason of the old ladies who used to knit beside the guillotine. She had to restrain herself from laughing at Winny's jokes because Christopher said they were puerile, which was a grown-up way of saying silly. Julia usually sat next to Eddie, who had the knack of putting anyone at their ease, and Julia grew less nervous and tongue-tied as she talked to him. Sometimes she would catch Eddie exchanging an approving raised eyebrow with Auntie Libby at the end of the table.

One rainy February Sunday after lunch, when it was too wet to go for a walk, Christopher took Julia to his bedroom in the private wing of the hotel. Although she'd spent half her childhood in and out of Adrian and Winny's room, and had run past Christopher's door on countless occasions, she had never been inside, and was surprised to see it was quite large, with windows on two sides and a double bed where Adrian and Winny had bunks. Christopher closed the door. There was a picture of a naked lady in a shell on the wall, which Julia pretended to be interested in because the double bed made her nervous. Christopher said it was by someone called Botticelli and Julia had to stop herself giggling at the rude-sounding name.

'Do you like it?' he asked.

'Oh, yes! It's very good,' Julia lied, not knowing where to look. Bed one way, naked woman the other.

She walked over to the window. It was already getting dark. Christopher's room was to the front elevation of the hotel, but visibility was poor and, at the far end of the Rhododendron Mile, she could only just make out the Swiss-cottage roof of the Summer House where she'd lived as a child.

Suddenly and quite unexpectedly Christopher kissed the back of her neck.

A shiver trickled all the way down Julia's spine.

'You're a very sweet girl,' he murmured.

Julia stared out of the window, hardly daring to breathe, remembering how as a child she had sat looking out of her bedroom window under the eaves, waiting for something to happen.

'There's something I've been meaning to ask you,' said Christopher.

Julia lost her virginity in Christopher's bedroom that rainy afternoon. It hurt a bit when his thing went into her, and she didn't really know what she was supposed to do with her hands as she lay spreadeagled underneath him, but she enjoyed the pleasure she seemed to be giving him as his breathing became faster and faster, and her happiness was finally complete when he shouted, 'Yes!' and shuddered to a standstill.

Afterwards, he fell asleep, but she lay wide awake wondering whether she dare ask him if she could have a bath in his en-suite facilities. When they'd done repro- duction at school, the Biology mistress had drawn a single little tadpole sperm on the blackboard with an arrow to the triangular cross section of womb where the egg was, but Julia had no idea that it would be swimming in at least a pint of sticky stuff.

On her return to the gatehouse that evening, she was sure that Cee and Bee would smell that it had happened, even if it wasn't obvious from her face. But both of them were glued to *Brideshead Revisited* on the television and barely looked up. After a lovely hot soak, Julia put on her dressing gown and went down to tell them that Christopher had proposed.

'And what did you say?' Bee asked sarcastically.

302

'I said, yes, please!'

As Cee rushed over to give her a hug, and Bee reluctantly offered congratulations, Julia couldn't help feeling a tiny bit superior. She was engaged to be married, the first one of them to become a proper, grown-up woman.

Iris was looking out of her office window on the twelfth floor. The cherry trees were in bloom in Regent's Park. From high above, it looked as if someone had scattered a bag of pink and white marshmallows on the bright-green grass. She promised herself that she would get a sandwich for lunch and go and sit under one of them in a peaceful canopy of blossom. She'd recently taken on a beautifully written crime novel, by an English woman who had lived in Japan, entitled, *The Cherry Blossom Murder.* Apparently, the flowering of the cherry tree was so significant to the Japanese that there was a blossom forecast on television during the brief flowering season. It was such a lovely idea, Iris wished the English weather would be enlivened by something similar. A bluebell forecast, perhaps, or a yellow arrow to show the drift of roadside daffodils up the country from the warm climes of the south coast towards the Lake District and on to the chilly highlands of Scotland. Was it really true there was a cherry forecast in Japan? Iris suddenly wondered, realizing that she had unquestioningly accepted it as fact although she had only learned about it in a novel.

Perhaps they should publish the book at cherry blossom time next year, and hold the launch party under a tree . . .

So far she had bought three first novels for her new imprint, which, after much thought and discussion, she had decided to call Capital Books because it went with the Portico logo of a classical column, sounded urban, and wouldn't limit her to publishing books by women. The plan was to launch the list with six books initially, and the temptation to buy something that would just about do, instead of something that was brilliant and original, was sometimes difficult to resist. But she knew she had been given a unique opportunity, and she didn't want to squander it.

A light tap on the half-glass wall of her office made her look up, but it was a rhetorical request for permission because Roman was already in the room. He pointed at the window as if to ask what was so fascinating out there that she had failed to register his presence.

'I was looking at the cherry trees,' Iris said. 'I thought I might go and sit under one with my sandwich.'

'Lovely idea. I would join you, but . . .' Roman checked his watch, 'I am due at the Savoy Grill in exactly two minutes . . .'

It crossed Iris's mind to point out that she hadn't actually invited him under her cherry tree anyway.

'Read your Irish short-story writer,' said Roman, perching on her desk. 'I do agree with you, but couldn't we do a novel first? Short stories are so difficult.'

'I was thinking of offering her a two-book deal. We would publish the stories, but only after a novel.'

'Excellent,' said Roman. 'Does she have an agent?'

'Not yet.'

'Ever more excellent,' said Roman.

Iris wasn't sure about the ethics of offering first-time authors derisory sums for their work in the knowledge that they would accept anything to be published. She wasn't even sure that it was a wise start to what was intended to be a long-term relationship, but she also recognized that she was not yet powerful enough to put this argument to her boss.

'Make sure you get world rights, and film. The Irish government are offering tax breaks for films made in Ireland. Could be an interesting place in the next few years.'

Iris admired the way Roman immediately saw the connection between things like economics and culture. Publishing was still a gentleman's profession in many senses of the word, and there was a general tendency to sneer at words like 'marketing' and 'margins'. Roman Stone had a gentleman's charm, but he was an entrepreneur by nature, anxious to make the most of any opportunity.

'By the way,' Roman turned to leave for his lunch, 'your father's sent me a short story. I wondered, perhaps, if you'd like to cast your eagle eye . . .'

'I imagine he would have sent it to me if he'd wanted my opinion.' Iris bristled with indignation. Roman's face lifted momentarily, unaware that her father hadn't shown her the story until she'd just told him, she realized, feeling slightly wrong-footed.

Iris knew that her father was writing again because she'd heard the old Remington typewriter rattling away when she went down to Kingshaven. When he emerged from his study, he was preoccupied, as she could remember him being when she was a child, as if there was another set of characters going on in his head that made it difficult for him to concentrate on the more mundane matter of real life. But when she asked him if it was a novel, he simply shook his head, and she'd been wary of further probing in case the work was at such a fragile stage that talking about it put a brake on his creativity.

'Well, I'll leave it up to you,' said Roman, checking his watch. 'It's on my desk, if you change your mind.'

And then he was gone.

The Zen calmness that Iris had been looking forward to achieving under the cherry tree refused to flow. The noise from the Euston Road, which was completely inaudible from her office up on the twelfth floor, was almost deafening at fifty yards; then there was the wasp that seemed to find her egg mayonnaise on granary more attractive than the nectar of a thousand flowers. Even if she could manage to block these physical irritants, there was the thought of her father's story, lying enticingly on the leather top of Roman's walnut desk.

Why did it matter that he hadn't told her? Iris asked herself. Perhaps he was only trying to protect her. What she didn't know, she wouldn't feel responsible for, and so there was no chance of her feeling awkward at work. And yet this seemed an improbably selfless motive. Iris thought her father's reasoning (if he had thought about it at all) was probably far more straightforward than that. It simply wouldn't occur to him that she might have any power in Portico Books. Although she was thirty, she was still his child, and female. She remembered telling him when she'd got her first job at Harridan, he'd said, 'As a secretary?'

Now she had a secretary of her own, and an office with a view, and still he didn't take her seriously! The resentment was exactly the same as Iris had felt as a teenager, and which she now recognized in Fiammetta. Your family was where you felt most needed (the peculiar thrill she had felt when her father had rung up at his wits' end, and said she was the only person who might be able to get through to Fiammetta), and most undervalued. Sometimes Iris felt she would only be a free person if she never had to see any of them ever again, but she knew that their physical presence would only be replaced by guilt. Family was an inescapable loop.

Maybe Josie had been right, Iris thought, when she had told her she should see an analyst. Josie always had a solution to everyone else's problems, and if they didn't take it, then they had only themselves to blame. To be fair, she'd offered to pay, when Iris had made the excuse that she couldn't possibly afford it, but it wasn't just the money. Analysis was all about finding things out about yourself, and Iris thought she knew enough about herself already. She'd had plenty of time to think about why she was like she was. Being aware of formative events didn't erase them. What good did talking about it endlessly do, apart from making you relive everything you were trying to forget?

All the staff on the fourteenth floor of the building were out at lunch. Even though he'd effectively given her permission, Iris felt slightly naughty as she went into Roman's office and closed the door behind her. Checking her watch, she was sure there was no chance of him returning for at least another half-hour, so she dared herself to sit in his comfortable padded swivel chair, the only modern piece of furniture in the room, and twirl a couple of times, like a child on a playground roundabout. Then she picked up the story, smiling at the title, 'The Romans in Britain'.

The previous year, there had been a furore about Howard Brenton's new play with the same title at the National Theatre, which featured a simulated homosexual rape of a Briton by a Roman soldier. The GLC had threatened to withdraw the theatre's grant; Mary Whitehouse had vowed to take it to court for obscenity. Michael's story used the discovery of an erotic mosaic under the turf of a very proper English middle-class town and the Establishment's efforts to cover it up as a metaphor for censorship. It was a funny piece, narrated in the third person, rather than the first person, as his novels had been.

'It's a shame there's nothing like the *New Yorker* in this country . . .'

Iris jumped at the sound of Roman's voice right behind her. She had been so engrossed she hadn't heard him enter the room, and she felt as if she'd been caught red-handed.

'That particular story would be perfect,' he said.

'Yes,' Iris agreed. 'Perhaps we should start a literary magazine like the *New Yorker* here.'

It was a throwaway comment, but she could immediately see from his eyes that Roman's interest was sparked.

'To showcase our new talent, and some of our old talent, of course . . . perhaps as a one-off . . .' she expanded, the idea taking shape in her head as she spoke.

'Why don't you bring it up at the next planning meeting?' Roman suggested.

Working with Roman was one of the most creative processes Iris had ever experienced. Even though he could sometimes be infuriatingly patronizing, his confidence in his own intellect enabled him to entertain ideas without being threatened by the fact he hadn't come up with them himself. She was aware that some of the more senior editors resented their rapport, and Trish, Iris's secretary, had even hinted that people thought they were sleeping together, which was ludicrous, but the buzz she got from working for him did make her feel alive and attractive in a way that no other job had ever done.

'So, are there dirty mosaics lurking under Kingshaven?' Roman pointed at the story.

'There was a discovery of Roman coins a while back,' Iris said. 'I think my father probably made the mosaics up.'

'Like he made up the affair in *The Right Thing*,' said Roman.

'And the runaway teenager in *Hide and Seek*,' Iris added, picking up on his reference to dialogue in Harold Pinter's recent play *Betrayal*, in which the publisher and the literary agent joke about the autobiographical nature of their successful novelist's latest work.

Roman put his hand on her arm and she suddenly felt a little panic-stricken by his closeness. She could smell that he had been drinking red wine at lunch. His eyes seemed to search hers for an answer, but she wasn't sure any more what question he was asking.

When a teacher, Mr Green, called from Lowhampton Comprehensive to ask whether Michael had received the note he'd sent home with Fiammetta, Michael was so perturbed he didn't think to ask what it was about, but instead agreed to come into the school straight away for a meeting.

He left the warehouse in a hurry to catch the twelve o'clock bus to Lowhampton, but halfway along the promenade stopped in his tracks, noticing that he was wearing flat navy espadrilles with the backs trodden down, and corduroy trousers with a black stain in the corner of one of the pockets where a biro had leaked. The one o'clock bus would still leave him plenty of time, he thought, quickly walking back to change, selecting his better pair of corduroy trousers, brown lace-up shoes, a checked Viyella shirt and a straight knitted tie. The impression was smart but unconventional, he hoped. It was important not to embarrass his children, but he didn't want to look too deferential either.

As the bus chugged along the coast road, Michael's mind whirled with possible scenarios. He couldn't imagine his daughter swearing at a teacher, or harming anyone. The school seemed perfectly happy with Fiammetta's progress. She had been diagnosed as dyslexic and was now given extra help with reading and writing. When he went to parents' evenings, the teachers all made a point of praising her verbal contributions. Privately, he'd wondered whether they were talking about the same child.

What could Fiammetta have done that was so bad it warranted calling him in? After the terrible time with Claudia's letter, when Michael had feared for her sanity, Fiammetta now seemed a little more at ease. He'd thought he'd detected a slight relaxation of the invisible rigid barriers she put up between herself and him. He'd dared to hope that things were improving.

Michael waited outside the staff room, as nervous and defensive as if he were a guilty pupil himself. The door opened, letting out a blast of cigarette smoke, and a man emerged who introduced himself as Steve Green. He had longish hair and wore glasses with small round wire frames. He looked far too young to be a teacher. Michael was acutely conscious of how old, at fifty, he must appear to him. They walked along empty corridors, which, even though it was a relatively new building, smelled like every school Michael had ever been in – a combination of chalk dust, rubber plimsoles and sweaty feet, with a humid hint of cabbage. Allowing himself a glance into the classrooms where lessons were in progress, Michael ducked out of the way when the children nearest the door looked back at him. Mr Green chatted on personably, giving no indication of why he had summoned him.

'What subject do you teach?' Michael asked.

'Didn't your daughter tell you?'

'My daughter tells me very little!' Michael tried to make

himself appear relaxed, but the attempted lightness only made him sound more stuffy and middle-aged.

'I teach Art,' said the young man, pushing his long black fringe back from his face. 'It's my first year at the school.'

Art. What could Fiammetta have possibly got up to in Art? For a moment, Michael thought of the thick grey and black paint she used to plaster all over her own drawings. Surely she hadn't done that to other people's work? How would he begin to explain that?

'Here we are, then,' said Mr Green, pushing open the art room door.

It was pleasantly disorganized, with easels from the previous lesson not yet cleared away, but the big teacher's table at the front was carefully laid out with a series of about twenty paintings, which Michael initially assumed to be the product of a whole class's attempt at the same assignment. From a distance, he could see they were all copies of the Edvard Munch painting *The Scream*, but as he drew closer it became clear that they were the work of one person; all, in effect, self-portraits. Almost like frames from a cartoon, the subtly changing expressions on the girl's face told the story of the scream, from dumbstruck fear through anger, anguish, darkness to final release. The background swirls of colour also changed through the sequence, from innocent pastels at the beginning through those dark, familiar blacks and greys, to a technicolour riot of fluorescent swirls that gave the final scream an almost joyous quality.

'Well, what do you think?' asked Mr Green gently.

'They're . . .' Michael felt he himself was being judged. He knew how important it was to choose the correct word. 'Disturbing,' he finally said.

'I suppose you're right,' said Mr Green, looking again, as if this was something that hadn't occurred to him.

'What do you think?' Michael threw the question back.

'I think your daughter has a prodigious talent, Mr Quinn. I'll come straight to the point. There's an exhibition of young local art students coming up at the Town

Hall. Fiammetta's much younger, of course, but I'd like to try to get her work in, if I have your permission . . . ?'

'That's what you brought me here for?'

His relief came out like impatience. Mr Green cowered slightly.

'I thought if you saw the work . . . I'm sorry if I've—'

'No! No!' Michael tried to reassure him. 'No, I'm very glad you did. Glad of the opportunity. My daughter's quite, well . . . I had no idea . . .'

He looked again. His knowledge of art was inadequate, gleaned from the meagre selection of books in Kingshaven library, a trip to Italy with Claudia, and a series of WEA lectures attended only by him and the unlikely fellow student Christopher King in the church hall a while back, but anyone could see that these were extraordinary paintings for a thirteen-year-old.

'I'll get her, shall I?' asked Mr Green, and was out of the art room before Michael had a chance to say that he didn't think it was necessarily a good idea for Fiammetta to know that he was there.

Michael stood staring at the paintings, examining each one, studying the tiny nuances she had managed to capture with such technical skill. Where did such talent come from? For a moment, he thought of Claudia's girlish watercolours. She had wanted to learn to paint properly, but there had never been the time. How proud she would be now! He tried to imagine her standing next to him, examining the paintings.

He could hear Mr Green's chatty voice approaching along the corridor.

'I've got a bit of a surprise for you,' he was saying.

'What sort of surprise?'

It was a shock to hear Fiammetta speak, not just a whole sentence, but a whole sentence spoken with smiling familiarity as if she was used to joking with the teacher.

'Someone I think was a bit surprised himself, actually.'

'Who?' A giggle. 'Who is it?'

And then Mr Green pushed open the door and held

311

it open with his arm, allowing Fiammetta to duck in under.

Her face, the same face as in the paintings, flipped rapidly through another range of emotions as she looked from Michael to her teacher, and back again. When she looked at her teacher, Michael observed, her expression was alive, but when she looked at him, the blankness returned.

'Hi, Dad!' she said, with an embarrassed kind of teenage shrug.

'You're a bit of a dark horse, aren't you?' said Michael, immediately regretting the clichéd choice of words. 'Mr Green seems to think you're very talented . . .' Now he sounded like an archetypal parent in a sitcom. 'I think you're very talented too. Bravo!' he tried again, but the moment had gone. He should have said it straight away.

'I wanted to ask your father's permission to put you in an exhibition,' Mr Green explained, as if he had picked up on the awkwardness between them.

'And what did he say?' Fiammetta addressed the teacher.

'I said yes, of course,' Michael told her.

'Oh, thank you! Thank you!' Fiammetta exclaimed.

But she was talking to Mr Green, not to him.

'I'll get back to you,' Mr Green said, offering his hand for Michael to shake as the bell went, and they could hear the next class lining up outside the art room.

'You can go home with your dad,' he told Fiammetta, as if it was a treat. 'Don't worry. I'll tell the office.'

The bus back from Lowhampton was virtually empty. Even though Michael thought his daughter would have preferred to sit on her own, she slumped reluctantly beside him, and the seat felt too small for both of them.

It was rare for the two of them to be alone together, and Michael knew he should take advantage of the opportunity, but he couldn't think of anything she might want him to say to her.

There were all sorts of questions he would have liked to

ask her about how she came up with ideas for her paintings and what she was going to do next. Would she like him to search out books on art for her? But Michael knew from experience that Fiammetta closed up even more when confronted with questions, her impassive face becoming almost panicky. Eventually, the intense pressure of wanting to say something overcame the fear of her displeasure.

'I'm so proud of you, you know. And your mother would have been too. Immensely proud.'

There was a long pregnant silence.

'And Barbara?' Fiammetta finally whispered.

Had she meant so much to her?

'I'm sure Barbara would have been thrilled to bits!' said Michael, not daring to look at his daughter directly, but aware of her looking at the side of his face, perhaps with an artist's eye, he thought, working out how she was going to put it on paper, which frightened him a little.

He turned his face away, and stared out of the window at the landscape of rolling green fields with its backdrop of rushing clouds, which made it look as if the whole world was in flux.

The town's delight at the announcement of Julia Allsop's engagement to Christopher King took everyone at the Palace by surprise. There had been a sense that the hotel's place as the principal focus of the town's identity had been eroded in recent years by the council's sale of several important amenities, such as the pier, to outside contractors who offered a more modern, commercial approach to tourism. Holidaymakers now had the choice of sweet and sour pork, or chicken biryani, as well as fish and chips. The opening of Mr Patel's first Sunny Stores Supermarket and the consequent closure of several long-established businesses, such as the greengrocery and the baker's, created a sense of unease that the town was sliding inexorably into a future it had no control over. A romantic union between the town's two most established native families was reassuringly traditional, and the announcement appeared in the local newspaper under the headline: 'Heir to the Palace to Wed Girl Next Door!'

A photographer was dispatched to take a photograph of Julia at Kingshaven's nursery school, where she posed shyly with some of the more photogenic children, and naïvely admitted that she had always believed in fairy tales and dreamed of living at the Palace.

Until she read it in the newspaper, Julia often wondered whether her relationship with Christopher was real or just wishful thinking. Now it was public, and people kept congratulating her in the street, she suddenly began to believe it was happening. She grew more confident, learning to say simply 'Thank you' instead of 'I hope so' when people told her she would make a lovely bride. She lost more weight and asked Daddy to lend her some money for appropriate clothes to wear at the Palace functions. Snubbing Sylvia's offer to design her wedding dress, Julia took herself off to London to try on dresses in the bridal department of John Lewis, and to purchase smart flat shoes in Russell & Bromley with Mummy, whose only question, when her daughter had told her the news, was a slightly disappointing, 'Are you sure he's tall enough for you?'

The wedding, once announced, seemed to have a momentum all of its own – the wording of the invitations, the choice of bridesmaids, the list, the flowers, the bridesmaids' dresses, the menu, the cake. Julia was up at the Palace sorting things out so regularly that Auntie Libby let her have use of one of the rooms, without a sea view, obviously, just down the corridor from Granny Ruby's permanent suite.

Although Christopher was extremely busy with his duties, which included responsibility for the grounds and the gardens, occasionally, there would be a knock on her door in the afternoon, and they would do it on the hotel bed, just like a proper honeymooning couple, which was much nicer and more comfortable than doing it outside. Julia was sick of trying to get the grass stains out of her skirts and finding bits of twig in her hair. Once, he'd even suggested they do it in the derelict railway station, which was about halfway between the Palace and the gatehouse, and she'd surprised herself by having the courage to tell him, no, she didn't think that would be suitable at all.

Iris fancied a drink, but she didn't want to ask Trish. Negotiating a balance of power with her secretary had been one of the things she'd found trickiest about her new job. She'd started off absolutely determined to treat Trish as a friend, but she found that made it difficult to ask her to do anything like type a letter. Going out for drinks after work had become a habit she'd also come to regret. In a big company, there was always going to be a 'them' and an 'us'. However much Iris wanted to think of herself as one of the workers, she was one of the bosses now. Trying to keep a foot in both camps ran the risk of making the bosses lose respect and the workers think she was a spy. Increasingly often Iris found herself picking up a bottle of white wine on her way home from work to drink with Vic. Except Vic was always out cruising, and so she ended up drinking it by herself.

Just as she was leaving the office, Iris's phone rang.

'Lyme Regis is your part of the world, isn't it?' said Roman's voice.

'It's a way down the coast,' said Iris.

'I've been invited to a screening of *The French Lieutenant's Woman*, do you want to come?'

'When?' Iris automatically began flipping through her diary.

'Now.'

'I'm not dressed,' said Iris, looking at the grey trouser suit she nearly always wore for work.

Roman said nothing, but she could almost hear his smile at the end of the phone.

'I meant for going out,' Iris expanded.

'It's only a screening, not a premiere,' he said, which made her feel she'd committed another *faux pas* for not knowing the difference.

The screening room was in a basement in Soho whose door Iris had walked past a thousand times without noticing. The carpeted staircase that led down from the street had a particular smell that took Iris back to the staircase down to the Zebra Crossing, the club Clive had managed before it was raided and closed down, a hint of damp mingling with stale alcohol and cigarettes. In the sixties, Iris had thought it the scent of glamour.

At the bottom of the stairs, there were about twenty people hovering in the lobby and a tray of glasses of red or white wine. Iris had the usual feeling she always had when she first went into a party, that she was the tallest person there and that she knew no one.

She was aware of someone coming down the stairs behind them just before the person said loudly, 'Iris?'

Iris spun round.

'Josie!'

'What are you doing here?' Josie demanded, always aggressive until she was in complete control of the facts.

'Roman asked me,' Iris said, unable to think of a stronger answer. 'Do you know Roman Stone?' She introduced them.

Now Roman was the one looking intrigued. Josie's column and her increasingly regular appearances on television had given her the dubious distinction of being the feminist whose sayings were most often mocked in *Private Eye*'s 'Wimmin' column.

'I've always considered Fowles's novel a massive act of masturbation,' Josie said loudly, as if people expected her to say something outrageous, like a modern-day Dorothy Parker.

Iris wondered if she was being particularly rude and controversial as a cover for her embarrassment at their unexpected meeting. Josie looked formidable, she thought, with her hair cut in a long bob and dyed the colour of an aubergine and her bright expressive eyes daring anyone to contradict her, but when you had lived with someone for six years, you knew when they were nervous.

'Can I get you a drink?' Roman offered, leaving them together.

'I heard you were one of his protégées,' Josie said a little more quietly, but with unmistakable innuendo.

'I'm a commissioning editor,' said Iris neutrally. 'You look well,' she added, unable to think of anything else.

'It's yoga,' said Josie.

'Yoga?'

'You should come. It's tremendously balancing,' said Josie, refusing the glass of wine Roman had brought back for her. 'Far better than alcohol,' she said, looking at the wine glass as Iris took hers.

Josie had always been a great proselytizer, insisting that everyone else must try whatever her latest solution to life's problems happened to be. For a while, it had been Jungian analysis, then it was not eating carbohydrates at the same time as protein, then feminism separatism, and now, clearly, it was yoga. The unifying theme, if there was one, seemed to be that in order to face the world, you had to be sorted out inside yourself, but Iris thought that numbing inner turmoil with a glass of wine was an equally effective, if lazier, option.

'I do hope they're not going to try to replicate the novel's pretentious post-modernism on the screen, or we are in for a tedious couple of hours,' said Josie, as Roman returned with his own wine and they went in to take their seats.

'Another Oscar for Streep,' she pronounced equally loudly, as they emerged into the still-light street at the end of the film, adding, as she waved down a cab, 'There's nothing Hollywood likes more than a mute woman.'

Without her, the street felt curiously empty for a moment or two.

'How do you two know each other?' Roman asked Iris.

'I used to live with her,' Iris told him.

He could make of that what he wanted. It seemed a very long time ago now.

They began to amble along side by side, as if neither of them were quite ready to go home.

'Would you like a drink?' Roman asked.

'OK, then,' said Iris, welcoming the chance to talk through the film, which she'd found absorbing if rather disturbing in its portrayal of a damaged red-headed loner in a place very similar to Kingshaven.

'I really liked the device of the film within the film,' she said, as they pushed their way through to an alcove in the crowded Salisbury pub. 'I thought it really worked, didn't you?'

'Yes,' Roman agreed, looking at her over the top of his glass. She could never quite tell whether he found her fascinating or banal.

'I've never quite known what we're meant to think of Sarah,' Iris went on. 'Is she a mad fantasist, or is she really a woman betrayed?'

'I suppose she could be both,' said Roman a little distractedly.

Was she boring him?

'Didn't you used to call yourself Sarah?' he asked, out of the blue, as if the memory had just occurred to him.

'Are you implying I'm a mad fantasist?' Iris asked.

'I'm interested in why someone should choose to live pseudonymously at such a young age.'

She wondered whether she wanted to tell him, whether she knew why herself.

'When I was a child I had an imaginary friend called Sarah Bird,' she began to explain. 'A kind of alter ego, I suppose. Sarah was the one who tore my skirt when I was climbing trees or who knocked over my glass of Ribena . . .'

'I see,' said Roman with a smile, as if he had learned something significant.

'When I ran away to London, I decided I would be Sarah. It's a more anonymous name than Iris.'

'And did Sarah continue to behave badly?'

One of the reasons for his power, Iris thought, was that he made you want to impress him. For a moment, she saw him as almost vampiric, sucking her secrets from her like blood. She was telling him things she had never told anyone else, not Josie, not even Vic, and it felt dangerous, but it was seductive.

'Most of the time, she was very good,' Iris said, affecting a demure look.

'But when she was bad . . .' he continued.

Iris felt herself colouring. They were playing a game. She was just as competitive as he, but he always just had the edge. Suddenly she felt she had revealed too much.

'Anyway, I'm Iris again now,' she said.

'Yes,' said Roman, picking up her glass. 'Another?'

'I'd better be getting back.'

'Someone waiting for you?' he asked.

'Yes,' she said, looking at him directly, knowing exactly what he meant and not knowing why she was lying.

The disused railway station had become their place, like a favourite hotel room, Christopher thought, although ironically a hotel room was the one place that had never been available to them. The railway station was his version of the Summer House in the grounds of the Palace, which had originally been used by his great-grandfather for romantic encounters. Christopher's great-grandfather had a notorious penchant for girls from the lower orders. It was even said that he'd built the Pier Theatre for one of his mistresses who'd been a music-hall actress. Was it possible that adultery ran in the King family? Christopher wasn't unaware that there were rumours about his own father, Eddie, implying his solo yachtsmanship wasn't quite as solo as he claimed.

The trouble was, Christopher thought, looking fondly down at his lover's flushed cheeks and the fan of golden hair spread over the dusty floorboards, it didn't feel like adultery with Milly. Adultery was what used to go on in the cheaper rooms at the back of a hotel in the days before divorces became easy to obtain. Adultery was women giggling as the men they were with signed the register 'Smith'. Adultery was what his sister Angela had made him watch from spyholes in strategic broom cupboards around the Palace Hotel when they were children.

There was nothing sordid about what he felt for Milly. He loved Milly, had always loved her. But this would be the last time they were together.

'What's the problem?' Milly's lips were always deliciously red after sex.

'The problem is I love you,' he said simply.

Her face was even more lovely when she smiled.

She put a finger up to his lips to shush him, but he knew that she liked hearing it.

'We've always known it would end,' she said, sitting up and putting a cigarette between her lips. 'I can't leave my kids or the pub, and you're about to get a nice young wife.'

'But I want you,' Christopher blurted. 'Granny Lily's the only one who'd never come round. And she's—' He stopped himself saying her age. He'd never wish harm to darling Granny Lily, but she surely couldn't go on much longer?

'No, you don't. Not really,' said Milly. 'We're worlds apart, you and me.'

Christopher stood up and perused the wooden panelling on which the initials of many sweethearts had been carved in the years since the railway station's sole use had been as a trysting place. An absurdly romantic impulse made him take out his car key and scratch their initials on the wood panelling. Beneath the dark stain, the wood was yellow and smelled of fresh sawdust.

'Vandal!' said Milly, coming up behind him.

He turned and kissed her on the nose.

'Is that right?' he asked, pointing at his initials carved above hers.

'People usually put a heart around,' she told him. 'Give me the key!'

With her tongue sticking out over her bottom lip in concentration, Milly carefully enclosed the initials in a heart and added another set of letters.

'What does that mean?' Christopher asked, trailing his finger over as if he was trying to decipher a code.

'Millicent Balls and Christopher King for ever,' she said.

He grabbed her hands, looked into her eyes. 'I can't bear to let you go!' he told her.

'We'll still be friends,' she said.

But in his heart, he doubted that would ever be enough. 'Milly . . . !'

She put a finger over his lips. 'You go now. I'll wait here and count to a hundred!' she told him, just like she always did.

The wedding date was set for the end of July, and on the last morning of the summer term, the nursery school children presented Julia with a huge collage card they had made of her in a white net wedding dress, with a round face, two single thick brown strands of wool hair, pearlized blue buttons for eyes and a curve of red felt for a smile. Julia had it under her arm together with the big box of Terry's All Gold and the frilly garter the dinner ladies had clubbed together to buy as her leaving present, and was feeling a little empty and sad after all the goodbyes, as she walked back to the gatehouse.

At the fork by the old railway station, Julia turned left into the lane that wound steeply up to the Castle and linked up with the main road that led down to the Harbour End. She was just passing the turning to the station when a white Hillman Imp came out so quickly Julia was forced back against the hedgerow. The car shot up the lane and over the humpback bridge so fast Julia couldn't see who was driving. Slightly shaken, she continued walking. From the crest of the humpback bridge over the little stream she looked back at the railway station. It was a perfectly peaceful summer day. The air was filled with birdsong. There was no one about. Suddenly, curiosity got the better of her.

Most of the windows were boarded up and covered with spray-painted graffiti, but the door opened with surprising ease. Inside, shafts of sunlight filtered in through the slits between the boards and lit up the dust motes dancing in the air. A slight smell of soot remained from the long-ago years of steam engines. The abandoned railway station had obviously been the venue for countless assignations over the years. Julia traced her finger over initials scratched into the wooden shutters of the ticket window.

In 1971 UTA loved SI and GB loved MB.

In 1972, GB was 4 ALK (was it the same GB, Julia wondered), because in 1973, the initials of GB and MB were back again with a big heart around them.

Slightly embarrassed to be intruding on other people's intimacies, Julia's eye was drawn to a recent inscription, still a pale straw colour exuding a faint smell of sawn timber as she sniffed it.

'1981 MB + ACCK 4ever'.

Surrounded by the simple record of other people's passion, the place suddenly seemed rather romantic and Julia regretted her own prudishness when her fiancé had suggested meeting here. Now she longed for him to take her in the pool of sunlight on the booking-hall floor and scratch CK loves JA on the floorboards afterwards.

And then it occurred to her.

Why not? He was her fiancé, after all!

Julia hurried home to the gatehouse, dumped her leaving presents, changed into a summer skirt, and, in an act of daring she thought even Bee would approve of, took off her panties. Today would mark a new beginning. She would let Christopher do whatever he wanted. They would go to the railway station and make love on the floor. Maybe she would even find the courage to do what the lady in the Roman mosaic had been doing as he had once hinted he would like her to. Julia had to fight the urge to be sick whenever she tried to brace herself to the idea of putting his thing in her mouth.

The lawns on either side of the hotel drive were as smooth as bowling greens and it was easy to forget that the trench had ever been there. Christopher was in the rose garden, staring out to sea, absently dead-heading the pink and yellow climbers on the pergola where the wedding photographs would be taken.

'I've finished work,' said Julia, adding, when he looked slightly mystified, 'It was my last day today.'

'Of course,' he said.

'So I'm now a lady of leisure!' Julia said, shifting her balance nervously from foot to foot. 'It's exciting, isn't it?' she asked, trying to hold his attention.

'What?'

'The wedding! Only two weeks now!'

'I'll be glad when it's over,' he said with his usual dry humour.

'Quite,' said Julia with a nervous giggle.

'Look,' Christopher was finally looking at her, 'are you absolutely sure you can bear to take on me and my family?'

Julia was startled. 'I love your family,' she assured him, and then, thinking that sounded a bit peculiar, she added quietly, 'and I love you.'

'I don't deserve you,' said Christopher.

What a sweet thing to say!

'Of course you do!' she enthused.

Now was the moment to be bold.

'It's such a lovely afternoon, I was wondering if you'd like to go for a walk.' She pulled in her tummy, smoothed the flimsy cotton skirt over her hips, attempting to look as sexy as she could.

'As you can see, I'm rather busy,' Christopher replied, waving vaguely at the pergola.

'It's just, well, we haven't really seen each other for days . . .' Julia did her best to flutter her eyelashes to give a heavy hint about what she had in mind.

'We'll be together all the time when we're married,' said Christopher.

On the way home, Julia kept going over the conversation again and again in her head. He said he didn't deserve her, which was nice if you looked at it one way, but taken with

323

what he said after, she couldn't help wondering if he was getting cold feet. All the insecurities she had managed to bury deep inside herself since he proposed now came shooting back up to the surface. Maybe she was too young and stupid for him. Maybe it had all been a dream as unreal as the one she used to have where David Cassidy was appearing at the Pier Theatre, noticed her sitting in the first row of the stalls, and fell instantly in love?

'We'll be together all the time when we're married.'

If it was his way of saying that they were going to live happily ever after, why had he made it sound like a life sentence?

As if to confirm all her worst fears, Christopher did not call that evening, nor the day after. On the third day, Julia began to panic. With no job to take her mind off it, and most of the preparations for the wedding made, Julia found she had nothing much to do except wait and stare at the giant picture of herself as a bride that the children had painted. After a while, the great round smiling face began to make her feel sad instead of happy. Still Christopher didn't call, and although she knew all his usual routes, she never bumped into him on one of his walks.

Cee and Bee sensed that there was a problem, but she told them she didn't want to talk about it, and, in the absence of another explanation, her friends assumed that Christopher had called the wedding off. They tried to say supportive things to cheer her up, like they were sure he was going bald and they'd always thought he was a bit of a wimp anyway, but that only made Julia feel more alone, more desperate, and even more in love with him.

Just when she had all but given up hope, a bouquet of flowers was delivered by a florist's van. Trembling as she opened the tiny envelope attached to the Cellophane, Julia's heart flipped with joy as she read six words written in the looping hand of a Lowhampton florist called Sally Ann.

'Looking forward to Saturday. Love, Christopher.'

The amazing thing about being in love, Julia thought,

was the way your emotions could seesaw from agony to ecstasy in seconds.

To be invited to one of Roman Stone's dinner parties was a mark of achieving a certain status on the London cultural scene and when Iris opened the envelope on her desk and pulled out a card with Roman's London address printed along the top and the scrawl of his distinctive handwriting in black ink asking if she was free on a particular evening, she couldn't help feeling she had reached a significant benchmark in her career.

The stucco-fronted house was one of a row of grand semi-detached villas, painted in ice-cream pastels, on a wide, tree-lined avenue in Belsize Park, a ten-minute walk from the tube. Most of the other houses had been converted into five flats, one for each floor, including the basement, and the porch of Roman's house was the only one with a single bell on the entryphone. The door buzzed as Iris announced herself. Pushing it open, she found herself in a hall with a tiled floor and a wide staircase. One wall was entirely covered in bookshelves, the other with framed drawings.

There were several coats hanging over the banister. Iris deposited a heavy carrier bag containing a manuscript she was going to read later beside them. There was no mirror in the hall. Moving from side to side trying to catch a reflection of herself in the glass in the picture frames, Iris noticed that the signatures on some of the drawings were the same as those on some of the eclectic collection of prints on the walls of her flat's art-gallery living room. Picasso. Matisse. Klimt.

'Come straight through!' Roman's voice came from beyond the slightly ajar door at the back of the hall.

Smoothing down her baggy linen suit, Iris took the bunch of Stargazer lilies she had bought at a flower stall beside the tube station out of the carrier bag. Whenever people had come to dinner at Josie's they always brought a bottle of wine, or a bunch of flowers. Iris didn't know enough about wine to bring a bottle, so she had opted for flowers for his wife instead.

Taking a deep breath, she pushed open the door at the back of the hall and found herself standing on a gallery two floors up overlooking a space like no other room she had ever seen. A huge Jackson Pollock painting covered most of the exposed brick of the side wall. The rest of the walls were entirely made of glass. The floor, at basement level, opened directly on to the garden. Three palm trees in very large terracotta pots rose almost to the ceiling, and hanging baskets of green foliage trailed down. The air in the room had the slightly humid quality of a conservatory in a botanical garden, but smelled incongruously of warm bread. Steps led down to a mezzanine kitchen, where Roman was standing beneath a hanging frame of kitchen utensils with a glass of white wine in one hand and a fish slice in the other.

'Iris! What lovely flowers!'

'I brought them for your wife,' Iris explained, a little embarrassed to hand them over to him.

'How very thoughtful! Pippa's in the country, I'm afraid,' he said. 'So, unfortunately, we're going to have to make do with my cooking.'

A huge two-handled saucepan of water was bubbling on a professional-looking hob with six rings. On the granite work surface stood a pestle and mortar with green paste in it, and a bowl of large grey uncooked prawns.

'Why don't you grab a vase and put them in water?' he said, pointing at a green glass vase on one of the high shelves with the fish slice.

Iris did as she was told.

'What a heavenly scent!' Roman said. 'Take them down and help yourself to a drink!'

'Iris Quinn,' he announced, leaning over the balustrade, to the four people already sitting at the large round table on the lower floor.

Carrying the large vase of flowers in front of her, Iris felt even more self-conscious than she normally did when meeting new people, especially as, when she put the flowers down, she noticed that some of the pollen had transferred on to her linen jacket making bright-orange stains on its natural canvas colour. She took the jacket off and hung it over the back of her chair, and, with a quick check that there was nothing on her white shirt, poured herself a glass of white wine, vowing only one, because she needed to be sober enough to read the manuscript later on.

The four other guests, picking at a painted ceramic dish of olives, were Wilf, a dour northern playwright of Iris's father's generation, who looked annoyed when Iris mentioned his first play, as he had written several since, none of which had achieved anywhere near the same iconic status; Gina, one of Portico's female authors, whose novels had been considered racy in the late sixties, but now seemed rather tame, who was wearing a lot of black eye make-up, and showing too much slightly crêpey cleavage; and Freddy, a documentary director who was about to direct his first feature film starring the other guest, a young actor just down from Oxford, with a long, fine-featured face, who looked intelligent but said nothing at all.

The supper of prawns with pasta and a fresh basil sauce was delicious, although Iris was acutely conscious of the danger of dropping green bits on her shirt or getting them between her teeth, which made her reluctant to talk very much.

Dinner party conversation was something Iris had yet to master, moving as it did between media gossip and discussion of current issues, but never really saying anything. Even though people in the media world were thought of as opinion formers, Iris was always astonished that it was considered *de trop* to express too strong an opinion about anything.

When the conversation inevitably turned to the Gang of Four and the recent formation of the SDP, Roman and Gina (who Iris thought had probably had an affair from the way she kept patting him) seemed to think the only matter of contention was how long it would take the party to build up an effective power base.

Unable to contain herself, Iris interjected, 'You don't really think anyone's stupid enough to vote for that bunch of egotists?'

Everyone looked surprised except Wilf, who chuckled and applauded her.

'No real Labour people will, and the Tories are hardly likely to embrace someone who abolished hanging and flogging when he was Home Secretary,' Iris argued.

'Surely you'd agree that this new brand of Tory thinking demands a new kind of opposition,' said Freddy, the film director.

'That's advertising speak,' Iris countered. 'They're not a new brand, they're the same old Tories . . .'

'Worse,' Wilf muttered beside her.

'Labour's won back control of the GLC,' Iris offered as evidence for her view that the traditional left was not yet as moribund as everyone seemed to assume.

'Isn't someone like Ken Livingstone more likely to make people turn towards the centre?' said Gina.

'You think policies of the centre will stop kids rioting in the inner cities, do you?'

Gina looked taken aback, as if she would not expect an employee of her publisher to disagree with her. But Iris noticed a slight smirk on Roman's face, as if, after a slow start, she was now performing as he'd hoped.

Roman collected up the plates and put out a plate of fresh raspberries and a dish of soft cheese called mascarpone that tasted like a much nicer version of tinned cream they'd had on very special occasions when Iris was a child, like Dad getting some money from his publisher.

Roman served very small glasses of delicious sweet wine, and little white cups of espresso coffee with hard almond biscuits to dip in.

The conversation turned to the well-worn theme of whether Golding or Burgess should have won the Booker the previous year, and what was likely to be on the shortlist this time round. Iris gazed around the room, wondering what her father must have made of it when he first came here. She could remember Sylvia wanting to know everything about his trip to London, and Michael being at his most maddeningly laconic.

'He's got a great big house,' he'd said, and that was more or less it.

If Iris still felt awkward in polite society after years of practice, how difficult it must have been for him, Iris thought, imagining him confronted by a roomful of Roman's publishing friends, trying to shrink behind a palm tree, or making the occasional acerbic contribution in his northern accent, unconsciously playing the role of angry young man as Roman wanted him to.

'So lovely to meet you,' Iris lied, as the actor was the first to leave with the film director, Freddy.

Then Wilf stood up to go.

Anxious not to be the one left, Iris stood up too.

'I have to go,' she said. 'Work!'

There was a slightly awkward moment with Roman standing at the foot of the staircase back up to the hall. Iris didn't know whether she should shake his hand, or kiss his cheek, and she decided to do neither.

'Darling Roman, such a treat, let me help you with the washing-up?' Gina was saying.

Iris picked up the carrier bag from the foot of the banister and let herself out of the front door. In the distance, she could see the orange lights of taxis on the main road. Checking her watch, she set off towards the tube station. After the hothouse humidity of the glass room, the evening air felt fresh and chill, and it occurred to her when she was nearly at the station that she had left her jacket over the back of her chair. The dilemma was whether to risk missing the last tube to go back, or have Roman bring it in to the office with all the gossip that would ensue.

Iris had to press the entryphone twice before it was answered.

'I forgot my jacket.' She spoke into the grille.

The door buzzed, and she went straight through the hall and into the glass room, expecting Roman and Gina still to be sitting at the round table where she'd left them, or standing side by side in the mezzanine kitchen area doing the washing-up. But the kitchen was still a mess and the room was now empty. Guessing that they had gone straight upstairs to bed together, Iris grabbed her jacket and was heading back up the staircase, taking the wooden steps two by two, when Roman suddenly appeared in the gallery. Iris froze guiltily as if she was the one caught *in flagrante*.

'You came back,' he observed neutrally.

She waggled the jacket around in explanation, still slightly out of breath from running. Standing a couple of steps down from where he was standing, she went to move past him, but he put a hand out to block her way, and smiled as if he was playing a game.

'The tube's about to close . . .' she said.

He peered at her as if he was examining a most precious piece of art.

'Gina . . . ?' Iris stammered.

'Gone. Along with the rather cross old man and the mime artist.'

A giggle blurted out of Iris.

'So you and I find ourselves alone,' said Roman, reaching for her hand. Her whole body jolted as if touched by a live cable.

The first kiss made Iris feel more beautiful than she had ever felt in her life. It was as if Roman was tasting something he had dreamed of tasting, finding it delicious and tasting again, wanting more. She opened her eyes and saw that his were closed, as if he was concentrating all his intelligence and power on her, and, feeling almost honoured, she began to kiss him back, arching her body against his. Like two people drowning, they suddenly broke apart and stopped for breath.

'Shall we go to bed?' he asked.

It wasn't an instruction, nor a command, but a request to an equal.

She nodded.

He led her upstairs and made love to her with exquisite intensity until, with delighted surprise, she was convulsed with pleasure so close to pain, she was unable to control her body, her voice or her mind. When the shudders finally died, Iris felt that she had lost part of herself to him.

'I thought you would be wonderful,' he whispered, stroking a strand of hair away from her face.

It was as if he was giving back what he had taken by allowing her to know that he had imagined this moment before.

'Why?' she asked.

'There's something uncompromising about you and your commitment to everything you do,' he said. 'Reckless, almost, and yet oddly puritan.'

The words were as precise as his lovemaking, she thought, gratified by a unique compliment that somehow seemed to affirm her existence.

Iris lay staring at the ceiling as he slept beside her, not knowing what she was supposed to do. Was there a certain form to be observed when you screwed the boss? Would he expect her to be there in the morning, to bring him a cup of coffee? Or was she supposed to slip away quietly and pretend that it hadn't happened?

One thing she was certain about was that it must not affect her work in any way. Jolted back to reality by the thought of the manuscript lying in the hall downstairs, Iris picked up her clothes, she dressed as quietly as she could, went downstairs and let herself out. The dark air was cold, her body was still flushed with the heat of sex, and she had to walk quickly to keep warm. It was too early for the tubes to be running, and in any case, she did not want to share a space with other bleary-eyed passengers and find herself creating stories about why they were up so early. Her own situation and all its ramifications required all her focus now. At the junction with Adelaide Road, a couple of taxis with orange lights on flashed past her, but Iris continued walking. In the bleak solitude of the moments just before dawn, there was no escaping the fact that what she had done was wrong in all sorts of ways, and yet her body continued to tingle with involuntary twinges of pleasure, her facial muscles seemed to be stuck in a stupid smile, and she couldn't persuade herself that she didn't want it to happen again. If it didn't, Iris thought, then she could live with that. She would keep the secret as if it were treasure, allowing herself very occasionally to remember, like the pearl earring she had once found in a rockpool in Kingshaven, which she knew she should have handed in, but was so pretty she'd wrapped it in her hanky and kept it for herself, changing the hiding place from time to time for fear of her mother going through her drawers, but sometimes, when she was quite sure everyone was out, allowing herself to roll the perfect little sphere in the tips of her fingers, feeling its curiously human warmth.

Back at the flat, Iris couldn't sleep or read, so she went into work early, and pretended to be busy, staring at the phone on her desk, yet still startled when it finally rang.

'Good morning,' Roman said.

'Good morning.'

'Are you free for lunch?'

'Where?'

'A little place I know.'

As she wrote down the address, her hands trembled with excitement, but when he rang off she was suddenly convinced that his plan was to buy her a nice meal and inform her that it had been a one-off.

Instead of a restaurant, she found herself outside a building in one of London's grand squares. Checking the scrap of paper, which she had carefully torn from the big diary on her desk where she made a record of all her calls, Iris walked up the steps into the impressive entrance hall.

The building was home to several private dentists' surgeries and had a distinctive clinical smell. Roman was waiting by the lift. The antiseptic silence as they rose through the building was punctuated sporadically by the high-pitched scream of a distant drill. Neither Roman nor

Iris spoke, but when they reached the fifth floor, the pit of her stomach seemed to bounce against her womb in the moment of stillness just before the lift doors opened.

The décor on the fifth floor was much more utilitarian than the deep-red carpet and gilded fittings of the entrance hall, the ceiling lower, making Iris wonder whether each floor was progressively less luxurious than the one below. Roman led her through a side door, which looked like a cupboard for brooms and mop buckets but instead revealed steps up to another door which he unlocked to let her into an attic flat under the roof, where there was a pine bed, which must have been assembled *in situ*, Iris found herself thinking, because it was far too big to manoeuvre up the stairs; a round pine table with a glass vase of Stargazer lilies on it, and two chairs with wicker seats, a small fridge, a two-ring cooker. At the far end of the room there was a bathroom with a sloping ceiling.

'I bought the place for my son when he started working for the BBC,' Roman explained. 'When he moved on to greater things, I was going to sell it, but I found I quite liked having somewhere nobody can get hold of me.'

'I bet you do,' Iris said, summoning cheekiness as a disguise for nerves.

'I'm not going to pretend you're the first person I've brought here,' Roman told her, taking her hand and leading her to the window, where she looked out on to the tops of the trees in the square. 'But it might interest you to know, you are only the third.'

'And the others?' she asked, fixing her eyes on a pigeon, who was preening himself just along the parapet, which obscured the view down to the street.

'History,' said Roman.

Iris's sensation of relief was tempered by the dismissal of two women in just one word.

'There are only two sets of keys,' Roman went on. 'If you like, I will give you one of them.'

She thought about it for a moment, and then turned to him and said neutrally, 'Yes, please.'

And it felt as if they had just negotiated a contract, the terms of which were quite clear to both of them.

Roman opened the little fridge and took out a bottle of white wine and a selection of sandwiches cut into quarters and arranged on a plate. She found the thought of him planning and preparing this lunch for her peculiarly touching, like the presence of the Stargazer lilies. She wanted to ask him whether they were the ones she had brought the previous evening – less than twenty-four hours before, she calculated. How could a life change in that time? – or whether he had purchased them this morning, but for some reason, she felt such a question would spoil the magic.

After eating, they made love, and it was even better, in this light room in the roof, where only the clouds could see them. Places in her body that he had gently awakened were now alert, ready for pleasure. His body seemed more substantial naked than it did clothed, his chest broad, hairy, his arms strong as they enfolded her.

Afterwards, they lay side by side, in silence, trying to stretch out the time before one of them would have to leave.

'Do you feel guilty?' Roman suddenly asked.

All the flames licking around Iris's conscience that she had been trying to dampen down flared up again. How could she so casually betray another woman? Unless, of course, you believed that marriage was a nonsense anyway, but wasn't that simply a way of ducking culpability? And even if she could get past that, wasn't it a terrible cliché to sleep with the boss?

'Yes,' Iris finally admitted. 'What about you?'

'I would never want Pippa to be hurt,' Roman replied carefully, which made Iris feel slightly irked, as if by mentioning his wife's name he had broken one of the conditions they had tacitly agreed. But then he kissed her, and she could think of nothing except his mouth, the delicacy of his touch, the weight of his body, the lightness of hers, as they rolled, first one way, then the other, locked in a loop of appetite and satisfaction.

Lying in a pool of sunshine, she could tell that the mellow temperature meant it was time to be back at the office. Reluctantly, she sat up and walked to the bathroom, knowing that his eyes were watching every movement of her naked body.

He was dressed when she emerged from washing herself.

Roman opened the door for her to leave.

'If anyone happens to see you coming out of here, they will assume you have been to the dentist,' he said.

'No, they won't,' Iris contradicted, delighted to elicit a twinkle of panic in his steady confident gaze. 'Anyone who knew me at all would know I'd never go to a private dentist.'

The wedding rehearsal was rather nerve-racking. Julia wanted only little girls from the nursery school as bridesmaids, but they were quite difficult to organize when they were overexcited, and her promise of Smarties for good behaviour proved unwise as damp little hands transferred unwanted streaks of colour on to their white dresses.

The seating arrangements were also less than straightforward. Churches were not designed to accommodate families who had transgressed vows made before God. It would be the first time Mummy had been in Kingshaven since she eloped. Although Julia had made arrangements for her to stay at a neutral guesthouse, there was still the question of where she would sit. Sylvia, as the current wife of the father of the bride, was insisting on being in the first pew, and as Daddy was still quite frail, nobody dared to argue with her. There was also the problem of what to do with Granny Ruby. According to protocol, Julia's grandmother should have been on the bride's side, but Ruby hadn't spoken to Mummy in the fourteen years since Mummy ran away, and Ruby also hated Sylvia because she considered she'd tricked her out of her shop. At the rehearsal Adrian, who had taken shore leave to act as best man, joked that Winny, who was chief usher, should offer three alternatives to the guests: bride, groom or battleground, which Julia didn't find very funny at all.

Her nerves were not soothed by the lateness of Mummy's arrival in Lowhampton. Luckily the station was a terminus because Mummy alighted without the wedding dress. Julia suspected Mummy had been drinking quite a lot in the buffet car because the John Lewis cardboard box was so huge she didn't see how anyone could forget it. It barely fitted in Cee's Metro, and blocked the view out of the rear-view mirror, so that Julia, who was wedged beside it in the back had to crane her neck and shout that it was all clear behind as Cee reversed cautiously out of the space in the station car park. As they ground up and down the hills along the coast road home, Mummy kept repeating that nobody was going to keep her away from her own daughter's wedding, which was a bit silly when they were making such an effort to get her there. As they approached Kingshaven, Mummy asked if there was an off-licence, and both Julia and Cee said, 'No!' so loudly and immediately, Mummy looked suspicious.

'It'll be closed now,' Julia lied, because in fact Mr Patel's Sunny Stores stayed open until ten o'clock during the summer season.

In the Bella Vista Guesthouse, Julia made her mother a cup of tea and tucked her under the pink candlewick bedspread in her room so that she could sleep it off. Then, with Mummy emitting gentle snores, Julia opened up the big white box, carefully unzipped the polythene cover and pulled out the beautiful white confection of silk, pearls and net which she would be wearing the next day.

The bodice, which had been tight in the shop, now felt roomy, making Julia slightly regret that she was not on better terms with Sylvia, who would most certainly know how to take it in. The skirt was so huge, there wasn't enough space for it to settle between the bed and the mirror on the door of the wardrobe. The tiara fitted perfectly. Julia looked in the mirror, touching her cheek to believe the vision of a fairy-tale princess in front of her was actually real.

On the bed behind her, Mummy suddenly opened her eyes and struggled to focus on the reflection.

'Oh, my darling,' she said eventually, 'you've become a swan!'

It was the knowledge that she looked beautiful that kept Julia going throughout her wedding day.

Being beautiful helped her to hold Daddy up as he tottered down the aisle beside her, and being beautiful made her remember to smile at the congregation as she passed. Being beautiful got her through the vows, even though she had to bite her tongue very hard to stop herself giggling when the vicar addressed Christopher as Albert Christopher Cyril King. She didn't know her husband's first name was Albert and it was such a shock, she said it the wrong way round when it was her turn to make her vows.

But none of that mattered, because she was beautiful in her beautiful dress.

As the organist played the rousing first notes of 'The Wedding March' and Julia turned to face the congregation, she realized that this was the moment she had been waiting for all her life. It was perfect. She smiled, and everyone in the church smiled back, even Sylvia, who was firmly linked to Daddy's arm in the first pew, and Mummy who was holding on to James in the second; even her envious sister Joanna. On her husband's side of the church, Auntie Libby was smiling and Eddie was smiling his half-flirty, half-avuncular smile, and Granny Ruby and Granny Liliana too. Even Pearl Snow, whose ex-husband, Tom, was taking the photographs, and their teenage children, Susannah and Damian. Adrian and Winny winked at Julia as she floated past. Angela even looked a little softer than usual as she picked little Piers up so that he could see the bride. In the rows behind her family, Julia's friends were smiling too; Cee standing alongside her fiancé, Justin, and Bee, looking very *femme fatale* in black and red, who kept glancing towards the back of the church where her former lover, Gerry Balls, was standing in the last row on the King side next to his wife, whom Julia always thought of as Millicent Bland.

GB loves MB, Julia suddenly thought.

Outside the church, it seemed as if the whole of Kingshaven was waiting to greet them.

Tom Snow fired off a battery of shots with the motordrive on his huge camera. They posed on the steps of the church, just the two of them, then with the bridesmaids, then with both families, and when Tom said, 'Come on, give her a kiss!'

Julia turned to her husband – husband! – and he kissed her quickly, just missing her mouth.

The round of applause from the town people who had come to look was so thunderous it sounded as if hailstones were raining down on the church roof, even though the churchyard was bright with summer sunshine. In defiance of the plea the vicar had made before the service, Christopher and Julia were pelted with showers of rice and a blizzard of confetti.

And then, all too quickly, it was over. The moment she had dreamed of all her life had come and gone, and Julia felt she'd hardly been aware of it. She had the strongest urge to shout, like a child demanding to be swung round in a great flying arc over the beach, 'Again!'

In the limousine on the way back to the Palace (Angela had offered, but Julia hadn't wanted horses at her own wedding), Christopher finally spoke, shattering the trance and bringing her back down to earth with a bump.

'Well, that wasn't as bad as I thought,' he said.

'Did I look all right?' Julia asked. It was a rhetorical question, but her husband – husband! – was the one person who hadn't yet told her how radiantly beautiful she looked.

'Sometimes less is more,' he said.

For a second, she felt totally demolished, but then she thought that perhaps it was his dry way of giving her a compliment, insinuating he'd rather see her in her underwear. Christopher was always saying how much he hated clichés, so it was probably silly to expect him to tell her how lovely she looked, as was normally expected of a husband – husband!

Christopher took a pressed white handkerchief from the inside pocket of his morning suit and mopped his brow. His initials were embroidered in claret in the corner. Julia wondered how it was that she had never noticed before. ACCK.

'I never knew you were called Albert!' she teased.

Then suddenly she shivered.

1981 MB + ACCK 4ever.

Surely . . .

'I wonder if we're technically married at all, since you said it all the wrong way round,' Christopher mused.

Feeling slightly sick as she sat down to the wedding break-fast, Julia struggled with the salmon, could barely swallow the potato salad, and waved away the raspberry parfait. When Adrian got up to make his best man's speech, Julia was so sure she was going to throw up, she excused herself and, not knowing where else to go, ran to her little room at the back of the hotel, where she vomited copiously into the vanity unit.

As the waves of nausea began to subside, Julia became aware that the room had been stripped of all the bits and pieces she had left there. The good luck teddy bear, the half-eaten box of All Gold and the various silver horse-shoes people had stopped her in the street to give, had all, presumably, been taken to Christopher's quarters, or thrown away. It hadn't occurred to her that she had lost the room that belonged just to her, and she suddenly felt tremendously sad to have given up something precious without properly saying goodbye.

Outside the door, Julia was aware of people approaching, and she found herself holding her breath as if she was playing Murder in the Dark. She'd always been the best at hiding when she'd played at Christmas with Adrian,

Winny and James when they were children, able to make herself invisible and quiet for much longer than the boys, but there was no way she was going to be able to get under the bed in her voluminous dress.

'Julia?'

The voice was Granny Ruby's. Julia wondered how it had been decided which one of them should go after her.

There was a knock at the door.

'Are you all right, Julia?'

'I'll be down in a minute,' she called.

'She says she'll be down in a minute,' Granny Ruby said, as if she was at the front of a delegation.

'Is there anything you want?'

'No, thank you,' said Julia.

She listened to the footsteps receding, then lay down on the single bed staring at a brown watermark she'd never previously noticed on the ceiling.

Just a few minutes on her own to steady herself. She'd been so caught up in the idea of her fairy-tale wedding (as the *Chronicle* always referred to it) that she hadn't really given a thought to what would happen after the actual day, and now it was here, it felt as if the colossal mass of her past had suddenly bumped up against her future and she was squeezed in the middle.

Suddenly it seemed completely incomprehensible to have given so much thought to dresses that would never be worn again, flowers that were already wilting, a cake that would be cut into tiny cubes and put into embossed boxes that would sit on people's mantelpieces gathering dust.

'Julia?' This time the voice was Bee's. 'Are you OK?'

Reluctantly, Julia sat up on the bed, composed herself and unlocked the door.

'I felt a bit funny, that's all,' she said. 'Is everything going all right downstairs?'

'The brief intermission has given everyone some much-needed drinking time,' Bee told her. Julia had no idea whether a minute or an hour had passed.

340

'Is Mummy OK?'

'She and Pearl Snow are vying to be crowned champion champagne drinkers.'

'I'd better come . . .'

Bee smiled at her, straightened her pencil skirt, then walked round Julia, making sure that the top skirt of her huge white dress was hanging smoothly over the net.

'As good as new,' she said, and went to open the door.

'Bee . . . did Christopher have an affair with Gerry's wife?' Julia suddenly asked.

Bee's face said it all without her uttering a word.

'Why didn't you tell me?' asked Julia.

'You'd hardly started seeing Christopher then. When Gerry said he was trying to make a go of his marriage, and then you got engaged, I just assumed they'd both stopped . . .'

'Is it still going on?' Julia asked.

'It bloody well better not be,' said Bee, outraged, as if she was the one who had been betrayed.

'I just can't imagine Christopher and . . .' Julia couldn't bear to say her name now.

'They go back a long way,' said Bee.

'Why didn't he marry her then?' said Julia.

'Because she was in love with Gerry. Nobody would want Christopher King if they could have Gerry.'

Julia tried to ignore the implications of this for the moment.

'So why did she . . .' Julia searched for an appropriately dignified word, 'go out with Christopher?'

Bee blushed. 'Gerry always had a roving eye.'

'You mean Christopher was her way of getting back at him? It was just a matter of tit for tat?' said Julia, outraged.

'So to speak,' said Bee wickedly.

They both suddenly burst into giggles, which made Julia feel much better.

'I don't want to feel I'm second best,' Julia said seriously, trying to inject a sense of decorum to the proceedings.

'You're not!' said Bee vehemently. 'You're the opposite from her. She's a barmaid and you're a lady. You
belong here. Anyway,' she added bluntly, nodding at the
ring on the third finger of Julia's left hand, 'it's a bit late
now.'

Chapter Twelve

1982

Iris had just pushed open the door of the ladies' toilet at work when she heard the Welsh lilt of the flirty receptionist call from one of the stalls, 'How is the Red Quinn these days?'

And Trish's voice reply, 'She's a lot better since she's been getting a regular shag.'

For a moment, Iris didn't know what to do. Should she duck into a stall herself and listen to find out how much they knew, or should she turn on the taps to let them know there was someone in the room? With an oddly guilty feeling, as if she was the one gossiping, rather than the by-stander, she elected to leave, giving the door a good push behind her so that they would be aware that someone had overheard.

When she looked at herself in the mirror, Iris couldn't see any visible change but she knew that she did look different in some way since the start of her affair with Roman. Men whistled at her in the street, which had never happened before, and flirted with her at parties. Sometimes she wondered if it was some kind of odourless scent, like an animal being on heat.

Iris was almost certain that nobody in the office knew who it was she was shagging, but sometimes she wondered whether Roman's absence from the twelfth floor, where he used to be a regular visitor, had been noted, or whether there was a way the receptionist could listen in to internal calls through the switchboard, her acute ear suspicious of the very terseness of their conversations, especially if she had eavesdropped on the rambling chats they used to have before they started sleeping together.

At lunchtime, just to be sure, Iris took a different route to the flat, dodging suddenly down alleyways to see if anyone from the office was following her, stopping at a bank to make a totally unnecessary withdrawal from her current account. She chose a different sandwich bar from her usual one and approached the building from the right instead of the left. Before running up the steps, she checked over her shoulder twice.

There was a rota of different doormen on the desk, who always greeted Iris with professional smiles, as they might do one of the staff, but Iris thought they probably swapped notes and knew exactly what was going on. Even someone who had sucked boiled sweets their entire life couldn't have enough decay to necessitate twice-weekly visits to the dentist for a period of over six months.

Roman was already there, already in bed. Iris kicked off her shoes and climbed on top of him, kissing him hard while simultaneously pulling her arms out of the sleeves of her jacket, only disengaging her mouth from his to pull her shirt over her head instead of undoing all the buttons. The first time was always greedy, ravenous, as if to satisfy an urgent hunger for each other. Afterwards, in the intimate cocoon of warm sheets, they talked about everything they'd done and seen and thought since the last time. She loved the way he constantly challenged her intelligence, the way they made each other laugh, the sheer competence he brought to everything he did, and she loved that he made her feel she was the person she was capable of being. Describing her journey to the flat, she made it sound like something from a thriller by John le Carré.

They ate cream cheese and cucumber sandwiches, which had become their standard lunch because they left few crumbs and no incriminating taint on their breath for the afternoon's editorial meeting.

'Have you found anything exciting this week?' Roman asked.

Iris took a sip of water to wash down the last of her sandwich. She never drank wine at lunch before an editorial meeting, fearing even the slightest misjudgement of a glance between them might be picked up by her colleagues.

'I've an idea I wanted to run past you first,' she said.

'OK,' said Roman.

'You're aware that what marks Capital Books out from its rival lists is that it combines critically acclaimed novels with novels that sell well.' Iris began her preamble as if she was speaking to a sales conference.

'And on rare occasions, novels that do both,' Roman added.

'Not that rare!' Iris protested, sitting up.

The series of Japanese crime novels were attracting a growing following and were now published in fourteen other languages; her female Irish novelist had been short-listed for the Booker Prize.

'Go on,' said Roman.

'I'm thinking of pushing into more nakedly commercial territory . . .'

Roman raised an eyebrow, and she thought how amazing it was to be sitting here with him, pitching a book with no clothes on. With belated modesty, she pulled a sheet around her chest.

'Do you know a book called *Scruples* by Judith Krantz?' she asked.

'I've heard of it, of course,' said Roman.

'I read it last weekend, and it's absolutely brilliant in its own terms.'

'Those terms being?'

'The sheer sinful joy of eating a whole box of hand-made chocolates yourself, or bathing in champagne . . . All right!' She held up her hands. 'So I've never bathed in champagne, but what I'm talking about is sheer escapism of the highest class – glamour, movie stars, shopping and sex – and I'd like to get a British author to do a huge, ambitious blockbuster.'

'Can this be the same Iris Quinn who helped to found that well-known feminist imprint Harridan Books?' Roman interrupted.

'I knew you'd say that! Because people always think that women's commercial fiction is about strong heroes and subservient women, but that's exactly what's different about *Scruples*. It's the women who are the strong characters, who make things happen, who consume, rather than being consumed. I'd argue that it's actually empowering . . .'

Roman's indulgent smile told her not to get too carried away, but his eyes made her think of a cartoon character with dollar signs instead of irises.

'But is it really possible to do an English version of that? Are we glamorous enough?' Roman asked. 'The Americans have oil and Hollywood and Bloomingdale's.'

'We have the class system,' Iris countered. 'And,' she added, 'everyone has sex.'

If Julia's marriage had a soundtrack, it would be 'Don't You Want Me' because that was what was playing every time she switched on the radio. If her marriage had a smell, it would be vomit. There wasn't a moment that hadn't tasted of sick, from the wedding itself, with all that rich food on an empty stomach, followed the next day by their ordeal on the *Brittany Anna*.

It had been generous of Eddie to offer them use of the precious yacht he spent most of his life polishing and scraping the barnacles off. It would have been rude to refuse, but Christopher wasn't as competent a yachtsman as his father, and Julia had never really enjoyed sailing since Adrian had taken her out in his first Mirror dinghy and capsized the boat seven times.

Christopher might just about have made it to harbour had the weather been kind, but a storm had blown up when they were halfway across Lyme Bay and they'd had to radio for assistance. An ignominious arrival in Torquay under tow hadn't felt like a very good omen for the future, although the crew of the lifeboat had been hilarious, and there'd really been no reason for Christopher to get in such a state about everything.

One of the first uncomfortable lessons Julia had learned about her husband was that he found it difficult to laugh at himself. She assumed it was because he was so clever, he hadn't had to learn to take a joke at school like she had.

Fun was another thing they had very different views about. Christopher's idea of a nice holiday was sitting on the balcony of their hotel room reading a book. He didn't seem to care if she went out shopping, but it didn't cross his mind to go with her. With her new slim figure, Julia quite enjoyed trying on things in places like Miss Selfridge, which she'd always felt too fat for before, but it was a bit lonely. Time seemed to pass very slowly as she tried to make tea in a department store cafeteria with a view of the sea last for more than ten minutes. Once, she even rang the gatehouse from a phone box in the hope of asking Bee whether this was normal behaviour for a honeymoon, but the call was unanswered, and Julia's eyes unaccountably filled with tears as she pictured the phone ringing in the empty little house.

On the last evening, Christopher reluctantly agreed to take her to the funfair. Amid bright flashing lights and pop music, they'd eaten hot dogs and she'd bought sticks of candyfloss, but he refused even to hold his because he said it was childish. Determined to make him smile, she'd dared him go on more and more exciting rides, but churned up by the pressure of trying to please him, and the rotation of the waltzer, her stomach had taken revenge, splattering her new husband's best casual jacket and engulfing them both in the smell of bile and spun sugar.

As Julia had packed her suitcase for the train journey home (Eddie had found one of his old Navy pals, now semi-retired, to sail the *Brittany Anna* back to Kingshaven),

347

she realized that she hadn't taken the skimpy peach nightie Bee had given her for the honeymoon out of the tissue paper it was wrapped in. Christopher probably would have disapproved anyway. They had had sex only twice, and Julia had been disappointed to find that it didn't feel any different once you were married from how it had done before.

Having always previously imagined that the act of conception would be so magical she would actually be aware of the miraculous fusion of essences within her, Julia had been astonished to discover a couple of months after they returned that the routine pumping of her husband's penis had resulted in a pregnancy.

Julia let her head loll upside down for a few seconds to make sure there was no more to come, then stood up straight and flushed the loo.

It didn't seem to matter whether she ate loads, or nothing at all, she was still sick. Sometimes she felt as if she was disintegrating inside and having to expel all the rotten bits of herself. Five months into her pregnancy, she weighed less than she had at the beginning. Her forehead was permanently sweaty and her eyes were always watery, so it looked as if she'd been crying even when she hadn't.

At first, Auntie Libby had been lovely and sympathetic. Everyone was sick in the first three months, she said, it was just one of those ghastly things women had to go through. But when it didn't stop, Julia could see that her mother-in-law thought she was making a meal of it.

When Auntie Libby and Uncle Eddie talked about the resilience of their own generation compared to young people nowadays, which they did a lot, Julia couldn't help thinking the comments were directed at her. She began to understand why Christopher always seemed so ill at ease with his parents. Previously, Julia had thought they were an exemplary family. Everything was in its proper place; the mummy and daddy looked after the children (unlike her family, where she'd sometimes felt she was the one doing the looking after) and set a good example (they'd been together for over thirty years!) and never had horrid arguments. But now she realized none of this was true.

She'd thought the Kings were perfect, but beneath the public face, tensions festered like sores. Sometimes Julia wondered if this was how all families were. Did anyone actually live happily ever after? Even in fairy tales, you never saw the Prince and the Princess sitting down for breakfast the morning after the wedding, nor the Princess getting fat and sick and pregnant. Julia had always thought that marriage was the happy ending, but she'd come to realize that it was only the beginning, and she wasn't in the least prepared for what came next.

'Julia? Julia? Are you all right in there?'

Adrian was the only one with a ready smile, the only she felt completely comfortable with, but Adrian was rarely home on leave, and now he was about to go away for an indefinite time. Julia didn't know if she could bear it.

Everyone else seemed to think that sending a task force to the Falklands was the perfectly obvious thing to do, but although Julia was the first to admit that she didn't know much about politics – let alone Argentine politics! – she did wonder if it was sensible to send the whole Navy thousands of miles to rescue a few people and sheep from a place nobody had even heard of before. If the Falklanders wanted to remain British so much, then why didn't they just come back to England, or Scotland if they preferred a bleaker climate? It seemed so unfair that Adrian and all his mates had to put themselves in danger just so a few islanders could fly the Union Jack over their windswept crofts.

'Julia?' Adrian's voice was full of concern.

'Just a minute,' she called.

Julia flushed the toilet again, cleaned her teeth, and patted her face with a towel. The nice thing about living in a hotel was that there were always clean, dry towels, unlike at the gatehouse, where they'd taken ages to dry over the back of a chair. Then she unlocked the bathroom door and emerged into the flat. Auntie Libby had let them have the rooms above the garage, which had belonged to the chauffeur in the days when the hotel still had a chauffeur. Christopher had left the decorating to Julia and although it was quite small, she'd made the main room as bright as possible, with curtains from Laura Ashley with a blue and yellow sweet pea design, and a matching border pasted around the lemon walls.

The sight of Adrian in his uniform, all ready to go, made Julia's eyes prickle with tears again.

He walked across the room, as if to give her a hug, but then stopped midway as her face crumpled.

'Cheer up! I don't want to remember you crying,' he attempted to jolly her up. 'You'll spoil your pretty face!'

Obediently, Julia tried hard to smile.

'I don't know what I'm going to do without you . . .' she sniffed.

'I'll be back.'

'Take care of yourself, won't you?'

'And you too.' He pointed at her bump. 'Make sure you eat enough.'

Julia felt the bile rising in her gullet and forced it back down, and then, as he turned to go, she said, 'Adrian?'

'Yes?'

'I love you, you know.'

For a moment, the mad thought came upon her that they should run away together. She could protect him from the war, he could protect her from everything. Just like when they were children and they'd planned to live in a gypsy caravan, and have ten children . . . She longed to rush to him and have his strong arms crush her against his uniform.

'I sort of thought we'd be together,' he said with a shrug.

She wanted to say, couldn't we still?

She was sure that if wives came with a money-back guarantee of satisfaction, Christopher would certainly have returned her. There had been several times when she walked into his office and he'd put the phone down quickly, which made her suspect that he'd been talking to Millicent Balls, although when she'd asked him point-blank, he'd accused her of having an overactive imagination. Which was probably true. When Julia had imagined what it would be like being married, she'd had a picture of herself and Christopher doing everything together, like hiring a pedalo and finding some deserted creek, just the two of them, or spending the day in a beach hut with the radio on, making each other cups of tea, or even just eating supper together in front of the television. Now all of that seemed like an absurd fantasy. The reality was that Christopher spent much of the day fretting in his office and they ate most of their meals with the family, which Julia had to concede made sense because the chef could cook much better than she could. But sometimes she thought it would be nice just to have a simple plate of beans on toast, and much easier to keep down than all that rich food. What she could never have imagined was how lonely it was possible to feel with your husband sleeping next to you.

'It's not goodbye,' said Adrian, sensing her despair. 'It's *au revoir.*'

He turned, waving the back of his hand at her, and then he was gone.

Julia watched him walking wearily across the gravel to the front of the hotel, where his father, Eddie, was waiting to drive him to Portsmouth in the car. She knew she couldn't join the rest of the family all assembled on the steps of the hotel without an unseemly display of emotion, which would be remarked upon. So she waved the car off silently from the window of the flat, whispering a private goodbye to her friend.

When the car turned out of the gate and was gone, Julia thought she'd never felt more alone and desperate. She longed to be able to tell someone, but there was no one. Her sisters, who'd always been astonished that Christopher had preferred her over them, would no doubt find it hilarious that she was miserable; James was up at Oxford and far too involved in a constant round of balls and punting parties to understand; she didn't want to upset Daddy and make him ill again; Mummy would just say she told her so. When the vicar had remarked in his sermon that the wedding was the stuff of fairy tales, everyone had heard Mummy mutter: 'Complete with a wicked stepmother, ugly sisters and a couple of old witches!'

Bee and Cee were bound to be sympathetic, but Julia wasn't sure she could bear the loss of face. It was all meant to be so perfect. Even people she didn't know, town people, seemed to have invested their faith in her. There was a picture of her in the *Chronicle* every week, joining in the nursery school Easter Egg hunt, talking to Mr Patel at the Regional Businessman of the Year Award, even buying an ice-cream cone on the first sunny day of the year. This year, she'd been the one invited to open the Flower Festival, a duty normally filled by Granny Liliana.

'A blooming Julia King,' the caption had read.

Sometimes when Julia saw the photos it took a second to register that she was the smiling, well-dressed lady. It reminded her of looking in the mirror when she was little, having to touch her cheek just to make sure it was her.

A sinister idea began to insinuate itself into Julia's troubled thoughts. Perhaps it would be easier just to end her life, rather than suffer the humiliation when people found out that she was nothing like they had thought she was. It would be simple enough to throw herself from the window of the Tower Suite, or lock herself in the garage downstairs and start the engine of the car. The idea was beginning to gather an almost attractive momentum, when Julia felt a sharp little nudge in her tummy.

Not realizing immediately what it was, she put a steadying hand on her belly, hoping to stop herself throwing up again. It was only when she felt another kick that she realized what it must be. She imagined her baby all curled up inside, feeling rather pleased with the first kick and wanting to try it again. It was almost as if it had sensed

352

her despair and was sending her the message: 'Here I am. Don't worry. I'll be your friend.'

Iris was watching the evening news when a dreaded ratatat-tat told her that Clive was outside. The television was probably loud enough for him to know that someone was there, so she reluctantly went to open the door.

'Fancy a pizza?' Clive thrust a printed leaflet into Iris's hand.

'PIZZA ON WHEELS'. There was a lurid picture of a pizza with two wheels with flames coming out of them and a telephone number underneath.

'I'm not hungry,' she said, trying to think of a reason not to let him in.

'But, if you were hungry, how much would you pay to have a delicious pizza delivered to your door?' Clive persisted, looking optimistically over her shoulder into the flat.

'It doesn't look very delicious,' she said, handing the flyer back.

His face fell. 'If I got a better picture, would you then?'

'You're selling pizza?' Iris asked in disbelief.

The only thing she'd ever seen Clive doing in the way of cooking was squirting brown sauce on to a bacon sandwich.

'Someone else is doing the making. I'm doing the delivering. Delivery is the future,' said Clive.

These days, a month didn't go by without Clive coming round to show off his latest money-making idea. There'd been the fake coins for parking meters, the telephone that lit up instead of ringing, a wipe-clean beer mat.

'Won't it be cold?' Iris asked.

'Insulated boxes,' said Clive.

'Won't it cost quite a lot in petrol?'

'The more orders, the lower the unit cost,' he replied.

Iris suspected he'd been reading one of the recent deluge of inspirational American business books with titles like *Get Rich Quick*, or *Risk A Dollar, Double a Dollar,*

353

but he wasn't a natural salesman, his only assets being persistence and his looks, she supposed. The years inside had coarsened Clive's youthfully fine features – his five o'clock shadow was more insistent, his black hair receding – but she thought that some women would still probably find him attractive even though she couldn't understand now how she ever had.

'Is Vic around?' Clive asked.

'No,' said Iris.

'He's never around these days, is he?'

'Not much,' said Iris, tired of the pretence and wishing now that Clive would find out that they weren't a real couple. Perhaps he already suspected.

'As a matter of fact I was on my way out,' Iris said, but he appeared not to have heard. He was peering over her shoulder at the news.

'We'll show those Argies!' he said.

Much as it pained Iris to let his right-wing views go un-challenged, she didn't want to invite him in.

'Nuke the bastards!' Clive shouted at the television.

'Isn't it a bit extreme to start World War Three over a minor territorial dispute?' Iris couldn't help herself. 'Thatcher's only having a war to divert attention from the mess the country's in, you know.'

'Someone needs to stand up for us,' said Clive.

'Oh, for God's sake!' said Iris.

'You've always been a bit of a peace lover, haven't you?' Clive said, as if it were a subversive quirk.

'Talking solves problems more effectively than killing,' said Iris, thinking how ridiculous it was having to explain herself to someone who'd been in prison for abetting a murder.

'That's what Chamberlain said about Hitler. If it'd been up to people like you, we'd all be *talking* German,' Clive told her.

'*Jawohl*,' said Iris flatly.

Suddenly Clive smiled. 'I was telling a mate about you the other day,' he said, as he turned to leave. 'I told him, you wouldn't believe this woman. She makes jokes like a man!'

Iris couldn't help feeling that from him this was a sort of compliment, but when Vic came back from work she pleaded with him, 'Can't we just tell Clive that we're not together? Then maybe he'll leave us alone.'

'You tell him if you want,' said Vic. 'It's you he's after.'

'He's not after me! He thinks I'm an appeaser!' said Iris hotly.

It was such a bizarre reason to cite, Vic started laughing.

'It's not that I have a problem with him knowing I'm gay,' he said, 'but he'll want to know who . . .'

'Is it serious?' Iris had detected a change in Vic's demeanour. There were long periods when he wasn't in the flat at all, and long periods when he was in every night, waiting for the phone to ring, then chatting for hours in his room.

'I think so,' said Vic.

'So, what's his name?'

'I'm sworn to secrecy. His job depends on people thinking he's straight,' said Vic. 'Believe me, I'd love to tell you, because I'm finding it a bit scary.'

'Scary?'

'He's famous,' said Vic.

'Is he a politician or something?' Iris asked.

Vic laughed. 'Can you really see me with a politician?'

'He might find it relaxing to be with someone who knows so little,' Iris speculated. 'Oh, come on,' she wheedled. 'I told you mine.'

Vic's sharp eyes had noticed that the sheets she was washing at the launderette were not the sheets she had on her bed, so she'd told him about the flat above the dentist's, and ever since she'd had to endure endless teasing along the lines of, 'Just a little prick! It won't hurt! Oh dear, I'm afraid you need a rather large filling!'

'Do you really promise to keep it a secret?' Vic asked.

'Cross my heart,' said Iris solemnly.

As if he didn't dare say it out loud, Vic leaned across and whispered the name of a flamboyant rock star into her ear.

'He's gorgeous!'

'I know,' Vic smiled bashfully.

'Wow! I thought he was a full-blooded heterosexual!'

'Like I said, that's what you're supposed to think,' said Vic.

'What's he like?'

'Full-blooded,' said Vic with a little private smile.

It was Saturday morning and it was sunny for the first time in weeks. Steve had set Fiammetta the exercise of producing a landscape in watercolour. Steve said it was important that she demonstrated skills in all different techniques for her portfolio if she wanted to go to art school and Fiammetta definitely wanted to go to art school. Each Saturday morning, when she woke up, the thought that art school was a week closer than it had been the previous Saturday morning was what made her get out of bed.

Fiammetta pictured art school as a Victorian building in some city far away from Kingshaven, with classrooms with tall windows, and corridors with lockers down each side where students would bump into each other in the bustle between lectures, a bit like the school for performing arts in the movie *Fame*. Her companions would be artists like her, with serious interests, who talked about proper things, not silly things like the other girls in her class at Lowhampton Comprehensive, such as whether Rive Gauche was sexier than Opium; would they rather go out with William Hurt or Richard Gere; or how they could get into a band like those two girls in the Human League.

The only music Fiammetta liked was John Lennon. John Lennon had been an artist, and he had fallen in love with an artist. Steve said that everything John Lennon had done since meeting Yoko Ono, like his bed protest, and his War Is Over poster campaign, was a conceptual work of art. When John Lennon was shot dead, Steve said he had felt as if he had lost a brother. The first single Fiammetta ever bought was 'Woman' by John Lennon and she played it over and over, until Bruno said that if he heard it again, he'd break it in two. Bruno said that Steve was an old hippy, Fiammetta didn't see what was wrong with that.

'Peace and Love, man,' Bruno taunted, making the peace sign, whenever he walked past the art room at lunchtime.

Whenever Fiammetta thought about art school, she imagined that Steve would come and visit her there. She'd be able to show him around, and then maybe they'd go out for a meal together.

She imagined sitting across a table from him, somewhere studenty, sharing a pizza or ribs, or some other trendy food, and him saying, 'I'd better be getting back.'

And her saying, 'You could doss at my pad if you wanted . . .'

And it would all happen from there.

Bruno didn't know what he was going to do when he left school. Bruno was top of the class in almost every subject, but he was very lazy about homework, and did sport all the time. Their father sometimes got cross with him because he said he was wasting his brain. If Bruno made a bit of effort, he could probably get into Oxford or Cambridge like James Allsop. Bruno said the last person he wanted to be like was James Allsop because he was a public school twit, but Michael said that wasn't the point and when he was a boy, he'd have given anything for the chances he had.

'And I'd give anything to get you off my case,' Bruno told him.

Fiammetta could still hear the murmur of conversation downstairs. Dad and Pascale were having breakfast. Bruno had already gone out to get the bus into Lowhampton for his football match. In a little while, Pascale would go down to mind the shop, and Dad would put the breakfast things in the sink, and go up to his writing room, and start typing. Sometimes the clatter was so fast and furious, Fiammetta thought her father was putting all his anger into the typewriter. She imagined him thumping the keys and swaying from side to side with his long swept-back fringe falling over his face, like a concert pianist playing Rachmaninov, or some other passionate Russian composer. Sometimes she was curious to know what it was her father was writing about, but the door to his writing room was always closed. As soon as the typing started, Fiammetta knew it was safe to go and eat her breakfast in peace. After that, she would take her sketchpad, her palette of watercolours and a jam jar full of water, and go for a walk along the cliffs. With any luck, the weather would stay fine, and she could be out all day.

From the top of the ridge Fiammetta looked down at the Castle. There was a flag of St George flying from the roof, a bright white flutter against the green and gold patchwork of fields. The pale grey stone Palladian building gleamed in the sunlight. There was now a crescent of black tarmac car park at the front of the house. At the back, the old orchard had made way for a mini golf course with bright green strips of lawn. There were yellow sunloungers and parasols around the azure rectangle of swimming pool. From this distance, her old home looked like a weird mix of David Hockney and Constable, Fiammetta thought, but she knew that it wasn't the kind of landscape Steve had in mind when he set her homework.

The sea was flat and just a couple of shades deeper blue than the cloudless sky. The town of Kingshaven was postcard pretty, but as Fiammetta sat on the South Cliffs trying to capture it in watercolour, she couldn't muster the enthusiasm to create a bland seascape like the ones they sold in the shop called the Artists' Gallery, which had recently opened on the High Street, showcasing the work of local painters and selling greetings cards from the Medici Gallery. From this vantage point, high up on the South Cliffs, the beach looked palely golden, as if it was made of the finest sand, but close up it was pebbly and spiked with sharp bits of shell. The paintings in the Artists' Gallery never attempted to capture the sudden shriek of a Harrier jet appearing from nowhere and dipping low over the sea, training to drop its payload of bombs on some foreign land. In those insipid watercolours, boats were always for pleasure, but a serious artist could not look at the sea at this moment in history without thinking of a ship full of sailors sacrificed in the South Atlantic.

Watercolour, Fiammetta decided, was far too polite a medium for her. She began to mix oranges and reds thickly to turn the sky to fire and the sea to blood, and painted an almost undiluted line of black for the outline of the harbour wall.

At the bottom of the paper, Fiammetta scrawled 'Sunset over Kingshaven', smiling at the irony that she was actually facing east and it could never look like this, feeling this added to the dystopian nature of the work.

Steve would like it, she decided, but he would give her one of his exasperated looks. The Artists' Gallery would refuse it, of course, as they had done all the other paintings she'd offered them.

It was almost the longest day of the year, Fiammetta realized, as she waited for the paper to dry before packing up and going home. The surface of the sea had now turned opaquely white in the pale rays of evening sunlight. She narrowed her eyes to focus solely on the colours and lines, working out whether it would be possible to convey the effect of the light on water simply by using white emulsion paint with tiny amounts of black mixed in to indicate the mercurial quiver of surface movement. Suddenly eager to go home and try it out in poster paint, she rinsed her brushes as best she could in the dirty water, then flung the contents of the jam jar over a stone wall as she walked back down the path to the harbour.

The railway station had been sold to a group of steam enthusiasts who'd boarded it up against further vandalism while they tried to raise the money to reopen the line, and so Milly said she'd meet Christopher on the South Cliffs, although he suspected that she'd only agreed to get him off the phone.

He'd stuck it out as long as he could, but after nearly a year, he'd found himself dialling the number of the pub. The first couple of times, her husband answered, and Christopher had quickly put down the phone. The third time, he had got Millicent.

'Uncle Cyril said it was always a mistake to settle for less,' Christopher told her now, as they sat with their backs against a dry-stone wall, looking at the wonderful view of the bay. Ironically, he remembered, his uncle had actually been referring to Milly at the time. Cyril had understood so much about him, but he had never understood that Christopher's love for Milly was sincere and deeply felt, that it wasn't just a question of rampant desire, more of profound contentment.

Milly was easy to be with. Julia Allsop, it turned out, was not.

Christopher had been fooled by the pretty English-rose complexion, those lovely round breasts, the shy smile, as devoted and obedient as one of his mother's King Charles spaniels. Everyone – even Milly! – had said she would be the perfect wife for him, but all his instincts had screamed no at him. In the end, he'd grown weary of the constant struggle against obvious good sense, and begun to ask himself the questions his mother, father and grandmother were always asking. Why did he always have to go against the grain? Why not settle for a simple life with someone who was obviously devoted to him and would be a lovely mother for any children they might have? Julia herself had told him that her sole ambition was to have a happy family. With no problems, she'd added with a little laugh, in what he'd taken to be a reference to her own rather complicated background.

Almost as soon as the ring was on her finger, however, the sweet, docile girl had transformed into a rather highly strung young woman who seemed to think that marriage gave her the right to act completely differently.

He'd assumed that having known him so long, she would have understood more about him, but, having been so in awe, suddenly she seemed to be demanding he changed. If he refused – he'd never been clothes shopping in his life and he was hardly going to start on his honeymoon, for goodness' sake! – she adopted a very petulant attitude. The solemn vows he'd made no longer seemed to be enough for her. He had never lied to her – even when she'd plucked up the courage to ask him point-blank whether he loved her, he'd been careful not to commit himself – but now she acted as if she'd been short-changed in some way, which was particularly ridiculous if one compared her previous circumstances – banished from her rightful home by an evil stepmother, as she herself had put it, and sharing a tiny house with two giggly girls – to where she was now. And she was always ill, when she had appeared such a picture of apple-cheeked good health. In the beginning, he'd tried to be sympathetic, but he'd begun to wonder if it wasn't just a way of getting his attention, and therefore best ignored. Then, of course, she accused him of being aloof and uncaring. It was a no-win situation.

As Christopher poured out his woes to Milly, he felt at ease for the first time in nearly a year. Just talking to her made the vice around his chest relax.

'A lot of women feel a bit ropey when they're pregnant,' Milly assured him.

'Not the whole time, surely?'

Tentatively he touched Milly's fingertips with his, but she drew her hand away.

'No,' said Milly.

'No, because I'm married?' he asked.

'No, because she's pregnant,' Milly explained. 'It's bad enough feeling fat and ugly without your husband getting his oats elsewhere . . . literally, in my case!'

Christopher admired the way Milly was always ready with a joke to mask her pain.

'After, then?' Christopher tried to push her, knowing he

361

could bear it, bear anything, if there was the glimmer of a prospect of seeing Milly again.

'Having a child changes things,' Milly informed him sagely. 'You'll probably feel differently about everything.'

'But if I don't?' he asked eagerly.

'I can't make any promises,' she said.

Christopher leaned towards her, closing his eyes in anticipation of a kiss, only to open them again suddenly as he felt a sudden smack of liquid on his face.

'What the . . . ?'

At first he thought it must be a seagull relieving itself above their heads, but there was far too much liquid for that. And when he wiped it away with the back of his hand, it was a strange charcoal-black colour, like the slippery grime on a city pavement when it rains after a long dry spell.

'Someone up there doesn't approve!' Milly pointed at the pale aquamarine sky.

'Actually, it was Fiammetta Dearchild,' said Christopher, kneeling up to look over the wall, seeing the small red-headed figure walking down the hill. 'I don't think she saw us.'

Millicent wiped the dirty water off his face with a hand-kerchief. Her face had escaped most of the dirty water, but there were a couple of blue-black spots on her cleavage, like the stigmata of sin, he thought.

'I think it's a sign,' said Milly. 'Don't you?'

'But after . . .' He tried to resume the conversation they'd been having before the interruption.

'Things will be different,' said Milly. 'You won't know what's hit you,' she laughed.

On the way back to the hotel, Christopher's step felt lighter. Even though the explanation that a young artist had inadvertently emptied some paint water on to him begged a good many questions about what he'd been doing, he couldn't seem to make himself worry about it. As it turned out, nobody was the slightest bit interested in why his shirt was covered in grey watermarks, or why his face looked as if it had been down a coalmine.

Christopher was greeted on the steps by his mother with a thunderous look on her face. Julia had gone into labour, and was not being very stoical about it. In Christopher's absence, they'd had to bring her into the hotel, because she couldn't really be left on her own in the flat. Granny Ruby was with her, but even she couldn't seem to calm her down. An ambulance had been called, but it would be appreciated if Christopher could try to make Julia scream a little more quietly because it was terribly off-putting for the guests who were eating dinner.

'Oh, for God's sake!' Christopher suddenly felt rather defensive on his wife's behalf. He could think of nothing worse than Granny Ruby if you were in pain.

'She's not the first woman in the world to give birth,' said Libby.

'She is having your grandchild,' Christopher pointed out.

'Angela never made all this fuss!' said Libby, reminding him yet again that his sister had provided their parents with the first grandchild, as well as the first wedding, as well as all her trophies and now her thriving business.

Christopher marched up the staircase and along the corridor to Granny Ruby's suite of rooms.

Julia was sitting on a hard chair, around which were spread out several large hotel towels. She hadn't got any make-up on, and she looked terribly young and vulnerable. Suddenly her face contorted with the pain of a contraction, and she let out a peculiar howl. It was a disturbing sound and the hotelier in Christopher couldn't help envisaging the Squadron Leader, a regular guest since the war, pre-paring to put a spoonful of trifle in his mouth, hearing the unholy shriek and missing. Christopher closed the door behind him.

'You poor thing,' he said, walking to Julia's side, not quite knowing whether to touch her or not. His hands remained suspended six inches from her body until the contraction subsided and he felt it was safe to stroke her back.

Christopher struggled to remember relevant passages from the book she'd made him read about childbirth. There'd been quite a lot about what to pack in the hospital bag, and a countdown of things to do as the intervals between contractions got shorter, but he had clearly missed the chance to run a nice hot bath for her or ask Chef to make some sandwiches. With intervals of less than five minutes, Christopher glanced anxiously at his watch. He thought they should probably be at the hospital by now.

'What do you want me to do?' he asked his wife.

'Stay with me, please,' she told him. 'I'm frightened.'

'You're going to be fine,' Christopher told her, patting her hand. 'I think I can hear the ambulance coming.'

Was that the distant wail of a siren, or was it just hope playing tricks on him? The idea that he might have to deliver the baby himself sent spasms of panic through his body. Should he boil some water, as they always did in films? What was the water actually for? Surely it would scald a newborn? It hadn't said anything about boiling water in the book. Perhaps he should fetch more towels from the laundry room?

'Don't leave me!' cried Julia.

'Do you think it would help if you stood up, or lay down?' Christopher asked, suddenly wondering why she was sitting on such an uncomfortable chair.

'If my waters break, it'll ruin the carpet, or any upholstered furniture,' said Julia, obviously repeating instructions.

'For God's sake!' said Christopher. 'What's wrong with everybody?'

Julia cowered.

'I don't mean you,' he told her. 'Bugger the bloody carpet!'

He didn't usually swear, and the words hung in the air, then Julia giggled, and as they smiled at each other like conspirators, he felt rather pleased with himself, and was tempted to swear again. Now he was sure he could hear the siren of the ambulance approaching; it wasn't an illusion.

It was the most visceral experience to see the bloody form of a new human being emerging from a woman's body, and the most humbling.

'A beautiful boy!' the midwife said, holding the baby by its ankles and giving it a good slap on its tiny puce bottom.

Christopher's first thought was that his son had been blessed with the most enormous penis. But then he realized it was the umbilical cord. The midwife clamped and cut it, then put the baby, still with its coating of gore, on Julia's chest.

'Hello!' she said, as if she already knew the baby, and then the image of the two of them – his wife, his son! – blurred. And Christopher realized he was crying.

'Why are you all dirty?' Julia suddenly asked, as if she'd only just noticed.

Michael's decision to leave the door of his study open, the last page of the story still in his old Remington electric typewriter, hadn't quite constituted an invitation for Fiammetta to read it, but when he walked past and saw his daughter bent over his desk, concentrating so hard on deciphering the words that she didn't hear him, his heartbeat quickened. It seemed like an age before she came down the spiral staircase into the big, open-plan living room with the typescript pages of the story in her hand.

'What's this?' Fiammetta said, flapping the pages at him.

'What?' Michael tried to feign ignorance.

'This,' said Fiammetta.

'It's a story I've written.'

'It's called "The Scream".'

'Yes.'

'Why?'

'Why what?' Michael asked.

'Why did you write it?' his daughter demanded.

It wasn't the reaction he had hoped for.

'I don't know why anyone writes anything. To try to illuminate something, to explain . . .'

'To whom?' she demanded.

'I don't know who to!' Michael shouted in exasperation. Then calming himself down, he asked, 'What did you think of it?'

'Doesn't matter what I think, does it?' Her voice was thick and she wouldn't look at him.

'Of course it does,' he said, risking a step towards her, a hand reaching out to touch her arm, but she stepped back.

'I suppose you thought you were writing about me, trying to explain me, but you weren't. You were writing about you. It's all about your emotions. It's so . . .' She struggled for the right word. 'It's so dishonest!' she finally said.

The word cut into him like a knife. He stared at her in shock. He hadn't heard her say so many words at once in years. Such precisely chosen words. His daughter stared back, full of rage. Now he was the one struggling for the right vocabulary.

'But don't you think,' he said eventually, in the hope of appealing to her on another level, 'don't you think that every artist is in some sense trying to understand themselves in their work?'

Fiammetta's face relaxed a little as if to acknowledge that his question was a serious one.

'Steve says that when you paint portraits of other people, the process is still fifty per cent about you,' Fiammetta conceded.

'Who's Steve?' Michael asked.

'Steve. Steve Green. You met him!' she said impatiently, when Michael still failed to respond. 'The one who arranged my show.'

Fiammetta's series of *Scream* paintings had been included in the exhibition in the Town Hall. The *Lowhampton Echo* had called her a darkly precocious talent.

'Your art teacher?'

Fiammetta nodded. There was a little smile on her face, almost a private smile. It was a look he hadn't seen before.

'You call your art teacher Steve?' he asked.

'It's his name,' she said.

'Don't you be cheeky with me, young lady!'

Fiammetta stared at him as if she couldn't quite believe he'd said that. Nor could he.

She was a teenager, he thought, and the last time he'd had to deal with a teenager was with Iris. Except he hadn't dealt with her, he'd left it mostly to Sylvia. And now he was talking as if he had suddenly transformed into Sylvia himself.

'Do you hang out with Steve, then?' he tried again, but he could see from Fiammetta's squirm of embarrassment that it was even worse when a parent tried to use teenager language.

'It's really none of your business, is it?' she said cockily.

'I think that rather depends on the nature of your relationship.' Michael rose to the bait. 'You're only four-teen . . .'

'You're not really in a position to advise anyone else about relationships, are you?' Fiammetta taunted. 'Especially not with inappropriately young women.'

Michael thought of all the times he had looked at Fiammetta, wishing she would speak, and now she was. From some distant place in his memory, he heard an echo of one of Sylvia's singsong platitudes: 'Be careful what you wish for, because it might just happen!'

For a long moment, they stared at each other, and then Fiammetta slammed his story down on the table and marched down the stairs.

'Where do you think you're going?' Michael called after her.

But she didn't reply.

He stood for a few minutes in a silence that felt hot with recrimination, and then he went upstairs to see if he could see from the top window which way she had gone. It was late, but the darkness was not quite complete because it was so close to the longest day. There was a gang of young people throwing a Frisbee on the beach. He could make out Bruno's form among them, not just because he was one of the taller ones, taller now than Michael, but because there was a particular energetic quality to his body shape, a determination to catch when he leaped, rather than flail indecisively in the air. Fiammetta was not with them.

There were a few couples on the promenade, one with a pushchair. For a moment Michael remembered another warm night rather like this one, when his children were babies and he'd taken them for an evening walk in their pram, trying to give Claudia a chance to sleep. But she must have woken alarmed to find them gone, and followed them down into town. In the shadowy twilight, he could almost see the silhouette of her now, running along the promenade looking for them, anxious, even then, about him being in charge.

What a mess he'd made of it! He'd promised Claudia that he'd cope and she'd said it wasn't enough. She wanted them to have wonderful lives. But now the children barely communicated with him.

Where was Fiammetta?

It was past eleven o'clock. Michael went to Pascale's room and knocked on the door.

'Did you hear?'

She nodded.

'Was I wrong?'

'You treat her like a child,' Pascale says.

'She behaves like one!' Michael defended himself.

'No. What she said – it is all true.'

Michael looked at the floor, shaking his head, as if Pascale was turning against him too.

'You also have to learn to talk,' she said.

A picture of Fiammetta's furious face was imprinted on his mind. It was not a childish tantrum, he realized. Since the last time they had said anything of significance to one another, his daughter had grown up. The ways in which he might try to assert his authority with a child were no longer appropriate.

'You're right,' he said, sighing. 'God! Who'd have children?'

When Pascale shrugged with a kind of resignation and dropped her gaze, he felt terrible again.

'I'm so sorry!' he said.

Fiammetta was standing at the end of the harbour wall, looking out to sea.

The relief at finding her so quickly made Michael want to laugh. What melodramatic daughters he had produced, he thought, trying to set his face into a more appropriate mood of seriousness.

'I apologize,' he called to her.

Obstinately, Fiammetta did not turn round.

'What for?' she asked eventually.

The insistence on precision reminded him curiously of Claudia. She never let him get away with sloppy thinking.

'For the things I've done that upset you. I've never intended to upset you.'

Still Fiammetta didn't turn round, but he sensed a relaxation in her tight little shoulders.

'Perhaps if we talked about a few things, you could explain how I could be a bit less of an embarrassing father, and a bit more of a friend,' he said.

Finally she turned round.

'I don't want you to be a friend,' she said coldly, but he thought it was probably a sign of progress.

'You can't call a baby Cyril!' Julia told her husband.

'He won't always be a baby,' Christopher pointed out.

'That's not the point!' Julia was as surprised with the vehemence of her response as Christopher clearly was.

'How about Basil? Granny Liliana would be thrilled!'

'It's not up to Granny Liliana!'

Julia found it easier sticking up for the baby than she did for herself. There was absolutely no way she was going to allow her son to suffer because of a stupid King tradition.

'Albert?' Christopher said.

'Only if we call him Bertie,' said Julia.

'Very well. Bertie it is,' Christopher agreed, to her astonishment, dropping a kiss on the baby's head.

From the window of their flat, Julia watched her husband walking over to the hotel with their baby in the pouch he insisted on wearing against the express wishes of his mother and father. Since the delivery room at the hospital, Christopher seemed to have changed into the sensitive and considerate person Julia had originally thought he was. Christopher loved his son and his obvious pride and gratitude made him much nicer to her too.

Bertie was a good-looking baby. Even Auntie Libby, when she first saw him, was moved to remark, 'Thank goodness he hasn't got his father's looks!'

Whenever Julia took him down into town in the pram, people remarked on how beautiful he was, often adding, 'He looks just like you!'

The *Chronicle* kept asking if they could come and take a family portrait.

Julia continually reminded herself that she was the luckiest girl in the world, with everything she ever wanted, but strangely, she didn't feel the joy she knew she should be feeling. The responsibility of looking after such a small, precious creature sometimes threatened to overwhelm her. She had never been more tired, and yet at night she kept waking with a start and rushing to the cot, having to touch Bertie's face to see that he was still alive, even picking him up and shaking him, just to hear him cry.

When a passing tramp climbed into Auntie Libby's bedroom window one summer evening, Julia felt as if danger was closing in around her. As it turned out, the tramp was harmless enough, and her mother-in-law as unruffled as ever. In fact, Libby had the presence of mind to ask the intruder whether he would like a cigarette and called down to order a packet of Benson and Hedges, hoping the night porter would put two and two together and call Sergeant Benson at the police station. Instead, a mystified Sid Farthing had delivered twenty Pure Gold on a silver salver, achieving more or less the same effect. For days afterwards, Julia lay awake at night, imagining every hooting owl or creaking floorboard indicated the presence of a dark stranger.

With Adrian away, there was no one in the King household she could talk to because she knew that they would say that she was being silly or ungrateful. The Kings thought it was peculiar enough wanting to breast-feed and look after the baby herself, but if she let on about her fears they would jump at the excuse to get a nanny in. The Kings took a dim view of instability, seeing it as a lack of self-control. Through all the births, marriages and deaths she'd seen them through, Julia couldn't recall a single tear. Struggling to keep her emotions in check seemed to make them burst out at the slightest excuse. On hearing the news that the IRA had blown up a detachment of guardsmen in Hyde Park, killing several horses, Julia couldn't stop crying. On that occasion, Libby, a keen horsewoman in her youth, was uncharacteristically sympathetic, patting Julia's heaving shoulders and saying, in an approving tone, 'I had no idea that horses meant so much to you.'

When Julia's oldest friend, Cee, dropped in unexpectedly after showing a prospective buyer one of the seafront cottages at the Harbour End, to tell Julia the happy news that she and Justin had finally set a date, Julia crumpled in the midst of congratulating her and the avalanche of weeping seemed to go on for ever.

'Marriage can't be that bad, surely?' Cee attempted a joke.

As if a dam had finally burst, all Julia's misery poured out in words. She told her friend about her doubts and worries and the awful compulsion she sometimes felt to take her own life, the way her mind always presented it to her as the obvious solution, how she found herself looking at Bertie as he slept his blissfully untroubled sleep, thinking that he would be far better off without her.

Julia sniffed and gasped to a pause, then looked fearfully at her friend. Could she trust Cee? Would she think, as Julia sometimes did herself, that she was going mad? Would she tell the Kings? Would they take Bertie away from her?

Cee looked remarkably unconcerned.

'It's all quite normal, you know,' she said. 'I read about it. It's called post-natal depression, and you'll be fine once all the hormones subside.'

'Really?'

Knowing that it was something proper, with a medical name, immediately made Julia feel much better.

'I'm not going mad?' she asked.

'Course you're not!' said Cee with complete confidence. 'But I really think you ought to get out more.'

As usual, Cee's advice was sensible and practical. The Mother and Baby Group at the church hall that took place every Monday morning quickly became one of the highlights of Julia's week.

There were plenty of bad things nobody told you about having a baby, but some unexpected good things too, one of which was the ease with which you could make friends. It was at the group that Julia learned that it wasn't weird or ridiculous to feel exhausted, or anxious about your baby's vaccinations, or to walk about with baby sick on your jumper, or even to find that sex with your husband was a chore rather than a pleasure. There was a ribald camaraderie between sleep-deprived mothers, a siege mentality rather like the wartime one people talked about, Julia thought. The fact of being a new mother meant she had everything in common with women she had absolutely nothing in common with.

As she watched Bertie rolling across a mat with another little boy, she slipped into conversation with the boy's mother, only to discover that she was talking to Denise Jones, whom she hadn't seen since leaving Kingshaven Junior School. Denise had married Joe Rocco, the son of Marco Rocco who ran the Expresso bar on the promenade.

She was a nurse at Lowhampton General and now working three night shifts a week, when her husband looked after baby Luca. Denise was worried that her son was developing epilepsy because he had suffered a couple of fits, which had frightened the wits out of her. Instinctively, Julia put a comforting hand on her arm, which, to her astonishment, Denise clung on to.

'I'm sorry,' she said, as tears poured down her face, and she tried to wipe them away with her sleeve.

Julia found a tissue in her bag and handed it to her, then fetched a cup of tea and a couple of HobNobs from the hatch where the mums took it in turns to do refreshments.

'Sorry,' said Denise, sniffing hard.

'Don't be,' said Julia. 'We're all in the same boat, aren't we?'

'But you're—' Denise began then stopped.

Julia knew what she was thinking. You're a King, not a town person. Kings didn't cry. But Julia had never felt as if she was a proper King.

The Frankfurt Book Fair was the most unlikely place to fall in love.

The publishing trade's annual convention took place in a vast complex of impersonal exhibition halls linked by glass tunnels with moving walkways. Inside, it felt a bit like being in a shopping mall, with no weather or traffic noise or birdsong. And no shops either. Instead, there were miles and miles of display stands, with photos of authors and blown-up prints of upcoming book jackets. Occasionally the grid of aisles was interrupted by a café selling bitter coffee or sweet white wine. The warm air was perpetually stale and carried a slight taint of German sausage, like a burp.

Each year, as well as the top money men, who stayed in the most prestigious hotel, the Frankfurter Hof, planeloads of women whose job it was to sell foreign rights flew in with capacious handbags full of lists, sample chapters and breath-freshener spray. A small selection of editors took it in turns to man the stand, or find their way to ten-minute meetings with their peers at foreign publishing houses, where they would pitch the company's upcoming list in the hope of getting translation or American sales of their books. This year Iris was one of them. There were two big challenges: the first was finding a way of making the stories about her books fresh and different the twentieth time she told them; the second was getting out of bed after only an hour or two's sleep.

After a couple of days Iris couldn't seem to remember what life before Frankfurt had been like. The Book Fair had a routine of its own. At the end of a day's back-to-back meetings, everyone went on to parties thrown by publishers in hotels round the centre of the city. After a frenzied orgy of canapés, champagne and chatter, disparate groups of Dutch and American, English and Japanese would go in search of more alcohol, more gossip, possibly even dancing in the seedy basement discos of Frankfurt's extensive red-light district, before staggering back to their hotels, and falling into their own, or someone else's bed. Frankfurt, Iris thought, was a kind of moral bubble, like a great cruise ship sailing in international waters, where the usual rules of human behaviour did not apply. The publishing hierarchies of wealth and power were replaced by stamina and capacity for alcohol. Journalists supped with editors; grandees flirted with lowly rights assistants. Once, Iris found herself dancing opposite a German author so legendary she had presumed him dead. Another evening, she drank cocktails with an American editor who knew Norman Mailer and regularly lunched with Jackie Onassis. Iris offered private thanks to Princess Diana for making flat shoes fashionable because she knew that she could never have coped with all the walking and standing and dancing in heels. As it was, she was asked her height on several occasions by Japanese men who stared at her as if she came from a different species. Once, when she replied that she was six feet tall, the questioner had asked her to convert it to centimetres, and she realized that a red-haired giantess was going to feature in tales of his wild adventures in the West.

Wherever she was, whoever she was with, Roman always seemed to find her in the early hours of the morning. In Frankfurt, there was nothing remarkable about Iris ambling back to the hotel alongside her boss. They always took separate lifts, Roman to his penthouse suite and Iris to the ninth floor, where she would grab her toothbrush and, after checking there was no one in the anonymous sound-proofed hotel corridor, take the emergency staircase to the penthouse, to spend what was left of the night with her lover. She got used to waking up beside him, and she found it curiously intimate to eat at the same breakfast table as him, even though they were surrounded by other Portico staff comparing hangovers, checking schedules and joking about degrees of constipation due to a diet of bratwurst and sauerkraut.

By the end of the week as everyone else was longing for home, longing for spinach or fresh fruit, Iris was wishing she could stay for ever in this peculiar capsule of unreality. In Frankfurt, her lover was her companion. In Frankfurt, nothing existed apart from the heady combination of work, alcohol and Roman. She began to entertain thoughts she had always vowed not to, and to imagine what it would be like if it were like this all the time.

'Sir John and Lady Allsop invite you to join them in their lovely country home . . .'

Libby King read from the brochure that had arrived in the morning's post.

'She's obviously set her sights on rich foreigners who don't know any better,' said Libby. 'She's even offering the dubious pleasure of dining with Jolly and herself.'

The brochure was printed on thick shiny card, with full-colour photographs and words written in italic script on a background featuring a coat of arms with a shell and a castle, which Julia had never seen before. How livid James would be! As the person who would eventually inherit the Castle, and the cleverest of the Allsop children, her brother had always been much more interested in the ancestral history than she or her sisters. Even to Julia's inexpert eye the refurbishment was hardly in keeping with the building, although it did look rather swish.

'One of us ought to go and have a look,' said Granny Liliana.

All eyes swivelled towards Julia.

'Take Bertie with you, so it doesn't look as if you're interested,' added Granny Liliana.

Julia had to fight back the urge to tell the old woman that she didn't need an excuse to visit her family home, thank you very much. Sometimes the Kings behaved as if they owned her.

When Julia arrived, the front door of the huge entrance hall was open, and she was surprised to find her father sitting behind a walnut table with a bell on it and a sign saying 'Reception'.

'Sign the visitors' book!' he said, turning a large leather-bound folder round to her side and handing her a fountain pen.

Julia obliged, taking the opportunity to read some of the comments.

Mr and Mrs Winthrop from Kentucky thought it was 'a peaceful haven'.

Mr and Mrs Ikehorn from Massachusetts thought the quaint English ambience was timeless.

'My wife tells me it's important to greet the guests personally,' he told Julia, proudly showing off the range of souvenirs from umbrellas to teaspoons to pots of strawberry jam, all with the new Castle Hotel crest.

'Sylvia thinks people will resist the temptation to filch if they're given the opportunity to purchase,' he explained.

In the drawing room, a smiling Japanese couple were sitting on the edge of a newly upholstered gilt Louis XVI settee balancing bone-china cups and saucers in their small hands, and Sylvia was making small talk with occasional reference to a copy of *Teach Yourself Japanese*. The guests oohed and aahed over Bertie, and nodded enthusiastically when Sylvia asked to be excused so she could give Julia a guided tour, only to have them follow round behind, like smiling, nodding shadows.

The newly redecorated bedrooms were unrecognizable with their deep-pile fitted carpets and abundant silk curtains with pelmets and tiebacks, all in varying shades of cream, coral and eau-de-Nil. The bathrooms featured onyx and gold taps and shower heads, and some of the baths had a whirlpool function, which Sylvia demonstrated, eliciting a little giggle from the Japanese lady.

'I'm thinking about putting a sauna in the poolhouse,' said Sylvia loftily.

'Wasn't it all terribly expensive?' Julia asked her step-mother in awe.

'We've had to sell a few more bits and pieces, but the economic climate's more favourable to investment now, and with all this unemployment you can get staff for almost nothing. I still know some of the features editors, so that's been useful on the publicity front. Our four-poster room was featured in *Good Housekeeping*, and we've got our first wedding reception next weekend.'

'Did you design it all yourself?' Julia asked, sneaking a feel of the fluffy white towelling robes with the Castle Hotel crest embroidered on the pocket in peach silk thread, which were hanging over a warm rail in the bathroom.

'Obviously,' said Sylvia, looking as radiant as Julia had ever seen her.

Julia knew she should offer her stepmother a compliment, but she couldn't quite bring herself to.

'Isn't Granny Sylvia clever?' she asked Bertie, bending over the pram to tuck the pale-blue cellular blanket under his chin.

Bertie smiled up at her.

'I don't know how she does it, do you?' Julia asked.

Another smile.

'He's a lovely baby,' Sylvia offered in return. 'Doesn't

look like a King at all, does he? And boys are much easier,' she continued. 'Until they grow up, of course!'

As they both stood looking into the pram, Julia felt strangely warm towards Sylvia, as if they had at last edged across the line between hostility and respect.

'Perhaps we could make the Palace all beautiful again?' Julia asked Bertie, as she pushed the pram home. 'What do you think?'

Even though he couldn't understand a word she was saying, Bertie smiled happily up at her. There was something intensely comforting about having a little companion with a friendly disposition. Even though the rest of Julia's life didn't match up to her dream, having a baby was much better than she had ever imagined it could be, now those first difficult months were over.

'The Castle is really lovely,' she reported enthusiastically to the King family at dinner.

'Flashy, I expect,' said Granny Ruby.

'They're getting a sauna and everything,' Julia persisted.

'How undignified,' said Libby.

'Perhaps we should think about updating the facilities we have here,' Julia ventured. 'Perhaps that's what people want these days . . .'

All the Kings glared at her.

'We're hardly going to change because that's what people want,' said Granny Liliana.

Iris loved coming to the flat almost as much when Roman wasn't there as when he was. At the beginning of the week she'd bought a bunch of Stargazer lilies and eaten her sandwich every day in their company. Now they were fully out and their glorious perfume filled the attic, blocking out the smell of mouth rinse and mild singeing that pervaded the building. Iris opened the window and leaned out, listening to the traffic below. The winter air had the same delicious taste as it had when as a teenager she'd sneaked out of Lowhampton Girls' Grammar School at lunchtime and walked along the canal to the docks, to stand watching the big ships loading and unloading their cargo, daring herself to stowaway to some exotic land and become a different person.

Roman had been in New York on business, but now he was on his way home. Perhaps that was even his plane she could see in the greying sky, gradually descending towards Heathrow. Iris imagined him in the window seat looking down over the misty city as the orange lights began to come on. If the plane was on time, he had promised to come into town for a couple of hours before leaving for the country, as he did every Friday afternoon. For a moment, she wished there was a phone in the flat, so that she could ring the airport to find out whether the plane had landed. After a while, she thought about going outside to the phone box across the square, but realized she had left it too late. If the plane was on time and he was in a taxi coming to see her, he might arrive in her brief absence and leave by the time she returned.

Iris waited until it was completely dark outside and the lights in the windows of office buildings around the square had gone out before she gave up hope that he would come.

Now there was going to be no chance of seeing him properly until after Christmas. There weren't any editorial meetings over the next couple of weeks, only the office party, at which they would ignore each other, and after that he would go to the country as he always did for the Christmas period. She imagined a big house like a stately home, a roaring fire, a mantelpiece lined with invitations, Roman and Pippa holding court beside a huge and tastefully decorated Christmas tree.

Iris decided to open one of the bottles of white wine in the fridge. The cool, crisp liquid washed away the muzzy taste of the central heating, which rose up through the dentists' surgeries, making the air in the attic dry and the perfume of the lilies almost suffocating. Iris poured another glass, trying to make up her mind whether to leave the Christmas present she had brought for Roman there, or take it with her. Presents for Roman were always a problem because there was no way she could begin to match his generosity. The first present he'd given her was an early edition of *Ulysses* casually wrapped in a brown paper bag. A few weeks later, there had been a flat package containing a line drawing by Matisse.

'Is it real?' she'd asked, marvelling at the way the artist could conjure a woman's body from a few curved lines.

'Yes, it's real,' he'd said, with a slight smile that made her feel that she had said the wrong thing.

Nobody, apart from Clive, had ever bought her gifts before. As a naïve sixteen-year-old, she had been thrilled with Clive's half-pound box of Milk Tray and the watch with a diamanté face, but rapidly the trinkets had come to symbolize the gulf between them, making Iris cross that he understood her so little he imagined she would wear a St Christopher charm, or hanker after an eternity ring from Ratners.

Roman's gifts had exactly the opposite affect, reinforcing her sense of the person she was, or would like to be. Now, she wondered whether there would be a present from New York. Something expensive like the Elsa Peretti silver bean pendant in a pale-blue Tiffany box he had brought last time, or kitsch like the snow dome with the Empire State Building from the previous Christmas. The thrill was not the item itself, but the knowledge that he had been thinking about her in that forest of skyscrapers three thousand miles away.

The previous Christmas, Iris had given him a slim little leather black book for telephone numbers from Smythson in Bond Street, with 'LITTLE BLACK BOOK' stamped in gold letters on the front. Roman clearly hadn't thought it was quite as good a joke as she had. This year, she had scoured antique shops for something small but affordable, but she wasn't confident enough in her taste to choose an ashtray for his desk, let alone a print. Eventually, she had decided on a fountain pen from the 1930s. It was not a personal gift, like a pair of cuff links or a tie, that would necessitate questions as to its provenance, but if he liked it (which she still wasn't completely sure about) it would be a kind of sign. She would see its distinctive marbled casing peeping out of his jacket pocket and know that he was carrying her around with him.

Iris decided to leave the gift-wrapped box on the bed, hoping that if he did stop by on the off chance, it would make him feel guilty for letting her down.

Had he missed her? Was somebody so powerful even capable of such an emotion? How long would she have to wait before the telephone on her desk rang with the three short bleeps denoting an internal call, and his voice said, 'Are you busy?'

There wasn't really enough wine to make it worth putting the bottle back in the fridge, so Iris swigged the rest down, directly from the neck, then she took the lilies out of the water jug, tipped the water down the sink in the bathroom and returned the jug to its usual place on the shelf. She took the lilies with her, shoving them in the nearest bin outside, not wanting Roman to know that she had bought flowers in his absence in case he saw it as a sign of nesting, which she knew would make him uncomfortable.

The air temperature was freezing, but her face felt hot. On Regent Street, myriad Christmas lights strung across the street blurred instead of twinkled and the shop windows danced with decorations. Iris wanted more wine. In the off-licence next to the Algerian coffee store, she bought the cheapest bottle they had in the fridge, and stumbled up the badly lit staircase, stopping at the top as she saw someone outside their flat looking through their letterbox.

'Thank God! I thought you'd moved, or something,' said Fiammetta.

'What are you doing here?' Iris asked.

'I'm on my way to Greenham Common,' said Fiammetta.

'Does Dad know?' asked Iris, getting out her key.

'No,' said Fiammetta, looking a little disappointed with Iris's less-than-enthusiastic reaction.

'You'd better come in,' said Iris, pushing open the door.

Suddenly sober, she put the wine in the fridge and put the kettle on to make a cup of tea. Fiammetta's face was white with cold. She was wearing her school uniform, with her skirt rolled up. Her hair was long but cut into layers, like a lion's mane.

'So what's going on?' said Iris, turning on the gas fire in the living room. They both sat beside it until the room warmed up.

'There was this school Christmas service thing at Lowhampton Cathedral,' Fiammetta explained. 'Peace on earth, goodwill to men and this stupid vicar in a frock going on about the true meaning of Christmas and how detestable war was. I suddenly thought about the Peace Camp at Greenham, and I thought that's where we should be . . . so I just left . . .'

'In your school uniform?'

'I knew if I asked Dad, he'd say no. I hoped I could borrow some clothes from you.'

Turning away to pour water into the teapot, Iris smiled to herself.

Fiammetta must be about the same age as she was when she ran away from home, but it was easier when you knew you had a big sister who would put you up and lend you some clothes.

'I was sure you would be going tomorrow . . . ?' Fiammetta stated. 'Embrace the Base?' she added, when Iris didn't immediately react.

Iris felt suddenly guilty that she had been so preoccupied with Roman's return, that she'd forgotten all about the major demonstration the women on the peace vigil were organizing. In her head, Iris began to list all the reasons why she couldn't go, most of which involved the remote chance that Roman would call. Then, recognizing the gleam of adolescent righteousness in Fiammetta's eyes, she realized there was no way she was going to get out of it.

'Here's the deal,' Iris said. 'We'll go, but you have to ring Dad and tell him where you are.'

'Why?' Fiammetta asked.

'It's not fair to leave someone not knowing,' Iris told her.

'You did!'

'That's why I know it's wrong. Look, I know you really hate Dad, but you really love him too, believe me.'

'How do you know?'

'Because I'm the same.'

'Even now?'

'Even now!' Iris admitted.

Fiammetta thought about this for a moment.

'You ring him, if you want,' Fiammetta offered the compromise, so Iris picked up the phone and called Michael, who was relieved.

'I would have taken her to Greenham,' he said. 'I'm just as against cruise missiles as she is. I was a member of CND before she was born!'

'It's only women,' Iris reminded him.

'But will you tell her that?'

'I'll tell her,' said Iris.

There was no cold quite like the cold of feet in wellington boots after hours of standing in a muddy field in winter, Iris thought. The women were pressed against the hostile fence like refugees, the air was dank with fog that didn't clear, buses full of policemen revved their engines occasionally, as if threatening to run the protestors down, and yet the simple peaceful bond of holding hands with fellow human beings made her feel warm, strong and free.

She had almost forgotten how uniquely supportive the company of women could be and it made her painfully aware of what she given up in pursuit of her own selfish desires. She worked on a different floor now from the women who struggled to keep Harridan going, and in the inevitable round of redundancies, she had deliberately kept her distance. The individual pursuit of her career had led her to disregard the principles she had once lived by. Even her secretary thought she was a tyrant. The habits of secrecy demanded by her relationship with Roman had infiltrated every aspect of her life, distancing her from other people.

Beneath the essential uniform of waterproof anoraks, jeans and woolly hats, there were all shapes and sizes of women present: young mothers with children, some of whom had wedged toys into the fence; serious older women with long grey hair, who appeared at every protest Iris had ever been on and never seemed to age; students with striped scarves in rainbow colours; the usual provocative contingent from the SWP; feminists she recognized, like Maeve, whom she hadn't seen since *Siren* days, who had been living under canvas for two months. Inevitably, Josie was there.

She greeted Iris with a warm hard hug and asked, 'Returning to the fold?'

But there was affection in her voice instead of the tight barbed sarcasm she usually employed on the occasions they bumped into each other at publishing parties.

'My God! Is this Fiammetta?' Josie asked, clasping her warmly as well. 'I'm glad to see your big sister's got you in training,' she said.

'It was Fiammetta's idea,' Iris felt bound to confess.

'Good girl!' said Josie. 'Claudia would have been proud of you! I remember her being furious with me when I ducked out of the first Aldermaston march. Never been too keen on the roughing-it aspect,' she whispered behind a gloved hand. 'But I've never dared miss another one!'

Fiammetta's eyes shone. 'It's like making a giant work of art, isn't it?' she said.

Iris recognized so well the desire to appear grown up, which sometimes made the things you thought profound sound excruciatingly naïve.

'It's not about art, honey,' Josie corrected her gently. 'It's about politics.'

Some women to the left began to sing 'We Shall

Overcome', but as the crowd began to sway gently, there was a sudden rough surge to their right as a couple of the more militant women started trying to clamber over the fence. The atmosphere changed shockingly rapidly from calm to violence, and the police seized the opportunity to move in and grab the ones they thought were the ringleaders, including Iris and Josie, who were the tallest women there.

'She wasn't doing anything!' Fiammetta screamed in protest, refusing to let go of Iris. A couple of policemen grabbed her too.

'Smile! You're being photographed!' Josie called out, as a man with a camera ducked in front of them as the police dragged them towards the van.

He had a long fair fringe, which fell across his eyes, and in the split second as he took his camera from his face to push the hair out of the way, Iris thought she knew him from somewhere.

Assuming he was either from the press or MI5, who always had agents photographing protestors, or mingling with the crowds, Iris shouted, 'Scum,' and stuck her tongue out just as the flashgun went off, only realizing afterwards that she'd unwittingly provided an image that might be splashed across the Sunday newspaper that Roman would read with his toast and marmalade at his country home the next morning.

Chapter Thirteen

1984

'A change is as good as a rest,' Granny Ruby always said, and although Julia was attracted by the idea of blue sky and sunshine in the Mediterranean, she was in the early stages of her second pregnancy, and couldn't face the prospect of terrible sanitation and oily food that Auntie Libby described whenever 'abroad' was mentioned. Christopher's preferred destination for their first holiday together was Scotland, having once been on a survival course there with his school. Eventually, they compromised on a cottage near Newquay in Cornwall, a much wilder coast than they were used to, with huge flat beaches where the tide went out for miles. The idea of being in a little house all of their own with their own front door filled Julia with excitement, as she dared to dream it would be like starting over again. Perhaps when they did all the normal things together, like cooking and washing up, they would become a normal, happy couple too.

After a couple of evenings, the fantasy quietly died. Having grown used to a chef to cook his food and a waiter to serve it, Christopher didn't greatly appreciate tinned spaghetti on toast, and when he proudly returned from a fishing trip with a brace of striped mackerel with a rainbow sheen like oil on a puddle, Julia had no idea what she was supposed to do with them.

'Grill them, I think,' said Christopher, leaving her to run himself a bath.

The wet round eyes of the fish stared at her balefully, and when she attempted to remove the guts, her fingers ran with red blood like a horror film. She only just made it to the bathroom to be sick, which Christopher, lying up to his neck in warm water and fiddling with himself under his flannel, wasn't very pleased about. However hard Julia scrubbed her hands, the smell wouldn't wash away all week, providing a reminder of her incompetence whenever her hands came near to her face to lick an ice cream, or blow her nose.

The small double bed sagged and smelled musty. Away from the familiar warmth and pastel colours of his room, Bertie kept waking up in the night and climbing in with them, which was hardly conducive to a good night's sleep.

Ironically, it was being a holidaymaker that gave Julia her big idea for the Palace Hotel. Had it been a lovely sunny week, then it might never have occurred to her, but it was typically English weather, with blustery showers and drizzle that didn't prevent Christopher from engaging in any of the leisure activities he enjoyed, but was quite wearing for the beach. Julia quickly tired of sitting huddled in an anorak, exclaiming her delight at every frond of seaweed or broken shell that Bertie carried up from the water's edge for her to look at.

Christopher had a plan for each day mostly involving steep walks to remote lighthouses, or sitting on harbour walls with a fishing rod, and when Julia declined to participate, he argued that if she and Bertie weren't prepared to join him, then it was their own fault if they were bored. Although Julia was sure there was something unfair about this, she never argued, because actually it was more fun alone with Bertie than with Christopher sulking beside them.

On the beach, Julia observed that most of the families around her were in more or less the same situation as she was. While the mother spent all day trying to entertain the children, keep sand out of the sandwiches, bribe a spell of good behaviour with ice-cream cornets, and still produce an evening meal and get towels and clothes dry enough to use again, the father sat behind his newspaper, with only an occasional display of energy to help his sons dam a stream and watch gleefully, arms akimbo, as the floodwaters crept towards families pitched higher up the beach.

For most mothers holidays were just the same as normal life, except in more difficult conditions. One afternoon, Julia exchanged a sympathetic glance with a mother of four who was sitting a few feet away.

'Why do we do this?' the woman called over to her. She beckoned Julia over to share the meagre shelter of her windbreak, and the last dribble of sweet tea from her tartan Thermos. 'Truth be told, the last people families want to see on their holidays is each other. Kids want to play with other kids, he wants to read the paper, we want to have a rest . . .'

'. . . enjoy a swim without anyone splashing us,' Julia added.

'. . . have a nice dinner someone else has cooked for us, and a hot bath, not a tepid one because the rest of them have used all the hot water!' the woman finished off.

They both laughed, shared experiences enough to make them immediate friends.

'Would you keep an eye on my stuff for a moment?' The woman suddenly leaped up in a late bid to stop her older boys stamping down the younger ones' sandcastle.

Julia sighed.

In times gone by, well-to-do couples, like her in-laws, had gone away without their children. She didn't think Christopher had ever got over it. To be fair, Libby and Eddie probably hadn't imagined leaving Christopher with his grandparents would do him any harm. In those days, they didn't really know about things like psychology, did they? Now, parents usually made the choice to take

388

their children with them on holiday, forsaking their own pleasure for family time together.

But why did a family holiday have to involve the sacrifice of grown-up pleasures? Julia suddenly asked herself. Why couldn't there be such a thing as a perfect family holiday where children could play safely, and parents could also enjoy a bit of the relaxation they craved? And why couldn't the Palace Hotel provide just such a service? It was the obvious solution to all their problems.

If they had a nursery for babies, and a kids' club for children, parents could sleep all day if they liked, or lie undisturbed and unsplashed by the pool. There could be two sittings for dinner: a buffet supper for the children, then a later setting with candles on the tables, waiters, maybe even a pianist, when couples could enjoy a romantic meal in the knowledge that their children were being monitored upstairs. The investment wouldn't have to be enormous. Redecoration, a baby-listening system, a few extra staff to run some clubs – but in the summer they could probably get students for next to nothing. For rainy weather, they could have a ball pond, and table tennis, treasure hunts, painting competitions, dance classes, or indoor football in the ballroom. It would be like being back at the nursery school!

Julia could hardly wait to tell Christopher, although afterwards she wished she had waited. After a lifetime of having his own ideas for the hotel overruled, Christopher was automatically hostile to anyone else's suggestions. If she'd been more subtle about it, then he probably wouldn't have felt as if the whole world was ganging up against him.

But, to Julia's astonishment, when she mentioned the idea to Libby on their return, her mother-in-law was not so instantly dismissive.

'Mothers getting rid of their children and husbands all day?' Libby repeated sternly. 'What an attractive thought!'

'I thought we might be able to offer horseriding,' Julia ventured.

'Extra business for Angela,' said Libby approvingly. 'And Adrian could give sailing lessons at the Yacht Club,' she added.

Her favourite son had recently completed his three years in the Navy and was at a bit of a loose end.

'A real family holiday.' Libby repeated the words Julia had chosen to describe her idea. 'It's what the Palace has always done best.'

'But adapted to the needs of today,' Julia added quickly.

'What does Christopher think?' Libby asked.

Julia loyally remained silent.

'The trouble with Christopher,' said Libby irritably, 'is that he never sees the way ahead.'

Since being arrested together with Fiammetta at Greenham, and later released without charge, Iris and Josie's brush with the law had renewed the bond of affection that had always existed between them. Sitting for hours in a cell together had made Iris realize how much she missed Josie's acerbic wit and her unique take on things. The hurt they had inflicted on each other would never be forgotten, but with the common enemy of injustice, they had tacitly decided to become cautious friends again.

'Did you ever think about having a baby?' Iris asked Josie one evening, during the interval of the National Theatre's production of *Guys and Dolls*.

'In my distant youth, you mean?' Josie enquired. 'No, I'm far too selfish.'

'Yes, it would be selfish, wouldn't it?' Iris agreed.

The world seemed a more dangerous place than it had ever been. There was a bloodbath in Beirut, war between Iraq and Iran, it was raining acid instead of water. In America, people were dying of a terrible new illness that, like a cruel metaphor for the climate of right-wing intolerance, seemed exclusively to target gay men. Gavin, whose room Iris had taken in Vic's flat, had been one of the first victims of the disease they were calling AIDS. It was not a world anyone in their right mind would want to bring a child into, and yet, unaccountably, the idea of having a baby increasingly preoccupied Iris.

'Is it the old biological clock?' Josie asked.

'I suppose,' Iris replied, wishing now she'd never raised the subject.

They were standing on one of the concrete balconies looking over the Thames. Iris could never understand why people made such a fuss about the functional minimalism of the National Theatre's architecture. When you were using the building, it was the most beautiful place in London.

'Depends why you want one . . .'

She should have known that Josie would pursue the train of thought to its conclusion.

'. . . If it's because you like your genes so much you think they ought to be duplicated, then I think that's a pretty good reason,' Josie said. 'But if it's because you want to be with a man, but you can't, and you think this is your way of having a piece of him, then probably it's not such a great idea.'

She gave Iris a penetrating look, but Iris would never confess her relationship with Roman to Josie, even though she suspected that Josie had probably guessed.

'It's just that sometimes, I think the time I felt happiest was when I was looking after the twins,' Iris offered in explanation.

The bell rang for the end of the interval.

'You've always been brilliant with children,' Josie said supportively. 'And you still are, even now they're teenagers.'

The sets for the musical were beautiful. A huge disc of Caribbean moon projected on to the back cloth brought a gasp from the audience, but as Iris watched the character Sarah singing silhouetted against it, she wasn't able to lose herself entirely in the magic of the production.

With her usual insight, Josie had identified the dilemma. It wasn't just a matter of wanting a baby, any baby, it was Roman's baby Iris wanted. Although she'd resisted admitting it, she knew she loved him. And it was a completely different feeling from anything she'd previously thought of as love. What she felt for him and how she felt about herself were all inextricably bound up. Sex with him was such a profound experience, it almost felt like making a baby. But was this just another challenge she had set herself, which would not miraculously solve her life even if she achieved it?

Iris was fulfilled by her job and by her lover. What more could a girl ask for? And yet, virtually every weekend, she found herself alone, reading in her Matisse bedroom, its bright-yellow walls dulled with grief since she and Vic had learned of Gav's death, wondering whether this was it. Was this how her life was going to be? Was it enough?

Occasionally, Fiammetta came up from Kingshaven for a demo. They returned to Greenham to participate in the fourteen-mile human chain between the air base and the nuclear weapons establishment at Aldermaston. In the autumn they went on the largest CND march for twenty years. But even then, walking beside her sister, united in common purpose, Iris caught herself staring at parents with small, solemn children in miniature wellington boots, thinking how much she would like to have a little gloved hand to hold, how it might give her a sense that her life was worthwhile.

Nineteen eighty-four was not the totalitarian nightmare George Orwell had envisaged, but a much more peculiar kind of horror no novelist could have made up, thought Michael Quinn. A B-movie actor who wanted to play *Star Wars* with nuclear warheads was the most powerful man in the world, and a blonde Britannia ruled the United Kingdom with a cruise missile in one hand and a handbag in the other. The changes to the language were as insidious as newspeak. Once noble words like 'nationalization' and 'union' had become taboo, others had taken new meanings. 'Increased productivity' meant those lucky enough still to have jobs had to work harder for less money. 'Freedom' meant individuals grabbing as much for themselves as they could.

From being an almost universally disliked zealot in her first year in office, Mrs Thatcher had developed near-Messianic status since the Falklands War, and it was difficult to see how an opposition in disarray would ever depose her. If proof was needed that those whom the gods wished to destroy they first made mad, the Labour Party supplied it by electing an eccentric old Fabian to oppose Mrs Thatcher at her second election. Even the most fervent admirers of Mr Foot, among whom Michael Quinn had numbered himself in his youth, hadn't thought he had a realistic chance of being Prime Minister.

The twins, who, for as long as they'd been aware of politics had only known the philosophy people were now calling Thatcherism, neatly reflected the sharp division in society, Michael thought, as he listened to their conversation at breakfast. Bruno, who charmed his way through life with the minimum of effort, now rode along on the tide, accepting the new status quo without question. Fiammetta, who had always been quiet, appeared to have found her voice in protest.

They were sparring about the A levels they would be starting in September. Bruno's choices included Business Studies and Economics.

'Boring!' said Fiammetta.

'What's the use of Art?' Bruno retaliated.

'Philistine!'

'That's a bit of a long word for a dyslexic,' Bruno joshed.

'I don't have to spell it to know what it means!'

'Nobody makes any money out of art or literature,' said Bruno with a contemptuous glance around the shabby interior of the warehouse.

'What about Iris?' Fiammetta asked.

'Do you know what Iris is paid? People in the City make ten times her salary, and more!' Bruno said.

'Money isn't everything,' said Fiammetta.

'I'll remember that next time you tap me for cash to go up to London for one of your marches,' said Bruno.

Fiammetta smiled ruefully. 'I regard it as conscience money you pay for not having one,' she said.

'I regard it as a loan,' said Bruno with a friendly smile, taking both of their cereal bowls to the sink. 'And now, if you'll excuse me, I've got two jobs to go to.'

Bruno worked as a lifeguard on the beach during the day. With his curly hair cut fashionably short for the summer, skin that seemed to tan as soon as he stepped out of the door, and laughing dark eyes, he resembled the Roman wall painting of a beautiful young man Michael had once seen in a book about Pompeii. His tall slim body was becoming muscly from all the sport he played, and Michael could always tell where he was on the beach from the swarm of teenage girls in bikinis around his look-out chair. Michael regularly opened the warehouse door to find girls with far too much eye make-up on, who had clearly spent a great deal of creative energy making up an excuse to drop by. Had Bruno left his pen on the bus, only they'd found one and thought it looked like his? Had Bruno seen the notice on the board that he'd been picked for the athletics meeting? These days, Michael just called 'Bruno!' when he opened the door, so the girl wouldn't have to stutter through her prepared speech twice. Bruno would swagger down to accept the proffered token, or grant a smile. Sometimes he would call, 'See you on the bus!' as they left, causing ankles in high heels to turn on the cobblestones, as they swivelled to acknowledge the favour with a blushing smile.

Michael suspected that his son had already had sex with a number of girls because when he had attempted to initiate a man-to-man talk, Bruno had casually remarked, 'Look, Dad, I know how to use a condom, if that's what you're getting at.'

And that was that.

As a father, Michael felt a kind of resigned exasperation. As a man, he couldn't help being slightly in awe of his son's charm. How could Bruno be so competent so young? He could remember himself at the same age, with an almost permanent erection, but no confidence to do anything about it. The only girl he had dared speak to was Sylvia, who lived next door to his aunt's house in Etherington, where he'd gone to live in the war. Where did Bruno get it from?

The answer came one day, when Michael happened to observe Bruno leaning on the promenade railing talking to a girl in a white bikini who had an ice-cream cone in her hand. She was not a local, because locals never did any of the seaside things, like eating rock or ice cream or having cream teas. The girl was clearly so captivated by Bruno's chat-up technique that the ice cream had begun to melt and a thin white line was inching down her forearm towards her elbow. As Bruno leaned forward, took her wrist and licked the trickle away, he noticed Michael watching and winked at him.

Michael shuddered with *déjà vu*. It was the exact same sequence of actions that his older brother, Frank, had performed once in Scarborough with a waitress in a lemon uniform making knickerbocker glories behind the counter of the milk bar.

Bruno looked so much Claudia's son, everyone had expected him to have inherited her character too. When he grew up an incorrigibly happy-go-lucky boy, unlike Claudia or himself, Michael had never been able to understand how it was the meeting of their genes could have produced him. Fiammetta was the one who had Claudia's seriousness, but she had Quinn features, with Frank's red-gold hair. When she was little she'd looked so much like Frank that Michael had almost felt Frank was sending him a message. Yet as she grew up her withdrawn character was so very unlike the expansive Frank, he had not seen his brother in her face for many years. But now he had turned up again, in Bruno: knowing, charming, a terrible ladies' man. Michael found it strangely comforting as well as slightly alarming.

In the evenings, Bruno worked in the kitchen of the

Ship, making crab sandwiches and toiling over the deep-fat fryer to produce endless baskets of scampi and chips. A cluster of his female fans would congregate in the forecourt of the Ship, with one or two of them occasionally daring to slip into the yard where the dustbins were and talk to Bruno through the open window of the kitchen, until the landlady, Millicent Balls, shooed them away. With two jobs and no spare time to spend any cash, Bruno was saving quite a lot of money, but he wouldn't tell anyone what it was for.

Fiammetta, on the other hand, worked as a waitress in Cobblestones in the afternoons and used the money to pay for her art materials. Any spare cash was converted to postal orders, which she currently sent to the funds of Women Against Pit Closures. Unlike Bruno, Fiammetta had never had a gang of friends, although she was always welcome to tag along with him, and it was clear to everyone else that Nikhil Patel was besotted with her. From snatches of overheard conversation, Michael knew Fiammetta still harboured a crush on her art teacher. On the last day of summer term, she had returned from school with bloodshot eyes.

'Mr Green's getting married,' Bruno explained quietly, and Michael was touched to see that the affection between brother and sister was still so strong that Bruno knew when to resist teasing her.

He had heard sporadic bouts of weeping coming from her room since then, but they seemed to be getting less frequent.

Today, unusually, his daughter remained at the breakfast table after Bruno had left for the beach. Michael sensed there was something she wanted to ask.

'Would you mind if I went to the Miners' Rally in London?' she finally said.

'With Iris?' Michael asked, his suspicion aroused by the fact that Fiammetta had posed it as a question. Usually she simply announced her intention.

'Well, actually, no. One of her most important authors is

speaking at the Edinburgh Festival and Iris has to go and hold her hand.'

'I see,' said Michael. 'Is there anyone else you could go with?'

Fiammetta shook her head.

'I'm not really happy about you going on your own,' Michael told her. 'The government's made it quite clear at Orgreave that they're prepared to use any means. There'll be police horses, and if something goes off, I just don't like the idea of you—'

'If people like you are frightened, then they've won,' Fiammetta interrupted.

He looked at her. Just like Claudia, he thought, with her clarity of thought, and her courage. He remembered the time they'd bumped into each other on the first Aldermaston march. A nun in a duffel coat, he'd thought.

'I'll come, if you like,' Michael heard himself responding to the challenge.

He'd long since grown cynical enough to know that marching with a banner never changed anything, but he recognized his younger daughter's wish to do something and thought it deserved his support.

He could see Fiammetta weighing up commitment to the cause against the potential embarrassment of having him with her.

'I'll pretend I'm not with you if you like,' he offered half jokingly. 'I'll sit in another compartment on the train and walk a safe distance behind. But I don't want you going on your own.'

'OK, then,' she said finally, as if she was the one who was doing the favour.

At Lowhampton Station the next day, after a quick glance round the carriage to check there was no one she knew, Fiammetta indicated that he could sit at the same table as her. The other passengers were mostly families going on day trips to London as a holiday treat.

'Nobody seems to care, do they?' said Fiammetta as the

train pulled out of the station. 'Even people who say they care, like Nikhil Patel, are too cowardly to do anything about it because their father wouldn't like it.'

'Don't be too hard on the Patels,' Michael said. 'It's often people who feel they are outsiders who feel they have to conform . . . be more British than the British, if you like. Especially in a place like Kingshaven.' He tried not to sound like he was lecturing.

'My wife Sylvia was just the same. When I went on the first Aldermaston march, her main worry was that someone would see me with my rucksack and ask where I was going. When I turned up on television, she never forgave me—'

'You appeared on television?' Fiammetta interrupted.

'Only on the news, as part of the crowd, but the way Sylvia went on you'd think I'd been carrying a banner saying, "Hello, Kingshaven!"'

Fiammetta granted him a small smile.

'Whatever made you come to a place like Kingshaven?' she asked.

Michael was enjoying the conversation and didn't want to spoil it by giving her an untruthful version of events.

'When I got my teaching qualification I applied to education authorities all over the place,' he said, carefully sticking to the bare facts, leaving out any mention of the reason they'd had to leave Etherington.

'I was offered a job in Kingshaven and I knew the name from a postcard my brother, Frank, sent me. He was billeted in the Palace Hotel for a period during the war. It looked a bit nicer than what we were used to. So Sylvia and I thought we'd give it a go, somewhere new. Lots of people felt like that after the war.'

'And then you met my mother,' Fiammetta cut in.

'Yes,' said Michael. 'We were both outsiders.'

'And you fell hopelessly in love?' she said.

'Yes,' said Michael, wondering where this was leading.

'I'm never going to fall in love again,' said Fiammetta categorically.

He wanted to say, 'You will, you will!' but daren't.

She turned her head and looked out of the window, making it clear that the conversation was over.

Tom Snow's photographic studio was in the flat above the shop that had once been Granny Ruby's, then Sylvia Quinn's, and was now the Happy Dragon Chinese restaurant and takeaway. The smell of garlic and Chinese spices was deliciously appetizing when you walked past, but Julia suspected you'd get sick of it if you worked here. In one of the diet books she and Cee and Bee used to follow rigorously for a few days at the gatehouse, before one of them cracked and brought home a giant bar of Cadbury's Dairy Milk, Julia remembered reading that 50 per cent of a person's sense of taste was in fact smell. Perhaps someone should write a diet book called *The Cooking Smells Diet*. It would be enormously popular because it didn't involve restricting yourself to beans, or searching for a constant supply of fresh pineapple, or even doing aerobic exercise. Perhaps she should even write it herself! People were always asking how she had got so thin. All you had to do was live near a restaurant, or hotel. If you woke every morning in a farty cloud of scrambled egg it was no problem at all to skip breakfast. If the smell of fish on Fridays was so strong you actually had to change your clothes before going out, you certainly didn't feel like eating lunch. Sitting in the small reception room of Tom's studio, Julia thought how much simpler it was to breathe a mouthful of sweet and sour pork coming up from the restaurant, than to eat it and throw it up later.

Tom's studio was in the long room that had originally been Granny Ruby's sitting room. Julia could just about remember visiting as a small child, sitting on the edge of the seat of a stiff armchair, with her hands in her lap and her knees together as Granny Ruby demanded. With net curtains and a dark patterned carpet, the room had seemed very dark then, so Julia had been surprised the first time she'd come to have a family portrait taken to see that there were two sets of French windows on to the balcony, and lots of natural light pouring in. The rooms at the back of the flat, looking over the yard where Mr Wong sometimes smoked a cigarette between customers, were now used as a dark room and reception area.

Julia thought the room she was sitting in had once been Mummy's bedroom. In those days, the walls had been lined with shelves of dolls wearing national costumes from every country in the world – except Germany and Japan – which Granny Ruby had stitched from off-cuts during the long lonely hours of blackout. The dolls had come with Mummy to the Summer House when she married Daddy, and Julia and her sisters had played with them over the years, often not as carefully as Granny Ruby would have liked. When they'd moved up to the Castle, the dolls must have been put in a box. They were probably still in one of the attics. It made Julia feel a bit sad to think of them all lying one on top of the other, trapped in the dark.

The walls of the reception area were covered with the best examples of Tom Snow's portraits over the years. Smiling couples with smiling children smiled down at Julia from every angle. The undertaker's daughter, Una, her husband, Simon Ironside, who was currently captain of the lifeboat, and their four boys trussed up in their Sea Scouts uniform; Angela and Miles Fogg with baby Piers; there was even a black-and-white photo of Tom Snow himself with a much younger and slimmer Pearl, and their two small children, Susannah and Damian, both adults now, all glowing with happiness. Julia tried to estimate how long it was after the photo was taken that Tom and Pearl had divorced. From such joy to such misery in so few years! She peered at the soft-focus shot. Had they really been happy even then? Perhaps one or other of them was already having an affair. Whoever it was who said that the camera never lied had been a liar.

Whenever pictures of Julia appeared in the paper, cutting the ribbon to open the Flower Festival, for example, or dressed up for the Rotary Dinner at the Yacht

Club, she was always amazed how different she looked from how she had actually felt. Now, as her eyes skimmed rows of familiar faces, both Kings and town people, their features ageing gradually over the years, it was like seeing a time-lapse history of Kingshaven's population: bald babies became children with cherubic curls; plump, embarrassed teenage girls become slim, confident brides, then reappeared as overweight mothers with taut smiles; men with hair a few shades greyer between portraits, or occasionally, a few shades darker; men with hair, and then without; crooked teeth replaced by gleaming dentures.

Julia's eyes stopped on a picture of herself in the black-and-white era, wearing her Guinevere dress, hair still matted from her dip in the sea, posing next to the hour-glass figure of Millicent Bland, her long white Roman dress slit almost to her waist, the Miss Kingshaven tiara slightly askew. There was a colour portrait of Millicent as a bride with a small but visible bump, and a family portrait of her with her husband, Gerry, fair hair shining in the studio lights like halos against the dark-blue velvet curtain, and in front of them two children, a boy smiling with no front teeth, and a pretty little girl. One of each. The perfect family, Julia thought bitterly.

'Here we are!'

Julia was startled as Tom came back in and presented her with a large brown envelope.

'I think it's come out very well,' he said, pulling out one of the smaller prints in a cardboard frame.

Julia examined the portrait. The morning the photo had been taken, her hair had been blow-dried by Tracy Dyer, who had taken over her mother's salon, changing the name from Get Set to Uptown Girl. Tracy had sprayed the big waves flicking away from Julia's face so much they had lasted the whole day. Julia was tipping their tiny new son, Archie, in his white christening robes towards the camera. Christopher, with a firm paternal hand preventing two-year-old Bertie from toddling off to investigate the toy the photographer held up, was smiling beside her. Anyone who saw the photo would be in no doubt that this was a vibrantly happy young family with a wonderful future ahead of them.

For a moment, the photo seemed almost more real than the reality of Julia's life. There it was in print. Proof that nothing was wrong. Maybe she *had* let her imagination get the better of her. Maybe Christopher *was* right to wonder if she was going a bit mad again, like she had after Bertie was born.

In the picture, there was no indication of disappointment on Christopher's face, no sign on hers of the sheer humiliation of the unholy row in the churchyard that had occurred less than an hour before the photo session, when Christopher had remarked to Mummy that he would have preferred a girl and Mummy had started screaming at him that he was an ungrateful bloody fool because her life had been ruined by having girls.

This picture would be the only memory that would remain of Archie's christening day, and Julia found that comforting. When they were grown up, her children would look at all the photos and think what a lovely childhood they'd had, and that was exactly how it should be.

In the end, Julia told herself, nothing else mattered as long as she could make her children happy. Even if marriage wasn't as lovely as she'd thought it would be, motherhood was infinitely better than she'd ever dreamed. There was no better feeling than being able to make Bertie laugh when he'd fallen over and scraped his knee, or smelling his hair after a bath, or watching little Archie sleeping. Just to be with them was luck enough, and she would always be there for them, and never leave them, as Mummy had left her and James.

Julia slipped the print back into the envelope.

'How much do we owe you?' she asked Tom Snow.

'On the house,' said Tom. 'It's family, after all.'

He winked at her. They both knew what it was like being married to a King, and yet, oddly, Tom was one of the few people who'd fallen out with a family member but was still welcomed at family occasions. It was as if everyone acknowledged how difficult it must have been to be married to Pearl and didn't blame him. And, of course, it was always useful to call upon the services of a professional photographer, especially if he didn't charge, a calculation that certainly wouldn't have escaped parsimonious Auntie Libby.

Out on the street, clutching the envelope to her chest, Julia felt a spring in her step. There was a cold wind blowing off the sea. The season was most definitely over for another year. The hotel had just about scraped through and soon would close for remodelling. The ballroom was to be stripped and painted like a jungle. Julia had ordered the soft play apparatus in bold primary colours. The baby monitoring system, operated from the reception desk, was already wired in. In order to finance the initial phase, the contracts of all the permanent staff except the night porter had been terminated. It had pained Libby King, who'd always considered herself a good employer, but as she herself had put it, 'We're all having to tighten our belts.'

Plans the architect had drawn up for the enclosure of a swimming pool in a modern conservatory with a retractable roof were going to have to be redrawn because Christopher was so adamantly opposed to what he called a blemish on the integrity of the building he had threatened to write a letter to the paper, if nobody took any notice of him. Otherwise, everything was going ahead. Julia could hardly believe it. Even though Auntie Libby was a different generation, she could see that they had to adapt or die, and though he didn't much enjoy the idea of change, Eddie King was resigned to it. Julia sometimes wished that Christopher could be as practical.

Walking past Cobblestones, the tea shop, Julia was aware of a tapping on the window, and she turned to see Bee sitting at the window table beckoning her in.

'What are you doing?' Julia asked.

'Reading my horoscope,' said Bee. 'Listen to this:

"Sometimes a setback is a blessing in disguise. With Venus in the ascendant, love may be found in unexpected places . . ."'

'Well, that sounds OK,' said Julia. 'Apart from the setback, of course. What do you think that might be?'

'I've been sacked,' said Bee.

'Oh! Why?'

'The official reason is that there isn't enough business during the winter to employ a full-time receptionist. The unofficial one is that Angela caught us . . .'

'Not Gerry?'

The last time they'd spoken about Bee's on-off affair, it was completely and finally over, and Bee was so angry she had squeezed superglue in the ignition of his motorbike. How could they be at it again? And if they were, did that mean that Millicent would be coming after Christopher? Julia wondered. Was that the reason for his almost constant dissatisfaction with her?

'Isn't a job more important than sex?' Julia asked prissily.

'Nobody who has had good sex would say that,' said Bee.

'So what's mine?' said Julia, trying to hide her discomfort by pointing at the horoscope.

'"Change begets change. You may not fully understand what you are letting yourself in for . . ."' Bee read.

'That doesn't sound very optimistic, does it?' said Julia despondently.

'At least you don't have to worry about getting a job right at the end of the season when everything's packing up. And Sylvia's chucking me out of the gatehouse. She wants to turn it into a honeymoon suite, apparently.'

Poor Bee. Her problems were much worse, Julia thought.

'Why don't you ask Adrian?' she suddenly asked. 'He's looking for someone to help him at the Yacht Club. The sailing lessons went really well this summer, and he's thinking of adding kayaking next year, maybe even windsurfing. You were always brilliant at sport.'

'But I don't really know Adrian,' said Bee dismally.

404

'I'll ask him then,' said Julia. 'I'm sure you'd get on.' Filled with renewed energy at the thought of helping two of her friends, she stood up. 'Don't worry,' she told Bee, understanding her apparent reluctance. 'He's not a bit like the rest of them!'

The leaves were falling and the air smelled slightly of smoke. The year was coming to an end. As Iris walked across the square, she tried to talk herself out of the conversation she was about to start. Her gut instinct, the talent that had drawn Roman to her, was screaming out that he would reject her ultimatum. Inevitably, their relationship would disintegrate as truths, once spoken, could not be retracted. It might even become impossible for her to work at Portico. The process might be agonizingly slow, like the drip drip of a tap before the washer fails, or instant. Roman was ruthless. In an hour's time, she could well have lost everything in her life that she had worked for and loved. It was completely mad to do this.

And yet she knew that she couldn't go on as she was, because the self-destructive part of her brain that had posed the question was clamouring for an answer. Faced with the choice of losing her, what would Roman do? If he didn't love her enough, then what was the point in going on?

Iris stood for a moment at the foot of the steps up to the attic, and then clattered up to meet her fate.

Roman was standing at the window, which immediately threw her, because she had expected him to be in bed, as usual. They would make love, as usual. Before she lost him, she wanted one last exquisite memory to keep. Perhaps it would be so wonderful, he would not be able to contemplate giving her up . . .

'Ah, Iris! Here you are!' he said, the timbre of his voice the same as he used at work.

'Here I am,' she repeated.

The distance between the door and the window suddenly seemed enormous.

'There's something I've been wanting to discuss. It's

a bit of a delicate subject. I don't know how to put it exactly . . .'

Iris had never seen Roman struggling like this.

'I've been having exactly the same trouble,' she said.

Had he guessed what she was going to say? Had she dropped clues? Was he going to pre-empt her? Maybe she had read him all wrong. Maybe he'd been as tormented as she had!

'Well?' Roman said.

'No, you!'

Negotiating with him was a bit like a chess game, and strategy had never been one of her strong points, but she had learned that it was better to let him speak first.

'I'll be frank,' Roman went on.

His clipped businesslike voice didn't sound as if he was about to suggest what she had in mind and she was suddenly terrified he was going to dump her.

'It's just, well, how can I put it discreetly? Do you think, in the light of present circumstances, we ought to be using . . . um . . . protection?'

Iris frowned. 'What do you mean?'

'I mean condoms,' said Roman.

'Condoms? I'm on the Pill!'

The conversation was suddenly so unlike the one she planned in her head, it felt like being in a nightmare, screaming but unable to make a sound.

'Yes, but . . . um. Well, it's a matter of life and death these days,' said Roman.

'You've lost me,' said Iris honestly.

'Oh, for goodness' sake!' Roman said impatiently. 'AIDS.'

He was joking, wasn't he? He wasn't.

'AIDS? You think I might have AIDS?' Iris asked, her voice rising.

'I wasn't suggesting . . . just a precaution . . .'

'But I don't. I haven't . . . the time before we . . . AIDS wasn't even invented!'

'Oh, come on, Iris!' said Roman.

He didn't believe her!

'I gave up sex in nineteen seventy-six. Too many complications . . . you see . . .'

How could she begin to explain herself? Why should she have to?

'You're the one who's sleeping with someone else!' she went on the attack.

The slight flush of colour on Roman's cheeks answered a question she had never dared to ask him. Did he still have sex with Pippa? The answer was clearly yes.

'For all I know, Pippa's got a team of rent boys giving her one!' she lashed out.

'For God's sake, Iris!'

Roman's expression of distaste was much worse than his anger.

'You can hardly claim the moral highground,' he said, infuriatingly cold. 'You're living with someone! You told me yourself . . .'

'What?' Iris was mystified.

Suddenly she remembered that time in the Salisbury pub, when she'd let him think that someone was waiting for her at home, deliberately misleading him because she wanted to make herself appear more mysterious. Had he only made his move on her because she was attached? Had he considered her safer that way?

'Do you feel guilty?' he'd asked, and she thought he meant about his wife. Did he really think she was the sort of person who would betray a man she was living with all this time?

'He's GAY!' she screamed. 'The man I live with is GAY!'

Roman flinched, the famous left-wing publisher not quite so liberal-minded now.

'You can't catch it from lavatory seats, you know,' she told him bitterly.

When they'd heard about Gav, Iris had asked Vic, 'You are careful. Aren't you?'

'I'm a one-man man these days,' he told her.

But she still worried that Vic wasn't taking it seriously enough.

Perhaps Roman was right to ask. Perhaps it was the responsible thing to do, in this day and age.

They stared at each other blankly, their minds trying to compute the bits and pieces of assumption and half-truth into a different reality from the one they had each constructed. For a moment, Iris could see them as a third party might, two characters playing out their little drama in this enclosed set, standing as far apart as the space would let them, as if one of the poles of magnetic attraction that had drawn them together had now turned, creating an almost tangible force field to keep them apart. The difference between a relationship and an affair, she thought, was mainly about space. Everything she and Roman had learned about each other, they had learned in this small room. The insidious necessity of secrecy had cut them off from the usual kind of social interaction that would have unveiled mistaken assumptions much earlier. She thought of the flat in Pinter's *Betrayal*, the play that Roman had urged her to see. Had that too been a discreet message, something he had expected her to understand?

'What was it you were going to say?' Roman finally asked.

His voice was soft, conciliatory, and Iris knew that if they stopped now, like sensible gamblers, took their losses, collected up the remaining chips, the possibility remained that they could return to the tables another day.

'Doesn't matter,' she said, putting her hand out behind her to open the door, turning to leave, but something inside her wouldn't let her go.

'There's something uncompromising about you and your commitment to everything you do,' he'd told her the first time. 'Reckless, almost . . .'

'What the hell!' she said, deciding to risk one last throw of the dice even though all the odds were stacked against her. 'I want to have a baby.'

The longer the words hung in the space between them, the surer she was that she had lost everything.

'Oh, Iris, Iris!' he said eventually, his voice half scolding, half exasperated, as if she was a child.

'Iris what?' she demanded.

'I can't. I can't give you what you want,' he said. 'I'm so sorry.'

'I wouldn't ask anything of you. I don't want your money . . .'

He was shaking his head.

'I could have done it without telling you,' she tried to appeal to his sense of justice, 'but I didn't think that would be fair . . .'

'Iris! Listen to me! I can't have a baby with you,' he told her firmly.

'Why? I'd be a good mother. I know I don't look as if I would, but you should have seen me with the twins, honestly, I'm much better than you'd think.'

'I have no doubt that you'd be a good mother,' said Roman.

'Why, then?' she asked.

'I've had the snip . . . a vasectomy . . . long before . . .'

Another twist of betrayal. Iris felt fury rising inside her.

'Why didn't you tell me?' she demanded.

'You never asked,' he countered.

'But I told you I was on the Pill. You've let me be on the Pill for three years for nothing?'

'I didn't think I was the only one.' He shrugged his shoulders, almost bashful, like a clever little smartarse schoolboy arriving at the simple conclusion of a maths problem. QED. He smiled at her.

'You bastard!' Iris shouted. 'You fucking smug bastard!'

Now she grabbed at the door handle, unable to leave the room fast enough, and ran down the steps to the fifth floor, punching the button, waiting for the lift, half expecting him to rush after her. He didn't. The lift was taking a ridiculously long time. She pushed the button again, then, unable to bear the thought of Roman emerging, assuming

409

the coast was clear, and finding her still standing there, she decided to take the stairs. Her footsteps clattered metallically in the echoey stairwell.

Just after the third-floor landing she became aware of quick light footsteps following her down. She could tell without looking round that the person behind was tall and in a hurry. She stopped at a corner and shifted to one side to let him pass.

'I thought it was you!' said Winston Allsop, standing on the narrow bit of the marble step beside her.

His smile was white enough to be an advertisement for the dentist he had just visited, and his voice so friendly, Iris felt her eyes welling.

'Hey!' said Winston, automatically putting his arm around her. 'Hey. What's up?'

Iris shook her head, unable to speak. Suddenly the lift shaft banged and the cage began to travel up the filigree shaft beside them. Determined to avoid an encounter with Roman in the entrance hall, Iris grabbed Winston's hand and started running down the remaining floors and past a surprised porter in the hall.

Outside, she hailed a cab, and, as Winston jumped in beside her, Iris swivelled to look out of the rear window to see if Roman came out of the building. Only when the cab turned into Regent Street did she face forward.

'What's going on?' Winston asked.

'I needed to get out of there,' Iris told him, getting her breath back.

'Not my favourite place, either,' said Winston. 'Did you have a filling?'

'Not today,' Iris smiled bitterly.

'Where to?' asked the cab driver.

Iris looked at her watch. It was only mid-afternoon, but it was already getting dark.

'I should go back to work, but I don't feel like it,' she said.

'My next appointment's not until five,' said Winston. 'Why don't you come and have a cup of tea at my place?' said Iris. 'It'll do you good to see how the other half lives.'

If Winston was surprised that she was still living in a council flat with a pile of filthy sleeping bags in the well of the staircase, where homeless people slept, he didn't show it, but as Iris opened the door and flicked on the light she was achingly conscious of the shabbiness of the flat's decoration, and the grime on the stove, which was too old to clean properly.

'Great location!' said Winston diplomatically. 'You'll make a killing when you exercise your right to buy. Place like this.'

'I'm not intending to exercise my right to buy,' said Iris, lighting the gas under the kettle with a match.

Winston looked slightly mystified. 'And I thought dinosaurs were extinct,' he remarked. 'I'd heard you were a bit of a capitalist yourself, these days.'

'Me?'

'You can't be a fan of *Dallas* and not be a capitalist, can you?'

'Oh, that!'

In a recent interview in *Publishing News*, Iris had tried to explain the different kinds of pleasure she got from books. Comparing the experience of reading with watching television, she was quoted as saying that sometimes she was in the mood for *The Jewel in the Crown*, and sometimes she craved the sinful escapism of *Dallas*, but everyone knew they were both really good, well-made programmes.

'All I was trying to say was just because a lot of people want to read something doesn't mean it's trash. People in publishing are such terrible snobs about commercial fiction. Especially if it's written by women.'

A flurry of disgusted letters had been sent to the editor, asking why anyone who was serious about books would be watching television anyway.

'I don't believe an old socialist like you enjoys *Dallas*,' said Winston.

'I find the message appealingly subversive,' argued Iris

411

self-mockingly, 'JR is the epitome of capitalism and we all hate him . . .'

Winston grinned at her. 'You haven't changed,' he said.

'Unfortunately not,' said Iris.

'And you look just the same!'

'You wouldn't say that unless thirty-four was so horribly old!'

'There's still no pleasing you, is there, Iris?'

She shook her head.

'What number wife are you on now?' she asked him sharply.

'Just the two. Candy and I have gone our separate ways . . .'

Now he was the one looking at the floor.

The lino was so old, she noticed, it was crumbling along the cracks.

'Children?' Iris asked.

'It never felt like the right time. What about you?'

The kettle started whistling.

'Who'd bring more children into this world?' said Iris, pouring hot water on a couple of tea bags in mugs.

The news recently had been full of footage of emaciated African children, their huge eyes shining with silent suffering.

'Quite,' said Winston. 'As a matter of fact, this meeting I'm going to is about raising money for the famine victims in Ethiopia.'

'How?' Iris asked.

'We're putting together a record. You'd be surprised by some of the names on board . . .'

'The music industry gets a political conscience, and I don't suppose it's bad for record sales either,' said Iris sarcastically.

'It's record sales that make these guys powerful. You can be as cynical as you want, but if everyone's singing a song about famine at Christmas, the government is going to look pretty uncharitable if they don't do something about it . . . what?'

'I thought I just caught a glimpse of a revolutionary I used to know when I was a teenager,' Iris said.

Winston laughed.

'How are the twins?' he asked, taking the cup of tea she offered him.

'Fiammetta is left wing and arty. Bruno likes sport, girls and money. They're quite normal really. You're very good at remembering their birthday, by the way. I don't suppose they write, but they do appreciate it. Money's quite tight, I think.'

'I'd like to see them again. Maybe when one of them's next in London. Do you think they'd like to have lunch at the Hard Rock? I've got a gold card. I can jump the queue,' he told her.

'Is there anywhere you don't have influence?' Iris asked him.

Winston smiled ruefully. 'It's good to see you, Iris,' he said, putting down his cup. 'Really good.'

He took a step towards her and enfolded her in a warm hug. She hugged him back, hard, then released him, but he was still holding her and the friendly gesture had suddenly become something else.

'I don't suppose . . . I could ask you to dinner?'

His lips were so close to her face she could feel his breath in her eyelashes. Her body felt as if it had frozen. She couldn't respond.

'Surely you can't still hate me because I once voted for Thatcher?' he said, pulling his face back to look at her.

'No, it's not political. It's personal.' Iris attempted a joke.

He looked a little crestfallen.

'Look, my life's a total mess right now. I'm screwing a married man in a shag pad and I've made the classic mistake of falling in love, and so it's all fucked up and I don't know what's going to happen . . . does that answer your question?'

'Totally,' said Winston, kissing the top of her head.

What a wonderfully safe and comforting feeling it

was, Iris thought, to be able to rest your head on a man's shoulder without bending your knees.

'I have one further question,' he said in a strict, formal voice, playing the barrister, she thought, because he was embarrassed that he'd asked and been rejected. 'The aforementioned shag pad, it wouldn't happen to be in the building where we just met?'

'How did you know?' she asked, amazed.

'I couldn't believe you would be going to a private dentist,' said Winston, with a smile.

Chapter Fourteen

1985

'I've just realized, today's the best day of my life!' shouted Bob Geldof into the mike. A huge cheer went up all over Wembley Stadium.

Nikhil Patel said something to Fiammetta but the noise was so loud, she couldn't hear him. He bent down and whispered in her ear.

'It's the best day of mine too!'

Fiammetta felt herself colouring, partly because the compliment was so guileless – she could never imagine Bruno saying anything so nice to any of the girls he went out with – and partly because she didn't know how to reply. She could hardly say it was the best day of her life because for one thing, it wasn't over yet, and for another, there might be lots of days in the future she would enjoy more. She knew it was just an expression people used, but still she didn't agree with saying things she didn't mean.

Winston Allsop had sent tickets for her and Bruno, but Bruno had pulled out at the last minute and given his ticket to Nikhil.

'There's no point in asking Nikhil. His father won't let him go to anything political,' Fiammetta had told him, slightly irked that her brother hadn't consulted her, although she couldn't immediately think of anyone else she would rather go with. Nikhil was, after all, supposed to be her boyfriend. She found it was quite convenient to be

415

officially 'going out' with someone, even if it only meant that he sat next to her on the school bus, because it stopped people thinking she was weird or lesbian when she said she was a feminist. They never actually went out anywhere because Mr Patel expected Nikhil to work in the shop in any spare time he had when he wasn't doing homework, so she was surprised when he said he would be able to come to Live Aid, having persuaded his father that it must be respectable because some members of the Royal Family would be attending.

At the beginning of the concert the Prince and Princess of Wales had appeared with a fanfare from the Coldstream Guards, which seemed a bit incongruous to Fiammetta, and she still wasn't quite sure about the ethics of people enjoying themselves so much in the midst of a major humanitarian crisis.

'It's a good way to raise money, isn't it?' Nikhil argued.

'And I suppose it must send some kind of sign to the government,' added Fiammetta hopefully. 'In the end poverty is never going to be eradicated by charity alone,' she told him.

Nikhil looked at her blankly just like Bruno did sometimes, but he didn't say, 'You think too much,' which Bruno always said.

She would have been cross if he had.

'You can come in now,' called Julia King from her office.

Bruno Dearchild stood up from the slightly threadbare upholstered chair and checked that the white shirt he had ironed that morning was pulled out exactly the right amount over the brown leather belt of his jeans. It didn't feel quite right to be wearing jeans at the Palace Hotel, but he wasn't going to wear his school trousers on a weekend, and he didn't have anything else.

'Hello, Bruno!' Julia King stood up and stretched her hand across the desk to shake his.

Although her picture was always in the local paper, it didn't give a true picture of how attractive Julia had

416

become. The last time Bruno had been this close to her he reckoned must be about ten years ago. She'd been a plump pubescent girl who always seemed to be shrinking into a corner, trying to make herself look smaller. Now she was almost as tall as he was, her body was willowy, like a model, and she emitted wafts of light fragrance as she moved. The soft roundness had gone from her facial features, revealing strong bone structure, but huge blue eyes still looked out from under her lashes like a shy adolescent. Her hair was too stiffly styled for his liking, all blow-dried and sprayed, and she was wearing a frumpy pale-blue summer frock with a dropped waist that was slightly too big for her. Curiously, he found himself thinking about what her shape must feel like underneath it. Sensing the beginning of a stirring in his groin, he tried to compensate by remembering how silly she'd been back in those days, how, even though the twins were much younger than she, they could always trick her into believing things, like telling her she was eating their pet goat when it was really just a turkey drumstick.

In the corner of the room, there was a small portable television with a circular aerial on top. Julia was watching the Live Aid concert. The reception was snowy and the sound was turned down, but he could just about hear Elvis Costello leading the crowd in a chorus of the Beatles' song 'All You Need is Love'.

'I had a ticket.' Bruno pointed at the screen.

'Really?' That impressed her. 'Why didn't you go?' she asked.

'Because I had arranged to see you,' he said, smiling straight at her and was gratified to receive a blush in response. Not quite so grown up, then.

She indicated that he should take the seat on the other side of the desk.

'Why do you want to work at the Palace?' she asked, picking up a pencil and looking down at her notepad.

'Same reason as everyone else, I expect,' he said.

Her eyebrows shot up.

'Money,' he said.

'Have you had other holiday jobs?' she asked.

'Last summer I worked at the Ship.'

'The Ship?' Julia frowned. 'And how was that?'

'I cooked so many chips, I felt deep fried by the end of it. Had to throw away a pair of jeans because I couldn't wash the smell of cooking oil out of them,' Bruno told her.

'Yuk!' said Julia, with a little giggle, but she seemed satisfied with the answer.

'So what appeals to you about this job?' she asked, glancing at her notes again, ticking off questions.

He had the feeling that she was new to the role of interviewer. It was pretty obvious that there wasn't exactly a great deal of choice in Kingshaven, but he thought he'd better make a bit of an effort.

'The advert in the *Chronicle* says you want team leaders with energy and enthusiasm who enjoy sport and are prepared to muck in. That sounds like me.'

'We might need some help in the kitchen too, in the evenings?'

'Fine.'

'And you have a life-saving qualification?'

Bruno was suddenly conscious of blue eyes skimming over his body, perhaps even imagining the contours of his chest inside his white shirt? Even though it was warm in the office, a shiver ran down his spine.

'Did you know I saved your life once?' Julia asked.

'Yeah, thanks,' he replied, catching her gaze and holding it. 'Perhaps I can do the same for you one day!'

It was a bit like a staring competition. The one who looked away first would in some strange way be the loser, even though he wasn't quite sure what the game was. Finally, Julia looked down at her notes again.

'What's your ambition?' she asked, making another tick.

'I want to own a Porsche by the time I'm twenty-five,' he replied recklessly. He'd never revealed this to anyone else before, not wanting to look a jerk if he didn't make it.

'You won't get one on what we're going to pay you,' said Julia quickly.

She was a little sharper than she used to be, thought Bruno, as well as a lot sexier.

'So I've got the job, have I?' he shot back.

She blushed again. 'When could you start?' she asked, determined to stick to the script.

'At the end of next week when school breaks up,' he said. 'But I could do evenings before that if you needed.'

'Tonight?' she asked. It sounded like a challenge.

'Fine.' He returned her gaze.

'Several of the staff have called in sick. I think,' she attempted a joke, 'that it's probably a severe case of Live Aids.'

Bruno didn't think it was in very good taste, but laughed none the less.

'Report to Chef at five. He'll tell you what to do,' said Julia, suddenly rather imperious. She shut her notebook and stood up to shake his hand again. The interview was over.

Standing in the entrance hall, Bruno was slightly at a loss. He hoped he hadn't just committed himself to another summer sweating over a deep-fat fryer. He should have asked what the job involved, but he couldn't seriously get his head round the idea of Julia as his boss.

As he stepped outside the building into sunshine, the volume on the television suddenly went up. He could hear her singing along with Sade.

'Your Love is King.'

In the kitchen of the Ship, Millicent watched Bernadette making a crab sandwich, and cursed her husband for allowing this sullen little piece, a distant relation of his, apparently, to come over from Ireland to spend the summer with them. She'd been here a couple of weeks already, but she hadn't yet got the hang of making a sandwich look generous by putting all the filling in the middle and cutting it crosswise, and she pressed the top slice down so hard that several customers had complained about thumbprints in the bread. Millicent had no idea how Bernadette would cope when business really stepped up in August, when Millicent would be too busy serving in the bar to oversee the kitchen. On big days, like the Carnival, they sometimes served over two hundred orders in a lunchtime. Last summer Bruno Dearchild had taken it in his stride, and managed to have a laugh at the same time. Bruno was good fun, as well as being nice to look at. Millicent had been looking forward to having him back.

Millicent sighed. At least they didn't have to pay Bernadette very much money because she was living in the spare room, having an extended holiday, truth be told, and Gerry seemed to like having her around. Charity begins at home, he said, although Millicent had never seen much sign of it before. Still, Sean's manners had got a lot better with a big girl sitting next to him at the dinner table, and Lucy idolized her, heaven knew why, and had even adopted her soft Irish way of saying things.

'Sprinkle a bit of cress over to make it look nice and fresh,' Millicent said as Bernadette handed her the squashed sandwich.

'Is that the last one?' asked Bernadette.

'It is,' said Millicent. Even she was falling into their way of speaking now. The Irish never said yes or no.

'It's not a usual kind of Saturday,' Millicent warned, trying to give the girl the idea that she'd have to get a move on if she was going to keep up. 'I think everyone must be at home watching Live Aid.'

'Can I go and watch now?' asked Bernadette sulkily.

Millicent looked at all the washing up and leftover debris from lunch. She'd do it twice as fast by herself.

'All right then,' Millicent agreed. 'Give us a shout when Bryan Ferry comes on!' she added, trying to find some common ground between them, but the girl gave her a contemptuous look that made her feel like she was past it.

*　　*　　*

It felt a bit funny to be singing 'Do They Know It's Christmas' on such a muggy summer afternoon. Julia stopped abruptly when Christopher put his head round the office door.

'Can you turn that infernal noise off? You can hear it in the public areas!'

'It is for charity!' she protested feebly.

'I very much doubt people want to think about starving children in Africa while they're eating their cream tea,' he said.

Obediently, Julia turned the volume down, then stuck her tongue out at the door as it closed behind him.

Why did he always have to be so grumpy? Why couldn't they have fun working together like Adrian and Bee did?

She shifted her chair nearer the television so she could hear Paul Young singing 'Everytime You Go Away', which was one of her favourites.

It could have been her larking about with Adrian at the Yacht Club, now renamed the Kingshaven Adventure Centre, Julia thought a little wistfully, but then, she consoled herself, she wouldn't be in charge of the hotel's summer programme, which looked like breaking even in its first year.

It had all started to come together at her brother, James's, twenty-first party in London. Even though the money for the party had come from James's trust fund, he had not invited their father because of Sylvia, and since Christopher didn't much care for parties Julia had gone by herself, and it had been much more fun with no grown-ups around – not that Christopher was technically a grown-up but he always behaved like one – not feeling she was being watched all the time in case she actually started enjoyed herself. She must have looked all right too, because lots of James's good-looking City friends asked him why he'd kept his beautiful sister a secret. But the luckiest thing had been meeting Melissa, James's new girlfriend, who had just got a job in PR and was keen to impress both James and her new employers.

Together, Melissa and Julia had planned the relaunch, brainstorming ideas for features in the holiday sections of upmarket magazines. The pitch 'We'll Take Care of the Kids, so You Can Forget About Them' featured two promotional photographs Tom Snow had taken, one of a tanned young woman in a bikini relaxing by the pool, the other of two laughing children sliding into the multicoloured ball pond. Julia had been confident enough to pose as the model herself, although since the picture had been taken on a bright winter's day, Tom had to use all his skill with the airbrush to iron out the goose bumps on her arms and colour in a golden tan.

Inevitably Christopher had disapproved. Instead of being grateful that she'd saved the fee for a real model, he'd said it was vulgar. Instead of being pleased that she seemed to have a gift for the hotel business, he seemed to resent her for it, as if she was only doing it to show him up, rather than trying to ensure their sons' future. Sometimes Julia wondered if she would ever find a way of making him proud of her.

'That's the Way Love is', Paul Young and Alison Moyet were singing on the television.

'Where are you off to looking so smart?' Michael asked Bruno as he came down the spiral staircase into the living room.

'Gotta job for the summer up at the Palace,' Bruno replied.

Although he hadn't expected his father to be particularly pleased – unlike his friends' fathers, Michael didn't seem to care whether he had a job or not – Bruno hadn't expected Michael's face to set into a dark frown that foretold trouble as inevitably as a purple-black cloud before a downpour.

'Why the Palace?' Michael enquired.

'I can get more hours there,' Bruno told him.

'Only because they've sacked most of their permanent staff, so they need casual labour.'

'You can't blame me for people being out of work,' protested Bruno.

'Look, I'd just rather you didn't work there, OK? I worked there once . . . there's a bit of history . . .'

Bruno didn't know which was worse, his father's outdated politics, or him trying to be mates.

'It's not the same now,' Bruno argued. 'It's got a whole new image.'

'It may have had a face-lift, but it's still the same institution, and the powers that be won't have your best interests at heart, I can tell you that.'

'The powers that be?' Bruno repeated incredulously. 'It's a business, for God's sake! I don't expect them to have my best interests at heart.'

'I don't want you going there,' Michael said angrily.

'And I don't really care what you want,' said Bruno, going to push past him but Michael stood firmly in the way at the top of the stairs.

They'd had arguments before, but it had never come to this, the two of them squaring up to each other, man to man. It was ridiculous, Bruno thought, because he was much taller and stronger and fitter than Dad. In a physical confrontation there could be only one winner, and, as if his father suddenly realized this, his body suddenly sagged, as if the fight had gone out of him, which made Bruno contrite, because he hadn't meant to humiliate him. He wanted to say sorry, but he knew it would only make it worse. They both stood for a moment, staring at each other, both losers, and then Michael stepped aside.

In the green room behind the stage at Wembley Stadium, Vic introduced Iris to his lover, Robbie Pluto.

'This is my best friend,' he said.

Robbie was wearing an almost identical outfit to Vic's. Tight jeans so faded they were almost white, a black leather belt with studs and a white vest. His shoulders were already gleaming with sweat. He smiled and shook Iris's hand, but she could tell he didn't really register who she was because his mind was focused somewhere else. It surprised her to feel how clammy his hand was. Did he get stage fright? The band played stadia all over the world. He was famous as a posturing, extrovert showman, and yet, if Iris had been given one word to describe him now, she would have said vulnerable.

'He gives everything to the performance,' Vic explained as he ushered her out of the dressing room. 'He's shattered when he comes home.'

Home for Vic had become wherever in the world the band was playing, Iris realized with a little jolt of loss.

'I'd better get back, see if he needs anything,' said Vic.

Iris thought it was touching that his super-rich, super-famous lover needed looking after like anyone else.

'Listen, if you see Clive, remember I'm a roadie,' Vic said.

'Clive?' she asked.

But Vic had already gone

It was really hot backstage, and it was so loud that after a short time you lost your hearing and your sense of time and place. Wherever Iris stood to watch she was always in the way of someone with a microphone, or a spare guitar, or a towel, or a man with a television camera, or a man following a man with a television camera around with a cable. When she finally found an empty space, she quickly began to smell scorching and narrowly avoided self-combustion from being too near a bank of lights.

When Winston had got her the backstage pass, he'd warned that he would probably be busy and might not be able to spend a lot of time with her.

'I don't need looking after!' Iris had told him. But now she thought she probably did.

Iris decided it would be safer to hang out in hospitality, where there was a television screen with a relay to the stage. The only cold thing to drink was beer, in big plastic cups. She noticed some of the girls serving food were wearing T-shirts with a familiar logo. And then she realized what Vic had meant about Clive.

How had he managed to wangle his way into the biggest pop concert ever? Knowing Clive, he'd have signs painted on the mopeds and delivery vans that were proliferating all over the city, saying 'We Feed the World!'

'I didn't know you knew Clive,' said Iris when Winston eventually found her.

'Clive?' Winston asked, distracted.

'Pizza bloke,' Iris explained.

'We use them for bringing stuff in if we're running over schedule at the recording studios. We used to send a runner out, now we just make a phone call . . . Why?'

'He's Vic's brother,' Iris told him.

'Vic, your friend, who's with . . . ?'

Iris nodded quickly, not wanting Winston to say Robbie's name in case that meant she'd broken her promise to Vic.

'Delivery's a big thing in the States. It's about time someone did it here,' said Winston. 'Wish I'd thought of it myself, as a matter of fact.'

Was pizza the only substance Clive supplied to Winston's bands, Iris wondered, feeling suddenly depressed at the idea of Winston and Clive doing business together, the former villain supplying the former idealist's demands.

'Queen's about to go on,' Winston told her. 'Do you want to come and watch?'

'Wherever I stand I seem to be in the way,' said Iris.

'Who said anything about standing?' said Winston. 'We've got the best seats in the house.'

Even as a child, Iris had never really trusted herself on climbing frames, so scaling the tower of scaffolding at the side of the stage with a pint of beer in a plastic cup was one of the most terrifying things she had done in her life, but it was worth it for the view, not just of the band below, but beyond to the sea of humanity bobbing and waving and clapping as far as the eye could see.

At the opening notes of 'Bohemian Rhapsody', Iris felt a thrill of nostalgia run through her body. She hadn't particularly liked the song when it came out, but it was part of the soundtrack to her life, an anthem everyone knew the words to, even though nobody had the slightest idea what they meant.

The performance was slickly professional, choreographed to the last note, with a roadie in tight shorts seamlessly swapping microphone for guitar, but it felt totally spontaneous. Freddie Mercury could work a crowd like no one she had ever seen before. In 'Radio Gaga', the sound of a hundred thousand hands clapping was so powerful, he lifted the crowd to a peak of unity and excitement so high that any higher would have tipped into mass hysteria.

Somewhere in that sea of people, far down below her, were Fiammetta and Nikhil. They'd said they'd try to hook up, but Iris knew there was no way she would find them in that crowd. She waved, hoping that one of them might spot her up on the scaffold, then she put her hand quickly back on the bar to steady herself as her bum slipped.

'You've just waved at a hundred million people,' Winston told her, pointing at the roving camera.

'This song is only dedicated to beautiful people here,' announced Freddie Mercury. 'Which means all of you . . .'

You could feel the energy in the stadium. It was totally exhilarating being part of a crowd that had become a single entity, more powerful than all the marches and demos Fiammetta had been on. There was no choice but to clap in time with everyone else, and sing and shout, as if they were no longer free individuals, but something much bigger.

She looked up at Nikhil, reached for his hand, and squeezed it briefly. He smiled his surprise at her, and then they couldn't seem to stop smiling at each other, as if congratulating each other on their good fortune and clapping along to 'Crazy Little Thing Called Love'.

Perhaps, thought Fiammetta suddenly, perhaps this is what love feels like. Perhaps love doesn't have to be about agony and complexity and longing, perhaps it can just be as simple and straightforward as the sharing of happiness.

*   *   *

Bruno couldn't work out whether Julia King had brought the portable television down into the Palace kitchen for the staff's benefit, or for her own, because she kept popping in and watching for a few minutes, then jumping up guiltily, as if remembering she wasn't supposed to be there, like a child who has sneaked down after bedtime and knows there'll be trouble if they're caught. There was nothing childlike about the dress she had changed into, a geranium-pink cocktail dress with spaghetti-thin straps that exposed flawless skin with a honey sheen of tan that looked as if it would feel both firm and soft at the same time.

'You can look, but you can't touch,' said Chef, as if he was reading Bruno's mind.

He was a younger man than Bruno had expected, still in his twenties, he guessed, and much more relaxed and chatty than was implied by his insistence on the title Chef (his name was Gary). Bruno had already learned that he was a stickler for detail, and capable of sustained colourful streams of abuse if a dish didn't conform to his very exact specifications.

Although he had a strong London accent, Chef had trained in Paris, and was a keen exponent of nouvelle cuisine, which he said was *de rigueur* in London restaurants, but had yet to arrive in Kingshaven.

The Kings were apparently divided about the wisdom of serving delicate portions of immaculate food in place of the traditional roast meat and two soggy veg. Apparently, in Chef's first week, Eddie King had stormed into the kitchen saying he wanted something to eat, not something to stick up in a bloody art gallery; and the Squadron Leader who had been a regular guest since the war had vociferously complained that it was worse than rations.

There was a bit of a battle going on upstairs, Chef informed Bruno, pointing at the ceiling of the kitchen. Mrs Julia King had got the idea that the people with money these days were the yuppies in the City who didn't want to see senile old military types dribbling into their spotted dick. The older women, Mrs Libby and Mrs Liliana, could see the cost benefit of smaller portions, but were reluctant to ditch the regulars who'd kept the place going over the years.

'And the men?' Bruno asked.

'They just shout a lot,' said Chef. 'It's always the women who—'

He stopped mid-sentence as Julia returned, danced in front of the television imitating the movements of David Bowie's backing singers as he sang 'Rebel Rebel', and then left again.

'It's not right the way they treat her,' Chef said, jerking his thumb at the ceiling. 'They should be grateful they've got her, not moaning all the time.'

When Julia returned, Bruno was scraping uneaten food off the plates from the children's sitting into the bin for the pigs. The television was now showing a film of starving children in Ethiopia, some of them barely able to move. There was no commentary, only the heart-rending soundtrack of 'Drive' by The Cars. Out of the corner of his eye, he watched as Julia sat perched on the stainless-steel counter with fat glistening tears sliding over her perfect smooth cheekbones. His instinct was to put his arm around her and draw her against his chest, pretending to offer comfort, but knowing it would be the fastest route to touching those peachy shoulders, taste those soft raspberry lips.

'Don't even think about it,' said Chef, behind him.

There was someone who looked like Jack Nicholson right next to Iris as she stood watching The Who. He grinned sideways at her, more *Terms of Endearment* than *The Shining*, as if it amused him to see her trying to work out whether it was him or not.

Then David Bowie was walking towards her smiling, and she smiled back and he said, 'Hey, Jack!'

And Jack said, 'Hey!'

And as these two icons walked off together, Iris suddenly

thought what an extraordinary day it was that all these giant egos had come together to work professionally, harmoniously and free of charge, for a good cause. The voice of outrage had found a new way of speaking to the world. She was so glad she'd been there to witness the shouting.

When Winston had offered her tickets, she had initially declined, imagining there would be nothing worse than being surrounded by sixty thousand people thinking they were doing something important. Then Vic had said he was going, and she should come. It would be like old times.

'Get a life!' he'd told her in his usual extrovert way.

In the months since her relationship with Roman had ended, Iris had buried herself in her work, living in just two boxes – her office and the shabby council flat – instead of three. When, after a couple of weeks, she decided to go back for one last look at the attic flat, the lock had been changed. Even then, standing at the top of the flight of stairs, jiggling her key for ages before it dawned on her what had happened, Iris hadn't cried. It was as if all the anger and regret had turned inside out, rendering her numb and unable to feel anything.

Today, she felt she'd got her senses back and it was thanks to Vic, and to Winston. Vic and Winston, her two closest friends, who always looked after her, even though she hated to admit it.

Iris could see Winston on the other side of the stage, deep in conversation with Elton John, his head inclined, listening seriously to a rocker in a magician's outfit, and she suddenly felt incredibly proud and fond of him.

Tonight, if he asked her out to dinner, she decided she would say yes.

What was there to lose? They'd been friends, and they'd fallen out, and now they were friends again. If they became lovers, and it all went wrong, surely they knew each other well enough to become friends again?

When he came round to her side of the stage, she gave him a spontaneous hug and was slightly put out when

Winston returned the embrace only politely. He ushered forward a leggy, beautiful girl wearing a pair of jeans shorts cut off just below the small tight cheeks of her buttocks and a Live Aid T-shirt.

'I don't think you've met Jazz! Jazz, this is Iris. My oldest friend.'

The girl had the same light cappuccino-colour skin as Winston, and masses of long brown curly hair streaked with gold.

'Jazz?' said Iris.

'Short for Jasmine,' said the girl.

'Lovely name,' said Iris.

'Winston's told me so much about you!' said the girl.

Iris didn't want to say that he had said nothing about her because she thought it might sound cruel. She guessed the girl was about nineteen.

'Isn't this the coolest?' said Jazz, slipping her arm through Winston's.

Elton John and Kiki Dee were singing 'Don't Go Breaking My Heart'.

And Winston's eyes were fixed on them.

Outside the stadium, it took a while for Iris's ears to adjust to the absence of sound. There were no cars, no people on the street. As she waited on the deserted platform of Wembley Park station for an overground Metropolitan Line into London, Iris could just make out the voice of George Michael singing 'Don't Let the Sun Go Down on Me'.

The train was virtually empty. It trundled down the line through the urban sprawl of Neasden and Dollis Hill and Iris could see little bright rectangles of television screens in the living rooms of houses backing on to the line. Even though she'd been told all day how many people were watching, it was all those little screens in all those houses that made her suddenly realize the enormity of the connection that had been made. Winston said they were making history. And he was right.

'Please, don't go!' he'd said.

'There's only so much compassion I can do,' she'd told him, trying to laugh off the acute humiliation of having allowed herself to feel usurped by someone half her age. 'And Paul McCartney was always my least favourite Beatle. You probably don't remember him,' she'd added to Jazz.

It had been a petty swipe. Unworthy, Iris thought. No wonder nobody loved her. Why would Winston want to be with an ugly bitch who picked fights all the time, when he could have an acquiescent beauty like Jazz? Why would anyone?

Iris got off the train at Finchley Road to wait for the Jubilee Line train to Charing Cross. The electronic board said the wait was seven minutes. After at least ten minutes had passed, it still said there were six minutes to go. It occurred to Iris that this was such a low point in her life there wasn't even a train to throw herself under.

As usual, Gerry had left it to Milly to wipe down the bar, make sure the doors were locked and check that there was no one asleep in the toilets. By the time Millicent got upstairs, the London part of Live Aid was long since over, but Phil Collins had arrived on Concorde and was singing on stage in America. What a small world it was, thought Millicent, peering at the flickering television from the door of the living room, although if it had been her choice, she wouldn't have had Phil Collins on twice. As her eyes grew used to the darkness in the living room, she could see that there were two people, not one, on the sofa. They were sitting close together. As Millicent came up closer behind them, she could see that Gerry had his arm round Bernadette's shoulder and she was leaning her head against his. They were both fast asleep. As if he sensed her presence behind him, Gerry emitted such a loud, extended snore it woke him up. He jumped up, looking as guilty as she'd ever seen him.

'For God's sake, Gerry!' shouted Millicent.

'It's not what you think!' he said automatically, cowering away from her.

431

Blearily, Bernadette woke up too.

'She's only sixteen!' said Millicent.

'It's not what you think,' he said again.

He'd been drinking. These days he was drinking so much he seemed to sweat alcohol.

'Well, what is it then?' demanded Millicent.

'I said she was a distant relation – well, she's not. Distant that is. Bernadette's my daughter,' he said. 'I swear it's the truth.'

The girl looked almost triumphant.

Both of them lying to her! Millicent could believe it of her husband, but not this useless, sulky girl. How dare they make a fool of her? In her own home!

'There,' said Gerry with a smile. 'I feel better for having told you.'

'You feel better? Everything I've put up with over the years . . . and all this time you've been lying.'

'Oh, come on, Milly Minx, you're not such an innocent yourself.'

It used to win her round, his pet name for her, but now it made her blood boil. Didn't he see this was different? This wasn't just another indiscretion, this was a different degree of misdemeanour, affecting not just her, but the children, their reputation in Kingshaven, where her family had always been respectable citizens, and both of them foreigners!

'How dare you bring her here?' Millicent screamed.

'She'd nowhere to go. Her mother's thrown her out. I thought you'd show a bit of compassion.'

'You didn't even tell me.'

'Can you blame me?' he said with a shrug of his shoulders, as if to add, if this is how you react.

This is what always happened, Milly thought. If she got angry with him, he'd somehow make it her fault. Not this time. This was different. It was not just another woman he'd been hiding from her, but another whole life. She'd thought she knew everything about him – that he was feckless and lazy, a drinker, a womanizer – and she'd found ways of putting up with that because she'd always assumed they were in it together and they loved each other, in their own way. Now, she looked at him and she didn't recognize him any more.

It was gone two in the morning, but Julia was still watching the pop concert on television in the living room of their flat.

'Could you turn it down?' Christopher asked, coming into the living room in his pyjamas, rubbing his eyes pointedly.

'I wish there was something more we could do,' Julia said, not looking up. 'I mean we're so privileged, when you think about it . . .'

'Make a donation, if you wish,' Christopher said.

It would be a small price to pay for some sleep.

'I've already done that!' said Julia impatiently.

'How much?' he asked.

'A hundred pounds.'

'A hundred pounds?' he repeated.

Had she gone mad? As usual, if he said anything, he would be the one who looked mean, even though it was his bank account the money would come out of.

'It just seems so terrible when we throw out so much food here.'

'Perhaps we wouldn't if we served something normal rather than – what was it this evening – hake in a pool of blackcurrant sauce . . .'

'It's actually called a coulis,' said Julia irritably. 'And you know that's not the point!'

The American singer on television was singing 'Imagine' when the phone started ringing.

Christopher picked it up.

'What?' he said impatiently, assuming it was Sid Farthing calling to report another bomb scare. Saturday nights in the summer were always the worst, when gangs of youths from the caravan site who had been swilling ale all evening in the pubs at the Harbour End thought it a huge joke to

433

make a call from the public phone box on the quay in a cod Irish accent and get all the guests at the Palace out of bed. Nobody had really taken it very seriously until the bomb in Brighton last year, but now there were strict procedures for evacuation, and the fire brigade had to be called to check the building.

There was silence at the other end of the phone. And then a little sniff.

'Who is this?' asked Christopher.

'I'm sorry to ring at this time . . .' It sounded as if Milly was crying on the other end of the phone. 'I need you!' she wailed.

'Oh! Of course,' said Christopher, putting down the phone so quickly his wife looked up suspiciously.

'Who was that?' Julia asked.

'Wrong number,' he said, shifting his weight from foot to foot. 'Look, since I'm obviously not going to be able to sleep, I think I might as well go for a walk.'

Chapter Fifteen

1987

In the silent bright stillness of a summer morning, the swimming pool was like a gleaming blue mirror shattering into glistening fragments as Julia dived in. Kaleidoscopic patterns of light danced around the bright turquoise mosaic-tile lining as she swam steady lengths. The pool was the one place she felt completely calm, the rhythm of her stroke bringing all her senses into balance.

Recently she had been sleeping badly. Half the night she lay awake fretting about why Christopher didn't seem to want to have sex with her any more, finally falling asleep to engage in bouts of rampant activity, often waking on the point of climax, confused and embarrassed to find her husband fast asleep beside her. She was almost certain that the man in her dreams was not Christopher, but she never saw his face because she was always blindfolded. Julia could only think she'd got the idea from seeing *9½ Weeks* with Bee at the Regal Cinema.

It was actually quite fun having Bee in the family, even though Julia had been slightly put out that Bee had got off with Adrian within weeks of starting work at the Kingshaven Adventure Centre without even asking Julia whether she minded. They had married the previous summer in the parish church.

It was good to have another King-who-wasn't-really-a-King around, and Bee was even less of a King than Julia.

435

Some of Bee's promotional ideas for the Adventure Centre, like the *It's A Knockout* competition on the beach, were so Butlins, they made Julia's plans for the hotel look like the Ritz in comparison. And when Bee and Adrian came up to dinner at the hotel, it was a relief to have someone else who said the wrong thing, like the other day, when Winny was moaning about being rejected by a majority of members of the lifeboat crew, Bee had remarked, 'At least you won't get dragged out of bed in the small hours by a load of beefy men trying to rescue some prat who doesn't know his boom from his rudder!'

Which Julia, though no expert on sailing, knew was simply not the way one spoke about the lifeboat.

Sometimes Julia envied Bee and Adrian's larks. Their marriage was fun. Or at least it looked that way. Who really knew what went on in a marriage?

After sixty lengths Julia got out, pulled off her goggles and wrapped herself in a towel. Usually, she made a dash for the greenhouse warmth of the indoor pool and health club, where she would steam away the goose bumps in a hot shower. Sometimes Denise Rocco gave her a relaxing shoulder massage. Denise had jumped at the chance to work for Julia as manageress of the new Wave Club because she had been finding the hours at Lowhampton General Hospital too difficult now she had three children. It was such a perfect morning, Julia decided instead to lie on a sunlounger for a moment and allow the sun to dry the droplets of water from her skin.

After a few moments of bliss enveloped in the scent of petunias and with only the distant rasp of waves breaking on shingle, Julia became aware of footsteps approaching the pool. She kept her eyes closed, clinging on to her solitude for a precious while longer, before preparing her best face for the guests at breakfast.

The footsteps stopped at the foot of the lounger, a shadow falling over her body. Shielding her eyes with her hand, Julia looked up.

He was wearing his usual white shirt and jeans, and his

shiny dark curls, much longer than the last time she'd seen him, looked crimson red with the early morning sun behind him.

'Bruno!'

'Mrs King!'

The way he said it, with a smile in his voice, made the formality far less respectful than if he'd called her Julia.

'I heard you might want people . . .' he said.

'I always want you!' Julia replied, and was covered in confusion as she realized how that sounded.

For the past two summers Bruno had worked at the hotel, as a tremendously popular leader of the older kids' club during the day, and often helping out in the kitchen or waiting tables in the evenings too. He was one of the few people who could slip easily across the battle lines between day staff and evening staff; kitchen staff and waiting staff. Bruno was so competent and easy-going, he was the kind of person who'd get on anywhere. At the end of last summer when he'd left for university, Julia hadn't expected to see him back in Kingshaven.

'How's London?' she asked.

'All right,' said Bruno, sitting down on the edge of the next lounger along. 'I'm not that keen on lectures and stuff, but I've got a great job in the evenings at a restaurant called Joe Allen's . . . you wouldn't believe the tips . . .'

'Still saving for your Porsche?' Julia remembered, sitting up, in an attempt to re-establish the hierarchy.

'I might just be able to afford my first tyre,' said Bruno.

'I'm surprised you've come back here then.'

'I miss the sea,' Bruno admitted. 'Footie on the beach and surfing and stuff. And you, obviously . . .' he added, with one of those flirty looks that always made her giggle.

'Welcome back!' she said, trying not to blush.

'So what do you want me to do?' Bruno asked her.

Julia sat up. 'I'll tell Gary you're here. You should find Denise, who's running the Wave Club for me, and introduce yourself.'

'The Wave Club?'

Julia was pleased he sounded impressed. 'We've had a logo designed and everything,' she told him excitedly.

In order to finance the indoor pool and gym, a management consultant friend of James's had suggested generating revenue all year round by opening the facilities as a members' club for local people with aerobics classes and circuit training, as well as use of the pools and Jacuzzi. Despite Christopher's opposition to opening up the hotel to just anybody, Libby King had cautiously given her support because all Julia's other ideas for modernizing the hotel had proved so spectacularly successful. The Wave Club was no exception. Take-up had far exceeded expectations. Summer activities for the younger children could now take place in an indoor pool if the weather was bad. Adrian came up each morning with a minibus to take the older children down to Kingshaven Adventure Centre.

Now Julia and Denise had plans to extend the facilities even further to include a beauty spa with manicures, pedicures, waxing and therapeutic massages, and appeal to wealthy yuppie parents with the slightly revised slogan: 'We'll take care of the children, so you can take care of yourself!'

In the low season, the hotel would offer pampering mini-breaks for stressed career women. James's girlfriend, Melissa, was already talking to one of the glossy magazines about a promotional competition.

Julia babbled on, only becoming aware of the time when the scent of petunias was overwhelmed by the smell of bacon drifting over the lawn from the kitchen. Two little boys were running towards them, the little one shouting, 'Mummy!' and the bigger one shouting, 'Bruno!'

Bruno picked Bertie up and swung him round in a looping circle over the neatly shaved grass.

'Have you come to play football with me?' Bertie asked breathlessly.

'And me?' asked Archie.

'You don't know how to play football,' Bertie told his brother dismissively.

'I do!'

'No you don't!'

'Boys!' Julia interrupted. 'Bruno's not here to play with you, he's come to work.'

'Work's boring. Daddy's always working,' said Bertie.

'Well, perhaps Bruno will give you a game later,' Julia said hopefully.

She was keen for them to grow up normal boys who did normal things. Christopher was a doting father, but he didn't do the rough and tumble that came naturally to most dads. Julia put it down to a childhood spent mostly with Granny Liliana, whose only game was bridge.

'Course I will,' Bruno agreed. 'Thanks, Mrs King!' he added, as she went into the house and he headed for the kitchen.

'What for?' Julia asked, glancing back at him over her bare shoulder.

'For wanting me,' he said, winking.

With a spoonful of muesli halfway between the serving bowl and his plate, Christopher watched from the dining-room window as his wife, wearing merely a towel around her body, chatted with Bruno Dearchild, their two children bouncing around their legs like puppies.

'Who is that fellow?' asked Granny Liliana behind him.

'Bruno Dearchild,' Christopher replied. 'He's worked here for the last two summers.'

'Good-looking boy,' said Granny Liliana. She made it sound like a question.

'Yes,' said Christopher, wondering what she was getting at. There was always an agenda with Granny Liliana.

'Do you think it wise to employ Michael Quinn's son?' Granny Liliana asked. So she did know who he was. She was only checking to see that Christopher did.

'He's very amenable, apparently,' said Christopher.

'I hope Julia will keep an eye on him,' said Granny Liliana.

'I'm sure she will,' said Christopher.

*   *   *

The party to celebrate thirty years of Portico Books was at the Groucho Club, a venue frequently mentioned in the review section of the *Observer* as a kind of shorthand for the hipper elements of publishing. Not having had a book published for over twenty years, Michael was surprised to receive an invitation, and his instinct had been to decline, remembering how uncomfortable he had always felt entering the exclusive domain of London literati, but he had allowed Pascale to change his mind.

'Of course you must go. For Iris!' she'd told him, reminding him gently that he was being selfish.

As part of the thirtieth birthday celebrations, Portico had published a paperback book of short stories by thirty of their most famous authors. Michael Quinn's story 'The Romans in Britain' was among those included. It had been good to see his work in print again and he'd had Iris to thank for that because the collection had been her idea and she had edited it. Editorial Director, it said beneath her name on the letter she'd sent with the proof.

As they entered the building on Dean Street, Michael knew that if Pascale had not been with him now, he would have kept the revolving door going all the way round and back out into the street again. Like most businesses in recent years, publishing had become slicker and more image-conscious. Pints in the Coach and Horses had been replaced by cocktails in private members' clubs. The publicity girl standing at the reception desk to greet guests was wearing a smart black suit with a very short skirt and high heels, and as she ticked Michael and Pascale's name off the list, and indicated disdainfully where they should leave their overnight bag, he was sure she hadn't the slightest idea who he was. Now he was relieved that Pascale had made him buy a suit because he would have felt even more out of place in his usual corduroy trousers. He had drawn the line at a tie.

As they entered the party room, Michael was acutely conscious of split-second judgements being made about whether he and Pascale were important enough to warrant interest, eyes averted again as their faces failed to register. Twenty years had not mitigated the sickening thump of inadequacy he felt at such gatherings.

'Look! It's you!' Pascale said, pointing at one of the large black-and-white author photos displayed around the walls of the room.

The grainy image of his younger self, taken by his friend Ivor Brown, stared critically across the room at Michael.

'You ought to get a better author photo,' Roman Stone's wife, Pippa, had told him long ago, but by then the photo had been on the back cover of Michael's first novel and had already gone out to all the newspapers to be reproduced alongside any article that appeared about Angry Young Men.

At the time, Michael had not recognized his expression in the photo, yet now, despite the fact that the line of his jaw was not as tight, his skin not as smooth, the pale eyes seemed to be reflecting back at him the bewilderment he had come to feel at life's uncertainties. Then, people had interpreted his look as defiance, now he recognized it as fear. In the monochrome photo, his fair hair looked as white as it had become. Perhaps Ivor had been a better, more insightful, photographer than he had given him credit for.

'Michael!' Roman Stone came over to greet them.

'This is Pascale.'

Michael felt a little fillip of pride as Roman's eyes assessed and approved of what he saw.

Pascale's slim body and serious face had not aged much in the time they'd been together. She wore her dark hair a little longer now, chin length, with a side parting and the hair pushed back behind her ears. Her plain black sleeveless dress was timelessly chic, and, even though she was in her mid-thirties now, the lightly tanned skin of her bare arms and legs was still taut and smooth as if she had been lightly polished.

'What a lucky man you are, Michael,' said Roman,

taking the hand Pascale held out for him to shake, bringing it to his lips to kiss it, his eyes fixed on hers.

'Yes,' said Michael, a little uneasy with Roman's attention, unsure suddenly how Pascale might react to the temptations of an urbane sophisticate.

He and Pascale sometimes talked about whether there were other things they wanted to do, now that the children were virtually independent – Fiammetta had just finished her foundation year at Lowhampton College, but would soon be off to art school for three years, and Bruno was already at university in London and only came back for the holidays – but neither yet seemed willing to alter the familiar pattern of their lives. Sometimes it crossed Michael's mind that it was cowardice that made them unadventurous, as if, having achieved a kind of stability after all the turmoil life had thrown at them, they daren't risk losing it. He wondered if they would come to regret that, but as Pascale pointed out the last time they'd spoken about it, a week didn't go by without somebody telling them that they had the perfect life. It seemed that a bookshop on a quay was the escapist dream of every weary middle-aged professional who visited Kingshaven.

Michael was happy – perhaps happier than he had ever been – now that the responsibility of parenthood was waning. Although neither Bruno nor Fiammetta had turned out as he had expected, they were both resourceful, good people, who seemed to be able to look after themselves. He didn't think he had done either of them any permanent harm, and that ultimately had been his one ambition since their mother died.

Roman was right. He was a lucky man. Having Pascale with him was a bonus he had neither dreamed of nor deserved. But when Roman made a statement, there was always a subtext, and the question why someone as young and beautiful as Pascale would want to be with him gnawed at Michael's mind, even though Roman hadn't asked it.

'Michael Quinn!'

Josie's hair was dyed as red as a pillarbox and her

statuesque figure was swathed in bold black and white striped jersey fabric.

'Don't tell me you've finally written another novel?' she asked.

'We're celebrating our history as much as our future on this occasion,' Roman interceded quickly.

'I am writing,' Michael replied evenly. 'Short stories . . .'

'There's no market for short stories, is there?' Josie asked Roman.

'It's difficult,' said the publisher. 'Although, of course, we'd love the opportunity to consider a collection,' he added diplomatically.

'Not yet,' Michael told him, and thought he detected relief on Roman's face.

'Where's Iris?' Josie demanded.

'I'm sure she's around somewhere,' said Roman, sliding away to greet another guest.

'There she is!' said Pascale.

Michael spotted his daughter at the bar. She'd cut her hair very short, which suited her, but was usually, he'd noticed, a sign that she was finding life difficult. She was talking to a woman Michael recognized as one of her bestselling authors, but her attention was distracted as Roman stepped up on to a podium that had been constructed to look like the Portico logo – a classical doorway, with a triangular pediment and two Doric columns on either side.

'Ladies and Gentlemen, it's lovely to see so many of you here, all my fantastic staff, all the lovely booksellers who stock our books, all the brilliantly talented critics who review them . . .'

Roman paused for people to acknowledge his outrageous flattery.

'And in particular so many of our authors from over the years without whom we would be nothing.'

There was a round of applause.

'When I founded Portico Books, I wanted it to be a forum for free speech, a home for new ideas to flourish, new voices to be heard, a place where the new agenda for the new society would be debated. Thirty years later, there is, apparently, no such thing as society . . .'

Roman held his hand up to quell the ripple of bitter laughter.

'Sadly, we have a government elected for a third term that threatens free speech, a government so powerful it can ban books it doesn't want us to read. Some people might see that as failure, but I say that it makes it even more imperative to continue, unbowed, uncensored, un-afraid . . .'

As people around him clapped and cheered, Michael watched Iris's face, expecting to see a great big smile of shared endeavour. This was the moment he'd come for. Not just to *be* proud of her, but, as Pascale had urged, to *show* her he was proud. But Iris didn't look across at him, and her face, which had always been the barometer of her soul, was reading depression. Her glazed eyes stared as Roman offered his hand to Pippa and pulled her up on to the podium to join him, like a politician's wife after the closing speech at a party conference.

Michael had learned not to ask his children about their love lives. He'd suspected that Iris was involved with some-one, but he'd never have guessed Roman. For a moment, he wanted to go and pull Roman down from his podium and punch him right in his self-satisfied face.

Michael turned to take a glass of wine from a passing waiter, and caught Josie's eye. She shrugged resignedly, as if she was thinking the same thought.

A jazz band suddenly started playing at the other end of the room. A few people began to dance.

Michael and Pascale threaded their way through the crowd to where Iris was standing. She kissed Pascale on both cheeks, and gave her father a hug. He held her tightly, the paternal urge to protect still strong, even though she was a grown woman of thirty-seven.

'It's a lovely party,' said Pascale.

'Yes,' said Iris without enthusiasm, draining her glass of wine.

Something about the hollowness of her eyes made Michael wonder how much she had already had. To his horror, he saw Roman's wife, Pippa, had spotted him and was bearing down from the other side of the room. She was still a handsome woman, but in the twenty years or so since he had last seen her, Pippa had aged much more noticeably than Roman. Pippa had a smoker's face. Michael had a fleeting flashback of kissing her in the hallway of their great big house in Belsize Park. She had tasted of Gauloises.

'Michael!' Pippa air-kissed him with loud 'mwaas'.

'This is Pascale.'

'How lovely . . . !' said Pippa, in that particular languid way the English upper classes have, as if they can't be fussed to finish a sentence.

She put her hand on Pascale's arm. 'We were so happy Michael found . . . we knew Claudia very well, of course . . .'

Pascale looked startled. 'I didn't,' she said.

'No, of course . . .'

Pippa turned her sights on Iris, her eyebrows raised, as if she expected an introduction. Surely they'd met, Michael thought.

'My daughter, Iris,' he said quickly.

'I've heard such a lot about Iris,' said Pippa archly.

The noise level in the room suddenly seemed to drop, no publishing gossip quite as entertaining as unfolding events at the party.

'Would you like to dance?' Michael asked Pippa, trying to draw her away.

The band continued to play. The song was 'Moonlight in Moscow', but the whole room heard Iris say to Roman, 'You can't even bring yourself to dance with me!'

Then Roman was dancing with Pascale, and when Michael next looked, Iris had gone.

At the end of the late dinner service, Julia usually came down to the kitchen to thank the staff.

'Only one who treats us like human beings,' said Chef.

Whenever Chef spoke about Julia, Bruno noticed that he got a sentimental look in his eye.

'Always taking care of other people,' Chef said. 'And nobody taking care of her.'

Bruno thought perhaps Chef would like to take care of her himself. Julia was attractive and stylish, but her insecurity was so near the surface it gave her an innocence that made you want to look after her. It crossed his mind that perhaps there was something going on between them but Bruno was pretty sure Chef was too common for her. If she wanted an affair, she could do a lot better than Gary.

Sometimes Julia stopped for a chat, perched on the corner of a spotless stainless-steel counter, eating a ball of ice cream directly off the scoop, or stuffing a handful of buttery biscuit curls that adorned Chef's puddings into her mouth, and another handful into her pocket.

'Don't know where she puts it,' said Chef. 'Beautiful figure like hers. I've seen her polish off a whole chocolate roulade.'

Bruno had an idea where Julia put it. He'd had a girl-friend, in his first term at college, who ate a lot, just like Julia did, but was stick thin. It was only when he'd started sleeping with her that he'd discovered her secret. She would wait till she thought he was asleep and then she'd go to the loo and make herself throw up. He'd caught her once, with her fingers down her throat, told her not to be so silly, but it was like an addiction. She would promise him solemnly she wouldn't do it again, but he'd still wake up to her tasting of sick. No amount of toothpaste got rid of it. In the end, he'd told her he'd had enough. You had to really love someone to put in all the work to get them through something like that.

Girls could be really strange about food. It was like they used it as a form of control, but then it started to control them. Fiammetta had been a bit like that after Barbara died. It had started as a kind of hunger strike, but then it had taken over, as if something inside wouldn't let her eat, as if she was trying to make herself disappear, and Bruno had been terrified because they'd always been together. He couldn't just let her go. He'd started preparing food himself because his sister wouldn't touch anything that his father or Pascale cooked. He'd spent hours trying all sorts of ploys to get her to eat tiny portions. It had taken a lot of patience, but gradually she'd got better, or transferred the obsession on to something else, he was never quite sure which. At least art wasn't unhealthy.

Sometimes, Bruno thought he detected the same gleam of mania in Julia's doe eyes.

Wednesday evening was dogs night at the racetrack in nearby Havenbourne when Chef went off smartly on his scooter leaving Bruno to clear up. Bruno had started both the dishwashers, which made such a noise he didn't hear Julia come in at first.

There was a big punnet of cherries on the table where desserts were prepared. Out of the corner of his eye, he could see her popping the fruit into her mouth, and popping out the stones into her hand, until her hand was so full of stones, they kept dropping on the floor he was trying to mop.

Eventually he stood with the mop under his armpit, until she became aware that he was watching her. She stopped guiltily, another cherry halfway to her mouth. He walked across to her and indicated she should open her hand. She did, like a child caught stealing. He cupped his hands so that she could tip the evidence in. Her palms were all purple with the juice. He took the stones to the bin that he'd just emptied. They clattered like a football rattle to the bottom.

'I know what you're doing,' Bruno told her, with a look.

'I'm sorry,' she replied guiltily, then burped.

Both of them laughed.

Bruno went back to his mopping.

'You won't tell?' she suddenly said.

'Who would I tell?' he said.

* * *

447

The Summer House, which stood at the far end of the Palace land, was originally a Victorian folly, a kind of grandiose playhouse for the dozens of children people had in those days. Outside, it looked like a Swiss chalet with the windows boarded up to stop tramps and vandals getting in. Inside, it was just like a normal house, although the ceilings were a bit low. The Summer House had most recently been lived in by Jolly Allsop and his family when they were waiting to move up to the Castle, but since then the downstairs had become a kind of glorified potting shed for the Palace grounds, housing various bits of equipment like a sit-on lawn mower and the Rotovator Christopher used to extend the kitchen garden he'd made on the back field. There was a strong, but not unpleasant, smell of petrol and grass cuttings.

Upstairs, under the eaves, wallpaper illustrated with boats indicated the rooms where the children had slept. The bigger central room was empty apart from a double divan bed, which had probably been left, Millicent thought, because the dusky-pink padded velour headboard wouldn't really have fitted in at the Castle.

Without thinking about it, she sat down and bounced a couple of times, testing the springs, and then stopped when Christopher entered the room.

Sex was a funny thing, Millicent thought. When she was young she couldn't get enough of it, but after the children it had become more of a duty than a pleasure, and then, one day, she just hadn't been able to bear the thought of it with Gerry any more, as if all the gears that had driven her to the heights of sensation had simply seized up. Sometimes she wondered if she'd made such a big deal out of the business with Bernadette as an excuse not to sleep with her husband. If she thought about it rationally, his decision to take in his daughter – who'd, after all, been just the result of youthful carelessness – was one of the better things Gerry had done in his life. But Millicent had never let him think she'd forgiven him, because she'd grown to like sleeping in a separate room, waking up to an alarm clock not a drunken snore, to the smell of Persil not beer in the sheets. To be fair, Gerry had accepted the arrangement with good heart, and they were as effective a team as they'd ever been. The pub was ticking over nicely. The children were happy enough. Bernadette had even learned to make a sandwich.

Women's magazines were full of articles about whether it was possible for women to have it all, and Millicent thought she wasn't doing so badly She was a wife and mother and she had a job. The only thing missing from her life was romance, and she got that from Christopher King.

Millicent didn't really know whether it was because she had been his first sexual partner, or whether it was because she had been the best, but Christopher loved her like no other man she had ever known. No woman could honestly say it wasn't nice to be adored. Whenever Millicent needed a bit of a boost, she'd ring him and they'd chat for ages. The Kings were all so stuffy, it was good for him to have someone normal to talk to, and his wife was so young and inexperienced, it didn't sound like she was much use. Millicent was the only one who understood that Christopher needed a great deal of patience. The knowledge that she could turn him on just by talking over the telephone made her feel powerful and sexy, without all the physical exertion and mess. But she'd always known that the time would inevitably come when he would want more.

'I'd love to see you,' he'd said the other day, oh so casually.

'Yes, but where?' She'd tried the usual excuse.

The railway station had been restored, the track to Coombe Minster was almost complete. All the enthusiasts from the Kingshaven Steam Company now needed was an engine to run up and down the line. The ramparts of the Iron Age fort, their other favourite venue, were overrun with holidaymakers during the summer months and, in any case, Millicent thought that an outdoor grope was a bit undignified when you were nearly forty.

'Have you ever been to the Summer House?' Christopher

had asked, adding, 'It's a remarkable piece of Victorian architecture,' as if he was offering a guided tour.

So, here they were, in a room with a double bed. In the fifteen or so years she'd known him, they'd never known such luxury.

Christopher sat down beside her on the bed. Then he took the cigarette she was smoking from between her fingers, and stubbed it out decisively in a china ashtray with the Palace Hotel crest on it. He turned her hand over and kissed it, gently, almost chivalrously. Milly was surprised to feel her body twitch with pleasure. Maybe the machinery still worked after all, she thought, as they both lay back on the mattress, staring into each other's eyes.

Bruno was out in the harbour with a group of children on kayaks when he heard Bee King's voice on the megaphone they used to call the pedalos in.

'Come in, Bruno Dearchild, your time is up,' she bellowed in a silly voice.

With all the kayaks tied to his, Bruno paddled the lot of them in. Bee had already donned a full-length wetsuit to take over from him. It was not the most flattering garment for her pear shape, but Bee's laughing eyes and long red hair blowing about in the wind gave the outfit a certain fetishistic raunchiness.

'What's the problem?' Bruno asked, splashing through the shallows to the slipway down from the Adventure Centre.

'Your boss wants a bit of service,' Bee replied with a wink.

Bruno got on fine with Bee, but sometimes her inability to say anything without a double entendre could get a bit tedious.

'Adrian will run you up,' said Bee. 'It seems Julia's need is quite urgent.'

Bruno could feel her eyes on his back as he stripped off his wetsuit and pulled navy-blue surfers' shorts on over his trunks, and a white T-shirt with the Wave Club logo.

When he arrived at the Palace, Julia was in the office, pacing up and down in front of the desk. It was clear from her blotched face that she'd been crying.

'What's up?' Bruno asked.

'It's Chef . . . he's come off his scooter on his way in, broken both his legs . . . he's in Lowhampton General . . . I don't know what I'm going to do!'

She started crying again, for Chef's pain or the inconvenience, Bruno wasn't sure. His instinct was to put his arms round her, allow her to sob against his chest, but her neediness was so raw, he didn't know if he could trust himself once they touched.

'It's OK,' Bruno told her. 'I'll step in for lunch.'

'But it's not just lunch,' Julia said, sniffing. 'He'll be out for the whole summer. Where am I going to get another chef at this point in the season?'

The question hung in the air between them.

'I don't suppose . . . ?' she asked.

'Me?' said Bruno.

'I *know* you can handle it,' she said in that lovely encouraging way she had when talking to her children.

Bruno had watched her the other day standing in the swimming pool stretching out her arms to little Archie as he stood shivering on the edge.

'I *know* you can do it!' she'd urged, giving him the courage to jump in.

Bruno wavered. Was it madness to think he probably could do it? The Palace dining room was busy, but the pace was much more sedate than Joe Allen's in London, where each table turned over at least three times an evening. It would be a lot of hard work, but he quite fancied the challenge. He might even get to experiment with a few of his own dishes.

'It'll cost you,' Bruno said, grinning at her.

'Perhaps we can talk about a pay rise once we've seen if you can do the job?' Julia said, suddenly a little haughty.

'I don't think you're really in a position to negotiate,' Bruno told her. 'If you want me . . .'

'You know I want you, Bruno,' Julia conceded, then blushed.

'Chef,' Bruno corrected her.

The degree courses Fiammetta liked the look of most were at Falmouth, Brighton and Etherington Schools of Art. When she'd gone to Falmouth, she'd found the ambience of the seaside town too much like a bigger version of Kingshaven, and it was so far away, it would be virtually impossible to see Nikhil, who was studying Medicine at Bart's Hospital, London, except during the holidays. She'd liked the cosmopolitan feeling of Brighton more. It was a different kind of resort from Kingshaven, much rougher and edgier, but you could still walk beside the sea and feel the salt wind through your hair, and it was only an hour from London by train. The interview had gone well, they had offered her a place, and Fiammetta had been so sure that it was right for her that travelling all the way to Etherington seemed a bit of a waste of time, but she didn't think it would be fair to make a decision without even taking a look. The photography course at Etherington was supposed to be one of the best in the country, and anyway, she was curious to see the town where her father had spent much of his youth.

As the train slowed towards the station she remembered her father's description.

'Not a bit like Kingshaven,' he'd said.

There were rows and rows of little terraced houses, each one, Fiammetta thought, containing a collection of lives and stories. She wondered how many removes her own story was from any one of them, how long it would take her to find someone who remembered her father or his aunt Jean (whom Fiammetta had always pictured as a colourful Rita Hayworth type).

The centre of the town had a solid monumental feeling, with large public buildings around the main square. With manufacturing industry in decline, a once-prosperous and proud community now had a deserted, neglected feeling, and there was litter blowing along the treeless streets.

The art school was housed in one of the institutional Victorian red-brick buildings. The legend above the entrance read 'Etherington School of Art and Textiles', but the textile industry had disappeared from the town, and the textile course with it. As Fiammetta walked along corridors and up and down endless flights of stairs, she couldn't imagine being inspired in a place of so little light. There was no one around. When she eventually found the designated room for her interview with Professor Barton, she didn't know whether she was supposed to sit on the row of chairs outside and wait, or knock on the door. She was half inclined to forget about the interview, turn straight round and take the next train back so that she wouldn't have to spend even one night in this depressing place.

Then the door opened, and a man in his mid-thirties, with longish fair hair and pale-blue eyes, looked out.

'Are you—' He stopped mid-sentence and frowned.

Fiammetta frowned back, trying to work out where they'd met before.

'Next?' he finally asked.

Fiammetta nodded.

'You'd better come in,' he said.

The room was full of light from the high windows. It was exactly as she'd imagined art school before she'd actually gone to one and discovered they were mostly sixties concrete buildings with big plate-glass windows. At the far end, there was a big untidy desk with a messy notice board behind it. The rest of the room was an explosion of bits of camera equipment, lights on stands, giant screen tubes, a projector, a lightbox, and piles of photographs all over the place.

The professor took a chair from a stack in the corner, swung it down on to an empty bit of floor in front of the desk and indicated that Fiammetta should sit down. Then he went behind the desk, swinging his legs up on to it, and looked at her, as if he was waiting for her to say something.

Fiammetta's eyes skimmed around the scuffed skirting board, as if she might find an opening sentence on the floor, with its untidy piles of books and boxes of slides. The silence seemed to go on for minutes. If this was a test, she knew she had failed. Eventually, she looked up at him in protest, and her eyes came to focus on a black-and-white photograph pinned on the notice board just behind his head.

Two very similar-looking women with unruly curly hair were staring defiantly at the camera. One had her tongue sticking out.

'That's me!' she said, pointing.

'Greenham Common, nineteen eighty-two,' said the man. 'When I saw you both, I cursed myself for not having colour film. I could have called the work *Reds*.'

'You weren't a press photographer?'

'Only an artist, I'm afraid.'

'It wasn't about art, it was about politics,' said Fiammetta firmly.

'Why can't it be about both?' said the professor.

Fiammetta stared at him.

'As a mere man, it was the only way I could be there that day.' He added, leaning across the desk, 'Clem Barton.'

'Fiammetta Dearchild,' she replied.

A spark of static electricity zapped between them as their hands touched.

'It's these bloody plastic chairs,' he said. 'There's no bloody funding for chairs. Tell me, Fiammetta Dearchild, do you really want to come to a place where there's no funding?'

'Yes,' Fiammetta heard herself saying.

He laughed. 'Tell me something about yourself,' he said.

Fiammetta could talk about the work in her portfolio, but she found it almost impossible to address the question he'd asked.

Clem Barton glanced back at the photo on the notice board again.

'Is that your mother?' he asked.

'Iris? No. My sister. Half-sister. My mother's dead,' said Fiammetta. Why on earth had she told him that?

'I'm sorry,' he said.

'It's OK. I was only two . . .' Now she felt fraudulent for eliciting his sympathy.

'Can you remember her?' Clem asked.

'I'm not sure,' Fiammetta told him.

It was an honest answer, but not a sufficient one, she realized, trying to elaborate. 'Sometimes I think I can remember, because people have painted a picture for me, and it's so strong it feels like I am remembering her, but it's always in the third person. Do you understand? There's a painting, in my portfolio . . .'

She pointed at the large folder she'd brought with her. He indicated that she should open it, and cleared away space, using his forearm to bulldoze marker pens, crisp packets, lenses and rolls of film right to the edge of the desk.

She opened the folder.

'This is her deathbed,' she said.

It was one of her first oil paintings. Only oils could capture the sheen on the black lacquer furniture, and hint at the delicacy of the gold inlay. In contrast to the intricate details of flowers and birds on the Persian carpet on the floor and the rich nap of the velvet cushion behind her head, the figures on the bed were drawn in very simple strokes, black features on white skin. A Madonna in the midst of pattern.

'Obviously, it's derivative . . . Matisse,' Fiammetta said, trying to pre-empt criticism, seeing the painting suddenly as Clem Barton might. 'And Chagall . . .'

'She looks so young,' he said.

'She was . . . thirty-two.'

'Cancer?'

Fiammetta nodded.

'And this is you?' he asked gently, pointing at the smiling baby floating above the woman, their only contact the baby's lips on the mother's face.

Fiammetta nodded.

'Do you like this painting?' he asked.

It was not a question she had ever considered. She looked at it again.

'I think I feel ultimately that it's probably dishonest,' she said eventually. 'I think that's why I'm interested in photography,' she added, trying to bring some coherence to the interview.

'We'll see you in September, then,' he said.

Iris stared out of the plate-glass window in Roman's office. It was pouring outside, and squalls of rain kept buffeting the window, like handfuls of soft sand thrown by an angry child.

'Your figures are down,' said Roman, putting his pen on the desk.

Not the pen she had given him.

'Fiction sales are down generally,' Iris said. 'In comparison, Capital's holding up quite well.'

'Nevertheless . . .'

'Have you considered my proposal to publish straight into paperback?' Iris asked. 'It's hardback figures that are really suffering, especially for first novels, and, quite honestly, I can see why. Why should anyone pay ten pounds for a hardback book that's heavy to carry around and difficult to read in bed, and they don't know whether it's going to be any good anyway?'

Usually she didn't have to work so hard to make him grasp her point.

'Nobody takes books published straight into paperback seriously,' said Roman.

'Only because we don't publish them properly. If we really put an effort into publishing original paperbacks, make them desirable objects, get some designers to come up with a look . . .'

'Reviewers won't review them,' he argued.

'They will if they feel they have to, if we carefully target our promotion . . .'

Iris was so sure she was right. It wasn't so much a matter of gut instinct as common sense. Now that there were so many competing media for people to spend their money on, like CDs, videos, Walkmans, publishing would have to think outside the box, as Winston put it, in order to survive.

Usually, when she was this determined, she infected Roman with her zeal, but today his face remained impassive.

'You don't feel there's any failure at an editorial level, then?' he said after a brief silence.

For a moment, Iris didn't understand what he meant, and then she realized that he was still talking about the short-term drop in Capital's figures, and hadn't been listening to her radical plans to break new ground and increase volume in the long term. Why was he so fixated on one bad quarter? There had been lean times before and Capital was still making a profit. Perhaps the rumours were true that Roman was planning to float Portico Books on the stock market, in which case the initial share price would very much depend on recent figures. But it was odd that he hadn't talked to her about it. She was his most senior editor.

'It's easier for me to defend the bad performance of good books, than the bad performance of bad books,' Roman continued.

His use of the word 'defend' confirmed her suspicions. Who did Roman have to defend himself against, except potential shareholders?

'Are you floating the company?' Iris asked him directly.

She took his failure to answer as a yes.

An uncomfortable silence stretched between them.

'I don't accept that any of the books I publish are bad,' she said finally.

'But you have to concede that the market's changing.'

'If you're looking to publish the next diet book or biography of the Duchess of Windsor, obviously I'm the wrong person . . .' Her words hung in the air.

Suddenly Iris realized what this chat was all about. How could she have been so stupid? He was ignoring her plans to make the future of Portico more successful, because he didn't see her as part of the future. Perhaps the future board of Portico plc had heard the rumours about their future chairman's past association with his editorial director, or perhaps Pippa was finally demanding revenge.

It had been totally self-destructive to challenge him at the party, allowing herself to drink so much that the momentary pleasure of embarrassing him and his snooty wife had taken precedence over all those years of careful subterfuge. She had expected the call as soon as she'd woken with a banging hangover. When it hadn't come, she'd convinced herself that nobody had heard, that it hadn't been as bad as she'd thought. But now she knew that it had been.

Against a backdrop of ominously black clouds, Roman in his office chair was like God on Judgement Day.

'Are you firing me?' Iris asked him, point-blank.

'I was hoping that it wouldn't come to—'

'You were hoping that you'd make me feel so bad, I'd resign,' Iris interrupted.

He said nothing. Wouldn't even look at her now.

'Perhaps you've been waiting all this time for me to go—' she asked.

'I was surprised . . .' Roman interrupted.

'I'm better at being an editor than a mistress,' Iris told him bluntly. 'I didn't see why I had to give up both.'

It was the first time either of them had referred to the past. She smiled at him, expecting to see if not shame, then regret, some sign that it had meant something, but he was frowning as if he had smelled a bad smell, that upper-class mannerism he must have learned from his wife, as if Iris had said something beyond the pale.

'I won't go quietly,' she said, suddenly boiling over with indignation. 'You ought to know me better than that. Some vestiges of workers' rights must still exist in this country.

I'm sure Winston Allsop can find me a good employment lawyer.'

It was a good name to be able to drop to the world's best name-dropper. Iris felt a small thrill of triumph at Roman's momentarily anxious look. She managed to hold his eyes squarely, determined he should know that she wasn't bluffing. She had learned a little from him about negotiation.

'OK. What do you want?' Roman finally asked.

'How can a grown man spend his entire life cultivating brassicas?' Libby King asked, peering over the top of her reading glasses out of the office window towards the back garden, where Christopher was pottering around his glorified allotment.

Julia wasn't sure whether her mother-in-law was hinting that something was going on, or whether it was just a straightforward question.

Julia's own suspicions had been aroused by Christopher's reaction to her plan to let the Summer House as a holiday chalet with full access to the hotel's facilities. It wasn't just that Christopher rejected the idea out of hand, which she was used to, but when she'd assured him that they could build a shed on the proceeds from just one season, he turned a horrible puce colour, and shouted, 'Why do you always have to argue with everything I say?'

The previous Sunday, when the King family were all out at church, Julia had feigned a headache, taken the keys from Christopher's gardening trousers and run all the way down the Rhododendron Mile to the Summer House.

It was rather odd to see hoes and rakes in the living room downstairs, where she'd spent so many hours playing with James. As a boy, James would have loved the little tractor thing Christopher used for ploughing up the land. Although it seemed a bit of a waste of the space, Julia felt slightly ashamed of herself for doubting Christopher when he told her he used the Summer House for his tools. Climbing the stairs for a nostalgic look out of her bedroom window, Julia found her own room exactly as it had always been. Then, feeling a bit like Goldilocks, because they'd never been allowed in there as children, Julia pushed open the door of her parents' room. The double bed was still there. The sheets were rumpled. Instinctively, Julia went to straighten the corners, then stopped. On the floor on the far side, there was a white china ashtray with the hotel crest containing several cigarette butts with smears of red lipstick. Scarlet Lady, Julia thought was the shade.

For a few moments, faced with the evidence, she was completely numb, then she sat down on the bed and wept.

It wasn't just that her husband had been lying to her, lying two-fold by telling her she was paranoid when she demanded to know who it was he was whispering to on the phone, but he'd compounded the deceit with the insult of carrying on in the place that had once been her home.

Betrayed and violated, Julia picked up a cigarette butt, and, holding it out in front of her, clattered down the stairs and ran all the way down the Rhododendron Mile in order to confront her husband with the evidence in front of the whole family, as the Kings processed back from church.

For once, Julia was grateful to the vicar for the length of his sermons, because, as she stood on the gravel drive, waiting for them, she began to collect herself and think about the consequences of open confrontation. Her husband would probably jump at the opportunity to get rid of her. She didn't think he'd ever really loved her and he felt threatened by her aptitude for the hotel business. So, where would she go? Not the Castle, not even the gatehouse, which was now the Castle's luxury honeymoon suite; and certainly not the Summer House. It suddenly dawned on Julia that her only home now was the Palace. There was nowhere else she could take the children, and she would never leave them.

She had made the decision that it would be better to say nothing at all, pretend that nothing was happening.

*　　　*　　　*

Julia observed her mother-in-law's face staring into the garden and tried to fathom whether Libby's expression was any more or less disapproving than usual.

'It certainly saves on our costs, growing our own vegetables,' Julia said loyally. 'Chef is very good at vegetables,' she added, hoping to elicit at least one favourable comment about her decision to promote Bruno. 'Have you seen the visitors' book?'

She opened it at the most recent page, pointing with pride at some of the comments.

'Our children didn't even realize Chef's Crispy Bacon Savoy was cabbage!'

'Dauphinoise to die for!'

Libby put on her reading glasses.

'It certainly makes a welcome change from mangetout,' she remarked, picking up Julia's new Dictaphone recorder.

'What's this?' she asked, in the suspicious tone the Kings reserved for new-fangled things.

'I dictate letters into it.' Julia demonstrated the record button and the rewind. 'It means we only need a part-time secretary,' she added.

Libby granted a grudging smile. She came from the frugal generation who'd lived through the war and felt guilty about making money and spending it. Julia could never imagine Libby, who still kept butter papers, shouting that greed was good, like her brother, James, and his City friends did as they sprayed each other with vintage champagne like Formula One drivers on the podium.

Now, Libby turned her attention to the accounts, poring over the figures with no reaction at all, even though they were better than ever.

Finally she took off her reading glasses.

'Very good, Julia,' she said. 'I realize it's not always easy for you.'

She glanced again out of the window in Christopher's direction, and then she was gone, and Julia was left, as she was so many afternoons, on her own in the office.

There was no lonelier place than a loveless marriage,

Julia thought, because when you were married, you couldn't talk to anyone about it. Not even Bee. She'd never completely trusted Bee since she'd failed to tell her about Christopher's affair before the wedding. The closest they'd come to a girly chat since they were both married women, was walking down the High Street after seeing *9½ Weeks*.

'Do you think people really do things like that, you know, with food?' Julia had ventured to ask.

Bee had laughed knowingly. 'There was nothing Gerry liked better than a pot of strawberry jam with his cream tea,' she'd replied enigmatically.

'What about Adrian?' Julia asked.

'Adrian's more of a meat and two veg man,' Bee said. 'Not that there's anything wrong with that.'

'No,' Julia agreed cautiously.

'What about Christopher?' Bee had asked.

'He's increasingly leaning towards vegetarianism,' Julia had replied, at which Bee had shrieked with laughter.

'Are we talking parsnip, or runner bean?' she'd asked.

Julia cast her eye over the reservation list for dinner. She always made little notes beside the people who arrived while she was on reception – 'Dyed blonde, roots showing'; 'Sloane, mole on right cheek'; 'Much older man, trophy wife', etc. – so that she would recognize the guests in the evening. It made such a difference if you greeted people by name, as long as you got the names right. She'd had to prevail on Christopher not to say anything after he'd asked one middle-aged woman how her son was liking the hotel when the relationship was clearly not in the least filial. That had sent him into another sulk.

Julia looked out of the window again, then she picked up the telephone on her desk and called the kitchen.

'Bruno? Can I come down and run through tonight's menu?'

'Cheer up! It may never happen!' said Clive.

He was about the last person Iris wanted to see right now.

'It just has,' she said.

Clive looked as if he was on his way to or from a business meeting, in his smart pinstripe suit and shiny leather shoes.

'How come I'm all wet, and you're not?' she asked him.

When she'd walked out of the Portico offices, the rain on her face had been cathartic, but now she was sodden and chilly. Puddles had gone right over the top of her sandals, and her bare feet felt slightly gritty. The spaces between her toes were rimmed with black grime that made it look like she hadn't had a bath for weeks.

'I've got a chauffeur,' Clive explained his pristine appearance. 'No parking worries.'

'Business is so good, you're even delivering yourself now?' said Iris.

Clive laughed more heartily than the feeble wit strictly merited.

'I suppose you could say that,' he said, giving each of his cuffs a little tweak.

'Want a drink?' Iris asked, opening the fridge and pulling the cork out of a half-full bottle of wine with her teeth.

Clive glanced at his ostentatiously large steel watch, which had all sorts of dials on the face giving information about the temperature, the time in Hong Kong, the depth of water he could dive to, stuff like that. He'd demonstrated it all at great length the last time he'd popped in, but Iris hadn't really been paying attention.

'I've just been made redundant,' Iris told him, excusing the need for alcohol so early in the day, and suddenly succumbing to tears.

It was so long since Iris last cried, it felt weird, like some alien thing had taken over her body and was shaking her and wouldn't stop. She stamped around lashing out at things in the flat – the fridge, the door, the sofa – then threw herself face down on her bed, kicking her legs like a frantic swimmer, pressing her face into her pillow as if to suffocate the pulsing, rabid presence inside her.

Clive stood looking bewildered and helpless in his smart suit.

'I'm sorry,' he said.

'It's not your fault,' Iris told him.

Tentatively, Clive approached the bed, kneeled down on the floor a little way away from her, as if uncertain whether it was safe to come any closer. He handed her a large white handkerchief.

'You deserve better than that job,' he said.

'What the fuck do you know about it?' Iris shouted at him.

She saw him wince. Even though Clive had lived his life amongst the hardest people, he still didn't like hearing a woman swear.

Iris could see he was searching for something to say to comfort her, but emotional vocabulary wasn't one of Clive's strengths. For a moment, the absurdity of the situation struck Iris as almost comic, and a bitter laugh blurted out of her.

'What?' Clive asked.

'Doesn't matter,' she said, sniffing loudly. 'Nothing bloody matters any more.'

'Don't be like that,' he said.

'Like what?'

'Sad,' he said. 'Here, look, I've got something that might cheer you up.'

Please not another business proposal, thought Iris, as Clive triumphantly produced a folded piece of paper from the breast pocket of his suit. Why did he always feel the need to consult them when he was clearly very good at business, and she and Vic were obviously not?

But it wasn't a business plan, it was an estate agent's details of a house in Chingford. A large mock-Tudor construction standing in half an acre, recently refurbished to a high standard and offering four bedrooms with an en-suite bathroom to the master suite. There was a conservatory and a kidney-shaped outdoor pool. In the photographs, the interiors were lavishly furnished and featured a 'medieval-

'style' dining room complete with an inglenook fireplace with log-effect gas fire. The kitchen had black granite work surfaces.

'Nice,' Iris lied, handing the piece of paper back.

'Look, I know now's probably not the time, but . . . you don't have to work any more, you know,' Clive stuttered.

'I'm sorry?'

'Obviously, you'd want to have a look yourself,' said Clive.

For a moment she wondered if this was his idea of a joke, but in all the time she'd known him, she couldn't remember Clive ever cracking a joke.

'What d'you mean?' she asked him.

'If you liked it . . .'

'If I liked it what?'

Clive looked embarrassed. 'I'm not going to ask you here,' he said, with a critical glance at the shabby surroundings. 'Even though I'm on my knees . . .'

She sat up, suddenly knowing she must stop him saying anything more.

This had to be a nightmare. It was as if she'd gone right back to the beginning, when she was seventeen and Clive had offered to take her to Mappin and Webb to buy her an engagement ring. Now he was offering a house instead of a solitaire diamond, but it was equally disturbing that he could have got her so wrong.

'I love you, Iris,' he said, stretching out his hand.

She shrank away from it. 'How can you say you love me when you don't even *like* anything about me?'

'I've always loved you,' said Clive simply.

'No! No! Stop it!' Iris held her hands over her ears. 'I don't love you!' she screamed.

He cowered as if he'd been hit and the flat seemed to echo with her words. For a moment she was terrified of what he would do.

'You loved me once,' he said.

'I had a teenage crush on you,' she told him.

'That must mean something.'

465

'Not now.'

'People change . . .'

If she'd changed from loving him to not, she could change back again, he seemed to be saying. How logical it all was when you were the one in love, Iris thought. Your brain made up a story to fit any version of the truth you were confronted with.

She tried another tactic. 'Look, I'm sure there are loads of women who'd love to be with you, Clive, but not me . . .'

'I knew it wasn't the right time,' Clive finally said, getting to his feet, brushing invisible dirt from the knees of his smart trousers.

'It's never going to be the right time,' Iris insisted.

'Say you'll think about it?'

Had Roman felt about her how she felt about Clive? Iris wondered. Had he thought her mad?

'I'll think about it,' she lied, knowing it was the quickest way to get him out of the flat, and, as she closed the door behind him and put the bolt across, redundancy suddenly seemed like the least of her problems.

Almost immediately, the phone started ringing. Startled, Iris watched it, trying to suppress the crazy thought that it was Roman calling to tell her it had all been a mistake. She let the answerphone take the call, then picked it up when she heard Fiammetta's voice talking from the bustle of a public phone.

'I'm at King's Cross . . . they said you'd gone home from work . . . hello?'

Half an hour later, they were sitting opposite each other in a booth at the back of the Luna Caprese.

'I thought you'd decided on Brighton?' Iris said, when Fiammetta revealed her news.

'I had, almost. But then, Etherington just felt like it was meant to be . . .'

Iris had never seen her sister's eyes shining with such excitement. It was so unlike Fiammetta to trust a feeling rather than logic.

Stefano brought them a bottle of house red and poured

two glasses. Iris took a big glug of hers, Fiammetta just sipped.

'Do you remember that photographer?' Fiammetta suddenly asked. 'The one who took a photo of us being arrested at Greenham?'

Even though it was almost five years before, Iris could picture him instantly. Fair hair flopping over pale-blue eyes. Very, very good-looking.

'He's a photographer. A professor of photography! He was the person who interviewed me and he's got that photo of us on his notice board at work.'

Now Iris thought she understood.

'How does Nikhil feel about you going?' she asked.

'I haven't told him yet,' said Fiammetta. 'Haven't told anyone. I wanted you to know first. Anyway, I can't fit my life around Nikhil. We were supposed to be doing Interrail this summer, but his dad's opened a new store in Havenbourne, so bang go our travel plans,' she added crossly.

Iris gazed at the mural of the Bay of Naples that covered the back wall of the café. The wine was beginning to seep into her veins now, calming her down, mellowing her out.

'We always said we'd go to Italy together, didn't we, if we ever got the time and money?' Iris said, speaking the idea that had just occurred to her out loud.

'Yes . . . ?' said Fiammetta cautiously.

'Well, you've got the time and I've got the money – what do you think?'

'Can you get the time off work?' Fiammetta asked.

'That's already been arranged,' said Iris, pouring herself another large glass of wine.

When Bruno passed the dessert preparation table on his way to the cold store there were seven profiteroles on a plate. When he came out, there were only four left, and Julia was standing with her arm inside the large jug containing the remains of the chocolate sauce. She heard him behind her, and quickly withdrew her hand, abandoning

467

the profiterole inside and leaving an incriminating trail of chocolate along the underside of her arm.

'Caught you!' said Bruno.

There was a little line of icing sugar along her top lip.

Bruno pulled a tea towel from the strings of his apron, and dabbed at her mouth. Then he nodded towards her arm, and Julia obediently offered it up to be wiped. As he held her hand, her trembling resonated with some frequency inside him, sending a shudder of lust through his body. His grip tightened on her hand as he dipped his head and licked away the chocolate from her pale delicate skin, the tip of his tongue tracing the delta of soft blue veins in her upturned wrist. Her free hand grabbed a fistful of his curls and yanked his head back up again, and they stared at each other for one long exhilarating moment of restraint, then his lips were on hers, tasting the sugar dust, the buttery sheen of choux pastry, the sweetness of vanilla *crème anglaise*. Her long taut body pressed against his as if she were trying to get inside him, her hands clawing at his hair, hurting him. He grabbed both her wrists, using all his force to prise them off and hold her arms rigidly away from him, like the bench press in the gym. She looked shocked, as if she hadn't been aware of what she was doing, and he couldn't resist kissing her again, tenderly now, watching those huge frightened eyes close, kissing her eyelids, the tip of her nose, her lips again, until he felt her limbs melt against him. He pushed the thin straps of her coral-pink cocktail dress down, kissing each of her golden shoulders, found the zip of her dress, looked at her for permission. Her eyes were still closed, but her mouth smiled, as if she was in the middle of a lovely dream, and didn't want to wake up.

'Come,' he said, leading her towards the walk-in cupboard where all the hotel plates were stacked on shelves. The door closed behind them, and then they were both blind. Slipping the stiff bodice down to her waist, his tongue traced first one puckered nipple, then the other, then ran down between her breasts to her belly button, and back up again. The dress slipped down to the floor. Automatically, she stepped out of it. In the claustrophobic heat of the cupboard, the scent of her lightly fragranced skin was overwhelmingly seductive. Bruno's tongue found the edge of brief silk panties, nudged them down, touched her clitoris, plump and salty, licked her to gasps of orgasm before unzipping himself, pushing into her, feeling her shudders become his, as the dinner plates rattled on the shelves around them, then were still again.

Julia's body lolled against his, her face against the starched white cotton chef's jacket. He propped her against the shelves, pulled her dress up over her body again. She was still pretending to be asleep. Not sleepwalking, he thought, sleepfucking.

Finally she spoke.

'So that's what all the fuss is about,' she said, her voice all smiles. 'I've never had one before.'

'A chef?' he asked.

'A . . . climax,' she said, suddenly coy.

'You were so ready . . .' he said.

'It was so amazing. You're amazing . . .'

'You're . . . delicious,' he said.

'Really?'

Now her eyes were wide open.

'I've been wondering what you tasted like for the last three years,' he told her.

In the soft humidity of a Florentine evening, Iris sat on a wall on the highest terrace of the Boboli Gardens, looking over the city and waiting for Fiammetta to emerge from the Pitti Palace. After a week of galleries in Venice and another in Florence, Iris's head was too full of art to look at any more. The self-contained quality that had made Fiammetta an enigmatic presence as a child, because you could never quite tell whether she was happy or sad, bored or entranced, made her a very good travelling companion as an adult. Fiammetta was happy to stand for hours in solitary contemplation of a painting, while Iris sat for

469

hours in a quiet square enjoying the luxury of not thinking at all.

There was a timeless quality about Florence that Iris loved. The view of the Duomo, the terracotta rooftops, and the shape of cypress trees had been the same for centuries. The intricacies of Iris's recent life seem to fade to insignificance in this ancient city that had nurtured so much of humanity's invention, inspiration and intrigue.

They were staying in a *pensione* on the Oltrarno, a stone's throw from the Ponte Vecchio in a quiet narrow street, with washing strung across from high windows, and little shops offering a few boxes of fruit outside, and inside, a few loaves of rough bread, a plump hemisphere of mortadella sausage, perhaps a yoghurt or two – just enough for a simple lunch.

While Fiammetta studied paintings, Iris walked through the olive groves outside the city walls all the way up to the pretty monastery of San Miniato al Monte, or wandered round the huge covered market of San Lorenzo, breathing the pungent smells of cheese and salami in its cool interior. One evening, she took a public bus to Fiesole, squashed in with old ladies in black, and workers going home, as the bus wound its way around hairpin bends up to the hill town. Sitting alone at a terrace table with a chequered cloth, sipping a neon-red aperitif, Iris gazed at the breathtaking pink of the city as the sun set over it, feeling a profound sense of peace.

Tonight, their last night, they had decided to eat in the warm ochre shadow of Santo Spirito. On the steps of the church, there was a group of students sitting talking, one of them strumming a guitar. The smell of oregano wafted around the outside tables of the restaurant.

'Home tomorrow,' said Iris, as they waited for their order to arrive, drinking red wine from little ceramic cups.

It occurred to Iris that the holiday was ending with the same taste as it had begun, although the wine was softer and warmer here, like the slightly damp air.

'Yes,' Fiammetta said, the regret in her voice leavened by excitement.

For Fiammetta, the holiday marked a watershed between two stages of her life, Iris thought. On her return, her sister would leave home and become an independent person. It had been a very special time for them both, but Fiammetta had so much to look forward to that she had reached that end-of-holiday moment when relaxation suddenly morphs into impatience to return to real life.

'What do you think you'll do now?' Fiammetta asked Iris.

Iris had found it surprisingly easy not to think, just look, taste, exist in a blur of a language she didn't understand. Now, when she said, 'I might stay here,' it wasn't something she had consciously considered, more like a fisherman throwing out a speculative line to see if anything would bite.

Fiammetta laughed, assuming she was joking.

'Why not, though?' Iris asked. 'What's to stop me?'

The waiter brought two gigantic pizzas flopping over the side of the plates.

What was there for her to go back to? Iris asked herself. Sure, she could get another job in publishing, start another list, get stressed, gossip at parties, drink too much, but what would be the point of that, except to earn enough to afford another holiday like this?

'You'd hate not working,' Fiammetta told her. 'You'd miss the buzz of discovering new talent.'

'I would . . .' Iris conceded. 'I would miss that. But that's about one per cent of my job.'

'Don't be silly,' Fiammetta said, anxious now, and crossly determined to return Iris from fantasy to logic.

'Why is it silly?' Iris asked.

'How would you survive?' Fiammetta asked more gently, as if to humour her.

'My redundancy money would keep me going a while . . . I could get a job . . .'

'What sort of job?' Fiammetta sounded like the older sister.

'Oh, I don't know,' said Iris.

471

She'd always fallen into things, never had a career plan like Thatcher's children did.

'But what would you do about the flat?' Fiammetta continued the interrogation.

'It's still Vic's.'

'You'd miss Vic . . .'

Yes, she would miss Vic, Iris admitted to herself, but not Clive. She definitely wouldn't miss Clive.

'Vic's hardly ever there now,' she said. 'Anyway he can come and see me. Everyone can!'

She was aware she'd slipped from the conditional to the future tense. Had she decided then, Iris wondered, in just a couple of minutes, to change the course of her life, to become passive instead of active; to go from having it all, to nothing at all? She smiled at Fiammetta, who shrugged, as if there was no reasoning with her.

'Here's to a room of my own!' Iris said, raising her cup.

'A room with a view!' said Fiammetta.

'And all other classic novels about English spinsters!'

As the evenings began to draw in and the holidaymakers went home, Bruno continued going up to the Palace every morning at nine o'clock, returning after midnight, sometimes later, to sleep.

'Aren't you cutting it a bit fine?' Michael asked him, the week after Fiammetta had left for Etherington to begin her degree course.

'What for?' said Bruno.

'For going back to university.'

Bruno sighed heavily. 'I'm not going back,' he said.

'Not going back?' Michael repeated.

'That's what I just said.'

'You mean, give up? I'd have given anything to go to university,' Michael suddenly shouted.

'But I'm not you, am I?' Bruno countered. 'I've decided to be a chef. In case you hadn't noticed, there's no university courses in Chefistry. I'm earning good money . . .'

'Money?' said Michael. 'Is that all you care about?'

'Money's not a bad thing in itself,' Bruno argued. 'Look what Winston does with his. Get real!'

'No, you get real,' said Michael, suddenly incandescent. 'You want to do your own thing. Fine. Just don't do it under my roof. Go to the Palace. And bloody stay there!'

'Fine!' said Bruno calmly. 'Now, if you've finished. I'm late for work.'

Michael stepped aside. Bruno walked past him.

Michael remained standing on the step for a few seconds, then he ran all the way up to the top floor and stood on tiptoe, watching Bruno walking along the promenade, wanting to call after him and tell him he didn't mean it. But Bruno didn't look back once.

'Did you hear?' Michael said, going down into the bookshop where Pascale was. 'A chef! How did I manage to produce a son who wants to be a chef?'

'In France, chefs are very important.'

'But there aren't any English chefs. They're all French.'

'But if he likes—'

'Cooking for the Kings!' Michael was almost crying with exasperation.

'But you push him into her arms!' Pascale exclaimed with very French impatience.

At first Michael thought she'd made a mistake with the possessive pronoun. Pascale still sometimes said his or her, when she meant their. But then she said, 'He's in love.'

'In love?' said Michael.

'With Julia King,' Pascale sighed. 'Didn't you see? At the Carnival? She presented him with the cup for the Swimathon. Are you so blind?'

He'd seen two attractive young people laughing. He hadn't thought anything of it.

A faint drumbeat of dread began to thump loudly in Michael's heart.

'You'll never guess what the owners are called,' his brother, Frank, had written. 'The Kings. The Kings in the Palace. One's a little princess, all right . . .'

Michael had never been able to get the idea out of his

473

head that the Kings had had a hand in what had happened to Frank. And then they'd seduced Michael too, threatened to ruin his life, and would have, if he hadn't ruined it himself. Now Bruno, his cocky confident son, with a charm just like Frank's, had been sucked in.

He didn't want to lose him to the Kings. It wasn't anger that had made him shout, Michael realized, but fear.

When she was little, Julia had always thought that if she was good enough and patient enough, then love would be her reward, just like the fortune-teller had told her. When Christopher had asked her to marry him she'd thought the waiting was over, but she'd been mistaken. She'd had to wait another six years.

It had been worth it, she thought, watching Bruno's sleeping face on the snowy-white pillowcase. There was something effortlessly sensual about him the way he lay sprawled, half on his front, half on his side, the hairless smoothness of his chest and back, his muscles strong and toned, but not yet bulky like a man. Any woman would kill to have eyelashes as long as his. His skin had a natural tan, unlike the pale pasty skin of her husband. Unable to resist touching Bruno, but not wanting to wake him, Julia fingered a single lock of his dark shiny hair. His nose wrinkled, and he shifted position.

'I love you.' She mouthed the words at him. 'I love you.'

The depth of the emotion almost made her cry.

'I love you.'

Outside it was already getting dark, and the wind was swirling around, rattling the small windows of the room at the top of the tower. It had been one of the maid's room, in the days when the hotel still had live-in staff. There was a trapdoor in the ceiling with a ladder so that workmen could get up into the attic to check the watertanks, which made it unsuitable for guests, but it had the best view in the hotel, Julia thought, as she got up and went to make sure the window was closed.

Chef was going to live in, she'd informed Christopher,

when he enquired why furniture was being taken up. There wasn't another available space, unless Christopher had changed his mind about the Summer House?

Sex had made Julia much more confident dealing with her husband. If he tried to be clever or mean, she found herself thinking about the smallness of his willy and, even though she never said anything, it was as if he picked up her thoughts, and backed down. There was a peculiar kind of truce between them now, a bit like the Cold War, she thought. They both had their weapons, but neither was going to use them. For the first time in her marriage, Julia felt secure.

Sex in the kitchen with Bruno had been furtively, dangerously thrilling. Once, she'd had to hide in the cold store when they heard someone coming and almost froze to death waiting for Eddie King to finish congratulating Bruno on his bread and butter pudding. Then Bruno had come in with her, kissing her face as her teeth chattered, his penis like a red-hot poker going into ice.

Every day he'd guided her, encouraging her to make demands, explore new ways. Once she'd asked him to blindfold her with a tea towel and he'd put a tiny taste of clotted cream on her tongue, then a dab of cinnamon, a single white currant, a feathery frond of dill, a dip of peanut butter. Driven wild by restraint, she grabbed his hand and sucked honey from his fingers.

In the kitchen, she had learned about sex. In his bedroom, it felt like making love. Afternoons were quiet in the hotel. When lunch was over, the kitchen washed down, cakes iced, just-baked scones cooling on racks, Bruno would leave the kitchen to his assistants and go to his room to shower away the sweat of the service, and catnap until Julia was able to join him. Now the season was over, the hotel virtually empty except at weekends, they spent more and more time together. Julia loved him so much that sometimes she thought she would burst with it.

'I love you,' she mouthed at him. She had not yet dared to break the spell by saying the words to him.

Bruno stretched, rubbed his eyes and smiled lazily at her.

'What's up?'

It felt like being in a fairy tale, up here at the top of the tower, like Rapunzel, Julia thought, except there was no need for her prince to climb the wall because he was already here. She turned and stared out of the window. He came and stood behind her, both of them naked in a lit window, but too high up to be seen. Below, the tops of the big trees swayed in the gusts, autumn leaves swirling in sudden eddies.

'Someone rang the BBC and said there was going to be a hurricane,' said Julia. 'But the weatherman said it was just a storm.'

The wind was so strong now she could feel the tower rocking. Outside, the air was full of dark moving shapes, like monsters, she thought. Suddenly frightened, she turned into Bruno's arms and breathed the warm, still-sleepy smell of him.

'Don't leave me,' she whispered.

'I'm not going to leave you,' he told her.

Chapter Sixteen

1989

'PHEW! What a scorcher!'

On the front page of the *Chronicle* there was a series of photographs of Kingshaven people doing their best to cool down in the hottest temperatures recorded since 1976: boys jumping off the pier; toddlers with ice-cream cones; a pensioner fast asleep in a deck chair; a woman with a big straw hat over her face, sunbathing topless.

'Apparently, there's to be a hosepipe ban,' said Libby King, reading the inside page. She lowered the newspaper and looked at Christopher over the top of her reading glasses. 'What will happen to your garden then?'

Libby always referred to the garden as if it were a trivial little hobby of Christopher's, rather than a serious occupation. Inevitably, Christopher's hackles rose.

'I shall have to find an alternative method of watering it,' he said.

'Chef's trying to source alternative lettuces,' Julia chipped in.

Her husband glared at her.

Libby sighed, and the paper went up again.

'Good God!' exclaimed Eddie King. 'What the hell is she up to now?'

'Who?' Libby King enquired wearily, lowering the newspaper again.

'The other daughter-in-law,' said Eddie, pointing at the photo of the topless woman.

'Is it Bee?' Libby asked, taking off her glasses and holding the paper very close to her face.

'Definitely!' said Eddie. Then, under the steady gaze of Granny Liliana, he explained, 'I recognize the hat.'

It was too hot to do anything, Julia thought, as she clambered down the steep steps at the end of the hotel's gardens to the beach, too hot even to think. The King family beach hut was like a furnace inside and there wasn't a whisper of breeze. She feared for her boys' skin in the searing sunshine, even with a coating of sun cream. The heat was making them fractious, so she suggested a walk along the beach to the Harbour End, half hoping that Adrian would volunteer to include them in some suitably sploshy activity, and she and Bee would be able chat somewhere nice and cool.

She found Bee in the flat above the Adventure Centre where she and Adrian lived with their baby daughter, in the room that had once been the Yacht Club bar and snooker room, but was now bright and airy and strewn with plastic toys. Baby Bethany was fast asleep in a travel cot, and Bee was lying on a bean bag next to an electric fan, with her long red hair flying about in the moving air. She was wearing only a bikini bottom, in more or less the same pose as she had been caught on the front of the *Chronicle*, except there appeared to be several pebbles lying on her very sunburned chest.

Julia had always envied the way Bee seemed to be at ease in her body, even though, she thought a little meanly, it wasn't the greatest body in the world.

'Don't tell me,' said Bee, opening one eye. 'The shit's hit the proverbial . . .' She waved at the fan. 'It's some new photographer at the *Chronicle*. I had a towel out in the yard, but he must have poked his head over the wall. They'd do anything to sell that newspaper.'

'At least you don't have Winny constantly pointing his lens at you,' said Julia.

Having been praised for his efforts videoing Adrian and Bee's wedding, the youngest King son, Winny, had got it into his head that he wanted to be a film director, and was always popping up unexpectedly with his video camera.

'I don't suppose we were amused?' Bee asked.

'Actually, it was quite funny.' Julia recounted the incident at breakfast.

'Trust Eddie!' said Bee, sitting up. 'You always get the feeling he's undressing you . . . unlike any of the other King men,' she said, flopping back down again despondently.

'I thought you and Adrian . . . ?'

'If he's not out all night with the lifeboat, he's too tired because he's been out all night with the bloody lifeboat,' Bee complained.

Julia said nothing.

'I suppose it's back to the deep freeze then,' said Bee.

'What?'

'Haven't you noticed? The Kings freeze you out if you step out of line,' said Bee. 'They're such hypocrites. It's fine to bonk the living daylights out of your secret lover, as long as you do it behind closed doors . . . but make the mistake of getting caught with your top off, and you're for it.' She opened both eyes to look at Julia.

'Why have you got three pebbles on your chest?' Julia asked, deciding to change the subject. She wasn't completely sure whether Bee was referring to Angela, against whom she still held a grudge, Christopher, or even herself, and she didn't really want to know.

'They're not pebbles, they're polished amethysts,' said Bee. 'It's supposed to have healing properties. I got them in the Crystal Circle, you know, where the butcher's used to be. Apparently, all crystals have powers. She's got something for everything.'

'Who has?'

'Sheila Silver. The lady who owns it.'

'Do they work?' asked Julia.

'I think they have taken away some of the heat,' said Bee, handing over one of the smooth stones.

It did feel surprisingly warm in Julia's hands.

'And the itching's died down, although it may be just that I'm concentrating so hard on keeping them from falling off,' Bee laughed. 'You should go and have a look. She does astrological charts and everything. Not stuff like you get in magazines that could apply to anyone, but proper personal ones just for you.'

'Have you had one done then?'

'Got to do something. Nobody tells you how incredibly boring it is looking after a baby, do they?'

As if she had heard her mother talking about her, Bethany woke up with a hot little whine.

Julia went to pick her up.

'Come on, darling, let's both sit by this nice fan,' she said. The baby stopped crying straight away and looked up into Julia's eyes.

There was nothing in the world as comforting as having a baby on your lap, Julia thought, enjoying the weight of this soft vulnerable bundle that suddenly became a vigorous little person when Julia pulled her up to standing, and stamped down with surprising vigour against Julia's thighs.

'Aren't you clever?' Julia said.

Bethany smiled at her, a long strand of drool dropping from her little mouth.

'I'm pregnant again,' said Bee.

'Oh, how lovely!' Julia said automatically, but inside she felt oddly resentful because Bee had just implied she wasn't having any sex, when actually she must be.

Julia's eyes filled with tears. The possibility of having another child wasn't available to her any more, because Christopher would be absolutely certain it wasn't his. She remembered telling him, in those wonderful first days after he proposed, when he was all over her like a rash, that she wanted to have lots of children, dozens and dozens, like the old woman who lived in a shoe. He'd laughed and said, 'Let's get started then!'

How naïve she'd been!

'Sheila Silver knew before me,' Bee went on. 'It was on my chart. There'll be a new arrival next year, she said, and then the Tarot confirmed it. Something to do with the World and the High Priestess together. So I bought a pregnancy test, and sure enough . . .'

'How amazing,' said Julia, trying very hard to concentrate on the present conversation, and not think about the past or the rosy future she had dreamed about.

'What else did you find out?' she enquired.

'She said that I would find my path in life, but it might not be the one I expected. She gave me some rose quartz, which aids peacefulness and calm in relationships. You really should go along,' said Bee. 'She's very good.'

'Maybe I will,' Julia said.

Sometimes she thought it was better not to know what the future had in store. For a moment she remembered the stifling heat of a gypsy tent long long ago.

A choice lies ahead.

Yes.

To follow the path of true love means turning away from what you most wish for.

Are you quite sure? her mother had asked.

In Bee's bright sunny living room, Julia suddenly shivered.

Fiammetta had left it right until the end of her second year at Etherington School of Art to choose what to specialize in. Torn between Fine Art and Photography, she knew the right choice in her brain, but her heart wouldn't let her make it.

The apprehension she felt waiting outside Professor Barton's studio was completely different from when she had sat in the same spot two years before. This time, when the professor opened the door, he smiled warmly at her, instead of frowning.

Unlike some of the other tutors, who occasionally fraternized with the students in the Union bar, or invited groups round for a decent meal at their homes, Clem Barton kept his distance. He was so scrupulously professional in tutorials that Fiammetta had been gutted to hear a rumour that he had been involved with a female student a couple of years before. So he was not happily married, or gay (as she had tried to persuade herself he might be), but perfectly capable of having a relationship with a woman. Just not with her.

Fiammetta tried to accept that his affection and respect was enough, but the love she felt for Clem Barton had been so instant and enduring she had not looked at another man since meeting him.

'You've broken Nikhil's heart,' Bruno told her when she went back to Kingshaven for the first Christmas holidays. 'He wanted to marry you!'

'His father would never have let him marry me,' said Fiammetta. 'Anyway, I don't love him.'

She hated hurting Nikhil, who had never done anything except adore her, but even though it would have been the sensible and logical thing to do, she had never managed to fall in love with him.

From the moment Fiammetta set eyes on Clem, she had understood for the first time in her life why artists traditionally depicted love by the firing of an arrow. Love was not warm and comfortable, it was shocking and acutely painful.

'What is it with you and art teachers?' Bruno had said, as they sat in the Victorian rain shelter about halfway along the promenade, an equal distance from the Palace, where he now lived, and the warehouse, where she went home in the vacation.

'This is different,' she tried to explain, staring at the grey, churning sea, inhaling its odour of seaweed, tasting the salt on her lips.

It wasn't just that her body was as giddy around Professor Barton as it had been around Mr Green, multiplied by a factor of about a million, it was the connection between their minds. She had listened uncritically to everything Steve Green had said, even though his so-called philosophy was, she could see now, a facile distillation of the lyrics of John Lennon. But she and Clem argued. He demanded intellectual rigour from her. She found that intensely sexy.

'You are weird,' Bruno told her.

'I didn't think someone who lived their life at a totally superficial level would understand,' Fiammetta teased him back.

Now Fiammetta picked her way through the usual fall-out in Clem's office to the desk and sat down with her hands folded in her lap.

'You wanted to see me?' Clem prompted.

'Yes . . .' Fiammetta tried to explain her dilemma.

While she had enjoyed the photography module more, she thought that ultimately her future might lie in painting.

'Yes. I think I'd agree,' Clem cut her off mid-sentence. 'If I were you I'd concentrate on that.'

'Why?' she asked, cursing her own ineptitude. What she had been hoping to achieve was Clem persuading her to stick with photography.

'Two reasons,' said Clem. 'Don't get me wrong. You're quite a good photographer. But lots of people can take a photograph. Very few people have the kind of focus needed to paint a really good portrait, that clarity of thought, that concentration.'

Fiammetta knew that it was high praise, but the words floated over the top of her head.

'Photography is often about capturing a moment. I don't know how good you are at moments . . . how much you trust in moments,' Clem continued.

'You're saying I'm not spontaneous,' said Fiammetta.

Was this the explanation of why he would never reciprocate her love?

'I'm saying that you are considered.' He tried to soften the criticism.

'And the other reason?' she asked, daring herself to look straight at him.

His slow smile made her aware that she had just proved everything he'd said. She was uptight, demanding. He had offered her two reasons, so she had to have them both.

'The other reason,' he said, 'is that I'd very much like to ask you out to lunch.'

'I'm sorry?'

'Would you like to have lunch with me?'

He was right, thought Fiammetta. She was useless at moments.

'Yes?' she said tentatively, suspecting there was a trick involved.

'Strawberry Fields for Only a Few More Days!'

Bruno looked at the flyer that had come with the delivery of potatoes. There was a place just outside Coombe Minster where you could pick your own strawberries, and the prices were being slashed as they tried to get rid of the fruit before the threatened drought restrictions.

'Can I borrow your car this afternoon?' he asked Julia, after the staff briefing about the lunch menu.

The Volvo estate she used had a large boot.

'Of course,' she told him.

'And can I borrow you to drive it?' he asked.

Julia's eyes flicked nervously from side to side, in case anyone might be listening, or watching.

These days you never knew when Winny might pop up with his video camera. Apparently they were letting him shoot a video of the hotel to sell to guests.

'Poor Winny,' Julia had explained when Bruno questioned the wisdom of this endeavour. 'He can't help out at the Adventure Centre because he gets seasick. Obviously nobody will buy the video, but it's a way of making him feel he's contributing . . .'

In Bruno's opinion, Winny was a total waste of space – what kind of a bloke would tolerate that nickname for a start? – but it was funny how Julia didn't quite approve of Bruno saying anything against the Kings, even though she complained about them all the time. Families were like that.

'I'd love to go strawberry picking with you, but I've promised to take the children to the gardens,' Julia whispered.

'The thing is,' said Bruno, catching her hand, stroking her wrist, 'I can't be without you.'

She looked at him with that startled innocent look she always had when he said something nice to her.

'You see, though it pains me to admit it, I . . . well, you see, I . . .' Bruno hesitated, milking the moment as she gazed at him expectantly. She was so easy to lead on.

'I . . . can't drive,' said Bruno.

'You can't . . . ? What about your Porsche?'

'Obviously I'll have to pass my test before!'

'You . . . you . . . fibber!' Julia said, hitting his arm quite hard.

Bruno laughed. 'We could always take the children with us?' he wheedled, knowing already he was going to get his way.

It was a hot afternoon and even with the windows down the car was so warm inside that Bertie and Archie were bickering in the back.

'I'm going to pick about a million strawberries and eat them all,' said Bertie.

'I'm going to pick more!' said Archie.

'I bet I'll pick more than both of you put together,' said Bruno.

'Bet you won't!' said Bertie.

'What's bet?' asked Archie.

'It's a kind of competition, darling,' said Julia.

'Is there a prize?' asked Archie.

'Is there a prize?' Bruno asked too, making her smile.

'It's a surprise,' she said.

'A surprise!' shouted Archie, delighted with this.

When Julia was with her children, she was different,

485

confident, Bruno thought. As a mother, she always seemed to know exactly the right thing to say.

'Shall we play I Spy?' she suggested.

'I spy something beginning with fee,' said Archie.

'Fee's not a letter,' Bruno pointed out.

'Doesn't have to be a letter in our game,' Julia explained. 'Is it field, darling?'

'Yup,' said Archie. 'Your turn!'

'Bruno can have my turn,' said Julia, wickedly passing the buck.

'I spy something beginning with L,' Bruno said.

'Elephant!' said Archie.

'Where?' asked Bertie.

'It's not elephant,' said Bruno. 'Elephant begins with E, anyway.'

'Give up!' said both boys.

'You're not really trying.'

'Give up anyway. What is it?'

'Lady,' said Bruno, looking at Julia, who took her eyes off the road to smile shyly back at him.

'Where?' asked Bertie.

'Your mummy,' said Bruno. 'She's a lady, isn't she?'

'No she's not!' said Archie. 'Lady Sylvia is a lady. Mummy's not like a lady at all!'

And then they were all laughing, but for different reasons, and Bruno thought how easy it was to please Julia, how she blossomed with the slightest attention, and how peculiar it was that her husband didn't even want to try. He couldn't imagine Christopher sitting in the front of the car making up daft games to entertain the boys, all of them laughing together.

The Kings were still a mystery to him. No upper lip was stiffer than theirs. The hotel would be nothing without Julia. She had a gift for making both staff and guests feel valued, and yet none of them ever seemed to acknowledge this. Sometimes, when she was feeling particularly fed up, Julia would refer to them as The Germans, and he'd initially thought that was because they ran the hotel like a concentration camp, but she'd laughed when he said this, and told him that they were originally German, although they hated anyone knowing. It reminded Bruno of something Dad once said about the Patels, how immigrants often tried to be more English than the English. The Kings set great store by the proper way of doing things, but it was all for show. There were plenty of rumours about their less-than-exemplary behaviour. Julia swore that Christopher was having an affair with Millicent Balls, but Bruno couldn't get his head around that one. He could see that for some men Millicent might have a certain dirty appeal, but it was beyond him how anyone could screw her when they had Julia in their bed.

They filled four shallow crates full of strawberries before the blistering heat of the afternoon became too much for the children and they began to whine. With the promise of an ice cream if they were good, Julia bribed them back into the hot car, now filled with the earthy smell of strawberries, and pulled up outside a thatched tea room with a yellow Wall's sign outside. There were pink roses clambering over the walls in the garden, and the only sound, apart from the occasional car driving past, was the hum of bees and the chink chink of tea being served.

Sitting at a table in the shade of a large green and white striped umbrella, Julia ordered a pot of tea for two, a slice of Victoria sponge, and dishes of ice cream for the boys, who took one spoonful before charging off to explore an incongruously garish plastic climbing frame in the shape of a giant caterpillar.

Bruno watched as Julia carefully cut the slice of cake into four, and ate each of her two pieces slowly. She was eating food for pleasure now, not because of some desperate craving for something – sex, he supposed. She had enough sex now.

As if she'd heard him, Julia looked at him from under her lashes, and smiled. Taking tea together fully dressed suddenly felt strangely intimate, even though they had not touched each other all afternoon.

'I'd like to live somewhere like this one day,' Julia said, pressing crumbs on the plate with the pad of her forefinger.

The question she hadn't asked hung in the air.

'It would be idyllic, wouldn't it?' she elaborated.

'I suppose,' Bruno said, knowing that it would make her happy if he went along with her game of happy ever after with roses round the door, but unwilling to join in. He wasn't even twenty-two. There was no way he was ready to settle down. He had been careful to give her no reason to think otherwise, but sometimes he suspected that she wanted him to sweep her up in his arms and carry her out of the hotel in his white chef's uniform, like Richard Gere at the end of *An Officer and a Gentleman*. But what would happen after this grand gesture, when they got to the bottom of the gravel drive and she suddenly became a bit heavy and he put her down, he thought. What then?

On the drive back to the hotel, the boys fell asleep in the back. Neither Julia nor Bruno spoke. Eventually, Julia leaned forwards and switched on the radio. The Pet Shop Boys were singing 'You Were Always on my Mind'.

It was amazing how a bit of sunshine could change the whole culture, thought Fiammetta. The central square of Etherington, usually a grim and forbidding place, had turned itself into a continental square. Office workers were sitting on patches of scrubby grass eating their sandwiches. Students were playing in the rainbow spray of the fountain, recklessly taking advantage before the threatened drought measures switched it off. The pubs seemed to be competing with each other for best window box. Restaurants she hadn't noticed before now had tables outside, with big parasols. One was grilling food on a huge open barbecue. The smell of charcoal reminded Fiammetta of the Ship's annual ram roast after the Carnival, a quintessentially summer smell.

'Here?' said Clem.

'Why not,' she agreed.

They ordered brochettes of steak and prawns called Surf and Turf accompanied by a big bowl of crisp *pommes frites* and a green salad dressed with walnut oil. As soon as Fiammetta bit into a blackened cube of meltingly tender meat she felt ravenous, unable to remember the last decent meal she had eaten.

Clem poured a glass of red wine. She sipped the soft warm blackberry taste, feeling instantly woozy, and told herself she must have no more. Because there was so little of her, even a very small quantity of alcohol had its effect. She had never been able to join in the marathon drinking sessions with her fellow students, nor the curries afterwards.

'Why?' Fiammetta asked, still unable to believe she was sitting across a restaurant table from him.

'Why what?' asked Clem.

'Why are we having lunch together?'

'It's lunchtime . . .'

'Yes.' Fiammetta told herself not to ask any more questions.

'I wanted to ask you to dinner,' Clem went on, 'but the opportunity arose for lunch, so I thought I might as well take it.'

'That wasn't really what I was asking,' she said.

He sighed, and she instantly wished that she hadn't pressed him. Why not just go along with this delicious surprise? Why did she always have to have reasons?

'There's a bit of history,' Clem said eventually, weighing his words carefully. 'A couple of years ago, one of my former students made a complaint of sexual harassment against me. I had to sign up to a code of ethics to keep my job.'

'Were you sexually harassing her?' Fiammetta asked, alarmed.

'I hope not. We had a relationship. It wasn't going anywhere. She was disappointed . . .'

Fiammetta thought that if she had read this in a newspaper, or seen it in a television drama, she would have thought it typical male rationalization of sexist behaviour – a simple reworking of 'Hell hath no fury like a woman scorned' – so why did she believe him?

'To be fair, I don't think she had any idea that it would put my job in jeopardy,' said Clem. 'But by the time she realized, it had all got a bit out of hand.'

'What happened to her?' Fiammetta asked.

'She got a first and now works in the fashion industry.'

Fiammetta imagined a willowy siren with shoulder pads and bright-red lipstick, and hated her.

'So I now make a point of not falling in love with my students,' Clem said.

'I see,' said Fiammetta. Was it the wine? She was getting all sorts of mixed signals.

'Technically, you don't count,' Clem went on.

Was he teasing her, like Bruno always did, or did he think she knew what he was talking about?

'Because when I first saw you, you weren't my student . . .'

'At Greenham . . . ?'

'I meant when you walked into my office, and looked so disdainfully at all the mess. I thought, who is this fearless little Pre-Raphaelite beauty, who sees into other people's souls with her paintbrush?'

'But I don't!' Fiammetta protested. 'I can't see into your soul at all!'

His pale-blue eyes locked with hers as his hand slid across the table. The touch was so shocking, her hand jumped, knocking over the glass of wine. She stared horrified at the purple liquid spreading into the white linen tablecloth.

'I think you can see, if you look,' he said gently.

She looked, saw, knew.

And then there were warm drops of wine dripping on to her bare leg, a waiter arriving with a change of tablecloth, a new glass, a napkin to mop it up.

'Can we get out of here?' she whispered.

490

They walked along the canal, past crumbling disused warehouses, under low bridges, over locks, along the backs of suburban gardens, and out, surprisingly quickly, into open fields with cattle grazing, horses in fields. Sitting on a lock gate, looking back at the hazy outline of the town, Fiammetta wondered, as she often did in Etherington, whether her father had been in this spot, seen this view.

'He was evacuated here in the war,' she told Clem.

'Odd place to be evacuated to,' said Clem. 'A lot of bombs fell on Etherington.'

She'd never really thought about that before.

'Maybe it was the only place he could go,' she said. 'He had an aunt here. He was from the North East and his mother and father were killed quite early on . . . and then his brother was killed in action.'

'And the aunt?'

'She went to live in Idaho after the war, I think.' Fiammetta realized how patchy her information was, how little her father spoke of the past.

When they were children, Michael had always been keen that they find out as much as possible about their mother's heritage, making them listen to all the professor's rambling stories, asking questions on their behalf, trying to extract as much as possible from that irascible depository of knowledge while he was still alive. But he had never spoken much about his own childhood, except recently to tell Bruno how lucky he was in comparison.

'I don't think he was happy here,' she said to Clem, wondering whether this was true. She pictured a lonely little boy roaming the bombsites, pedalling along this canal on his bike. Sylvia had been the girl next door. Fiammetta simply couldn't picture Lady Allsop as a girl, her hair not in a stiff chignon; her feet not in court shoes that tapped, and without the pervasive drift of perfume that gave advance warning of her presence. Fiammetta decided she would ask her father about his time here when she next saw him, find out a little more.

'I didn't really speak to my father for years,' she tried to

491

explain to Clem. 'People thought it was my way of punishing him for falling in love with Pascale, but it wasn't that. I couldn't speak . . . physically. I stopped being able to talk to anyone except my brother Bruno . . .'

Clem said nothing.

'There was this wonderful woman called Barbara who really loved us . . .' Fiammetta still found it difficult to think about Barbara without gulping. 'She drowned . . . and just before, there was this party, in our new house, and it was really hot and crowded, and she asked me if I wanted to go out for a breath of fresh air, and I said no . . . I don't know why I said no . . . and then she went out herself . . . and . . .'

'You think you could have saved her?' Clem prompted.

'Not physically pulled her out of the sea, but if I'd have gone, then everything would have been different, wouldn't it? She might not have gone in.'

'Why did she go in?'

'It was so hot . . . I don't know. I think she probably loved my father, perhaps she realized that my father had fallen in love . . . Pascale moved in the next day . . .'

'You think she might have killed herself?'

The words had always been too terrible to say out loud, but now Clem had spoken them Fiammetta felt strangely unburdened. Tears streamed down her face, and her nose was running, and she didn't want him to see her with snot all down her face, but she didn't have a tissue.

'So you couldn't talk, in case you gave the wrong answer, and inadvertently killed someone?' Clem said, putting into words something that she had never admitted, even to herself, for fear of it being true.

'Yes!' said Fiammetta.

He put his arm around her, held her, and she felt completely safe with him, wiping her nose on his T-shirt, smelling his smell for the first time.

He lived in one of the streets of terraced houses she had passed on the train when she first came into Etherington. As he opened the door, kicking aside letters and flyers on

492

the hall floor (some of them bills, Fiammetta couldn't help noticing, with red writing instructing the recipient to open immediately) she thought how strange it was that her own story had brought her here, as if she had unconsciously foretold it.

She sat in the kitchen as he crushed garlic and set a big saucepan of water on to boil. The house was as crazily messy as his office. A line of prints was strung across, like washing hanging up to dry. The bathroom, which led off the kitchen at the back, doubled as a darkroom, with a blackout curtain nailed over the small window, and various containers of developing agents lined up alongside aerosols of shaving cream and bottles of shampoo. On the kitchen table there were camera lenses alongside unwashed coffee cups. Automatically, Fiammetta's hand began sweeping up toast crumbs, then stopped as she saw that he was looking at her.

'It's OK, go ahead. I would have cleared up a bit if I'd known . . .'

'But you did know . . .'

There was still a tiny glimmer of suspicion that this was all a ploy. Did he choose a suitably naïve female student at the end of each year, and enact this elaborate chat-up ritual?

Clem turned round, holding a fistful of dry spaghetti. The water was bubbling in the big saucepan now.

'We both knew, didn't we?' he said.

They ate the spaghetti, simply dressed with olive oil and garlic, and then went out to the pub at the end of the street and stood outside talking while Clem drank a pint of beer. When they returned to his house, Fiammetta washed up two cups, made coffee and they sat at either end of the squashy leather sofa that took up most of the front room, with their shoes kicked off and feet up, facing each other, but not touching.

The sofa had come from his parents' house, Clem explained, and he hadn't let it go when they were clearing out, because it reminded him of his mother more than any photo could. He put his face against the leather, and Fiammetta did too, detecting a faint smell of alcohol and cigarettes beyond the smell of leather.

His mother was always inviting new people back to the house for impromptu parties, stinking the house out with smoke, making too much noise.

'We were the teenagers,' Clem said, 'and we were the ones saying, Mum, do you have to have music on so loudly?'

Fiammetta smiled.

'Sometimes she would come down in the morning with a hangover and snap at everyone, and go on about how much she hated Etherington and all the small-minded people. She was always setting up protest groups, women's groups . . . putting every bit of her personality and charisma in, but nothing ever lived up to her expectations, so then she'd move on to the next thing. The house was always full of people, and yet I always felt she was lonely, and she was trying to fill a kind of emptiness . . .'

'And your father?' Fiammetta asked.

'He was just terrific,' Clem said, and she could see instantly that his feelings for his father were much more straightforward than those for his mother. 'He loved her so much. And us. And he was always there . . .'

'And did she love him?'

'She needed him. She recognized that. And that's a kind of love, I think.'

Clem looked at her, as if searching for confirmation, and for a moment he looked more like a child than a man, and Fiammetta loved him even more for that. Tentatively, she let her toe touch his, then the sole of her foot, pressing it lightly against his, as if their feet were kissing. He opened his arms, and she moved across the sofa into his embrace, resting her head against his chest, as he ran his fingers through her ringlets, occasionally pulling one gently away from her head like stretching a spring to see how long it was. After a little while she became aware of his body relaxing under hers, and the evenness of his breathing, and she realized he was sleeping, and she thought how much more intimate this felt than all the times she had imagined what it would be like to kiss him, and then she drifted into sleep too.

At some point in the night, probably around dawn, Fiammetta thought, because the air was suddenly chilly, they woke up and he took her hand and led her upstairs to bed, when they slept some more, waking in the heat of another blisteringly hot day. Pretending to be still asleep, Fiammetta listened as he padded downstairs, clattered about in the kitchen, swearing, then brought her a mug of tea. She smiled drowsily up at him, opened her arms, half stretching, half pulling him down on to her and then they made love in the blinding glare of sunshine, and it was more beautiful than she could possibly have imagined.

The downturn came when the weather broke, although even before that, Julia felt a chill run through her soul when James rang to tell her that several of his friends had died in the sinking of the *Marchioness* in the Thames. The thought of all those bright hedonistic people she knew from her brother's parties, drinking champagne and dancing under twinkling coloured lights one minute, then cast to the murky dark depths the next, made Julia shiver with foreboding.

There was a definite feeling in the air that it was the end of an era.

Decades were like seasons, Julia thought. As the end approached, the natural response was to reflect on what had happened, think about what the future might bring. On the television news, people even seemed to be expressing doubts about Mrs Thatcher now the eighties were drawing to an end. Suddenly the future seemed much less assured.

Granny Liliana's repeated warnings that good times didn't go on for ever had grown more frequent recently, like the scratched old 78s Julia could remember Sir John and the professor listening to, and, following the record-breaking summer, just as she prophesied, business suddenly dried up.

The end of the season was always a period of reorganization at the Palace. Most of the casual staff left, with only Denise retaining both her assistants at the Wave Club. Sid Farthing was told to recruit porters as and when he saw fit; chambermaids doubled as waitresses, and Bruno's staff was cut to just a sous-chef and a dishwasher.

With Bertie and Archie both at school, afternoons in bed with Bruno were less rushed, and yet though the sex was still blissful, the little attic room seemed full of preoccupation afterwards, as if there were hundreds of words floating about neither he nor Julia dared to pin down. She detected a fidgety restlessness in her lover, like one of the leaves on the beech tree, now turning to parched copper, flickering about in the chilly September gusts, impatient to separate from the branch.

Julia was shopping in Kingshaven when she walked past the shop that had been the butcher's. In the wake of mad cow disease, people seemed more inclined to trust the hygiene of Sunny Stores Supermarket, where the meat came cut into convenient portions and sealed in Cellophane, rather than an old-fashioned butcher with blood on his apron. Now the shop was called the Crystal Circle, and instead of steel trays of pink pork chops and slippery brown liver in the window, there were ammonites graded by size, and baskets of polished semi-precious gems labelled with handwritten descriptions of their healing properties.

Julia stopped to read. Aquamarine was soothing and could banish phobias. Citrine raised self-esteem. Hematite enhanced personal magnetism. She was suddenly filled with the urge to buy one of each to ward off the stirrings of unease.

As she pushed open the door to the shop, wind chimes in all shapes and sizes suspended from the ceiling jangled, then trembled to silence as she closed the door behind her.

A middle-aged woman with long white hair, wearing lots

of silver jewellery, watched as Julia carefully selected glossy pebbles of jasper, amethyst, and a piece of tiger eye 'the confidence stone', as golden and stripy as a humbug.

'You have a pure and radiant aura,' the woman suddenly said.

'Me?' Julia asked, pointing at her chest, as if there was someone else in the shop. She fished around for the right money in her purse.

'Take some lapis as well,' the woman advised.

'What does that do?' asked Julia.

'It's the stone of friendship, and it matches your eyes!'

Julia laughed a little nervously. Bee hadn't mentioned that the woman was a bit weird.

'Sheila Silver.' She extended her hand.

Silver hair and silver jewellery, Julia thought. The handshake was warm and firm.

'Have you had a good season?' Julia asked, trying to keep the encounter on a businesslike plane.

'Not bad,' Sheila Silver replied.

'You should do well. Something different for the foreigners to take home – the visitors, I mean,' Julia corrected herself. Embarrassed, she found her eyes focusing on the sign behind the counter offering tarot readings for ten pounds.

'Would you like a reading?'

'I'm not sure if there's time.' Julia glanced anxiously at her watch, but there was still an hour before she had to pick up the children, so it wasn't a very good excuse.

'You should make time for yourself . . .' Sheila Silver said. 'You always make time for other people.'

Had she seen Julia's picture in the paper presenting a giant charity cheque, or in the mums' race at the boys' sports day?

'Actually, why not?' Julia agreed, following her behind the curtain at the back of the shop where there was a table with a fake Tiffany lamp on it, which bathed the space in warm red light.

Unable now to think of a way of getting out of it without

appearing rude, or mad, Julia shuffled the cards and cut the stack, as Sheila instructed, with her left hand, then passed it across the table. She watched as Sheila laid out the cards.

'This one tells us about the past, which is currently influencing you.'

The card Sheila turned over was called the Wheel.

'But it is reversed,' Sheila said. 'Which might mean that other people have been in control of your life.'

'Well, that's certainly true!' said Julia with a wry laugh, relaxing a little against the hard back of her chair.

'The Hermit and the Tower suggest that you're still suffering from a lack of trust, because you've been wounded in the past.'

Sheila could probably work that out from what she'd just revealed about herself by butting in, thought Julia.

'This card will give an indication of your future . . .' Sheila turned it over.

Julia gasped.

Death. Not even reversed, which was obviously the Tarot way of saying upside down.

'Don't worry, you're not the first person to have that reaction,' Sheila said reassuringly. 'It doesn't mean what you think. It does signify an ending and it could well mean that something bad is about to end, something bright about to begin.'

Julia tried not to look at the Death card. But her eyes kept returning to it as the reading became more and more uncannily accurate.

'Now, this line,' Sheila pointed at the top line of yet unturned cards, 'represents the mind and the internal life. The Temperance card suggests that you're good at putting on a brave face. You've previously experienced happiness as fleeting, but now it could be more sustained. Look at all these cups! You're obviously a very caring and sensitive person . . . but the down side of that is that you sometimes delude yourself . . . the World confirms what the Death card has indicated.'

'What's that?' Julia was on the edge of her seat.

'There are new beginnings, transformations . . . optimism and renewal. The message coming through to me . . .' Sheila Silver hesitated and looked up at Julia for a long silent moment.

'Yes?'

'Giving love may be more fulfilling than receiving it,' she pronounced.

Julia laughed, relieved that it wasn't something terrible.

'You've trusted people in the past and you're finding it difficult to do so again, aren't you?' Sheila said.

Julia nodded, chewing her lip.

'The Chariot reversed indicates there may a setback. Be careful how you travel . . . But it's all pointing to a future full of renewal and trust . . . which is only what you deserve.'

Julia smiled. For a moment, in the womb-like space, she was suspended in a happy, safe place.

Then at the front of the shop, the door opened and the draught tinkled the wind chimes.

The reading was over, and Julia was slightly flustered to realize she had lost all account of the time. She recognized from the school playground the young woman who had come in. She was one of the council house mums with pushchairs, who gossiped and smoked while their toddlers tore about making a nuisance of themselves. Julia thought the pasty little girl might be in Archie's class. The child had seen a bracelet of rose quartz beads in the window and was threatening to throw a wobbler if her mother didn't buy it for her.

It was a tense moment. Julia was sure the mother couldn't afford it, but then, to her huge surprise, Sheila Silver leaned into the window and took the bracelet out.

'Is this the one you want?' she asked the little girl.

The child nodded.

'Here you are then!'

She wouldn't stay in business long like that, Julia thought, as she left, and it was never a good idea to reward bad behaviour. As she hurried up towards the school, Julia wondered whether the Kings had a point about the type of children Bertie and Archie were mixing with. Julia had insisted on them having a normal school life, instead of being sent away to suffer the harsh regime of prep school that had so clearly scarred Christopher, but perhaps it was time for a rethink.

A new beginning, she thought, repeating the words over and over in her head to the rhythm of her hurrying footsteps. Optimism and renewal.

Julia's back arched and she threw her head so far back Bruno couldn't see her face. He held on to his own climax for as long as possible with her bucking and shouting, 'Oh yes! Oh yes! Oh yes!', her long strong thighs astride him, until finally, he allowed himself to let go, the specific, exquisite release of his own orgasm ultimately anticlimactic after the enveloping totality of making love to her.

Her slim body, her stomach flat and toned from the workout she did each morning, smacked down on to his chest, her accelerated heartbeat pumping against his ribs. Her hair, all messed up from thrashing about, fell over his face. He blew strands of it out of his mouth as her breathing slowed down, and she dropped grateful kisses all over his face. He wondered how he could even think about giving this up.

'Julia?' he whispered.

'Yes?' she murmured.

'I don't think I can stay like this any more.'

'Sorry!' She shifted her weight back on to her arms. 'Am I crushing you?'

She rolled off him, and lay with her face against his chest.

The sun was already low and mellow. The days were drawing in.

He took a deep breath, tried again.

'I'm thinking of getting another job,' he said.

'Aren't the perks good enough here?' she replied, not taking him seriously.

It was one of the things that had begun to get to him. The way that he had allowed her to believe that she was the boss of his life as well as his work. The balance of power had shifted and he wasn't sure how to shift it back without hurting her now.

'I want more,' he said.

'I'll try to oblige,' she giggled.

Suddenly Bruno didn't want her skin stuck to his any more. He sat up.

'No, listen, I want to train as a chef,' he said.

'But you are . . .'

'No. I'm not. I'm a hotel cook. In the back of beyond.'

'But you can't leave me!' she said, her eyes immediately brimming with tears.

'I don't want to leave you, but—'

'You don't love me,' she said.

'Of course I love you,' he said.

Her sudden, ecstatic smile made him realize that it was the first time he'd told her.

'I promise things will change,' she said. 'Next summer when things pick up, we'll open the restaurant to non-residents. You could go on a course, if you like – not that I think you need it. We could even call it something – Chez Bruno? How does that sound?'

They were running out of time, Bruno thought, looking at the alarm clock on the floor beside his bed. In ten minutes he would have to start on dinner. He didn't want to argue with her now. He wasn't sure he knew what he wanted any more. Nobody got a restaurant, just like that. And he knew she was planning to attract more guests down from London, sophisticated types who knew about food. He might get a reputation. It might help when he eventually went to London. It would be crazy to leave.

'You probably just need a holiday,' Julia said, stroking his hair away from his face. 'Why don't you go and see Iris when the hotel closes?'

There was something Bruno didn't quite like about Julia dictating what he should do, and where he should do it, and yet in her almost telepathic way she had hit upon something he had been wanting to do almost without realizing it.

The teachers of English as a Foreign Language at the school where Iris worked divided into two distinct groups. There were the recent graduates, who wanted to see the world before settling into a career, and had done a four-week course to get the International House Certificate. They sat in the school common room during breaks ticking off the sights they had seen in their *Rough Guide to Italy*. Then there were the others, a motley crew of world-weary English and Irish flotsam and jetsam, who'd washed up in Florence, for reasons they never talked about, and nobody ever asked.

The fresh-faced graduates were young enough to socialize with the students, who were mostly spoiled young middle-class Italians, still living at home, unable, or unwilling, to find work after the many years they'd spent at university. The other teachers, including Iris, kept themselves to themselves, except, occasionally, on Friday, when they all went out, got drunk together and exchanged cynical observations about the younger teachers. Sometimes Iris would get a glimpse of a colleague's past, what had brought them to this place. Several of the women were slightly raddled divorcées, and Iris suspected they had come to the warm Mediterranean climate in search of love, like Shirley Valentine, and then become addicted, as she was, to the freedom of anonymity. Without a history, life was so much easier.

If she had been given notice Iris might even have been tempted to put Bruno off when he wrote to say that he was coming to see her but, due to the erratic behaviour of the Italian postal service, Bruno turned up before the letter did. She came home from work late one evening to find him sitting on the step outside her door and was overwhelmed by joy at the surprise.

Iris had worked the busy months of the summer and the school was happy to let her take unpaid leave in a slow time. Since Bruno wasn't much interested at looking at frescoes in churches, or giving the Uffizi more than an hour's walkabout, they borrowed a Fiat Cinquecento from one of Iris's colleagues, and drove out of the city to explore Tuscany, stalling on every hill until Bruno got the hang of the gears.

'When did you learn to drive?' Iris asked him, as they puttered towards the hilltop town of Monteriggioni.

'Nikhil's dad bought him a car as a reward for his A levels,' Bruno told her. 'He gave me a couple of lessons.'

'You passed your test on just two lessons?' Iris was not surprised. Bruno had always been practical and well co-ordinated.

'Nearly . . .'

'You didn't pass your test?' Iris asked.

'I didn't not pass. I just didn't take it yet . . .'

There were two alternatives, Iris thought. One was to say, stop the car immediately, but that seemed a very English reaction, and she seemed to think it was quite a long way since they'd passed anywhere that looked as if it might have a phone.

'I don't even know if you need a licence to drive in Italy,' she said, smiling sideways at Bruno, as the tiny car ground its way up towards the walled fortress town. 'Why are we coming here, by the way?'

'I recognized the name from a bottle of wine,' said Bruno.

'As good a reason as any!' said Iris, relaxing back in her seat with her feet up on the dashboard.

The holiday was to be a gastronomic tour, a sensory exploration of taste and texture. Each day they found themselves in another little cobbled street with a slightly fruitier, or sharper-tasting beaker of wine, a dish of young citrusy olives, or fat ripe ones, their soft, almost rotting flesh oozing with oil. Bruno, who spoke no Italian at all, was as good at communicating as Iris, sometimes better, because the women who cooked pasta in the little trattorias loved to ruffle his hair and give him a squeeze. They offered him tastes of soup, crostini with smears of strongly flavoured pâtés on top, little nicks of salami and cheese. Bruno would discover which milk the cheese was made from by making animal noises. His imitation of a goat was so funny and accurate, he was made to repeat it again and again while an audience gathered, laughing, patting him on the back, making him one of their own.

Sometimes when they were driving along, he would veer off the road without warning, divining with some sixth sense that there would be a farmhouse down the track where Sangiovese grapes were being crushed, or olives being brought for their first pressing. Once, Bruno rang the great iron doorbell of a castle that looked deserted, only to find a family of aristocrats in residence. They too succumbed to Bruno's charm and invited him and Iris to dinner in a vast medieval hall, with tapestries on the walls that looked as if they had hung there for centuries.

Bruno was great company, but although he was more attuned to the physical than the cerebral, Iris could tell that his interest wasn't just about tasting and eating the food. He was all the time making mental notes on ingredients and flavours.

'What are *pomodori secchi*?' he asked one day in a shop where they were buying ingredients for a picnic lunch.

'Tomatoes dried in the sun, then preserved in olive oil,' she told him.

'Sun-dried tomatoes,' said Bruno, savouring the words.

They bought a jar and ate them, with country bread and a quivering mozzarella that came in a bag of whey, sitting on a stone wall and looking over a smoky autumn view that might have been the backdrop for a painting by Piero della Francesca.

'Do you think this would taste as delicious in England?' Bruno asked Iris. 'I don't think Kingshaven's ready for sun-dried tomatoes, do you?'

It was the only time he had mentioned his life in

England, and Iris found herself wanting to know what his plans were, but she kept herself from asking, knowing the unique irritation of a family member prying into your personal life. It seemed unlikely that this beautiful young man, who could charm peasants and aristocrats alike, even when he didn't speak the language, could be happy in an insular little place like Kingshaven. She thought there must be a woman involved.

When Iris asked him about his ambitions as a chef, Bruno could wax lyrical about pasta made from chestnut flour, or the freshness of lemons required to make the perfect sorbet, or the zabaglione cream inside the delicate choux buns sold in the pretty little patisserie that every village, however remote, seemed to support, but he didn't seem to have a specific plan to utilize all his culinary ideas.

'I want to make Loadsamoney!' he told her, gesticulating with his fist as if it had a wad of notes in it. 'Loadsamoney!' he repeated, explaining, when Iris didn't get it, that it was a catchphrase from some satirical comedy programme on television.

In Italy, Iris didn't really watch television. She got her news from the *Corriere della Sera* and occasionally bought the weekly *Guardian*. Although she had read about the relaxing of border controls between East Germany and Hungary, and the traffic jams of people leaving, it was with some surprise that one evening, sitting in a bar in Lucca, dunking hard almond biscuits into strong black coffee, she and Bruno both suddenly stopped talking as a news flash broke into the loud game show on the screen above the bar.

The caption said the images were live from Berlin. There were people hacking bits out of the Wall.

'Wow!' said Bruno. 'This is like watching history! In the future people will say, where were you when the Berlin Wall came down?'

He shifted his chair to see the television better.

Iris could remember when the Wall went up. Her father had showed her the photograph in the paper, and Sylvia had said, 'She's far too young to understand politics!'

But Iris *had* understood, because it had been much like a child's solution to a problem. If you didn't like your neighbour then you built a big wall. It had made perfect sense.

Bruno had been about the same age as she was then when Mrs Thatcher came to power, Iris thought. To Bruno's generation liberation meant the ability to make 'loadsamoney', but she wondered whether all the people dancing and celebrating their freedom on the television would ultimately find that their lives were any better.

'At least they can make their own choices now,' said Bruno.

Iris didn't bother to push the argument. Cynicism had no place in this *Zeitgeist*. The Italian commentator was getting increasingly excited, like the football commentary Iris sometimes heard filtering out of bars on her way home from work, when two of the big teams such as Inter and Juventus were playing each other. She felt about as distant from the politics as she did from the football.

When they returned to the Oltrarno, having delivered the Cinquecento back to its owner with only a scratch or two, Iris's landlady, who lived on the ground floor, handed her a clutch of letters, and stood firmly in the doorway, with her arms folded, as if she wasn't going to let Bruno pass without good reason.

'My brother Bruno from England,' Iris explained.

His Italian looks and name appeared to make the landlady even more suspicious.

'She thinks you're my toy boy,' Iris giggled as they climbed the five flights of stairs to her one-bedroom flat.

Iris looked through the envelopes. The only one addressed to her was Bruno's brief note announcing his arrival. The rest of the letters, written in a girlish looping hand, were addressed to Bruno.

The flat was so small, that however much Iris tried to busy herself with unpacking, and watering the plants on the window ledge, she couldn't altogether avoid noticing

Bruno's reaction as he read. The smile showed he was clearly fond of the woman, the frown that he was alarmed. Five letters in fourteen days did seem a little excessive, especially since the Italian postal service could well have mislaid several more.

'Someone likes you,' Iris said, wanting to give him the opportunity to talk about it, but promising herself she wouldn't press further if he didn't take it up.

'Yeah,' said Bruno, sighing. 'Your landlady wasn't too far off about me being a toy boy. I'm having an affair with Julia King.'

'Julia King?'

'You wouldn't believe how different she is . . .' he said, seeing Iris's mystified expression.

Iris's image of Julia was a fat little posh girl, as thick as a plank, but always eager to please.

'She saved your life once,' she said, searching for a positive memory.

'Yes, she told me that.' Bruno smiled. 'She's lovely . . . and, well, it's kind of fun . . . and her husband treats her like shit . . .' he added, as if to appeal to Iris's feminist instincts.

'And you thought you'd save her?' Iris guessed.

'Something like that,' said Bruno with a sheepish smile. 'But now it's got a bit full on . . . and, well . . . look!'

He handed the letters to her. Even a cursory glance gave Iris the impression more of obsession than love, although sometimes she thought that love was just another name for obsession, the way it made you mad, the way it made you let yourself down. Iris stared at the border of hearts and crosses Julia had drawn all round the paper, feeling a little sorry for her.

'It's kind of hard to tell what it would be like in the real world because we're always sneaking around,' said Bruno.

'Doesn't she have kids?' Iris asked shortly.

'Yes. Two boys.'

'She's got a lot invested in Kingshaven, then.'

'Yes . . .'

'You could always have the flat in Soho, you know,' Iris said to Bruno, guessing he might need an escape route. 'Vic's never there, and there's my old room . . .'

'I can't just run away.'

There was such sweetness in Bruno, she thought, underneath all his macho swagger.

'I used to think that running away was a bad thing,' Iris told him. 'Everyone's always going on about how you should face up to your problems, but I've found it's just as good to leave them behind.'

Fiammetta moved in with Clem the first day. It was obvious. She had to give up her room in hall anyway. The third-year students were expected to find their own accommodation. Sometimes Fiammetta wondered whether she had in some peculiar way known what was going to happen, because she had never got around to looking for anywhere, never put her name on any of the notes that went up on the JCR notice board about possible flat shares. Nor had she given any thought to what she would do in the summer, knowing only that she couldn't bear the thought of another vacation waitressing in Cobblestones, with Nikhil Patel occasionally walking casually past and waving at her hopefully. When she called her father to say that she was staying on in Etherington, he seemed surprised, but did not question her, which was a relief because he had been so illogically judgemental about Bruno's life, Fiammetta did not want to offer up details of her own for him to criticize.

Clem allowed her to clear up a little, but after a while she didn't mind the mess. The tidy, precise person she had been disappeared with her virginity.

As the weather turned and the new term approached, Fiammetta began to worry that the idyllic bubble of love would pop as they went back to being professor and student, but the time they spent together only seemed more precious now there were hours spent apart.

The best room for her to paint in was the bedroom at the front, although, with the days drawing in, the only natural light was in the morning. One day she got up early to sketch her lover sleeping, feeling almost as if she was taking advantage of him, but pleased enough with the drawing to let him see it.

'Do I sleep with my mouth open?' he'd asked, horrified.

'Yes! Can I paint you awake?' she asked.

'Perhaps you'd better.'

'Now?'

She wanted to capture that moment of surprise in his eyes when he woke up and found her there, but it was such a fleeting unconscious look it wouldn't be transferred to canvas. The man in the painting had all Clem's features, the untidy fair hair, with natural streaks of white blond, the blue eyes, the ironic twist of smile, but it wasn't him somehow.

'Is that how I look?' Clem asked.

'Not really!' Fiammetta told him, laughing, but it disturbed her that she couldn't paint him as she saw him. Maybe there had to be some separation between an artist and her subject, she thought. Maybe she could no longer see what Clem looked like because it felt like he was part of her now.

It was an exciting time to be alive. The winds of change were blowing through Eastern Europe. At home, the Iron Lady's grip on power and sanity seemed to be slipping as the big beasts abandoned her and she appointed unknown yes-men in their stead. The turn of the decade offered hope to people who had felt uneasy with the greed and consumerism of the eighties.

Historic injustices were unravelling. Clem was keen to capture the turning of the tide on film, driving all the way down to London one night to stand outside the appeal court in order to capture the moment when the Guildford Four were released; predicting as the regime in Hungary fell that East Germany would be next, and making an impulsive decision to take a train to Berlin.

They were there when the Wall was breached.

It felt like being part of the greatest demo ever, but

Clem took very few photographs because it just felt wrong to spy on people who had been oppressed by other people spying on them. The atmosphere was so extraordinary, it had to be experienced. And it was intensely intimate to experience it together, in the midst of wildly celebrating thousands.

'Marry me?' Clem said, picking Fiammetta up in his arms as if the moment demanded some grand gesture.

'Yes!' Fiammetta shouted without hesitation.

Sometimes Julia missed Bruno so much she used the master key to open his room at the top of the tower and lie on his bed, eyes closed, as if wanting him enough might make him materialize again. When, after the first week, she realized from the crispness and the smell of starch that the chambermaid had changed his sheets, she howled with anguish and pounded her fists against the mattress.

Bruno's only communication was a postcard with just eight words scrawled on the back.

'Having a great holiday. See you soon! Bruno.'

Aware that the Kings opened their post at breakfast, it would have been indiscreet of him to say any more – and yet just eight words! Julia read them again and again, searching for hidden meaning, taking comfort from 'see you soon', interpreting his choice of picture – the leaning tower of Pisa – as a subtle sexy message that he was missing her. Bruno's ever-readiness for sex was such a relief after the endless ministrations that had been required to get her husband's member erect. Not that Millicent Balls seemed to have a problem about that, Julia thought, allowing herself to imagine Millicent's lipsticked mouth around something other than a cigarette, then feeling nauseous.

Bruno's absence made it harder to dispel the resentment Julia felt about Christopher's affair. With little to occupy her mind, she seemed unable to stop running over the history of her marriage. Even when she tried to distract herself by working out hard in the gym, jealous thoughts would float to the forefront of her brain. Sometimes she doubted whether Christopher had ever stopped bonking Millicent, even at the beginning.

As a naïve teenager, who had believed that Christopher was the One, Julia had been too eager to put his mumbling equivocations about love down to superior intelligence. When she had eventually plucked up the courage to ask him directly, 'Do you love me?' he had winced as if it was such an unsophisticated question, it didn't deserve a response, and Julia had never pushed for a proper answer, fearing that he'd decide she was far too stupid to be his wife.

In those days she'd assumed his convoluted way of saying things meant that he was deep; now she recognized it as cowardice. She had taken his gentleness as kindness; now she saw that it was weakness. Had she witnessed one of his red-faced fits of pique, she probably wouldn't have married him at all, because her husband looked so much like Daddy had done when he used to shout at Mummy. When Bruno asked why she didn't stick up for herself, he didn't understand that it wasn't because she wasn't brave enough, it was more that confrontation reduced her to the little girl she had been then, powerless to do anything except cry. And as soon as she started crying, it made her situation even worse, because the Kings had no time for people who cried.

Julia grabbed the pillow on Bruno's bed and held it tight against her, imagining him here, stroking her hair, telling her she was beautiful, making everything all right.

'Julia? Julia! Where is she?'

Julia was suddenly aware of her name being called from the bottom of the steps. She held her breath, just like she used to as a child when they played Murder in the Dark at Christmas, until she eventually heard Libby's footsteps retreating.

'Oh, there you are!' said Eddie King, when Julia bumped into him later on her way out to pick the children up from their new prep school. 'We were looking for you everywhere.'

Julia visualized the page in the desk diary where she wrote her appointments down. She was sure there was nothing, nothing all week until the boys' Nativity Play.

'There's been an accident,' Eddie informed her.

For a moment, Julia's heart stopped beating. Had the school rung while she was lying on Bruno's bed?

'We thought you might take him to the hospital . . . bloody ambulance strike!' said Eddie.

'Is it Bertie?' Julia interrupted.

'It's not Bertie.'

'Archie?' Julia almost screamed.

'No, no!' Eddie laughed. 'Christopher's Rotovator hit a stone, bloody thing turned over, threw him off, then fell on top of him.'

'Thank God!' said Julia.

'He's broken his arm, quite badly,' said Eddie. 'Apparently they're keeping him in overnight.'

'Oh dear,' said Julia, belatedly ashamed of her reaction.

'Sid Farthing drove him to Lowhampton General. With you gone AWOL, we didn't think we could leave the place solely to Liliana.'

Granny Liliana, though still remarkably good for her age, was getting a little forgetful. Only the previous week, after ringing the kitchen for a bacon sandwich, she had got it into her head she would prepare one for herself, abandoning the attempt when she was unable to find where the bacon was kept. It was only when the fire alarm had gone off that Julia had found a frying pan red hot and smoking on the hob, although Granny Liliana categorically denied lighting the gas underneath it.

'Why don't I pick the boys up from school and drive them over to see Christopher?' Julia volunteered, feeling she ought to do something to make up for her perceived failure.

'Attagirl!' said Eddie, slapping her bottom to indicate his approval.

As she drove along the coast road towards Havenbourne, Julia wondered if life would be easier if she could bring herself to act the devoted wife a little more often, but she didn't see why she should always pretend when Christopher wasn't prepared to. She was sick of his ignoring her at family meals, sick of not ever being given credit for saving the Palace from a slow death, sick of his snide remarks about her being sick, which had started to happen again without Bruno around to cheer her up.

She just about managed to keep up a pretence in front of the children, although she had been doubly sad recently when, after locking herself in the bathroom to have a discreet cry, a tissue had been pushed under the door together with a note written in Bertie's childish hand that read, 'DO NT BE SAD MUMMY. I LUV YOO.'

When they were born Julia would have bet her life against ever sending her children away to boarding school, now it crossed her mind that it might be easier for them. Her own schooldays had been happy compared to holidays. But, she reminded herself, that was because she and James were always traipsing between Mummy and Daddy, straining to put on a happy face so that neither parent thought they preferred one to the other. At least her boys didn't have that to contend with, and never would have, because she would never leave them, Julia vowed, as she swung the Volvo into the school drive.

'Daddy's had to go to hospital because he's hurt his arm,' she told them once they were safely belted into the back seats. 'So we're going to visit him.'

'Will there be lots of blood?' Archie wanted to know.

'Will he have an operation?' asked Bertie.

'Is he going to die?' asked Archie brightly.

'No! He's not,' said Julia.

'Some people do die in hospital, don't they, Mummy?' said Archie.

Where had he picked that up from? Perhaps she ought to be stricter about what she let them watch on television.

'Daddy's perfectly well, but he's just got a bit of a sore arm,' she explained.

'So why do we have to go and see him?' Bertie wanted to know.

He was a perceptive little boy, Julia thought.

'Because, well, because it's what people do,' she said.

At Accident and Emergency, Julia was told that Christopher had been taken up to Men's Surgical and was directed down a long, glass-sided corridor, past the florists, the canteen and the sweetshop where the boys chose Smarties as the sweeties that Daddy would like most.

When they finally arrived at the ward and asked for Mr King, the nurse bent down to the children's level and said, 'What a lot of visitors for Mr King. Isn't he a lucky man?'

Which Julia thought was very sweet of her, even though the boys didn't seem to need a great deal of reassuring.

Christopher was sitting up in bed with his arm in a sling. When he looked up and saw them come in, his face was aghast. There was already another visitor sitting beside the bed.

'At least it wasn't your leg,' she was saying in her loud town-person accent. 'That would have taken a lot more getting over!'

For a moment Christopher and Julia stared at each other, then Julia put one hand on each of the boys' shoulders, swivelled them round, and said, 'I think we ought to go and eat tea in that nice cafeteria we passed, don't you?'

'But I want to say hello to Daddy and the lady,' protested Archie.

'If we don't go now, it might close, and then you'd be hungry,' Julia told him, practically dragging him along the corridor and down in the big lift, hoping that once the boys had the distraction of food, they wouldn't notice that the canteen showed no sign of imminent closure.

The boys had plates of sausages and chips. Julia chose a big bowl of lasagne and an enormous slice of Black Forest gateau, then put both back, knowing that the slightest mouthful would make her throw up. As the boys ate, she stared through the glass side of the canteen at the hospital world passing by: doctors in white coats – why bother wearing them, Julia wondered, if they never buttoned them up? – nurses with lumpy legs in black tights under their pale-blue uniforms; a man on crutches with an unlit cigarette in his mouth and a lighter in his hand, hopping along as fast as he could to the hospital entrance to have a smoke; harassed-looking visitors hurrying to be with loved ones after working all day; a child with a bald head pedalling hard on a tricycle, pulling an IV trolley along behind it, and a mother shouting, 'Not too fast, Kylie!'

One of the little girl's arms was attached by a long plastic tube to the IV, the other had a bracelet of rose quartz beads around it.

'Kylie!' shouted Archie, sliding off his chair and running after her.

'Stay there!' Julia warned Bertie.

'She knows not to go out the door,' said Kylie's mother, as Julia watched Archie running along next to the little girl as she pedalled down the long corridor. The woman had aged considerably more than the three or four months since Julia had seen her in the Crystal Circle.

'It's nice for her to see someone she knows,' the young mother added.

Julia didn't have the heart to run after Archie and drag him back.

'How long has she been in?' she asked.

'Eleven weeks now,' said her mother. 'Her friends came to see her at the beginning, but they soon forget at that age, and I think some of the parents don't want them getting too close . . . in case . . .'

Julia remembered what Archie had said in the car.

'Some people do die in hospital, don't they, Mummy?'

'What is it?' Julia asked.

'Leukaemia,' said the mother.

'How awful!'

'She seems full of life at the moment,' said the mother, her eyes bright with tears she didn't want to shed for fear of embarrassing herself in front of a stranger.

'I'm so sorry you're having to go through this,' Julia told her. 'I'm Julia, by the way.'

'I'm Sharon,' said the woman. 'Who have you come to see, then?'

'My husband . . . oh, don't worry, there's nothing wrong with him really,' Julia said, now even more annoyed with Christopher. It felt fraudulent to be visiting someone with just a broken arm.

'You won't have to come again, then, hopefully,' said Sharon.

'No,' said Julia. 'But I will bring Archie, if you think Kylie would like to see him? They seem to be getting on pretty well,' she said, as the children came hurtling back towards them.

'See how you're fixed, eh?' said Sharon, and Julia knew that she didn't believe that she would come back, which made her even more determined.

'It's quite a coincidence that Mrs Balls happened to be visiting someone else when I was brought in . . .' Christopher said as Julia bent to kiss his cheek for the children's benefit.

'I'm not a complete idiot, you know,' she hissed into his ear. 'How are you feeling?' she asked out loud.

'Actually I'm in a lot of pain,' Christopher sulked.

'For God's sake. It's only a broken arm!' Julia was so angry, the words were out before she could stop them.

Bertie and Archie looked mystified at her apparent indifference. Usually Mummy was the best person in the world for making you all better.

'Have you brought me some pyjamas?' Christopher asked.

'No, I forgot,' said Julia.

In fact there was a pair in her shoulder bag, but she decided she'd prefer him to suffer the indignity of a backless hospital gown a little longer.

'We've brought you some Smarties!' said Archie. 'But you have to share,' he warned severely, repeating what Julia always told him.

516

'Are you going to have an operation?' Bertie asked his father.

'I am, as a matter of fact,' said Christopher, shooting a glance at Julia. 'Apparently, it is quite a complicated break. They say I may have to be in for a few days.'

'Can we come again?' said Archie, as if the hospital was as exciting as the theme park they sometimes went to as a treat.

'We'll see,' said Julia, which was her standard response to such demands.

Fiammetta didn't know why she had been apprehensive when Bruno invited himself for Christmas because he and Clem hit it off straight away. They all went to the pub at the end of the road when he arrived, and Bruno told them about Italy, and they told him about Berlin, without revealing that they had decided to get married because Clem wanted to wait until his sister was there too.

When they got home, and Fiammetta showed Bruno up to the back room where he was going to be sleeping, she couldn't wait till they got to the top of the stairs before asking, 'Well? What do think?'

'He's a good bloke,' Bruno said unequivocally. 'And he seems very fond of you.'

'I've never been so happy!'

Bruno squashed her in a great big hug, and when he pulled away, she noticed that his eyes were sad.

'How is it going with Julia?' she asked him.

'Don't ask,' he said.

'Oh, I'm sorry . . .'

'We're having a bit of a break from each other. I'm not sure how long we can go on like this. I don't know what either of us really wants. I thought it would become clearer . . . but it hasn't . . . anyway . . . don't let me put a dampener on your domesticated bliss!'

'You couldn't!' said Fiammetta, pushing open the door to the back room, where she had made up the single bed, and stacked her paintings as neatly as possible, so that Bruno would have a bit of room.

'Is this your recent stuff?' Bruno said, flipping through the canvases, and stopping at the one of Clem.

Fiammetta nodded.

'When did you last see Dad?' he asked.

'I suppose it must have been Easter,' said Fiammetta.

'So did you paint this from memory?'

'It's not Dad, it's Clem!' said Fiammetta, exasperated. 'I knew it looked like someone . . .' she said, holding the painting out at arm's length to look at it again.

'It's very good,' said Bruno.

'Just not like Clem! Clem doesn't look like Dad, does he?' Fiammetta suddenly asked, hoping there wasn't some weird Freudian thing going on.

'I suppose he looks a bit like Dad did when he was young,' Bruno said. 'That Steve McQueen kind of look.'

'God, do you think Clem looks like Steve McQueen?' said Fiammetta.

'That's what Iris said,' said Bruno. 'I think she must have fancied him herself.'

'How is she doing?' Fiammetta asked.

'She's fine,' said Bruno, but Fiammetta wondered whether he would have known if she wasn't. Bruno always took people at face value.

On Christmas morning, Clem sat in the kitchen watching Bruno preparing lunch, asking questions and getting tips, and Fiammetta thought how amazingly uncompetitive Clem was compared to the other men she knew, how little he let his ego dictate the mood. She felt a little sentimental at the sight of the two men she loved most in the world joking and laughing together.

Bruno boned the turkey and rolled it up with a stuffing made from dried porcini mushrooms, which had been his Christmas present to Clem, breadcrumbs, rosemary and bacon. He used more bacon to wrap the joint, then tied it all up with string and put it in the oven to roast along with the potatoes. Then he set about making a rich stock from the bones and offal left over from the turkey, along with the liquor he had soaked the mushrooms in.

Clem opened a bottle of wine.

When Clem's sister Clare arrived, she was not at all as Fiammetta expected. A headteacher at a big comprehensive school in Manchester, Clare looked as if she devoted all her care to her job, and gave little thought to her appearance. She was quite plain and was wearing trousers and an unflattering blouse with a ruffle at the neck that made her look very middle-aged. Clare had the level stare of a headteacher, and standing on the doorstep, Fiammetta had a moment's anxiety that Clare would deem her undeserving of her precious younger brother, but once Clem had given her a hug and a glass of wine, his sister seemed to relax, and Fiammetta wondered whether she wasn't in fact just a bit shy herself.

As the four of them sat down to eat, pulling the crackers she had bought and grimacing at the awful jokes, Fiammetta realized that it was the first Christmas she had ever spent as a grown-up. The Christmases of her childhood when they'd lived at the Castle were swirling riots of colour in her memory, but when they'd moved down to the warehouse, the festive season had always been grey. Last year, it had been even worse because neither Bruno nor Iris had been there, so it was just her and Dad and Pascale, and Fiammetta had automatically reverted to a sulky teenage state. She'd promised herself afterwards that she'd never spend another Christmas there.

Everyone agreed that Bruno's turkey was the best Christmas dinner they had ever eaten, and Fiammetta swelled with pride as Clem, a purple paper crown at a wonky angle on his head, proposed a toast to the chef and Bruno stood up theatrically to take a bow.

Clem remained standing and beckoned Fiammetta, who was sitting opposite, to join him.

'Now we've got you both here,' he said, putting his arm round her, and giving her a little squeeze, 'I'd like you to drink a toast to us too, because we're getting married.'

Fiammetta glanced nervously over at Clare, and was relieved to see that she was smiling with genuine warmth.

'To you two!' Clare said, raising her glass.

'To you two! Congratulations!' said Bruno, shaking Clem's hand manfully, and planting a kiss on Fiammetta's cheek.

'Have you told Dad?' he asked.

'Of course not! Not before telling you. We were thinking of driving down for a couple of days. We'll give you a lift back if you want.'

'Great stuff!' said Bruno.

Clem poured the rest of the wine, clinking the bottle against the glasses. He had consumed most of it for courage, and Fiammetta thought it was touching that he'd been so nervous about making their announcement.

'Where does your father live?' Clare asked.

'Kingshaven. On the South Coast,' Clem replied for Fiammetta. 'Didn't we go there once?'

'Yes, we did,' said Clare.

'We went to a pop festival,' Clem explained to Bruno. 'You were already a teacher, weren't you, sis? And I was still at school, I think. When was it?'

'Nineteen sixty-nine,' said Clare.

'Of course! It was the day Neil Armstrong walked on the moon. I remember lying on the grass looking up at the moon and thinking how weird it was that this spacecraft was up there, circling.'

'Our mother died that day,' said Bruno.

'Oh, I'm sorry . . .' Clem said.

There was suddenly a slight awkwardness at the table. Why had Bruno said that, Fiammetta wondered, feeling irrationally cross with him.

'Our mother died that year too,' Clare said, as if to re-balance the atmosphere, but it only made it worse. Now nobody knew how to restart the conversation.

'I'm sorry,' said Bruno, looking at Fiammetta apologetically.

'Do you remember that bloke who cried?' Clem sud-

520

denly asked Clare. 'We were at the Festival and there was this bloke we bumped into,' he explained to Bruno and Fiammetta. 'He was a friend of Mum's, and when we told her she was dead, he sank to his knees and cried and cried, in front of everyone!'

'Michael Quinn,' said Clare quietly.

'Michael Quinn?' repeated Bruno loudly. 'That's our dad!'

Only Fiammetta seemed to notice the look of sheer terror pass across Clare's face.

'But your name's Dearchild,' Clare corrected, in head-mistress mode.

'That's our mother's name. They were never married,' Bruno explained.

'Your dad knew our mother?' asked Clem, the wine making him a little slow on the uptake. 'Well, what do you make of that?'

Fiammetta stared out of the front window at the street outside, one of a hundred similar streets of terraced houses with families inside, all celebrating Christmas together. She thought about coming into Etherington on the train that first day, and looking at all those rows of houses containing all those lives, and wondering how long it would take to find someone whose story connected with hers. And now she had, and she knew just from looking at Clare's face, although neither of the men were yet aware, that the story did not have a happy ending.

'What is it?' she asked Clare.

'I'm sorry.' Clare got up. 'I'm so sorry . . .'

'You're not going already?' Clem said.

He still hadn't got it, hadn't picked up on Clare's fear. His senses, normally so finely attuned, were blurred by the wine.

'What's up?' he asked, still affable, still innocent.

'There's dessert,' said Bruno. 'I've steeped some figs in Marsala. Unfortunately, mascarpone hasn't yet arrived in Etherington . . .'

'Oh shut up!' Fiammetta screamed at him.

'What is it? Please tell me what it is . . .' She tried to hold Clare's arm to stop her leaving the house.

'I can't tell you,' said Clare. 'I promised not to tell. You must ask him. Ask Michael Quinn!'

The Kings had always played charades after their Christmas lunch, but this year there was little enthusiasm for it. Granny Liliana was a stickler for the traditional form rather than the modern version on the popular television programme *Give Us a Clue*, and the great-grandchildren soon lost interest and asked permission to play with their new toys.

'I know!' said Bee, who was now heavily pregnant, to the remaining adults. 'Why don't we play Scruples!'

'What's Scruples then?' asked Eddie King.

'It's this great new board game where you have to say what you would do in compromising situations, like, say, if you found out that your best friend's husband was having an affair . . . you know, a bit like Humiliation . . . oh, come on, you must have played Humiliation . . . it's absolutely hilarious . . . I say something like, well, say, "I've never had sex hanging from a chandelier," and then I get points for anyone who has . . . doesn't have to be sex, obviously . . .' Her voice trailed away. 'It's only a bit of fun . . .'

'Would anyone like to see my film?' asked Winny, in the never-ending moment of disapproving silence.

'What a good idea!' said Libby.

'How lovely! A film show!' said Granny Liliana with uncharacteristic enthusiasm.

Bee and Julia exchanged bored glances across the room as Winny slotted a video into the machine.

'Is it on television, then?' asked Granny Ruby.

'It's not actually on television,' Eddie explained to her. 'It's just the way it's done nowadays.'

'Well, I never!' said the old woman.

Winny turned the lights out.

On the screen Bertie and Archie were standing looking rather embarrassed holding up a handwritten sign that said, 'WELCOME TO THE PALACE HOTEL!'

In the background, Winny's voice could be heard.

'Action!' There was a pause. 'Come on . . . say it!'

Bertie looked anxiously from side to side, mumbled, 'Welcome to the Palace!' Then ran off.

The camera tilted up to the ceiling.

'Bless him!' said Granny Ruby.

On the screen, Archie was walking down the steps to the swimming pool.

Even before he said his line, Julia knew what was going to happen, and gripped the arms of her chair as if she might even now be able to stop it.

'This is our garden!' said Archie, concentrating so hard on his words that he tripped and fell over. There was a moment of silence like an intake of breath, and then Archie opened his mouth very wide and screamed, 'Mummy . . . !'

The video cut again.

'Never work with children or animals,' Winny said to the assembled audience.

'Is he all right?' asked Granny Ruby.

'Of course he's all right. It was filmed in the summer!' Granny Liliana told her.

'But it looked like quite a nasty fall . . .'

'He knocked his front teeth out and grazed his knee quite badly, but it was fine once we'd cleaned it up and put a plaster on,' Julia assured her.

'For heaven's sake!' hissed Winny impatiently.

The video now zoomed in on a close-up of a massive courgette, pulling out to reveal Christopher's garden.

'This is where we grow all our vegetables . . .'

The camera panned slowly round 360 degrees to show the extent of the grounds.

'The Swiss Cottage is actually the Summer House,' said Winny's voiceover.

As the camera zoomed in to close-up, the door of the Summer House opened, and out of it walked the instantly recognizable figure of Millicent Balls, completely unaware she was being caught on camera, and smiling rather like the lady in the weather house Julia had owned as a child, who used to come out when it was going to be sunny.

The camera swung away quickly, pulling out to a long shot.

Julia stole a glance at the impassive faces of Libby and Liliana King. Had they seen what she just had? Christopher, who was sitting on the other side of the room, wriggled uncomfortably in his seat.

'The Rhododendron Mile . . .' continued Winny's commentary, '. . . is not in fact a mile but less than five hundred yards.'

There was an awkward cut to the King family standing on the steps of the hotel with the front door open behind them.

'I remember this bit,' said Eddie.

As the members of the family were introduced, they each stepped forward and waved, a bit like the characters used to at the beginning of *Camberwick Green*, Julia thought.

There was another awkward cut to the beach where Bee, dressed up as a giant onion, was chasing after Adrian, dressed in a rubber carrot suit.

'Vegetables seem to have become a bit of a theme, I'm not sure why,' Winny explained.

'This is the King family having fun!' said his voiceover.

'How much more of this is there?' Libby asked.

'About another ten minutes,' said Winny.

Libby sighed heavily.

'I'm enjoying it!' said Granny Ruby.

Suddenly Bruno was on the screen, waving a fish slice at the camera.

Julia held her breath. He looked so utterly gorgeous in his white jacket, his long hair pushed back from his face with a blue and white spotted bandana, like a pirate.

'Don't you have a scarf rather like that, Julia?' Granny Liliana asked.

'What?' Julia pretended not to have been paying attention.

'They sell them in the chandlery at the Harbour End.

Loads of people have them,' Bee jumped in loyally, but the fact that she was so obviously trying to cover made it worse.

'Can you at least do me the courtesy of watching, when I've gone to so much trouble?' Winny interrupted crossly.

'This is the Wave Club,' said the voiceover. 'A state-of-the-art gymnasium . . . in short, all you could ever want for a fun, relaxing holiday.'

The screen suddenly went blank.

Granny Ruby started clapping loudly.

'Very professional!' she said. 'I'd like to be in the next one, wouldn't you, Liliana?'

'I doubt you and I would fit in with the new image,' said Granny Liliana brusquely.

'Well?' Winny switched on the lights. 'What did you think?' he demanded.

'I don't think Martin Scorsese need have any sleepless nights,' said Adrian.

Bee laughed loudly.

'Who's Martin whatshisname?' asked Granny Ruby.

'Perhaps with a little more practice, Winny,' Libby began diplomatically.

'Oh, bloody hell! That's absolutely typical, isn't it? I go to a great deal of trouble and all any of you can do is laugh and sneer!' Winny stormed out of the room, leaving everyone feeling rather shell-shocked.

'Poor Winny,' said Julia finally.

Libby nodded sympathetically.

'We really must do something with the Summer House,' she said, changing the subject abruptly. 'It's such a waste to leave it empty.' She shot an icy glance at Christopher.

'Actually,' Julia said, snatching the opportunity, 'I've had an idea.'

She knew she was unlikely to find another window of opportunity like this, on the very day when they were under orders from the vicar to think of others less fortunate.

All of them turned to look at her. Christopher glared malevolently across the room.

525

'When we were visiting Christopher in hospital, we discovered that one of Archie's little friends was there being treated for leukaemia,' Julia began to explain.

The Kings adopted appropriately grim facial expressions.

'The thing is,' Julia pressed on, 'I got talking to the nurses in the children's wards, asking if there was anything we could do at Christmas.'

'Good for you!' said Eddie encouragingly.

'But the nurses said that they never really need anything at Christmas, because everyone sends in toys, the local radio does an appeal and they're awash with teddy bears, but in the summer it's a different matter. Nobody thinks about sick children when they're on the beach, do they? But the children can't have a holiday because they need nurses and specialist equipment . . . and it got me thinking that maybe that's something we could help with. I hadn't actually thought of the Summer House,' she added disingenuously, 'but since you said . . . ?' She looked at Libby.

'Ridiculous!' scoffed Christopher immediately. 'It would cost a fortune!'

'Not necessarily. I've spoken to the local radio station and they said that in principle they'd run an appeal – collect at their summer road shows,' Julia said.

'I'm sure the lifeboat crew would get involved. We're very good at fund-raising . . .' Adrian jumped in unexpectedly.

Julia smiled at him. Good old Adrian! Sometimes it was difficult to believe that he was the same family as the rest of them.

'Denise is a trained paediatric nurse and she's keen to help,' Julia went on.

'Presumably the costs of equipping the Summer House would be tax deductible?' Libby asked.

'We'd set up a charitable trust,' said Julia. 'There would in fact be quite a few tax benefits.'

'You've done your homework!' Christopher remarked sourly.

'Julia always did her homework,' Granny Ruby chipped in. 'It's a mystery to me why everyone's always thought she's thick.'

Now everyone looked to Granny Liliana for her reaction.

'Some charitable work would undoubtedly be good for the hotel's reputation,' she said, making Julia's heart turn a somersault of triumph.

Christopher stood up and walked out of the room.

For a moment, Julia felt sorry for him. Granny Liliana was the one who always made allowances for him, and now he must think that Julia had turned even her against him

Instinctively, she ran after him, catching up with him in the hall.

'Christopher! I didn't mean . . . !'

He spun round. 'Yes you did!' he spat with such anger that a spot of his spittle landed on Julia's face just under her eye.

She put her hand to her cheek, shocked.

'Just exactly who do you think you are?' he shouted. 'Suffer the little children! You're not exactly a saint, Julia, are you?'

'I don't know what you mean,' she said, eyes downcast.

'Oh yes you do!' he said, storming away, leaving her standing alone next to the enormous decorated Christmas tree.

So he knew then. He knew, but he'd never mentioned it, never challenged her. In fact, he thought so little of her that he didn't even care that she was sleeping with someone else. And now she'd made him hate her. His flushed, apoplectic face was just like Daddy's used to be. Weak men could be very cruel if publicly humiliated. Now that she'd effectively closed down his love nest, Christopher would demand revenge. Wishing that she could rewind the last ten minutes like one of Winny's videos and record something different over the top, Julia ran down to the kitchen and started stuffing her mouth with leftover

527

turkey, spooning in mouthfuls of bread sauce, sprouts, a mince pie, two forcemeat balls, a glug of custard. It was easy being sick. She didn't even have to force two fingers down her throat. Shivery and weak with self-loathing, Julia climbed the steps up to Bruno's room, and lay face down on the bed, sobbing.

When she eventually came down, she had no idea what the time was, but from the canned laughter coming from the Kings' private sitting room, she thought they must all be watching the repeat of *Fawlty Towers*.

Unable to face sitting with them, she went back to the flat.

There was a message flashing on the answerphone. For one excited second Julia thought that Bruno must have called to wish her Happy Christmas, but when she pressed playback, she was mystified to hear Christopher's voice. He sounded a little breathless, as if he'd run for the phone. He'd obviously picked up the receiver after the tape had clicked on.

'*Hello? Hello?*'

'*Darling!*'

'*Oh, darling. It's you!*'

'*Happy Christmas, darling!*'

'*Would that it were,*' said Christopher gloomily. '*I can't bear it without you . . .*'

'*Me too. I need you all the time.*'

'*Do you?*' Christopher's voice was getting husky. '*I want to feel my way along you.*'

'*You're awfully good at feeling your way along . . .*'

'*All over you, and up and down you and in and out . . .*'

'*Oh!*'

'*Particularly in and out . . .*'

'*Oh! That's just what I need!*'

'*The trouble is, I need you several times a week, all the time.*'

'*Mmm. So do I. I need you all the week. All the time.*'

'*Oh God! I'd like to live inside you. Like a tampon . . . !*'

Julia had to stop herself throwing up all over again. Her

finger hovered over the rewind button to erase the tape. But then, in a moment of sheer wickedness, she pressed eject instead.

They had to wait until Boxing Day before making the journey to Kingshaven, because Clem had drunk too much to drive. He drank a lot more when Fiammetta went upstairs and locked herself in their bedroom. Bruno decided it would be tactful to go out for a walk and spent so long wandering round the unfamiliar city that when he returned Clem had fallen asleep on the huge sofa in the living room. Catching a glimpse of himself in the hall mirror, Bruno saw that he was still wearing a yellow paper crown on his head. He knocked several times on Fiammetta's bedroom door, knowing she was in there, awake, but she wouldn't open the door.

It was only when Bruno went into the back room where he was supposed to be sleeping and saw the picture his sister had painted of her lover, that he realized what both the women already seemed to know.

On the drive down to Kingshaven, the interior of the car felt as if it would explode with the tension. Clem was hungover, simmering with indignation at Fiammetta's silence. It was as if she had just closed down. Sitting in the back seat, Bruno felt like a naughty child, who'd rather be anywhere else while his parents were having a row.

When they finally arrived, it was dark. There was nowhere to park on the narrow streets of the Harbour End, so they left the car just up the road on the way to the Castle. Bruno ran towards the warehouse, wanting at least to warn his father of their arrival.

It was only when Michael opened the door that Bruno remembered that they weren't supposed to be speaking to each other.

'Well! Merry Christmas!' said Michael. He looked delighted to see him.

'Dad . . . we're all here,' Bruno managed to say, before Fiammetta and Clem rushed up.

He watched his father's face mutate from surprise to disbelief, as he looked from one face to the other.

And then Fiammetta finally broke her silence with a terrible scream.

'Oh my GOD! You *KNEW*!'

For the first time in his life, Bruno felt separate from his sister. This was about Dad and her and Clem and there was nothing he could do to help her. Holding his hands up, he began to back away, leaving the three of them standing staring at each other. Then he started running along the promenade.

The entrance hall of the Palace was surprisingly dark when Bee King opened the door.

'Chef!' she said. 'We're playing Murder in the Dark. A very good place to hide might be the Windsor Suite,' she added, with a wink.

Bruno took the stairs two by two and knocked softly on the door of the Windsor Suite.

He tried the handle. It opened.

The room was totally dark apart from the tiny red light of the clock radio next to the bed.

He sniffed the air, smelling the perfume Julia always wore that sent a signal straight from his nostrils to his groin.

'Julia?' he whispered. 'Julia? It's me.'

With his hands stretched out in front of him, he stumbled around, feeling each chair, patting the heavy curtains for her shape behind, stubbing his toe on the leg of the big bed. But she wasn't on it, nor under the heavy counterpane. As his eyes became more used to the dark, he heard a tiny muffled giggle. Kneeling down, he lifted the counterpane, stretched his hand as far as he could, jumping when she suddenly grabbed it and pulled him under the bed with her.

He found her mouth, tasted the sourness of bile, kissed her deeply, drowning all his muddled thoughts in the sensuousness of her body, the long sweep of muscle, the soft melting flesh.

The door of the room opened a crack. A triangle of light spread over the floor.

They both held their breath.

'Julia?' Adrian's voice asked.

'I've already looked there,' said Bee, behind him.

The door closed and they breathed again.

'Lock the door!' Bruno instructed.

'What if someone comes?' Julia asked.

'They'll have to break it down, won't they?'

She wriggled out from under the bed, and tiptoed across the room.

Bruno waited until the key had turned, then rolled out and switched on the bedside light.

Julia was wearing one of those big bright shapeless jumpers with a silly pattern on, but underneath just a black silk camisole. He kissed each of her beautiful shoulders, let the thin straps fall down, kissed her breasts, reverently, just as he had done the first time. Then he pulled back the heavy cover on the bed. They lay side by side for a moment, wallowing in the coolness of the sheets, and then they made love more tenderly than they had ever done before, slowly erasing every sad moment of separation.

Afterwards, his fingers sought hers, knotted them tightly in his.

'I can't go on like this, Julia,' he said.

'What do you mean?' she asked.

'I can't be your toy boy for ever . . .'

She laughed a little nervously. 'No,' she said. 'Apparently, you're past your prime. Yours was at eighteen. I haven't reached mine yet!'

It was the sort of women's-magazine information Bee was always coming up with. Had they been talking about younger men generally, Bruno wondered, or about him in particular?

'Julia. I'm not kidding,' he said, sitting up. 'I want more . . .'

'More than me?'

'I want you, and I want other things,' he quickly re-phrased it.

'You can't leave me again! I hate it when you're not here!'

'Come with me, then.'

As soon as he had said it, he wondered if he meant it. The silence seemed never ending.

'I can't,' she said eventually. 'I couldn't do that to the boys, couldn't let them suffer like I did . . .'

'Isn't it just as bad for them to live a lie?' Bruno asked, trying not to think about the terrible scene he had just run away from at the other end of town.

'It's better than being without a mother.'

'But you'd get custody,' he argued.

'Mummy didn't.'

'It's all changed since then . . . divorce is much easier . . . you'd probably get half the hotel too.'

Bruno wondered why he was saying all this. He couldn't make her any promises. He had nothing to offer her or her children. He told himself to stop.

'But what if you were wrong?' she demanded. 'You've no idea what it's like to grow up with only one of your parents . . .'

'I have, actually,' said Bruno.

'Oh God! I'm so sorry!' she said, mortified.

'It's OK,' Bruno told her, getting out of bed.

'Please don't go!' she pleaded with him. 'Look, even if you're right, and I got a divorce, there's no half of the hotel for me to get because it's not even worth as much as the mortgage.'

'Mortgage?'

'James said it was the best way to borrow money for the refurbishment, and it was all going so well, and then it just stopped. The only way of getting any money out of this place right now would be to burn it down and collect the insurance!'

'So you lied about opening a restaurant?'

'I didn't want you to go . . .' she faltered.

'Look,' said Bruno, getting dressed, 'I've decided what I want. Now you have to decide what you want.'

'But you promised not to leave me!' she said.

He was sure he never had. He bent down to do up the laces on his trainers.

'I saved your life!' she screamed at him.

She was clutching at straws now, trying to make him feel guilty, and he did. He wanted to help her, but if he stayed, he would just be perpetuating a fantasy.

'I can't save yours,' he told her.

'But that's not fair!'

'Please don't cry,' he said, relenting for a minute, sitting down on the bed.

She sniffed, tried to smile at him. 'Where will you go?' she asked.

'London.'

'Can we still see each other?'

'Sure,' he said.

'Do you think we'd still like each other in real life?' she asked timidly.

Chapter Seventeen

1992

'Why did you move to Rome?' Josie asked, ever the journalist looking for the story.

They were sitting at a pavement table outside a restaurant on the Via Veneto. It was the sort of place rich ladies with large sunglasses and small dogs took their lunch.

'Florence was beginning to feel a bit Disneyland.'

Iris wondered whether you stayed at the same emotional age as you were when you first met a person. She must have been twenty-one when Josie arrived in her life, and Josie thirty-five. Now that over twenty years had passed the age gap seemed almost negligible, but Iris's first impulse was still to try to impress her friend with a clever response.

The queues of American tourists in Florence had been annoying, but it was when Iris had realized that she couldn't walk down any street without bumping into someone she knew that she had begun to feel hemmed in by the medieval city walls rather than protected. She had come to Rome for a weekend, liked it, and decided it was time to move on. Rome felt more like a proper city, with pollution and police sirens, and sprawling suburbs where she was always a tram ride away from losing herself.

She found a job in a language school near Termini Station, taking a room in a cheap *pensione*, before realizing that it wasn't an area you wanted to be around in the evenings unless you were a transvestite prostitute. She had fallen lucky with a one-bedroom flat in the Trastevere area, taking it over from a couple who worked at the language school, who were moving on to Cairo. The bedroom was small, with only a sink to wash in, and a shared toilet two storeys down, but the flat had a roof terrace with a canopy of vine leaves, where she could sit in complete privacy, listening to the hum of the city.

'What brings you here?' Iris asked Josie.

'When you've worked for the paper as long as I have, you deserve the occasional little treat. I suggested European city breaks for the "High Life and Low Life" bit of the Travel section. I've already established where the nice shops are . . .'

'And you want me to fill you in on the flea markets?'

Josie smiled at her. She had aged, Iris thought. With her hair dyed almost black now, her skin looked too dry and white, and her lips were painted with a hard line of dark lipstick. Iris couldn't imagine, or remember, what it would feel like to kiss them.

'What do you miss?' Josie wanted to know.

'Eating in restaurants like this,' Iris replied, with an ironic smile.

In fact, eating in expensive restaurants with unctuous waiters was one of the things Iris missed least because she associated it with expense-account lunches, the small talk you were supposed to make before getting down to the business reason you were there. She'd never been very good at that.

'But you must miss your career?' Josie pressed.

For Josie, a career wasn't just the work, it was the prestige of being someone. For years, Iris had tried to be someone too, but she'd discovered that she was happier being no one. She was still curious about the books people brought with them on holiday, but she now thought Roman had probably been right to question her editorial judgement.

'There seems to be a new genre of commercial women's fiction, with pretty watercolour covers, about the marital dilemmas of middle-class women who live in the country,' she said.

'Aga sagas?' said Josie.

'I wouldn't have been any good at publishing those,' said Iris. 'I'm not even sure what an Aga is.'

Josie laughed. 'You must miss the twins?'

Iris nodded, but actually she'd been relieved not to be drawn into the row between her father and Fiammetta. It was such an intractable mess, and she knew that if she'd been in England she'd have felt responsible for sorting it out, and guilty when she couldn't. Now Fiammetta was cross with her for not condemning Michael more strongly, but Iris didn't see the point of adding her remonstrations when he was so clearly devastated by the misery he'd unintentionally wrought. Perhaps she was getting mellower in middle age?

'Is Michael still with that French girl?' Josie asked.

'No,' Iris replied carefully. 'She went back to France.'

Pascale had written to explain. A Frenchman had come into the shop one day and they had got talking. She hadn't realized how much she had missed speaking her native language. Iris wasn't convinced by the reason, but she sympathized. She knew how impossible Michael was to be with when he was miserable, how his gloom seemed to pervade everything. Pascale had probably been glad to speak to anyone in any language at all, she thought.

'I wonder what Michael thinks about Anthony,' said Josie.

'What about Anthony?' Iris asked.

The only communication she had with her brother these days was at Christmas when she sent him a suitably tasteful card of a Botticelli Nativity, and Marie sent a photograph of their ever-increasing family looking suitably relaxed and Christmassy standing in front of their fireplace. He now lived only a stone's throw away from Josie in trendy Tufnell Park.

'He's got himself a seat to fight at the next election,' said Josie.

'For which party?' Iris asked.

'Labour!'

'Labour?' repeated Iris.

'The Labour Party is changing,' Josie told her.

'It must be, if Anthony's a candidate.'

'He calls himself Tony now,' said Josie, which, for some reason, made them both roar with laughter.

'I can't believe that Anthony's the one who's ended up in politics,' said Iris.

'Politics is about managing the media these days,' Josie told her. 'It's not about ideals.'

'One thing I did miss was being there to see Thatcher stabbed in the back by her own henchmen,' admitted Iris.

'There was a bit in the Travel section about your mother the other day,' Josie said, as if the thought of Mrs Thatcher had somehow brought Sylvia to mind. 'Something about romantic places to spend St Valentine's Day.'

'Sylvia has everything she ever wanted,' said Iris. 'An adoring husband, a title, a lovely house and rich people paying money to associate with her.'

'Sometimes I think that Sylvia was the best feminist of us all,' Josie remarked. 'Rising like a phoenix from the ashes of a repressive marriage, and getting everything she wanted on her own terms.'

'But she'd hate you for calling her that,' said Iris with a wry smile.

The waiter deposited a plate of antipasti in front of them, each morsel costing as much as Iris's usual lunch.

'Don't you miss your friends?' Josie asked.

'I do miss Vic,' Iris said.

The only time she'd felt at all like going back to London was when Vic's lover had died the previous year. She should have been there to support him. But the first she'd known of it was when she'd seen an out-of-date newspaper in the staff common room with his picture in. Before Robbie died, he'd admitted to having AIDS. In the photo he was a skeletal shadow, barely recognizable as the vital physical presence she remembered at the Live Aid concert.

When Iris had eventually managed to speak to Vic on the telephone, the funeral was already over. Vic seemed sad, but calm.

'We've had quite a long time to get used to it,' he said. 'It's his parents who were devastated. Finding out he was gay and about to die on the same day . . .'

'But are you all right?' Iris pressed, asking more about his physical than his mental state of health. 'I'll come back if you need me.'

'I'm OK,' Vic told her. 'Maybe I'll get round to coming to see you now, when I've got things sorted here.'

She must call him again soon, Iris thought, then looked up, saw the expectant look on Josie's face.

'And of course I miss you,' she said.

Josie was one of the few people in her life who had really loved her, Iris thought.

'So what do you *do* all day?' Josie asked briskly, as if to cover up any perceived soppiness.

'In the mornings, I teach. I usually have lunch. If it's a fine day, I sometimes go for a walk in the Villa Borghese or read a book up on the Palatine. See a film. There's an English Language cinema right near where I live where they show a lot of old films . . .'

'Are you with anyone?' Josie wanted to know.

'I enjoy the occasional zipless fuck,' Iris told her, rather pleased to see Josie glancing round anxiously to see if she had offended any of the lunching ladies and their pooches.

'Erica Jong was absolutely right,' Iris continued. 'It is the best . . . brief, free from power games, curiously pure . . .'

'And I thought it was supposed to be a fantasy,' said Josie.

'Not in Rome,' said Iris. 'You have sex, and then he goes home to Mamma!'

The temptation to impress had once again made Iris slightly economical with the truth. There was a student, Fabio, who'd come back to her flat a couple of times after end-of-week drinking sessions at the local bar. He was beautiful, and said lovely things he didn't mean, and they had great sex, but Iris had made it sound like she was bonking every second man who zipped past on a Vespa.

The Friday evening pitch was sought after by everyone, and Fiammetta had arrived too late. A caricaturist called Malcolm was already there with a small queue. Fiammetta preferred Friday evenings because the people milling around the Covent Garden piazza were mainly adults with something to celebrate – couples on a first date, tourists on their last night in London – and adults were easier to draw than children. Children's faces were flatter, rounder, more amorphous, and sometimes she found herself searching their parents' faces to find the distinctive feature – an unusually broad forehead, a thin, long nose – that would give her the likeness. She could tell that the parents were never quite as pleased as they expected to be with her sketches. Sometimes she wanted to say that it was probably how their children would look in a few years' time. Often, she didn't charge. She'd learned to work quickly, and to finish a drawing with lightning speed as policemen approached to move her on, but the most difficult bit of being a street artist was having to ask for money. Bruno got so cross with her about it that on his day off he stood next to her, collecting the cash.

With a mixture of irritation and relief, Fiammetta propped her folding easel against the railing and pulled off her beret (another of Bruno's marketing ideas), which itched. There was a soprano singing the drinking song from *La Traviata* in the well of the old market, where the wine bar was. Her voice was so strong, the orchestral accompaniment pounding from her ghetto blaster so familiar that a crowd of people had gathered. Pressed against the railing, Fiammetta felt a little tap on her shoulder. Two young women she did not know looked embarrassed when she turned round.

'Oh, I'm sorry . . . we thought you were someone . . .'

'No,' Fiammetta told them. 'No. I'm not. Sorry.' She quickly pulled her beret back on.

After Clem, Fiammetta had shaved all her hair off. Her hair had defined her. With it gone, she felt cleansed of genetics and gender. She took a photo of herself before and after, with her head like a wig stand. Being a bald woman took away your identity. People looked the other way. A bald woman was either a victim of chemotherapy, or a freak, both to be quietly passed by. But in the last few months since Sinead O'Connor had appeared on the pop scene, people had started humming 'Nothing Compares 2U' as Fiammetta walked past, and she constantly found herself apologizing for not being someone, when not being anyone was what she craved.

Perhaps it was time to let her hair grow back, Fiammetta thought. It wouldn't mean that she was over it. She'd never get over it.

Nobody, not even Iris, seemed to understand that it wasn't shame or guilt she felt, but grief. She'd had to give up the man she loved.

Had she though? Sometimes she wondered why she couldn't just have left it, let them carry on in ignorance. Recently, Fiammetta had read an article in a newspaper about the attraction between blood relatives who have been separated most of their lives. It wasn't so unusual. It even had a name. Genetic Sexual Attraction. Those who experienced the phenomenon described it as awesomely powerful, intensely moving, like perfect romantic love. One of the explanations put forward was missed bonding between a mother and infant. It was natural, then, only wrong if you knew about it. But because she always had to demand the truth, she had made it impossible, ruined her own life and his.

'You KNEW!' she had screamed at her father.

'No!' he had protested. 'I didn't. Not like you think!'

And Clem had just stood there, saying, 'What are you talking about? I know who my father was. You've got it all wrong . . .'

Fiammetta could still see his face, his limpid blue eyes, but she realized with a shock that she could no longer remember what his voice sounded like.

The final note of the soprano's aria filled the air with its purity, and all around Fiammetta, people were applauding and cheering. She felt a smile spreading across her face, which sometimes happened these days.

Jolly Allsop had never fully recovered after his stroke in the late seventies, and for several years he engaged in nothing more strenuous than a short walk in the Castle grounds. When he failed one spring morning to emerge from his bedroom to have lunch with a party of Japanese, Sylvia feared something was amiss. Dr Ferry, the GP, immediately summoned an ambulance and Jolly was admitted to Lowhampton General Hospital with suspected pneumonia. Although he appeared to be making a good recovery, he suffered a heart attack and died the day before he was due to be discharged.

Grief took people in different ways, Julia observed, in the days before the funeral. Sylvia seemed to direct all her sadness into hunting for the right black outfit; James arrived from London steaming with anger. As the new incumbent at the Castle, he issued orders for the staff to pack his hated stepmother's things, and when they'd done that, he sacked most of them.

Julia herself felt numb, almost unable to believe that the old man she had seen sitting up in bed so recently no longer existed. When she'd popped in to see him on her weekly visit to the children's ward, her father's face had lit up, just as it always did when she brought her boys to see him at the Castle and they played cricket together, with Bertie bowling, Daddy batting from his wicker chair and Archie running for him. It had always been acknowledged that Julia's birth had been a disappointment to him, being a girl when he had desperately wanted an heir, but in recent years, Julia knew she had become his favourite child, the only one who didn't answer him back, the closest to him.

It was only when she entered St Mary's church for the funeral, saw the stark reality of the coffin on the catafalque, and realized that she was the one who would be sitting nearest to it in the pew – the closest to him – that Julia suddenly started shaking. As she walked down the aisle – the same aisle that her father had walked her down on her wedding day (although in truth, he had still been so frail from his stroke that Julia had been the one supporting him), the same aisle from which he had watched Bertie and Archie being christened – her sobbing became louder and more hysterical. She was aware of a terrible gasping, wailing noise coming from her, and there was nothing she could do to stop it.

She sensed Christopher's hand hovering beside her arm, uncertain what to do.

'Don't you dare touch me!' She suddenly rounded on him, unable to bear the hypocrisy or the pretence any longer.

Daddy had been so pleased when she married a King, and he would have been so angry if he'd known how Christopher had treated her. He hadn't known, had he?

Julia had told her husband not to come to Daddy's funeral, but then Libby had pointed out that it would only be distraction from the proper respect and dignified departure that Jolly deserved. Now she'd ruined that too, Julia thought miserably, as she sobbed her way through all the hymns and readings, until her father's coffin was lifted on to the shoulders of the pall-bearers, with James taking one corner, and she stared as it moved away from her, crying, 'Daddy!'

As if she would bring him back.

Julia's two older sisters and their husbands followed behind the coffin. Suddenly Julia realized that she was meant to be next, but she simply couldn't bear to walk out beside Christopher in a ghastly parody of their wedding march.

Sylvia was standing in the opposite pew on her own, waiting as James had told her to. The children always follow the coffin, he'd insisted, inventing another aristocratic protocol to humiliate her.

Julia's heart went out to her stepmother. Black was no

longer a good colour for her. It made her look drawn and old, pathetic really, as if all her youth had gone with Daddy no longer there in comparison. Sylvia was the only person, Julia suddenly thought, who had actually made Jolly jolly. He'd enjoyed playing lord of the manor with the awed foreigners who stayed at the Castle, enjoyed having soft carpets to pad about on and a lift installed when he began to find the stairs difficult. The Castle might not be exactly how it was meant to be when it was built, but it was a good deal warmer and more comfortable. And if that had meant selling off a few dark old paintings, so what? It had been a home, which it had never been before Sylvia's arrival, and Daddy had been happy there, and he wouldn't be happy at all now if he knew that his beloved wife was standing alone, ridiculed and excluded by his family.

Impulsively, Julia extended her hand across the aisle. Sylvia's eyes opened wide, suspecting a trick, but Julia nodded at her reassuringly, then stepped towards her and took her hand, and they walked out of the church together.

It helped to hold someone's hand, someone who had loved Daddy, as his coffin was lowered into the Allsop grave. Once James had shovelled a symbolic spadeful of earth in, Julia felt a kind of release, as if she wouldn't cry any more.

'Where will you go?' Julia asked Sylvia, as the people around the graveside began to disperse.

'Don't you worry about me,' Sylvia told her, giving her arm a little squeeze before releasing it. 'You've got enough to worry about with that lot . . .'

Julia wasn't quite sure whether she was referring to the Allsops or the Kings, or both. They exchanged furtive little smiles, and then Sylvia opened her handbag, took out a compact, checked her mascara and reapplied a slick of lipstick.

'Onwards and upwards, as Jolly always used to say,' she said, squaring her shoulders, and walking determinedly out of the churchyard, as if she had another pressing appointment to attend.

Christopher and the rest of the Kings departed tactfully for the Palace, leaving Julia to get a lift with her older sister back up to the Castle.

They arrived to find eight bewildered Canadians standing by the reception desk, watching James kicking bin liners of Sylvia's clothes down the curved marble staircase. Then her brother picked up a cardboard box, and went round removing photographs of Sylvia from every mantelpiece, unable to rest until every last trace of her was gone.

He was so pink in the face that nobody dared get in his way, but when he'd finished, he came back into the hall with a big smile, clapped his hands together and said, 'Coffee, anyone?' as if it were a perfectly normal day.

The Canadians – two Second World War veterans, Julia established, with their wives, sons and sons' wives – looked decidedly uneasy. They were at pains to explain – as if it were their own fault that they had intruded on this private family gathering – that they must have already left British Columbia on the first leg of their vacation to the Normandy beaches when Julia had attempted to contact them. Anxious not to reignite James's wrath, they willingly agreed to Julia's suggestion that they spend the rest of their holiday at the Palace.

'The Palace! That's it!' one of the older men said. 'That's the name of the place we were in. I knew it was something royal . . .'

'So, we're going to be staying in the place we thought we were staying in all along!' said one of the wives, eager to demonstrate that it had all turned out for the best.

There would be no charge, Julia assured them, and of course there would be a full refund from the Castle. She glanced at James for confirmation. Her brother nodded, but she could see that he was tight-lipped with rage again.

'Just you remember,' James whispered to her, as she ushered the Canadians out of the door, offering to show them the way if there was room for her in one of their rented cars, 'whose side you're on.'

Did he mean the Allsops' side against the Kings', or was he referring to the hand of sympathy she'd extended to Sylvia, Julia wondered, her heart sinking because she'd naïvely hoped that now Daddy was gone, there wouldn't have to be so many sides any more.

It was a spectacularly sunny morning and for the first time in as long as she could remember, Sylvia had absolutely nothing to do. It was ages since she'd walked along the promenade, breathing the fresh air coming off the sea. The sun was so unseasonally warm, Sylvia undid the large gold knot buttons on her black Chanel-style bouclé jacket, allowing the breeze to blow right through the fine black wool dress underneath. The sensation of cool sea air on her skin was so refreshing, Sylvia removed the jacket and, slipping her finger through the little chain at the collar, slung it over her shoulder. It probably wasn't properly respectful to have bare arms on the day of a funeral, but she was sure Jolly wouldn't mind, and the rest of them could go to hell.

Sylvia had never been much of a one for the beach, even when her children were little. Whenever they brought a picnic down, Sylvia had always insisted they eat it sitting up nicely on a park bench. Even the sandwiches were better behaved in the Victoria Gardens, whereas on the beach they couldn't wait to jump out of the greaseproof paper and hurl themselves, filling side up, into the sand. Iris and Anthony had soon stopped clamouring for her to go with them, which had suited her, because there was always lots to get on with, and Sylvia was never happy sitting idly and trying to look pleased when Iris brought her back pebbles, which were beautiful shiny colours when wet, but always dried to the same dull grey.

Today, after the oppressive atmosphere of the church, and with only a small room with a single bed with a candlewick bedspread to go back to, the empty beach looked strangely inviting. Removing her new black patent court shoes, Sylvia picked her way gingerly over the shingle to the wet sandy bit where sea meets land, her feet deliciously soothed as the freezing water soaked through her tights and lapped her blistered toes.

Sylvia closed her eyes and tilted her face towards the sun. The pull of the waves dragging the shingle back was like the sound of tyres on the gravel when people arrived at the Castle. It reminded Sylvia of quick, anxious checks in the mirror, deep breath and Smile! before opening the door to greet new arrivals. No more of that, thought Sylvia, unpinning her chignon and letting her long fair hair blow about in the wind. She wouldn't miss it. You welcomed people into your home, treated them as friends, but they still stole the little bottles of shampoo and hand lotion from the bathrooms, often a towel or two as well, and were the first to complain when the loo was blocked with their tampons, or the steak wasn't cooked quite rare enough. It was no wonder really that the Kings always looked like they were sucking on lemons.

The hotel business had been fun when it was still a novelty, and she'd enjoyed the sheer achievement of making it happen, but quite soon it had become routine in a way her shop never had. Fashions changed every season, whereas one rich Japanese was very much like another. All in all, Sylvia thought, she was glad to be rid of the place without the loss of face of having to shut up and sell. The debts would be her leaving present to the new Sir James.

Sylvia was suddenly aware of the crunch, crunch, crunch of approaching footsteps. The sun was so bright, she had to shield her eyes with her hand to see who it was.

'Having a paddle?' asked Michael.

'My feet are so cold I can't feel them,' Sylvia said with a little laugh.

He was frowning as if slightly worried about her state of mind. Perhaps he thought she'd gone mad with grief, she thought, and was about to wade into the sea. It was nice to think he still cared a little bit.

'I was sorry to hear . . .' Michael began awkwardly.

Sylvia hadn't yet come up with the right thing to say

when people extended their condolences. Her natural instinct was to say, 'It's all right,' when people said they were sorry, but they looked at you a bit oddly if you did.

'Well, anyway, it was quick,' said Sylvia.

So quick, Sylvia had popped out for an hour to look round the shops, only to come back and find curtains round the bed. She was upset that Jolly had died alone, because she knew he would have been frightened without her there. She felt she had let him down at the end.

'You've moved out of the Castle?' Michael enquired.

'Chuffed about that, are you?' Sylvia snapped.

'Not at all,' said Michael, and she instantly regretted her tone. Whatever his other faults, Michael wasn't the type to carp.

'I'm staying at the Riviera for the time being,' said Sylvia, trying to sound dignified. 'Until I can get my flat back.'

'I see,' said Michael, shifting awkwardly from foot to foot.

Sylvia thought he was probably regretting making the walk down to the shoreline now. It wasn't like passing someone on the promenade, exchanging the time of day, then continuing on. Down here at the water's edge, one of them moving off would make more of a statement, and walking up the beach together would feel significant in a different way.

'Both of us on our own now then,' Sylvia observed, unable to think of anything else to say.

She wasn't sure what had happened to Michael's French girl. People said there'd been a big argument with his daughter Fiammetta. Her name meant Little Flame apparently, but Sylvia always thought of her as Little Miss Firebrand.

'Yes,' said Michael, giving nothing away.

'Perhaps we should have stuck together?' said Sylvia.

She only meant it as a joke, so was a little bit offended to see panic flash across his eyes.

'I don't think you'd have achieved everything you have if I'd stuck around,' said Michael.

It annoyed Sylvia intensely that he'd made it sound as if he had somehow stepped aside in order to let her get on, when in fact he hadn't thought about anyone except himself when he deserted her.

'You're right, I wouldn't,' she retaliated. 'Because you always did have a deadening effect.' And then she realized what she'd just said; how much worse it sounded than she had intended. 'I didn't mean—' she said.

'It's all right, Sylvia,' he said, with a shrug. 'You're probably right.'

Michael's hair was quite white now, but it wasn't that that made him look old, she thought, it was the air of defeat around him. She was suddenly desperate to say something to cheer him up, make him smile.

'Writing anything these days?' she asked brightly.

'As a matter of fact I am,' he said.

There was light in his eyes again, which made her feel much better.

'What's that then?' she asked.

'It's a kind of novel . . . more a series of linked short stories set in a little town on the South Coast, from the Roman invasion to the present day,' he said, looking at her as if expecting a reaction. 'I'm calling it *Foreigners*.'

Sylvia didn't think it was a very appealing title, but she knew he wouldn't appreciate her telling him that.

'I've often thought I've got a book in me,' she said. 'I'd call it something like *Ragtrade to Riches*. Then I could do a sequel, *Back to Rags*,' she added self-deprecatingly, and was rewarded with a smile from him.

'You know,' she prattled on, not wanting him to go back to gloom again, 'like those big books Iris used to publish . . . sex and shopping, people called them. I could definitely write about the shopping,' she said.

For a moment, she felt wonderful lightness at making Michael laugh.

'I didn't know you followed Iris's career,' he said approvingly.

'Anthony keeps me up to date,' said Sylvia. 'He bought

me some of the books too. I enjoyed them. I thought it was a shame Iris gave it all up—'

'She seems to like Italy,' Michael cut in defensively.

Sylvia could see he was still unwilling to countenance the slightest criticism of their headstrong daughter.

'What do you think of Anthony's new job, then?' Sylvia asked.

In the recent General Election, Anthony had been one of the new MPs elected to the House of Commons.

'I'm astonished!' said Michael.

'A Labour MP!' said Sylvia.

'It isn't like the Labour Party I belonged to,' said Michael.

Typical of Michael never to be satisfied, thought Sylvia. She still wasn't quite able to believe that the son she'd brought up virtually alone, sent to public school and everything, had given up a thriving career in Law to go into politics, and, if that wasn't bad enough, he'd chosen the Labour Party, who hadn't even won, even though Anthony had assured her they would.

'Families, eh?' she said, deciding it was time to move on.

She and Michael had come to the end of what they had in common, and her freezing feet, ankle-deep now in the rising tide, felt as if they were being sliced to ribbons by the sharp shingle.

'Tolstoy said that all happy families resemble one another, but each unhappy family is unhappy in its own way,' said Michael.

Sylvia thought about that one for a minute.

'Sometimes I wonder whether there's such a thing as a happy family at all,' she said.

Michael was looking at her as if she'd said something interesting, and then, quite unexpectedly, he kissed her on the cheek.

'Take care of yourself, Syl,' he said, as he walked away.

'You too,' she replied, her voice suddenly thick with emotion.

He looked back at her, and for a moment she could hardly stop herself asking, 'Couldn't we take care of each other for a bit . . . see how it goes . . . ?'

But she knew what his answer would be, and she didn't know if she'd be able to stop herself crying, what with her feet so cold and everything.

Bruno had the radio on loud and was shouting along with The Clash's 'Should I Stay or Should I Go' as he slipped the skins off plum tomatoes that had been immersed in boiling water, discarding the seeds, roughly chopping the flesh and sweeping it from the wooden chopping board into another bowl.

Among the changes he'd made to the flat – which he still thought of as Vic's, even though Vic now owned the huge house in Notting Hill he had shared with Robbie – were taking out the old cupboards and cooker, and installing a separate hob and oven and stainless-steel work surfaces. He had painted everything white, ripped up the carpet in the living room and tiled the concrete floor with quarry tiles that were cheap but looked pretty good. The old sofa had gone on a skip, a new red leather one bought, along with a state-of-the-art widescreen television connected to a satellite dish on the outside wall for watching sport, and a glass dining table and steel chairs for dinner parties.

Fiammetta called it bachelor-pad minimalism.

Bruno sawed through a loaf of bread he had bought in Lina's, pausing for a second to inhale its sour yeasty aroma. He ground some sea salt into the chopped tomato flesh. The flat was beginning to fill with the aroma of chicken roasting with fennel. Bruno checked his watch. The onion was chopped finely for the risotto, the veal stock prepared and ready to heat, Parmesan grated, white wine opened. The secret of successful Italian cooking was to leave everything to the last minute. Risotto must be creamy not sticky, bruschetta crisp, not chewy, and newly rubbed with garlic, the tomatoes freshly drizzled with pungent olive oil, not semi stewed in it. Only the chicken would be improved by sitting in its juices, the citrus flavours of lemon and green olives sweetened by the warm aniseed scent of fennel seeds.

Bruno liked people watching him cook. He'd had a rectangular hole knocked through from the kitchen to the living room. Since he'd been in London his vision of the professional kitchen he'd like to run had changed from the invisible domain of a Michelin-starred chef, to an open counter in a converted Victorian pub like the one he'd been to on Farringdon Road, where the food was freshly cooked from organic ingredients. The intention behind tonight's dinner party was to take him one step closer to fulfilling his ambition.

At the Compton Club, the private members' club on Old Compton Street, where he was now assistant chef, Bruno had begun to introduce some of his dishes as specials for the lunchtimes when he was in charge. The head chef's style was more New York Grill, with club sandwiches, home-made burgers and Caesar salad among the most-ordered items, but Bruno's butternut squash and pancetta risotto had been so successful, it now had a place on the permanent menu.

It was on the stairs of the Compton Club that Bruno had run into this evening's dinner guest. He was one of the founder members of the club, and looking to expand the brand. Further sites in London were being explored, as well as the idea of a country retreat for members. He had heard a lot of good things about Bruno, he'd said, giving Bruno a big wink, and there were some ideas he'd like to throw around with him, so Bruno had invited him to dinner at the flat on his night off.

Satisfied that everything was just about ready, Bruno was about to take a shower when the sound of a key in the lock startled him, but it was only Fiammetta.

'Mmm. Smells good,' she said, slipping past him and into Iris's old room, which seemed much bigger now that all the faux-Matisse wallpaper and *trompe-l'œil* furniture had disappeared under several coats of white emulsion.

For Bruno, his twin was the ideal flat share, someone who had tolerated his mess all her life, and even cleaned up after him. They rarely coincided, but when they did, he sometimes felt a bit guilty, as if he should be looking after her more. He didn't think his sister had a friend in London.

'You're welcome to join us,' said Bruno, standing at her bedroom door with only a towel around his waist.

'No, thanks,' said Fiammetta.

Her navy-blue eyes looked even bigger with her head shaved. Bruno thought it had probably been an attempt to make herself look sexless – like Joan of Arc or something – but curiously it had exactly the opposite effect, making her even prettier than she had been with a mass of red curls.

'Actually, it would really help me out,' Bruno tried again. 'Otherwise it's just going to be me and my guest.'

'Why don't you invite one of your many girlfriends?' Fiammetta asked.

'Because, well, it's business,' said Bruno.

'I don't see how I would help then.'

'But you would.'

'Who is it?' Fiammetta asked.

'You'll see.'

'I won't, because I'm not coming,' said Fiammetta.

'Oh, come on!' said Bruno impatiently. 'How long is this going to go on? It's been almost three years now. Isn't that a long enough seclusion?'

'I don't think you have any idea what it is to love someone, really love them, not just bonk yourself stupid with a different waitress every night,' Fiammetta suddenly shouted at him, and he felt he'd achieved something by getting a reaction out of her.

'I had no idea you followed my love life so closely!' he said, trying to make a joke of it, but her outburst made him wonder whether his promiscuity and his sister's frigidity were just their different ways of coping with the same feeling of emptiness.

He missed Julia. In the first few months after he'd

arrived in London, they'd talked on the phone late at night when he'd come in from work, with her whispering so as not to wake the children. Once, she'd come up to go to the sales, and they'd spent the whole afternoon having sex in the flat. As he walked her back over Waterloo Bridge to the station, he'd thought how nice it would be if she could have stayed, and they could have done some normal things together, like rowing on the Serpentine, or even just getting a takeaway and watching television.

They'd kissed passionately on the platform, and she'd promised to come up again as soon as she could. But after that she had never called again. And he'd wondered whether she'd picked up what he was feeling, as they walked hand in hand for the first time, because she was intuitive like that. Perhaps what he had been feeling – was it love? – had frightened her off. Or perhaps she'd found she didn't like him so much in real life.

Bruno sighed. 'I think life is probably easier without love,' he said to Fiammetta.

'How tremendously profound!' said Fiammetta sarcastically.

There was a knock at the door.

Bruno looked at the towel round his waist.

'Now look what you've made me do with all your talking!' he said archly.

Fiammetta grinned. 'It's all right,' she said. 'You get your shower and I'll entertain your guest. But I'm not joining you for dinner!'

Bruno stepped into the bathroom, straining to hear the encounter through the door before turning the shower on.

'Fiammetta?' said the loud voice of Sir James Allsop. 'My word, you look absolutely stunning!'

For months after Bruno had gone, Julia had waited, looking out at every new car that arrived in the Palace drive, paying particular attention to Porsches. When she'd seen him in London, she felt so in love she would have stayed, if he'd asked, just bolted, like her mother before her. But she'd arrived back to the news that Bertie was in hospital, and she had known it was a punishment from God for even thinking of leaving her children. There'd been an accident at his boarding school with a cricket ball. Bertie's skull was fractured and he was going to need an operation. Julia had sat outside the operating theatre in Lowhampton Hospital, making a pact with God that if he saved Bertie, she would give up Bruno. And Bertie had been fine. In fact, he'd recovered so quickly that Julia had wondered whether it had really been necessary to offer God quite so much in the negotiation, but she'd still kept her promise.

Sometimes Julia recalled what she had heard the gypsy fortune-teller saying to Mummy all those years ago: *To follow the path of true love means turning away from what you most wish for.*

And she wondered whether Mummy hadn't got it wrong. Perhaps she was meant to give up her lover for the children, not the other way round.

Julia knew in her heart she had made the right decision. As her own tarot reading had foretold, giving love was more fulfilling than receiving it. After Bertie's stay in hospital, she had concentrated even more of her efforts into the Summer House Hospice for Sick Children.

But occasionally Julia still found herself looking down the drive, wishing that Bruno would appear in a convertible Carrera, with opera blaring out, like Richard Gere in *Pretty Woman*, and take her away from all this.

There was no such thing as a family hotel any more. Apart from a few well-heeled visitors from abroad, whose details Julia had retrieved from the Castle reservations book, the main business of the Palace Hotel during the recession was medium-sized conferences. The hotel had recently played host to the South Western Association of Psychics, a group of surprisingly ordinary-looking elderly women in cardigans, who were virtually indistinguishable from the members of the Society of Crime Writers, who had held a Mystery Weekend at the Palace, in recognition of its place in the novels of the late Daphne W. Smythe, once a regular guest. Though not nearly big enough for a full party conference, this week the Palace was the discreet venue for a think tank of Tory Eurosceptics, although Julia was hoping that the call she'd just received from the local television station asking her to confirm whether Norman Tebbit was in residence (he wasn't), didn't mean that they were about to be swamped by reporters, which might spoil the scheduled opening of the Summer House Hospice. It had rained in the night, but this morning it was bright, if chilly. Everything was prepared. The ribbon across the front door was ready to be cut by one of the hospice's first little patients. Two huge boxes of fireworks had been delivered and Winny had promised to set them up by the evening. The last thing the celebrations needed was the media descending in a bid for some new angle on the ERM.

Preoccupied by what she should do in the event of journalists arriving – the Palace gates could be shut, but how long would it be before reporters discovered access from the beach? Christopher would have to be deployed to head them off at the pergola – Julia assumed that this was what Eddie King was referring to when he waved the newspaper at her as she walked into breakfast.

'Where the hell did they get this from?'

But closer inspection showed it was only the local paper.

Under a photograph of the hotel, the headline on the front page read: 'A NEW FUTURE FOR THE PALACE?'

Eddie read the rest of the front page out loud:

Does the opening this weekend of the Summer House Hospice for Sick Children signal a new direction for one of Kingshaven's oldest institutions? In an exclusive interview with the *Chronicle*, proprietor Julia King says, 'If it were up to me, I'd turn the whole hotel into a place of healing . . .' Full story inside . . .

Julia couldn't deny that they were her words, but it had been an off-the-cuff remark. Most of the interview she'd given had concerned the amazing generosity of local people raising the money for the Summer House in less than three years.

Eddie King opened up the second page and read the slightly smaller headline.

Charity begins at home? In a frank interview, Julia King speaks of putting her troubled past behind her and her plans for the future . . .

All the King family glowered at Julia as Eddie read on:

Popular hotelier Julia King's large blue eyes shone with tears as I asked her where the original idea for her Children's Hospice came from. 'When you have known unhappiness in your life, it's easy to sympathize with other people's pain,' said Mrs King, 31. 'The Summer House is where I lived as a child, and I wanted other children to be able to use it. Children matter more to me than anything in the world, so I'm prepared to fight for them.'

And what a fight it's been!

Eddie continued reading, his voice getting more shrill with increasing disbelief.

A close friend who didn't wish to be named said, 'Julia's had to battle everyone, even her husband, because he wanted to continue using the Summer House as a place to meet his special friends . . .'

Rumour has it that the Summer House was built by the oldest son of the original proprietor of the Palace Hotel as a romantic hideaway for his mistress.

'The Kings are very keen on keeping up family traditions,' claims a source close to the family. 'But Julia was determined to put a stop to that particular one.'

'For me, children are a constant inspiration,' Julia confessed. 'When you see their bravery in the face of terrible illness, everyday problems LIKE NEGA-TIVE EQUITY OR YOUR HUSBAND'S AFFAIR WITH A BARMAID SEEM TRIVIAL.'

Eddie shouted out the last sentence.

Libby King's mouth was a thin line of disapproval.

'I didn't say that!' Julia protested.

If she had, she'd only meant it as a joke. The journalist was a nice young man with glasses. She didn't think he'd even taken it in. He certainly hadn't said he was speaking to other sources – Bee, Julia presumed, who was probably only trying to help, but had put her foot in it, as usual.

Now all of the Kings were arrayed against her, like a court martial, where there could be only one outcome. Julia would be taken outside and shot.

'Well, it is true, after all!' Julia said indignantly.

Christopher snatched the paper from his father's hands, reading out the final paragraph in a mocking voice.

'I've had more satisfaction from creating this children's hospice than any of the improvements I've made to the hotel. If I had my way, the whole place would become a holiday home for the less fortunate . . . somewhere people could be healed.'

'I don't actually see what's wrong with that,' said Julia. 'I wasn't saying that was on the cards. Just that it would be a nice idea.'

'I suppose you were flattered by someone telling you how marvellous you were,' said Libby sadly.

'Well, none of you ever do, do you?' Julia tried to defend herself. 'I've tried so hard to please you, and what do I get? Nothing!'

'You get a home, security, children. I thought children were the most important thing . . .' Christopher threw the quote back at her mockingly.

'But I don't get love,' she challenged him. 'Love's supposed to go with marriage, isn't it?'

'Like a horse and carriage!' sang Granny Ruby, proving beyond doubt that she was really losing it.

The Kings lowered their eyes.

'Love!' scoffed Christopher. 'What does love mean anyway?'

'That's the trouble with you,' Julia suddenly shouted. 'All of you! None of you knows what love means . . .'

She threw her napkin down and rushed out and down to the kitchen, ordering the astonished chef, who was preparing a soup for lunch, to take a break, then cramming what remained of the hotel breakfast into her mouth: leftover scrambled eggs, flaccid triangles of damp toast, cold croissants . . .

'Who do you think you are, Mother Teresa?' Christopher was behind her.

She turned round to face him. 'I was only trying to do good!' she said, her mouth full of Danish pastry. 'What good have you ever done apart from build a compost heap?'

Christopher's puny body seemed to inflate like one of the helium balloons they were planning to let off at this afternoon's celebrations, but then deflate again, appearing to shrink before her eyes.

Maybe she should have shouted at him before, Julia thought. Maybe things would never have got to this point if she'd been a bit braver. But it was too late now. The man she thought she loved was a wimp.

'Even when our son was under general anaesthetic, you went to see *The Mikado*!' she said, realizing only now that the last vestiges of love she had for him had disappeared when Christopher had kept his annual appointment with Kingshaven Amateur Dramatic Society rather than wait with her at the hospital for Bertie to come round.

'The consultant assured me there was little danger . . .' Christopher started to excuse himself.

'Oh, why don't you just piss off?' Julia shouted.

Suddenly, she didn't feel hungry any more. She grabbed a tea towel, wiped her mouth, and turned to leave.

'And, by the way, you've got a minuscule willy,' she added.

'Wow!' said Millicent Balls, as Christopher threw open the door to the Windsor Suite. He looked so pleased with himself, she half expected him to pick her up and carry her over the threshold like a just-married couple. Instead, he took a step back, politely indicating that she should go first.

Perhaps Julia had done her a favour, Millicent thought, taking in the lavish surroundings. If it was openly acknowledged she and Christopher were an item, then maybe they wouldn't have to sneak around like teenagers. This was certainly an improvement on the beach hut they'd had to use since his wife had commandeered the Summer House for her charity work.

The Windsor Suite was one of the few rooms in the Palace that had been preserved exactly as it was in its heyday in the 1920s, Christopher explained, pointing out the original features with pride.

The en-suite bathroom had twin basins in onyx marble. The bath was the size of a small swimming pool.

'So how come you've brought me here?' Millicent asked.

'My family are all over at the opening of the Hospice,' he replied.

'Weren't you welcome?' Millicent wanted to know.

'In the light of the newspaper article, I declined to attend.'

'Why are the rest of them there, then?'

'If they weren't, it might look as if the stuff in the paper was true.'

'But it is.'

'That's not the point.'

'It's all about putting on a show with you lot, isn't it?' said Milly, flopping down on the eau-de-Nil silk bedspread.

'I'm here,' Christopher said simply.

'Bloody nerve, her calling me a barmaid when I'm the landlady,' said Milly.

She looked up at the ornate Venetian chandelier above her. From the door, it looked like an upside-down palm tree, but when you were underneath, you could see that the fronds were peacock feathers made of coloured glass. It was the sort of luxury you could easily get used to, she thought. Christopher lay down beside her. She reached across and felt the hard bump under his flies.

There was something a bit naughty about making love in the afternoon, like coming out of the cinema when it was still light. Milly and her friend Una had been to see *The Bodyguard* at the Regal the previous afternoon, and Milly still couldn't get the theme tune out of her head.

'What Julia said . . .' Christopher asked nervously, when they'd finished.

'How many times do I have to tell you, it's the quality, not the quantity!'

Milly thought that if she'd had a pound for every time she'd had to tell Christopher that over the past twenty years, she'd be a rich woman. She quite fancied being a rich woman too. It was only what she deserved. Now that Sean and Lucy were both teenagers, and Bernadette engaged, she was beginning to see a time when she would just be left on her own, in the pub, with Gerry. What kind of a life was that?

The French windows on to the balcony were open, and there was a slight breeze coming in off the sea, bringing with it a hint of vanilla cigar smoke.

'We've got a former cabinet minister next door,' Christopher told her, then sitting up quickly, he said, 'Oh God, you don't think he heard?'

'It's nothing he won't have heard before.' Milly laughed.

Christopher propped himself up on his elbows and looked at her.

'I do love you, you know,' he said.

'Why don't you tell Mrs Bountiful to push off, then?' Milly asked him.

'I would,' said Christopher, lying down again, staring at the ceiling. 'It's just . . . well . . . the children . . . and it would kill my grandmother . . .'

'It wouldn't kill her!' exclaimed Milly. 'She's survived two world wars! She's a tough old bird.'

'It's not just the matter of my wife . . . Granny Liliana was awfully fond of your husband too.'

'Yeah. She gave him an engraved silver cocktail stick. I sometimes wonder what he gave her . . .'

'Please!' Christopher looked horrified.

'The trouble with you is you're soft,' Milly taunted him. 'You don't want to offend people, and you end up offending everyone. Including me, if you're not careful.'

'I'm not soft.'

Milly lit a cigarette and blew a funnel of smoke straight up towards the chandelier.

'I wish you wouldn't smoke,' Christopher said.

'Why should I give up, when you won't give up anything for me?' Milly demanded.

'I will. I promise.'

'That's what you always say!' Milly defiantly took another long drag.

Christopher took the cigarette from her fingers and rested it in the ashtray on the bedside table. She blew out the smoke so that he could kiss her.

'Stay,' he whispered.

'What?'

'Stay with me, here, tonight . . .'

'You must come down to the Castle one weekend!' James Allsop had declared, when Fiammetta explained what she did for a living. 'I need to have my portrait painted.'

She had assumed he was joking. Nobody their age had their portrait painted. But the following day she had arrived back at the flat to find an enormous bouquet of orange lilies by the door, and a card, which read: 'Can't wait to sit for you. Are you free this weekend?'

She had declined that weekend, and the next, even

though Bruno told her, only half-joking, she was ruining his prospect of financing his gastropub.

Then the following Friday evening, she looked up from her pitch in Covent Garden to see James waiting in her queue to be sketched.

'Twenty pounds seems rather a bargain,' he said, appraising the work.

As usual, she was hopeless about taking the money.

'Let me buy you dinner instead,' he insisted, picking up her easel and her folder of paper, and carrying it for her as they walked towards Soho.

James was full of talk about his plans for the Castle, and because she knew it so well, it felt strangely as if they had a lot in common, although really, Fiammetta kept reminding herself, they couldn't be more different. James was loud, rich, insufferably right wing, but he was very funny too, and a brilliant mimic. His imitations of Kingshaven people were so spot on, Fiammetta found herself laughing almost despite herself.

They stood for quite a long time talking at the bottom of the steps up to the flat. It had gone past the point where she could invite him up for a coffee, and yet she was in no hurry to part.

When he said, 'Come and see for yourself! We'll have dinner on the way down!' she suddenly couldn't think of a reason why not.

They ate in a Little Chef on the motorway.

'Not quite what I had in mind,' James told her, but she quite liked the incongruity of his posh voice against the background of muzak, and the nostalgic taste of packet apple pie with a puff of aerosol cream that melted immediately to a white dribble.

By the time they arrived in Kingshaven, it was late and it felt colder inside the Castle than out. James showed Fiammetta to the room that had once been the nursery, unrecognizable now with its coral and cream décor.

'Ghastly, isn't it?' he said, switching on the light for her. 'My petit bourgeois stepmother's taste, I'm afraid, but it won't be like this for long. See you in the morning.'

She felt oddly disappointed that he didn't even try to kiss her. Not that she wanted him to, she told herself.

Fiammetta found it difficult to get to sleep. With the lights out and the wind swirling round outside, the Castle sounded just as it had when she was little, but she missed Bruno's even breathing across the room to lull her. Even now, in the flat, she found she slept better knowing that her brother was sleeping just the other side of the wall from her.

The house was very quiet when Fiammetta woke up in the morning. She could tell that it was sunny outside from the slice of light at the edge of the curtains. James was nowhere to be found. His car was gone from the drive.

Feeling almost as if she was trespassing, Fiammetta opened the back door and stepped out into the garden. There was a swimming pool where the walled garden had been, and even though it was now drained, there was still a whiff of chlorine in the air. The wrong smell. Fiammetta closed her eyes and inclined her face to the sun, receiving a peaceful anointment of warmth on her skin. For a moment, she could smell the lavender again and hear the quiet hum of bees. Then a squall of chill breeze returned her to the present, as the sun disappeared behind clouds. Fiammetta remembered how as a child she always thought the weather inside the walled garden was different from the outside world, that it was an enchanted place.

She heard her name being called from the house.

'Here you are!' James shouted, bounding over to her like an enthusiastic Labrador.

'I've been out for provisions!' he said, as if they were on a camping adventure together, like the Famous Five, or something. 'Bacon, eggs . . . whatever you like!'

Fiammetta followed him back into the house and dutifully ate the breakfast of eggs and burned toast he cooked for her, sitting in the empty restaurant, a huge modern conservatory Sylvia had added to the house and furnished with bamboo chairs with William Morris-print cushions.

'The only bit she hasn't completely ruined is the entrance hall,' James told Fiammetta. 'And that's where I should like you to paint me!'

James Allsop's natural way of standing was rather like the subject of an eighteenth-century portrait, thought Fiammetta, his thick wavy fair hair, the distinctive round blue eyes of the Allsops, and his full lips giving him the indulged, rakish look of a Reynolds.

Fiammetta's own internal portrait of him, the image that kept jumping into her mind as she tried to judge how she would like to paint him, was more of a close-up, his face only the distance of a dinner table away, his eyes locked on hers, his foot – accidentally or opportunistically? – touching her ankle beneath the table. A look, as lascivious as a satyr, that had made her feel as if she was blushing all the way through her flesh to her core.

Now, as he struck poses on the grand staircase, Fiammetta had a wicked urge to draw him naked, in half profile, like the Roman sculptures of Mars and Mercury that stood in niches on the side of the staircase. She glanced up from her sketchpad, alarmed that he might be able to read what she was thinking.

James smiled, a slow, knowing smile, and she felt a shiver of pure lust down her spine.

What on earth was wrong with her? James Allsop was the total antithesis of any man she had ever liked. He was aristocratic, haughty and with a distinct potential for cruelty. He had always been a naughty boy, she remembered, and now he was a dangerous man.

'I . . . I think that's enough for now,' she said.

'Can I look?' James asked, coming down the stairs towards her.

'No,' she said, closing the sketchpad.

'As you wish!'

'I'm . . . I'm just not sure this is going to work,' Fiammetta stuttered, unable to look at him now.

'Why?' he asked.

She said nothing.

He reached out a hand, tilted her chin so she was forced to confront his icy round blue eyes. Fiammetta felt as if all her nerve endings had suddenly been magnetically pulled towards the point just above her throat where the tip of his finger met her skin.

'Why?' he asked again, more firmly.

'Because I keep thinking about how you would look naked,' she said, trying to make a joke of it.

'Do you think you would be able to capture me better if you knew?' he asked, as if it were an entirely academic conversation they were having.

'Possibly,' said Fiammetta coyly.

'Shall we find out?'

'Why not?' she said, still looking into his eyes.

He kissed her hard, pushing her down on to the floor, and they made fast, furious love with the Roman gods looking down at them. Then he left her there, winded, panting, shocked by the ferocity of her desire. The marble was very cold and flat under her body, her flesh hot and bruised with his imprint. Fiammetta stared at the stucco ceiling. Then James returned with a bottle of cold champagne, his naked body firm and shameless. He kneeled beside her and, taking a gulp from the foaming neck of the bottle, placed his lips on hers, transferring some of the cool bubbling liquid to her mouth.

'The only way to drink champagne,' he said, smiling down at her.

The sky lit up with pink, green, orange bursts of tiny, brilliant stars as the fireworks popped like champagne corks and filled the air with the smell of gunpowder . . .

Julia woke up, knowing instantly that something wasn't right. Her brain tracked back through the evening. There were no fireworks. The matron of the new hospice had vetoed Winny's *son et lumière* on the grounds that poorly children shouldn't be up after dark. They were excited enough with all the fizzy drinks and the visit from the local television newsreader.

Julia sniffed the air. Something *was* burning. She leaped out of bed and ran to the boys' bedroom, her reaction as instinctive as when her children were babies and she used to jump awake in the night, fearing the worst, and have to put her head right inside their cots to feel tiny damp puffs of their breath against her cheek.

Now, seeing their beds empty, Julia panicked, her heart racing, and then she remembered they were at school. Safe!

Julia rubbed her eyes. Something wasn't right. She was sure she hadn't slept long enough for it to be dawn, but the flat seemed brighter than it should, the room had a strange orange glow. Julia pulled back one of the Laura Ashley curtains and gasped . . .

The bell started ringing and Christopher stretched his arm out blearily to bang the alarm clock, but couldn't reach it. His hand flapped around ineffectively for a moment or two before his brain registered that the alarm was much louder than usual.

The fire alarm!

Christopher sat bolt upright, disorientated. Where the hell was he?

The Windsor Suite!

Millicent was sleeping so peacefully beside him, he could hardly bear to wake her. He nuzzled in behind her, blowing gently in her ear, loving the feeling of her warm back against his chest, pulling the heavy coverlet up over their heads to block out the noise.

'What's happening?' Milly suddenly asked, sitting up.

'It's probably just a bomb scare. Bloody drunks!' Christopher murmured.

'Shouldn't we evacuate?'

Christopher sighed and sat up reluctantly.

'You stay here. I'll investigate.'

He got out of bed, pulled his shirt and trousers on, walked over to the door, opened it, then banged it shut again immediately, as a thick wall of smoke advanced into the room, making him choke.

Millicent was already in the bathroom running the bath tap on a pile of towels.

'Here, put these round the door!' she ordered him. 'Where's the fire escape?'

Christopher's legs felt like jelly, as they did in dreams, except that he was pretty sure that this wasn't a dream. He pointed towards the door.

'Well, that's a load of use. We'll have to go out on the balcony,' said Millicent.

'You can't go out there!' Christopher suddenly found his voice.

'Why not?' asked Millicent.

The bedroom door was beginning to buckle.

'People will see you!'

The door creaked alarmingly.

Millicent screamed, grabbed him by the hand and dragged him out on to the balcony, closing the French doors behind them.

'Quick!' she said. 'We'll climb all the way along!'

'But you're in your underwear!' he cried.

Fiammetta felt as if her blood had been replaced with champagne, her body and mind erased of all sensation.

The sound of explosions startled her out of a stupefied slumber.

'Fireworks,' muttered James. 'Some charity thing of Julia's.'

He turned over, yanking the sheet from Fiammetta's body.

She got out of bed, and went to the window, drawn by the glow of the sky.

Across the valley, the sky was as red and orange as her painting long ago of sunset over Kingshaven. But the sun had gone down hours ago. The sea was red and slate grey, undulating like molten lava, the town bathed in a strange pink light. There were random explosions, as if the Palace were a great box of fireworks, as windows shattered and yellow tongues of flame leaped out.

'James?' Fiammetta called.

He grunted.

'James! The Palace is on fire!'

In the misty, grey dawn, with the acrid smell of burning still hanging in the air, Libby King picked her way through the piles of wet rubble that had been the hall. The charred remains of the grand staircase stopped at the first landing, the Tudor-style oak banister now just a blackened stump. The fire had completely destroyed the main body of the hotel, leaving the private wing and the Tower virtually intact.

'I'm afraid I must ask you to vacate the area, now, Mrs King,' Sergeant Benson said to her. 'We are treating it as a crime scene.'

Escorted from her own home by the police, thought Libby. What greater indignity could there be?

'A crime scene?' she echoed. 'You suspect arson?'

'Nothing is ruled in, and nothing is ruled out at this stage. The majority of hotel fires are caused by careless smokers, I'm afraid, but I am advised that preliminary investigations suggest the presence of explosives. The building is insured, of course?' asked the policeman.

'My son attends to all that,' said Libby.

Fortunately, the evacuation procedures had gone like clockwork, with every member of the family and every guest accounted for, along with a couple of extra women in skimpy nightdresses, who were not on the register but had appeared with one of the Tory grandees in his pyjamas.

They would have to be more selective with guests in future, thought Libby, if there was to be a future. Who could tell? One would have thought the psychics could have at least dropped a hint about an imminent conflagration. It was certainly always best to steer clear of politicians. Unfortunately, the rumoured presence of former cabinet ministers had brought an excitable camera crew from the local television station.

'You've had a bit of a year,' said Sergeant Benson.

'Not one I'll look back on with undiluted pleasure,' said Libby with a tight little smile.

It had been a horrible year, she thought, a year in which the foundations on which she built her life had been destroyed. The fire seemed like a physical manifestation of the turmoil that had rocked the house. And it had all happened in the name of love.

'You don't know what love means!' her daughter-in-law had declared, but the fact of the matter was that Julia's generation, the children of the sixties, had changed the meaning.

In her day, Libby thought, love had been a sacred vow, a solemn commitment. *Brief Encounter* was the love story that women of her age had wept over. No sex at all in that. Only a woman remembering her duty, returning to her husband.

He might be boring, or worse, have a roving eye, but that's what you did. That's how it worked. Love was like the froth on the top of a cappuccino that people seemed so keen on drinking these days, but it was no use at all without the stronger stuff to hold it up. Women were the glue of the family, the home, the whole fabric of society. Today's women seemed to expect so much more, for giving so little.

Libby shuddered at the thought of the small ad that had appeared in the *Chronicle* earlier that summer: 'Bored housewife seeks afternoon fun!'

And underneath, Bee's full name and the address of the Yacht Club instead of a box number. (Was it a mistake? Libby hadn't been convinced by the protestations of innocence by the editor. She'd made a formal complaint to the chief executive of the Echo Group. He'd issued a public apology, but, with hindsight, that had probably made things worse. He was Australian, didn't really understand the status quo as dear Mr Otterway always had.)

When Adrian had confronted Bee, she'd had the brazen

nerve to demand he ask himself why she might be looking outside the 'relationship'. Another dreadful word, in Libby's opinion.

That was marriage number one, over.

Then Angela, who'd done her best, had finally succumbed to terminal boredom. Poor old Miles. Thick and wet like his name.

Marriage number two. Finished.

Now the ongoing saga of Christopher and Julia had surely reached the point of no return. Anyone watching the live television bulletins of the Palace fire would clearly have seen the unedifying spectacle of Millicent Balls in her lingerie being carried down a long ladder by a fireman.

It had been a dreadful year, Libby thought. Three children safely launched, now limping back to port with masts broken. Libby didn't even want to think about what love held in store for Winny.

And now this. The Palace, not just her home, but everything she'd worked for and believed in. Gone.

Women of her generation never cried, Libby told herself firmly, unlike her intemperate daughter-in-law, who blubbed at the least provocation.

When she was a little girl, Julia had listened carefully to the story of 'The Princess and the Pea' when Mrs Evans read it to the nursery class. She'd borrowed one of James's marbles and put it under her mattress to see if she was a real princess, then woken early in the morning, disappointed to find no bruises at all.

She'd asked Mummy, 'Do you think the princess was staying at the Palace?'

'Which princess, darling?' Mummy asked. 'The one who never laughs?'

'No, silly, that's the story of the Golden Goose. I mean 'The Princess and the Pea'. There's ever so many mattresses at the Palace . . . perhaps the princess fell off a big pile and that's why she was black and blue!'

Mummy had laughed. 'It's just a fairy story, darling.'

But Julia had insisted, 'When I grow up I'm going to marry Adrian and be princess of the Palace.'

'You'll probably have to marry Christopher if you want to do that!' her mother had told her.

Now, the fairy tale was finally over, Julia thought. There was no marriage any more. No proper family that she'd dreamed of being part of. There wasn't even much of a Palace.

Julia took a deep breath. Better get it over with.

It seemed ages since the previous day, almost as if a whole life had been lived in the last twenty-four hours. The triumphant opening of the hospice, then the fire, had overshadowed the events at yesterday's breakfast table, but Julia had known then that her time was up. The Kings could tolerate bad behaviour, but not if it was splashed all over the paper, as Bee had found out to her cost earlier in the summer.

'The Kings can't stand you being *too* anything,' her friend had said. 'It's the English way. I am way too bad, and you are far too good.'

Julia knocked on the door.

Julia had never been in the Kings' bedroom suite before. The view over the Palace gardens towards the bay was particularly fine. The sparkling sunshine outside didn't really go with the horrible smell of burning that pervaded what remained of the building. Julia longed to be in the fresh air. How wonderful it must be to be a white seagull, she thought, soaring, swooping, free.

Libby had turned her dressing table into a makeshift desk, giving up all pretence of letting Christopher attend to anything now.

'Ah, Julia, there you are! How did the boys take the news?'

'It's difficult for them to understand when they're away,' said Julia, who'd just spoken to Bertie and Archie on the phone. Once she'd assured them that their rooms were unaffected and the swimming pool was OK, they'd been

571

eager to get back to the game of football they'd been called away from.

'Perhaps just as well that they are, in the circumstances?'

'Yes,' Julia agreed.

'I think we both know why we're here,' Libby went on. 'It's become all too clear that you and Christopher have irreconcilable differences.'

'The trouble is, there are three people in the marriage,' Julia said. 'As everyone who was watching the local news last night will have seen. So it's been a little crowded,' she added with a shy laugh.

It didn't feel right to be speaking out loud about adultery to the woman she still thought of as her honorary auntie.

'At times there have even been four, I understand,' said Libby evenly.

So they all knew! Julia kicked herself for playing the wronged-wife card so early. There had been many occasions when Granny Liliana and Granny Ruby had attempted to teach her bridge. Julia had always been quite good at the bidding, but she'd never got the hang of playing out her hand.

'He started it,' she said defiantly. 'He was with Millicent Balls before and during the marriage, and will no doubt be with her after as well!'

She realized it was the first time she'd admitted that it would end, even to herself.

'I put up with it for a long time. I did everything I could . . . I wanted to make a happy home for the children—'

'I don't deny there's fault on both sides,' Libby interrupted with a pained look on her face. 'Which is why I propose that you are given a fair settlement and that you share custody of the children.'

The words took a moment to sink in.

No. No. No.

'But I don't want to share custody,' said Julia. 'I want to stay here with them. It's me that's saved this place, after

572

all, and I'm the only one with the slightest chance of rebuilding it . . .'

She realized immediately that she'd overstepped the mark.

Libby King's mouth was so thin, it had almost disappeared.

'I'm beginning to think that Christopher is right in some of the things he says about you,' she said. 'You really have got a little beyond yourself, Julia. This place, as you call it, had been running perfectly well for over a hundred years before you graced us with your presence, thank you very much. And if you want to continue to dabble in the hotel business, I'm sure your brother will appreciate your undoubted gifts.'

'But you can't just kick me out! I want sole custody of the boys and I'll get it too!' said Julia. 'I won't go quietly!'

Out of her handbag she withdrew her Dictaphone recorder and flicked the button to Play.

I want to feel my way along you, said Christopher's voice.

You're awfully good at feeling your way along . . . Millicent's town-person accent was unmistakable.

All over you, and up and down you and in and out . . .
Oh!
Particularly in and out . . .
Oh! That's just what I need!
The trouble is, I need you several times a week, all the time.
Mmm. So do I. I need you all the week. All the time.
Oh God! I'd like to live inside you. Like a tampon . . .

'That's enough!' said Libby.

Julia stopped the tape, allowed herself a small smile.

Libby stared at her levelly.

'I'm sad that it has to come to this,' she said, suddenly looking rather old and grey, which made Julia feel ashamed. Auntie Libby had always been kind to her when she was little, and in her own way she was trying to be fair. She waited, her heart beating in her head, as Libby fished around for something in her capacious handbag, a tissue, her reading glasses, perhaps? Julia was surprised when

Libby eventually produced an identical Dictaphone to the one Julia was holding.

'You remember we always play Murder in the Dark on Boxing Day?' Libby asked.

Julia nodded, unable to think where this was leading.

'I always find it quite convenient to hide in the reception area,' Libby smiled, as if she was letting her in on a little secret. 'There's quite a bit space, under the counter and for some reason, people never think of looking there. Of course, since your brilliant idea of installing baby listening, one can hear what's going on in all the bedrooms. I suppose it gives one an unfair advantage . . .' she mused. 'Of course, one sometimes hears things one's not supposed to . . .'

Libby pressed the Play button.

Please don't go! Julia heard herself saying.

Look, even if you're right, and I got a divorce, there's no half of the hotel for me to get because it's not even worth as much as the mortgage . . .

Mortgage?

Julia took a sharp intake of breath at the sound of Bruno's voice.

James said it was the best way to borrow money for the refurbishment, and it was all going so well, and then it just stopped . . . the only way of getting any money out of this place right now would be to burn it down and collect the insurance!

Libby clicked the Stop button.

'I do wonder how the police, who haven't yet ruled arson out of their investigations, would react to hearing this,' she said, looking straight at Julia. 'Of course, as the boys' grandmother the last thing I'd want is for their mother to come to any harm,' she added brightly.

Chapter Eighteen

1993

Iris wished women had a little of whatever it was that made men sleep after sex. She could tell by the absence of noise that it wasn't yet dawn, but she knew she would remain awake now. Careful not to disturb the sheets, Iris swung her legs out of bed.

In the kitchen, she poured hot water on to a Lipton's tea bag, only now remembering she should have asked Vic to bring some proper English tea with him. She sat down at the small Formica table and started absently correcting the homework Fabio had been working on, making several underlinings and omission marks in red pen on the paper before it occurred to her that it was not homework, but a poem.

> *You tell me go*
> *Youre friend he come*
> *A man you love*
> *He not loves you*
> *I do love*
> *And I no like*

The sentiment was all the more touching for the uncharacteristic effort Fabio had put in, and although its simplicity probably owed more to his laziness learning vocabulary than any latent poetic gift, it lent a purity to the verse that reminded Iris a little of the Roman poet Catullus, whose work she had been reading in a Penguin Classic. Iris loved the way the poem ended so abruptly, and wondered whether this was an artistic decision, or whether Fabio just ran out of ideas. She folded the piece of paper and slipped it into her wallet.

The clanking of the refuse truck told her that it was now around six o'clock, and she wanted to head out for the airport early to avoid getting stuck in the morning rush hour.

In the bedroom, she kissed Fabio softly on his temple. He turned over, frowned, rubbed his eyes, stretched up his arms to pull her back on top of him. But she was already dressed, ready to go and keen to get him out of the flat. She didn't want an overlap between her old life and her new, couldn't bear the thought of Vic teasing her about Fabio's age, or worse, trying to get off with him. For Vic to meet Fabio would make the relationship much more than what it was. A zipless fuck. Fabio was spending too much time at her place anyway.

As they parted at the door and Iris watched her lover walking away, sulking, not looking back at her, she had a sudden shiver of presentiment that she would not see him again, and was tempted to run after him, kiss his face, make him smile at her one last time. She told herself not to be so melodramatic. The little cobbled street with three-wheeler vans puttering along, and old women sitting in the doorways, always gave her the slight feeling she was living in a film.

The taxi was waiting outside and Julia was all ready to go – suitcase, passports, tickets – when the postman arrived.

Along with a postcard from Bee from some Caribbean island, which said simply: 'This is the life!' there was an official-looking envelope, franked with the Sunny Stores logo.

Inside, Julia quickly scanned the typed letter from Mr Patel.

After a formal expression of sympathy regarding her separation, Mr Patel went on to say that he had been impressed with her charity work in recent years, and in particular the Summer House Hospice Charitable Trust. The purpose of the letter was to enquire whether she might be interested in discussing ways in which Sunny Stores Ltd might make an ongoing contribution to further charitable endeavours.

With a little leap of excitement, Julia put the heavy cream sheet of paper back in its envelope and stuffed it into her handbag to read properly on the plane.

'Good news?'

Sid Farthing was now driving a taxi, since there was no job for him as night porter while the Palace was closed.

Julia was fizzing with the need to share Mr Patel's letter with someone, but she'd never really liked Mr Farthing, who was a particular favourite of Granny Liliana's.

'Possibly,' she said, closing the door of the taxi.

Mr Farthing drove too fast, and she could feel him watching her in the rear-view mirror, almost as if he knew she was slightly scared, and was enjoying it. Julia decided not to give him the satisfaction of asking him to slow down.

The boys were waiting on the gravel drive, so she didn't have to get out of the cab.

'Mummy!' Archie shouted, throwing himself along the back seat to hug her.

'Have you been having a nice time?' Julia asked as the taxi pulled away.

'Yes, thank you,' said Bertie politely.

Nearly twelve, and on the cusp of puberty, Bertie had grown tall in recent months, and Julia recognized the awkwardness that accompanies the beginning of adulthood.

'No way! It was BORING!' shouted Archie.

'Well, we're going to have a lovely time! Are you excited about going on a plane?' said Julia, putting her arm around both boys, who automatically snuggled against her chest.

Buoyed up by their love, she stared defiantly in the rear-view mirror at Mr Farthing, wishing he would keep his eyes on the road.

Iris stood scanning the passengers as they came through the Arrivals gate. She couldn't help noticing that there was a uniformed chauffeur with a handwritten sign saying 'SIGNOR VICTOR', which she thought would amuse Vic, so she went and stood next to it. There were quite a few tourists, families with children blinking bewildered at the directions for the Metro and struggling to take off their jackets in the sudden change of temperature; more nuns than usual, probably because it was Easter, Iris thought. No one who looked remotely like Vic. She hadn't seen him for five years, and was beginning to think, as the surge of arrivals became a straggle, that perhaps he'd changed, or she'd changed so much that they'd missed each other. Then she heard him calling out, and she recognized his voice before his face. She'd been looking at eye level. Nothing could have prepared her for the emaciated skeletal figure in a wheelchair being pushed by one of the airline staff.

'My nurse said he should come with me,' Vic said, trying to reassure her with a brittle joke. 'But I told him three's a crowd. Still, I thought we'd need a driver.'

The chauffeur with the sign, whose name was Mauro, pushed Vic to a black limousine parked illegally just outside the concourse. Vic was just strong enough to stand up and get into the car, while Mauro folded the wheelchair and put it with his suitcase in the capacious boot.

The limousine had tinted windows and air conditioning. It was like getting into a fridge. Murmuring the theme tune to *The Godfather*, Vic played with all the buttons, making the windows go up and down, the fan go on and off.

'Champagne?' he asked, opening a little fridge as they drove into the city. 'I never got used to all this. Better than the number 38 bus, though, eh?'

Iris's brain tried to work out what to do. Everything she had planned for his visit was now redundant.

'Where's nice for lunch?' Vic asked.

Unable to think of somewhere more suitable, Iris directed Mauro to the Trevi Fountain where she had planned to take him. The limousine could barely squeeze down the narrow streets and tourists had to squash into doorways. Iris took Vic's arm firmly, and helped him over the cobbles to the little trattoria. He felt as frail and bony as a bird, but his grip was strong and desperate, as Claudia's had been, Iris suddenly thought, as she'd shifted her up on her pillows, the only other dying person Iris had known.

Vic pointed at the tourists who were having their picture taken as they threw coins over their shoulders.

'Just like Audrey Hepburn and Gregory Peck in *Roman Holiday*,' he said.

'If you throw in a coin, you'll come back to Rome,' Iris told him, then couldn't bear to look him in the eye, knowing that the superstition wasn't going to work for him.

In the midst of the shock, there was a little bit of her that was cross with him for not telling her about his condition. She had planned an itinerary, borrowed a camp bed from one of her colleagues, but she'd never be able to get him up all the stairs to her rooftop flat.

'The thing is,' she began, 'I'm not sure my place is really suitable . . .'

'Don't worry,' said Vic. 'Life is easy when you've got money. Course, it's better if you've got life too,' he added blackly.

Iris laughed.

'I've got all the money in the world,' Vic told her. 'I could live the rest of my life – the rest of your life, even – at the Ritz if I wanted, and I'd still have more money tomorrow than I have today . . . so let's spend some of it, eh?'

Iris nodded.

Accustomed to living on an English teacher's salary, it was quite difficult to get into the mindset of automatically sitting at the expensive tables outside, ordering every single flavour of ice cream at Gioliti just because you could, buying a handbag from a street vendor and leaving him disappointed that you hadn't haggled over the price, or shopping for a Pucci silk top that cost what Iris earned in a month, then horrifying the snooty assistant by walking out on to the Via Condotti wearing it with jeans. But no amount of money could get Vic's wheelchair up to the Palatine to see the view, nor lift him on to the number 26 tram that trundled all the way round the city.

'You know what I'd really like to do?' Vic said, as they sat in a café on the Piazza di Spagna, looking the flower-decked Spanish Steps, but unable to climb them.

'What?' Iris asked.

'Do you remember that mural in the Luna Caprese?' Vic asked her.

The best and most expensive hotel in Sorrento was called the Palace, the travel agent told them. The drive down was only a few hours. When they arrived, Mauro carried Vic in to the cool marble reception like a *pietà*, and laid him on a vast leather chesterfield, as Iris checked them in.

When they opened the shutters of their suite on to a vast terrace, the view of the bay was so exactly like the mural, with Vesuvius looming dark in the background and the blue of the sea garishly blue, Iris felt tears in her eyes. There were even lemon trees!

'See Naples and die!' said Vic.

Julia had expected better shops. They were all full of painted ceramics, lace tablecloths, or miniature bottles of Limoncello for the tourists to take home as souvenirs.

The boys were keen to go to Pompeii because Archie was doing the Romans at school.

'There's real dead bodies,' he said ghoulishly. 'They got caught in all the ash and died just like that!'

'We'll go tomorrow,' Julia promised, her heart sinking at

the thought of trailing round a dusty old ruin. 'Why don't we spend this afternoon in the pool?'

The swimming pool looked even better than it had in the brochure, cut into the sheer rock and with a perfect picture-postcard view of the Bay of Naples, but it wasn't customary in Italy to heat the water. The waiter who brought a coffee to Julia's sunlounger seemed mystified as to why anyone would want to swim before the summer months.

The boys dived in and swore manfully that it wasn't a bit cold once you got used to it, but were very quickly out with teeth chattering, demanding to know what they were going to do next.

The holiday, which Julia had secretly hoped to spend beside the pool in the sunshine, despite having emphasized the archaeological aspect of the trip to Christopher, was beginning to look more trouble than staying at home.

'We always like to eat with this view!' said Vic, as the waiter showed them to a window table.

Darkness was beginning to fall, the bright-blue sky fading to grey, the lights of the distant city twinkling weakly.

The restaurant was gloriously opulent. Marble palm trees with golden glass fronds supported the baroquely frescoed ceiling. The inlaid marble floor seemed to magnify the clatter of knives and forks and the chatter of the hotel guests. The busy tableau reminded Iris of the dining-room scene in *Death in Venice*, and, as she glanced at Vic, she was almost certain that he was thinking the same thing.

In just twenty-four hours, Iris had grown so used to his skeletal features she found it difficult to remember Vic looking any other way now. She picked up the menu.

'Do you know what you're having?'

'*Spaghetti alle vongole*, of course,' he replied.

Iris looked up to beckon over a waiter, then quickly ducked her head down again.

'What?' asked Vic.

'I think I've just seen someone I know,' she said.

'Who?'

'Julia King. She's a silly Sloane Ranger from Kingshaven.'

To Iris's horror, at that very moment Julia looked in their direction, did a double take, then smiled and approached.

Iris performed the introductions, relieved that Julia took Vic's hand and shook it warmly, because she had noticed people shrinking away, as if his illness might be contagious. Julia's boys, though clearly somewhat reluctant, also stepped forward politely to shake hands.

'What brings you here?' Vic asked Julia.

'It's the boys' holidays,' says Julia. 'Technically, it was their father's turn, but it's all repair work, so I was granted leave to take them away on a suitably educational trip. So here we are.'

'Why don't you join us for dinner?' Vic suddenly suggested.

'Are you sure?' said Julia, immediately pulling out a chair.

Iris never felt comfortable when bits of her past intruded on her new life, let alone two separate bits coinciding and threatening to take over the last precious days she had with her oldest friend, but Vic seemed to be in a sociable mood, and she didn't really feel she could object.

'How odd we should meet up at the Palace!' Julia chatted on. 'I chose it specially for the name. Just because I'm banished from one Palace doesn't mean I'm banished from them all, does it? Sadly, it looks as if we'll have to go to Pompeii tomorrow—'

'Why sadly?' Iris interrupted.

'I'm not particularly keen on all that Roman mosaic stuff,' said Julia, colouring.

'I'll take them if you like,' Iris found herself volunteering since it was clear that Vic couldn't go and Julia didn't want to.

*　　　*　　　*

582

It was an exhausting day, but interesting, despite her misgivings. Since living in Rome she'd become fascinated by Ancient Roman civilization, finding it difficult to believe that the vain and lazily beautiful young men she taught at the language school could have come from the same stock as soldiers who'd conquered most of the known world.

Despite their prep-school accents, Julia's boys were nice enough kids, not very bright, but perfectly happy charging up and down the steeply raked seats of the amphitheatre while she'd read the guidebook.

When she mentioned her brother, Bruno, Bertie asked hesitantly, 'Do you mean Chef Bruno?'

And Iris laughed and said she supposed she did.

'Bruno taught us to play football,' Archie told her.

'We're not supposed to talk about Bruno,' Bertie admonished him. 'Daddy says.'

'But I like him,' Archie proclaimed.

'So do I!' Iris told him, astonished when the little boy rammed his head against her tummy, which she thought was probably his way of signalling affection.

It was fun having them around, and, waiting on the station for the train back to Sorrento, Iris realized that she was dreading going back to Vic's constant camp jokes, which made her think he was trying to trick death by not letting it get a word in edgeways.

Vic was full of the day he'd spent gossiping with Julia in the bar.

'I think she's an angel. She's such a great listener! She wanted to know all about Robbie,' he said, making Iris feel as if she hadn't talked about his boyfriend enough. 'She was his biggest fan,' he went on. 'And she's been telling me all about her hospice for sick children, and now she's thinking about making a place by the sea for people with AIDS too. I said I'd leave her some money. She's a really beautiful person . . .'

'Oh, for God's sake!' said Iris, feeling suddenly jealous of his new-found friendship.

She drank quite a lot of wine at dinner and, after seeing Vic safely up to their suite, came back down in search of more alcohol. There was a piano playing in the lounge, and two or three couples were dancing. The room was even more kitschly ornate than the dining room, with huge chandeliers of multicoloured flowers, gilded rococo furniture, a ceiling painted with cherubs festooning ribbons.

Too late, Iris realized that Julia was sitting at a table alone on the other side of the dance floor and had spotted her. To turn around would be rude, to sit at another table even ruder. Reluctantly, Iris walked across the parquet floor, dodging the waltzing couples.

'Your boy safely tucked up too?' asked Julia brightly.

Iris nodded.

'I'm drinking Limoncello,' said Julia. 'Vic and I discovered a taste for it this afternoon.'

'What's it like?' Iris asked, sitting down.

'Like alcoholic lemon curd.'

'I'd better stick to wine,' Iris said, calling a waiter over.

Julia ordered a glass of water. 'I think I've probably had enough,' she said. 'You can have too much of a good thing, can't you?'

Iris winced at the cliché.

'Oh, I'm sorry,' said Julia. 'I expect you're sick of me barging in on your holiday.'

'Not at all,' Iris felt obliged to say.

'The boys had a lovely day with you,' said Julia.

'Good!' said Iris. 'And Vic enjoyed himself with you.'

'Good,' said Julia.

There was a small silence, and then Julia said, 'You must be terrified . . .'

The steam of crossness that had been building up in Iris's head all evening suddenly seemed to condense just behind her eyes, and she had to look out of the window and stare at the lights of Naples in the blackness. Terror was exactly what she felt. She'd been terrified ever since she set eyes on Vic in his wheelchair. And now she was even more terrified that she was going to ruin this last time together with her crossness. And that made her even crosser, and it just seemed to be an inexorable cycle that could only have one ending.

'I'm sorry,' she said, blinking away a single tear. 'I'm sorry, I never cry.'

'Don't you?' said Julia. 'God! I cry all the time! I didn't think I could cry any more. But now I'm in therapy, it's virtually non-stop . . . I have an eating disorder,' she told Iris in a rather childlike way, as if she had been encouraged to admit it. 'I used to think it was about not wanting to be fat, but it's really about lots of other things . . .'

'But you seem . . .' Iris searched for the right word – jaunty, smiley, would that sound offensive?

'I've always been good at putting on a brave face,' said Julia, guessing what Iris was going to say. 'I had to learn from an early age.'

'I've always been good at putting on a cross face,' said Iris.

The tension seemed to bubble away.

'You and I have quite a lot in common, don't we?' Julia said.

Iris couldn't think of a single thing. Perhaps she was a little drunk?

'We're women, I suppose,' she said.

'We both come from broken families,' Julia added.

'Sylvia!' Iris exclaimed suddenly. 'My mother. Your step-mother!'

'I feel quite sorry for Sylvia, actually,' said Julia.

'So do I,' said Iris. 'But . . .'

'I still don't like her!' they chorused, just as the pianist came to the end of the piece. Their laughter echoed round the lounge.

Iris was beginning to see why Vic liked Julia so much. She was guileless and refreshingly open.

'Bruno was always talking about you.' Julia blushed.

Someone else they had in common.

'Was he?' Iris felt a little swell of pride.

'Are you with anyone?' Julia asked, pushing the intimacy a little further.

An image of Fabio walking away down the street sprang to Iris's mind.

'Not really,' she said.

'Bruno always said that you should be with Winston,' Julia told her.

'Winston?' Iris scoffed. 'I'm far too old for Winston! You're even too old for Winston!'

Julia giggled.

'What about you?' Iris asked, suddenly realizing that she was the one answering all the questions. 'Are you with anyone now?'

'No,' said Julia. 'No. I'm just trying to get myself together. Make it as all right as possible for my boys. I'm still in Kingshaven. James has let me have the gatehouse, for the time being. You know about him and . . . ?'

'Fiammetta?' said Iris.

Iris couldn't imagine anyone less suitable for Fiammetta than James Allsop, but perhaps that was the point. Perhaps that was exactly what Fiammetta needed.

'Fiammetta's helping him with the house. They're restoring the walled garden,' said Julia.

'Ahh . . .' said Iris, thinking of the lavender, the roses rambling along the wall, her father lifting Fiammetta up to sniff their heavenly perfume. Now she thought she understood.

Iris waved the waiter across to order another drink.

'Did you ever want children yourself?' Julia asked suddenly.

Iris froze. 'I didn't want to run the risk of making a child unhappy, like I was,' she replied carefully.

'My therapist says that there are two reactions to broken families,' Julia told her. 'Some people, like me, spend their lives trying to repair the damage, from dolls' houses onwards, really. They have children and try to make their lives perfect . . .'

'Do you ever wish you hadn't?' Iris interrupted.

'What?'

'Had children.'

'Never,' said Julia categorically. 'I don't think anyone who had children could wish they hadn't . . .'

'What about the others?' Iris interrupted. 'The other reaction . . .'

'Oh, they spend their lives running away from any situation that feels remotely like a family,' said Julia.

Normally Iris had little time for people who offered psychobabble to explain why she was like she was, but Julia had uncannily struck a chord.

Every time Iris had fallen in love, the relationship had been doomed to fail: Clive; Josie; Roman . . . the image of Fabio walking away from her flashed through her brain again. Not Fabio. Fabio was her zipless fuck, not a proper relationship.

Now a tenor had joined the piano player. He was singing 'Return to Sorrento'.

It was so unreal being seranaded by Italian love songs in this camp, celestial room, looking at the lights of a distant city twinkling like stars.

'I did have a child,' Iris heard herself saying and then she wondered if she had actually said it out loud. 'Nineteen sixty-eight,' she continued. 'I was a crazy sixties chick and my boyfriend was a good-looking geezer with cash to flash and an enormous dong. People think the sixties were all about the Pill, but women still got pregnant by mistake, and despite all those liberal values, being a single mother wasn't acceptable . . . and he was a drug dealer, possibly a murderer . . .'

How easy it was suddenly in this alien place to unburden herself to someone she would probably never see again. Iris wondered if Julia had any idea she was the first person she had ever told.

She looked at Julia, caught her startled expression.

'You think I'm making it up?' Iris asked with a shrug. 'Sometimes I wonder myself . . . he went to prison . . . didn't know anything about it. I was going to have an abortion, but when it came to it, I couldn't.'

'But the baby . . . ?' Julia stuttered.

'Adopted. I had a life to get on with, didn't I?' Iris let out a short, bitter laugh.

'But wasn't it around then that you came back to Kingshaven?' Julia recalled.

'That was the irony,' Iris admitted. 'I gave up my baby, and a few months later I was handed two more . . . and I couldn't get out of looking after them . . .'

'You were lovely with them . . .' said Julia.

'Maybe I wouldn't have been such a bad mother, then . . .' Iris tried to make light of it, but her face didn't seem to want to smile as bidden.

'I always wished you were my big sister,' Julia told her with touching fervour.

'Did you? Perhaps that's what I'm good at, being a sister . . .' Iris looked out of the window again, into the night.

Instinctively, Julia reached across the table.

Iris didn't know how long it was she sat there, clasping Julia's hand. There were so many tears, they were in her mouth and ears and running down her chin and neck. She couldn't tell if the singer was still singing or the piano player playing.

'A little girl,' she finally blurted.

She could still see the tiny scrunched-up face, little lips moving as if she was trying to say something in her sleep; strands of damp black hair across her head; astonished blue eyes when she woke; the way she had looked at Iris, as if she trusted her to do the right thing.

'She was perfect . . .' Iris said, 'my baby . . . but it didn't feel as if she had anything to do with me! I didn't know how to look after a baby! Far too much responsibility . . . I didn't think I'd be any good at it. I thought . . .' she struggled to describe the emotion, 'I thought I could never do her justice.'

'But that's how everyone feels with their first baby!'

588

Julia exclaimed. 'At least, I did,' she qualified quickly as Iris stared at her in disbelief.

'Do you ever think of looking for her?' Julia asked gently.

'No,' said Iris, with a loud, decisive sniff. 'Definitely not. Better not do any more damage, don't you think?'

THE END

Acknowledgements

During the course of researching this novel I have found the following books enjoyable and useful: *Diana: Her True Story* and *Diana In Pursuit of Love* by Andrew Morton; *Diana* by Sarah Bradford; *Charles and Camilla: Portrait of a Love Affair* by Gyles Brandreth; *Shadows of a Princess* by P. D. Jephson; *The Diana Chronicles* by Tina Brown; *Royal* by Robert Lacey; *Blood Royal* by John Pearson; *Raine and Johnnie* by Angela Levin; *Mrs Simpson* by Charles Higham; *Elizabeth, The Queen Mother* by Hugo Vickers; *Hello! The 20th Century in Pictures*; *Guinness World Records: British Hit Singles (16th Edition)*; *The Best of Jackie*, Prion Books; *The Seventies: Good Times Bad Taste* ed. Allison Pressley; *The French Lieutenant's Woman* by John Fowles; *Kinflicks* by Lisa Alther; *Valley of the Dolls* by Jacqueline Susann; *Fear of Flying* by Erica Jong; *Scruples* by Judith Krantz. I am grateful to Audrey Cox for lending me her collection of royal memorabilia.

Thank you to all the people who wrote or talked to me about *The Time of Our Lives*, especially Stan Barstow and Alan Sillitoe, and to all readers at the Devon Libraries Day in Dartmouth, who gave me such encouraging feedback at a crucial stage in the trilogy.

Writing this book was much more difficult than I imagined it would be, but my life was made easier by the help of good friends. I particularly want to thank

Martha Kearney, Felicity Bryan, Steve Wilkinson, Rod McNeil and Debra Isaac for their practical support and astonishing enthusiasm, and Carlos Acosta for providing sunshine on dark days.

I am so lucky to be published by Transworld, and I'm particularly grateful to Claire Ward for the beautiful covers, to Linda Evans for her patience and understanding, to Vivien Garrett and Judith Welsh, for making the proof-reading fun. My agent, Mark Lucas, is always a generous and intelligent reader, and great company. I thank him and everyone at LAW, especially Alice Saunders, for their support. Thanks also to Nicki Kennedy and Sam Edenborough at ILA for all their hard work on my behalf.

This is a book about families and the way they shape a person's destiny. My mum, Kath, has always been there for me, my sister Becky is my dream reader as well as my best friend, my brother-in-law Peter offers a great technical support service, and my niece, Caitie, is a delightful source of inspiration. But as usual, it is to my lovely husband, Nick, and my brilliant and beautiful son, Connor, that I owe the greatest debt of gratitude, for their love and laughter, and for reminding me what it's all for.